To Anthony, Addison & Alexis

THE CRIES OF SAN SEBASTIAN

A Novel By
Anthony Ramos

PublishAmerica
Baltimore

First printing

Hardcover 978-1-4560-5569-1
Softcover 978-1-4560-5567-7
PUBLISHED BY PUBLISHAMERICA, LLLP
www.publishamerica.com
Baltimore

Printed in the United States of America

PROLOGUE

Dr. Betances stared at the sheet of paper for the better part of an hour. Dark, brooding eyes squinted thoughtfully, while a trembling right hand barely held on to a fountain pen. Standing pensively before his desk, an equally tremulous left hand reached for a pair of round spectacles. The wire frames, bearing thick lenses, smeared by worn and debilitated fingers, rested near two bottles of black ink that sat perilously near the edge of his antique, but favorite writing table.

Dr. Betances had crossed out the first two sentences of his latest work, and had given up on yet another attempt at writing an opening statement when he paused shortly to look across his small, nondescript room. He gazed wistfully at an unkempt bed; the wrinkled sheets, pulled halfway down, and the stained pillow marking a clear indentation of his head, seemed to beckon the doctor's return. On top of an old night table, wedged between the rickety bed and a beige stucco wall, sat a Bible. Next to the Holy Scriptures, the fading light of a candlestick flickered intermittently—the wax melted down to its base.

Fighting off the conflicting desires within, and carefully weighing the matter for several moments, Dr. Betances reasoned that one more hour of sleep that morning offered him nothing more than the loss of precious time. Altering his approach, he tasked his mind for a title, but then he quickly abandoned the idea and decided to make a fourth attempt at writing his essay; he would think about a title later. Titles never seemed to bother him much because he knew they would always emerge through the work itself. A good measure of what he needed right then was patience—patience and a good hook with which to ensnare his readers. His most recent work was an essay about *Alexander Petion*, Haiti's revolutionary first President, titled *Washington Haitiano.* He had published the essay fifteen years earlier, but he was 61 now and had not written anything of real importance since. Painfully aware of his monthly financial obligations, especially to the owner of the tenement building where he had lived for a number of years, and the fact that food was not a cheap commodity either, he decided it was time to write again.

Dr. Betances's medical office was only a few blocks down the street from his flat, on Rue de Saint-Dominique, but since most of his patients were poor, more often than not he found himself offering his services pro-bono. Fortunately, his connections to a local publisher brought in desperately needed cash from time to time; enough cash to maintain a roof over his head and food in his stomach.

Through the window of his small flat, a warm breeze ushered in the scent of freshly baked bread. The bakery, with its dual ovens operating at full capacity and a long queue of impatient customers, had been open since dawn. Though situated some three blocks from his tiny flat, strong northeasterly winds carried the aroma from *Le Petite Pain* to Dr. Betances's nostrils in just a matter of seconds, forcing him to pause all over again.

Dr. Betances placed the fountain pen down on the blotter, and walked over to the open window, placing both hands firmly on the sill. He took in a deep breath, and while savoring the aroma of baking dough, his dark brown eyes stared contemplatively at the narrow, cobblestone streets and morning people going about their business. Directly below his window, he noted the owner of the five-story brick building, Madam Eloise Dubois. Before losing her husband last year, Eloise was an exuberant woman, full of life and happiness—a true bon-vivant. Now she was just another plump, grey-haired woman, who owned a tenement building and mostly kept to herself. Watching from his window, Betances could not help but to feel Eloise's pain; a pain he had been all too familiar with throughout his tumultuous life. He observed Madame Dubois as she swept garbage off the sidewalk with a sense of purpose, oblivious to her surroundings, as if it were the most important task of the day. He found the scene strangely amusing, but it did not cause him to crack a smile. In fact, he could not recollect with any degree of certainty the last time he smiled. Betances turned his attention back on the horizon.

The panoramic view of the city, as the sun slowly emerged from its dark repose, brought a smile to Dr. Betances's otherwise stoic face. The scene, reminiscent of Puerto Rico's capital, suddenly rekindled the deep love he still felt for his homeland, an emotion his saddened heart struggled to maintain dormant. He sighed heavily and whispered, "*Oh, my old San Juan, how much I miss you.*"

He brought his frail fingers to his face and navigated through a thick blanket of platinum-colored hair. He dug his fingers deep into his beard and scratched vigorously. The large bags under his eyes and that far away stare often noted by many of his friends, gave clear evidence of the sleepless nights, and the worries and anxieties he had suffered over the consequences of his life's passion.

From the small window of his flat, gazing toward the west, Betances could see hundreds of workers and scaffolds and the faint image of a steel tower rising into the air, as if it were a large tree sprouting from the ground. The low hum of men riveting steel girders and people bustling, working like busy ants in an effort to complete Gustave Eiffel's steel monument in time for the World Exposition, came across clearly to Betances's ears.

Dr. Betances marveled at the industrious nature of his adopted country, her progress toward modernization and her determination to become a world leader. He frowned right away, though, because such reflections would invariably force him to drift backward in time, to a place he hated going; a place that compelled him to dwell on past memories of his beloved Puerto Rico. And like the weighted force of a ship's anchor, his heart would sink into a deep sea of depression because he knew that his country was no more than a backwater civilization, a small, insignificant speck of land that nobody cared about or even knew existed. Yet while in Paris, Dr. Betances's persistence had yielded numerous meetings with members of the National Assembly and people of prominence, and although the sessions never bore fruit, the good doctor refused to give up hope in his life-long quest to seek international support for a free and independent Puerto Rico. Oh how his heart yearned to be in Puerto Rico at that very moment, his place of birth and the only thing on earth that made him feel truly happy.

They called Puerto Rico *La Isla Del Encanto,* The Island of Enchantment. Puerto Rico was part of a chain of islands along the Caribbean Sea called the Greater Antilles. Conquered by the Spanish in the 15th century, it had been under their rule for nearly four hundred years. Oftentimes, Dr. Betances would sit in his flat and wonder how Puerto Rico might have looked to the first Spaniards arriving on her shores. They must have been awestruck at first sight of her pristine beaches, gentle waves and tropical birds; a scene further complemented by a canopy of green, lush vegetation. The interior of the island, with its rolling hills and thick rainforests, had to have been God's gift to the inhabitants for their natural piety and for their deep communion with earth; and from a poet's conception, it was the manifestation of true paradise, a veritable Eden.

Weakened by the overpowering scent of leavened wheat, Dr. Betances finally yielded to the sounds of his gurgling stomach. Holding tightly to the frail banister, he walked down five flights of stairs and began walking towards the bakery, his nose trained on the persistent but delightful aroma of fresh dough. As he lumbered past his landlady, he uttered, "*Bon jour*." He could see that despite her willingness to become a recluse and though she appeared to have lost her zeal for life, her blue eyes were still vibrant and full of energy. She turned, looked up at Betances and smiled, "*Bon jour, Docteur. Allez-vous pour une promenade ce matin?"* Betances did not break his stride but found it strange that she had taken the time to ask him if he was taking a walk that morning. It was never more than a 'good morning' or a 'good afternoon' and sometimes, if she was still up, even a 'good night'. Betances answered politely. *"Oui, je vais acheter pain"*

Gingerly holding a warm baguette in one hand and a flask of milk in the other, Dr. Betances walked back to his flat. He sat before his desk and stared at the same sheet of paper that still lay innocently on his desk. Hampered by the frustrations of a mental block, he picked up the paper and crumpled it, and as he shook his head submissively, he finally understood why he was unable to write. Though it did not happen too often, there were moments when Dr. Betances's mind would drift back twenty years earlier, forcing him to recall perhaps one of the most disappointing times of his life.

It was a different era back then, a time when many of his peers shared and articulated the same dreams and hopes, a time when the political and social divide between the rich and poor had grown to abysmal proportions, a time rife with intrigue and betrayal, and a time ripe for change.

Twenty years ago, in the spring of 1868, Dr. Betances found himself exiled in the Dominican Republic because of his devotion to the independence of Puerto Rico. He wrote passionate articles and spoke fervently against Spanish colonialism and repression, and over time, the people would come to recognize him as the leader of Spanish opposition. Advocating ideals contrary to those of the mother country was a very dangerous mission for any creole to undertake at the time. With heightened fears of igniting a Puerto Rican revolution like the one occurring in Santo Domingo at the time, Spanish colonial authorities accused Dr. Betances of sedition and banned him from his beloved country.

Times were hard those days for the creoles of Puerto Rico; children lacked education, food was scarce and Cholera had been plaguing the islanders for many years. As if dwelling in a land with such terrible conditions were not enough, African men, women and children still found themselves bound by the shackles of slavery. Despite the island's disastrous economy, which forced the creoles into absolute dependency on Spain, the agricultural industry was still producing goods, and slaves were very much an integral part of it. Lurking in the background, like wolves encircling their prey, the wealthy *Peninsulares* perpetuated that misery behind their financial and political machinations.

Peninsulares was the term creoles gave to recent arrivals on the island—men and women born in Spain. They either arrived from the Iberian Peninsula or, as loyalists, forced to flee the Dominican Republic's revolutionary war. Peninsulares arrived on the island colony with money, and the Spanish authorities of Puerto Rico enthusiastically embraced them and immediately began to favor them more than they did the creoles. In a few short years, they owned practically all land in sight.

There were also significant numbers of foreign nationals who had settled on the island at the invitation of Spanish officials, and they too found favor with the government.

The creoles saw the Peninsulares coming by the boatload and still they could do nothing to stop them from opening up shops and export companies throughout the western part of the island. Before long, peninsulares began lending money to cash-strapped *hacendados*. Hacendados were creole landowners and farmers who, in recent years, had been suffering great hardships at the hands of Spanish tax collectors. The government of Spain had caused the hardship by imposing heavy assessments on their properties and capital gains in order to fund the counter-insurgency plan against the Dominican rebels. The shortfall of cash forced the majority of Hacendados to seek loans from Peninsulares, who happily obliged them but offered them high interest-bearing notes. Having exhausted all means by which to obtain additional capital, the hacendados found it impossible to repay their loans. Of the many creoles that put their lands and homes up as collateral, nearly all of them lost their properties by default.

The son of a wealthy landowner himself, Ramón Emeterio Betances was born on August 8, 1827 and was one of the few fortunate creoles to receive the benefit of a good education. He studied in France, where he received a medical degree from the University of Paris in 1855. Upon his return to Puerto Rico, he settled in Mayagüez where he founded a hospital and worked tirelessly to eradicate the dreadful Cholera epidemic.

To Dr. Betances in the early part of 1867, the future of Puerto Rico, if allowed to continue under Spanish rule, looked bleak and hopeless. The creoles of Spanish descent, the freed people of color and the slaves were being systematically choked by a repressive regime that, prior to Simon Bolivar's South American revolution in the 1820's, had placed little or no value on the island except to serve as a military outpost.

Dr. Betances had a profound admiration for the founding fathers of the United States and their noble visions of a free and democratic nation. His admiration for the United States never faltered, not even during the darkest days of the Civil War, when all appeared lost. During the four long years of the American conflict, Dr. Betances had amassed a collection of newspaper articles and accounts about the war. Finally, in November of 1865, one of his friends had recently returned from New York with news that the North had won the war. Betances took great comfort in the news and prayed that the Union would uphold President Lincoln's Emancipation Proclamation. Slavery was anathema to him, as was the class structure; a repressive system that choked the islanders' will into abject dependence on the motherland. Conditions in Puerto Rico had to change, thought the then forty-year-old doctor, because only a select group of people was reaping the profits of the current economic situation.

It was in the latter part of 1863 that Dr. Betances gave serious thought to the notion of independence, but the issue that needed attention first, before any thoughts of independence could ever materialize, was the issue of slavery. Following President Lincoln's proclamation, Dr. Betances and a few friends founded a society dedicated to the abolition of slavery. Over the next few years, their society met in several Masonic lodges in Mayagüez, where they agreed to print and circulate leaflets condemning slavery. Their vocal opposition to slavery and to Spain's stronghold on the island was so powerful that it forced the colonial authorities to take note of their movement. The Spanish declared that anyone advocating independence or speaking out against slavery would be considered a subversive and a danger to the colony. Subsequent to the declaration, the Spanish ordered the militia to arrest all suspected agitators. Finally, in 1867, the governor of Puerto Rico exiled Dr. Betances and his group of radical friends to Spain.

Refusing to spend an indefinite amount of time in a prison three thousand miles away, and fearing a future that seemed uncertain, Dr. Betances and Segundo Ruiz Belvis—his long time friend and fellow Freemason, decided to flee to the Dominican Republic, where they founded the Revolutionary Committee of Puerto Rico. While in the Dominican Republic, they sought money to fund their movement from people in the neighboring islands, as well as countries in South America. From their base in the Dominican Republic, they planned a revolution to free the African slaves and free Puerto Rico from the ever-tightening Spanish yoke.

Betances cut the warm baguette in half, poured milk into a glass and ate his meager breakfast. As he chewed on a morsel of bread, a host of memories flashed through his mind; of the places that he had been to and people he had met over the years. Of the many people with whom he had associated over his long lifespan though, there was one person who stood out more than anyone else did on that particular morning. Although she had not been directly involved in the Lares uprising that took place on the night of September 23-24, 1868, she had become a vocal opponent of Spanish rule. Dr. Betances did not meet her until she paid him a visit in France years after the Lares uprising. In fact, he had no idea who she was, or that in some way her family might have played a role in the events leading up to the fatal confrontation. In spite of her efforts to show her enthusiasm at meeting him, Dr. Betances noted her sadness, as if she had been bitterly heartbroken and had never gotten over it.

While on her way to Spain in the fall of 1883, the woman took the opportunity to travel to France and pay Dr. Betances a long overdue visit. They had dinner in a quiet café, where they immersed themselves in several conversations ranging from economics to philosophy, science and history. Dr. Betances got to know the woman and liked her from the start. After dinner, they strolled along the Champs-Elysées, toward the Arc de Triomphe where they sat on a bench dimly lit by an overhead gas lantern. Her name was Rosalía, and for the next four hours, she told Dr. Betances where she was on that fateful night and her story as it related to the Lares incident so many years ago.

Dr. Betances grinned with a good measure of satisfaction as he reached into the side drawer of his desk, pulling out a fresh sheet of paper. He concluded that the only way to clear his mind was to write about Rosalía's story, and this effort, though painful for him to recollect, would flush the mental block out of his head. Unlike all of his prior works, however, he would never publish this one. This work he would do for himself, for his benefit and for his sense of redemption. Filling his fountain pen with fresh ink, he began to write the story that would never be.

CHAPTER 1

Nothing could have prepared Rosalía Luz Hernández well enough to confront the horrible events of September 23 and 24, 1868. But then again, Rosalía had lived a sheltered life up to that point. For the first eighteen years of her life, Rosalía lived in a world of opulence, attended to by many servants and slaves, pampered and educated by personal tutors from Spain. The auburn-haired beauty was the daughter of Rodolfo and Maria Hernández, and her family was one of the few members of Puerto Rican aristocracy.

Rosalía's father was a wealthy landowner, a peninsular, and her mother was the daughter of a minor count in Spain. Members of San Juan's elite society viewed their marriage as a good union between two well-to-do families, a good combination of old and new money. Rosalía was the youngest of the three Hernández children. Laura, at twenty-three, was the eldest, and Anita, at twenty, was the middle child.

The Hernández family owned thousands of acres of land in the towns of San Sebastián and Lares, and Rodolfo's leasing of the land to local farmers brought him vast sums of money over the years. Known as *Jíbaros*, hicks from the mountains, the farmers were all poor, uneducated and considered lowly peasants by the upper class. Nevertheless, they were wise country folk, and, aside from knowing how to farm the land, they were well aware of the current political climate on the island as well as the poor economic conditions, from which a small percentage of the population found exemption.

Contribution to Rodolfo's wealth also came by way of money he lent to the hacendados of San Sebastián and Lares. Although many creole hacendados owned their lands, and in spite of the fact that Spain considered them citizens of the realm, to be treated equally in the eyes of the court, peninsulares never regarded them as their equals and exploited them harshly for nothing more than financial gain.

It was on the third day of February 1868 that Rodolfo Hernández planned to bring his family to San Sebastián, and this fateful decision would change Rosalía Hernández and her entire family forever. The family owned a country estate in the outskirts of San Sebastián but Rodolfo never took his family there, preferring instead to travel alone and conclude all of his business transactions as quickly as possible. He enjoyed city life far too much to be venturing into the hinterland on a regular basis, but since the hinterland was where the source of his wealth flowed, like the uninterrupted flow of a river, he viewed making the journey to San Sebastián as part of his pecuniary obligations. For reasons Rosalía could never explain, Rodolfo decided to take his family on holiday and bring them to their hacienda in San Sebastián for several weeks.

While in San Sebastián, Rodolfo always took the opportunity to call on his solicitor and obtain the *libretas* on everyone who owed him money, and this occasion, though he had brought his family with him, would be no different from all previous occasions.

Between the years 1830 and 1848, the people of Puerto Rico had been under a system known as the *Reglamento de Jornaleros (Laborers' Rules and Regulations).* Created by then governor, Don Miguel Lopez de Baños, the harsh system wrought increased misery to creole life. Under the Reglamento, persons owning no property or lacking the financial means with which to meet their needs were obligated to seek employment. Upon reaching the age of 16, citizens were required to register with the municipal board closest to their homes and seek employment at once. If they remained unemployed for more than a month, the Reglamento forced them to work for the state at half pay or, in some extreme cases, sent them to jail. Although the Reglamento raised productivity, it also caused many *jornaleros* to escape the law and avoid jail time, resulting in an unceasing wave of complaints from many of their land-owning employers. By 1849, the complaints flooding the new governor's office were so many that they forced him into rewriting the Reglamento. Governor de la Pezuela's revision would manifest into the Libreta system. Under the Libreta system, jornaleros received identification papers, which they had to produce upon demand and inspected every month by local municipalities. The libreta would detail a jornalero's work history and current employment, thus ensuring the government that they were indeed working. The Spanish merchants of the island, however, took the governor's idea and created a different and more effective libreta system. They were books and documents that recorded debts owed to the Spanish merchants by farmers and landowners, and the main reason for Rodolfo Hernández's frequent visits to San Sebastián.

Visits to these rural areas always seemed to bring out the worst in Rodolfo Hernández, and the closer he got to his campestral destination the more his persona would change, evolve, morph into a hideous disposition. Despite his best efforts to keep his dark side away from the general public, everyone knew all too well how ruthless a man he was. To the people of San Sebastián and Lares, the fifty-five-year-old Rodolfo Hernández personified evil, thus they began calling him *El Demonio*, the Demon. His five-foot-ten-inch frame sported a muscular physique that was an extreme rarity among his peers. He kept his fine brown hair cropped short and took great measures to keep it as neatly as he did his long beard, which, unlike many of his friends' beards, was untainted by grey. In San Sebastián four years earlier, he suffered the consequences of prodding an enraged mule and felt the blunt force of its powerful hind legs before dropping to the ground in agonizing pain. Despite being in traction for several weeks, the wound to his knee never healed properly, and so his limp became more prominent over the years, forcing the occasional use of a walking cane. His almond-shaped brown eyes, with their long eyelashes, caused the envy of women, and above the hairline of his dark beard, his high cheekbones were still visible and one could discern that Rodolfo, in his younger years, had been a strikingly handsome man. But the awful limp caused by the injury, negated any hint of sexual attraction a woman might have otherwise had because of his rugged good looks. Perhaps that is why he hated going to San Sebastián, because every time he went there it reminded him of the day of his injury.

At home, Rodolfo Hernández was just as domineering and demanding on his wife and daughters as he was on his slaves and those who worked for him, and though he wished his wife and daughters would truly love him he knew they feared him terribly. On the outside, the Hernández family portrayed themselves as a caring and loving family, but only they knew how difficult it was to live under Rodolfo Hernández's roof.

This was the world of Rosalía Hernández when she came to San Sebastián in February 1868.

The morning of Monday, February 3, began with a wave of anxiety in the Hernández home in San Juan. The servants were busy rushing upstairs and downstairs with Maria's last minute requests, while she made certain she had accounted for all bags and trunks. The house always seemed to come alive on the day of a Hernández journey and every member of the household, whether they liked it or not, found it hard to avoid the excitement. But it was in the faces of slaves and servants that a profound sense of exuberance dwelled because the master of the house would not be home for weeks and possibly, to their great expectations, for months.

The stately house, built largely of wood, sat on a foundation of stone. Arched windows and hallways, and a pastel yellow siding were complemented by a terracotta-tiled roof. A manicured front lawn and trees lining the road into the house made it the most visible home in San Juan. The Hernández home boasted six bedrooms, study, kitchen, sitting room and a large living room that sometimes doubled as a modest ballroom. Toward the back of the mansion, a pump with a long metal lever, gushed out fresh water, and further into the woods the dark silhouettes of two outhouses stood out like sentinels protecting the rear. A winding dirt road led to the front of the mansion, where two African slaves were busy loading a wagon with bags and trunks. Another slave, a much younger man than the two slaves loading the wagons, silently harnessed the team of four horses while the rest of the slaves remained inside the mansion catering to the whims of Maria Hernández.

Rosalía had just finished packing her trunk and had taken a moment to look out of her bedroom window. As she gazed at the coach and wagon parked in front of the house, her supple young body swayed nervously. A curtain of lacy auburn hair draped nearly all of her back, and it moved gently in response to her body's rhythm. Thrilled at the notion of traveling beyond the confines of San Juan, her heart was beating rapidly, just as it had three years earlier when she sailed across the Atlantic Ocean accompanying her father on her first voyage to Spain. Her thin eyebrows furrowed as she imagined the many adventures that lay ahead in the coming days.

Heeding her mother's words during her prepubescent days, Rosalía would wash her angular face daily and now, her olive skin, unblemished by acne, was smooth to the touch. Her perfectly shaped nose complemented her bright red lips and her smile produced a perfect set of white teeth that drew immediate attention. She was a beautiful, sensual and desirable young woman, and because of her stark beauty, Rosalía had surpassed her elder sisters in the number of suitors that would come around the house to call on her. Unfortunately, for Rosalía, she had never seen any of them because Rodolfo, insisting she was too young for courtship, would chase them all away.

This was the first time Rosalía would be venturing into the main island, and she had been looking forward to the trip ever since her father had made the announcement two weeks ago. The family planned to take a ferry from San Juan to Cataño where they would stay the night at Don Jimenez's house, and then set out for San Sebastián the next day.

Anita Hernández, Rosalía's middle sister, had just finished packing her trunk, and as she walked the long hallway toward the spiraling white staircase, she went past Rosalía's room. Anita stopped suddenly, reversed her steps and noticed her younger sister staring aimlessly out the window, her body fidgeting. She walked into Rosalía's room and stared curiously. "Rosa, are you done packing? Father said we have to leave by nine this morning."

Rosalía turned and with a huge smile pranced toward her sister, her ocean blue eyes flashing with anticipation. "Ana, aren't you excited?"

"Excited is hardly the word *I* would use. No, I am not excited and I cannot believe that Father wants all of us to go with him. I have been dreading the idea of traveling into the mountains for days. What's in San Sebastián but heat, mosquitoes and snakes?"

Rosalía reached for Anita's hands and held them tightly. "That's not the reason why you've been so reluctant to leave San Juan, now is it?"

"What do you mean?"

"You know what I mean. The reason why you want to stay in San Juan is because of Ruben De La Cruz. You're afraid he'll come around to call on you only to find the house empty."

Anita hesitated but then her light-brown eyes blinked twice and her round face stretched with a wide grin. Then she laughed and hugged her sister. "You know me so well, Rosa. Yes, Ruben wrote to me and told me he would be arriving from Cuba by Wednesday. I wrote back to him and told him I wouldn't be here when he arrived but since the mail is so slow, I don't think he's received my letter yet."

"Well, if Ruben is serious about courting you then he will wait for you."

"You think so? I still can't believe Father agreed to his courtship and Mother seems to like him, too."

Rosalía held her breath for a split second. She sensed confusion in Anita's mind and felt her elder sister could do with a little cautioning. Rosalía shook her head disappointedly and said, "Oh Ana, you poor thing, Father agreed to his courting you because Ruben is a De La Cruz, and the De La Cruz family owns practically everything in Yauco. He comes from money, and money makes Father a very happy man. On the other hand, Mother will go along with anything, so long as she doesn't have to hear Father's voice."

"You don't think much of Ruben, either, do you? You don't think he's genuinely in love with me and that Father and Mother do not care one way or another. You and everybody else in this family seem to have already passed judgment on my relationship with Ruben, but why is it always Ruben? Why not Laura's fiancé? Why is it always me?"

"I didn't say all that, Ana. All I'm saying is that Father has not taken a moment to know Ruben. All he knows is that Ruben comes from a wealthy family and that just about sums up our Father's requirements.

But it doesn't matter what Father and Mother think, right? What's important is how *you* feel. Does Ruben make *you* happy?"

"Of course he does, Rosa. Why do you ask me as though I'm not sure of what I'm doing?"

"Are you?"

"Damn it, Rosa, you're my younger sister but you're acting like an old woman! *I* should be the one asking you these kinds of questions."

"I'm not the one who's being courted by Don Ruben De La Cruz now am I? Are you sure it's not because you want to leave home so badly that you're willing to marry the first suitor that comes along?"

"Rosa, I'm not going to get into this conversation with you again. I am attracted to Ruben and he is attracted to me. Father and Mother have approved the courtship and that's the end of it!"

Neither Rosalía nor Anita noticed that Laura had entered the room and had heard their entire conversation. Leaning against the threshold with arms folded as if she were a schoolteacher expressing disappointment at a couple of unruly students, Laura chuckled sarcastically. Her curly, dark brown hair swirled and covered her green eyes momentarily as she shook her head. The eldest sibling then glared contemptuously at Anita. "You're a silly girl. If Ruben De La Cruz has not asked Father for your hand in marriage by now, then it is obvious he is not interested in you. It's been what, almost one year? Ruben's been away for almost a year now and he's not even taken the time to visit you? What does that tell you, Ana?"

Rosalía felt the heat of anger rising within her as she watched Laura's attempts at destroying Anita's last vestiges of hope. Rosalía rushed over to Laura so that she could face her eye to eye. "Why are you always putting us down? Why do you feel that only you should deserve all the happiness? Can't you let us be for once in your rotten life?"

"Oh hush now, you spoiled brat!" fired back Laura. "You're just Father's little girl and you've always gotten away with everything! But I'm not Father and that little girl charm will not work on me!"

Anita darted over to Laura, and in defense of her younger sister she yelled, "Why don't you just leave us alone! More and more each day I see Father in you, Laura. You're exactly like him! You have no sympathy and no love, just abhorrence for everyone except yourself."

At that moment, Maria Hernández walked into Rosalía's room shouting. "You three are at it again? Your father told us last night that he wanted everyone in front of the house by nine. Now gather all your things and get yourselves downstairs!" Too angered by Laura's comments, neither Anita nor Rosalía acknowledged their mother. They kept their eyes focused on Laura's face with so much contempt that even Maria felt the heat of their anger from where she stood. Failing to get their attention, Maria turned to Laura and said scornfully, "What are you three arguing about now? For once in your lives, can you three do something without having to fight? It simply amazes me that you are all sisters! If your father hears you three arguing again, he will lose his temper and beat you silly like the last time. I hope that you have not forgotten about the leather belt he used on all of you. Now I will not tell you again!"

Laura ignored her mother's command, and stared right back at Anita and Rosalía, but unlike her younger sisters, she was not angry at all. In fact, Laura felt good inside because she had done some kind of damage to Anita. To Laura, it did not matter what form of damage it was so long as she had been the first to attack. She slowly turned and left the room. Anita and Rosalía waited for a long while, until they were completely certain that Laura had cleared the stairway. Fully satisfied, they quietly departed the room, ignoring their mother as if she was never there. Maria shook her head and sighed heavily, unable to control the frustration she felt over her failure to get through to any of her daughters. Deep down inside though, Maria felt relieved, as if a terrible burden had lifted off her shoulders. She had not seen Rodolfo since he had gotten up out of bed at 4:30 that morning but she was grateful that he had not heard his daughters arguing again. At the same time, though, Maria wondered where Rodolfo was at that precise moment, and that's when it hit her: she knew exactly where he was!

During construction of the Hernández house, twenty-five years ago, Rodolfo had instructed the builders to make a secret room. The tiny room could only accommodate a small bed and a night table, but its secrecy was of paramount concern to the master of the house. It was located on the first floor, inside the study. The entrance, concealed by a large bookshelf with a metal lever behind it, was difficult to detect. Depressing a particular book on the shelf lowered the lever and unlocked the bookshelf, thus causing it to swing open to reveal the room. From inside the room, Rodolfo would raise the lever and the bookshelf would swing closed, allowing him all the privacy he would need to do his secretive business.

Rodolfo had company in his secret room. She was a beautiful young woman, no more than twenty years old. Her name was Berta and she was a muláta, a slave born into the Hernández household. He had deflowered her two years earlier, and she had made numerous trips into the secret room at the behest of her master. On this particular morning, Rodolfo had been fornicating with enough energy to make the sexual liaison linger in his mind for weeks. With each thrust, Berta moaned to show her master how well he was pleasing her. But since Rodolfo had buried his face into Berta's neck, pressing his lips on her soft and sweaty brown skin, kissing her passionately, he never saw the outright disgust pervading her face—a contemptuous repulsion that made her face cringe with nausea. Rodolfo raised his head and placed both hands on the bed so that he could thrust harder, droplets of sweat raining down on Berta's small but firm breasts. When she saw her master's face, Berta suddenly changed her look of disgust to pleasing smile. Rodolfo pushed harder and harder and then released his energies into Berta. Ever fearful of her master, especially after their sexual act, Berta would continue to press into him as if she wanted more even though she knew he was drained of all energy. In reality, she hated her master so passionately that many times she thought about killing him during one of their sinful encounters.

A fully spent Rodolfo rolled over, and, as he breathed heavily, lying spread-eagled on the bed, he heard his wife's voice calling out for him. Raising his eyebrows in a sort of mild shock, he quickly turned to the side and looked at Berta. He put his index finger to his mouth in a hushing gesture and simply waited. Sweat beads rolled down his forehead as his breathing slowly returned to normal.

Maria walked into Rodolfo's study and squinted as if trying to put to reason a faint, muffled sound that emanated from beyond the wall just a few seconds ago. There was nothing but silence now, and though she stood in the room for a while, straining her ears, she remained unconvinced. She knew exactly where he was, right behind that awful shelf full of books Rodolfo had never taken the time to read. As much as Maria's husband had taken measures to maintain the room's secrecy, he was careless, and one day, in November of last year, Maria heard sexual moans coming from behind the bookshelf. Fully aware that her husband was inside that awful den of sin, she called out his name loudly to make sure he knew she was there looking for him. Having interrupted her husband's carnal pleasures that morning, Maria felt no further need to remain inside that dreadful study. She feigned the idea that she was still looking for him, and continued to call out her husband's name.

Rodolfo waited for several minutes until he was certain his wife was gone, and then he quickly hopped out of bed. Fully naked, he looked at Berta with a smile. "That was great! I will miss you, Berta, but I will be back soon! How was it for you?"

"As always, Patrón, your manliness has pleased me greatly," Berta replied with a nervous smile. "I shall look forward to seeing you again."

"Thank you, Berta!" said Rodolfo, smiling. All of a sudden, his smile vanished and his eyes turned dark and cold. He jumped back on the bed and grabbed Berta by the hair, pulling hard enough to get her undivided attention. Though she was in obvious pain, the young slave said nothing, not even a whimper. "You are a worthless negra, but you know something? Of the many slave bitches I've had over the years, you've been the best one so far! Now, I'm going to finish dressing and leave soon. You will stay in the room and wait until we leave the mansion, is that clear?"

"Si Patrón," replied Berta, painfully. She tried desperately to keep her eyes from tearing, but failed miserably. One tear managed to roll down her cheek.

"That's right," said Rodolfo with an evil grin. "I *am* your Patrón!" He let go of her hair and sprung off the bed. As he tucked his shirt into his trousers, he looked down at Berta and said, "Do you know the reason why that beautiful, soft back of yours has never felt the sting of a whip?" He watched Berta shake her head. "It's because when I fuck slaves, I don't like to feel scars. Besides, I think one day you're going to fetch me a handsome price. There is a young man in Santo Domingo, a distant cousin of mine, who's interested in buying a woman slave. You should see his wife, Berta, she looks like a pig. I think I know why he wants to buy you, so when I return from San Sebastián I'm going to sell you to him. I'm sure you'll give him many years of pleasure."

Berta was born into the Hernández family and her mother and father, as well as her three brothers, were still together. The only world she had ever known was the Hernández household. The thought of someone buying her and forcing her to leave that familial world, had never entered her mind until now, and she began to dread it. There was time, though, time enough to plan an escape before the master's return from San Sebastián. Berta looked up at Rodolfo with inquisitive but humble brown eyes. "Have I not pleased you well, Patrón?"

Rodolfo smiled and chuckled. "Of course you have, but I've grown tired of you and I think Mrs. Hernández is starting to suspect something. I cannot have her knowing about this, now can I? You have to go Berta. Take the next few weeks and spend it wisely with your family, and when I come back I will ship you to Santo Domingo." Rodolfo buckled his belt, pushed down the lever and the bookshelf swung open. He poked his head out and made sure no one was in his study. Then he turned back and took one more look at Berta. "I will miss you, Berta." He stepped out and depressed the book. Moments later, the bookshelf swung closed, leaving Berta alone in the room. Berta slowly rose and pushed her hair back to make it as neatly as possible. She sat up, brought her hands to her face and began to cry.

CHAPTER 2

It was nine thirty, and the Hernández family was already late for their journey. Maria and her three well-dressed daughters were outside overseeing the storage of trunks onto the wagon. One of the male slaves was still busy harnessing the horses, but it was far too late for him because Rodolfo Hernández had just stepped out of the house. Sensing Rodolfo's presence, as if suddenly confronted by an evil spirit, the young slave quickened his pace.

"Don't tell me you're still fiddling around with the horses, Manolo!" shouted Rodolfo. The young slave hesitated for a split second but continued to work, fully aware that his master had been in a foul mood that morning. "Manolo, you piece of shit!" shouted Rodolfo as he approached the coach.

"Come girls, get inside!" said Maria, attempting to shield her daughters from what was sure to come. The three young women hurriedly entered the coach, as their father's voice grew stronger. Maria took only a brief moment to see Rodolfo's face flushed with anger, and that was all she needed to know. She quickly stepped into the coach and slammed the door closed. Then she heard the awful sound of smacking skin. Although Maria was a product of aristocracy, she kept her negative views on slavery a secret, refusing to give Rodolfo another weapon with which to use against her. The fact was that Maria had always detested slavery, but lacking the nerve to oppose her father and later her husband, she resigned herself to the idea of letting things go on as they always had.

At fifty, Maria showed no signs of age; her slim figure had not changed despite bearing three children and her skin was smooth and lacking the sun-dried wrinkles so prevalent among women her age in San Juan. Her blue eyes radiated a sense of benevolence and her graceful movements confirmed her aristocratic upbringing, high education and refinement. Her auburn hair was longer than Rosalía's was, and she took great care to maintain its silky appearance.

Rodolfo grabbed Manolo by his neck and spun him around. Then he smacked his face several times before thrusting a punch at him. Manolo fell to the ground while nursing his swelling cheekbone. "These goddamn horses were supposed to be harnessed hours ago! You fucking slaves are nothing but lazy sons of bitches! If I didn't have to leave soon, Manolo, I swear I would have you flogged until your skin bled. Now get up and finish your task!"

From inside the windowless, secret room, Berta could hear her master shouting at her brother and wondered how bad the situation was. As she put on her dress, which was merely a rotting piece of fabric now, she convinced herself that escape was the only way to free herself of her nightmare. She planned on broaching the subject with her brother, but since Manolo was more level-headed than she was, she doubted he would entertain such a senseless idea. Uncertain whether Manolo would indeed follow her, she vowed that she would find a way to escape with or without him. While Manolo rushed to complete his task, his two older brothers, Candelario and Agustín, emerged from the stable. Rodolfo had charged them with the task of driving the Hernández family to San Sebastián, and though they immediately noticed their younger brother smarting from Rodolfo Hernández's assault, they showed Manolo no reaction.

At precisely ten thirty, the Hernández family finally began their journey. The coach pulled out first, followed by the trunk-laden wagon. As the horse-drawn vehicles slowly made their way out of the mansion through the winding dirt road, the rumbling of horse hooves, the squeaking of springs and the grinding of wheels against the dirt road, seemed like music to the poor souls left behind to oversee the mansion. One such poor soul was Manolo who stood watching the wagons. A long line of Ceiba trees flanked the dirt pathway on either side, its long, leafy branches extended outward so that opposing sides met at the center of the pathway, blotting out any glimpses of sunlight. Manolo could not open his left eye because of the swelling, but as he watched the wagons disappear into virtual darkness, he was grateful not to have received a flogging, for that was far worse than a punch to the face. As the coach and wagon disappeared from Manolo's view, he sensed his beloved sister standing behind him and spoke without turning around to face her. "Do not worry, Berta, I'm fine."

"I hate that miserable pig! Every time he comes to me I want to kill him!"

"You kill him, Berta, and you kill all of us," replied Manolo, slowly turning to face his sister. A sudden breeze rushed in the gentle, aromatic scent from the nearby garden. The flower garden, set to the side of the mansion, was Maria's pride and joy and on a windy day, the smell of ylang-ylang and ginger lilies was overpowering and hard to ignore.

Berta closed her eyes in despair when she noted Manolo's swollen face. "I've got to leave this hell, my brother. I just can't stand to be here any longer."

"What are you saying Berta? You cannot escape. They'll hunt you down and flog you until your skin bleeds raw." Manolo was shorter than his two brothers were, about the same height as Berta, but his body was compact and muscular. The short, curly brown hairs over his head gleamed with sweat, and droplets of perspiration streamed down his smooth black skin. As he took in the garden's fragrance with a disproportionate nose, he exhaled in frustration. Manolo loved his sister and he would do anything for her, but up until that very moment, he had never contemplated the idea of escaping. He cast his anxiety-filled ebony eyes at Berta and pursed his brown lips.

"That devil is planning to sell me to a cousin of his in Santo Domingo!" yelled Berta. "I don't want to be sold to anyone, Manolo. I'm no one's property. I am a human being! I am not an animal!" She felt Manolo's arms embracing her and placed her head on his chest, weeping uncontrollably. "It's not fair, Manolo. Why do they make us suffer like this? Who gave them the right to make us slaves? Why do they think they are better than us?"

"Hush now, Berta," said Manolo, stroking her back, trying to console her. "How serious are you about escaping?"

"Very serious, and I'm going to do it well before that monster returns. Will you come with me?" Berta looked at her older brother with hopeful eyes.

"You know that once we flee, we can never return," cautioned Manolo. "We will never see Mamíta and Papá again, or our two brothers. We will have to live off the earth, and times will be very hard for us. No one will take us in and word about our escape will spread throughout the island."

"We can take a boat and flee to an unpopulated island. We can even sail to America, where it is said they abolished slavery three years ago. Maybe an American ship will see us and take us in, it's worth a try."

"All right, Berta, I will join you," said Manolo. He, too, had suffered at the hands of his brutal master and he, too, had had enough. "The Hernández family will be gone for more than a month," Manolo said optimistically, "so we have plenty of time to gather food and plan an escape. We must tell our family of our plan and ask them to keep it a secret."

"You think that demon will take reprisals on Mamíta and Papá?"

"I don't know, Berta, and that's the reason why I want to tell them of our plan. I want their blessing, for without their blessing I'm not going anywhere."

Berta nodded and said, "All right, Manolo, let's go talk to them.

Manolo nodded, smiled and held his sister's hand while walking back to the mansion. All the time he wondered why his sister never questioned why her skin was so much lighter than that of her siblings, or that her hair grew long and lacy and unlike that of her family's hair. He remembered the day he found out the truth. Standing behind a thick oak tree, near the mansion one day, he heard his two older brothers talking privately. He listened and learned that on a rainy day in December, when Manolo was a two-year-old toddler and sleeping in a bed of hay next to a dwindling fire, Don Rodolfo Hernández had come around their wooden shack. He had fought with his wife earlier that day and had been in a drunken stupor that night. Rodolfo pounded on the weak door and broke it down after thrusting his body into it several times. Manolo's eldest brother, Candelario, who was seven-years-old, was the first to see Don Hernández. Ever fearful of Rodolfo's wrath, he pulled on his mother's arms, which were cradling his five-year-old brother, Agustín, but she did not wake.

Rodolfo stormed into the shack and grabbed Mamíta by her shoulders, shaking her arms loose of Agustín who then fell to the floor crying. With tears rolling down his face, Candelario rushed over to his brother and picked him up off the floor. As he rose to his feet, looking for a safe place to put his brother in, he never saw Don Hernández's foot, but felt it when it landed across his back, forcing him to crash down on the floor. Candelario's back was hurting badly but as he fell to the floor, he never let go of Agustín, who was still crying. While on the floor, he turned to the side and noted that his youngest brother, Manolo, was all right and sleeping on his bed comfortably. He looked at Don Hernández again and wished he had been a grown man so that he could fight and kill his master. Then he watched Don Hernández beat and rape his mother on that rainy night so many years ago. While being forced to witness his mother's agony, Candelario quickly understood the reason why two days earlier Don Hernández had lent his father out to Don Santana who lived in Camuy. As Candelario grew older, he realized that Don Hernández had ordered his father, Claudio, to Don Santana's plantation under the pretext of helping his friend out with his sugar cane harvest. In reality, Don Hernández had been planning Mamíta's rape all the time, volunteering Claudio's services so many times that Don Santana finally agreed just to shut him up. Waiting for the right moment, Don Hernández pounced on Candelario's mother, and nine months later, Berta was born. Upon Papá Claudio's return from Camuy, all Candelario could hear was his father crying and asking the Lord why? Manolo would never tell his sister that her real father was Don Hernández and not Claudio. If his mother and father and his two older brothers thought it was necessary to let Berta know, they would have said something years ago. Manolo saw no benefit in making Berta aware of it either but deep down inside, it hurt him to deceive his sister. And if Don Hernández would ever find out that he had been having sexual intercourse with his own daughter for more than two years…

CHAPTER 3

The coach and wagon rumbled along the dirt road and went past the main gate. Inside the coach, Laura sat next to Rodolfo facing Maria and her two sisters. While holding his cane in between his legs, Rodolfo masticated a worn out wad of tobacco. Gazing through the open window, his body vibrated to the coach's movement. As the coach turned right and onto the main road, Rodolfo reached into his jacket pocket and drew a clean, white handkerchief. All of a sudden, he stuck his head out the window, spat out the tasteless brown ball of tobacco and wiped his lips clean with his handkerchief. He slowly turned, sat up straight and noticed Maria looking aimlessly out of her window. His eyebrows furrowed for an instant and his mouth contorted to show his displeasure. "I told you never to wear that awful dress again; it makes you look old and fat!"

"Everything else was packed, Rodolfo, what else was I going to wear?"

"Oh stop it Maria, you had a lot of time to change. You wanted to wear that dress just to upset me because you know how much I hate that fucking dress! I have a mind to rip it off right now!"

"If that pleases you, Rodolfo then go ahead, do it!"

Rodolfo sighed and frowned, and then he turned his sights on Anita who was staring at him with vengeful eyes. "What are you looking at?" Anita said nothing and looked the other way. Rodolfo then narrowed his eyes at Laura. "I heard you three arguing again. What was it this time, the color of shoes or the size of a handbag? You three argue about the dumbest things, and the next time I hear another petty and pointless argument from you three, I am going to beat all of you. I'm tired of this nonsense. It's bad enough that I've got to run a business, let alone do your mother's work."

"I told them to stop arguing," yelled Maria in her defense. "What else could I do, it's not like they're little children!"

Rodolfo turned back to his wife, and widened his eyes to show his anger. "Don't raise your voice at me, Maria, you know better than that! When it comes to our children, you've always been a weakling. You have never gained the respect of your daughters, and now they do as they damn well please."

Rosalía did not look at her father, but her anger was growing steadily as he berated her mother. She wisely kept her mouth shut. In fact, all three daughters kept quiet, fully aware of the consequences of speaking without his addressing them first. She turned away and looked through her window. Anita, who was wedged in between Maria and Rosalía, also turned to look out the window from her mother's side of the coach.

"Why couldn't you have given me a son?" Rodolfo went on in frustration. "All you gave me was three daughters, three troublesome daughters!"

"That's not true, Father," interjected Laura, risking the act of speaking out of turn. "I've never given you any trouble."

Rodolfo chose to remain silent. The heat of the day was slowly rising and his face began to gleam with perspiration. After a long while, Rodolfo redirected his rage at Laura. "So, when is Don Sánchez planning to marry you? Is he ever going to marry you? Or will you become a spinster like your tía Angelica?"

"Of course he will, Father," replied Laura, unable to hide her sudden embarrassment; but she felt angry too, angry that her father had broached the subject of marriage in front of Anita and Rosalía. Custom on the island dictated that by the age of twenty-three, Laura was to have been married already, with a child or two. Laura put on her best face and rose above her anger and embarrassment. "He wrote to me and told me he will be arriving in November after his tour of duty is over in Santo Domingo."

"If he doesn't get himself killed," said Rodolfo. "We should have sent troops there years ago, before any hint of a revolution ever got started. We should have killed all of them, burned everything in sight and started over again. There are too many Africans there and the fucking island has turned to shit." Maria and her three daughters remained silent, allowing Rodolfo to spew his anger. "I hope for your sake that Captain Sánchez comes back alive. I hear the fighting is fierce over there and that Spain is just too slow to see what's going on."

Determined not to lose hope and not to reveal her anger, especially in front of her two sisters, Laura forced a smile at her father. "He is an able officer, Father, and he will claim his inheritance upon his return."

"By the grace of God, that is my one consolation, Laura. You've chosen well and I'm looking forward to meeting his family." Rodolfo glanced at his wife but ignored her as she looked out of her window. He turned to Anita, and with angry eyes said, "And what about that fool, Ana? When is he going to ask me for your hand? That weasel's been away for so long I can't remember the last time he came around the house or what he even looks like. Where the devil is he?"

Anita cleared her throat, turned slowly to face her father and replied nervously, fully aware that Laura was now smiling and gloating. "Father, you know very well that Ruben is in Cuba. I told you that I wanted to stay home because he will be arriving on Wednesday. But since you insisted that we should all go with you to San Sebastián, he will come to the house and find it empty."

"So! All he has to do when he gets to the house is ask one of my prietos where we've gone. Then he should place his skinny ass on his horse and ride to San Sebastián. Or has he no cojónes to face me?"

Anita sighed, wanting to cuss at her father for making her suffer so many years with his verbal abuse, but she took her time and allowed her anger to subside. But even if she had dared to vent her anger out on her father, she knew it would not have changed his mind at all. "Of course Father, he will do just that," she replied gracefully. "He will find out where we have gone then ride to San Sebastián, I'm sure of it."

Rodolfo grunted and then finally turned to his youngest child. "Rosalía, my pretty Rosalía, don't follow in your sisters' footsteps. I will see to it that once your preliminary schooling is complete here in Puerto Rico that you enroll at the University of Madrid. Then I will make certain you marry a nobleman. You, my dear child, will not disappoint me!"

Across Rosalía, Laura's pale green eyes, festering with hatred and jealousy, beamed at her youngest sister. How could Father dote on such a whimpering child? Out of all three children, Laura physically resembled her father the most, and even her stout personality was like that of Rodolfo's. Why her father chose to ignore something so obvious was a mystery to her. From that moment on, Laura decided that Rosalía was her enemy. She would strive to bring her youngest sister down from that pedestal upon which her father had placed her since birth. Laura would make Rosalía a total disappointment in her father's eyes and she would wait for an opportunity to ambush her like a snake in the ground.

No one said a word for the next hour until the rumbling coaches finally reached the shore. As soon as they arrived at the calm shores of San Juan Bay, the Hernández family entered a boat that would ferry them across the bay to Cataño, where they would finally take up residence for the night at Casa Jimenez.

That night, while Rodolfo drank rum in the company of Don Jimenez, Maria sat on the bed and pouted. She knelt before her bed, holding her rosary beads tightly, and prayed for a long while. Unable to purge her misery and humiliation through prayer, she cried at hearing Rodolfo's cruel words repeatedly in her mind. Maria slowly rose to her feet, and in a fit of anger, ripped her dress to shreds.

In the room next to Maria's, Rosalía lay still in her bed. In the silence of the bedroom, she could hear her mother ripping her dress and crying. Anita was on the bed next to hers, sleeping, and Rosalía turned to the side to make sure she was still asleep. Rosalía turned again, and in the bed across from her, she confronted two eyes staring right back at her. A tear rolled down Rosalía's young cheeks.

"Stop crying, you sniveling brat!" whispered Laura. "Why do you cry for her? Father was right. Mother is nothing but a weakling, and let us be truthful: her choice of clothes today was utterly ridiculous. It was all her doing. Now she sits in her room weeping and ripping her dress like a spoiled child, a dress she knew she shouldn't have worn."

"Oh shut your mouth, Laura!" answered Rosalía, wiping her cheeks. "How can you say that? Why is it that you have no respect for the woman that bore you, fed you, cared for you and loves you? Mother looked just fine in her dress today! Father is the one who hates that dress. It's *always* Father!" Anita turned in bed and moaned several times but she never woke up. Having made sure again that Anita was still asleep Rosalía glared at Laura. "Doesn't he have enough on his mind ruling over his financial empire that he must rule over our lives as well? Must he have the final decision on what we wear, eat and do?"

"If that is his wish, then as the head of the family, it is his prerogative. It is because of Father that you enjoy a privileged life, Rosa, or would you rather be a peasant jornalera, a jíbara from the mountains?"

Rosalía, unafraid, fired right back her oldest sister. "If it means that I can make my own decisions and live my life how I please, then I would rather be a peasant."

"You don't know what you're saying, you're just a child! You don't know what it is to live in poverty."

"And what, do you?"

"No," Laura replied defensively.

"So why do you talk about it as if you're an authority on the subject?"

"I do not know what it is to live in poverty, but I don't have to be an authority on the subject to understand it. I have gone on many trips into the hinterland, Rosalía, and I have seen the harsh realities of poverty. Believe me, Rosa, when you see the things I have been a witness to, you will be grateful that we are on the other side of society. So be thankful that Father is the way he is because he is making sure that we do not end up on the poor side."

"Father is the way he is because of his greed and nothing more."

Laura grew incensed at how callously Rosalía characterized her father, and she could not believe what she was hearing. "You should speak of Father in that way, Rosa, you of all people? You're the one he dotes on, yet you have the nerve to talk so bad about him?"

"It's the truth."

"The truth? The truth is that if I had my father's eye, I would make the best of it. The truth is that you're an ingrate and that is why you will displease Father greatly. The day will come, I'm sure of it."

Refusing to continue their nocturnal conversation, Rosalía shook her head and whispered, “Good night, Laura.” She turned around, pulled the bed sheet over her head and closed her eyes.

CHAPTER 4

Miguel Pítre's only moment of happiness out of his long and torturous day, occurred while standing atop a hill, just minutes before sunrise. Every day he would rise at four in the morning and don his usual garbs—an ensemble consisting of nothing more than a pair of soiled white trousers, a filthy and odorous shirt, and a rickety straw *pava* that barely offered protection from the searing heat of the day. Walking barefoot along the soft, red soil of his father's leased *finca*, he would head straight for the corral. After milking their only cow, collecting a handful of fresh eggs from the henhouse and feeding the pigs, he would grind a handful of coffee beans and brew the first pot of the morning. Before beginning the real work of the day, Miguel Pítre would climb to the summit of a neighboring hill—a green mound that rose steadily before his shanty home—to gaze across the ebon skies and spend just a few moments in meditation.

On the summit of the hill there was a large, partially exposed, rock. Miguel would stand on that rock and breathe in the morning dew, the smell of nearby pine trees, and the aroma of thousands of plants that graced the fourteen *cuerdas* of land earmarked for the cultivation of coffee beans. Veiled by the darkness of night, Miguel could not see the land but he could still feel its presence, as if it were close to him, as if it were a living creature needing attention, love and respect. During those peaceful, solitary interludes, brief as they often were, he would take a moment or two to pray. As the coquís and crickets sang their nocturnal music, he would beg the Lord to make this year's harvest bountiful enough to earn them lots of money so that his father could pay off most, if not all, of the debt owed to the proprietor of the land.

At twenty years of age, Miguel Pítre stood five feet ten and his robust body was the result of years of harsh mountain farming. He was a creole, the son of Juan Pítre and the grandson of Bonifacio Pítre.

Grandfather Pítre was born in 1787, in Catalonia, Spain. When Bonifacio's father died, he inherited enough money with which to make his lifelong dream a reality, and that dream was the New World. He sailed to western Puerto Rico, bought land from the Spanish government and settled in Mayagüez to begin a new life as a farmer. Within three years, he sold the land at a profit and moved east, resettling in San Sebastián at the age of 24. He purchased fifty-two cuerdas of the best fertile land in that part of western Puerto Rico, and later married Dorotea Ramirez. Seven years later, in 1818, their only son, Juan Pítre, was born.

During the 1820's and early part of the 1830's, the Pítre family was so well rooted on the island and had become one of the wealthiest in San Sebastián that there was talk of making Bonifacio the *Alcalde*. Nothing in Juan Pítre's mind, however, could have foreseen the tragedies that would befall his family just a few years later.

In the summer of 1838, Bonifacio and Dorotea fell victims to the Cholera epidemic and died quickly, leaving the twenty-year-old Juan Pítre the sole heir to the estate. Three years later, the Cholera epidemic had spread beyond San Sebastián and had ravaged the workforce necessary to run the fifty-two cuerdas of land. By 1850, Juan Pítre had no choice but to sell large chunks of his property in order to satisfy the enormous debt he had incurred while his land remained idle. By 1860, when Miguel was 12 years old, Juan Pítre sold the last fourteen cuerdas in his possession to Don Rodolfo Hernández, and then began leasing the land from him. Over the next eight years, Juan grew very poor and had grown to rely on the meager harvest of coffee beans his little farm produced.

That was the only world Miguel Pítre had ever known in February of 1868.

In every sense of the word, Miguel and Juan Pítre were the quintessential jíbaros. There were thousands of such jíbaros in the western part of Puerto Rico, from Camuy to Lares, from Mayagüez to

Ponce, and from Utuado to San Sebastián. The jíbaro was a poor farmer, a creole, mostly uneducated and dependent on whatever he could sell at the market. Jíbaros planted all sorts of crops, from *yucca* to *ñame, platano, batata* and *guineo, yautia*, coffee, red and white beans, and so on. From their far away farms, they loaded their donkeys and wooden wagons with their harvested crops and traveled on a dirt road. The rocky, uneven thoroughfare, carved out over the years by wagons and mule trains, ran for many winding miles and led them to the pueblo's market where they sold their bounty to shop owners or directly to the miniscule number of cash-paying customers.

Jíbaros lived a hard life and by the sweat of their brow became the backbone of Puerto Rico's small and insignificant agricultural economy. Their hands were rough and calloused, and their skins were tanned dark by a sixteen-hour workday, exposed to an unforgiving, tropical sun. Their days were long and their nights were short, but they willingly gave up their hearts and souls to the never-ending quest of a good harvest, for without it they would cease to exist. Jíbaros lived mostly in shacks built of wood and covered by flimsy roofs. There were no doors in front of their houses and no private rooms in which to sleep. Their latrines were just a few feet away from the house and on a windy day, the foul odors of human excrement blanketed all breathable air.

Once a month, in the barrio of Pepinos, jíbaros, slaves and freed people of color gathered at the Comisario's hall to socialize. Musicians brought *maracas, güiros, cuatros* and guitars and sang *Aguinaldos.* The music had been evolving over the years into a fusion of Spanish and African rhythms that became distinctive to the people; it had become their outlet, their way of releasing their blues and their way to forget about their harsh existence for a brief moment. They danced, drank beer or rum and joked all night long. During those intervals of refuge, they would forget about debts owed to peninsulares, forget that once they were the original owners of their land, and forget that hunger and depravity of sleep were their main staples in life. The Comisario's hall was their oasis, a private place where they could come to free their minds of worries and anxieties. But no matter how much they danced and sang, they could never completely forget their desperate situations.

Eventually they would have to return to their homes and in the morning begin their work all over again.

Atop the hill, Miguel Pítre stood still for a long moment, taking in a deep breath of mountain air. He smiled, and as he exhaled, he nodded approvingly. Today would not be as hot as yesterday. Though Miguel had no access to the prognostication of weather, he just felt it would not be hot. Living on the farm for all of his life, his body seemed to sense these things, as if he had melded souls with the land, as if he and the land had become one.

He trained his green eyes down the hill and toward his home, where he saw his father emerging with a lantern in hand. The skies were starting to brighten by now and Miguel slowly prepared himself for the worst. Today, he was to take the mule out and plow the four cuerdas of land to the extreme left of the farm, the ones next to Don Rafael Blanco's farm. If there was one thing Miguel hated most, it was plowing land. His feet would sink into the deep red soil and his trousers would get wet with ground moisture, but those were just minor inconveniences. Candela was the real reason why Miguel hated plowing day; the mere thought of it would always give him the jitters. The temperamental mule often refused to work and sometimes would kick fiercely, whinny and grunt ferociously. As Miguel turned upward to gaze at the star-filled skies, he sighed heavily and nodded again. He had to do it. There was nobody else.

A light breeze suddenly rushed in from the north and gently stroked the swirls of curly, light-brown hair on Miguel's round head. Patches of scraggily reddish-brown whiskers filled certain parts of his face, and though Miguel tried to grow a full beard since he turned seventeen, he found that even an experienced farmer couldn't do that.

As he made his way down the hill, Miguel remembered the image of his mother and the last time he saw her. Miguel was ten years old when he heard the last argument between his mother and father. Rosario hated the country, despised farming and blamed Juan Pítre every day for her miserable existence. Rosario and Juan argued frequently and sometimes their arguments would turn physical, knocking to the floor what little furniture they possessed. She would throw plates at Juan, pots and pans or anything she could get her hands on just to make him feel her pain. Juan would grab her hands to stop her from breaking things but she would free herself and slap him or dig her nails into his face. Despite her physical abuse, Juan would never lay a hand on her because somehow he understood her misery; somehow, he felt the same anger and the same hurt. In the end, there was nothing he could do stop her from leaving him. Rosario blamed him for selling the land at such discounts and for not having the sense and courage to seek financial aid from banks or even the government. She could never understand the government's reluctance to recognize creoles as true Spanish citizens; or the fact that banks would always manage to come up with an excuse to reject their loan applications. Rosario never understood that all the Spanish merchants wanted was to squeeze the creoles out of everything they owned. Juan could never make it clear to Rosario that the odds of survival were stacked heavily against them. Finally, on a rainy and dank day, Rosario vanished. Several weeks later, Juan received a letter post-marked out of San Juan. In the letter Rosario explained her reasons for abandoning Juan and Miguel, but at ten years old, Miguel could not comprehend his mother's reasoning. All he was able to understand was that his mother was not going to be there for him and he hated her for that. By the age of twenty though, he had reconsidered his position and finally understood why Rosario had left San Sebastián. For one whole year, Rosario wrote weekly. Then she met a man and her letters became less frequent until one day they stopped arriving. Juan and Miguel knew exactly where, in San Juan, Rosario had taken up residence, but neither of them bothered to go see her. It wasn't because they were angry with her for abandoning them, but for other reasons. For Juan Pítre, it was the mere thought of seeing his ex-wife again and re-opening the old wounds in his heart. He still loved her, but he could not bear to see her again and not be able to hold her in his arms in the same manner as he dreamed every night. He could not stand the notion of seeing her with another man, either, a thought that gnawed at him constantly. For Miguel it was the simple fact that over the years he had lost the image of his mother. Rosario had long ago severed the maternal connection with her son and the damage was irreparable. Miguel could no longer recall the tone of her voice or recollect in detail her personality, and to Miguel, Rosario was just another woman.

The elder Pítre poured milk into his cup of coffee and waited patiently for Miguel. He sat on an old school chair that he had found on the street last year. He brought the chair home with the intentions of repairing it but Juan never had the time to fix it, and so it stood right where he had left it in the front porch a year ago. Juan tilted his head backwards and gazed at the brightening, cobalt skies. He pinned his head against the wall's uneven wooden planks and allowed the chips of white paint to fall on his graying hair. Then he straightened himself and placed the cup on top of a rickety wooden crate that served as a table. He knew that Miguel had been up on the hill and he would always give his son that 'alone' time, never even brought up the subject or made arguments to the contrary.

As he approached his father, Miguel took notice of his graying hair and the hump starting to form on his back. At fifty, Juan Pítre was far too young to look so old. "Buenos Dias, Pápi. I think you should go back to sleep and let me handle the work today. You look very tired."

"Nonsense, I cannot let you do it alone," replied Juan with a smile. "Come and sit next to your old man." He waved his hand at Miguel, beckoning his son toward him. "Besides, you know Candela's a nasty and lazy bastard."

"I don't think he's lazy," replied Miguel optimistically. "He just needs to be coaxed into working."

"You know what I think?" said Juan grinning. "I think Candela needs a woman!" He turned to Miguel and both men laughed. Their echoes of laughter carried far in the silence of the morning and for a brief moment seemed to drown out the nightly duet sung by thousands of coquís and crickets.

Miguel picked up a cup and poured coffee as the sun slowly rose and began to peek over the hill. Juan took another sip of his coffee and gazed across the brightening field. "I was planning to go to the pueblo tonight."

"Why?"

"Because today is Tuesday, Miguelito, and you know what we do on the first Tuesday of every month! Everyone's going to be there, aren't you going?" He watched Miguel frown and shake his head. "Why do you never go to these social events?"

"I'm meeting Carlos Peña tonight."

"I told you not to get mixed up with that slave, didn't I?"

"Pápi, Carlos is not a slave. He is a freed man and he is my friend."

"Carlos Peña is nothing but trouble, Miguel, and you should steer clear away from him." Juan never raised his voice at his son and never had much cause to admonish him not even when Miguel was a boy, but seeing his son associating with the likes of Carlos Peña frightened him to no end.

Miguel had never argued with his father. He respected and loved his father very much and he would never do anything to hurt him. At the same time, though, he could not understand why his father always seemed edgy at the mere mention of Carlos's name or why he reacted so negatively at the idea of his befriending the former slave. It was an unsettling feeling for Carlos, too, causing him to limit the number of visits to the Pítre farm. "Why do you hate Carlos so much, Pápi? Is it because of the color of his skin?"

"Miguelito, you know I'm not that way. Though I had plenty of opportunities and though your mother wished that I had, I never owned a slave. That's not the reason." Juan placed his cup down on the wooden crate next to the pot and leaned back on his chair.

"What is the reason then?" insisted Miguel. "Carlos has made the most of his freedom. He has educated himself, he can read and write and he is very wise. He has taught me how to read and write and for that I am grateful."

"Carlos Peña is a good man, I do agree with you," Juan answered quickly. "I cannot blame you for wanting to establish a close relationship with him, but Carlos Peña is a very dangerous man. He is part of that rebel group led by Manuel Rojas—you know the one I'm talking about."

"No, Pápi, I don't," replied Miguel.

Juan Pítre gazed at his son and searched his green eyes for truth. Miguel's eyes were the same color as those of Rosario's and when Juan looked at Miguel he couldn't help but to see the image of his ex-wife, a woman he still loved with all of his heart. Juan took a long moment to study his son's face until he convinced himself that Miguel had no idea of what he was talking about. "Carlos Peña is a dangerous revolutionist," Juan clarified in a fatherly tone. "There is talk in the pueblo that he is forming his own rebel cell in the barrio of Pepinos, and he is doing it with the blessings of Manuel Rojas and that Mathias Brugman fellow."

"Pápi, I don't know any of the names you've mentioned and I don't get their connection to Carlos."

"Well you should, Miguelito, because they are dangerous people." Juan leaned forward to pick up his cup again, and slowly sipped the dark, steaming liquid. Without turning to face his son, Juan spoke his mind. "And the ring leader is none other than Dr. Betances."

"Is he the one who was exiled to Spain?"

"Yes, but he is not in Spain. He and his partner fled to Santo Domingo, where they created the Revolutionary Committee of Puerto Rico. They have agents here dedicated to Puerto Rico's independence by violent means, if necessary. Carlos Peña is one of their agents, and he's been given the task of creating a new cell right here in San Sebastián."

Miguel rubbed his chin out of curiosity. "How do you know all this?"

"José Morales invited me to a late night meeting in Lares, where I heard Manuel Rojas speak the words of revolution. It was there that I learned how big the movement is and how dangerous it can become not only to them, but to all of us as well. I saw Carlos Peña that night, too. Rojas himself introduced Carlos as one of the new leaders of the rebel movement. So please, do your old man a favor and stay away from Carlos Peña."

"Pápi, take a look around you, I mean take a good look. What do you see?" said Miguel, leaning forward, trying to get his father to look at him. Juan remained steadfast and gazed across his plantation. "What do you see, Pápi?"

"I see nothing but a field that needs tending to."

"You know what I see? I see a vast field of fertile land that once belonged to the Pítre family. I see how the high tax burden and terrible trade deficits have forced the Pítres and other creole families like us to sell their lands and become dependent on Spain. I see how the people of Puerto Rico have no say in the governing of their own land. I see—"

"You see nothing! That's Carlos Peña talking, not you!"

"No, Pápi, I don't need Carlos Peña to put words in my mouth. I can think for myself. I can see for myself."

"Please, Miguelito, tell me you haven't gone to those meetings. Tell me you're not a member of a rebel cell or anything of the like, please."

"Why have you become so complacent?" Miguel said disappointedly. "Why have you chosen to live under these poor conditions and why do you stand so vehemently opposed to change? Please tell me, Father, why is it that you refuse to stand up for your rights as a human being? Is that what you want me to do? The answer to your question is no. I have not received an invitation from Carlos. Honestly, I don't know any of the names you mentioned, except for Betances, and Carlos Peña has never raised the topic of revolution with me. Look, Pápi, all we do is talk. When we get together, Carlos has me read books and newspapers. He has me write extensively and then corrects my grammar. He's been a good friend to me and I will always appreciate that."

Juan finally turned to Miguel and placed a hand on his shoulder. "Beware of strangers bearing gifts, my son." Juan slowly rose to his feet and looked down at his son. "Come, Miguelito, we've got a lot of work to do today and time's a wasting."

CHAPTER 5

Carlos Peña was blacker than most Africans on the island. His nappy hair was grotesquely unkempt, and his teeth were so white that anyone could see them in the dead of night with but the faintest of light. His six-foot-four frame held a lanky body, and most peninsulares who did not have the honor of knowing him, at first sight, thought him a spent slave, a beast of burden that had run its useful course. Contrary to his outward appearance, though, Carlos Peña was a strong man, imbued with a never-ending passion for life. Endowed with a wide nose, large brown lips and a deep voice, Carlos stood out in a crowd much like a lighthouse in the midst of a dense fog. But when he spoke, all manners of ill will one might have thought against him because of his outward appearance ceased immediately. Over the years, Carlos developed a strong vocabulary and tirelessly worked on his speech until he no longer spoke creole slang but perfect Spanish. Dwelling on an island-colony dominated by European settlers, his flawless diction and sophisticated palaver drew immediate attention not only from his creole counterparts but also from astounded peninsulares. Neither creole nor peninsular would ever know that Carlos Peña was a self-taught man who had struggled all of his life to destroy the shackles of slavery, to become a free man in every sense of the word.

Ten years earlier, a twenty-nine year old Carlos Peña had saved enough money to buy his freedom off the Peña plantation in Arecibo. He toiled on the sugar cane plantation all day but toward late afternoon, after Master Peña's reaping of the fields, Carlos would pick up the scraps of canes left on the ground. With a sharp machete that he kept hidden below a Ceiba tree near the Peña hacienda, Carlos would chop the long stalks into foot-long canes. Then he would fill several straw bags with the precious merchandise and strap them over his shoulders before traveling into town to sell his bounty. As if leaving the plantation without permission from his master and without his papers was not risky enough, his undercutting the price of a sugar cane incurred the wrath of many stand-owners at the market. But since Carlos would always arrive minutes before closing time, it wasn't worth their efforts to stop him. After selling his products, he would risk a visit to Doctor Mauricio Ortega's home. Dr. Ortega was a known abolitionist who also risked his life by teaching African slaves and freed people how to read and write. Carlos, by far, had been his brightest student, but there was something more between student and teacher. There was mutual respect and admiration, and both men struck an amiable friendship, a strong bond that would last for many years. Within a year, Carlos had become so proficient in Spanish that he stopped visiting the doctor and decided to continue his education on his own. Over the next five years, he had accumulated enough money with which to buy his freedom but when his master suddenly died of influenza his hopes for freedom quickly vanished.

Upon the death of his master, Carlos Peña learned that the magistrate planned to sell him and ship him to Camuy. On the night before Carlos was to travel, an overseer, jobless because of Master Peña's death, stormed into Carlos's shack and bound him. Then, while Carlos watched, the overseer ransacked his shanty home and stole his life's savings. The next day, while still bound, Carlos noticed that the overseer had left the plantation. Though he tried desperately to loosen his bindings and escape before the authorities arrived, he found that he could not free himself. On the way to Camuy and uncertain of his future then, he prayed to God that his new master would not be as vicious and cruel as his former master was. To his great surprise, Carlos ended his travel at a small farm in Camuy, a ten-cuerda estate recently purchased by none other than his old friend, Doctor Mauricio Ortega. When he saw Carlos, Dr. Ortega immediately granted him his freedom but the proud Carlos Peña refused the offer. Instead, he told Dr. Ortega that he would give him an honest day's work for an honest day's wages, and when he had accumulated enough money, he would legitimately buy off his freedom. The doctor quickly agreed, and one year later,

Carlos Peña became a free man. Leaving Camuy, Carlos Peña traveled to San Sebastián where he heard there were many coffee plantations that desperately needed jornaleros. He came to work on Don Santiago Duran's plantation, a stretch of 40 cuerdas adjacent to Don Rafael Blanco's plantation, which, in turn, ran parallel to the Pítre farm.

The February sun was riding toward its midday position when Carlos Peña, sitting atop his horse, took a moment to rest his steed. His dark eyes spanned the breadth of the Duran plantation and captured sight of a great number of Africans working the land. Sadly, they were still slaves. He closed his eyes briefly and shook his head. The scene reminded him of the time when he was a child growing up on the Peña plantation, a perpetual nightmare from which he had finally awoken. He could almost hear the women on the field singing songs from their homeland as they chopped down sugar canes with their machetes. Turning to the side, he could see the image of an overseer sitting on his horse like an army general inspecting his troops. A leather whip tied to the saddle, and a pistol tucked into the waist of his trousers gave him all the authority and respect he required. Turning to the other side of the field, his mind flashed images of a young Carlos with his arms wrapped around a tree and hands bound by a rope. He could see the fourteen-year-old Carlito's back, exposed, gleaming from sweat and receiving twenty lashes for not fulfilling his quota of sugar canes. Carlos Peña closed his eyes, almost feeling the stinging pain of those lashes upon his back, remembering that day as clear as if it had happened yesterday. But that was a long time ago, and now he was a free man.

He took great comfort that Don Santiago Duran was a good man, who never beat any of his slaves, but Don Santiago Duran was still a slave owner and despite Carlos truly liking the man, the fact that he still exploited African men and women was a source of discomfort, like a rose thorn impaled on a finger. Over the past ten years, Don Santiago Duran came to rely heavily on Carlos Peña. He had given Carlos the task of overseeing the fieldwork and traveling into town with wagonloads of his precious harvest of coffee beans. Santiago Duran had no children because his wife had run off with another man twenty years earlier and he vowed never to marry again. He was not a rich man, but, at the very least, he was debt-free and beholden to no peninsular on the island. In fact, Santiago Duran was a stubborn hacendado who refused to sell his land and despised the way Spaniards treated creoles.

It was through Don Santiago Duran that Carlos Peña became a revolutionist. He would spend hours sitting on the porch, listening to Duran's fiery opposition to Spanish rule and discussing Puerto Rico's future. At fifty-six, Duran suffered terribly from arthritis and he could barely move his hands or even walk without the use of a cane. He hated living like an invalid but his passion for farming never died and with the valuable help of his African jornalero, he was able to continue with his life-long work. Many times, he wished he were twenty years younger so that he could join the revolutionary committee, but more often than not, he settled on living vicariously through Carlos Peña and his involvement with the rebel forces. Every day, the two men would sit on the porch and discuss the movement's daily activities. Carlos would brief Santiago on the progress they were making, and both men would dream about the day their work would bear fruit.

Carlos Peña spurred his horse into a light trot and rode back to the Hacienda Duran. As usual, Don Santiago Duran sat on a wicker chair, smoking a cigar and waiting patiently for his valued employee. Carlos reined in and the horse grunted several times, cocking its head before it stopped. The tall African nodded at Santiago and then dismounted quietly.

Santiago Duran took in a huge puff and blew out a thick, white smoke that lingered over his head for a while before dissipating into the humid air. "Come Carlos, tell me the news." Duran's hazel eyes followed Carlos's every movement. His fair skin, reddened by the blazing sun, was beginning to show lines of age, but the coffee planter paid no heed to any of that. In fact, ever since his wife disappeared from his life, he stopped caring about his appearance. He had blown up over the years until a prodigious belly prevented him from the simple task of tying his shoelaces.

Carlos tethered the horse to a post and slowly walked toward the porch. He sat on a wicker chair next to Santiago, stretching his face with a smile. "They did it."

"No, they didn't."

"Yes they did, Don Santiago, they certainly did."

Santiago Duran's mouth widened at first, and then, genuinely revealing his enthusiasm, a hearty laugh bellowed from the depths of his enormous belly. "They made you a leader! I cannot believe it! That *is* good news! Go get that bottle of rum, Carlos, today we will celebrate."

Carlos slowly rose from his chair and disappeared into the house. Moments later, he returned holding a brown jug in one hand and two glasses in the other. He poured the rum into both glasses and handed a drink to Santiago. The old man slowly and painfully rose to his feet, took the glass, raised it and smiled. "Here's to the success of your cell, Carlos, good luck!" The men drank several shots of rum before sitting back on their wicker chairs to contemplate the field and celebrate their recent success. "I know several men, right here in San Sebastián, that are ready to commit to the cause," uttered Duran. "I will give you their names and where you can find them." Carlos nodded and said nothing, but Santiago immediately noticed his reticence. "What is it? What's bothering you, Carlos?"

Carlos turned to Santiago, raising his bushy eyebrows. "I had rather hoped you would allow the men here to join my cell."

Santiago frowned. "You mean the slaves, don't you? Carlos, you know I cannot do that. You know that without them, I cannot farm the land. If I cannot farm the land, I cannot sell coffee beans. And if I'm unable to produce my only source of income, then I cannot afford to pay the taxes imposed by the government or pay you the wages you so much deserve."

"And if our mission succeeds, Don Santiago, what then?"

"If our mission succeeds, then we will never again be forced into giving up nearly all of our income in taxes. It would mean that I could truly afford to free all of your African brothers and sisters on the plantation and pay them their just wages. That is why your role as a leader is so important, Carlos, because you must see the cause through to completion." Don Santiago Duran smoked the last of his cigar and flung the butt into the brush by the side of the house. He took several moments to study his protégé, but he could not discern what Carlos was thinking. "Trust me on this, Carlos."

"I would like to, Don Santiago, truly I would, but I've been made to believe many things over the years only to be disappointed in the final analysis. How can I be sure?"

"Well that's a fine question to ask me. I have been good to you, and you know that. You also know that I have been kind to all of the slaves here, on the plantation. By God, Carlos, have I not shown you what I'm all about?"

"Yes, Don Santiago, you have done that on many occasions, but you are still a business man and a slave owner. Parting with slaves is not an easy thing for a hacendado to do."

"That is true, Carlos, very true. However, I am willing to make that commitment because I strongly believe in a free and independent Puerto Rico. I believe in my heart that *all* men should be free. And when the time comes, and I do pray it does, I promise I will free all of them."

Carlos Peña looked at Don Santiago Duran and sensed his honesty. Other than Don Mauricio Ortega, his mentor and educator, there was no other man on earth he trusted. Although he liked Santiago Duran, he felt he could not fully trust him or any other creole for that matter. Suffering the indignities of abuse, persecution and brutality at the hands of those associated with the malignancy of slavery, had sharpened Carlos's cynicism. He discovered early on in life that he could never be free of that deep-seated sense of pessimism and mistrust. No one was above suspicion, and that foreboding sense of distrust had hardened his heart against all creoles and made nebulous all manners of sound judgment on seemingly benevolent people. Santiago Duran might well have been one of those honest and selfless people, but Carlos could not bring himself to place his faith entirely in him. "Do not make promises you can't keep, Don Duran."

Santiago leaned forward with difficulty and grimaced in pain as he picked up the brown jug and poured into both glasses. He handed Carlos his glass and said, "I know you've lived a hard life and I can certainly understand why you're so distrustful. But you're just going to have to trust me, Carlos, that's all I can say to you."

"All right, Don Santiago, we shall take it one day at a time. Now tell me about the men you spoke of, are they reliable?"

CHAPTER 6

By five in the afternoon, Miguel had completed plowing the last cuerdas of land. Tomorrow he would plant as many seeds as possible and hope for a good harvest. It turned out that Candela had cooperated all day and not once did he fight Miguel. Miguel was grateful for that.

Miguel Pítre unhitched the plow and walked Candela back to the stable. He picked up a handful of hay and tossed it on the ground next to Candela's hooves. Miguel was tired and felt uncharacteristically sleepy, and as he watched Candela eat his meal, he yawned. He never realized that his father had been standing just a few feet away, contemplating him.

"You're a good son," said Juan, admiringly.

Startled for a split second, Miguel turned to face his father. "I didn't know you were here, Pápi. Should I go get the seeds?"

"No," said Juan shaking his head. "You've done enough for today. I'm going to get dressed. Have you changed your mind?"

"No, Pápi. There's nothing for me in town."

"What are you talking about? There are many young women in the pueblo. You're twenty-years-old, and by now you should be looking for a woman."

"Pápi, I'm just not in the mood. I'm tired and I don't feel like going to the pueblo tonight. Besides, I just don't feel like carrying my libreta into town and having it inspected by a snot-nosed government lackey."

"We all have to carry our libretas—it is the way of things," replied Juan sadly. Then he nodded, resigning to the notion that he could not convince Miguel otherwise. "All right, then please get some rest."

Before Juan Pítre could take a step toward the house, his eyes caught sight of a tall, dark figure silhouetted against the setting sun. The figure was that of a man atop his horse, and he was trotting slowly toward the

Pítre field. Juan Pítre froze for an instant, but then he quickly turned around to face his son. "What the devil is that man doing here? Doesn't he have anywhere else to go?"

"Stop it, Pápi."

"Why? Is it because I don't want you to associate with that man? Is it because you don't want to know the truth?"

"Pápi, what *is* the truth?"

"Don't get me started, Miguel, not now, not in front of that man." Juan desperately feared for his son's safety and he would do anything to prevent him from joining any rebel cell.

"What *is* the truth?" insisted Miguel, eyes aimed directly at his father.

"The truth is that you're going to get yourself in trouble, and that the Spanish government will capture, torture and hang you for sedition. That…is the truth! The truth is that these so-called rebels have no clue of what they're doing or of the consequences of their actions. There is not an ounce of common sense in any of them! If they had any common sense, they wouldn't even think about a revolution."

"That is your version of the truth, not mine," countered Miguel. "The truth, the reality is that you're afraid to take a stand. The truth is that you would prefer to live a subservient existence under the Spanish, rather than take matters into your own hands and do something about it. The truth is that our people are suffering at the hands of ruthless peninsulares and that the Spanish government is working in concert with those goddamn vultures. Look how we live, Pápi! I have only one pair of shoes and two sets of clothing. I use one set for work and the other for church. We never have any money and sometimes we go hungry for days. Our home is a wooden shack that can barely stand and we spend all day on a field that hardly produces anything of value. The truth is that the peninsulares are choking us to the point of death. There is no compassion whatsoever and they keep squeezing us!"

"That's enough!" yelled Juan. His voice was so loud that even Carlos, who was several hundred feet away, could hear it.

Miguel's eyes enlarged out of sudden shock. That was the first time his father had ever yelled at him and it did not sit too well with him.

Miguel lowered his head and trained his eyes on the ground. "Forgive me, Pápi. I didn't mean to upset you."

Juan blinked twice and sighed, immediately regretting his outburst. "Miguelito, I understand how you feel, and I know how difficult it is to live like this, especially for a young man. Your notion of independence, though, however noble as it may seem, will only serve to get you jailed or killed. I do not want that to happen to you. You are my only treasure and if you are killed, my life will end."

"But Pápi, there is no other way."

"Yes there is," replied Juan with a glimmer of hope. "You say that Carlos has been teaching you, right?" He watched Miguel nod affirmatively. "Then take that education and build upon it. Get into politics and become a representative at the Cortes in Madrid, and then get your independence through diplomacy."

"But Pápi, that takes time and money, and we have neither of the two. Besides, we have sent many representatives to Madrid and nothing ever changes. Diplomacy simply does not work."

"And so what, revolution does?"

"It worked for the United States, didn't it?"

"Yes but at a great cost, and besides, they had help from France."

"We could get help."

"Now who would want to help us?" said Juan skeptically.

"The United States would. I'm sure we could send a delegation to Washington and plea our case to the President."

"So why don't you do it now?"

"Because we must show the United States that we have succeeded in our revolt. Upon the success of our revolt, we will create a provisional government so that they can recognize our independence. Only then will the United States help." Miguel took a moment to study his father just to see if he had changed his mind. By now, Carlos Peña's horse was so close that they could hear its thudding hooves.

Not wanting to argue or give away his position in front of Carlos Peña, Juan Pítre relented. "Just do me a favor, Miguelito. Before you do anything, please consult with me first."

"I promise I will, Pápi," said Miguel with an appreciative smile. He looked over his father's head and shouted. "Carlos! How are you my friend?"

Juan Pítre sighed, and with a smirk turned to face Miguel's friend. He nodded at Carlos and uttered, "Buenas Tardes, Don Peña?"

"Buenas Tardes, Don Pítre."

Juan Pítre nodded and then slowly walked back to the house.

As Carlos Peña dismounted, he turned to look at Miguel's father and noted the disappointment on his face, the lines of age more visible, and brown eyes filled with apprehension. He grabbed hold of the reins and walked his beast toward Miguel. "Is everything all right?"

"No Carlos."

"Sounds like you two were arguing—were you?"

"Yes. He thinks you're a dangerous man and feels that associating with you is going to get me killed. He thinks rebellion will not work."

Raising his dark, bushy eyebrows, Carlos nodded. "I see. He fears for you, Miguel. And if he is the way he is, it's because he loves you very much, so please, don't be too hard on your old man."

"I'm not, Carlos, I just want to make him understand is all."

"You can't," replied Carlos consolingly. "In this situation you are either for or against; there is no middle ground."

"So what can I do?"

"There is nothing else you can do that would change your father's mind right now. But after we succeed with the revolution, he will appreciate the fact that his son will have had a vital role in the reshaping of Puerto Rico's future. Until then, just let your father be."

"As usual, Carlos, you are the voice of reason. So, how did it go?"

"Are you ready?" asked Carlos, gleaming with excitement. "The council at Centro Bravo made me a leader."

"Are you kidding me?"

"No, Miguel, it's the honest truth! I have been instructed to organize a cell, right here in San Sebastián!"

Miguel's eyes lit up, and he jumped in the air. "Thank God! Carlos, I am so happy for you! Your dream has come true!"

"Not my dream, *our* dream, Miguel! *Our* dream!" shouted back Carlos. The two men embraced each other in brotherly love. Then Miguel pushed him back and with a set of curious green eyes, stared intensely at Carlos. "So who's going to be your second in command?"

Carlos folded his arms and looked up at the skies. "Hmm…I was thinking about Don Francisco Salazar. He's a good organizer and a fiery speaker."

Miguel frowned, openly displaying his disappointment, but never realizing Carlos was merely playing with him. "He's a good choice, Carlos, I'm sure you thought good and hard about him."

"Are you kidding, Miguel? Do you think I would choose fat man Salazar over you? Hell no, you are my second in command!"

Miguel's face stretched to reveal a handsome smile, a smile filled with relief. "I thought you were serious."

"I am. I want you."

"No, I meant I thought you were serious about Salazar."

"Come on, after all we've been through, do you honestly think I would have offended you like that? No, you are the logical choice. You know me and you know my politics. You and I think the same way and we are both revolutionists at heart. And if anything should happen to me, I would be happy to know that you are there to assume leadership of the cell. That is why I want you to go with me to Manuel Rojas's plantation in Lares. The council at Centro Bravo must know who you are."

"You want me to meet Rojas, *the* Rojas? My father will have a fit! I played it off that I did not know about Rojas or any of the rebels. He thinks Rojas is out of his mind."

"To live as we are currently living, we must all be out of our minds, Miguel."

"Indeed. So, when are we going to Lares?"

"Soon, but first I have to meet with several men in town tonight."

"You're going to the pueblo?"

"I'm not going to the celebration, if that's what you're thinking. No, I am meeting secretly with these men. They are friends of Santiago Duran and I have to enlist them as members of the cell. Want to come?"

"Oh yes, Carlos, yes!"

"But we must be careful," cautioned Peña. "The town is full of loyalists and peninsulares, so when we walk through San Sebastián, we must keep vigilant."

"How can you tell who's who?" Miguel asked.

Carlos smiled, as if he were a schoolmaster revealing a bottomless pit of tolerance at a child's innocent question. "How can I tell? I can tell by the look in their eyes. In time, you will come to discern that look, too, and that knowledge may serve to be the difference between life and death."

"Then teach me, Carlos."

"Indeed, I shall."

CHAPTER 7

Mathias Brugman had been riding for several hours with plans of reaching Lares by nightfall. Baldomero Baurer, the cell's secretary, rode alongside Brugman, and, as always, kept vigilant for enemies along the way. The cell's vice-president, Juan de Mata Terreforte, also rode in Brugman's company, along with another cohort named Pablo Antonio Beauchamp. The rebels, whose Corsican and Dutch ancestry had taken root in Mayagüez in the late 1700's, rode wide-eyed and with ears attuned to the faintest sounds of the forest, fully aware of how dangerous a journey they had undertaken.

In the midst of the rebel group were two very important men, and the sole reason why Brugman was so hard-pressed in arriving at Lares without incident. The two men of importance had arrived secretly at the port of Guánica in a boat that had departed Santo Domingo two days earlier, and their presence on the island of Puerto Rico had proven to be a stressful dilemma for Brugman and his associates. As members of the first revolutionary cell in Puerto Rico, however, they would fulfill their obligations and follow orders as true soldiers were supposed to do.

Mathias Brugman's strong hands held tightly to the reins of his horse as it climbed steep hills, crossed valleys, streams and creeks. His lean body had not suffered the hardships of a long journey by horse but his angular face, which sported a well-trimmed mustache, revealed the constant worries of a leader. Although his receding hairline gave away his age, his face still seemed to have a youthful appearance about it. Brugman kept his deep-set eyes trained on the path before him, concentrating deeply on the task ahead, eyes hardly blinking. Yet, as intense as his pupils seemed to appear, his light-brown eyes had a warm quality about them, as if radiating compassion and love. His eyebrows were short and thin and though his nose stood out, its prominence did not take away from his good looks.

The fifty-seven-year-old revolutionist was born on January 11, 1811 in New Orleans, Louisiana. His father, Pierre Brugman, was a native of Curacao, and his mother, Isabel Duliebre, was a native of Puerto Rico. Pierre and Isabel met in New Orleans, where they courted for a while and later married. At the time of their courtship, the Louisiana territory was under the rule of Spain. The Spaniards had held the region since 1762, the year in which France had ceded the land to the Iberians. To Pierre Brugman's dismay, Spanish rule did not last long because under the secret treaty of San Ildefonso, in 1800, Spain ceded control of the territory back to France.

By the turn of the 19th century, there were many Spanish citizens living among French nationals in New Orleans. Undaunted, the Brugmans decided that the growing coastal city would prove ideal for rearing and educating their children. Their children would learn Spanish from their mother and he would teach them French. But in 1803, the United States purchased the Louisiana territory from France and everything changed dramatically for the Brugmans. Though Pierre and Isabel made a reasonable attempt at living under a new government, they found that coping with a new language and a rapidly changing culture proved more difficult than they had anticipated. Finally, Pierre Brugman moved his family to Puerto Rico shortly after Isabel gave birth to Mathias.

Mathias Brugman was raised and educated in Puerto Rico and later came to settle in Mayagüez where he opened a *colmado*, a grocery store, and became very successful. During the 1840's Mathias Brugman had had enough of Spain's politics and harsh treatment of the creoles, and in the early 1850's, began to speak out against the mother country. His fiery speeches attracted many people and made him a figure of notoriety, watched and scrutinized by powerful peninsulares who quickly alerted Spanish agents about his rebellious nature. It did not take very long before Doctor Emeterio Betances and Segundo Ruiz Belvis took notice of the passionate speaker, and all three became very close friends. Under the tutelage of Betances and Ruiz, Brugman's incendiary speeches against Spanish exploitation and calls for independence made him a popular figure among many disenchanted creoles living in Mayagüez and soon attracted the likes of Manuel and Miguel Rojas, as well as Mariana Bracetti.

Under the auspices of Doctor Betances and Segundo Ruiz Belvis, Mathias Brugman, along with Manuel and Miguel Rojas, formed the two most important rebel cells in Puerto Rico. Brugman began to use his store as the headquarters for the revolutionary movement and later codenamed it Capa Prieto. Situated thirty miles northwest of the port of Guánica, the rebels saw Capa Prieto as the ideal staging point for all revolutionary actions. Weeks later, Brugman assisted the Rojas brothers in the formation of the second most important revolutionary cell called Centro Bravo.

Having placed all confidence in the Rojas brothers, Mathias Brugman never saw a need to visit his fellow freedom fighters. Pressing into service the lower echelon members of his cell as messengers, there was constant communication between the two parties and the two factions kept each other well informed.

Brugman and his associates needed to discuss very important matters with Manuel Rojas and felt the occasion this time was different from all previous communications put together. The high level of communication, combined with the recent arrival of two important figures, could not take place at Capa Prieto because of its notoriety with the loyalists. For these reasons Brugman decided it was safer to conduct their clandestine meeting in a less noticeable locale such as Centro Bravo in Lares. The rebels had not shown this much excitement and fuss over a gathering since the formation of the Revolutionary Committee back on January 3; there seemed a giddiness about them, an excitement compared only to that of a child about to receive a gift.

Utilizing their underground network, Mathias Brugman had informed all collaborators of the burgeoning rebellion that both Emeterio Betances and Segundo Ruiz Belvis would secretly make their way into Puerto Rico and would make a rare appearance to discuss the overall progress in the revolution. It was highly dangerous for the two men to be seen in Puerto Rico and equally dangerous for any citizen to be seen associating with them.

Fully aware of the inherent danger, Mathias Brugman and his associates made sure Betances and Belvis would reach their destination safely. Brugman was a very cautious man by nature who never took unnecessary chances. He sent a group of riders ahead to scout the forward trails and provide ample warning should the Spanish discover their secret journey. Bruno Chabrier, another of Brugman's long time friends, was leading the well-armed advance whose job it was to clear a safe path for the leaders of the cell. Capa Prieto had sent the call out to all corners of western Puerto Rico on February 1, and many would come out from hiding, risking exposure, so that they could finally see the two leaders of the revolution. The date for that historic meeting was set for the night of Saturday, February 8.

CHAPTER 8

One hundred miles east of Mayagüez, in the Capital city of San Juan, Governor Julián Juan Pavía sat before his stately desk. His dark brown eyes concentrated on a document that had arrived only two hours earlier. He had read it two times already and was in the middle of reading it for the third time when Lieutenant Colonel Juan Manuel de Ibarreta entered his office. The middle-aged governor looked up and greeted the colonel. "Buenos Dias, Manuel."

The colonel stood at attention and saluted the governor. "Buenos Dias." The governor's eyelids appeared as narrow slits, and Colonel Ibarreta could barely see his pupils. Sporting a well-trimmed but slowly graying beard and a neatly waxed handlebar mustache, the governor exuded a world class appearance, as though he might have served as an ambassador to some great foreign nation in the distant past, or had been a member of the royal court of Spain.

"Please, Colonel, take a seat," said Pavía, motioning with his hand at the vacant seat in front of his desk. Ibarreta read the governor's face and sensed there was more to the usual morning meeting. What was different about it was that the governor had sent for him twice that morning and that was something he had never done before. Besides dispatching two messengers to the colonel's house, the governor took no steps to shield his face from anxiety, the intensity of his squinted eyes foreshadowing gloom and prompting the colonel into complete attention. The colonel removed his cap and sat. There was no hint of fear on the battle-hardened colonel, and Pavía immediately noticed the aura of self-confidence surrounding Ibarreta's six-foot-two frame.

The governor had recently appointed Ibarreta commander of the militia of San Juan as a reward for successfully completing two tours of duty in the Dominican war. As commanding officer of a regiment,

Ibarreta led his men into the thick of war and won every battle and skirmish in Santo Domingo. For his victories and for keeping his men alive during the battles, the Caribbean Viceroy gave the forty-two-year-old a choice for his next assignment. Ibarreta chose Puerto Rico because he had visited the island on previous occasions and it had found a special place in his heart. It was not only the island's beauty that endeared itself to the colonel, but its peacefulness, too, a place where there was no hint of revolutionists or their incendiary propaganda. After witnessing the horrors of war, Ibarreta's ideals had changed. He no longer felt compelled to see the land and rivers flow red with blood or see the entrails of men while still alive, or hear the cry of pain and the dreadful sound of gun and cannon fire. Two tours of duty had been enough for him and he would wait out the final six months of his term on the peaceful island of Puerto Rico. Then he would buy fifty cuerdas of land in Yauco, find a good Spanish woman to settle down with and become a farmer.

The governor kept the colonel waiting while he read the document for the third time, as if somehow the contents would miraculously change and finally find favor with him. Unfortunately, the letter did not change. He finally placed the document on the desk and looked straight into Ibarreta's pale blue eyes. "It would seem that your appointment as commander has been a timely stroke of good fortune."

"What do you mean, Governor?" Ibarreta asked curiously, raising both eyebrows at the same time. The ends of his thick, black mustache stretched out and nearly touched the lobes of his ears.

"Here, read this." The governor handed the document to Ibarreta.

6th February 1868

To His Excellency, Governor Julián Juan Pavía,

On the 28th of January, following your orders, I witnessed the arrival of Doctor Betances and Señor Belvis at the port of Guánica. Don Mathias Brugman and several armed men were there to greet them. I followed the conspirators from Guánica back to Mayagüez, where Señores Betances and Belvis stayed at Brugman's hacienda on the night of February 3rd. They left at dawn on the 4th of February, heading east, presumably toward Lares or San Sebastián. I am not certain about their final destination because I could not get past their armed militia without giving myself away. I have no further intelligence as to their current whereabouts and shall await your further instructions.

Your faithful servant,

DR

Colonel Ibarreta handed the letter back to Governor Pavía but chose to remain silent. Pavía leaned back on his chair and folded his arms. "You know those men don't you?"

Ibarreta nodded. "I know *of* them but I have neither met nor seen them. I know that they've been hiding somewhere in Santo Domingo but they're as elusive as rats on a ship, Governor. They have many friends in Santo Domingo but what little I know about them, I don't think they were involved in the uprising there."

"But you can bet your ass they're heavily involved here," replied the governor quickly.

"How reliable is your informant?"

"Very reliable, Colonel, the spy is very close to infiltrating a rebel cell."

Ibarreta cleared his throat. "So what do you want me to do?"

The governor unfolded his arms and stood. He walked over to the window behind his desk, and while gazing at the empty streets of old San Juan, he answered the colonel. "I want you to go to San Sebastián and find out what's going on there."

"What exactly do you want me to do, Governor?" Ibarreta inquired, but somehow he knew what the governor wanted. It was almost as if he could read the governor's mind, and it began to sicken him. The governor's reactions reminded the colonel of how similar they were to Governor Baez's reactions in the years preceding the Dominican revolution. Rather than talking to disgruntled creoles and learning what their grievances were, the Dominican governor ignored their concerns and went on the offensive. His actions exacerbated an already tense situation, which irrevocably climaxed into a violent revolutionary war.

"I want you to establish contact with all of the military commanders of western Puerto Rico and press Gamir's plan into action should the situation require it. I also want you to meet with the alcaldes of

San Sebastián, Camuy and Lares and coordinate a resolution for the eradication of this insurrection. Can you handle this, Colonel?"

"But Governor, I know of no such insurrection in Puerto Rico. How big is this movement? How many people are involved?" The colonel took no steps to hide his skepticism, and his lack of positive reaction seemed to bother the governor, a man accustomed to having his orders followed without question. Ibarreta sensed his annoyance, but chose not to make an issue of it until he heard what the governor wanted of him.

The governor sighed, as if the need for explanation to a subordinate was unnecessary. "From the reports I have received the past two months, it appears that the movement is fairly large. There are revolutionary cells all over the western part of the island beginning in Mayagüez and stretching as far as Lares, San Sebastián and Camuy. You might do well to check in with the militia of Arecibo, too, you may need Colonel Iturriaga's help."

"Help, for what?"

"In case there is an armed confrontation."

"Governor, from what I have heard, there are only a handful of mindless men who are talking about a revolution. There are no conspiracies and no organizations large enough to pose a threat to Spain."

"When did you arrive here, Colonel?" The governor asked bluntly. The heat of the day was already unbearable and sweat beads began to roll down his forehead.

"Two months ago, Governor."

Governor Pavía turned around to face the colonel and smiled sardonically. "Two months ago…well, there you have it. In two month's time, you have figured it all out, Colonel. Let me give you a piece of advice: never presume to know everything, especially about the goddamn creoles who think they have a right to do as they please. They are not even Spaniards, for God's sake! And who knows how much of their blood is already tainted by the Negroes and Indians?"

This time Ibarreta was the one to sigh heavily. "But hasn't the Cortes in Madrid recognized the creoles as Spanish citizens? Or am I wrong?"

"If you ask me publicly, I'll tell you that I support the Cortes and embrace the creoles as my fellow Spaniards. Privately, I will tell you that they are no better than the slaves! We cannot afford to trust them. They are deceptive and dangerous, and if you're not up to the task, then tell me right now, Colonel, and I'll appoint someone else, someone... more reliable."

Ibarreta immediately resented the governor's remarks. He stood up firmly and walked toward the governor to face him eye to eye. "Not up to the task, governor? Tell me, have you ever served in the military? Have you ever suffered the pangs of hunger, or crept so low to the ground that you are forced to taste dirt? Have you ever writhed in the misery of sweat and depravity of sleep or agonized over the constant fear of death? Have you felt the burning sting of lead buried into your skin? Have you ever killed a man, or held a dying man in your arms? I don't think so, Governor. I'm certain that you have never felt the need for the comforts of a soft bed or a decent meal. Yet you sit in your gubernatorial office and dictate orders without the benefit of knowing the consequences and hardships of accomplishing such orders. So do not stand there, looking high and mighty, and ask me if I am not up to the task. I am a soldier and a loyalist, and I will do whatever is required of me."

Governor Pavía recoiled and held his breath, but nothing happened. Realizing the colonel was not going to strike him, he regained his composure, nodded with a sheepish grin, and quickly gave the colonel the respect he deserved. "I apologize for my presumptions, Colonel, but you must not take this growing movement too lightly."

"Governor, I will leave for San Sebastián tomorrow morning and I will investigate this insurrection. If there is a conspiracy, I will root it out and eradicate it."

"Very well, that is all I ask from you, Colonel."

CHAPTER 9

Night came rapidly but the heat and humidity still lingered in the air and stubbornly refused to dissipate. Along their fifty-three mile, four-day journey from Cataño to Camuy, the Hernández family stayed in roadside inns, but since they were accustomed to the finer things in life, they found the inns appalling. When they arrived at Don Ignacio De La Torre's hacienda in Camuy, Maria and her three daughters were grateful that Rodolfo decided to call on his friend. From De La Torre's house, they were only nineteen miles from their country estate in San Sebastián.

The Hernández family had grown weary and tired from their exhaustive journey and felt grimy, too, from all the sweat. Rodolfo would usually ignore his family's discomfort, but since the heat of the day brought him a good measure of misery, as well, he decided De La Torre's house would be a good place to stay the night. He had done business with Ignacio before on several occasions but his friendship never went beyond business, and he wondered whether staying at De La Torre's house was a prudent idea. He quickly dispensed with the thought, stuck his head out the window and shouted orders at Candelario.

To Rodolfo's relief, De La Torre received his family with open arms and insisted on their staying the night. De La Torre had not seen Rodolfo for more than two months, and at 5:30 that afternoon, he could not hide the overwhelming joy that an opportune moment had presented itself. For a while now De La Torre had wanted to discuss some business opportunities with Rodolfo and had planned to contact him. Now that Rodolfo had unexpectedly called on him, he felt that fate had intervened. The impromptu visit could not have been timelier for De La Torre, and the landowner would cater shamelessly to the Hernández family, making them feel as comfortable as humanly possible. De La Torre ordered his servants to prepare a feast of extraordinary proportions, and he would see to it that Rodolfo and his family would go to sleep that night with their bellies full.

De La Torre ordered the house slaves to draw water from the pump outside their grand hacienda and fill the two bathtubs in the house with hot water so that his guests could bathe before dinner. By eight o'clock that evening, the Hernández family, bathed and dressed elegantly, slowly took their seats at the dinner table. At eight fifteen, Rosalía was the last to arrive at the dining room. The flavorful aroma of roast pork, yellow rice with pigeon peas, shrimp soup and an assortment of greens carried through to Rosalía's nostrils and stirred her famished stomach with gurgling sounds. Though she was hungry, she took comfort in the fact that her tight corset would prevent her from overeating. She wondered at the same time whether Anita and Laura had donned their corsets also. Rosalía noted how everyone was so elegantly dressed, and as she made her way toward the dining room, she tried to ignore her feelings of disgust. She had grown to despise the pomp in such dining rituals, as well as the panoply of such excesses of food and drink. She would have been content with but a tiny piece of bread and a small glass of water.

Don Ignacio De La Torre moved his tall and lean figure toward the head of the table and asked Don Rodolfo Hernández to sit on the chair to his immediate left. Brushing back his long, curly brown hair over his shoulders, he cast his large grey eyes over the dining room to make sure everything was in order. The square-jawed landowner's face grinned satisfactorily; everything was moving according to plan. Maria sat next to Rodolfo and faced Doña Inez De La Torre. Laura sat next to Maria while Anita sat further down the table far from her father and mother. Doña Inez's two stepsons took seats across the table facing Anita. No one said a word as Rosalía slowly made her way to the dinner table. To Rosalía, it was obvious that all conversations were held in deference to Rodolfo's apparent discomfort. Rosalía had been the last member of his family to arrive at the dinner table, and that was an embarrassment to him. She could sense Father's disappointment, but Rosalía could not have cared any less about how he felt. Rodolfo shot a glaring look at Rosalía and pulled out his pocket watch to note the time. Then he sighed and put the watch back into his jacket pocket.

Rosalía studied the seating arrangements and quickly decided to sit next to Anita and be as far away from Laura and her father as she could possibly be. A black servant, dressed elegantly, rushed over to Rosalía and pulled the chair back so that she could sit. Rosalía thanked the servant, looked around the table and watched everyone silently looking at her. As she sat, she heard her father clearing his throat—a subtle communication of his intolerance for lateness and general rudeness.

Don Ignacio De La Torre, certain now that Rosalía was sitting comfortably, nodded to the head servant. "You may begin." The head servant bowed and disappeared through two swinging doors. A few moments later, other well-dressed slaves came through the swinging doors bearing silver trays of steaming food.

One servant poured red wine into crystal glasses, and then went around the table placing drinks. Across the table, Ignacio's two sons gawked at Anita and Rosalía as if they never before in their young lives saw women. It was very rare for the sixteen-year-old Pedro and his fourteen-year-old brother, Josefíno, to host another family at their home. In fact, the last time the De La Torre family had hosted a dinner party was when they were nine and seven years old.

The slim and fair-skinned Inez De La Torre felt and truly looked like the most awkward of the group because she was Ignacio's second wife, and she did not know the Hernández as well as Ignacio's first wife did. Nevertheless, she would make the best of her situation and be the good hostess her husband demanded her to be.

Ignacio De La Torre raised his glass in the air and toasted reverently, "To Queen Isabel!" He watched everyone at the table raise their glasses and waited for their unified response. "God save the Queen." they all said. The Camuyan peninsular sipped some wine, and then turned to look at his guests. He raised his glass again and said with a huge smile, "To friends!"

Rodolfo smiled appreciatively. "To friends," he said softly, almost whispering. He removed the linen cloth off the table and placed it on his lap. All the while, the servants kept placing on the table large oval-shaped silver trays filled with steaming food. The aroma was enough to make anyone with hunger faint.

De La Torre watched Rodolfo's eyes as they gleamed in ravenous anticipation. "Eat whatever you want and as much as you need, my friend. Just tell Porfidio, my head servant, what you want and he will fill your plate."

For most of the meal, the two families ate in silence, and the only interruption of that dining serenity came from the occasional clatter of plates from the kitchen or the scraping of servants' shoes against the wooden floor. The families finished their meals nearly at the same time, and from the looks of the empty plates, Ignacio knew they had enjoyed a well-deserved dinner. The male host leaned back on his chair and motioned Porfidio to fill his and Rodolfo's glass with wine. As Porfidio poured wine into the glasses, Rodolfo completely ignored him and looked directly into De La Torre's eyes. "You've made a few improvements, Ignacio, the hacienda looks great."

"Thank you, Rodolfo. It wasn't cheap either, but I feel it was worth it."

"Indeed," replied Rodolfo grinning, fully aware that De La Torre was a low-ranking member in the social pecking order. "Having a magnificent home is a testament to one's character and financial status. I would like to thank you for putting us up for the night."

"No need," replied De La Torre, waving his hand at Rodolfo.

"No, I mean it, Ignacio." Hernández noted De La Torre's smile as he nodded back at him. "I would like to extend to you an open invitation to my home in San Juan or if you like, why don't you come to my estate in San Sebastián. We'll be there for about a month and we'd love to have you come over for dinner."

"Thank you, Rodolfo. I will take you up on the offer." De La Torre flashed a genuine smile at Rodolfo but doubted he would ever venture into San Sebastián. He had known Rodolfo for more than ten years and knew all about his ruthless business tactics. Yet, though he was leery of involving himself and his family with the likes of Hernández, a financial opportunity had presented itself and he knew there was no other man with the right qualifications for this venture other than Rodolfo. And by right qualifications, he meant a decent amount of money.

"I think your coming here was a godsend, Rodolfo," said De La Torre with a twinkle in his eyes. He said nothing else and watched Rodolfo slowly put his glass down on the table. De La Torre wanted to bait Rodolfo like a fish and then reel him in slowly. Naturally, Rodolfo obliged.

"How so?"

"Do you know a man by the name of Don Francisco Frontera?"

Rodolfo nodded. "I met him a few years ago in Lares, why do you ask?"

De La Torre purposefully took his time to respond. He picked up his glass and sipped some wine. Placing the glass back on the table, he said, "Señor Frontera is a good friend of Don Juan Marquez. Do you know the Marquez?"

"Yes…well, who doesn't? Don Juan Marquez's life mirrors that of my own. He arrived on this island in the late 30's. He saved every peso he earned and then invested his money wisely. He purchased a store, made good money from it, and then began leasing it to others at a huge profit. Juan Marquez became a prominent member of Lares's elite, and by 1844 had become an Alderman. A few years later, he became the mayor of Lares. By the late 1840's he had sent for his brothers and together they formed Casa Marquez & Co., one of the most successful exporting companies on the island. I met all of his brothers, Ignacio, and they're all bright, talented and savvy businessmen."

Maria looked across the table and noted everyone listening to the conversation between Ignacio and Rodolfo. Uninterested in their conversation, Maria turned to Inez and said, "I love the color of your curtains."

"Thank you," replied Inez nervously, hoping her husband would not publically reveal his anger at her for talking to Maria. Contrary to her fears, Ignacio seemed to welcome the discussion because he made no fuss about it as he had made on other occasions. As the men continued their conversation, Rosalía and her sisters turned to their mother and Inez to listen to their conversation.

"So why do you ask me if I know those men?" Rodolfo said, placing his glass on the table.

"The Marquez brothers are looking for investors to expand their business and to better compete against Amell, Julia & Co. I've known for some time that the Marquez brothers have asked Don Pedro Mayol and Don Francisco Frontera to come on board as investors." De La Torre watched Rodolfo's eyes widening with curiosity, and knew that he had hooked his fish. Now he needed to reel him in slowly.

"So how does that partnership bring *you* into the picture? How does it bring *me* into the picture?" Rodolfo immediately recognized a financial opportunity was in the making. He had generated all his wealth through land acquisitions but he had always wanted to diversify. He knew just how wealthy and powerful the Marquez family had become over the years and if an opportunity arose for Rodolfo to join that prestigious circle, he would not hesitate in doing so.

"How do I come into the picture? Señor Frontera is my compadre. I am the godfather of his eldest son, Felipe, and his wife is first cousin to my wife. That's how I come into the picture." There was more, of course, but he wanted to make Rodolfo very curious.

"All right, Ignacio," Rodolfo finally responded. "You are related to Don Frontera, who's been asked by the Marquez brothers to invest in their company. How is my coming to your hacienda a godsend for you?"

"Don Frontera wants to invest a large portion of money into Casa Marquez & Company. On paper Frontera will appear as an investor and partner but he came to me a couple of weeks ago wanting to cover a part of that investment."

"I see," said Rodolfo, eyes glinting with interest. "He's not too sure about that upfront investment, right?" De La Torre nodded affirmatively. "But if you or I invest money in Casa Marquez & Co., our names will not appear on the company documents."

"That's exactly correct, Rodolfo. Don Frontera, through his solicitor, will draw papers to create a separate investing company listing me, and a few others, as partners. The combined capital will be invested in Casa Marquez & Co. by Don Frontera."

Rodolfo nodded to acknowledge what De La Torre wanted of him. He then eyed De La Torre with a broad smile. "How many investors is Frontera looking for, Ignacio?"

"Not many. He's looking for about four to five investors."

"And how much money does he want?"

Ignacio de la Torre hesitated, cleared his throat and then uttered, "Ten thousand pesos to match his ten thousand." De La Torre waited to see Rodolfo's reaction, but the opportunistic entrepreneur showed him only a placid face. Rodolfo picked up his glass and finished the wine.

"You can put up two thousand," suggested De La Torre.

"No, Ignacio."

"But why not? I think it would be a good opportunity for you, a sound investment that you simply cannot pass up."

"No, I didn't mean that. I meant no to more investors. Can you handle five thousand pesos? If you can, then I will put up five thousand."

"Unfortunately, I am not as well off as you are, Rodolfo. I can only invest about two thousand pesos."

Rodolfo nodded to acknowledge De La Torre. He rubbed his chin while mulling over the sudden opportunity. Then, as Rodolfo leaned back on his chair, ignoring the chatter between Maria and Inez, the head servant poured more wine into his glass. All of a sudden, Rodolfo turned to De La Torre and squinted, "All right, your two thousand pesos and my eight thousand."

"That's a lot of money, Rodolfo. Are you sure you want to invest eight thousand pesos? Why don't you take your time and think about it?"

"No need, Ignacio, but first I would like to meet with Don Francisco Frontera. Can you arrange that?"

"Yes, I think I can do that."

At the other end of the table, Laura watched a small black boy, no more than eight years old, as he walked into the dining room nervously holding a silver tray filled with diced fruits. While the two men continued their conversation and while Maria and Inez talked about the latest fashions from Spain, Laura shook her head in disgust. There was no one in the De La Torre household with whom she could engage in a conversation worthy of her interests, and her boredom plainly revealed itself in her unblinking eyes. To Laura's left, separated by two chairs, Anita had started a conversation with Pedro and Josefíno, while Rosalía took notice of the young boy for the first time.

The boy was not wholly black. He was a muláto who, because of his lighter skin color, had been taken off the field to work inside the house—a servant in training, so to speak. Having been around slaves all of her life, Rosalía immediately detected something about the boy. Though his innocent face appeared calm, his tiny eyes were emitting fear, a kind of fear that could only be compared to one who was about to receive a good thrashing with a leather whip. Rosalía could see his little hands shaking as he held the silver tray bearing fruits. It might have been his first day as a house servant or maybe he had never served at a dinner party, or maybe he was so afraid to be in the company of his master that it made his hands quiver. Whatever the reason, Rosalía felt sorry for that boy because she saw primal fear in those small brown eyes.

De La Torre suddenly cut his conversation off with Rodolfo and then turned to the little boy. "Ah…our dessert has arrived!" He turned to the youthful servant and commanded, "Go around the table and place fruits on each of the plates, boy!"

The young man obediently performed his task as the master commanded. With the greatest of care, he picked up several slices of mango with a set of tongs and gingerly placed them on Rodolfo's plate. Rodolfo, as always, seemed impatient as the boy went about his business. The boy then advanced toward Maria, and when she asked for sliced bananas, the boy humbly obliged. As he carefully placed cut bananas onto Maria's plate, Laura watched him. Her gleaming aqua-green eyes appeared to be concentrating on the boy, her mind calculating something devious. She was bored and she needed some kind of excitement. As the boy finally approached Laura, Rosalía contemplated him, imagining he would grow up to become a very handsome man one day. Deep inside, though, Rosalía prayed the boy would complete his task without incident. On the other hand, Laura looked at the boy with nothing but utter contempt, repulsed by his appearance as though his skin roiled over with boils or suffered the affliction of leprosy. She gestured with her eyes at the mango on the tray and the boy placed several slices on her plate. Laura waited until he was done. Then, as he moved past her, Laura stuck her foot out and the boy tripped and fell, dropping the tray to the floor. The silver tray made a crashing sound forcing everyone at the table to focus their attention on the boy.

"Goddamn you!" shouted De La Torre. He rose from his chair and rushed over to the boy. The young man, though aware that he'd been the victim of someone's cruel joke, still felt embarrassed. Determined not to let it affect the completion of his task, the boy got up off the floor only to receive two slaps across his face from Ignacio's hand. Rosalía noticed Laura's devilish smile as Ignacio slapped the boy again, cursing at him, belittling him in front of all his guests. Yet, through it all, the boy never whimpered and never showed any reaction to pain. Rosalía admired his tenacity but when she turned to Laura, she could feel her face grow hot with anger. To Laura it had been a harmless prank, something with which to bemuse herself and lift her out of her boredom. On the other hand, Rosalía knew that Laura's little prank would cost that boy dearly. Before Ignacio could raise his hand again, Rosalía jumped out of her chair, ran to the other side of the table and stood in front of the boy. She looked up at Ignacio and said, "Señor De La Torre, it was an accident!"

"Rosalía!" shouted Rodolfo, rising to his feet. "What the devil do you think you're doing?"

"Father, it was an accident. There's no reason to beat this little boy for a simple accident!"

"Mind your business, Rosalía! Or have you forgotten that this is not our home and that we are guests of Don De La Torre?"

De La Torre nodded at Rosalía, and then gave Rodolfo an apologetic smile. "It's all right, Don Hernández." He focused his eyes on the swinging doors and noticed Porfidio standing nervously. "Porfidio, clean up this mess right now and take this little monkey back to the field!" Thinking no more of the situation, De La Torre walked back to his chair and resumed his conversation with Rodolfo. For a few moments, Rodolfo could not give the host his complete attention because he feared Rosalía would do something impulsive and stupid, and he would not tolerate another embarrassment. As De La Torre continued to talk, Rodolfo gradually returned to the conversation.

The head servant rushed to the side of the table where Laura sat. He bent his knees to the floor and began to pick up pieces of fruit. The boy remained standing behind Rosalía, looking at Porfidio's hands as the head servant placed the fruits back on the silver tray.

As Maria and Inez resumed their conversation and while Pedro and Josefíno conversed with Anita, Laura turned from her chair and saw the young boy poking his head from behind Rosalía "You are a pathetic piece of shit!" she whispered at him. Rosalía heard Laura's voice clearly, and angrily looked down at her. She wanted to lash out at her sister right then but she knew that her father was still infuriated with her for embarrassing him, and, though he did not show it at the moment, he would store his anger, like all the money he so carefully stored in the vault at home, and would draw it out later. She didn't want to exacerbate her father's anger but she could not help herself. She whispered at Laura "You should call this boy a piece of shit? *You* are the piece of shit, you bitch!"

Laura turned her eyes away from the boy, looked up at Rosalía and whispered back at her. "Careful, little sister, Father's not too happy with you right now." She raised her right hand at Rosalía and curled her index finger to meet with her thumb, leaving a tiny space between the tips of her fingers. "And you are just about this much away from a public beating."

"You'd like that wouldn't you?" replied Rosalía angrily.

"Nothing would give me more pleasure on this boring evening."

"I saw what you did, Laura. You are a cruel and miserable person."

"So I tripped him, so what? He's just a fucking slave."

Porfidio, clearly hearing their conversation, finished his task, grabbed the boy's hand and ushered him out of the dining room. By the concerned look on his face, Rosalía sensed Porfidio wanted to put him back in the field immediately. It wasn't because he was angry with the boy, but because he wanted to save him from a certain beating. Porfidio knew that no benefit would come from beating a boy so young, and being the recipient of countless beatings and whippings himself, he wanted to spare him of the experience.

Rosalía remained standing until Porfidio and the boy disappeared through the swinging doors. Then she took her seat again and kept her silence until the dinner party was over.

CHAPTER 10

Miguel and Carlos arrived at San Sebastián by seven that evening. The two men rode their horses toward the Comisario's hall, and as they dismounted, they could hear strumming guitars and singing voices. The run down hall stood across the street from Don Emilio Pagan's bar, the refined and prestigious tavern where all peninsulares gathered and where creoles were not welcomed. Despite the Hall's rundown appearance, many creoles attended the celebration, and Miguel could hear shouts of merriment, women and men conversing and the stomping of feet as people danced the night away.

"It simply amazes me," Carlos wondered as he wrapped the reins around the wooden post. "The way they come here to celebrate every month boggles my mind. They are content with the way things are. They are content to live under the heels of their Spanish masters and like dogs feed on the crumbs off their tables." Carlos shook his head in bitter contemplation. "It's a wonder to me."

"Where are we going, Carlos?" Miguel inquired with a concerned look.

"Just down the street, to the colmado at the end of the block."

"Don Ramirez's store? Don Sinecio Ramirez? I never thought Don Ramirez to be a separatist—that is a surprise."

"Indeed, it *would* be a complete surprise to you, and maybe it's because Don Ramirez is a devout loyalist."

Miguel crunched his eyebrows out of curiosity, "I don't understand. If Ramirez is a loyalist, then why are we going to his colmado?"

"Because his two sons are separatists who'd like nothing better than to see Puerto Rico a free and independent nation."

Closed for business, the colmado was dark inside and seemed very quiet. Fully determined, Carlos Peña walked to the doors. He knocked three times, paused and then knocked two more times. The music from the hall was faint now but it was still loud enough to let Carlos know that old man Ramirez was still there celebrating with his creole friends even though they knew he stood opposed to their revolutionary ideals. Carlos and Miguel heard two knocks, a pause, and then three knocks. Carlos knocked one more time, and then the doors opened to reveal a young man's face. Enrique Ramirez held the door ajar and raised his head to look up at the dark figure appearing before him. He opened the door wider and said hurriedly, "Come in!"

Miguel followed Carlos into the dark establishment, where he saw Enrique strike a match and light a gas lantern. The young man nervously brought the lantern to his face so that Carlos and Miguel could see him. "Follow me."

Enrique Ramirez led Carlos and Miguel to a room in the back of the store. The room faced an intricate pattern of woodlands that masked the rear of the colmado, and so there was no need to turn out the lights. The room was packed with men; faces that both Miguel and Carlos immediately recognized. They sat on chairs, crates or on the floor and waited for Carlos to initiate the meeting. Carlos smiled and nodded at his audience. "I didn't think so many would attend tonight's meeting. We have in our company, Don Manuel Cebollero Aguilar and Don Eusebio Ibarra, two prominent members of San Sebastián's militia. Gentlemen, your presence here tonight gives credence to the seriousness of our cause." Carlos looked around the room and smiled. "I also see Don Cristobal Castro and the four Font brothers, as well as Don Cesareo Martínez. Thank you all for taking such a risk to be here tonight."

"So what is the word, Carlos?" Aguilar said impatiently.

"The word is: go!" replied Carlos with a genuine smile. Then he took a brief moment to acknowledge a fearful and muted applause. Carlos turned to Miguel and flashed a confident smile. He stepped to the side to reveal his friend to the audience. He gestured at Miguel with his huge hand and said, "You all know Miguel Pítre. He will be joining our cell."

"What will we call our cell?" said Aguilar sounding impatient again.

"Let us first discuss the rules and regulations before we decide on a name," replied Carlos.

"This is preposterous!" shouted Aguilar, "How can this cell be led by a *negro*? No one else will want to join us."

Ramon Font angrily rose to his feet, turned and looked directly at Aguilar, "Carlos has been appointed the leader of this cell by the Revolutionary Committee and we will adhere to the committee's choice, the choice made by Doctor Betances!"

All of a sudden, there was uproar in the small gathering and everyone began talking, arguing and shouting at the same time. Some members demanded that a white creole lead the cell, some wanted no Black members at all, some shouted equality for all men, and a small number remained quiet, indifferent. Carlos, visibly frustrated, shook his head and frowned. He raised his hands in the air and shouted. "Gentlemen please: be silent!" Carlos widened his eyes and fixed a stern gaze at his audience. His face, taut with utter conviction, had somehow captured their immediate attention, as if they could easily read his face and feel his passion and his belief in the cause. When Carlos opened his mouth to speak, the deep vibrato of his voice resonated in their ears, and his abounding confidence made the words flow out of his lips without hesitation, as if his belief in the cause had equaled or even supplanted his belief in the Almighty.

Carlos brought his arms down to the side. "If this cause of ours is to take root," he thundered at the audience, "it must take root with the people, with us, right here, right now!" Carlos paused for a short moment. He gradually raised his right arm and clenched his hand into a tight fist. "If we are to sow the seeds of revolution, then as proven farmers we must do it properly so that later we can reap freedom's bountiful harvest. If Puerto Rico is to become free, then *all* Puerto Ricans must become free, and that means all of us. The same freedom our white counterparts enjoy and take for granted must also be enjoyed by Puerto Ricans, whether Indian Taino, African, Muláto or Creole. All races—mixed or unmixed—must unite to achieve that precious commodity, that God-given right we call freedom!" The members slowly sat back on their crates, showing more reverence now to the chosen leader. "Freedom is pure!" shouted Carlos, lowering his arm, "and it does not draw a line based upon the color of a person's skin! Freedom is not an exclusive club, where only white people can become members. If you cut my skin, you will see that my blood is just a red as yours!" Carlos thumped his chest with both fists, and shouted, "The heart that pumps my blood is the same heart that pumps the blood of our Spanish masters! The lungs that take in the air I breathe are also the same. The only difference is the color of my skin." He shook his head and cast his eyes to the floor, heavy hearted, replete with acrimony. "How much it would task my soul with utter satisfaction," continued Carlos, "if anyone of you white creoles, sitting on your wooden crates, could switch bodies with me for just one day; that would be something, wouldn't it? Alas, it is but a wish, so you will never know how it feels to be regarded with contempt and utter revulsion, treated worse than a street dog because of the color of one's skin. But in spite of your bigotry, and with a profound sense of humility, I forgive all of you because I take stock in the notion that you will become better men after the rebellion succeeds. Remember this too, the way you see me now is the way you will see me all the time. I promise that I will make no efforts to beguile you or serve you worthless platitudes. My goal is to win freedom for our nation. I promise you that as leader of this cell, I will make it my business to achieve that freedom for every one of you…or die trying. I have made a covenant with God and under His eyes I have pledged my heart and soul to the cause for liberty! However, my vows notwithstanding, if you feel that I do not represent the manifestation of that dream, then I will step aside and you may vote for a new leader…a white leader."

There was absolute silence as Carlos stood nearly at attention, eyes still opened wide, fully determined to challenge anyone in an argument. His hand was still clenched in a tight fist. No one dared open his mouth, not even the vocal Aguilar who seemed impressed with Carlos's speech. "That won't be necessary," said Aguilar. He slowly stood to address the gathering. "I, too, share the same dreams and passions as those of Don Peña and I am willing to do whatever is necessary to achieve our freedom. However, we should vote on a vice-president and secretary."

"Well, I have decided on appointing Miguel Pítre as vice-president," replied Carlos, but somehow he knew the appointment would not sit well with the members of his audience, and he was right. For one thing, he needed as many members as he could get, so he had to appease them. Then, the cell needed to draft and incorporate the rules and regulations. Finally, they had to cast votes for Carlos officially, and all votes had to be recorded by member name. Despite the odds, he was determined to argue for Miguel.

"No, Don Peña, we will not accept that," said Aguilar vehemently. "We will either vote for the cabinet or we will all walk out of here right now!"

Carlos felt Miguel's hand grasping his elbow and turned to face him. "Carlos, it's all right. They should vote properly and wisely."

Carlos squinted at Miguel and whispered so that no one else could hear. "Are you sure about that, Miguel? Are you sure you just want to be a regular member and be on the outside of every decision?"

"The cause is greater than my pride, Carlos. It is greater than you or this cell, and we must *all* make sacrifices."

Carlos nodded at Miguel and reluctantly accepted his friend's decision. He turned to face the audience and nodded. "All right, who will make the nomination?"

"I will," said Eusebio Ibarra, rushing to his feet. "I nominate as vice-president, Don Manuel Cebollero Aguilar."

"I second the nomination!" shouted Miguel from behind Carlos. Carlos heard Miguel's voice clearly and deep in his heart, he felt powerless to do anything for his friend now. Without batting an eye in response, he shouted. "All in favor say aye." He nodded and reluctantly smiled. "The ayes have it. Don Aguilar, please stand and be recognized as the vice-president of the cell." The short applause for Aguilar preceded the nomination for secretary, which Don Eusebio Ibarra easily won. The rebels spent the next two hours drafting the cell's rules and regulations and finished the tedious work of transcribing the texts at around nine that evening.

"Now that our rules and regulations have been drawn, the last item on the agenda is to name the cell. Are there any suggestions?"

Aguilar, as always, was the first to speak. "How about: *Soldados de la Libertad*?" Everyone immediately dismissed Aguilar's suggestion.

"*Lanzador de los Pepinos*!" shouted Rodrigo Font.

"No," replied Carlos. "*Lanzador* is already taken by the cell in Camuy."

"How about: *Borinquen Libre*?" someone in the back suggested.

"That's too close to *Cuba Libre,*" said Carlos shaking his head.

"What about *Porvenir*?" Miguel uttered.

Everyone turned their heads at Miguel, theirs eyes filled with interest. Even Carlos seemed to like the name. He turned to Miguel and smiled, almost knowing what his young protégé's was thinking. "And why should we call our cell *Porvenir*, Miguel?"

Miguel slowly faced the audience. "Because *Porvenir* means the future, and the future is like a blank sheet of paper that stands ready to be inked. We have all sworn to change our future and the destiny of our beloved Puerto Rico. *Porvenir* represents our hopes and dreams, my brothers, and we will make those hopes and dreams a reality!"

The small gathering of men all rose to their feet and gave Miguel a standing ovation, their hope-filled faces beaming with dreams—impossible dreams of removing the terrible yoke the Spanish had placed over their necks for four hundred years. Miguel's speech forced them to forget about their differences and to stand united against their common enemy. For the moment, they were of one mind and one heart.

After the long ovation subsided, Carlos turned back to the audience and smiled with satisfaction. "Is anyone here opposed to calling our cell *Porvenir*?" No one said a word. In fact, they were surprised that Carlos had even dared to call out an opposing view, but as president of the cell Carlos had to make sure there was no hint of disagreement. After a long pause, he smiled again and said, "By your silence I hereby move to ratify the name of our cell as *Porvenir*."

The meeting ended at nine-thirty.

As the members filtered out of the colmado, Carlos Peña and Manuel Cebollero Aguilar stood by the door, bidding everyone goodnight. Miguel stood outside, waiting for Carlos but he kept himself busy by looking out for spies. While scanning the streets, he could hear the conversation between Carlos and Manuel. "I will be traveling to Centro Bravo and hope to arrive there by Saturday the 8th," Carlos said to Manuel. "Very important people will be there so I want you to come with me."

Aguilar nodded. "All right, where will we meet?"

"Let's meet up at Miguel's place on Friday the 7th."

Miguel suddenly turned and looked up at Carlos inquisitively. "Father must not know, Carlos. I don't think we could trust him."

Carlos quickly agreed. "Very well, then let's meet at Don Santiago Duran's plantation at six Friday morning."

Carlos and Miguel made their way across town, untied their horses and rode back home. It was very dark outside, but lanterns, posted every few hundred feet, lit up their path every now and then. During one of those lighted intervals, Carlos turned to Miguel. "Where did that speech come from?"

Miguel smiled, placing no significance on Carlos's praise. "I don't know. I guess a little bit of your speech rubbed off on me."

"I don't think so, Miguel. I think you're a natural-born speaker and you should cultivate that talent."

Miguel shook his head. "No, I'm not an orator, but I think you are, Carlos. You should have seen their faces as you spoke. You had them in the palm of your hand and you could have led them in any which way. I have never seen anyone speak so passionately and so genuinely. It is you, my beloved Carlos, you are the one with real talent. I'm just going along for the ride."

"Thank you so very much, Miguel. I am sorry that I could not make you my second in command."

"No need to apologize, Carlos. You have been good to me and I know your heart. I just want you to know that I will be there for you as you have been there for me."

Miguel arrived at his home just minutes before his father did and he was grateful for that. As he swung on the hammock, snuggling into a comfortable sleeping posture, he could hear the low thudding of horse hooves. His father was slowly approaching the house. Ten minutes later, Juan Pítre entered the house reeking of booze. He took notice of his son who had fallen asleep and contemplated his youthful face for a while. Then he staggered to his cot on the floor and passed out. Minutes after Juan closed his eyes for the night Miguel opened his eyes and looked at his father with a saddened heart.

The future belonged to the rebels, and they would change Puerto Rico's future or die trying.

CHAPTER 11

The nineteen-mile journey from Camuy to San Sebastián was a challenging task for the occasional traveler, but even the most seasoned traveler found ways to avoid the trip. The narrow horse trail was rocky and full of water-filled ditches festering with mosquitoes. The trail rose gradually and wound around a few hilltops before descending into a thick rainforest where bandits usually hid at night, poised to ambush unsuspecting travelers. Since Rodolfo decided to leave Camuy at dawn, when most of the bandits scattered around the forest had bedded down, the coach and wagon rumbled along the dark pathway quietly and without incident.

Although Rodolfo had unwittingly spared his family of the terror of robbery at gunpoint, he could not spare them much of anything else, and for the rest of their journey they fought against all sorts of insects that keenly found their way into and out of the coach. The ladies also endured a long, bumpy ride on a foliage-covered trail that reeked of mud and horse manure.

Thankfully, the Hernández finally arrived in San Sebastián by mid morning. The second the young women captured sight of their country estate, their eyes stirred with the same alacrity as that of prisoners about to be released from jail.

As the coach and wagon approached a clearing, Candelario recognized the house. The dwelling was much smaller than the mansion back in San Juan, but still, it was larger than any other house in San Sebastián. Its wooden siding, painted in a pastel yellow hue was bright enough that anyone could see it with but the faintest of light.

As Candelario eased the coach towards the house, he thought about the previous evening and smiled with satisfaction. Last night had been very good for Candelario and Agustín. They were guests of De La

Torre's head servant, Porfidio, and stayed at his slave quarters. Playing the perfect host, Porfidio offered his two guests plenty of leftover food, real food that he also shared with the rest of the slaves crammed into the small shack. Large banquets at the De La Torre household were rare but when they occurred, Porfidio would always see to it that everybody enjoyed the meal. Porfidio would perform this humble task at great risk because Don Ignacio De La Torre thought it a waste in offering leftovers to his slaves, rather than to his precious pigs. Candelario and Agustín thanked their host and slept very well last night.

Candelario tugged hard on the reins, forcing the team of four horses to come to a sudden halt. Behind him, he could hear Agustín's wagon also coming to a halt, the horses grunting with fatigue. Rodolfo opened the door of the stagecoach and stepped outside, only to confront the fierce heat of the morning. He nodded satisfactorily and uttered, "Thank God." He looked at Maria, who was still inside the stagecoach, and openly revealed his disappointment. "Well, are you waiting for a special invitation?" Maria said nothing. She stepped out of the coach hoping Rodolfo would, at the very least, extend his hand to help her down, but her husband showed her no such courtesy. Instead, he turned to Agustín and yelled, "Take the trunks into the house!"

No one had been more grateful to arrive than Rosalía. She had been looking forward to the trip for so long she could not wait to step out of the coach. She opened the door on the other side of the coach, the side facing the woods, and jumped down. Anita and Laura soon followed her but their faces showed no interest in arriving at San Sebastián. Their minds and hearts were set firmly on their future husbands, their future lives, a world separated from their domineering father.

Rosalía took in a deep breath and exhaled slowly. "The countryside is so beautiful," she said contemplatively. "I love the way the house was built so deep inside the forest. Isn't it lovely, Ana?"

Anita remained stoic and silent. She was still sore at her father because of what he said about Ruben De La Cruz. Deep in her heart, she still felt Ruben would come around the house in San Juan, find no one there and then turn around and leave. Her hopes of marrying Ruben were quickly vanishing. She dreaded the idea of becoming a spinster and the subject of her father's ridicule much like Tía Angelica was. Rosalía turned to Anita, waiting for her response, but when she noted her sister's melancholy, she toned down her enthusiasm. Standing alongside her sisters, Laura fixed her wide bonnet and straightened her dress. Then she glanced at Anita, and while noting her sister's silent disappointment, shook her head disapprovingly. "You're deluding yourself if you think Ruben will ride to San Sebastián just to see you. Whatever gave you the idea that he would ever come here just to see you? It's been over a year since he last saw you. Why don't you come to your senses, Ana, and forget about that man?"

Anita remained quiet as the music of the forest consumed the air around her. Birds, veiled by a curtain of forest greens, chirped their private tunes. Macaws and parrots, soaring above the trees, shrieked arias of life. The pinging chords of coquís and crickets combined with the occasional breeze that fluttered the trees and rattled the leaves, added to the melodies of a forest symphony. At times, strong gusts of wind would shake loose the fronds of nearby palm trees and they would come hissing down on the foliage-covered ground, sounding like the cymbals of an orchestra.

Anita refused to dignify Laura's comment with a response, and remained silent. On the other hand, Rosalía could not let Laura get away with it, especially after the stunt she pulled last night on that poor, defenseless boy. Rosalía had just about all she could take from Laura, and found herself confronting her eldest sister once again. "You just won't let anybody be, Laura. Why must you make everyone around you feel as miserable as you do? You talk about Ruben De La Cruz but what makes you think your precious Captain Sanchez will even survive his tour of duty in Santo Domingo?"

All of a sudden, Laura whipped around to face Rosalía, narrowed eyes defining her rage. "That wasn't necessary, Rosalía. It almost sounds as if you wish Gregorio would die. You better watch your mouth!"

"Aha! You don't like it when someone turns the table on you," said Rosalía smiling triumphantly. Rodolfo and Maria were making their way to the front of the house but since Rosalía and her two sisters were on the other side of the stagecoach, they neither saw nor heard their daughters arguing.

"My situation is totally different than that of Anita's," replied Laura angrily. "Captain Gregorio Sanchez has already asked for my hand in marriage. All I was saying to Ana is that a year has passed and she has not heard from Ruben, that's all."

Anita finally turned to face Laura. "That's not true and you know it, cabróna!"

Laura eyed Anita so contemptuously that she almost let her hands swing at her middle sister. She turned back to Rosalía and raised her eyebrows. "You see, now she insults me by calling me a cabróna. I'm just showing my concern for her. I do not want to see her get hurt by waiting for a man who will never call on her. I want to spare her of that misery."

"You, Laura, concerned about someone other than yourself?" Rosalía said almost laughing now. "I don't believe that for one second and I'm sure Ana doesn't either."

"I, sure as hell, don't believe it," added Anita while looking at Rosalía. "And I'll be damned if ever let her console me or try to help me." She turned back to face Laura. "Your help does not come unconditionally or straight from the heart. Your help comes with a baggage load of strings attached to it. You're still a pig and goddamn cabróna!"

Laura's patience could not hold out any longer and her actions took Anita and Rosalía by surprise. "Why you bitch!" Laura said angrily. Her nostrils were flaring just as her father's nostrils would flair whenever he got angry. Laura swung her hand and slapped Anita's face so hard she almost knocked her to the ground. The sound of the smack against Anita's soft skin seemed to linger inside Rosalía's ears, as if it were a cloud of cigar smoke circling above her head. Anita twisted her head in response to Laura's violent attack, but then she turned right back and stared deeply into her malevolent eyes. Anita then took two steps forward, grabbed a handful of Laura's hair and pulled hard enough to cause her elder sister to fall to her knees. Laura's brand new bonnet easily slipped off her head and fell to the ground.

Rosalía immediately jumped into the fray, but fighting Laura was not her intention. All she wanted was to pull Anita away from Laura and keep all three sisters away from a certain beating. "Stop pulling my hair you bitch! Let go of my hair!" shouted Laura.

"No!" shouted back Anita. Her eyes glared at Laura with hatred. The adrenaline coursing through her blood like the rapids of a river, gave her new-found strength, allowing Anita to keep at bay the much stronger Laura. "You have to pay for all of the insults and for all of the misery you have caused me!" Anita kept one hand firmly in control of Laura's hair and with the other hand slapped her face hard.

When Rosalía saw this, she took hold of Anita's hand to remove her grip from Laura's hair. "Ana, stop it!"

"Why should I? You hate this pig as much as I do, so let me finish this!"

"No Ana, please stop it!" shouted back Rosalía. Rosalía knew now that the incident had reached a point of no return. It had been a full-blown fight between two sisters and one that they could not keep a secret like so many of their other fights.

Laura's hairdo had taken an over an hour to prepare, but Anita took only seconds to destroy it. Strands of Laura's beautiful, lacy brown hair went in every direction, most of it covering her face. While kneeling on the ground at the mercy of Anita and her powerful grip, Laura did manage to see Rosalía's face. "Don't do me any favors, Rosa, I can handle her and I can handle you, too!"

Rosalía ignored Laura and continued to pull Anita's hand away from Laura's hair. Feeling Rosalía's prying hand, Anita cried out, "No Rosa! Let me deal with this rotten whore!" Rosalía struggled with Anita until finally she was able to pry her fingers loose. Forced to let go of Laura's hair, Anita now came across with a slap so hard her fingers were painted across Laura's cheek. In response, Laura reeled back with her arm and punched Anita in the belly. Anita gasped in pain and fell to her knees facing Laura eye to eye. Rosalía lost control of Anita's hand and she, too, fell to her knees. Rosalía struggled to rise but before she could stand, she felt Laura's hand across her face. It felt like a flat plank of wood. "Why did you hit me?" Rosalía shouted angrily.

"Because I felt like it, puta, and besides, I've wanted to do it ever since our last fight."

Rosalía shook her head as blood began to trickle out of her mouth. Anita, who was slowly recovering and rising off the ground, failed to see Laura coming back at her with a closed fist. Anita felt Laura's knuckles against her lips, and then sensed a trickle of blood oozing down her chin. Laura then rose to her feet and pounced on her two sisters at the same time, pinning them to the ground.

"Get off of me, Laura!" shouted Rosalía.

"No! I'm going to make the both of you pay!"

Recovering quickly Anita turned to confront her elder sister. "If you don't get off of us, I swear I'm going to scratch your face!"

The second those terror-filled words came out of Anita's mouth all three women froze instantly. Laura then turned her attention from Rosalía to Anita and her eyes instantly lit up in fear. "You bitch! We all agreed never to scratch our faces! If you scratch my face I will have to scratch yours!"

Even Rosalía was surprised. She turned to Anita and while feeling Laura's knee pinning her down, she said, "Ana, you know we made a pact never to scratch each other's faces. As much as I hate this bitch, she's right."

"Then tell her to get her smelly body off me!" Anita shouted. Anita waited for some sort of response from Rosalía but she quickly noticed her youngest sister's eyes focusing not on her but on something just past her. Anita followed her sister's eyes, turned her head to face the other side and saw the tips of expensive leather boots; boots that could only have been worn by her father.

CHAPTER 12

Standing above them with his arms folded, Rodolfo Hernández yelled, "What the hell is going on here?" He left Maria standing at the porch but she was still unable to see what was happening on the other side of the coach. Despite not being able to see, Maria had a good sense of what was taking place. She also had a good idea of what Rodolfo was going to do to his three daughters. She disappeared into the house, pulled out her rosary beads and decided to deal with the situation with prayer.

All three women let go of each other and quickly rose to their feet; their beautiful dresses torn, raggedy and tarnished by dirt. Their expensive bonnets sat crushed on the ground and the delicate strands of hair that only moments earlier had adorned their heads went in every direction. Their faces had bruises and each of the women spat out blood. Remarkably, though, none of their faces had a scratch on it!

"Father," pleaded Laura, "This was Ana's fault."

"I don't give a damn whose fault it was! I warned all three of you the last time," said Rodolfo with angry eyes. "Didn't I warn you?" He watched his three daughters nod their heads collectively and fearfully. Then Rodolfo unfolded his arms and pointed toward the porch. "Get going!" he commanded thunderously.

While the three women ran toward the porch, Rodolfo looked around and found a good tree-limb with which to teach his lesson. He quickly removed the excess limbs and left only the stubs so that it could cause more pain. Very calmly, Rodolfo walked back to the house and confronted his three daughters. Their faces revealed a kind of fear that Rodolfo could only compare to that of a slave about to receive a lashing. Rodolfo climbed the three steps onto the porch and looked at his three daughters with anger and with a determination to teach them a thorough lesson this time; a lesson they would remember for the rest of their lives. Holding the limb firmly with his right hand, Rodolfo pointed to the railing and commanded. "Bend over!"

"But Father!" shouted Laura, "It wasn't my fault!"

"Like hell it wasn't!" retorted Rosalía.

"I don't care!" shouted Rodolfo more angrily than before. "I'll not tell you again, now bend over the railing!"

The three women reluctantly walked toward the porch's wooden railing and arched their bodies. Rodolfo then walked over to them and raised each of the dresses to expose the white petticoats. He stretched his right hand all the way back and swung the tree-limb across Anita's buttocks. Anita let out a howling yell. It was like the howling of a hungry dog in the dark forests of San Sebastián. Rodolfo decided to let Anita simmer in pain, and then he took a step toward Laura. He swung again and thrashed his limb across her buttocks. She, too, let out a painful yell.

In her room, Maria could not escape the dreadful cries of her daughters and she, too, began to weep. She had never before felt so helpless, so weak and so inadequate. Maria prayed that one day God would give her the courage to stand up to Rodolfo.

Rodolfo took another step, swung his right hand backwards and with all of his strength whacked Rosalía's buttocks, but he noticed something right away. Even though he had swung the tree-limb harder than he had done at Anita and Laura, Rosalía did not shout or cry. He admired that. He walked over to Anita and saw tears streaming down her cheeks. "You're a goddamn weakling, Ana, just like your mother!" He swung again and Anita cried out in pain. Agustín and Candelario, who were busy removing the trunks off the wagon, heard the whirring pitch of Rodolfo's tree-limb and could almost feel the stinging sensation. Every time they heard the whacking sound, they flinched, as if they were the ones receiving the beating. To Candelario, it did not matter *who* the recipient of the beating was. It was the act itself that disgusted him, a cruel, evil and vile manner in which to show someone's superiority.

In her bedroom, Maria kept pacing back and forth, rubbing her hands, shaking her head and wondering when Rodolfo would cease the heartless punishment. Every second seemed like an hour and every whack of the tree-limb became louder inside Maria's head.

Thin red streaks of blood began to appear across the seat of the women's petticoats and as their petticoats turned red with seeping blood, the shrill of his daughters' cries echoed through the depths of the forest.

Rodolfo swung the tree-limb repeatedly but by the seventh or eighth time, he felt Maria's hand grabbing hold of his arm. It wasn't a strong grip, and Rodolfo did not read any animosity in Maria's eyes when he turned to face her. "Rodolfo," pleaded Maria in a passive tone. "I think the girls have had enough. I think they've learned their lesson."

Rodolfo turned back to his three daughters and realized Anita and Laura were near to collapsing. Then he turned to Rosalía and noticed her staring directly at him with unflinching eyes, face taut with anger and without any hint of fear. He could almost feel her anger as if she were communicating mentally with him. Yet, despite his obvious disappointment, Rodolfo seemed to welcome Rosalía's anger because her bravado reminded him of his fearless mother. Rodolfo dropped the tree-limb onto the porch and yelled. "Now get the hell out of my sight!"

Anita and Laura quickly straightened themselves, pushed down their dresses with as much dignity as they could muster under those circumstances, and then rushed into the house. Rosalía slowly erected her young body, pushed down her dress and in deep pain slowly walked past her father and mother. Rodolfo watched Rosalía as she went past him. He held on to the fierce expression he had shown his daughters while beating them but found that he could not fight the admiration he was suddenly feeling for Rosalía. So far, she had demonstrated to Rodolfo that she had the will and the strength of character to take over the family business. All she needed now was a weakling of a husband, a man that Rosalía could control with the aid of his teaching. He had not planned on beating his daughters today, and he certainly did not want to beat Rosalía, but he could not reveal any hint of favoritism, and so he felt he had to beat her, too. "Let that be a lesson to you, Rosa. Now you will heed my warning."

Rosalía closed her eyes in anger, sighed heavily but instead of letting the matter go, she turned back to face her father. Maria closed her eyes and shook her head, knowing Rosalía was not going to keep quiet. "You think that by beating us you will change us?" said Rosalía angrily. "All you are doing is showing how much of a bully you really are, Father, and nothing more. All you are doing is making the separation wider between yourself and your daughters. Do you think I fear you? Do you think I respect you? I do not fear you, Father, and I certainly do not respect you! How can I respect a man who beats his wife?"

"Silence you imprudent bitch!" shouted Rodolfo. All instances of favoritism vanished in a split-second. He glared at Rosalía, and then arched his body to pick up the tree-limb. "Silence or I'll thrash you to death!"

"Go ahead, Father! Do it! Release me of this nightmare!"

"You are an ungrateful little bitch, Rosa!" yelled Rodolfo. He swung back and tried to whack Rosalía in the face, but Rosalía reacted quickly and raised her arms to her face. She felt the pain of the tree-limb as it thrashed against her forearms. Rodolfo quickly dropped the limb and grabbed hold of Rosalía's hair, pulling her head backwards. He closed his fist and swung hard but Rosalía quickly bent her head and Rodolfo's fist landed right on top of her crown. Rodolfo let out a yell while holding on to his right wrist with his left hand. "You little brat, you've broken my wrist!"

The blow to the head was so severe it caused Rosalía to stagger. While trying to balance herself she curiously saw hundreds of tiny dots of light, flashing and dancing merrily before her eyes. She felt light-headed and within seconds came crashing down on the wooden porch floor. Holding on to his wrist, Rodolfo looked down at Rosalía and uttered, "Serves you right." He turned to Maria and commanded, "Help me tie a sling to my wrist. That little bitch of yours broke my hand!"

Candelario and Agustín had taken the last of the trunks upstairs and had begun to walk to the servant quarters next to the stable when they heard Rodolfo's voice. Tilting his head upwards, Candelario's eyes focused on a window in the second floor and noticed his patrón. "Candelario!" shouted Rodolfo, his right arm in a makeshift sling. "Take Rosalía into the house and put her in bed! Then I want you to ride into town and fetch my solicitor. His name is Don Diego Redondo and his office is at the end of Calle Las Flores. If you get lost, ask anyone in town to show you how to get there."

"Si Patrón!" yelled back Candelario. He watched Rodolfo Hernández disappear into the house but then almost immediately heard his voice again.

"One more thing, Candelario, do you have your walking papers?"

"Si Patrón!"

Maria had spent the last two hours placing cold compresses on Rosalía's head. Holding on to her rosary beads, she prayed for her daughter to regain consciousness. Two hours earlier, Maria had removed Rosalía's dress and tended to the crimson stripes that crisscrossed her buttocks. It would be a while before Rosalía could sit again, thought Maria but she wondered if her daughter would ever learn her lesson. After taking care of Rosalía, Maria checked on Anita and Laura and while they lied face down on their beds, mother undressed them and tended to their wounds. It was a great start to their vacation, Maria pondered sarcastically; perhaps it was an omen of things to come. She could not have been more prophetic.

CHAPTER 13

A little past four in the afternoon, a well-dressed man, atop a brown stallion, galloped along the winding path leading to the Hernández hacienda. He reined in hard and the beast halted just inches before Agustín's face. "Is Don Hernández here?" he said demandingly, a superior tone of voice characteristic of a slave owner. His long, brown hair fell down to his shoulders and his chestnut colored eyes beamed at Agustín with authority. The six-foot tall solicitor secretly hoped to come across in a firm manner that Agustín would recognize immediately, and while placing both hands firmly on his waist, expectantly, his light-brown beard shone brightly against the fading sunlight.

"Si señor," replied Agustín cautiously. "He is upstairs."

"Good, then tell him that his solicitor, Don Diego Redondo, is here." Redondo dismounted and turned over the reins to Candelario who had just stepped out of the hacienda. "Here, give him fresh water and grain. I will be here for a spell, so I expect you to take care of my horse. Do you understand me, *prieto*?"

Candelario nodded without looking at Redondo. As Redondo stepped onto the porch, Candelario saw Agustín's face and recognized his anger. Agustín hated that condescending tone of voice, that superior timbre in the intonation of words, that aristocratic cadence that characterized the peninsulares into a single group of fat-bellied patricians whose only role in life was to achieve wealth at the expense and domination of others.

Agustín's repulsion and disdain for the peninsulares came together in a single moment just by hearing Don Diego Redondo's voice. And like his younger siblings, Manolo and Berta, he could not live any longer under the current conditions in Puerto Rico, especially after the United States of America had joined England and most of Europe in finally abolishing slavery. The winds of change were starting to blow towards the island of Borinquen, and Agustín somehow sensed the era of slavery was at its end. That is why he and his older brother, Candelario, were members of *La Cruzada,* a revolutionary cell based in Santurce. Founded two years ago, long before Betances and Ruiz had founded the Revolutionary Committee of Puerto Rico, it had been growing in membership. It was comprised of slaves only and they had been secretly storing machetes, knives and a few pistols and rifles. It was a slow stockpiling of arms but while they amassed their weapons, they recruited more slaves into their fold with the promise that one day they would surprise their white masters.

Don Diego Redondo removed his leather gloves and his top hat, and as he approached the hacienda, Rodolfo stepped outside to greet him. "Buenas Tardes, Don Redondo," said Rodolfo with a pleasant smile, as if the incident with his daughters had happened weeks ago.

"I received your message but I didn't think you'd arrive so quickly, Don Hernández."

"Yes, we did better than expected, but, here we are. Well, what's the status?"

"Right down to business, eh?"

"That is why I'm here, Don Redondo," replied Rodolfo, in a sudden change of demeanor. "Or would you prefer I go into town, spend half the night at a tavern, and then come see you in the morning?"

Diego had forgotten that Hernández was an impatient son-of-a-bitch, and though he always tried to become Rodolfo's friend, the fact was that Hernández only saw him as someone who worked for him and nothing more. "Spending the night at a tavern was not what I meant, Don Hernández," said Diego meekly.

Rodolfo nodded, and stared at his solicitor without batting an eye. "I have no time for socializing. I am here on business, and I have one month to complete all transactions. Are we clear on this, Don Redondo?"

"Si señor, very clear," replied Diego with a dry mouth.

"Follow me," ordered Rodolfo. He led his solicitor to a brightly lit parlor adorned with wicker furniture. The parlor smelled of freshly picked flowers and its brightness came from brilliant sunlight that penetrated the many large windows surrounding the social room. "Please, take a seat," said Rodolfo.

Diego Redondo sat on a wicker chair and reached into his leather bag. He retrieved a thick notebook and handed it to Rodolfo. "I present you with the ledger." Rodolfo took the notebook and placed it on the wicker table.

"I will study it later, just give me a summary," grunted Rodolfo, slowly beginning to lose patience.

Diego Redondo cleared his throat, but it was a nervous reaction to Rodolfo's request. "You currently own an estancia of 852 cuerdas in San Sebastián and an estancia of 625 cuerdas in Lares. You have a total of 43 leases."

"What about Camuy and Añasco?"

"I do not represent you in those municipalities, Don Hernández," replied Redondo nervously.

"That's right, I seem to have forgotten," replied Hernández scratching his head. "All right, you may continue."

"Of the 43 leases, 15 are in delinquency."

"How much did you say?" Rodolfo asked, but he heard his solicitor's voice clearly.

"Fifteen, señor," uttered Diego. "The debts vary in size, but I have summarized and written the amounts in that ledger. I have also written the names of the people who owe you money."

"Give me the names of the ones who owe me the most," demanded Rodolfo, eyes now glaring at his subordinate.

"May I?" Diego asked while gesturing to the ledger lying on the wicker table. He waited until Rodolfo nodded his approval. Diego then reached for the ledger, turned to the summary page and read. "At the top of the list, owing you 6,217 pesos is Don Ricardo Pérez, and he is followed by Don Guillermo Martínez who owes you 4,353 pesos. Third on the list is Don Juan Pítre who owes you a total of 3,237 pesos. Next on the list is Don Eduardo Sant—"

"Enough!" yelled Rodolfo, waving his hand at Diego. "I'll go through the list later but what I want for you to do is to meet me here tomorrow morning at eight. I want you to accompany me to everyone who owes me money. Bring enough paper to document our conversations in case we have to serve papers in court. If these goddamn creoles refuse to pay me, I will evict them! Do you understand me, Don Redondo? Am I clear on this issue? Is there any doubt over what I am asking you to do?"

"No, Don Hernández, I understand exactly what you want me to do."

Rodolfo rose to his feet right away and looked down at his solicitor. "Good day to you, Don Redondo." He turned and walked out of the parlor.

Diego remained sitting and staring at the ledger he still clutched in his shaking hands. For a brief moment, he thought Hernández would fire him. He had only three clients but Rodolfo, by far, was his biggest one, and the thought of losing the Hernández business sent a fearful chill up his spine. Tomorrow he would gather enough paper and ink, and document every word, every nuance and every expression of the face. He would leave no doubt about any of Rodolfo's conversations and he would use those documents in court as though his life depended on them. At the same time, he wondered about the creoles that owed Rodolfo money, and felt sorry for them.

Diego Redondo had long ago realized that he would never become a great solicitor, and he often wondered why Hernández kept him on retainer when there were so many other notable solicitors in Puerto Rico. Perhaps it was because Diego was so accommodating, so willing to cave in to Rodolfo's whims that he found himself kept on retainer. Perhaps that weakness is what Governor Pavía saw in him, too, when he threatened to suspend Diego's license and destroy his law practice if he did not cooperate. Pavía had dispatched him to Lares and ordered him to infiltrate Centro Bravo, something Diego thought he would never do. It was a dangerous mission and he hated everything about it, especially the part where he had to betray the members. It made him feel like a low down two-face, and it drained him of all self-respect, but he had to cooperate because he was not a member of the elite, because he was more of a workingman who depended on their business, but most of all because he owed money to the local criminal.

Through a mutual acquaintance, Pavía learned about Diego's loan and agreed to pay off the debt. With Pavia as his new creditor and with the fear of losing his license, Diego quickly agreed to spy for the governor. For several weeks, Diego tried to make a connection with an active member of Centro Bravo but was unsuccessful. He left Lares and decided to reconnoiter his hometown of San Sebastián where he finally made contact and befriended the unsuspecting and quick-to-trust Eusebio Ibarra.

Diego Redondo kept staring at the ledger in his hands, and while shaking his head in obvious disappointment he realized that he was in total control of all gathered intelligence. He was also in control of how much information he could give to Pavía. That would become a tool for him, something he could put away for now and use later for his benefit. Right now, he had to prepare himself mentally for tomorrow. He had to prepare his conscience to witness Rodolfo Hernández's cruelty and he was not really looking forward to that. He placed the ledger back on the wicker table and said under his breath, "You bastard." He sat there for several moments more, and just before rising to his feet, he felt Rodolfo's powerful hand on his shoulder. Diego closed his eyes, wondering if Rodolfo had heard him.

"I've had a change of mind, Don Redondo. Please look in the ledger and tell me which lessee is the closest to me."

Redondo opened the green book and read aloud. "That would be Juan Pítre. He leases from you a stretch of 14 cuerdas. The property lies near barrio Pepinos and it runs next to the Blanco and Duran plantations."

"Did you say Duran? Is that son-of-a-bitch still around? I remember a couple of years ago I offered him good money for his land but the bastard refused to sell. Does he owe me any money? Does he owe anybody money? Perhaps I could pay off the debt and have him owe me. Then maybe it will change his mind. Does he owe anybody?"

"No, señor, Don Duran is completely debt-free and beholden to no one. So, too, is Don Blanco, whose farm runs adjacent to Don Duran's."

"Blanco's debt-free, too? I see. Well then, I will just have to wait. Sooner or later they will lose their money; it's just a matter of time."

CHAPTER 14

Sunday, February 9, began just like any other Sunday on the Pítre farm. It was church day, and farm work would not begin until after Mass. Only one thing was different: Juan Pítre felt under the weather that morning and simply could not accompany Miguel to church, as he had always done. Juan stayed in bed all morning long and did not rise until two in the afternoon. Sensing that Miguel was on his way back from Mass, though, and realizing his son was probably famished, Juan decided to cut a few plantains and fry them just in time for Miguel's arrival.

Juan stepped out into the afternoon sun and hunched over a burlap sack filled with plantains he purchased three days earlier at the market. Slowly reaching into the sack, he felt the pain in his lower back rising up through his spine. It felt like his back was splitting into two pieces, and he staggered briefly as he grabbed hold of a couple of plantains. He straightened himself, but grimaced from the awful pain as a result. The elder Pítre looked at the plantains he was holding and noticed they were starting to turn yellow. Miguel was going to eat ripe plantains that afternoon.

As Juan returned to his threadbare dwelling, he heard the unmistakable sound of horses whinnying far off into the distance. He turned and saw two figures heading toward his home, apparently coming from the direction of Don Blanco's farm. Juan frowned right away because he was not in the mood to entertain Miguel's guest, or anyone else for that matter. It wasn't that Juan harbored ill feelings for Carlos Peña; in fact, he was eternally grateful to Carlos for teaching Miguel how to read and write. It was the thought that Carlos had somehow made Miguel grow up too fast, crowding his mind too quickly with thoughts of rebellion, and making him think that the only means by which to achieve independence was through violence. Independence! Now that was a word Juan kept hearing ever since he was a child. Over the years he had seen them come and go. Every now and then, young visionaries, filled with dreams, hopes and fiery convictions, would come out to Juan Pítre's farm and preach the gospel of freedom to him. Nothing would ever come of it, though, because they could never overcome the great lack of will among the people, the abject resignation, and the futility they collectively felt in opposing the motherland. He saw the same dreams and hopes for independence in Carlos Peña that he had seen in young men so many times before, and Juan's experiences with the likes of Carlos had taught him that he was just another *independista* who had no idea of the kind of trouble into which his passions would lead both he and his son. Juan shook his head as the two figures grew larger, and decided that today he would boldly confront Carlos and tell him to keep away from Miguel. Juan realized this would be a difficult thing to do because he feared that his opposition to Carlos would drive a deeper wedge of separation between father and son, but it was something that Juan felt compelled to do.

All of a sudden, Juan Pítre dropped the plantains to the floor and stood frozen, opened-mouthed, as he recognized the two figures now. They were not Miguel and Carlos. They were Don Rodolfo Hernández and his solicitor, and their faces did not register any emotion, only a business-like expression that told Juan Pítre this was not going to be a social call.

Juan Pítre stepped down from the porch, and, as the two men finally arrived, he looked up and forced a smile. "Buenas Tardes, señores."

Rodolfo eyed Juan Pítre with utter disdain as he slowly dismounted. Following his master's orders, Don Redondo remained atop his horse and reached for a notebook with which to write.

Juan forced another smile. "Buenos Dias. To what do I owe this visit, Don Hernández?"

"Spare me the pleasantries, Pítre! You know why I'm here. You owe me money. What other reason could get me to come out to this god-awful place?" Rodolfo turned and looked up at Don Redondo. "How much does this man owe me?'

Don Diego Redondo dismounted, and then retrieved the libreta from the bag attached to his pommel. He walked nervously toward Don Hernández, opened the libreta and spoke timidly. "Señor Pítre owes a sum of 3,237 pesos as of last month."

Don Hernández turned back to Juan and looked straight into his ashen face. Juan could see the sheer hatred in Don Hernández's eyes, and it gave Juan the impression that there was no compassion in Rodolfo's heart. "I have been meaning to talk to you about that, señor." Almost immediately, Juan regretted his response. He could not think of anything plausible enough to explain his delinquency; he simply did not have the money.

Rodolfo squinted impatiently at Juan. "What in the world could you possibly have to say to me, Pítre? Either you have the money or you do not, no talking. Talking is for women! You are six months in arrears, and I have been more than patient and kinder to you than I have been to all of my lessees. This is not a charity, Pítre, this is a business!"

"But señor, my last harvest did not yield as much as I expected, and I wasn't able to meet the monthly payment to your solicitor. I do expect a good harvest this season, señor, and I will give you all of the money earned from it."

"There you go again, Pítre, talk, talk, and talk!" shouted Hernández. "That's all I hear from you: nothing but horseshit! What is the matter with you goddamn creoles? You people are lazy and stupid, and lack the motivation to better yourselves. That is why we stand above the likes of you, Pítre. That is why *we* are the masters and *you* are the servants!" Rodolfo took his eyes away from Juan and gazed at his house. "Look at how you people live! You call that a house? You fucking peasants know absolutely nothing, care about nothing, and live in nothing!" Diego kept quiet as Rodolfo stood there berating a helpless Juan Pítre. The fearful solicitor wrote down every word of their conversation, just as Rodolfo had ordered him to do. In the distance, heading toward the farm, Miguel was returning from church, and he could see that his father had company, but who were they?

Rodolfo Hernández kept his tirade in full swing because he knew that his trip so far had yielded nothing. Juan Pítre had no money for him that day—and Rodolfo could do nothing about it. Rodolfo drew closer to Juan and poked his chest hard with his index finger. "You are in serious debt, Pítre, and I have just about run out of patience! Now, I'm going to give you a month's time, thirty days with which to meet your financial obligations to me. I will send Don Redondo out to you on the 9th of March, and if you do not have the money, I will evict you."

Juan could not hide his frustration and fear, and unaware that Miguel was drawing closer, he tried to plea with Hernández. "But how much money do you want?"

"All of it, Pítre, all of it!" Rodolfo snapped.

"Señor, there is no way that I can up with 3,000 pesos, not even with a bumper crop!"

"That's not my problem, Pítre!" replied Rodolfo. He had already been in talks with another farmer that morning, a young man who had expressed his desire to move into the Pítre farm. Finding new tenants had never been a problem for Rodolfo, but since he had purchased the land from Juan years ago, he felt he should give him just one more chance to pay the back rent. Other than that, he felt nothing else for Juan Pítre. "Now, standing before my solicitor, Don Diego Redondo, I want you to promise me that you will have all of my money by March 9 of this year."

Juan turned to Diego, who had just finished writing down Rodolfo's last words. Diego looked up and saw the outright fear in Juan's eyes, but he kept his own fears well hidden, and showed Juan nothing but a placid face. Juan turned back to Rodolfo and sighed heavily, as if he had to deal with yet another burden, one more yoke over his neck. "All right, Don Hernández, I will pay you the money. And if I am unable to pay you, come March 9, I will move out of the farm."

It was only then that Rodolfo finally managed a smile, but the gesture did not come from amusement or gratification. The smile came from his sense of victory, a smile that confirmed his superiority over Juan Pítre. "Very well," said Rodolfo. Without taking his eyes away from Juan's face, he said, "Don Redondo, did you record this conversation like I told you to do?"

"Si, señor Hernández, I wrote down every word."

"Good," said Rodolfo, nodding his head. Then, he gave Juan a dismissive look and turned back to mount his horse. As he climbed onto his horse, Rodolfo noticed Miguel's image for the first time. Rodolfo stared at Juan Pítre's son, as he drew closer to the house, and nodded to himself, as if a sudden thought had just crept into his mind. Preoccupied with the sudden turn of events, though, Juan Pítre never noticed that his son had been steadily approaching his home. While Don Redondo mounted his horse, Rodolfo looked down at his boots and saw the clumps of dirt on the tips. Holding true to his devious nature, he waited until he was certain Miguel was close enough to see him. There was a brief moment of silence as Rodolfo thought deeply, calculated and devised. Juan removed the worn out pava from his head and held it tightly against his chest. He cast his humble, grey eyes up at Rodolfo, whose face now reflected a sense of satisfaction. Rodolfo glanced one more time at Miguel, and then looked down at Juan. "Remove the dirt from my boots, Pítre!"

Diego turned to the side and noted Rodolfo's face. There was pleasure in that wicked face, thought Diego; a kind of pleasure only an elite, an aristocrat could display. He wondered right then on which side he thought he should be. Did he want to become a member of the elite, as he had always strived to become, or was he just another commoner who had no business being involved with the aristocracy? He knew that he had to make a decision soon.

Juan Pítre shook his head. "I will not wipe your boots, señor. Though I may be a peasant to you, I do have my pride."

Rodolfo needed to make a statement to Juan's son; a silent statement, which he would have to invest with money. Rodolfo knew that the statement would yield a far better harvest than Juan's farm could ever yield. "Consider my request a job, Pítre. I will remove 300 hundred pesos from your debt right now if you remove the dirt from my boots." He turned to Redondo and commanded. "Deduct three hundred pesos from Pítre's debt right away!" He watched his solicitor write furiously.

"Don Juan Pítre now owes you 2,937 pesos," said Redondo.

Hearing Redondo's confirmation, Juan considered the offer, and thought it would benefit him greatly. It was merely a simple act of cleaning someone's boot, and he would receive money for it at the same time, a simple job that would only take a few seconds worth of time. He nodded at Rodolfo, and then humbly reached with his hand to wipe the dirt from off the proprietor's boot. Then he heard Rodolfo's powerful voice. "No, damn it! Wipe the dirt off my boots with your shirt!"

Juan hesitated at first, wondering why Rodolfo had made such a request, but he did not understand Rodolfo's way of thinking and fell right into the landowner's web of malice.

Miguel tugged the reins and stopped his horse to watch the events taking place only a few feet away from him now. He watched curiously as his father pulled the tail of his shirt out of his trousers. Then he saw his father use his shirt to wipe the dirt off one of Rodolfo Hernández's boots. Witnessing such an act of humiliation sickened Miguel so much that he could not hide his anger. While Juan Pítre walked around Rodolfo's horse to wipe the dirt off the other boot, Rodolfo took that moment to watch Miguel's face. Realizing Miguel had been watching the scene, Rodolfo's face stretched with a wide smile. "Is that your son, Pítre?" he asked as if he did not know. But he knew it was Miguel, and he had directed that scene carefully, like a maestro with an orchestra. Rodolfo felt he needed to make a statement strong enough so that the next generation of peasants would know their place in society.

Juan Pítre froze again, and closed his eyes briefly in a moment of sudden realization. He knew right then that he had fallen into Rodolfo's subtle trap, and he was angry—angry for being so stupid. He scraped the last clumps of dirt off Rodolfo's boot, straightened himself and looked up at Rodolfo. "Yes, Don Hernández, that's Miguel."

"Good, then he should see this so that he could know his place!"

Having understood now the reason for Rodolfo's request, Juan nodded at Rodolfo with half a smile. "By the grace of God, Miguel is a much different person than I am, a better man, wiser, too, and fearless."

"How so is your son fearless?" Rodolfo asked curiously, a sense of deflation suddenly overcoming him.

"Let me put it to you this way," replied Juan with a tone of satisfaction, "he will not end up like me."

Rodolfo smirked at Juan. "Is that a fact? Well, only time will tell." Rodolfo spurred his horse, and, as the beast turned around, it dug its hooves deep into the soil and kicked out dirt onto Juan Pítre's face. Diego watched Juan remove the dirt from his face, and shook his head in helpless frustration. He spurred his own horse and followed his client.

As Rodolfo approached Miguel, he nodded at him. Miguel stood atop his horse, holding the reins tightly in outright anger, but he offered Rodolfo no response. As Rodolfo rode past Miguel, though, he saw the anger and resentment in the young man's eyes; something he had never before seen in a peasant. Miguel displayed green, fiery eyes that showed no fear, none of the humility Rodolfo had come to recognize in peasants and certainly no respect, a look that Rodolfo had to take seriously. Catching up to Rodolfo, Don Diego Redondo tipped his head at Miguel, and without pausing, said, "Buenas Tardes."

Miguel watched him, too, but said nothing. As the pounding of hooves slowly faded away, only the sounds of birds and crickets filled the air. Miguel remained atop his horse, watching the still image of his father—a broken man, a man without money and a man without an ounce of pride. How could he respect his father now after witnessing such humiliation? Despite how he felt about his father, he still loved the old man. He struggled internally with his own convictions and felt that no matter what he and Carlos did for the creoles of Puerto Rico it would never amount to anything because they just did not want to change things. Though Miguel agreed to help his father after church, he could not erase his father's shame from his mind. He refused to see his father's apologetic face, and clamored at the thought of hearing him justify his humiliation. He turned his horse around and rode off toward Don Santiago Duran's plantation.

Juan Pítre stood in the middle of the field watching his son's image fade into the distance. He sighed deeply, and then removed the small clumps of dirt from the tail of his shirt. How could he explain all this to Miguel? How could he tell his son that by cleaning Don Hernández's boots he was able to reduce his debt by 300 pesos? That narrow wedge that existed between father and son, that tiny political divide that he feared so much, had grown into a social divide, a separation caused by the evil machinations of Rodolfo Hernández and by his own stupidity. Juan realized it was too late to narrow the ideological gap between them, and no way that he could convince his son to stay away from Carlos Peña now. On the other hand, perhaps there might have been some calculation on Juan Pítre's side, too. Perhaps somewhere, deep in the recesses of his heart, lying dormant like a volcano was Juan's passion and visions of seeing Puerto Rico free. Perhaps he *wanted* Miguel to see him in the act of subservience. Whatever he thought at that moment, however, did not matter now.

CHAPTER 15

Miguel rode out to Don Duran's plantation and met up with Carlos Peña that early afternoon. Carlos was saddling his horse with plans on traveling into town on behalf of Duran, when he noticed Miguel slowly approaching the farm. Though he was pleased to see him, Carlos could not help but notice the sad look on Miguel's youthful face. He tried several times to get Miguel to talk to him but Miguel wasn't in the mood to reveal his deepest emotions at the time. Finally, Carlos asked Miguel to accompany him into town. Any distraction, thought Carlos, would probably get Miguel out of the fog he was in and perhaps get him to open up.

The two men arrived in San Sebastián a short while later, and as they tethered their horses to a nearby post, Carlos could see that something had disturbed his protégé greatly; something that must have hurt him deeply. They kept silent as they walked slowly through a dirt road that bisected the town. Every now and then, they would see a jíbaro pulling his donkey behind him. The jíbaro would make his way to the tiny market at the end of the road, and with a hopeful look about his face, stand all day until he sold all of his crops. Carlos and Miguel witnessed the townsfolk, mostly dressed in white clothing, bustling in and out of shops or standing in the middle of the road to talk about their individual hardships.

Walking side by side with Miguel, Carlos thought it wise not to pry his young friend anymore, and just let him be. He watched the townsfolk with the keen eyes of a rebel and sighed heavily out of frustration. "Look at them, Miguel. Look how they struggle to make ends meet. There is not an ounce of pride in any of them. Do you see all of those shops lining the street? Who owns those shops? Who owns most of the land, too? Who runs the country? The goddamn peninsulares do,

Miguelito! Complacency is a dangerous thing for the Puerto Rican people these days. It must be eradicated and replaced with pride; pride for oneself and pride for one's country." Miguel followed Carlos's eyes and let his friend talk away. "Just look at them, Miguel, I am willing to wager that if I ask all of them to dig into their pockets there would be no more than five pesos between them. The government forces them to walk around with a libreta and produce it upon demand to one of their sniveling bureaucrats just fresh off the boat looking to exploit a helpless jíbaro for his own gain. Yet nothing that we do will ever change them or their way of thinking! That is why we must resort to revolution; it is the only way."

"Up until today," Miguel broke his silence, "my heart was never one hundred percent convinced about revolution. But now, I am in total agreement with you, Carlos."

Carlos did not turn to look at Miguel, but was glad that his friend had finally opened his mouth to speak. "I've never seen you this downtrodden before, Miguelito. What happened? Did you have another fight with your father?"

"No, but I wish I had; it would have been easier to deal with. No, Carlos, it wasn't that at all. Rodolfo Hernández came around to the finca today, probably looking for money. But I witnessed something awful, Carlos, something that hurt me so much that I cannot bring myself to go home right now." Carlos stopped abruptly and turned to face Miguel. "I actually saw my father stooping like a slave to wipe dirt off Hernández's boots with his shirt! I could not believe my eyes! My father never looked at me, either, and that bothered me. All the while, I saw a calculating look upon that bastard's face, as if he knew I was watching and knew what I was thinking at that moment. Carlos, I have never hated anybody before, but today I wanted to beat the living daylights out of Rodolfo Hernández. It was as if a dark cloud of sheer hatred overcame me and consumed my heart with vengeance. You should have seen him, sitting atop his horse with that pompous look on his face, showing the world that he was a master. As he rode past me, I was tempted to jump on top of him and drag him through the dirt, beat his face with my fists until he bled the ground through and through. But what held me from my inclinations, what held me back from seeking retribution for my father's humiliation *was* my father. I knew that if I had laid a hand on Hernández, you would be talking to me through cell bars right now, and that bombastic devil would have evicted my father. After that bastard left, I looked at my father and saw his apologetic face. I knew that if I'd come home, he would try to justify the reason why he had humbled himself to Hernández, and try to convince me how the people of Puerto Rico are powerless to overcome their peninsular masters. My stomach knotted at the thought, and rather than engaging my father in another argument, I chose to leave."

Carlos gazed at Miguel but decided to say nothing to him, no consolation, no pity, and no kind of encouragement. The final piece in the construction of a rebel was finally in place, and Carlos surprisingly had nothing to do with it. Miguel Pítre was ready. Carlos's prior doubts about his young protégé instantly vanished, and now he looked upon Miguel with nothing but utter confidence. There was nothing else to do. He put a hand on Miguel's shoulder and nodded with a smile. "Come, Miguelito, let's go get something to eat."

CHAPTER 16

The gathering was supposed to take place on Saturday, February 8, but the journey to Lares had taken longer than the leaders expected. Along the way, they heard rumors about loyalists spies reporting their movements back to the authorities. Forced to take alternate routes, the rebels finally assembled two days later, on Monday, February 10, at the Rojas plantation.

There was a mood of excitement amongst the rebels because the two leaders were going to make a rare appearance at the gathering. The rebels came from all parts of the western countryside, answering the call as if both Betances and Ruiz were the pied pipers of their day. Fearful of a premature discovery, Rojas decided to wait until nightfall, until all loyalists and peninsulares had bedded down for the night.

The rebels came in bunches, and sometimes one at a time. Some had never seen the leaders before and some came out of curiosity. In all, there were about one hundred and fifty rebels. They gathered behind Rojas's hacienda, away from curious passersby, and sat down on the ground. Their faces glimmered against the glowing light of hand-held torches or lanterns fixed upon wooden posts. The murmur of the crowd grew intensely, as they waited for the leaders to show themselves.

At the front of the gathering sat Carlos Peña, Aguilar, Ibarra, and Miguel Pítre. Although Aguilar fought hard to hide his feelings from Carlos, the African leader knew that Aguilar wasn't thrilled with the idea of Miguel being there. Despite Aguilar's feelings, Carlos insisted on Miguel's presence at the meeting, and he took no steps to hide the fact that he had more confidence in Miguel than he had in his own vice-president. As far as Carlos was concerned, Aguilar had to sit there and take it like a man. On the other hand, Ibarra remained quiet and looked up at the front porch, where Manual Rojas finally emerged out of his tiny house.

"Ladies and gentlemen," Rojas said. "I thank you all for coming here tonight. It shows your belief in the cause and your determination to overcome your fear in the dangers of this illegal gathering." As Rojas spoke, Mathias Brugman, along with Baldomero Baurer stepped out onto the porch. A few seconds later, Miguel Rojas and his wife stepped outside, followed by Juan De Mata Terreforte and Pablo Antonio Beauchamp. "And now, without further delay, I call on señores Betances and Belvis!"

The moment Dr. Betances stepped onto the porch there was a resounding ovation. The applause and cheers were so loud, that Rojas had to step in front of Betances to wave his hand at the crowd in a hushing gesture. Moments later, Belvis stepped out and he, too, received an ovation.

Carlos could not suppress his excitement, either, because ever since he joined the movement he wanted to meet Dr. Betances, his hero. To Carlos, Dr. Betances was an abolitionist first, and then a revolutionary. Miguel turned to look at Carlos and noted a boyish smile from the otherwise stern and focused man. It was as if Carlos had seen the three Magi—a little-boy look that confirmed to Miguel that Carlos revered Betances as Puerto Rico's savior. Whatever the reason, Miguel was glad to see Carlos filled with genuine happiness that night.

"Please, tone down your applause, lest the loyalists wake and come snooping around!" said Rojas, his mouth barely noticeable against his thick, dark beard. The ovation continued, however, until Dr. Betances was forced to step in and raise his hands in a quieting gesture. All of a sudden, like a warm breeze in the afternoon, a reverent silence transcended the plantation. The rebellion's Messiah trained his sights upon the crowd and spoke with the tone of an aging sage.

There was a tired look on Betances's face, as if he had not slept in days. Bags were starting to form under his eyes and his beard was starting to turn grey. In spite of his privation, though, he knew that he had to muster all of his strength and show his audience that he was a still a strong man. As the gathering waited in silence, the pinging sound of crickets and coquís began to dominate the airwaves. "Ladies and gentlemen," said Betances in a sermon-like delivery, "tonight is a special night. I bring glad tidings to all of you. As many of you know, Governor Pavía exiled Segundo and me from Puerto Rico and, although we were supposed to go to Spain voluntarily, we decided that it would better serve the cause if we were to disobey the governor's command and exile ourselves to Santo Domingo. While in our sister colony, we met with the Dominican rebel leaders and with their help we were introduced to many important people from South America. Over sixty years ago, the South Americans fought against Spanish tyranny and successfully removed their colonial yoke. Presently, they have expressed a keen interest in what is taking place in Santo Domingo, and have supplied the Dominican rebels with food and arms. They also stand poised to lend troops if necessary.

"A group of Cuban revolutionists, exiled from their country as well, were among our group and together we made the South Americans aware of our plans to revolt. The plan is simple. Currently, the Spanish have their hands full quelling the rebellion in Santo Domingo. At the given time, we will start our own rebellion, here, in Puerto Rico. Once our Cuban rebel friends confirm that the rebellion has started in Puerto Rico, they will commence their own rebellion in Cuba. According to our Chilean friends, Spain will have no choice but to divide their forces in order to combat all three fronts.

"Señor Belvis will travel to South America, as our Ambassador, to secure desperately needed financial and political help. The South Americans have promised to provide us with a ship stocked with rifles and pistols. I will arrive on that ship at the port of Guánica on the eve of the revolution and distribute arms to everyone. Every one of you will have a specific duty that day, and you all know what we expect from you. It is a dangerous thing that we are doing, but if we succeed, Puerto Rico and Cuba will be free and independent states. If we fail, we will all hang."

The crowd remained silent for a few moments, but then someone in the back started to clap his hands. Then, everyone in the crowd stood up and gave Dr. Betances an ovation. All of a sudden, Belvis stepped forth and waved his hands at the crowd. He waited until the applause faded. "I and I alone will be undertaking this dangerous voyage to South America. The Spanish navy has many warships patrolling the Caribbean Sea, and I will have to exercise extreme caution. Aside from this, I want to promise you that I will secure the arms deal at all costs, and that I will have the weapons ready in Caracas, Venezuela, where we will load them into Doctor Betances's ship. You will have arms with which to defeat the Spanish imperialists! Que viva la revolucion! Viva Puerto Rico Libre!"

The crowd, much to Manuel Rojas's obvious disappointment, cheered on the cry of freedom. It continued for two whole minutes until Dr. Betances raised his arms in the air. "Please!" he yelled. The crowd hushed again into a venerable silence. "Segundo and I came here tonight because we felt you needed to see and hear us. We wanted to give you hope and give you encouragement to keep our cause alive. Now, it is up to you. It is your task now to recruit more people. You must be careful in this endeavor because you must know to whom you can speak. Do not worry because I have instructed señores Rojas and Brugman on how to recognize a potential recruit. They will instruct their leaders and their leaders will instruct you. Remember that total secrecy is of paramount importance. The Spanish authorities must never find out about the rebellion until the appointed time. Now, we must take our leave of you and set the course for Puerto Rico's destiny. Good night and God bless each and every one of you."

This time, there was no applause, only silence. Ruiz followed Betances into the Rojas house and soon after, the rest of the leaders disappeared into the house. Only Manuel Rojas stood outside. He smiled briefly before addressing the crowd. "I want to thank you all for coming tonight. Good night!"

The crackle of burning torches pierced the stillness of night, and as the crowd of people, whispering excitedly about their rebellion began to disperse, Carlos, Miguel, Aguilar and Ibarra stood still, watching Manuel enter the house. The door slammed closed and the noise caused Carlos to snap out of his reverie. He stood looking at the closed door, shaking his head. "I wish I could have met him, shaken his hand, and tell him just how much he has meant to me."

"Perhaps one day you will," said Aguilar. "If we all survive, that is."

Carlos turned and looked down at Aguilar, dark eyes beaming intensely. "We must succeed, Manuel, or we will forever remain under the Spanish yoke." He turned around to face Miguel Pítre. "Well, what do you think? I told you he was something special, didn't I?"

"Indeed, Carlos, now, more than ever, we must see this thing through," replied Miguel.

Carlos nodded at him, and then eyed both Ibarra and Aguilar. "You heard the man, we must recruit more people. I have several men in mind. They are Don Duran's slaves but they are willing to join the cause."

"Slaves?" Aguilar asked rhetorically. "What makes you think Don Duran will let his slaves join the rebellion?"

"I will ask him and he will allow them to join. Although, Don Duran is not a member of the rebellion, he is sympathetic to the cause. And when the time is right, he will let the slaves join us."

"We shouldn't go around recruiting slaves, Carlos," growled Aguilar. "What we should be doing is recruiting creoles, working men with money to help out the cause; committed men who will fight!"

"There is no greater commitment than a slave's desire to be a free man, Manuel," replied Carlos angrily. "Believe me, I should know. Don Duran's slaves *will* fight!"

"Very well, what do you want Eusebio and me to do?"

"I want you to inform the other members of Porvenir about the meeting tonight. Then, after I meet with Manuel Rojas, I will come into town and instruct you on how to recruit a potential rebel. Then you two will split up and go into the barrios of San Sebastián. Keep in mind that there are many loyalists and peninsulares in San Sebastián, so you must proceed with extreme caution."

"And what are *you* going to do?" Aguilar asked with a tone of skepticism.

"I will meet up again with Manuel Rojas, after giving you instructions."

"Why?"

"I want to discuss the details of the plan and what role Porvenir will play on the day of the revolution. At this time, the date has not been set but I feel word will come down any day, so we must be ready. How are we doing in terms of arms?"

Eusebio Ibarra looked up at Carlos. "We have about twenty rifles and a few pistols but we are low in ammunition. Although we have been buying bullets in town, we do this every third or fourth day, sometimes once a week. This we do so as not to draw any attention from the damn peninsular gunsmith, who's a nosy bastard."

Carlos sighed. "Then we must depend on Dr. Betances and his ship. In the meantime, continue what you are doing. It might be wise if you could send some of the men into other towns to buy ammunition; this will further avoid suspicion."

The four men of Porvenir were the last to leave the Rojas plantation that night. They mounted their horses and undertook the ten mile journey back to San Sebastián.

CHAPTER 17

After a two-day absence, Miguel finally decided to return home. For two days Juan waited for Miguel, desperately clinging to the hope that he could convince his son that what he did, he did for money. By one o'clock in the morning on February 11, though, Juan began to realize that his son might never come home, and a great sense of loss suddenly overtook his senses.

Miguel did not arrive until three that morning and thought his father had been sleeping. Instead, he saw the bright light of a lantern and the image of his father emerging from their shack of a home. Hopes and dreams, and visions of a free Puerto Rico now filled Miguel's heart and had quickly supplanted the rage that had consumed him two days before, when he witnessed his father's humiliation. If the rebellion succeeded, his father would never again have to stoop to wipe dirt off a Spaniard's boot. The rebellion, if successful, would restore Juan Pítre's dignity and self-respect. This, above all others, was the reason why Miguel would become the fiercest rebel on the island. He took up the mantle for redemption on his father's behalf, and he would return all 52 cuerdas of land, once owned by the Pítre family, back to its rightful owner. Miguel was no longer a child. He was a focused man who now knew the reason why God put him on earth. He would become the champion of freedom, the liberator of oppression and the paragon by which history would judge all rebels.

He dismounted and tied his horse to a post just outside his house. As he slowly walked to his home, Miguel saw the lantern swinging back and forth, occasionally illuminating Juan's face. "Where the devil have you been, Miguelito?"

"I was staying with Carlos. I have also been to Centro Bravo," said Miguel confidently. He no longer felt the need to hide his feelings from his father or further deceive him. He was a man full of conviction and pride, and if his father disagreed with his feelings, then he was all right with that, too. He knew that his father would benefit greatly from the rebellion, even though he had been against the cause from the start. Miguel looked at his father expecting a barrage of obscenities but no words came out of his mouth. "Well, aren't you going to say anything?"

"What do you want me to say, that I am happy? That I wish you good fortune in your endeavors?"

"Yes!"

"Look, Miguelito, what you saw yesterday was—"

"You don't have to explain anything to me, Pápi."

"Yes, I do. Don Rodolfo Hernández paid me to clean his boots. I didn't do it because he ordered me to do so, you must believe me."

"Yes, and I bet he didn't ask you to clean his boots with your shirt, either, right?" Juan did not say a word. Miguel had spoken the truth, and Juan could not deny it either. "He knew I was heading home, Pápi. He saw me. It was his way of showing me who is the master and who is the servant. He also knew that he count on you, too, Pápi, and you didn't disappoint the man."

"Enough, Miguel!" yelled Juan, a tear rolling down his cheek, unable to hide the terrible pain in his heart. All those years of suffering the misery of poverty, loneliness and deprivation seemed to converge in that one single moment. Though he struggled valiantly against succumbing to self-pity, he failed miserably because that was all he had left in the world. He placed the lantern down on the porch floor and walk into the field of coffee plants. While gazing into the darkness he resorted to the only thing a loser against such a battle could do, and that was to cry. He wiped the tears from his eyes, looked at Miguel and shouted. "Are you happy now? Are you happy in seeing your father a broken man? I have lost my wife to another man, and not a day goes by that I do not think of her! I have lost all of my money and cannot afford to buy food or clothes or send you to school! I have lost my lands! And now…I seem to have lost you, too!" Juan fell to his knees and began to weep.

Miguel closed his eyes, in a feeble attempt to hide his own tears, but the sight of his father crying in misery, clawed away at his self-control. He tilted his head upwards and with eyes widened, gave in to his emotions. He shouted from the depths of his lungs, but his outburst wasn't out of pity but from the release of all the frustration and anger pent up in his soul for years. Miguel shouted repeatedly while his father buried his face into the red soil, crying and begging God to take his soul away. Juan moaned eerily, a sound of hurt that came from the recesses of his being. While Juan released his misery, Miguel kept shouting into the blackened skies in total agony, frustration and sheer abhorrence at his father's situation.

When Miguel released all of his frustrations, he ran to his father, grabbed hold of him and easily lifted him off the ground. "Do not cry, Pápi! Please do not cry!"

"Forgive me, Miguelito. Forgive me for bringing you into this wicked world! Tomorrow I will leave the finca and you will never see me again. I will never embarrass you again!"

"Oh Pápi, you don't have to apologize. You were never an embarrassment to me! I just hated to see you work so hard and show nothing for all of your efforts. I hated the fact that you had no choice but to sell your lands. I hated that you were miserable, though you tried never to show me your pain. All I ever wanted was for you to welcome a change. All I wanted was to change Puerto Rico's future for you. I want to see these lands back in your hands as the rightful owner. My dream is to see you as a successful plantation owner, with lots of money so that you can come back to Mámi and show her your success. My dream is to see you and Mámi together again. I know how much you suffer every day; I can see it in your eyes. I know how much you long to see Mámi and it makes me sad to know this. By heaven, I swear to you that I will see the rebellion through to completion. You will have your lands back and you will have your dignity restored—this I promise you!"

Juan finally managed to smile at his son, and then he opened his arms to hug him. Miguel wiped the tears from his father's face and returned the hug. The two men wept uncontrollably for nearly a quarter of an hour. After several moments more, Miguel let go of his father and smiled at him. "Let us talk no more about this, Pápi. From now on, you will let me deal with this Rodolfo Hernández character. From now on, *I* will take over. You will rest now. You will no longer have to worry about the day-to-day operations, or worry about money. As a member of Porvenir, I am eligible for emergency funds if warranted. These funds have been set aside to help poor farmers, and to help with recruitment. I will talk to Carlos and he will help us out, Pápi."

"But what will you do about Rodolfo Hernández?"

"I said you don't have to worry about that anymore, Pápi. I will deal with that bastard!"

"Son, don't do anything you might regret."

"The rebellion will succeed, Pápi, and the first thing we will do is get rid of all the peninsulares! They will leave by choice or we will force them to leave. In either case, the lands you once owned will be yours once again. We will begin trading with other Caribbean nations, as well as with countries in South America. Then we will make contact with the United States of America and seek their support for our independence. We will begin trade with them, too. Oh Pápi, the future is wide open for us, and all you have to do is believe. You must believe in the cause with all your heart and all your soul."

"Thank you, Miguelito. Thank you for opening the eyes of an old man, and setting him straight."

"So, you're with me then?"

"Yes, Miguelito, I am with you."

"Thank you, Pápi." Miguel looked up at the skies again and smiled. "In one hour I must get up to do the chores. Let's go get some sleep." Miguel picked up the lantern, and placed his arm under his father's shoulder. The two men silently entered their home, and moments later, the lantern faded to black.

CHAPTER 18

On the morning of Wednesday, February 12, Maria Hernández had sent her three daughters into town to buy fruits and vegetables. Rodolfo had returned late the previous night and would sleep most of the morning. Maria knew that the moment he woke up, Rodolfo would start demanding food as though he were the king of Spain. Before setting out to San Sebastián, Rodolfo had decided against the idea of bringing their cook along on the trip, and this meant that for the duration of their stay, Maria would have to do all of the cooking. That did not bother her, though. What bothered her was the fact that Rodolfo had gotten so used to Bernicia's cooking that he would probably reject Maria's cooking and hurt her with his awful comments. The one thing in Maria's favor was that while Bernicia cooked, she would watch how she prepared the meals. Maria felt confident that Rodolfo would like her cooking just as much as he did Bernicia's cooking. Nevertheless, Maria sent Agustín to San Sebastián in search of a local cook.

The morning sun cast brilliant streaks of light on the porch of their country house, and while Maria waited for her daughters to return, she contemplated the slivers of sunlight piercing the vegetation and falling on a nearby orange tree. While gazing at the orange tree, her mind drifted back to her courtship days with Rodolfo.

Rodolfo was a much different man those days so many years ago. Rodolfo was never an introvert; in fact, he was quite the opposite. Garrulous and full of energy Rodolfo made jokes and laughed heartily. He was the life of the party wherever he went, and most of Maria's friends and family liked him immediately. From the start, he impressed Maria with poems and songs, kindness and devotion. He slowly drew her into his tender arms with a gentle disposition she could not ignore. His affection and love for Maria was so profound that he simply swept

Maria off her feet. Not long after the marriage, Rodolfo began to exhibit change, another side of him that was dark and mean. It felt to Maria as if Rodolfo had played a good game of charade during their courtship days, an elaborate ruse on her and her father so that he could gain their love, respect and, most of all, their trust—the keys that would eventually facilitate Rodolfo's entry into nobility. To Rodolfo, marriage into the De Valera family was a convenient arrangement for him because it was a virtual guarantee for opening doors, making connections and paving the way toward limitless wealth. The young and naïve Maria never knew that a monster would come to replace that kind and gentle man she had married. Once married, she could no longer go home, and when she complained to her father about Rodolfo's abuse he turned a deaf ear because, coming from a devout Catholic family, the idea of divorce was simply out of the question. He told Maria to go back to her husband and make the best of it. That was the last time she saw her father, and shortly thereafter, Rodolfo decided to venture to the colonies to seek his fortune.

Laura, Anita and Rosalía held their parasols over their heads to shun the brutal sunlight. As they walked down San Sebastián's main thoroughfare, Rosalía, for the first time in her life, saw how other people lived. The town that morning teemed with jíbaros, standing by their wooden wagons selling their crops, and peasant creoles shopping along with their children. The men wore straw hats called pavas, and when the daughters of Rodolfo Hernández walked by them, they removed them and tipped their heads in homage. The jíbaro and creole peasants knew who they were; it was a rarity to see such nobility in a farming town such as San Sebastián, and so word of the Hernández's arrival spread quickly.

Something captured Rosalía's attention that morning; something she had never before seen in her young life. Rosalía stopped suddenly and turned to gaze across the dirt road. Her two sisters continued walking ahead, unaware that Rosalía was no longer with them. Rosalía slowly brought down her parasol and closed it. Across the dirt road, Rosalía saw a young woman holding a baby in her arms. The baby had no shirt and no pants, only a cotton sheet that served as a diaper.

Trailing behind her were two other children, a boy and a girl. They had no shoes, and their feet were dirty from walking on the road. The girl's knotted hair made it seem like she had never combed it before and the boy was extremely thin and malnourished. The young woman walked past an old man with missing teeth, who was standing next to his donkey. A plump woman stood beside the old man, shouting out her prices for the bananas she held in her hands. Rosalía saw another woman crossing the dirt thoroughfare, and four children following her closely—all were barefoot and wore ragged clothing. Rosalía turned to the northern end of town and saw a group of men in tattered clothing. They were unloading bundles of sugar canes out of a wooden wagon. A plantation owner stood above them and screamed obscenities at them for taking too much time to unload the perishable goods.

Rosalía turned her head to gaze at the small shops lining the street, and noticed a well-dressed man emerging out of one of the shops. He was the shop's proprietor, and he was a peninsular. He wore an expensive jacket and a neat vest, where he kept his gold pocket-watch. His beard was thick and curly but was well trimmed. As he took in a deep breath of fresh air, he contemplated the bustle of people outside his shop, and Rosalía immediately noticed the disdain in his eyes. Rosalía shook her head at the man, but the man never noticed Rosalía staring at him. The unassuming peninsular went back into his shop when a peasant woman entered.

Rosalía took in all of the sights and happenings of an average day in the town of San Sebastián, and never heard Laura calling out her name. Rosalía finally snapped out of her seeming trance when she felt Laura grasping her arm. "Are you deaf now, Rosa? Didn't you hear me calling you?"

"No, I was busy marveling at the sights."

"What sights?" Laura demanded impatiently. "There are no sights in San Sebastián; it's just another goddamn farming town and nothing more! Besides, you are not on a sightseeing trip but on an errand. We must get home before father wakes up!"

Rosalía turned back to look across the dirt road and noticed the same woman that was holding the baby moments earlier. She was no longer holding her baby, and she seemed to be crying. Trailing behind the woman was her two other children and they, too, were crying. Laura took that moment to watch her sister carefully. Anita, who was standing next to Laura, turned and looked across the street, at what Rosalía's eyes were capturing.

Laura scrutinized Rosalía's face and sensed her emotions, as if she could read her mind. "Well, well," said Laura in a moment of realization.

Rosalía turned to look at her sister. "Well, well, what?"

Laura smiled, and, while looking at Anita, said, "It would seem that our young sister, here, is concerned about that peasant woman across the street."

Rosalía shot Laura a curious stare, wondering why her eldest sister's heart was so hardened against compassion. "Look at her," she said with genuine empathy. Both Laura and Anita, while still holding their parasols over their heads, turned to look at the woman. Rosalía shook her head as she studied the young woman. "Look how she wears no bonnet and uses no parasol against this unforgiving sunlight. Look at her brown hair all tied up in a bun behind her head, and her skin, darkened by the tropical sun but dry and worn out by brutal work on someone's plantation. Notice the bags under her eyes, and that far away stare, as if her mind were somewhere else. See how she suffers so greatly at the terrible pain of having to give up her baby. I must tell you, my sisters: this sad sight has deeply moved me. I am saddened to see how the peasant creoles live, and more so by the fact that we live our lives shielded from all this." Rosalía turned back to her sisters and noticed they were staring at her, open-mouthed and in total disbelief. "What's the matter? What's wrong with you two?"

Laura glared at Rosalía with utter contempt. "Have you forgotten who you are, Rosa? You are a Hernández and a De Valera, and one day you will have to deal with the likes of those peasants you contemplate with such sadness. Somehow I am sensing that you are feeling sorry for them, is this true?"

"What's wrong with showing a little sympathy, Laura? I mean, just look at how they live and compare it to how we live. Is it fair?"

"Life's not fair, you naïve bitch!" Laura retorted.

Anita finally put in her opinion. "As much as I hate to agree with Laura, she may have a point, Rosa. We are much different than they are, because we are true Spaniards. They are the lower class, peasants whose only purpose is to serve us."

"Anita! I can't believe I'm hearing this from you!" Rosalía said alarmingly. "They are human beings, and they are no different from us. Those are Father's words, not yours! We are Christians, brought up in the Holy Roman Catholic Church and taught to be compassionate, caring and generous."

"I don't believe this bullshit!" Laura cried out. "Come, Ana, let's get to the market and leave this awful town before Father wakes up. Are you coming, Rosa? Or are you just going to stand there and cry your heart out for every peasant you see?"

Rosalía opened her parasol and brought it over her head. She followed her two sisters to the market, where they made several purchases and returned home before their father woke.

CHAPTER 19

Rodolfo Hernández woke at 10:30 that morning and just like Maria predicted, he was ravenous and demanded his breakfast immediately. Rodolfo washed his face and mouth and nodded his approval at seeing a plate full of eggs, tostones and bread. A cup of steaming coffee next to the plate was the first thing Rodolfo grabbed. He ate in silence while Maria sat at the table, expecting him to converse with her. Rodolfo said nothing at all, though, and simply ate his meal. After drinking the last drops of coffee, he stood and reached for his cane.

"Where are you going today?" Maria asked humbly.

"Into town to see Redondo, what's it to you?"

"Nothing, I'd rather hoped we could have dinner tonight in town, at a local restaurant."

"Maria," said Rodolfo in a tone of frustration, "I didn't come here for pleasure. I'm here on business."

"I know that, Rodolfo, I just wanted for us to enjoy at least one night out, without having to discuss business or anything else." Maria looked at her husband with hopeful eyes.

Rodolfo thought about her suggestion for a moment, but then shook his head. "I don't know, maybe, if there's time. We'll see."

Maria frowned. "Make some time, Rodolfo."

"Goddamit, Maria, I don't have time for that nonsense!" shouted Rodolfo. "I said I will see, now why can't you be satisfied with that?"

"All right, I shall wait for you," replied Maria meekly.

Rodolfo grunted but offered nothing more to his wife. As he stepped outside the house, he saw Laura standing by the porch. "Are you going into town, Father?" Laura asked in a hopeful tone.

"What the hell's going on here today? Why is everybody so interested in where I'm going?"

"I just wanted to know if you needed company, is all."

"Look Laura, I'm going to be making my rounds today with Don Diego Redondo. It is business, and something that would bore you. Besides, shouldn't you be planning your wedding?"

"Why can't you teach me about your business?" insisted Laura.

"Because you're a woman, and a woman's job is to marry and tend to her husband, though I really can't say that about your mother!"

"Then who will take over the family business if not your eldest child?"

"When the time comes, and I hope it's not for a very long time, I will decide. I may turn the reins over to your husband, if he turns out to be a capable man. If not, then I will have to consider either Ana's or Rosa's husband, but there is not much potential there either. Look, now is not the time to talk about this."

"All right, Father," replied Laura disappointedly. Shifting her disposition, she said, "We were in town early this morning, all three of us."

"Against my wishes, as always," said Rodolfo impatiently. "No doubt it was your mother's idea, so what about your trip into town?"

"I have nothing much to tell, Father, except that I saw something strange in Rosa."

Rodolfo sighed impatiently. "What? What did you see?"

"I saw Rosa fixated on the local population."

"So? What's so important about that?"

"You should have seen her, Father, she almost cried when she saw the peasants in town."

"What do you mean she almost cried? What are you talking about, Laura?"

"She started talking about how unfair we are to the peasants and that they have a right to be our equals. I had to stop her, Father, because she was carrying on about feeling guilty that we are so rich and the peasants so poor. It was awful."

"I see," uttered Rodolfo. "Well, you did the right thing, Laura. You must keep a close watch on Rosa from now on, and even Ana, too. There are dangerous elements out there that would like nothing more than to topple the government, independistas that espouse nothing but rebellion and anarchy. We must not let Rosa get too close to these individuals because if you are right about her, they may easily sway her into their camp. That would be a major embarrassment for the Hernández family, and a terrific blow to our family business. Let us keep this matter between us, and maybe next week, I'll take you into town and perhaps teach you a few things about my business." Rodolfo walked down off the porch and mounted his horse. Within minutes, he vanished into the woods.

Moments later, Maria stepped out onto the porch, unable to veil the hurt on her face. "So, I'm not much of a wife?"

Laura turned to face her mother. "You heard our conversation?"

"I heard every word. Just what are you up to, Laura? Are you trying to curry your father's favor by sacrificing Rosa?"

"I told him the truth, Mother. I told him that Rosa is becoming more rebellious every day. He told me to keep a watch on Rosa and Ana, so I will do as he says."

"And who is going to watch you?"

Later that day, towards early evening, Rodolfo had returned from his long day in town. He had arrived with a rare smile on his face. The reason for his uncommon happiness was that through Don Redondo, he was able to recover a great deal of money from farmers that owed him. Rodolfo tied his horse and walked up to the porch, where he noticed Rosalía and Anita sitting on wicker rocking chairs, enjoying the early evening breeze. The pounding of Rodolfo's boots on the porch's wooden planks sounded deep and resonated inside Rosalía's ears. Rodolfo placed both hands on his hips and simply gazed at his two daughters.

"Good evening, Father," said Ana. Rosalía said nothing, and she did not make an effort to acknowledge her father either.

Rodolfo sighed in frustration, but the joy in today's successes had far outweighed any rage he might have otherwise harbored. "Ana, can you give us a moment please?"

Anita was surprised to hear her father's polite request and took it for all it was worth. She knew that he would probably never ask her like that again. She smiled courteously and said, "Certainly, Father."

Rodolfo waited until Anita entered the house. Then, he sat on the wicker chair next to Rosalía and looked at his daughter. Neither he nor Anita, who had just entered the house, suspected that Laura was standing near the open door, just out of view. Laura had waited all day just to hear her father lash out at Rosalía for being sympathetic to the peasants of San Sebastián, and now the moment was drawing closer.

"Rosa, Laura told me that your mother sent all three of you into town this morning…against my wishes." Rosalía chose to remain silent. Still sore at him for the beating he gave her, she was not about to forgive him. "I know that you saw many things in town today, things that you never saw before. I know that for a young person like you, it may be difficult to grasp a full understanding of how life truly is, Rosa. But life is not that colorful and carefree world that you enjoy, and that I have provided to all my children. Life is hard, and success is measured by the degree of sacrifice one makes. I have given all of my life and energies to the family business so that you will never suffer the want for anything. Yet, you have now seen how other people live and it has saddened you. It is all right to feel that way, Rosa, but you must know one thing, too. They have not sacrificed as much as I have and that is why they are peasants. What you saw today *should* be indelibly etched in your mind because that is what lies in store for you if you reject our way of life. The rich cannot populate the world alone; the world must have street cleaners, too, shoe repairers, household servants, butlers and jornaleros. Because of my hard work, we have become wealthy people, and members of the social elite. I will not apologize for that, Rosa. I will not apologize for the hard work and the sacrifices I've made in order to get to where we are. And I tell you right now, Rosa, if any one of those peasants you saw today were to have the same ambition as I had, then they too would reach the same goal that I reached. You have felt sympathy for the peasant—I can understand that because you are a good Christian. But this is as far as you should go, Rosa. You must keep in mind that you are on the right side of society. You are a privileged child and hated by the peasants. Be very careful, Rosa, because I sense danger in the air. San Sebastián is a den of revolutionists, a beehive of anarchists and warmongers. Never go into town alone." Rodolfo rose to his feet and placed his hands on his hips, expecting his daughter to argue against his thoughts. From inside the house, Laura was seething in anger. She could not believe how kind and gentle her father was behaving with Rosa. She had hoped that he would arrive with the devil himself and beat Rosa for showing such sympathy for the peasants of San Sebastián. Instead, Rodolfo had made money that day, and, fortunately for Rosalía, had arrived home in a terribly good mood. Laura's eyes reflected nothing but utter hatred for Rosalía and she began to plot another downfall for her youngest sister. Rodolfo gazed at his daughter. "Well, aren't you going to say anything?"

Rosalía kept looking aimlessly at the darkening woods. The sun had set moments earlier and dusk was quickly overtaking the day. Rodolfo nodded to himself, certain in his mind that he had reached Rosalía, and then he turned and entered the house. Rosalía remained sitting on her wicker chair, rocking back and forth. The creaking shrills of crickets began to fill the air and a steady breeze brought a sense of calmness to her. Then she smiled and opened her mouth. "Nice try, *pendéja sucia*."

Frustrated that Rosalía somehow knew she had been hiding behind the door all the time, Laura emerged from the darkened house, unable to hide her chagrin. "What are you talking about, bitch?"

"I know it was you. You told father everything that happened in town today. It's all right, though, because I expected you to do that. You're so goddamn predictable it's no longer any fun."

"So are you," replied Laura, now standing before Rosalía ready for yet another fistfight. "I knew how you were going to react in town today, in fact, I counted on it. It's just too bad that Father was in a good mood tonight. But, there will be many more opportunities, and you will not fail me!"

"Oh Laura, why don't you just disappear? Shoo! You're just like a bothersome mosquito!"

"You'd like that wouldn't you. Then you'd have the family business all to yourself!"

"The family business all to myself, are you kidding me? That's the way you think and the way you perceive everybody else thinks, but thank God, that's not true. Besides, what about Ana or Mother, do you think I would cut them off?"

"You and I both know that Ana isn't fit to run a candy store, let alone our real estate business. She's a weakling just like Mother."

Rosalía finally looked up at her sister. "I hate you! I truly despise you, and I'm ashamed to call you my sister!"

"I hate you, too, with all of my heart! I wish you would die!"

Rosalía rose to her feet and met Laura eye-to-eye, rage filling every part of her young body. "Then kill me!"

Laura swung her arm and slapped Rosalía hard across her face. When she saw Rosalía falling back into the wicker chair, Laura pounced on her. Rosalía grabbed a handful of Laura's hair and pulled so hard it made her scream in pain. "Ouch! Stop pulling my hair you bitch!"

"No!" yelled back Rosalía. She quickly raised her legs and kicked Laura's belly. Laura reeled backwards and fell on the wooden porch. Rosalía quickly rose and then jumped on top of Laura, slapping her face repeatedly.

Upstairs, in the master bedroom, Maria was about to turn in for sleep. By a sliver of moonlight, filtering through the open window, she looked at her husband. Rodolfo was facing the other way—head buried into the pillow. Maria gently nudged his shoulder. "Rodolfo, I think Laura and Rosa are fighting downstairs!" Rodolfo was not sleeping though but he refused to respond to his wife's concerns. A slow grin began to form on his face as he heard the rumble downstairs. "Rodolfo, aren't you going to do something about this?"

Rodolfo turned over and looked at Maria's silhouette. "Nah, let them fight it out. It'll make them stronger."

Laura managed to roll out from under Rosalía's knees, and quickly rose to her feet. Then she swung her fist at Rosalía's face and landed a hard blow that made Rosalía queasy. Rosalía shook her head and managed to stand to her feet. The two women grabbed each other, one trying to get an advantage over the other, but since they matched in size and strength neither gained the upper hand. As they struggled with each other, they fell over the porch's three steps and landed on the dirt. In a tight and violent embrace, they rolled over in the dirt numerous times, pulling hair, slapping, punching, but never scratching each other's face. "Get off me you whore!" yelled Laura.

"No!" yelled back Rosalía.

In one of the smaller bedrooms, Anita was fast asleep. No sound in the world could ever wake her once she fell asleep, not even thunder from a rainstorm.

The two women fought each other like two wild beasts; strands of mussed hair going in every direction and nightgowns dingy from rolling so fiercely upon the dirt. Their bruised and reddened faces could not hide the number of blows they gave to each other, but neither of them refused to yield. Laura managed to stand first but Rosalía quickly followed. Standing with her back to the house, Rosalía glared at Laura, "Had enough, bitch?" Facing her sister, though, Laura noticed her father right away. He was holding a club in his hand, and as he stepped down off the porch, Laura knew Rosalía was in for it. Rosalía uttered again, "Well?" All of sudden she felt a thud upon her head and everything went dark—down went Rosalía; lights out!

Witnessing her youngest sister fall to the ground brought a smile to Laura's face. She walked closer to her father and nodded. "Thank you, Father, she got what she deserved." All of sudden Laura felt a thump on her head, and she too dropped to the ground unconscious; lights out for her, as well.

"Now I can get some sleep," muttered Rodolfo to himself. For one fleeting second, Rodolfo thought to pick up his daughters and bring them to their respective bedrooms. Then he threw the club onto the porch and entered the house. Rodolfo had not nestled quite right into his bed when Maria suddenly sat up. "Is everything all right? Are the girls all right?"

"Oh yes, they're all right," replied Rodolfo. He turned over and closed his eyes. He could not sleep though, because he did not know how much of his speech had gotten through to Rosalía.

As Rodolfo closed his eyes, memories of his former life flashed vividly through his open mind. Rodolfo had a big secret; a secret so big that he could not share it with anyone, not even his wife. Rodolfo had come from a very poor family in Barcelona, Spain. And even the name, Rodolfo Hernández, wasn't real. His father was a blacksmith who lost a duel with a much better swordsman and died at thirty-two years of age, leaving his family penniless. His mother was a house servant for a rich family. She worked long hours and never saw her son. The burden of raising the young boy was borne by his grandparents, who were also poor. But grandpa Santos was a mean son-of-a-bitch, who was always drunk and beat his grandson constantly. He warned the boy that if he ever told his mother or grandmother, he would kill him. Fearing his grandpa terribly, he kept quiet and took every beating until he grew to absorb the pain. At fourteen, and tired of the physical abuse, the young man finally ran away from home and vowed never to return. He traveled to Madrid where he fell into the company of scam-artists and con men. By the time he was twenty, Rodolfo had become a proficient pickpocket and thief, a man fully transformed into an opportunist. That is when he first saw the De Valera family and their entourage in a long procession on their way to the royal court. It was as if everything stood still, everything crystallized into a single moment of realization. When he saw how much attention and respect the people gave Count De Valera and his family, he knew right then that that is what he wanted to be. He vowed from that moment on to force his way into nobility.

As a pickpocket and professional thief, and never caught by the authorities, the young criminal had accumulated a tidy sum of money. He would have been content with living out his existence as a thief had he not seen that procession so many years ago. But he did see it, and it became the focal point of his second transformation. Several weeks later, he contacted his con men friends and they helped him establish a new identity. He was no longer Jorge Santos, from Barcelona, but Rodolfo Hernández, a distant cousin of the noble Hernández family of Seville. With the earnings from his former life as a thief, he purchased very expensive clothing, held lavish parties and began making connections with the social elite of Madrid. His newly acquired friends finally arranged for him to meet with Count De Valera at a card game. During the game, ran by his con men friends, of course, Rodolfo made sure to bet high and lose high, too. A masterful artist at deceit, he never showed one bit of regret when losing money, and that lack of reaction impressed the notion in Count De Valera's mind that Rodolfo Hernández was a very wealthy man. But the Count was completely unaware that he was the only person at that table who lost money that night. Weeks later, Rodolfo received an invitation to the Count's mansion, where he met Maria De Valera for the first time. The moment he walked into the De Valera mansion and met the Count's daughter, Jorge Santos died and Rodolfo Hernández was born. He knew that marriage to nobility was the only means by which he could purge his former life, wash away his prior existence as baptism would the sins of the impious. That is why he was so hard on his daughters and on everyone else who served under him. He never wanted to go back to that way of life and was so fearful of it, that he would resort to violence in order to preserve his transformed existence.

CHAPTER 20

On Sunday, February 16, Maria and her three daughters were on their way to the church. The tiny church, bordered by a square plaza and adorned by hundreds of pigeons, was at the center of town and had stood there for more than sixty years. It would be their first visit to a church other that the one in their hometown of San Juan, where they attended every Sunday without fail. Candelario led the team of four horses at a slow pace, through a long, winding dirt trail. The trail eventually led to a wider road, which finally brought them to the outskirts of the tiny pueblo of San Sebastián.

Along the way, Rosalía, who sat on the left side of the coach, stared out of her open window, and contemplated with pity the long line of shanty homes. The houses were made of uneven planks of wood, painted in different colors, and apparently removed from other condemned houses. The roofs were nothing more than a sheet of corrugated steel, rusted to the point where a mere shake would crumble it into dust. Outside the houses, flocks of chicken roamed in random patterns, clucking incessantly. Behind the houses, Rosalía saw a cow or two or goats tied to wooden posts. She could hear a chorus of women shouting inside their homes, and their husbands sitting passively on the porches drinking whiskey or rum. As the stagecoach rumbled along the road, Rosalía noticed several men sitting at a makeshift table playing a round of dominos. She could feel the intensity in their faces, as if their lives depended on winning the game. Around the side of a house, she saw a naked boy urinating happily into the reddish ground. Rosalía locked the images in her mind—a mosaic of Puerto Rico's bucolic life, and there it would remain in the same manner as an artist would the vision of his masterpiece. Was this how the masses actually lived? They did not live in mansions, like her family did, and they did not own any slaves either? Sadly, Rodolfo's youngest daughter had come to the hard realization that the preponderant number of Puerto Ricans did not consist of rich people but of poor workers.

As they finally entered town, the three women could feel the rumble of wheels against the uneven dirt, and the coach vibrating and bouncing in response. A few hundred yards outside the plaza walls, just several hundred feet to the left, Rosalía noticed a small gathering of people standing in front of a young man. The youthful orator, with a scraggily beard, was perched on a stump. His white shirt and trousers were filthy and his face appeared unwashed, but behind that veneer of dirt, there hid an extremely handsome young man, thought Rosalía at first. As she watched the young man, she could not deny the fact that his appearance gave clear evidence of peasantry. Nevertheless, she kept watching him, admiring his confidence, his mannerisms, and his strong voice. All of a sudden, Candelario tugged harshly at the reins and the women inside the coach jerked forward. Another stagecoach was crossing the street, forcing Candelario to yield to it. By sheer coincidence, Rosalía's stagecoach had come to rest right in front of the young speaker.

Standing on the stump overlooking the gathering, Miguel continued his speech, unaware that new listeners had unwittingly arrived. "That is why we must change the way we live!" shouted Miguel at his audience. "Why must we allow the Spanish, who are three thousand miles away, to rule us here? Why do we allow Spaniards to come here and take away our land, our businesses and our livelihoods? We let them because we do nothing about it!" Standing next to the young speaker, Rosalía, noticed a very tall African man nodding his approval at the young man's message. The crowd cheered on as the speaker spewed his words of rebellion. Rosalía listened to his every word, and because she had been a witness to the poverty, she found that she agreed with most of the young man's speech. Miguel continued his volcanic oratory, shouting at times and raising his hands in a powerful, gesturing plea to rally the people. He looked up and over the heads of his audience where he finally noticed the idle stagecoach. Narrowing his eyes to sharpen his view, he noted a very pretty woman looking at him through her window. He crunched his eyebrows and pointed with his index finger at the coach, not really thinking. "And it's people like them, over there!" The audience members all turned around at the same time, and took notice of the coach and its occupants. "Just look at them, and see how they dress. See how they ride into town with those fancy coaches and look down at each and every one of you!"

Maria Hernández sensed it immediately, almost as if she were reading their minds. It was the silent stirring of a mob; a palpable air of evil that caused Maria to fear for her family's safety. The sudden shift in the crowd swayed the gathering toward the stagecoach like an unstoppable tidal wave. The gathering of mostly peasant men all turned toward the idle stagecoach and began to draw closer to it. On the other hand, Rosalía had no inkling of what was about to take place, which is why she found her mother's reaction a little strange. Maria quickly picked up her parasol and banged on the roof several times. Candelario, who knew why the crowd was fast approaching, took his time. He waited until the crowd was only inches away from Rosalía's window before snapping the reins. The first people to reach the coach were three young men, who tried to reach for the door handle. Rosalía smiled at them, thinking they were trying to be friendly, but when they spat out cuss words and when she saw the fire in their eyes, she instinctively moved away from the window. All the time, Maria kept jabbing her parasol tip into the roof, until finally the coach jerked the three women backwards.

"What was that all about?" Rosalía asked.

Laura, who was sitting in the middle, next to her mother, looked at Rosalía while shaking her head. "What did you think, Rosa? That they were going to welcome you into their town?"

"They looked friendly to me," replied Rosalía.

"Friendly? Oh Rosa, you're so fucking stupid! They despise us!"

"That's enough!" yelled Maria. "I don't care for the use of foul language, Laura, especially before going to church." She turned to Rosalía, leaned forward and said, "But Laura's right, it is dangerous to think of them as one of us. Be mindful of that, Rosa." Maria leaned back, looked across the inside of the coach, to the other side, and noticed Anita looking out of her window, oblivious to the tragedy that nearly happened.

CHAPTER 21

While his family attended church that morning, Rodolfo rode into town with different plans. A frequent visitor of San Sebastián, and fully aware of the sentiments toward his kind, Rodolfo never traveled without his rifle, which he straddled on the side of his saddle, and never without his two ivory-handled pistols that he brazenly displayed.

Rodolfo tied his horse to a wooden post, and walked up the five stairs leading to the large, wooden doors of the mayor's house. He knocked several times and waited until the mayor's butler opened the doors. There was no need for introduction because the butler, an elderly black man, recognized *El Demonio* immediately. Rodolfo placed his riding baton under his arm, removed his leather gloves and his top hat and gave all three items to the butler without saying a word to him.

"Alcalde Chiesa is in the study, señor Hernández, I shall escort you."

"No need," Rodolfo said authoritatively. "I know exactly where it is. Just tend to my horse; give him fresh water and some grain."

Rodolfo entered the mayor's study, where the smooth politician was sitting behind his desk, apparently entertaining another guest. The mayor's avuncular appearance had been the secret to his success as a local politician. His balding scalp was tanned dark by the tropical sun, and his round face bore a thin mustache, which had been turning gray over the years. He was a short and plump fifty-two-year-old man, whose innocuous disposition concealed his real persona. But Rodolfo knew the mayor for what he really was, a conniving, sneaky, and self-serving son-of-a-bitch; a man who had no interest in politics at all—a man who took up politics for the sole reason of exploiting his public office in order to line his own pockets.

The mayor's other guest that morning was Lieutenant Colonel Juan Manuel de Ibarreta, who had just arrived from San Juan. Both men stood up and greeted Rodolfo Hernández. Rodolfo shook hands with the mayor, and then with Ibarreta. "Have we met before, Colonel?"

"I don't think so. I've just recently arrived from San Juan, and prior to that I led a battalion in Santo Domingo."

Rodolfo raised his eyebrows and gave the colonel an acknowledging nod of the head, "How's the fighting over there?"

"It's brutally savage, señor. We may lose the colony."

All three men sat down quietly. Rodolfo shook his head, openly revealing his disappointment. "I just cannot understand why Spain won't send more soldiers to quell the uprising there; it boggles my mind."

"Let us not forget that the mother country has had its own rebellions to deal with," said the mayor. "It has seen several coups, and every regime that comes to power has had to first deal with internal strife before turning to the colonies. Regrettably, we must make do with whatever resources we have available—it's that simple."

"It would seem so, señor Alcalde," said Rodolfo in utter resignation. "The same thing that is happening in Santo Domingo could very well happen here. We must take every precaution that rebellion does not take root in Puerto Rico."

"That is precisely why I have invited you here today, señor Hernández," replied the mayor with an appreciative smile. "That is why Lieutenant Colonel Ibarreta is here, too."

Rodolfo turned to Ibarreta with a curious expression. "What do you know, Colonel?"

"Nothing much, except that Governor Pavía has reason to suspect that many rebel cells have already formed on the island, and that it is only a matter of time before a rebellion catches wind."

"Colonel," said Rodolfo with a stern expression. "I know the governor personally, and he does not come to such conclusions without good reason. Is there any intelligence on this matter?"

"The intelligence comes from a note apparently written by a spy; someone who has infiltrated a rebel cell and has been communicating its activities back to the governor."

Rodolfo scratched his long beard. "How reliable is this informant?"

"I'm not sure, but it has given the governor enough reason to send me here. The note states that señores Betances and Ruiz were seen several days ago in Guánica, and the presumption that both men were on their way here or possibly to Lares."

Rodolfo sighed heavily while turning to the mayor. "I told him. I told Pavía to have them all arrested and executed for sedition, but he refused to listen to me. He felt that executing them would make martyrs of them. Instead, he exiled them to Spain. And now look—they have suddenly resurfaced." The mayor said nothing in response to Rodolfo's comments. Rodolfo turned back to the Colonel and said forcefully, "Who is this spy? Maybe we can get a hold of him and get more intelligence out of him."

"The spy signs off his reports with the initials: D.R. I do not know if the spy is a man or a woman."

"Is there any way to go searching for those two goddamn rebel bastards?" Rodolfo asked the mayor.

The mayor leaned forward. "We don't have the manpower necessary to canvas the countryside, señor Hernández. Besides, the rebels communicate so well that before we could mount any decent effort to go looking for Betances and Ruiz, they'd be long gone."

"Then how does the Colonel's presence help?" Rodolfo challenged the mayor.

"It doesn't," answered the mayor quickly. "That is why I've asked you to come here today."

"All right, then what do you want from me?"

The mayor glanced at Ibarreta before fixing his eyes directly at Rodolfo. "Señor Hernández, you are a very successful businessman. You have many people that work for you, and you hold many libretas over the local peasant population—isn't this so?" The mayor watched as Rodolfo nodded to agree with his statement. "Couldn't you enlist the services of one of your debtors to gather intelligence for us?"

"You mean spy for us, don't you?"

"Yes," said the mayor. "You have, shall we say, the disposition to force anyone of them to spy for us, and maybe we could eradicate any rebellion before it has time enough to start. You can threaten them by telling them that if they do not cooperate, you will enforce their debt and incarcerate them. Of course, I will support you by pressuring the circuit judges to rule in your favor." Rodolfo remained silent, assessing the mayor's request for a short while. Then he smiled sardonically and laughed by himself. The mayor furrowed his eyebrows. "What's so funny, señor?"

"The local population would like nothing more than to see me hanging from a tree, Alcalde. They would rather go to jail before agreeing to spy for me."

"Surely there must be someone out there that you could use," insisted the mayor.

"I don't know, but if I could find someone willing to betray his people, I would have to negate his debt as an incentive, and not enforce it as you suggest. That will cost me money, and I don't foresee the local municipality reimbursing my expense."

"A rebellion will wipe you out, señor," said the mayor. "So it is in your best interest, as well as our best interest to invest money in this venture."

"All right," replied Rodolfo reluctantly. "Give me a little time and I will get back to you. I want you to know that I am a loyalist, and I will do whatever is necessary to root out this so-called rebellion." Rodolfo rose to his feet, shook hands with the mayor and the colonel, and then quietly departed.

After Rodolfo left, the mayor looked at Ibarreta and smiled while shaking his head. "He is a loyalist—that is true, but he is a businessman first. He has a lot to lose if the rebellion succeeds."

Rodolfo could not hide his frustration as he reached for the reins of his horse. So far, this month's visit had yielded only 1200 pesos, not enough even to cover his traveling expenses to San Sebastián. Now, on top of everything else, he had to go looking for a spy. As he mounted his horse, he turned his attention to a crowd of people that was slowly dispersing. Then he recognized Miguel Pítre, jumping down from the stump he occupied only moments earlier. Rodolfo also saw a tall black man, reaching with his long arms to catch Miguel. "Great, another rebel peasant!" he uttered to himself. Then, as he turned his horse around, an idea suddenly flashed through his mind, and he pulled hard on the reins. He turned his horse back around to gaze at Miguel. He had found the spy he needed, but it was not Miguel—it was his father, Juan! Rodolfo smiled with satisfaction; that was too easy! He kept staring at Miguel and Carlos as they crossed the dirt street, and nodded with a small measure of delight. Then, he cast his sights upon the church, as the tower bell began to ring, and frowned. Aware that his wife and daughters would soon be exiting the church, he turned his beast around and spurred it into action. The steed galloped furiously, creating a swirl of dust from its pounding hooves, and disappeared into the forest.

CHAPTER 22

Carlos and Miguel slowly crossed the street and entered a colmado to get a drink of water, or whatever cool refreshments were available. As they entered the tiny establishment, Carlos turned to Miguel with admiration. "You are getting a lot better. You no longer flinch and your eyes remain steady as you speak. I am very proud of you. Did you see how the crowd responded when you poked your finger at that stagecoach? For a split second, I thought we had started the rebellion, right here in San Sebastián."

Miguel did not respond to Carlos's praises but walked over to the wooden counter instead, where the proprietor gave him a sneer. "Can I help you?"

"May we have a glass of water, señor?" Miguel requested humbly.

"We have no water," the owner replied tersely.

Miguel looked down into a wooden crate near the counter. The open crate contained several flasks of fresh orange juice. Miguel reached into the crate, pulled out two flasks and placed them on top of the counter. The owner took the flasks and put them on the counter behind him. "There is no juice here, either."

Carlos laughed mockingly. "Then we must be imagining things because those two flasks you put on the counter behind you sure look real to us."

The colmado owner, a recent arrival from Santo Domingo, looked up at Carlos and gave him that familiar disdainful look of a peninsular. "You must be imagining because there isn't anything for you here at *this* colmado. There is nothing here for rebel scum!"

"You piece of shit!" yelled Miguel, reaching for the owner. He managed to grab his apron and pulled it hard enough to rip it off the man. But he felt Carlos's long arms, wrapping around his body, and pulling him back. "Let go of me, Carlos. Let me give this filth a lesson in humility!"

"No Miguelito!" yelled Carlos. "That's exactly what he wants you to do, can't you see that? He'd like nothing more than a good reason to have us arrested, so don't give him the satisfaction."

Carlos finally succeeded in pulling Miguel away. He flashed an apologetic smile at the owner and said, "We're sorry for the inconvenience, señor." He pulled out several coins from his pocket and slammed them on the counter. "That's for your apron, señor, and for your troubles."

"I don't want your money, you goddamn peasant! Just get the hell out of my store!"

Carlos left the money on the counter, and then forced Miguel completely out of the colmado. "What's with you today, Miguel?" Carlos said, head shaking. "I swear, boy, you look as if you got the devil in you, and after such a lovely speech—why?"

Miguel threw the apron on the ground and began to cross the street. Carlos followed his protégé, wondering what had been bothering him. "It's nothing, Carlos. I'm just fed up with their attitude towards us."

"Forget it! The time will come when all this will be but a faint memory," said Carlos as the church bells continued to ring. Then he saw Miguel suddenly stop and spin his eyes toward the church doors.

"She's beautiful," said Miguel.

"What, the church?"

"Not the church Carlos. I'm talking about the lady that was sitting in the stagecoach—wasn't she beautiful?"

"Who? What are you talking about, Miguel?"

"You didn't see her?"

"See who?"

"The woman inside that coach—you know, the coach the mob almost attacked."

"No Miguelito, I did not see her."

"Well I did, and she's in church right now," said Miguel, focusing his eyes on the church doors. All of a sudden, Miguel abandoned Carlos and darted toward the church. Carlos wisely stood his ground and simply watched Miguel rush across the plaza, startling hundreds of pigeons into a hasty flight.

Carlos shook his head and uttered to himself, "Miguelito, you're in for a rude awakening. This you must deal with on your own." Carlos turned his back on Miguel, walked to his horse, mounted and then departed San Sebastián.

Speeding through the center of the plaza, Miguel recognized his friend, Lolita. She was a blind old woman who owned a flower stand, and her cantankerous windpipe covered all corners of town. Miguel strode toward the blind woman and hastily eyed the many flowerpots on the ground. "Quick, Lolita, how much for a rose?"

Lolita immediately recognized the voice, and smiled. "Miguelito, for you a rose will cost three centavos, just pick one to your liking."

"Thank you, Lolita," responded Miguel. He reached into the long clay vase and pulled out a rose with a long stem; its petals still closed. He pressed three centavos into Lolita's frail hand, thanked her again, and then made the final dash toward the church.

As Miguel approached the house of worship, the doors suddenly swung open, and a tiny priest stepped out onto the front steps. He greeted every parishioner with a smile. Miguel stood there for a short while, and although many people emerged from the church, he did not see the young woman he was searching for with such enthusiasm. He waited patiently, however, but she did not step outside. When he saw the priest shaking hands with the last of the parishioners, he sighed heavily. The priest re-entered the church, but left the doors wide open. Miguel kept his hand across his chest, holding the rose in an upright position, but then he slowly began to lose his enthusiasm and dropped his hand to the side, dangling the rose he had just purchased. He stood in front of the church looking up at the open doors, waiting, but no one came forth.

Miguel had just about given up all hopes when he finally saw the priest again. Directly behind the priest, Maria Hernández and her daughters slowly emerged from the church. As the priest and Maria engaged in a deep conversation, and as Laura and Anita stood behind them, Rosalía finally emerged. It was then that Miguel's face stretched with a wide grin. He brought his hand back across his chest, kept the rose in an upright position, and then slowly walked over to Rosalía.

Laura was the first to notice the young man's determined face, as if he had a secret mission to complete. At first she wondered where Miguel was going in such haste, especially when Mass was over, but when she noticed that Miguel's eyes were completely focused on Rosalía, she smiled wickedly.

Although Maria's prudent upbringing forced her to maintain eye contact with the priest, out of the corner of her eye she noticed an approaching figure. As the priest spoke, Maria turned to the side and caught sight of Miguel for the first time. Confirming her suspicions, she cast a motherly frown on the young peasant. Miguel kept his eyes trained Rosalía. The lion had marked its prey, but his beautiful target, who was standing behind her middle sister, did not even notice Miguel. Realizing Maria was no longer paying him any attention, the priest turned to where she was looking.

Miguel finally reached the top stair, and came face to face with Rosalía. "Buenos Dias, señorita." Miguel extended his hand to give Rosalía the rose.

Completely startled and at a loss for words, Rosalía took a step backwards.

"Oh look, Mother, Rosa finally has suitor!" said Laura in her usual sarcastic tone. "Won't Father be proud today?"

"Young man, what do you think you're doing," said Maria alarmingly, as if Miguel had a strange disease from which she felt compelled to shield her family. Maria rushed over to Miguel and confronted him eye to eye. She snatched the rose from Miguel's hand, threw it on the front step and crushed it underneath her shoe. Under normal circumstances, she would never have been so rude, but she saw Miguel Pítre as a threat, a dangerous threat to the already tenuous situation in the Hernández family.

"Señora, the rose was not meant for you. It was meant for her," said Miguel, gesturing with his head at Rosalía.

Laura began to laugh uncontrollably, and Rosalía sensed that her father would somehow learn about this incident. It made her angry that

Laura made a mockery of Miguel's honorable intentions. It angered her, too, that her own mother stepped in to quash Miguel's hopeful expectations. But then again, Rosalía noticed that Miguel seemed unfazed by both, Laura's mockery and her mother's intervention. It was the look on Miguel's face that told her he was no pushover peasant; a look of supreme confidence that struck a chord in her, and she admired that very quickly.

"I know the rose was not meant for me, young man," Maria answered back. "But what you are doing, and what you think is going to happen can never be. Do you know who we are?"

"Yes. You are señora Hernández, and you are the wife of *El Demonio*," said Miguel with an even expression.

"Why you goddamn peasant!" shouted Laura, stepping out from behind her mother to confront Miguel. "How dare you call my father a demon?"

Rosalía finally regained her composure and realized her sister was at it again.

"Miguelito, please go home," insisted the priest, face contorting.

"No, Padre, I will not!" replied Miguel. He glared at Laura and fired away. "We call your father *El Demonio*, because that is what your father is; he and every peninsular vampire that comes to my country to suck our blood!"

Maria tilted her head and looked over Miguel's shoulder, across the plaza, to see if her husband was anywhere in sight. Allaying her worst fears for the moment, she turned back to face Miguel. "Then if you know who we are, and if you know my husband, you would be wise to leave right now, before you suffer great consequences."

"Señora Hernández, I am not afraid of your husband!"

"Miguelito! Stop this immediately!" yelled the priest. "Go home!"

Laura took a step closer to Miguel and swung her hand across his face, leaving the red image of her fingers imprinted on Miguel's cheek. "There! How do you feel now, you fucking jíbaro low-life! How dare you come to us in your shabby appearance and think we will give you our attention? Go back to that shit-hole you crawled out of and leave us alone!"

"Señorita," Miguel said calmly. "Enjoy this moment, for the time will come when your existence here will have vanished—this I promise you!"

All of a sudden, Rosalía stepped forth from behind Anita, who was standing in total shock, and gave Miguel a pitiful look. "I apologize for my sister's behavior, señor. We're not at all like that." Then she stooped to the concrete step and picked up the crushed rose. Most of the petals had fallen off the rose, but she held it firmly in her hands. "Thank you, for your kind gesture."

"My name is Miguel, señorita."

"My name is Rosalía, but they call me Rosa, just like this rose you gave me."

"That's quite enough!" yelled Maria. "Candelario, bring the coach!"

Candelario, who had parked the coach across the street and had been watching the scene with great interest, suddenly stirred into action.

Unable to resist herself, Laura opened her mouth again. "That's right, Rosa, bring this peasant home to meet Father. I'm sure he will impress Father greatly."

Rosalía turned to her sister with hateful eyes. "Shut your mouth! You're the reason why everybody hates us. Look how you treat them, Laura!"

"I treat them the way Father treats them, like all peasants, whose only existence is to serve our kind, ought to be treated," fired back Laura.

"Señorita," said Miguel with a smile. "You treat us that way because of your fear!"

"Fear? I have no fear of you peasants!"

"Yes you do, I can see it in your eyes; I can see it written all over your face. Well, you *should* be afraid, *very* afraid because the tables will turn, and you will become the shabby ones."

The coach rumbled toward the front steps of the church, the horses grunting and whinnying. Maria caught sight of the coach, and quickly grabbed Rosalía's hand, dragging her down the stairs. Rosalía kept her eyes on Miguel, as she felt her mother tugging at her hand. "Good day to you, Miguel."

Miguel smiled pleasantly, "Good-day to you, señorita Rosa."

When Miguel turned back, he confronted Laura's cold, dark eyes. "Don't even think about it, peasant, you will never, ever, marry the likes of us! My father will hear about this incident, so you better prepare yourself!"

Miguel looked at Laura with so much contempt that Laura could feel his anger like the heat of the sun. "Señorita, tell your father that my name is Miguel Pítre. My father is Juan Pítre, and our farm lies next to Don Blanco's farm. Tell him that we live on the lands he stole from us. Tell him señorita! Tell *El Demonio* that one day we will take our lands back in the same manner he took them from us. Tell him where I am, and that I will be waiting for him."

Laura realized that the peasant standing before her was different, very different from the usual peasant. He refused to show her any respect, fear, or courtesy. He stood up to her like no peasant had ever done before, and so it frustrated her that she could not respond to him as she was used to responding to peasants. Laura remained silent, unable to say anything meaningful to Miguel. Infuriated, she turned and headed down the church steps toward the awaiting coach.

The priest shook his head out of disappointment and walked over to Miguel. Both men stood on the top stair and watched the women enter the coach. The priest shook his head one more time. "Miguelito, you have stirred the viper's nest. Now you must suffer the consequences."

"Don't you worry about me, Padre; I can take care of myself!"

"It is not for you that I worry, Miguelito. It is for your father."

Miguel stared at the coach as it pulled away from the church. He never looked at the priest as he replied. "Well, don't you worry about my father, either; he's in good hands."

Rodolfo rode to Don Redondo's modest house situated in the barrio of San Lucas. He knocked several times until he forced Diego Redondo to wake up and answer the door. Diego Redondo opened the door and confronted a very determined-looking Rodolfo Hernández. "I see you're not much of a religious man, either," said Diego. "Buenos Dias, señor Hernández."

"I don't have time to sit in church listening to the same old message week after week," replied Rodolfo, stepping into Redondo's house. "My time in San Sebastián is very limited, so I must take advantage of every minute of the day."

"Would you like some coffee?"

"No, thank you. I just want your opinion on something; do you feel up to the task?"

"Yes."

"All right, then tell me: what do you think about Juan Pítre?"

Redondo let out a morning yawn, and then gave Rodolfo a curious look. "In what way señor?"

"Just tell me about the man, goddamn it!"

Clearly taken aback by Rodolfo's indomitable disposition, Redondo cleared his throat. "Not much, señor. He is penniless, as you well know, and by law you have every right to evict him from your land."

"Sometimes, Redondo, I wonder why I keep you on retainer. I already know that, but that's not what I am interested in!"

Unsure of what information his master was seeking, Redondo looked utterly helpless. "I don't know what you want, señor."

"Is the man sympathetic to this absurd notion of rebellion?"

Redondo shook his head. "No. Juan Pítre is too old to get involved with any form of resistance. He'd rather not rock the boat, as it were."

"Can he be approached to serve as a spy?"

"A spy, señor?"

"Yes, Redondo—a fucking spy!" Rodolfo yelled impatiently.

Redondo cleared his throat again, clearly revealing his lack of confidence, but it was more the fear of losing the monthly retainer that kept a roof over his head and food in his stomach. "He is a well-known jíbaro, and though he is not involved with the current political mood in these parts, he will not willingly go against it, unless…"

"Unless what?"

"Unless you talk to him and present a terribly good incentive to have him go work for you, señor."

"Like money, right? I have already thought about that. Is there anything else I could do to force him into spying for me?"

"No, not really, but instead of offering him money, perhaps you could offer to write-off the entire debt from his libreta."

"Are you mad, Redondo? It's the same goddamn thing as giving money to him!"

Diego Redondo hated the fact that Rodolfo treated him no better than a jíbaro, and he resented Rodolfo's impromptu visits, too. Nevertheless, he had to knuckle under Hernández's will because without his money, Redondo might just as well have been a jíbaro. But this morning, Redondo was in no mood to hear Rodolfo's annoying voice, and he lashed out at his employer for the first time. "No, señor Hernández, I'm not mad. I'm just telling you the simple truth—that *is* why you keep me on retainer, right?"

Rodolfo gave Diego a sudden look of shock, before nodding back at him. "All right, Diego, if that is what you think I should do, then we will pay Don Juan Pítre a visit.

CHAPTER 23

On the morning of Wednesday, February 19, the local cook Maria hired two days ago for the remainder of the stay in San Sebastián took ill, and there was no one Maria could entrust with the task of purchasing food at the market.

Rodolfo had left the house early that morning with hopes of accomplishing his daily goals early, and Maria knew that without that fatherly restraint, her daughters would not miss an opportunity to resume hostilities. Maria was afraid of another brawl between them, and that was the sole reason why she asked Laura to go into town alone.

Laura immediately rejected her mother's request and Maria found it impossible to sway her daughter. Refusing to embroil herself in yet another argument with Laura, Maria felt completely helpless. That is until Rosalía heard her mother's pleas and volunteered, but Maria was too wise to allow Rosalía to venture into town alone, especially after what happened in front of the church a few days ago. Maria argued against the idea until Rosalía convinced her that Anita would accompany her. It was then that Maria finally acquiesced and gave her money. In the end, though, Maria made sure that Candelario would accompany her as well.

Candelario brought the women into San Sebastián as Maria ordered him to do, but at Rosalía's insistence, he did not accompany them into the market.

The market was a tightly packed collection of wooden stands lined along either side of Orejola and San Cristobal streets. Hundreds of people filled the small market, shopping for fruits, vegetables, linen, blankets, pots and pans, lard, eggs, and all sorts of merchandise. Rosalía could feel the market teeming with buzzing customers, speculating over the price of a fruit or its conditions for consumption. Mothers held their children by the hand while their husbands, toting canvas bags filled with the day's purchases, dutifully kept pace with them.

Toward the end of Orejola Street, Rosalía saw a fish stand, and men gutting out the catch of the day. The cries of stand owners calling out for potential customers or displaying their wares resonated in Rosalía's ears as if it were the smooth, melodic tones of an orchestra. Through her young eyes, Rosalía could plainly see that the townsfolk were poor and, seemingly, without hope. In contrast to their outward appearance, though, Rosalía felt a vibrant mood among them, as if the task of shopping for food was the greatest thing in the world. She wanted to feel the mood, too, and threw herself into the sea of human consumers.

Unlike Rosalía, Anita had no inclinations whatsoever to go on a shopping errand on behalf of her mother, even though she would benefit from it. The only reason why Anita had agreed to accompany Rosalía was to get away from Laura, even though she had not spoken to her since the big fight outside their country estate. Anita felt convinced that her father had punished her the most, and she hated Laura for that. She hated Laura with all of her heart, and jumped at the opportunity to get away from her elder sister that morning.

The two young women moved along the stands, purchasing tomatoes, lettuce and pigeon peas. On occasion, Rosalía would stop at a jewelry stand and admire its many necklaces. Some necklaces bore colorful beads mixed with seashells, and some were made of gold or silver. As they moved along the stands, the bag that Anita carried was starting to fill up quickly, and soon her face began to show signs of stress.

The sun was fierce that early morning, and the two women began to regret their decision to leave their parasols at the house. Unwilling to draw unnecessary attention to their presence in San Sebastián, they felt that parasols would be too obvious in public. They had even changed into what they thought best represented the local attire. Rosalía wanted to be as inconspicuous as possible and thought she had achieved her goal. Then someone recognized her.

"That necklace would look wonderful on you, señorita."

She had heard that voice once before, a smooth, tenor tone that immediately drew her attention. She turned around quickly and recognized a pair of wondrous green eyes; eyes that seemed to penetrate her very soul. She offered no kind of emotion, although something about him had clearly moved her. Was it pity for the young man's shabby appearance? Was it empathy for the jíbaro's daily struggles, to which she had been a first-hand witness, or was it something else; something so dangerous that even she had to deny it to herself? Rosalía narrowed her eyes. "Thank you, señor Pítre." She felt Anita so close behind her she could feel her body heat.

"Rosa, what are you doing?" cautioned Anita.

Without turning to confront her sister, Rosalía answered back. "Nothing, Ana, I am having a conversation with this gentleman. Señor Pítre, this is my sister, Anita."

Miguel Pítre removed his pava, revealing his short, curly and light-brown hair. Holding the pava tightly in his hands, he nodded and smiled. "Muy encantado, señorita." Miguel extended his hand in a shaking gesture, but Anita took a step backwards, wide eyes defining a well-justified apprehension. "I will not bite you, señorita."

Disturbed by her sister's unusual behavior, and with a curious set of blue eyes, Rosalía said, "Ana? Where are your manners?"

Anita moved her eyes away from Rosalía and trained them on Miguel's humble face. "Señor, I don't mean to be rude, but you must remember what happened at the church the other day. You should leave my sister alone. If you know my father, you know that he has many spies in town who'd love nothing better than to curry his favor."

Miguel sighed deeply; it was a kind of sigh, though, that seemed to sum up all of the years of frustration into a single moment of disgust. He shook his head, and though he wanted to lash out at Anita, he held his emotions in check. He turned back to Rosalía and flashed a broad smile at her, showing a perfect set of white teeth. "Señorita Rosa, I would like to get to know you a little better, if it's all right with you." He sensed Anita moving away, allowing her younger sister a brief moment of privacy.

"Why, señor Pítre?"

"Please, call me Miguel. Why? Because you seem different from the rest of the peninsulares, because in spite of your social standing and contrary to your mother's wishes that day, you took a moment to speak to me. I liked that. It showed me that there is good in you, and that there is compassion in your heart. That's the reason, señorita Hernández."

"You may call me Rosa. Thank you for your kind words, but I fear that what happened in the church that day was merely a taste of what you would receive, should you pursue friendship with me, Miguel. We come from different worlds, you and I, and I feel that your attempts to befriend me would be an exercise in futility, not that I mind at all. You know my father well, and you know the extremes he will go through in order to protect his family."

"Protect his family, from what, from whom?" Miguel asked while furrowing his eyebrows.

"From the likes of you, Miguel."

"I see. Heaven forbid that one of Rodolfo's daughters should have the misfortune of befriending a jíbaro from San Sebastián. But what do *you* think? What does your heart tell you, Rosa?"

"I don't know, Miguel, I don't think that—" Before Rosalía could finish her response, she felt Anita's firm grasp on her elbow.

"Rosa, we had better leave. I just saw father's solicitor, Don Redondo, at one of the fruit stands."

Rosalía looked across the street and recognized Don Redondo. She nodded back at Anita, and then gazed wistfully at Miguel. "I must take my leave of you, Miguel. It was nice chatting with you."

"Likewise, Rosa, and I hope that we get another opportunity to speak again."

"Señor Pítre," said Anita, moving in front of Rosalía. "Please, forget about making friends with Rosa. For your safety, please stay away from her."

Miguel smiled at Anita, but the gesture was not out of amusement but because of her attempt to warn him about her father and her belief in the notion that she was protecting him. He smiled again at the thought, but the daughters of Don Rodolfo Hernández had no clue that Miguel Pítre was a fearless man. They had no idea about the plans for revolution. In his mind, it was they and their kind who needed to be fearful, not him. He calmly put on his pava and tipped his head at the two women. "Buenos Dias."

Rosalía stretched her beautiful face, gave Miguel a grand smile, and then joined her sister.

Miguel simply watched as the young women disappeared into the sea of human shoppers. Then he sensed someone standing next to him. "You don't give up, do you?" The deep cadence of Carlos's voice vibrated inside Miguel's ears, like chords from a bass, a distinctive pattern that no one could mistake for any other person's voice.

"There is something about her that I like, Carlos. Besides her beauty, she is intelligent, reasonable and compassionate."

"You know all that about her in just two, very brief encounters?"

"I cannot explain it. I just know it in my heart. Rosa is a very sincere person, and I do not see that façade that I see in so many of the peninsulares with whom I come across. Yes, Carlos, all that in just two brief encounters; I like her—I like her a lot."

"And what happened at the church doesn't have any meaning for you?"

"You mean other than the impossibility of establishing a friendship with her?"

"Friendship, is that all? I sense something more, Miguelito, something very dangerous."

"I know what you're thinking, Carlos, but I'm smart enough to know that I cannot court that woman."

"That is your brain talking, but it is not what your heart is telling you, now is it? Miguelito, you cannot fall in love with her. You must resist that temptation because when the revolution starts, you will have to take sides and—"

"Carlos, you don't have to lecture me about this," interrupted Miguel. "I know what I have to do." Carlos said nothing more, and just stood silently beside his protégé. Miguel, however, gazed into the crowd, but his eyes could not betray what his heart was feeling at that precise moment. Rosalía was gone, and somehow he felt as if he would never see her again—a dreadful sense of loss that he could not explain. What was it that he was feeling right then? He felt excited, giddy, and melancholy all at the same time. He had no inkling that he was beginning to fall in love with Rosalía Hernández, an impossible love, a dangerous affair that might result in his death. Miguel shrugged his shoulders. "Let's get out of here, Carlos."

CHAPTER 24

Rodolfo Hernández had been riding all day in the hills of San Sebastián, inspecting his land holdings, and collecting money. Riding along with him that day was Don Vicente Gaudier, a wealthy peninsular who had emigrated from the Basque region of Spain and had settled in Camuy. Gaudier took great pains to look and sound like an aristocrat. His thin and frail body wore nothing but the best and newest apparels imported from Spain, France and Italy. His gaunt face could not grow a full beard, as many of his contemporaries did, but an outlandish mustache that hid his lips entirely, helped offset the physical shortcoming. His dark brown eyes, matching the color of his hair, were set deeply into his sockets, and the dark area around his eyes testified to a great deal of sleep deprivation. He strived to make his mannerisms appear as though he was the product of nobility but to the creole psyche, he was just another Spanish settler who had enriched himself at their expense.

The two men took the narrow dirt trail that ran along the Duran, Blanco and Pítre farms, and while slowing their horses to a comfortable trot, they took a moment to gaze at one particular piece of land.

"How do you do it, Rodolfo?" Gaudier said with admiration.

"Do what?"

"You've just evicted two families from your properties without so much as batting an eye. How do you not feel guilty?"

"It's quite simple, Vicente, I'm a businessman. I have no time for feeling guilty. I'm surprised that you have not yet conquered those silly emotions."

"I do not own as much land as you do, Don Hernández. My money comes from my export companies."

"Don't you have to deal harshly with those who serve under you?"

"Yes, sometimes."

"It is no different being a landowner."

"Still, I don't believe that I can look into someone's eyes and evict them from their homes."

"Then perhaps landowning might not be a profitable venture for you, señor."

"Perhaps, but I *would* like to dabble in real estate. What about this farm?" Gaudier said, gesturing with his head at the farm directly to their left.

"That farm there? It belongs to Don Santiago Duran, a stubborn creole hacendado."

"Why stubborn?"

"I've offered to buy his forty cuerdas but he refuses to sell. He owes no one any money, so I cannot buy a libreta for him. It's a beautiful stretch of land, rich and perfect for growing coffee."

"Indeed. Perhaps we could talk to him."

"We could try. Are you interested?" Rodolfo watched Gaudier nodding with interest. "Well, if we're successful, you will pay me a finder's fee, right?"

"No problem," said Gaudier animatedly.

The two peninsulares moved their horses along a narrow rocky pathway that led to Don Duran's hacienda. As the horses trotted slowly, the men kept their eyes trained on the white house, ignoring the many slaves that toiled the bountiful land. The afternoon skies were dotted by thick puffs of clouds, and the sun emerged every now and then to cast narrow streams of light on the porch. Following the beam of sunlight, the peninsulares slowly trotted atop their horses until they finally came to a halt in front of Don Duran's hacienda.

As usual, Don Santiago Duran was sitting on his favorite wicker chair contemplating his estate. He recognized *El Demonio* right away, but he could not place the other visitor. While the two men dismounted, Duran figured exactly what the purpose for their unexpected arrival was.

"Buenas Tardes, señor Duran," said Rodolfo, forcing a smile.

"Buenas Tardes, señor Hernández. To what do I owe this unannounced visit? And who is that?"

"This is Don Vicente Gaudier, from Camuy."

The two men approached Don Duran, shook hands with him and stood looming over him.

"Please, señores, take a seat," Duran said invitingly. At first, he thought to offer them a drink of rum but passed up on the idea because he did not want the slaves or neighboring hacendados to think he was socializing with peninsulares.

"You have a nice piece of property here, Don Duran," said Rodolfo with gleam in his eyes. "I'm sure it is a profitable farm."

"As you have told me on numerous occasions, señor Hernández, I suppose I do all right. Is that why you came here, to compliment my farm?"

"Right down to business, Don Duran, I like that," said Rodolfo, unaware that Duran immediately sensed his patronizing compliment and resented it about as much as he did all peninsulares.

"What do you want, Hernández?" insisted Duran.

Rodolfo glanced uneasily at Gaudier, but then eyed Don Duran with a serious expression. "Don Gaudier is very interested in purchasing these lands from you."

Duran shook his head, clearly revealing his frustration at the two men. "How many times have you asked me that question, and how many times have I responded to you? This land is not for sale."

"Everything has a price, señor Duran," said Gaudier confidently.

"Not *this* property."

"The fair-market-value for these forty cuerdas is roughly ten thousand pesos," Gaudier persisted. "I know that Don Hernández has offered you fifteen thousand."

"That's right, and I turned him down."

"I am prepared to offer you forty thousand pesos—that's one thousand pesos per cuerda."

Don Duran furrowed his eyebrows at Gaudier's offer, and even Rodolfo turned to him in utter shock. But Rodolfo, keeping his mind focused on the finder's fee, allowed Gaudier to continue.

"Are you mad, señor Gaudier?" Duran said wide-eyed. "No cuerda in San Sebastián is worth a thousand pesos. You must be a very wealthy person to make such an offer."

"I own several export companies in San Juan, Camuy and in Mayagüez. I can back up my offer, Don Duran."

Rodolfo said nothing, and just sat on his wicker chair, dumbfounded. Gaudier's offer had blown his offer of fifteen thousand pesos out of the water, and that made Rodolfo feel less of an aristocrat than Gaudier. In fact, no one had ever made such a ridiculous offer for land in San Sebastián. But Gaudier *had* made the offer, so Don Duran *had* to take it seriously. Forty-thousand pesos was enough to force the staunchest of creoles into selling just about everything, including their souls. Despite his contempt for peninsulares, as well as the repugnance of doing business with them, Duran found it very difficult to ignore Gaudier. "Señor Gaudier, why do you make such a substantial offer? Clearly, you must be aware that you have overpriced this land. Why? Why me? Why do I deserve such an offer?"

"I am a businessman, Don Duran, and I need to invest my money. Your land is profitable and very attractive to my interests. I hope that the sale of land will include your slaves, too."

"If I were to consider your offer, the slaves would never be a part of the sale. I know how you bastards treat slaves, and I will not place them in your hands; I would rather free them than turn them over to you."

"It doesn't matter, Don Duran, I could always purchase new ones."

There was a long moment of silence as Don Duran studied the offer. He rubbed his bearded chin, and then turned to the side to contemplate his farm. He turned back to face Don Gaudier and shook his head. "No, señor, this land is not for sale."

Don Gaudier removed his top hat and held it firmly upon his lap. His eyes never blinked and his body never flinched at Duran's rejection. Instead, Gaudier looked straight at Duran and said, "How about fifty thousand pesos?"

Now it was time for Rodolfo to step in. "Vicente, I cannot allow you to do this. This land is only worth fifteen thousand pesos, perhaps twenty, but that's all. Don't give this fool any more money than the land is worth."

Duran sensed a jealous tone in Rodolfo's voice that Gaudier, who was too preoccupied with the deal, did not recognize. It tickled Duran that Rodolfo Hernández showed his frustration so openly, and he wanted to stretch that moment of satisfaction for a little while longer. He turned to Rodolfo and said, "Let the man be, Don Hernández, if he wants to make an offer of fifty thousand pesos to me, then it's his prerogative, not yours."

"Fifty thousand pesos would make you a very wealthy man, Duran."

"So what? Can't stand the idea that a creole could have that much money?"

Rodolfo stood up and cast angry eyes at Don Duran. Then he looked down at his friend. "We don't need this bullshit, Don Gaudier. There are many other fincas in San Sebastián that you could purchase for less than ten thousand pesos."

"Yes, but not like this one, and you know that, Don Hernández," fired back Duran, looking straight up at Rodolfo. "That's why you keep offering to buy this land, right?"

Rodolfo could not answer him, because Duran was right—he did want the land for himself.

"Then will you consider my offer?" Gaudier asked humbly, expecting a quick response.

"Let me think about it. Come back next week, and we will talk some more. I cannot ignore your offer, señor, so I must give it due consideration. In the meantime, please take a moment to ride up and down the property and get familiarized with it."

"You fucking bastard!" yelled Rodolfo at Duran.

"Tsk, tsk, señor Hernández, such vulgar words from the mouth of an aristocrat? Good Lord, you sound just like a jornalero! Have you been associating with field workers lately?"

Rodolfo knew he could not get his way with Duran, not in the same manner as he did with other creoles of San Sebastián. He shot a glaring sneer at Duran and then looked at Gaudier. "Come, Vicente, there's nothing for you here."

Don Vicente Gaudier rose to his feet, put on his top hat and looked down at Duran with a smile. "Think about my offer, Don Duran. I will come back next week with my solicitor."

Duran nodded at Gaudier but offered no verbal response. He took in the moment with absolute glee. As Rodolfo climbed onto his horse, Duran could see Rodolfo's anger seething through a pair of glaring brown eyes. Rodolfo took hold of the reins and sneered again at Don Duran. Then he turned his beast around and spurred it furiously into a fast gallop. Gaudier mounted his horse, and as Rodolfo began to fade away, he tipped his head at Duran. "Just think about the offer señor. Buenas Tardes." A few moments later, Gaudier joined Hernández, and he too disappeared from Duran's view. All of a sudden, Duran let out a boisterous laugh. He reached underneath his wicker chair and pulled out a bottle of rum. He put the spout to his mouth and drank feverishly.

That evening, as Carlos Peña was returning from town, Don Duran could not hide his enthusiasm. There was no doubt in his mind that if he accepted Gaudier's offer, it would make him a very wealthy man. As Carlos drew closer, Duran watched the weary look upon the former slave and quickly stifled his excitement. How could he tell Carlos that he was considering an offer to sell the property to a peninsular, the very people he swore to Carlos he would never do business with? How could Duran tell Carlos that once he sold the property, Carlos would have to make his own way? Yet, as much as the idea of selling his property to a peninsular went against every fiber of his reasoning, he simply could not afford to ignore its financial appeal. Duran had abandoned his honorable values, his idealistic notions, and succumbed to what Carlos referred to as the vilest of human temptations: greed!

CHAPTER 25

Carlos left the Duran plantation early the following day, and headed toward the Pítre farm to fetch Miguel. The two men took off for San Sebastián that morning to meet with the other members of the Porvenir cell. After the meeting, Carlos and Miguel decided to venture into town, and arrived at the market at midday.

Carlos felt exuberant. Porvenir's membership had been steadily growing over the past few days, the plans for revolution were starting to form, and he was starting to feel like a true pioneer. He likened himself to the founding fathers of the United States. He had read accounts of the American Revolution, and tried to emulate his hero, John Adams—a man whose noble visions he had come to respect. For Carlos Peña, the future of Puerto Rico was like a blank sheet of paper, waiting for ink, waiting for an author, and he would become one of its authors.

"I think things are going very well," said Carlos, while inspecting an orange he took from a fruit stand. "We have recruited Angel Luis Pagan, whose father owns the printing press in town. With his help now, we could print leaflets and papers in support of the revolution!" Carlos glanced at Miguel, and looked at the stand owner. "How much?"

"Tres centavos," the owner replied.

Carlos paid for the orange, and then turned back to Miguel. "There is still so much to do. I must make a trip to Lares and speak with Don Manuel Rojas. Do you want to join me?"

Miguel looked up at Carlos with hopeful eyes, but then frowned. "What about Aguilar and Ibarra?"

"What about them?"

"If they find out that you went to see Manuel Rojas without them and took me along instead, it may cause you unwanted trouble. You know Aguilar's a hot head."

"I don't care what Aguilar or Ibarra think. I am the leader of this cell, and if they do not like it, it's just too bad. You're coming with me and that's the end of it."

Miguel nodded at Carlos with satisfaction. Carlos never vacillated; he was quick to think and quick to decide and that was one of the many traits Miguel admired in his friend.

Miguel purchased a banana, and as he began to peel his fruit, he looked across the market and noticed her again. What a beautiful sight! She was like an angel, sent down by God to please Miguel's eyes. Sadly, though, Rosalía Hernández was an untouchable! The wall that separated her and Miguel was thick, filled with contempt and utter disdain; a wall that Miguel could never breach. The young man held his banana and stared at the incredible beauty standing just a few yards away. Accompanying her today, however, was that other sister of hers, that dreadful woman who chastised him in front of the church.

Carlos, being an astute man, sensed Miguel's woes. "You might as well forget about her, Miguelito, she's not for you."

"Why? Why is it impossible?" replied Miguel. "My friend, you have taught me to follow my heart. You have taught me to pursue my dreams no matter what obstacle lay before me. And now, you ask me to forget about her?"

"This is something different, Miguelito because you're putting yourself in a terrible place. I do not want to see you suffer for something you will never have. Listen to me on this, Miguelito."

All of a sudden, a voice cried out from within the market crowd. Someone had been shouting out Carlos's name in a frantic tone, as if he were dying. Both Carlos and Miguel searched the crowd, but no one emerged. The voice fell silent, and Carlos looked at Miguel, shrugging his shoulders dismissively. The two men thought nothing more about it and began to walk to their horses when the voice cried out again. This time it was louder and more focused. "Carlos! Carlos!"

It was Pedro Torres, one of Don Duran's jornaleros, a field hand. He was running toward Carlos and Miguel as though his life were in danger. The look of exasperation and determination caused Carlos to take him very seriously. Pedro finally reached Carlos and Miguel, panting and sweating. He looked up at Carlos with saddened eyes. "Carlos, I have grave news for you!"

"What is it Pedro, is Don Duran all right?"

"Yes. But the news I bring to you is dreadful!"

"What? What is it, man! Speak!"

"Don Santiago Duran has sold the farm!"

Miguel had never seen the look of fear on Carlos's face. It was if Carlos's world had suddenly ended. Carlos grabbed Pedro by his shoulders and held him firmly in his huge hands. "What the hell are you talking about, Pedro? Duran would never sell his property!"

"He did, and to a rich peninsular from Camuy!"

"Who is this peninsular?" Carlos asked, unable to hide his worst fears.

"I do not know him, but he was accompanied by *El Demonio*!"

Miguel sensed Carlos's reluctance to accept the truth of Pedro's words. Carlos kept Pedro firmly wrapped in his arms. "That's a goddamn lie! Don Duran would never sell his property, especially to a peninsular!"

"Well he did, Carlos, and if you don't believe me, why don't you go ask him yourself?"

Carlos let go of Pedro, dropped his orange to the ground and ran to his horse. He mounted quickly and galloped out of town in a fit of rage. Miguel had no time to react. He shouted at Carlos to wait for him, but Carlos just disappeared from sight, totally ignoring his friend.

Miguel was angry now. He glared at Pedro. "This had better not be a lie, Pedro. I swear I will beat you to a pulp if you're lying. Are you sure that Rodolfo Hernández was there?"

"Miguel, Don Duran has sold the property. And yes, Hernández was there, too."

Miguel said nothing more to Pedro Torres, and as he ruminated the terrible events that had taken place over the past few days, his emotions seemed to crystallize into a single moment of absolute rage. As Rosalía and Laura moved past him, Miguel saw them, not as young women but as symbols of what he detested most in his life. He walked up to

Rosalía and raised his index finger at her as if she were a child. "Your father has done it again, hasn't he?" he shouted.

"Don't yell at me!" shouted back Rosalía. "I don't know what you're talking about, Miguel. What has my father done?"

"Don't act so surprised, señorita; you know what your father's done! He's conspired with another goddamn peninsular to drive yet another one of us to sell his land, and because of your father's evil work, many decent people will suffer. My friend, Carlos, is one of them! How can you people do this without blinking an eye, without any form of compassion?"

"How dare you?" shouted Rosalía, clearly taken aback by Miguel's outburst. "How dare you presume that about me; you don't even know me, señor!"

"I don't need to know you because you're all the same; cut by the same mold!"

"That's enough!" interjected Laura, stepping in between Miguel and Rosalía.

"No, that's not enough! I have not even started! You will pay for all the misery you have caused us! You goddamn peninsulares think you own the world and that you can have your way as you please without regard to the consequences! No, it's not nearly enough!"

Laura was not about to let a peasant shout at her as if she were a common jíbara. She began to swing her arm back to smack Miguel's face, but when Miguel saw what she was doing, he looked straight into her eyes. "I let you smack me once, señorita. But if you raise your hand at me again, I will not hesitate in responding to you!"

Laura noticed the fire in his eyes and quickly realized Miguel was not bluffing. She brought her arm down and stared right back at him. "You have caused my sister a lot of grief for no reason, and my father will deal with you!"

"I don't give a damn about your father!"

It was then that Rosalía finally regained her composure. She pushed Laura back and looked directly at Miguel's angry face, tears beginning to well in her eyes. "I had thought highly about you, señor Pítre. But you've shown me that you're no different from any other peasant in San

Sebastián. It is clear in my eyes that your hatred for us runs deep, and I am very sorry to have met you. I don't ever want to see you again!"

"I don't want to see you, either!" shouted back Miguel, but as he watched Rosalía and Laura turn to head back to their stagecoach, he immediately began to regret his outburst. What caused the sudden change in Miguel's temperament was the finality in Rosalía's voice. Rosalía was gone and she never wanted to see him again. He simply stood there, regretting his outburst at the one thing that in recent days had brought a ray of light and hope into his darkened soul. "My God, what have I done?" Miguel uttered to himself.

Carlos jumped off his horse and ran toward Don Santiago Duran, who sat on his wicker chair with an expectant look, as if he had been waiting for Carlos all day. "Is it true?" yelled Carlos, straining every ounce of fiber in his body.

"Calm down, Carlos."

"No! Tell me, Santiago, is it true?"

"Yes, Carlos, I sold the farm. I had not planned on it but it did happen. I was supposed to sell it next week, but since the offer was so good, I felt no need in prolonging the inevitable. I sent for Don Gaudier and we signed the papers this morning, while you were in town."

Carlos dropped to his knees, digging his long fingers into his thick, brittle hair.

"Why do you despair? You should know that I will take care of you, Carlos. I will give you money from this deal. It will not make you a rich man, but you will have enough money so that you will never go hungry. Haven't I always taken care of you?"

Carlos dug his knees further into the soil while clenching hands into tight fists. "That's not the point, Santiago! I was never interested in money! I was happy living here! Why did you sell? Why did you sell the farm to a peninsular? Don't you know what's going to happen now, especially to the slaves?"

"They are not part of the sale. In fact, I have just drawn papers for their freedom. I was hoping you could go into town to have them ratified. I thought you would be happy in doing that."

"What about all those noble ideals that you spoke of so eloquently, so profoundly, so passionately? What about the suffering of our people, did you forget that? Did you forget about the revolution? Did you forget about the future of Puerto Rico? You've sold out, Don Duran; you've sold us all out! You are no better than those peninsular vultures are! In fact, you're worse, because you've sold out your principles for money!"

"Now wait a minute, Carlos, I never gave you any indication that I would be involved in a revolution!"

"No you never did, but you pushed *me* towards it, and you made *me* feel as though you were sympathetic to the cause. But the only thing you seem to be sympathetic about is money!"

"Carlos, don't be this way. Come here and let us discuss this in a civilized manner!"

"No Santiago, I'm through with you! I will gather my stuff and leave immediately. You can deliver those freedom documents all by yourself—you don't need me for that!"

"You're being unreasonable, Carlos!"

Carlos could not help feeling the sting of Duran's idealistic betrayal. What hypocrisy! It was all bullshit from the start, and Carlos regretted ever setting foot on Duran's farm. His world had come crashing down on him, as if it were a boulder rolling down a mountainside. And if such a turnaround were the ideological manifestation of Carlos's mentor, then perhaps, everyone in Puerto Rico would end up the same way. A revolution would never get a foothold on the island because in time everyone would sell out; it was just a matter of setting the price. Carlos finally rose to his feet and mounted his horse. He took a long moment to study his former friend. Then his face changed from utter sadness to complete stoicism. "I'll come back for my things tomorrow morning."

Don Duran reached for his bottle of rum and took several swigs before entering his house.

CHAPTER 26

The morning of Friday, February 28, began with a torrential downpour that quickly saturated the ground and brought nothing but misery to the local wagon drivers. Many of them struggled in vain, prying the wheels of their wagons out of the rain-soaked mud. Miguel and Carlos had set out to meet up with other members of the Porvenir cell early that morning, and as they made their way through the muddied road, they could hear the wagon drivers cussing aloud. A week earlier, Carlos had requested a meeting with all of the cell members, but the gathering could not take place until Carlos was reassured that Don Ramirez, a loyalist and the owner of the store where the meeting was to take place, would not be around. The night before, Enrique, Don Ramirez's son, sent word to Carlos that his father was traveling to Camuy the next day and that the colmado would be available for the meeting. Carlos immediately sent word to the members of the cell in San Sebastián, informing them the meeting would take place the next morning.

The past week had given Miguel enough time to reconsider the awful actions he took against Rosalía Hernández. As he rode his horse into town, he suddenly felt sickened by it because he had allowed his anger to control him, and had disregarded the teachings of his mentor. During that one moment of rage, he did not see Rosalía as a human being but as a symbol that represented the daily miseries under which all Puerto Rican creoles lived. As Miguel rode past several stalled wagons along the road, he could hear Rosalía's words in his mind over and again: *It is clear in my eyes that your hatred for us runs deep, and I am very sorry to have met you. I don't ever want to see you again!*

The door to the Ramirez colmado opened slowly, and after taking a brief moment to acknowledge Carlos, Enrique nodded approvingly.

Now that the leader had finally arrived, Enrique grinned and beckoned Carlos toward the back of the store. Carlos had not slept much the past few days, but it wasn't because he had taken up residence at Don Blanco's farm and was now sleeping in a barn alongside farm animals, but because of Don Duran's reversal. It hurt him so much every time he thought about it. Every night Carlos lay down to sleep, images of the day he learned about the sale of Duran's farm flashed through his mind. He could not believe how easily Duran had allowed Gaudier to sway him with money. Every night, though, he convinced himself that not every creole was like Duran. He pinned his hopes on that thought because that was all he had now.

Carlos entered the back room of the colmado and was utterly surprised at how much the membership had blossomed. He did not recognize nearly half of the audience but he trusted Aguilar and Ibarra, and relied heavily upon their judgment of character. In all, there were twenty-three members, all of whom approached Carlos to shake hands. While Carlos greeted everyone personally, Miguel finally made his appearance.

After acquainting themselves, the members remained standing and focused their attention on Carlos. Carlos began to address his audience in that powerful deep voice of his, and while he spoke, Miguel took the time to study the new members. One face, out of all of the members, stood out like a gold peseta sitting on the road reflecting sunlight. It took Miguel several minutes to place that face and after several more minutes, he was certain he had seen it once before and where he had seen it. The man, whose image Miguel scrutinized with alarming concern, kept his eyes on Carlos and never noticed that someone had been watching him.

"I wanted to update everyone today on our current situation," began Carlos. It did not take too long for Aguilar and Ibarra to notice that Carlos was lacking the fire he once had in his speeches. It seemed as if Carlos had lost his zeal for the revolution, and the notion brought instant fears upon the two men. "I have received word from our friend, Don Manuel Rojas, that our leader, Don Betances has indeed secured an arms deal. The arms and ammunition will be coming from South America, aboard *El Telégrafo*, which will dock in the port of Guánica."

Aguilar stepped forth and said, "When?"

"I don't know the answer to that, only that the deal has not yet been consummated."

"What do you mean?" Aguilar inquired.

"I mean that the deal has not yet been funded," replied Carlos emotionless. "But rest assured, gentlemen, Dr. Betances *will* make it happen." He looked down at Aguilar. "How are you doing with securing arms for the cell?"

"We're not doing well, Carlos. The loyalists and peninsulares simply do not trust us. They will not sell us any rifles or pistols and continue turning us away. We have gone as far as Utuado but even there they will not sell us arms. It's like they know who we are."

"Then we will have to depend totally upon Dr. Betances's shipment whenever it arrives. How about machetes and knives, have you gathered them?"

"We have plenty of that, Carlos," Ibarra lamented, "But what can machetes and knives do against rifles and cannons?"

Carlos sighed heavily and looked across his audience. "We must be patient and allow Betances and Ruiz to do their work. They will not fail us, and they will not fail the cause." Although Carlos made a valiant attempt at reassuring the members, even he knew that his words were weak, lacking the confidence and determination they once had.

The meeting was over as quickly as it had started, and, to no one's surprise, Aguilar began to espouse his version of how to lead a rebellion. But Carlos had no time to argue with Aguilar that morning and cut him off immediately, much to Miguel's content. As the members filtered out of the store one by one, Carlos, Aguilar, Ibarra and Miguel shook hands with them.

The last member to exit the colmado was the one Miguel had studied with keen interest. The man shook hands with Aguilar first, then with Ibarra, but as he moved forward to shake hands with Carlos, Miguel put out his hand. "Thank you for coming, señor. And you are?" Carlos was surprised at Miguel's sudden forwardness; he had never done that before. On the other hand, he knew Miguel, and reasoned there must have been a purpose behind his abrupt behavior. He said nothing, and for the moment allowed Miguel the liberty. Both Aguilar and Ibarra watched and listened but neither of them had a clue as to the reason for Miguel's sudden action.

"My name is Redondo, Diego Redondo," answered the man, taking in Miguel's firm handshake.

"You look familiar to me, señor, have we met before?" Miguel said, narrowing his eyes at the solicitor.

"I don't think so," replied Redondo nervously. Carlos immediately sensed Redondo's uneasiness, as if he were hiding something.

"I'm sure I have seen you before, aren't you a lawyer or something?" insisted Miguel, drawing even closer to Redondo.

"I am a lawyer, yes."

"And you're from San Sebastián?"

"Yes," answered Diego, glancing at Aguilar who stood only inches away. "I was born and raised in San Sebastián, but I studied in Spain, where I received a degree in Jurisprudence. I came back to San Sebastián after graduation and opened a law office."

"A lawyer, huh?" said Miguel with untrusting eyes.

Aguilar, who was paying close attention to Miguel's sudden inquisition, took a step forward and gave Miguel a disapproving look. "We already know that señor Redondo is a solicitor, Miguel, we investigate every man before he is made a member." He turned to look up at Carlos. "That is what you've entrusted us to do, right Carlos?" Carlos nodded at Aguilar in total agreement. Aguilar then turned back and gave Miguel a sharp stare, as if telling him to mind his business.

Miguel took his eyes away from Redondo's face and trained them on Aguilar. "No one's questioning your recruiting methods, Manuel, or yours, Eusebio, I just thought I recognized the man, is all." Carlos kept his eyes on Redondo while Aguilar and Miguel spoke, but the man's edginess spoke volumes. Such blatant apprehension had to account for something, reasoned Carlos. Miguel then turned his attention back onto Redondo's face. "I thought I had seen you in the company of Don Rodolfo Hernández—you know who I'm talking about, right,

El Demonio?" Miguel measured Redondo's facial gestures and eye movements for truth.

"I provide legal services to señor Hernández from time to time," said Redondo in his own defense, "as I do with everybody else, whether creole or peninsular. I am a solicitor and this is what I do for a living. I've already disclosed this information to señores Aguilar and Ibarra."

Carlos raised his hand in the air to halt the conversation. "And I trust in their wisdom, señor Redondo." He shook hands with the lawyer and stretched his face with a grand smile. "Welcome to Porvenir, señor, in time we might have need for your legal services. I am glad that you have joined our cause."

Redondo shook hands with Carlos, and then glanced at Miguel before leaving the colmado. Standing outside the colmado, the leaders watched Diego Redondo mount his horse and waited until he left town. "What the hell was all that about?" Aguilar said, shaking his head at Miguel.

Miguel shrugged his shoulders and gave Aguilar a smug look. "Nothing—nothing at all."

Aguilar gestured dismissively at Miguel and then turned to face Carlos. "Better put a leash on your young friend here, we need every member we can get. And Don Diego Redondo could be a useful ally."

Carlos nodded to appease Aguilar. He shook hands with him and Ibarra and bid them good day. Aguilar and Ibarra mounted their horses, and as their pounding hooves faded into silence, Carlos eyed Miguel. Fully aware that Miguel was hiding something, he waited for the right time to address that concern. After leaving the colmado, and while riding their horses on their way back to Miguel's home, Carlos finally broached the matter with his dear friend. "All right, Miguel, now can you tell me? Why so much fuss over Diego Redondo's membership?"

"I saw him the day Hernández had my father wipe dirt off his boots. He was with *El Demonio* that day and I bet he is Hernández's permanent lawyer here, in San Sebastián. I just don't believe that he simply works for that monster from time to time."

"That's your anger talking," Carlos rebutted. "What have I told you about acting out of anger?"

"I am not acting out of anger," Miguel replied defensively, "but out of common sense. I don't trust anyone who freely associates with peninsulares, especially lawyers."

CHAPTER 27

The following day, Maria and her three daughters went into town to shop for new dresses for the gala at the mayor's home that evening. Rosalía lagged behind her family as they window-shopped along the streets of the small town. Rosalía's melancholy had overtaken her for more than a week, and during that time, she remained mostly in her bedroom, staring aimlessly through her window. It pained her heart to see how Miguel had suddenly turned on her and made her feel guilty about something for which she was not responsible. Yet, in spite of Miguel's sudden turnaround, Rosalía clung to the notion that he had acted out of anger, and perhaps had vented his rage out on her. But she had to deal with the fact that she had dismissed him, and told him she never wanted to see him again. In her heart, though, it was a lie. She did want to see him, and she did want to talk to him. Rosalía finally caught up to her family as they stopped to observe a window display.

After browsing briefly at the window display, Laura shook her head in obvious disappointment. "I can't believe they're still selling these kinds of dresses. That's what we were wearing five years ago."

Maria sighed. "There is no fashion, here, Laura. We must make do with whatever is available in San Sebastián."

"Rags, they're all rags, Mother," replied Laura angrily. "Everyone will know that we bought those dresses in town. We cannot wear those rags."

Anita, as always, stood behind her mother and took no pains to hide her indifference. All she thought about was Ruben De La Cruz and the moment he would ask her to marry him.

"All right, then," answered Maria in a motherly tone of voice. "We will walk up the street and look at other stores. If we cannot buy new dresses, then we will have to wear whatever evening attire we brought with us."

As Maria spoke, Rosalía's blue eyes widened to reveal her surprise. Standing across the narrow street was Miguel Pítre and his African friend, Carlos. Rosalía found that she couldn't keep her eyes away from Miguel despite the harsh treatment he had given her over a week ago and despite how much his actions had broken her heart. What was it that she was feeling at that precise moment? She felt a pang in her gut that she had never before felt in her life. She felt excitement and fear, happiness and melancholy all at the same time, and during that brief moment, the convergence of such conflicting and palpable emotions drove her insane with confusion. It seemed to Rosalía as if time were moving slowly, because every second she took to look at Miguel had taken an eternity. As Rosalía watched Miguel, she could not deny the fact that she found him terribly attractive. His confidence came forth naturally through his face and body movements. He had a self-assured swagger that, at least in Rosalía's eyes, was very attractive, as well as exhilarating. But most of all, she loved the way Miguel spoke. She loved his gentle voice and the way his green eyes would penetrate her heart while the words came whispering out of his mouth. Is that what falling in love felt like? Was she starting to fall in love with Miguel? How could she have allowed herself to fall in love with a peasant? It was wrong. It was dangerous to exhibit such carnal inclinations of the heart.

As Rosalía contemplated Miguel from across the street, she was oblivious to the fact that Laura had been staring at her for a long while. Not wasting the opportunity, Laura slowly walked over to where Rosalía was standing. Laura nearly burst in laughter because while Rosalía watched Miguel, she was mimicking her youngest sister. Maria shook her head at Laura but Anita, who was watching Laura, felt nothing but anger. All of a sudden, Laura's voice broke Rosalía's reverie. "Look, Mother!" Laura said, pointing her index finger across the street. "It's Rosalía's suitor!"

Maria and Anita both turned their heads and focused their eyes on the young creole standing across the street, inspecting vegetables at a stand. Rosalía quickly faced Laura and with contempt spewed her response. "He is not my suitor!"

"You could have fooled me. The way you were gazing at him suggests something else," replied Laura, calculating as always.

Maria quickly moved toward Rosalía and with a skeptical expression said, "What is Laura talking about, Rosa?"

"Nothing, Mother, Laura's just trying to make trouble. She cannot help it; she's just a troublemaker—a wrecker of happiness. It's in her blood, Father's blood."

"Don't talk that way about your father, Rosa; he is a good man and a good husband!" Maria admonished.

"It's the truth, Mother, and you know it! Why do you protect him, especially knowing how badly he treats you?"

"Silly brat!" Laura said with fire in her eyes. "You just don't know how good you have it! Father should be made aware of all this."

"It surprises me that you have not already told him, Laura. Why have you not told him?"

"Because of me, that's why," interjected Maria, eyebrows furrowed. "Laura told me what happened in town between you and that peasant. She said that you told him you never wanted to see him again. I believed that, and so because of that I asked Laura not to tell your father."

"I'm not a child, Mother. And I really don't care one way or another if Father should know."

"You see, Mother?" Laura said angrily. "She doesn't appreciate a thing."

"Come girls," insisted Maria. "Let's go home! Things are starting to get out of control, and the further we're away from that peasant, the better."

Rosalía reluctantly followed her mother and sisters toward the awaiting stagecoach, but before entering the vehicle, she took one last look at Miguel. This time, however, Miguel was looking right back at her. Rosalía blinked twice, raised her eyebrows, and then entered the coach.

Though Miguel remained aloof, his heart was fluttering for some time now, and Carlos was quick to detect that veiled excitement. Miguel stood there for a long while before he heard the sound of an old man making some sort of an announcement. There were about ten to twelve young men facing the speaker, listening with brightened and hopeful eyes. Curious, Miguel crossed the street toward the old man so that he could hear what he was saying.

"The mayor needs waiters for his gala this evening," announced the elder man. The pay is two centavos an hour!" The old man was the mayor's head servant.

Miguel looked over his shoulders at Carlos, who was still watching him from across the street, and then turned back to face the speaker. The moment he saw Miguel raising his arm to accept the job, Carlos shook his head in frustration. Minutes later, he watched Miguel cross with a huge smile, as if he were a little boy who'd been given a handful of candy. "What do you think you're doing, Miguelito?"

"She'll be there tonight."

"And?"

"And what, Carlos? I just want to talk to her."

"And tell her what, that you're sorry? You're going to apologize and lower yourself to a peninsular bitch?"

Miguel's smile suddenly vanished and rage overtook his senses—green eyes beaming unobstructed anger at his mentor for the first time in their friendship. "Her name is Rosalía, and I don't ever want to hear you talk about her like that again, you hear me? We cannot blame her for her father's misdeeds! We cannot blame her for being born into wealth any more than we could blame you for being black or me for being poor! She is different! And if you speak about her like that again, I will end our friendship!"

Carlos stared silently at Miguel and for the first time in five years of friendship, he began to question his friend's true intentions. "I apologize for my remark, Miguel. Are you in love with her?"

Miguel sighed deeply and shrugged his shoulders. "I don't know. I do find her attractive, and I believe in my soul that she is a good person. Perhaps I *am* in love...but I really don't know for sure."

Carlos placed his huge hands on Miguel's shoulders. "I just don't want to see you get hurt while chasing an impossible dream. You must not forget about the cause. You must stay focused and alert. But if you feel a need to apologize to her, then you must do whatever your heart tells you." He took his heavy hands off Miguel's shoulders.

"Thank you, my friend," answered Miguel, appreciatively.

CHAPTER 28

The night rushed in a wave of steamy humidity that brought discomfort even to the locals of San Sebastián. Seeking refuge from the infernal moisture, most of the townsfolk had decided to spend the early evening hours outside, in front of their meager abodes.

Although the townsfolk made their presence known by their loud chatter and by vocalizing their misery about the weather, Miguel would not see any of them or hear their commiseration. Miguel had a singular vision that night, a mission so important that he did not even feel the sudden change in climate. Unencumbered by the natural elements, he joined the four other selected men at the mayor's house that evening.

Arriving promptly at six, Miguel stood shoulder to shoulder with his fellow servants, looking up at the mayor's butler who was standing in the back porch of the house. The butler had a large black canvas bag on the floor next to his feet, and in one of his hands, a leather pouch. For the next ten minutes, the butler went on to explain the serving rules to the eager men. They were to remain silent at all times, and if asked to do something by any one of the mayor's guests, they were to oblige them politely. If a request was something out of the ordinary, they were to pass along the request to the butler.

To Miguel, it seemed as if the butler had a long list of rules and regulations, and that he would stand there on the porch all night long until he read every rule to the young men. When the butler finally finished his rambling speech, he looked at every one of the men and scratched his neatly trimmed beard in deep thought. Reaching a quick solution, the butler ordered the young men into the woods behind the house. They walked past an old out-house, that stunk to high heaven, and down a small ridge to a creek. The five young men were clueless as to why the butler had brought them down there but they followed him nonetheless. Standing above the men, on the crest of the northern bank, the butler ordered the young men to strip and bathe. He flung the leather pouch at them and told them there were razors and soap inside it.

Miguel's beard had never fully grown, and some areas of his face would not grow any hair. Lacking the means to keep his whiskers in good order, his beard grew wildly, but then nobody really complained about it, at least not until that very moment. Well, if shaving and bathing in a creek was what it was going to take to see Rosalía again, then that is what he was going to do.

The butler patiently waited as the men shaved and bathed, and when they finally emerged with clean bodies and boyish faces, the butler threw only two towels at them and insisted they share them. Their bodies still naked, the five young men stood on the edge of the creek looking up at the butler, expectantly. The butler then arched and reached for the black canvas bag. He threw the bag at the men and told them it contained suitable trousers, shirts and ties, and bade them haste in putting on their temporary apparel.

Not being quick enough, Miguel had been the last to retrieve the clothes inside the bag. To his great regret, the trousers were too short; the hem falling just above his ankles. As if that were not enough, the sleeves of his shirt were also too short and the collar as tight as a hangman's noose. But what had given him the worst discomfort of all was the set of shoes he had to wear; they were tiny and they crimped his toes, forcing him to walk awkwardly. He was grateful that the pair of socks he wore at least covered the space between the hem of his trousers and his ankles.

When the five young men finished dressing, the butler nodded with some satisfaction, and then he told them to leave their clothes by the creek and fetch them after their duties were over that night. He told the men to climb up the ridge and escorted them to the mayor's house.

The butler assigned Miguel the task of serving beverages. It wasn't because the butler specifically chose him, but because Miguel just happened to be the first man on line. Miguel stood inside the kitchen, holding a silver tray, while the butler placed wine glasses on it. The butler poured slowly and deliberately until he filled the glasses. Then he gave Miguel final instructions and ordered him into the dining hall.

The moment Miguel stepped into the dining hall he took a few seconds to acquaint himself with everything and everyone. Mayor Chiesa took pride in the long oak dining table imported from France, and he often bragged that it was one of his finer investments. The table held twenty-two chairs, ten on either side and two on each end. The guests occupied every seat and filled the hall with their seemingly endless chatter. At the head of the table sat the mayor, and at the other end sat his prudish wife. Rodolfo Hernández sat to the right of the mayor and Maria sat to the right of the mayor's wife. Next to Rodolfo sat Don Francisco Frontera and across from him sat Don Juan Marquez—two of Puerto Rico's most prominent businessmen. Sitting at the mayor's dining table also, wearing his formal military uniform, was Colonel Juan Manuel de Ibarreta. Other guests included bankers and plantation owners.

The daughters of Rodolfo and Maria Hernández sat separately, just as Rodolfo had ordered them to do. Earlier in the day, he vowed that his daughters would not get an opportunity to embarrass him as they had done so at Don Ignacio De La Torre's house weeks ago. Rosalía sat in the middle of the table, and to her greatest regret and discomfort, Laura sat directly across from her. Anita sat on the same side of Laura but several chairs away.

Rosalía had a look of boredom, and while she struggled to maintain a polite conversation with some of the guests, inside she wanted to scream. For the sake of her father and his rage, however, she would use her best charm and do what high society expected of her. Sitting next to Rosalía, Don Pedro Mancuso, a banker, began a conversation with her about the current banking situation on the island. On occasion, Rosalía would nod as if she understood him and was truly interested in his conversation, but she did not know anything about banking and felt repulsed by the man's awful breath. She cringed inside at the foul order emanating from the mouth of what was supposed to be a refined man.

When the kitchen door opened most of the people glanced up at the young man holding a tray full of wine glasses, but other than the mere glance, they all returned to their conversations. Rosalía was the only patron that kept her eyes on the young man. At first, she could not place his clean-shaven face, but when she saw his green eyes, staring right back at her, her young heart began to palpitate.

Rosalía turned back to the banker and smiled politely but kept glancing back at Miguel who was steadily approaching the table. Sensing Rosalía's disinterest, the banker turned to the guest sitting on his right and began a new conversation. Laura was quick to notice her sister, and by the look in Rosalía's excited eyes, she knew something was afoot. She followed her sister's eyes, turned her head and noticed a young man holding a tray. Laura could not place the face at first, but then she studied the young man for a while and concluded he was none other than Miguel Pítre! She nodded devilishly and realized a great opportunity had presented itself. Now, all she had to do was calculate. But would she get an opportunity to wreak havoc that night? What Laura didn't know was that Maria Hernández was also watching Rosalía, and she too recognized the young man. Though she maintained her conversation with the mayor's wife, she kept glancing at Rosalía.

Miguel placed each wine glass down on the table as instructed by the butler. He went around the table until he finally came upon Rosalía. Despite her anger at Miguel's unmitigated outburst, she still felt something for him, and when he arched his body to place the glass down, their eyes locked. "Buen provecho, señorita, or, as they say in France, '*bon appetite*'." Miguel said courteously.

Rosalía smiled. "Gracias…Miguel."

Miguel straightened up slowly but kept his eyes firmly on Rosalía's beautiful face. He smiled at her and whispered. "Rosalía, I want to apologize to you for my behavior, I was wrong about you. Can you find it in your heart to forgive me? Can we start over again?"

Rosalía's heart fluttered for a few seconds, but then she gave Miguel a kind of smile that told him right then that she had forgiven him. Still, Miguel wanted to hear her say it. He wanted to hear her angelic voice just one more time.

Miguel's hopes were thwarted for the moment. Rodolfo, too astute to let anything go unnoticed, realized right away that the young man had taken much too long to place a simple glass of wine on the table. He found it strange also that a servant had even dared to talk to one of the mayor's guests or one of his daughters, for that matter.

While Laura watched her sister and calculated her downfall, and while Maria grew more concerned about the situation, they were all suddenly distracted when Rodolfo commanded. "Boy, come here!"

The mayor gave Rodolfo a strange look, wondering why his guest had called out for one of his hired servants. The mayor looked at his butler and gestured to him to take control of the situation. The butler nodded back at the mayor, and then made his way around the table, toward Miguel.

Ignoring Rodolfo's voice, Miguel kept his eyes on Rosalía. "Do you forgive me, Rosa, I must know."

"Miguel, that's my father calling for you!" Rosalía insisted, voice crackling with panic.

"I know."

"Go to him, he wants a glass of wine."

"He can wait."

"Miguel, you're going to get fired!"

Across the table, Laura's face reflected nothing but glee because she didn't have to do a thing that night. Rosalía was causing her own damage. This time, she sat back on her chair and simply watched the events as they quickly unfolded.

"Do you forgive me, Rosa? I will not leave you until I hear you say it."

"Miguel you're going to get into a lot of trouble. Please go to my father!"

All of a sudden, Miguel felt the butler's hand reaching out and squeezing his elbow. "You impertinent fool! Do as you're told, and leave this young woman alone."

Miguel took his eyes away from Rosalía and locked them on the butler's weary face. He whispered so that nobody else could hear him. "Take your filthy hand off me, you subservient dog, before I smash this tray over your head!"

The butler took just one look at Miguel's fiery eyes and quickly let go of Miguel's arm. He turned his head and shot a helpless glance at the mayor.

Miguel looked down at Rosalía and said, "Forgive me, Rosa, I didn't mean to upset you that day in town. I was just angry that Carlos had lost his home because a rich peninsular had bought Don Duran's farm. I took it out on you and I should not have done so; you were not at fault. Please forgive me."

The mayor finally rose to his feet, and by his action brought a sudden hush across the dining hall. "Felipe!" the Mayor cried out.

The butler looked at the mayor but all he could muster was a helpless expression.

Miguel kept his eyes on Rosalía and waited for her answer. "Will you forgive me?"

Fearing for Miguel's safety now, Rosalía, nodded. "Yes, yes, yes, Miguel, I forgive you now go!" From across the table, Rosalía heard Laura chuckling, as if she were watching a stage comedy. Rosalía ignored Laura and looked into Miguel's green eyes, fear now pervading her face.

"Thank you, Rosalía, that's all I wanted from you. Now we can start over again or, if it pleases you, I will leave you alone and never bother you again." Miguel finally turned around and while closely followed by the butler, sensed everyone's frowning gesture.

When Miguel approached the head of the table, the mayor, who was still standing with a seething look on his face, demanded, "What is the meaning of this, Felipe?"

"Señor Alcalde, I didn't—"

"Oh it's nothing," interrupted Rodolfo, waving his hand at the mayor. "Please, señor Alcalde, take your seat. All I wanted was a refill." Rodolfo looked at Felipe with glaring eyes. "Can your boy do this simple task without having to disturb the mayor's guests?"

"Si señor!" said the butler nervously.

Rodolfo nodded at the butler, and then he narrowed his eyes at Miguel. "All right then, get to it, boy."

Miguel calmly walked to Rodolfo and began to pour wine into the empty glass. As he poured the wine, Rodolfo studied him. "I know who you are. You are Juan Pítre's boy, aren't you? Helping your father out with his debt?"

Miguel said nothing. He kept filling the wine glass until it overflowed and ran off the table into Rodolfo's lap. Rodolfo felt the wine drip down onto his trousers and immediately rose from his chair. "You incompetent son-of-a-bitch!" he yelled. He looked at the mayor. "Señor Alcalde, you should have your butler do a better job of hiring. Clearly this boy has no training."

Following Rodolfo's remarks, the mayor rose to his feet and turned to Felipe in a fit of anger. "Felipe! Take this idiot out of here!" He cast an apologetic face at Rodolfo and uttered. "Señor Hernández, please forgive me."

"It is not your fault, Alcalde. It is your butler's fault, and you should deal with him."

"Indeed, señor," added Don Frontera who was outraged at Miguel's lack of respect and training.

But the mayor valued Felipe's service, and realizing good help was hard to come by, refused to fire the butler. He knew that Rodolfo expected no less than a good firing, but he would not let go of Felipe so easily, no matter what his guests felt. He took a few moments to reprimand Felipe and then chased him away.

Miguel entered the kitchen and placed the tray on the table. Felipe quickly followed him into the kitchen and by the look on the butler's face Miguel knew he feared for his job. "What are you so afraid of?"

"He may fire me because of what you did," replied Felipe with a look of resignation. "You never really wanted a job, did you? All you wanted was to talk to that young woman. Well, I'm glad you accomplished your goal at my expense."

"Relax, Felipe," said Miguel calmly. "If the mayor wanted to fire you, he would have done so right in front of that piece of shit, Hernández. Trust me: he will not fire you. Besides, aren't you sick and tired of those bastards coming here from Spain and taking over everything? Are you not sick and tired of being a servant for those peninsular cabrónes? Isn't it time for you to wake up and do something about your country, señor, about yourself? Isn't it time for you to choose sides? I invite you to join the revolution. I invite you to take a stand against Spanish imperialism and tyranny."

"Revolution?" the Butler said skeptically. Miguel had come to recognize that skepticism in so many of the older creoles, like a dreadful disease, and he deplored it. "That's a pipe dream, young man. Now get out of my kitchen. I don't ever want to you see again."

Miguel knew the kind so well that he didn't even bother to voice a rebuttal. He nodded, and then headed straight for the back door. "Wait!" said the butler's voice. For an instant, Miguel thought the butler might have had a change of mind. He turned around slowly and confronted Felipe. Felipe looked at Miguel up and down before opening his mouth again. "Take off your clothes and leave them here, in the kitchen."

"What did you say?" said Miguel incredulously.

"I said take your clothes off and leave them here. You think I'm going to let you walk out with those clothes? I'll probably never see them again. No, take off your clothes and walk back to the creek naked. Find your clothes and leave immediately."

Miguel chuckled to himself, as the other young men barged in and out of the kitchen leaving or taking new trays of food or drinks. Miguel nodded at Felipe. "All right, old man."

At the dining hall, Rosalía could not hide the euphoria in her blue eyes. Miguel had come to see her in spite of all the inherent dangers. Miguel had come to renew Rosalía's hopes and make her feel happy once again. As she immersed herself in thought about Miguel, she moved her eyes around the table, looking at each face, knowing in her heart that no one at the table was as happy as she was at that moment. Then her eyes met her father's eyes looking back at her, and the euphoria came to a sudden end. Her father sat, holding a cigar in one hand and a drink in the other, looking directly at her with contemptuous eyes. Rosalía knew that she would probably get the worst beating of her life, now that her father knew there was something between her and Miguel. She was sure that if he did not know the whole story, Laura would happily fill in all the blanks. In reality, Rosalía did not care one way or another. Miguel had come to see her and that was the only thing that mattered to her.

At around eleven thirty that evening, Miguel had stopped by Carlos's new digs at Don Blanco's farm. The two men sat on a couple of bales of hay as Miguel recounted his experiences earlier in the evening. As the two men laughed at Rodolfo's expense, the evening air carried their sound of laughter out from the barn and into the silent hills of San Sebastián. In the middle of laughter, Miguel concluded his story. "You should have seen the look on his face, Carlos, when the wine fell all over his pants; it was priceless!"

"If old man Rodolfo didn't know you then, he certainly knows you now—that's for sure!" Carlos said. Then the laughter subsided and both men kept their silence for a long while. During that moment, Carlos contemplated his dear friend. He admired Miguel's tenacity and wished there were more men in Porvenir like him. "I'm glad that she forgave you, Miguel. So what are you going to do next?"

"Nothing. I told her that all I wanted was to be forgiven and that once she forgave me, she would never see me again."

Carlos was too smart to allow Miguel to fool him. He sensed a lack of conviction in Miguel's tone, and nodded to himself. "If that were only true, my friend."

"You don't believe me?"

"I believe your mind's intentions, but your heart may think differently."

Miguel turned to look at his friend. "Trust me, Carlos, after tonight la señorita Rosalía will be a faint memory."

"So are you with us again?"

"I never left you."

"You must stay focused now, Miguelito. Things are starting to move very quickly, and the day for revolution will be upon us soon."

CHAPTER 29

The morning of Tuesday, March 3, saw Rosalía sitting restlessly on her bed, unable to think of anything else except for Miguel Pítre. Rosalía admired Miguel's courage and his determination to succeed against all odds, and by his actions, Rosalía knew in her heart that he was attracted to her. There were so many things left unsaid between them, and she wanted to get it all out in the open. Though he promised her she would never see him again, she refused to take stock in his words; every fiber in her body told her otherwise. For one thing, Miguel's voice lacked the confidence that Rosalía felt separated him from all other creoles on the island; a trait that immediately attracted her and one to which she had already become accustomed. Behind Miguel's emotional veneer, Rosalía detected hope and sincerity the likes of which she had never before sensed in a human being. Rosalía would think of nothing else because she wanted Miguel to come back into her life.

By the sound of rattling pots and pans, Rosalía knew her mother had been in the kitchen that morning preparing breakfast for the family, and while she was certain her mother would toil away until late morning, she was equally certain Anita was sleeping comfortably upstairs. She was already aware that her father, as always, had left the house en route to his financial conquests of the day, and would not return until nightfall. But Rosalía had no clue as to Laura's whereabouts, and it bothered her that she could not figure out where her eldest sister was. Laura was so sneaky, thought Rosalía, perhaps she was hiding somewhere in the house and watching Rosalía's every move. Rosalía shook her head, angry with herself because she had given her sister too much thought, too much credit. The anxieties in Rosalía were gradually consuming her, and she was powerless to overcome them. The need in her to see

Miguel's face once again was so overwhelming, that she finally decided to do the unthinkable.

Rosalía quietly opened the front door of the house and began walking down the dirt road. Driven by a compelling desire to see Miguel, she ventured into town alone and fully aware that she would have to deal with the consequences upon her return. From her window upstairs, Laura stared aimlessly, counting the number of days she had already spent in total boredom when all of a sudden, she saw Rosalía walking away from the house. At last, there was something to do, Laura thought. She smiled wickedly as she watched Rosalía breaking the strict orders her father had issued to everyone in the household. Laura squinted at the sight of her sister walking away and, while her sister's image slowly faded into the woods, Laura came to a quick resolution. A few moments later, Laura walked out of the house and began trailing her sister.

CHAPTER 30

Eighty miles northeast of San Sebastián, in the outskirts of San Juan, Berta and her brother Manolo, made their best efforts to hide in the woods. Brother and sister had gotten their parents' blessing to run away from the Hernández estate several days earlier, and wasted no time in consummating their deliverance. At first, they tried to stow away in the bowels of a Spanish merchant ship, but there were so many stevedores and anglers in and around the docks, that they could not approach the ship without someone seeing them. Next, they tried to steal a rowboat, but several fishermen nearly caught sight of them. They decided to leave San Juan and try elsewhere.

Berta knew that no one had sounded the call for runaway slaves because the Hernández were many miles away and therefore had no clue about their escape. By 1868, though, Berta and many of her slave peers knew that peninsulares had stopped employing the use of ruthless overseers. Ten years earlier, however, it would have been a much different situation. They would not have made it past the road without confronting an overseer. Then, even if they did manage to avoid an overseer, the nightly slave count would have discovered their escape and all overseers, including those of the surrounding plantations, would have banded together in a posse to hunt them down. Finally, the thought of capture and subsequent punishment for their attempted escape would have put too much fear in them to act out their intentions. It was different now because there were very few overseers left. In her mind, Berta felt the overseers' demise came as a result of the abolitionist movement. What she did not know was that slave masters all thought overseers were not only lazy, but too sadistic to be trusted with such prized properties, not to mention their high salaries. Berta also sensed the tide of change had finally reached the shores of Puerto Rico because the abolition of slavery had been a hot topic among many creoles for the past few years. Some of the peninsulares, although they were not legally bound to do so, even paid their slaves—all in an effort to fall out from under the abolitionists' scrutiny. In spite of these small gains, even the dumbest peninsular knew that slavery would not last for much longer. England had abolished slavery years earlier and only recently, the United States had come to good reason, though it did take a civil war to settle the issue. Berta and Manolo reasoned that they needed to get as close to American waters as possible, close enough so that a United States ship could see them and take them in as freed people.

Emerging from their wooded shelter, Berta and Manolo doubled back to the Hernández mansion and changed their direction towards San Juan Bay. Since the docks on the bay side of San Juan were less guarded and less populated, perhaps they could steal a sailboat. Manolo and Berta walked for hours until they caught sight of a tiny marina and counted a dozen or so sailboats. Towards the end of the marina, Manolo noticed a very small rowboat tied to a narrow pier. He tugged at Berta and she followed him toward the vessel. As they crossed the tiny village, the few creoles that saw them, thinking they were on an errand for their master, made no fuss about them. Taking advantage of the moment, Berta and Manolo crept along the shoreline until they saw the rowboat, bobbing up and down in rhythm to the rolling waves.

Brother and sister were frightened so much that neither of them had the nerve to walk to the boat. They feared a creole would discover them and have them arrested. All of a sudden, they heard a deep voice. "You want that boat, don't you?" Manolo turned his head to the side and noticed a dirty set of shoes, partially buried into the hot sand. He looked up, and, against the bright sunlight, managed to see the face of a black man. The man placed his hands on his hips in an authoritative manner. The creases on his forehead and his white, receding hair, unwittingly gave the man an air of wisdom. Manolo kept silent and held his sister's hand tightly, waiting for the black man to announce the discovery of runaway slaves. But the man just stood there, looking down at the two frightened individuals. "Rise, my young friends, and do not fear me, for I am not the owner of that boat."

"Forgive me, señor, for not rising. My sister and I have run away from our master and if we are seen…"

"I was a slave, too, a long time ago," the man interrupted. "But I am a free man now." He crouched to the sand and looked at both Manolo and Berta. "Tell me, what were you going to do with that boat?"

"We were going to use it to get to the other side of the bay," said Manolo, a twinge of apprehension in his voice.

"The bay is too rough for a tiny boat like that one, young man; you would have capsized and drowned. And even if you managed not to capsize, it would have taken you forever to cross the bay. What you need is a bigger boat, a sail boat that can get you to Cataño more quickly."

"But how can we do that, señor? We have no money and we are runaway slaves."

"Do you want to get out of San Juan or not?" demanded the old man impatiently, slowly standing. He looked up to make sure no one had been watching. Then he looked down at Manolo. "Well?"

Manolo nodded to say yes but there was still a great deal of uncertainty in his mind. His eyes could not hide it from the experienced human smuggler. Would the old man betray him and his sister? It was too late for that now. Manolo stood up, and as he reached for his sister's hand, he heard the deep voice again. "Follow me, quickly."

The old man led Manolo and Berta towards a small bungalow at the far end of the marina. The southern wind began to stir and brought with it a cool breeze that swayed the rows of palm trees above the marina, soothing the three Africans as they neared the bungalow. They entered the house only to confront a creole with a set of piercing brown eyes that seemed to penetrate their minds in that one instant. Unable to detect any emotions in the creole's eyes, Manolo and Berta braced for the worst. Despite his outward appearance, his gentle voice instantly quashed their fears. "Ah Cirilo, what have you brought me today, huh?"

"Two runaways, señor Serrano," replied Cirilo with a heartfelt smile. "They seek passage to Cataño but have no money." Cirilo gazed at Manolo and Berta and flashed a comforting smile at them; a warm, heartfelt smile that told them everything was going to be all right. "This is Don Justicio Serrano," said Cirilo in a prideful tone. "He is the owner of the boat you wanted to steal. This kind man purchased my freedom ten years ago and set me free. I have been working for señor Serrano since then in the fishing business. You must also know that Don Serrano has not only freed me, but many other Africans, too. He is an avowed abolitionist who is willing to help you today."

Serrano nodded happily. "Thank you Cirilo. Now, the best thing to do right away is to keep you safe until nightfall. You two will stay here in my home until tonight while I secure the aid of my friend who owns a nice, big, sailboat. Tonight, we will be moving about sixty men and women to Cataño. Upon reaching Cataño, other members of our movement will meet us there and get you to a safe house in the outskirts of San Sebastián. From there, other members will guide you towards the port of Guánica, where you will take another boat to America." Serrano noted their silent but apprehensive faces, and added, "Please do not worry about your safety, for I will guarantee that nothing will happen to you. All I want is for you two to rest a bit because the voyage to Cataño and later to San Sebastián will be a long and arduous trip."

Manolo turned to Berta and took her smile as an approval. He turned back to face Serrano. "Thank you señor, thank you so very much."

"Don't thank me, thank Cirilo; *he's* the one who found you."

For the first time in days, brother and sister would sleep the entire night. For this one time, Manolo and Berta would not have to take turns keeping watch during the long and frightful hours of the night. But little did they know that their journey to the port of Guánica, the staging point for their journey toward freedom, would take them through the town of San Sebastián, where their fate would once again intersect with that of their unforgiving master.

CHAPTER 31

The walk to San Sebastián took much longer than Rosalía thought it would. After nearly one hour of trudging along the uneven dirt road, she finally reached the outskirts of the growing pueblo. Two hundred yards away, Laura cussed silently at her sister and at the long walk into town. But her desire to see what her sister was up to far outweighed her current misery, and she would endure it just as Rosalía was enduring it.

Rosalía crossed several streets, searching constantly for Miguel, until she finally caught sight of him. She stood at the edge of Orejola Street, where it intersected an unnamed alley, and simply contemplated Miguel. Miguel was standing behind a wooden cart filled with ripe bananas, oranges and other fruits. He had been arguing with a man who kept insisting the scales were incorrect. Fearing the man would go to another fruit stand Miguel reduced the price on the bunch of bananas and thanked the man courteously. He moved slowly towards the front of his stand and organized the fruit display, happily arranging them for presentation. As he moved several oranges, he heard that beautiful, angelic voice again; a blissful melody he thought he would never hear again.

"I thought you were in the coffee business?"

Miguel kept arranging the fruits and never turned around to face Rosalía, but as he went about his business, his face began to stretch with a smile. "I make extra money at this fruit stand; not much but enough to buy bread and a little meat." As he turned to face Rosalía, he looked around the market square to see where her mother and sisters were, but soon realized they were nowhere to be seen. He looked down at Rosalía, bearing a hopeful grin, but his eyes could not hide his curiosity. "You traveled into town all by yourself?"

"I did."

Miguel gazed into Rosalía's blue eyes and nodded with another smile. "Your parents will not be too happy about that."

"My mother asked me to buy some fresh fruits for tonight's dinner. How fresh are your fruits?"

"This stand belongs to Don Blanco, and he picked these fruits just this morning, there are none fresher anywhere in town."

"Then I wish to purchase a pound of oranges, one pound of bananas and three mangoes, if you don't mind."

Miguel walked behind his stand and carefully chose the best of the banana bunches, oranges and mangoes. He placed the fruits into a brown paper bag and handed the goods to Rosalía. "That'll be medio peso, señorita."

Rosalía reached into her purse, picked out several coins and handed them to Miguel. She hesitated for a just a brief moment, and waited for something to happen. But Miguel simply looked at her and said nothing more. While staring at his face, Rosalía surmised that any feelings Miguel might have had for her vanished on the awful day when he met her mother and Laura in San Sebastián. Rosalía gave Miguel a courteous smile. "Thank you, señor Pítre." She turned around dejectedly and began walking back to the main road, away from the market square. Standing near a jewelry stand several yards away, Laura had been watching the scene with interest. Her eyes narrowed with contentment when she saw Rosalía walking away from the stand. It seemed to her that Miguel had heeded the warning set forth by Maria Hernández, and had summarily dismissed Rosalía.

Feeling more dejected now, Rosalía held her brown bag tightly and began her trek back to the Hernández country estate. All of a sudden, she heard Miguel's wonderful voice again.

"Señorita Hernández!" shouted Miguel. "May I walk with you?"

Rosalía did not turn around to face Miguel. With a great measure of satisfaction, she nodded her approval, and then heard Miguel's footsteps as he approached her. They walked for several paces before Rosalía got the nerve to turn her head and look up at Miguel. "It is not safe for you to walk alone, Rosa, especially in a town where most of the creoles hate your father."

"I know my father's strong disposition is not an easy thing to deal with," replied Rosalía, fixing her gaze back on the narrow sidewalk. "After all, he is a businessman."

"Your father and many like him have been exploiting the creoles of Puerto Rico for many, many years. Through their financial craftiness and shady political deals they have taken the lands away from the creoles and left them virtually penniless. They come here from Spain or from the colonies with a limitless supply of money. They open up exporting companies, real estate firms and gobble up everything in sight, and when they've had their fill, they leave with all the riches in their pockets, leaving us to our misery."

"I cannot believe that every creole in Puerto Rico has suffered the same fate," replied Rosalía confidently.

"There are but only a handful of exceptions but even those few can be swayed when a peninsular dangles a wad of cash in front of their noses." Miguel turned again to look at Rosalía, and noted her shaking head, as if she found it difficult to accept Miguel's cynicism. As the young couple walked through the busy sidewalk, the townsfolk stared at them curiously. Miguel could do nothing about their staring and sighed out of frustration. If the townsfolk found their walking side by side a little strange, then he imagined high society would also find it strange. The creoles had cast their judgmental eyes upon the young couple, and had already made their decision, but he didn't care what the creoles or peninsulares thought at that moment. All he cared about was that he had finally gotten an opportunity to see Rosalía again, and talk to her, and that was far better than anything else was at that moment. "You amaze me sometimes, señorita Hernández, you really do."

"What do you mean by that, señor Pítre?"

"I meant nothing. I do not wish to offend you."

"Oh no, you cannot make a statement like that, and then refuse to qualify it on the basis of offending me. It is not like you, señor."

"All right, señorita. You amaze me because on the one hand, you are an educated person, and I sense that you are wise, too. On the other hand, I perceive that you are very naïve. You have lived all of your life in wealth and have never had the want for anything. You have been sheltered from the poor side of society because your parents wish you to believe it does not exist. But it does, Rosa, it is real and the people of Puerto Rico are suffering."

"And yet, when I come into town," replied Rosalía, "I see the market square and observe the people buying food, clothing and other merchandise."

"What you see is different from what I see."

"How so?"

"You will never see the same people the next day. They come once a month or maybe even longer than a month. They work hard to make a few centavos so that they can come into town to buy a loaf of bread, or a few vegetables and fruits. Maybe with enough money they can purchase a decent pair of shoes, but they would have to work for more than two months for that. And even if they did save the money for a decent pair of shoes, they probably wouldn't make such a frivolous purchase because a pair of shoes is a luxury. Aside from that, they'd have to make sure to bring their libretas along with them so that a government lackey might inspect their employment history, and then send them on their merry way."

"I simply cannot agree with you, Miguel, we are not all monsters."

"I didn't say you were, Rosa," said Miguel with saddened eyes. He couldn't comprehend why Rosalía was being so stubborn, especially after she had seen so much in town. He sighed again, and then nodded at her. "The only way I can make you understand is to show you. Would you like to see how we really live?"

Rosalía stopped abruptly and then turned to look up at Miguel, gazing at his beautiful green eyes. "Very well then, show me."

Miguel escorted Rosalía to his horse and together they rode into the woods using an old dirt trail. Behind them, Laura carefully took note of the developing situation.

CHAPTER 32

Don Pedro Gutierrez had been pleading with Rodolfo Hernández for the better part of an hour, but the staunch real estate mogul refused to listen. From atop his horse, Rodolfo yelled at Don Gutierrez, as if he were admonishing a child. Alongside Hernández, Don Diego Redondo sat atop his horse and watched Rodolfo in silence. Pedro Gutierrez was a young creole, too young to have taken on the burden of farming and supporting a family. The twenty-year-old Pedro was the only son of Simon Gutierrez, a once wealthy creole dentist whose love of rum and gambling far exceeded his love for his son and wife. One night, Simon Gutierrez got into a fight over cards and later died of his injuries, leaving his wife and ten-year-old son in poverty. Following his father's death, Pedro quit school and became a jornalero. He worked on various farms over the years until his late teen-age years, when he was able to secure a lease from Rodolfo Hernández. Pedro's dark, reddish complexion hinted a mixture of Taino blood, but no one talked about it. His almond-shaped brown eyes, though youthful, showed maturity and an amazing clarity to realize that he was in a precarious situation. "But Don Hernández," pleaded Gutierrez. "If you evict me from the farm, I will have no other means to support my wife and three children. All I ask is that you extend the deadline. Just look around you, señor and see that the finca has yielded a great harvest of bananas and plantains; all I need is a little time to reap the harvest. A good bounty is hard to come by, but this one will fetch enough money not only to pay you for the three months I owe you, but also support my family for the next two months. I implore you, señor, and I entreat your compassion."

"Entreat my compassion? That's all I have shown you for three months, Gutierrez!"

Pedro then turned to Redondo, hoping the young solicitor would help him. "Diego, we were neighbors once, and our parents were good friends, can't you intercede on my behalf?"

"Don Redondo is not here to plead your case!" shouted Rodolfo. "He is *my* solicitor!"

Ignoring Rodolfo for the moment, Pedro kept his hopeful brown eyes on his former neighbor. "Are you not indebted, too, señor? You must know how terrible a situation this has become for me and my family."

Rodolfo's sharp ears and keen mind took careful note of Gutierrez's last statement, and while Pedro spoke, the shrewd entrepreneur crunched his eyebrows in deep thought. *Don Diego Redondo is indebted? Hmm, to whom does my cunning solicitor owe money?* All of a sudden, Pedro Gutierrez's debt no longer felt important to Rodolfo. Pedro had unwittingly presented something more valuable to the landowner. It was not the promise of money, but a single piece of information; a tiny fragment of a puzzle that Rodolfo had been trying to construct for a long time. As Pedro chatted away, Rodolfo could sense Diego's face stiffen with fear. The young farmer had given away Diego's great secret; it was out in the open now and Rodolfo was too astute to have simply ignored it. The perceptive landowner waved his hand dismissively at Pedro, as if he were an annoying mosquito. "That's enough, Gutierrez! Very well, I will give you three weeks to reap your harvest. If I do not receive your payment in three week's time, I will come here with the militia and magistrate to formally evict you."

Pedro rushed over to Rodolfo, grabbed hold of his hand and kissed it several times. "Thank you, señor Hernández! You will not regret this decision!"

Rodolfo quickly removed his hand from Pedro's grip. Repulsed by Pedro's act of gratitude, he yelled, "Get your filthy mouth off my hand, you goddamn peasant!" He turned to Redondo, nodded at him and then spurred his horse into action.

As Rodolfo drew further away and the thumping beat of his horse grew fainter, Diego kept his eyes on Pedro, shaking his head in disappointment. "You have sealed my fate, Pedro. Now he knows I'm in debt."

"What about *my* fate? What about the fate of the rest of the creoles in Puerto Rico or have you forgotten us already? Besides, what are you doing in the company of that monster? Haven't you suffered enough, too?"

"I'm trying to survive, just like you."

"No Diego, not like me at all. Unlike me, you have a good education, you're a respected solicitor, and you've found employment. By God, Diego, if I had an education such as yours, I would do something to better the lives of our people. But that's not in you, is it?"

"And neither is groveling."

"Sometimes people have to do what they have to do to survive. I am a proud man, but I have a wife and children, and where there are mouths to feed, pride takes a second seat."

Realizing Diego was not following him Rodolfo halted and turned his horse around. He yelled for Redondo several times.

Pedro and Diego stared silently at each other as Rodolfo kept yelling for his solicitor. Finally Pedro said, "The master is calling for his dog, Diego, you better go." Diego said nothing for a few seconds before spurring his horse.

Diego and Rodolfo trotted along the dirt road for several moments in total silence. Behind that silence, though, Rodolfo had been reasoning, formulating, and manipulating. Finally, he turned to Redondo with a smile. "So, Diego, how much do you owe, and to whom are you indebted?"

"Nothing escapes you, does it?" Redondo said dryly.

"You should already know that."

"I'm indebted to none other than Governor Pavía who purchased my debt from Don Carlos Pizarro about a year ago."

"Pizarro, huh? So how much did you owe the local vice lord, and what was it for, gambling or prostitution?"

"Does it matter? I owed that bastard five thousand two hundred pesos."

"A tall figure," said Rodolfo, contemplatively. "What would you say if I agreed to settle half of that debt with the governor?"

"I wouldn't say much, Don Hernández, except for the fact that I would owe two men instead of one. You wouldn't be doing me any favors."

"What would you say then if I signed papers that would release you from my half of the debt?"

"Then I'd have to ask you what you wanted in return."

Rodolfo flashed a smile at Diego, but the solicitor knew that smile all too well. Diego had already figured what the opportunistic Hernández wanted from him.

Rodolfo turned away from Diego and concentrated on the road ahead. "A few weeks ago I met with the mayor of San Sebastián and his guest, Colonel Ibarreta," Rodolfo said. "The good colonel had recently arrived from San Juan with news that Governor Pavía possessed intelligence about rebel activities here, on this part of the island. He further told me that this intelligence came from someone, a spy, who had infiltrated a rebel cell, someone trustworthy enough to make Governor Pavía realize the truth of the current situation. Colonel Ibarreta also told me that the spy signed off the reports with the initials D.R. So I wondered: who could that person be?"

"What do you want, Don Hernández?" Diego said impatiently.

"Straight to the point, very good, Diego; I like that. What I want is for you to let me read your reports before you dispatch them to the governor. If you do this, I will legally absolve half of your debt. You're a lawyer, Diego; you can even draft the papers for me."

"And lay in bed with two devils."

"That's a little harsh, don't you think? I'm trying to help you, son."

"No you're not, Don Hernández, and stop pretending that you are; it doesn't fit your character."

"Clearly, but the offer still stands," replied Rodolfo patiently.

"Let me think about it."

"Alright, that's good enough for me. Come, and let us ride to our next destination. Who's next on the list?"

"That would be la señora Jimenez," replied Diego. As he rode alongside Rodolfo, he shook his head in frustration. Now he had two masters to whom he would betray his people. How did it ever come to this? Why was he so weak against peninsulares? Why was he betraying his own people? All vestiges of pride, and what little measure of self-respect he was clinging to, vanished in an instant, swept away by the winds of betrayal.

CHAPTER 33

Miguel gently helped Rosalía off the horse they'd been riding for the past hour. He had first taken her through a barrio dotted with shanty homes made of rotten wood and roofs covered with rusted corrugated steel. He had shown Rosalía naked children and young men in idle despair, waiting for jobs to come to them, as if by some miracle they'd come raining down from heaven. Miguel showed Rosalía mothers crying over their hungry children, and husbands consoling their wives. He showed his young friend the meager food that lay on many of the tables, or the absence of food in many of the homes. But the house they were heading to would prove to be much different from what Rosalía had already witnessed, and Miguel had to make sure that she would see it.

Miguel escorted Rosalía to the front of a tiny house, where she heard a rooster crowing and saw several hens running about. A very slim cow, tethered to a nearby tree, could barely move, moo or even produce a bucket-full of milk. The laughter of children from nearby homes echoed from a distance. Miguel removed his straw pava and held it tightly in one hand. Using the other hand, he knocked twice on the side of the house. As with many of the creole homes, this one had no door upon which Miguel could knock, but a drab, wrinkled curtain that stretched across the threshold for privacy.

A young man, not much older than thirty, emerged from inside the house. "Miguelito!" he said nervously. "Tell your father I will be there later today."

"That's not why I'm here, Rafael," Miguel quickly answered. Turning to Rosalía, he said, "I am giving señorita Hernández a tour of your quaint barrio. May we come inside?"

"Of course, you are welcome Miguel, and so is your guest. Please, come inside. I'll heat up some coffee."

To say that Rosalía was appalled at the sight of Rafael Cintron's house is to put it mildly. In fact, she was flabbergasted to the point of nausea. The house was a just one big room. There were no beds, only blankets to cushion them against the floor's wooden planks. Rosalía saw an ancient cast-iron stove, filled with wooden branches. On top of a wooden crate that served as a dining table sat two bananas, darkened to the point of rotting. Flies hovered around the rotting bananas, as well as the eyelids of his two young boys. There was a musty smell about the house, as if they never washed the blankets they slept in or mopped the grime and caked up mud off the floor. Yet, through all the filth and putrid odors emanating from that dreadful shack, and despite Rafael Cintron's shabby appearance, Rosalía noted a sense of pride. Rafael smiled at Rosalía, as if there was nothing to be ashamed of, as if this was how everybody lived. Rosalía, in turn, tried valiantly to stave off her emotions. How could Miguel do this to her?

"Here, señorita Hernández, I brewed this coffee yesterday; but it's still fresh," said Rafael humbly. "Here, Miguelito, take some."

The coffee tasted horrible, but Rosalía and Miguel drank every drop of it, hoping not to offend their host. "So are we going to work on the plantation today or not?"

"Yes, Rafael, we are. Where is your wife?"

"Mariana took on a maid's job at a peninsular's house; a recent arrival from Spain. Mariana lives in his house all the time, but she comes around every Sunday to look in on us. She gives me a little money to buy food."

"Please, give her my regards," offered Miguel. Then, he placed his pava over his head, thanked Rafael Cintron for the coffee, and escorted Rosalía out of the house.

While Rafael Cintron looked on, Miguel climbed onto his horse and extended his hand at Rosalía. Rosalía grabbed Miguel's hand and straddled the horse. "Señorita, are you the daughter of Don Rodolfo Hernández?" Rafael asked excitedly.

Rosalía looked down at Cintron and nodded at him. "Yes, I am."

"Then it was a pleasure to have met you."

Rosalía smiled at Cintron, but before Miguel could spur the horse, she reached into the leather saddlebag. She pulled out the brown paper bag with the fruits she had purchased from Miguel, and handed it to Rafael. "Please, señor Cintron, take these fruits."

Rafael Cintron glanced at Miguel, and then reached for the bag. "Thank you, señorita Hernández, for your kindness."

Rosalía smiled at Rafael, and then felt a sudden jerk when the horse began to gallop. She quickly wrapped her arms around Miguel's waist and began to bounce up and down.

Miguel pulled on the reins until the horse came to a slow walk but Rosalía still kept her arms wrapped tightly around Miguel. "Why did you take me to that house?"

"I took you there to show you the extremes under which many of us live, and to show you the differences between peninsulares and creoles, and, finally, to open your eyes."

Rosalía pressed her face onto Miguel's back and with saddened eyes, uttered, "I had no idea, Miguelito, no idea at all. You must believe me."

"I believed that about you from the moment I first laid eyes on you," replied Miguel, feeling the warmth of her face on his back. "That is why I asked you to come here. Now you can see how things truly are and that they will never change unless we make the determination and effort to change them. Now you can see that the only way to change things is through a revolution; only through armed conflict will we ever resolve the current situation in Puerto Rico."

"Stop the horse, Miguel. I want to get off!"

Miguel pulled on the reins and the horse whinnied before coming to a stop. He dismounted, and then helped Rosalía off the horse. "You wish to walk all the way back to town?"

"No. I just want to talk to you face to face. Why do you insist on the idea of revolution? Spain will never allow that to happen and neither will the peninsulares who live here, you must know that. You will be arrested for sedition and spend a very long time in jail, or worse, you may die in battle."

"I would rather die in battle, fighting for freedom, than live in misery under the Spanish yolk; a regime that cares nothing about the people of this island. I've had my fill of it and can stand no more."

"Miguel!" cried out Rosalía, unaware that she had thrown herself into his arms. Miguel held her gingerly, as if he were holding an infant. As she pressed herself further into his chest, Miguel closed his eyes passionately, smelling her perfume and feeling the heat of her body. All of a sudden, Rosalía quickly removed herself from Miguel's hold. "I apologize, Miguel, I didn't mean to—"

Miguel stepped forward and took hold of Rosalía before she could utter another word. He held her tightly in his arms this time, and Rosalía willingly allowed him. He wanted to hold her for the longest time and now that the moment was right for it, he would not squander the opportunity. He moved his right hand toward her chin and gently forced her to look up at him. Then he bent his head and planted a kiss on her beautiful, red lips. They kissed for what seemed like hours.

They stood in the middle of the woods, holding each other as the birds chirped away, and coquís sang their indigenous songs. Miguel wanted this moment to last forever, but the thought of someone seeing them so close together gnawed at his reasoning. He released her abruptly, as if realizing he had broken a taboo. "I must ask you to forgive my indiscretion, Rosa. That is not the reason why I brought you here."

"Even if it wasn't your reason, I'm still glad you kissed me, Miguelito."

Miguel shook his head and closed his eyes. This time he felt Rosalía's lips upon his lips, and they kissed again for a long time. After a few moments more, Miguel let go of Rosalía for the second time. "This is madness. We cannot be together. Rosa, you and I come from two very different worlds."

"You're right, Miguelito," said Rosalía firmly, "but there is no law against our seeing each other, is there?" She watched Miguel turn completely around, casting a wistful gaze at the woods ahead of him. Rosalía uttered curiously, "What's the matter?"

Miguel turned back around and gazed into Rosalía's magical blue eyes. "Can I trust you?"

"Of course you can."

"I'm involved with the rebel movement, and I have committed myself to fight against Spain, against everything that your family stands for. In time, I will become your enemy. Let us part ways, now before it is too late."

"My love," said Rosalía, throwing herself back into Miguel's eager arms again, "It is already too late!"

Having no horse with which to trail her sister, Laura had to follow her on foot. She had lost sight of the young couple immediately, but she remembered the narrow dirt road they had taken, and she followed that road until it led her into a filthy barrio. Laura had not witnessed everything Miguel and Rosalía had done during their tour of the barrio, and only arrived there after Rosalía completed her eye-opening mission. In fact, Laura had arrived at the very moment Miguel and Rosalía were holding each other and kissing each other passionately, but that was all she needed to see. Now Laura had enough ammunition with which to make a powerful assault upon her youngest sister. She stood behind a thick tree and watched as they rode past her back toward town.

As Miguel steered the horse along the trail, his feelings for Rosalía were beginning to grow stronger, and deep inside he just could not leave her in town all by herself. He decided to accompany Rosalía all the way to her house.

Stopping several hundred yards away from the pathway leading to the house, Miguel dismounted, and then helped Rosalía off the horse. They kissed passionately before parting ways. As Miguel trotted along the dirt road, a sense of wonder overcame his being, lifting his spirits to new heights; it was a feeling he had never before experienced in his young life, a powerful transportation to a place of wonderment and excitement.

Consumed by the power of ecstasy, Miguel had lost the track of time and had not realized that he had already reached the outskirts of San Sebastián. His mind swirled with images of him holding Rosalía, kissing her, and as he rode along, he could not hear the townsfolk greeting him good day. All of a sudden, a horrible sight across the street abruptly snapped Miguel out of his reverie. Laura Hernández had been standing in front of a coach she had just hired for the return trip home, and her eyes stared at Miguel with hatred. From that distance, Miguel could feel her evil. Had she been in town all day? Had Laura witnessed him and Rosalía talking, or worse, could she have followed them into the barrio and seen them kissing? Impossible; it was clear that she did not ride a horse into town. Besides, if she had followed them by horse or by coach, he would have heard her riding behind him. He quickly dispensed with his doubts and rode out of town.

CHAPTER 34

Miguel reached Don Rafael Blanco's plantation late in the afternoon and saw Carlos unhitching a plow off a mule. He rode steadily toward Carlos, who by now sensed he had company. The sun was in its final stages, and soon dusk would cover the tropical skies. "Where have you been?" Carlos asked without turning to face Miguel. He heard Miguel dismount and walk slowly toward him.

"I was in town selling fruits, and guess who came to my stand?"

"The governor?" Carlos said.

"No. La señorita Rosalía Hernández," replied Miguel, happily. Carlos said nothing in response. The tall African man pulled the harness off the mule and began walking the beast back to the barn. Miguel followed him but he was curious as to why Carlos remained silent. "Did you hear me? I said Rosa—"

"I heard you," interrupted Carlos. "So what was she doing in town?"

"She came to buy fruits. We talked and got to know each other very well."

Carlos sighed. "What did you talk about?"

"We talked about conditions in Puerto Rico. In fact, we argued about the differences between the peninsulares and creoles. I even took her to the barrios of Pepino, and showed her how creoles really live. You'll be happy to know that she has had a change of mind."

Carlos could not hide his skepticism or fears of being exposed. "And what else did you do?"

"I took her to meet Rafael Cintron."

"Well, if anything could change a peninsular's mind, it's certainly Cintron's house," answered Carlos. Then he turned to Miguel with a smirk, exposing his suspicions to the young man. "And what else?"

"Nothing else, Carlos, except that the tour I gave Rosalía seemed to have opened her eyes."

"You spent all day with her, and all you did was talk?" Carlos said. He watched Miguel's face and studied his protégé's eyes for a long moment. Then Carlos raised his eyebrows in sudden shock. "Oh no! Oh my God!"

"What, Carlos, what are you thinking."

"You're in love with her!" cried out Carlos. "I could read it all over your face, Miguelito! Now tell me the truth! What really happened today?"

Miguel's face stretched to show his dear friend a wide smile. "We kissed. It was the best experience of my life! I held her in my arms, Carlos, and her skin felt soft and she is—"

"Stop it!" yelled Carlos, placing his hands over his ears. Mortified with the thought, he shook his head at Miguel before dropping his arms to the side. Then Carlos took two steps forward and placed his gargantuan hands on Miguel's shoulders. "You cannot allow yourself to fall in love with the daughter of a peninsular, Carlos. Have you forgotten your promise to the cell and to the revolution? For God's sake, get a hold of yourself! Come to your senses, boy, and realize that they are the enemy!"

"I know what I'm doing," Miguel countered, but even he knew how weak his response was.

"No you don't, my young friend," answered Carlos, terribly frustrated. "We don't need for this to happen, especially with her being the daughter of the most ruthless man in all of San Sebastián. We don't need to give that man an excuse or a reason to expose our cell. You may have jeopardized our cause before it even got the chance to get started." Carlos let go of Miguel and stared directly into his love-filled eyes. "She knows about you, doesn't she?"

"I told her," uttered Miguel. He watched Carlos shake his head in disappointment. "Trust me, Carlos, she is different. Rosa has changed her opinion and in time, she may come to join our cause. I will convince her."

Carlos sighed heavily. “I hope that none of the members of our cell find out about your relationship with that woman. You may have placed your life, as well as mine, in danger. Just do me a favor, please, keep silent about the revolution the next time you see her. In the meantime, I will probe the members in my own way to see if they suspect anything.”

Night had fallen quickly, and a gentle breeze rushed through the front porch of the Hernández country home. Sitting on a wicker chair, below a lighted gas lantern, Laura waited for her father’s arrival. She could hear the faint rumble of her father’s horse, and could see the light of his hand-held lantern bouncing in the darkness. As the pounding of Rodolfo’s horse grew louder, so too did the pounding of Laura’s heart.

Rodolfo seemed tired that night, more so than Laura had ever seen him. But there was a certain aura about him, which somehow betrayed the fatigued look on his face. Laura was quick to pick up that subtle glint of good humor in him. Father had had a good day. Rodolfo dismounted and tied the horse to the porch railing. He didn’t notice his daughter until he stepped onto the porch. “Good evening, Father.”

“Good evening, Laura. Why aren’t you in bed?”

“I was waiting up for you.”

“Why?”

“I have something very important to tell you.”

CHAPTER 35

The morning of Wednesday, March 4, began with a torrential, three-hour downpour. The most memorable or forgettable part of that morning was the awful humidity that suddenly surfaced after the rainstorm.

Rodolfo had risen early and was waiting for his youngest daughter to wake. Sweat beads poured down his forehead and collected above his eyebrows, but he ignored the usual morning discomfort. Though Maria had offered to make him breakfast, Rodolfo was too preoccupied with Laura's news last night to eat anything that morning. He turned Maria's offer down and simply stood by the stairs waiting. There were still many items in his agenda that needed closure. First on his list was Rosalía. He needed to find out exactly what she had been up to and whether her actions had caused embarrassment to the Hernández reputation. Then he had to visit three more leaseholders before wrapping things up in San Sebastián. Finally, he had to comply with the mayor's request that he recruit a spy. Although he had found his spy and had broached the subject with him, there was no firm agreement between them, and he still needed to see Diego Redondo's reports.

Laura had already been up that morning but she was too scared of her father's wrath. Instead, she stayed in her bedroom but kept the door ajar so that she could hear. Her mother, as always, had no clue as to what was going to happen once Rosalía rose out of bed.

Running out of patience, Rodolfo shouted for his wife. Maria emerged humbly from the kitchen, expecting her husband's request for breakfast. "Go get Rosalía up out of bed!" he commanded. Maria nodded and obediently rushed up the stairs. A few moments later, Rodolfo saw Rosalía in her nightgown making her way down the stairs, rubbing her eyes from sleep.

"You sent for me, Father?"

"Indeed I did. Sit down!" Rodolfo commanded. "You were seen in town yesterday," began Rodolfo.

Maria, who was standing at the top of the stairs, came rushing down. "What were you doing in town? Haven't I told you not to—"

"Be silent, Maria!" yelled Rodolfo. "You've got your head so far up your ass that you don't even know what the hell is happening in your own home! Now get back in the kitchen and let me handle this!" He watched Maria's eyes flickering at him with sheer anger, but she kept her silence. Maria turned and headed straight for the kitchen. Rodolfo looked down at Rosalía who was now sitting on the wicker couch, looking up at her father. "You were also seen in the company of that peasant, Miguel Pítre."

"We were just talking, Father," replied Rosalía unafraid.

"You cannot be seen associating with jíbaros, Rosa, especially here in San Sebastián."

"Of course, Father, I wouldn't want to ruin your reputation."

"That's right! My reputation is what puts the fear of God in the jíbaro's heart. It is not only my reputation, but yours, too. You come from an aristocratic family and you must marry your own kind, not some two-bit peasant who can only offer you a life of misery, poverty and despair."

"Look at you, Father! You speak of the peasant with such disdain, as if they were lepers or animals, but they are just as human as you are, and they deserve something better. You speak of being an aristocrat, but all you have done is to enrich yourself off their backs, off the sweat of their brow and off their hardship. How can you look at me, pass judgment over me, and feel proud about yourself and your accomplishments?"

"I *am* proud of my accomplishments," said Rodolfo defensively. He walked closer to Rosalía and gazed into her blue eyes with a fatherly appeal. "And you have been the beneficiary of those accomplishments, dear daughter. Or would you rather live in a wooden shack and suffer the pangs of hunger?"

"The reason why they live in hunger is because people like you have taken everything away from them. I wonder how life would be in Puerto Rico without peninsulares and without Spain's stronghold."

"Careful, Rosa, those words smack of sedition and rebellion, and I will not have you associated with that kind of talk."

"Perhaps that is the only way for the creoles to be rid of us and Spain."

Rodolfo's first impulse was to smack his daughter in the face and erase the rebellious pollution from her mind. Then he calmed himself quickly and sat down next to her.

Sitting on the floor pointing her ear through the door opening, Laura's frustrations were starting to show on her angered face. Laura reasoned that by now Rosalía should have been in the middle of a brutal beating at the hands of her father. Anger began to fester deep in the pit of her heart, and she had to make sure that Rosalía would fall out of her father's favor. She emerged from her room and quietly walked to the top of the stairs so that she could clearly hear the conversation. "Listen to me, Rosa, if you persist in these kinds of thoughts, and if you continue to see that jíbaro, you'll force me to send you back to San Juan. You will force me to enroll you at that convent you hate so much. Is that what you want me to do?"

"Of course not, Father," replied Rosalía with a tear welling in her eye. "But I have gone into town, and I have personally seen the poverty and despair that you speak of with such fear in your eyes."

"Fear? Is that what you see in my eyes? Then you are correct, but it is not for me that I fear but for you. If you lend your sentiments to those ideological fools, they will use you, but after you have served their purpose, they will abandon you. We will find your body in some alleyway, dead from hunger, or we will see you hanged by the government. You might even be murdered by the very same rebels for whom you sympathize." Rodolfo placed an arm around Rosalía's shoulder. "I don't want that to happen to you. I want you to be happy."

Rosalía wiped the dripping tear off her check and looked up at her father. "How can I be happy, when I know that our family thrives upon the backs of these people? How can I live so duplicitously and without a care in the world?"

"Rosa, you have not received any suitors because I have forbidden it. I know that you have never associated with the opposite sex, but it is because I have tried to shelter you from that. I have big plans for you, Rosa. I want to marry you to one of the best families of Spain. I know that this was perhaps the first time you've ever felt something for a man, and maybe he is charming and full of intoxicating ideas. Maybe his disposition and his ways of thinking have swayed you. All that will pass, my dear child, and when you become a fully mature woman, you will realize that I was right all along. Has your relationship with that jíbaro gone beyond friendship?"

"All we do is talk, Father, and nothing more."

"No Father!" shouted Laura while running down the stairs, unable to control her anger.

Both Rodolfo and Rosalía tilted their heads up to see Laura running down the stairs, shouting. Rodolfo rose to his feet and narrowed his eyes at Laura, "What the devil were you doing up there, eavesdropping?"

"Yes, Father, because I wanted to see if Rosa would tell you the whole truth, but it is obvious that she did not tell you everything. Father, there is something she did not tell you, something I, too, held back from you last night."

Rosalía stood up and fixed a steely glare at her sister. "I might have known it was you, Laura!"

"Well, what is it?" demanded Rodolfo, ignoring Rosalía for the moment.

"I followed Rosa and that peasant all the way into a dirty barrio, where I saw them kissing and holding each other. Rosa's friendship with that boy has blossomed into a full-blown romance! And you should not be deceived, Father!"

Rosalía placed a hand over her mouth in shock, and then she closed her eyes before feeling the back of Rodolfo's hand. Rosalía fell back onto the couch and simply lost count of Rodolfo's swings across her face. She felt a strong punch to her jaw and then another to the top of her head. Then there was numbness before everything went dark.

CHAPTER 36

Juan Pítre had spent the entire morning, watering the plantation and caring for each of his coffee plants as though they were his little children. The extreme care he took showed the infinite patience, knowledge, love and respect he had for his work. Several days ago, a family of rodents had taken up residence deep within the finca, and they were starting to threaten the harvest. Juan had taken his rifle out that morning to see whether he could shoot the rodents and save the desperately needed harvest. As Juan carefully nurtured his plants, he kept watching for rodents and took comfort that his rifle was nearby, strapped to the pommel of his saddle. Occasionally, Juan's mind would drift to his son. Miguel's increasing absence on the finca was starting to take a toll not only on the coming coffee harvest but also on his heart. More and more each day, Miguel would find ways to avoid working on the coffee plantation, and Juan's fears over his whereabouts were beginning to gnaw at his reasoning. He was grateful that at least Rafael Cintron was there to help him, but he truly desired his son's company. Rafael had been working clear across the other side of the plantation, on the north end, and Juan could barely see his image. Though he took some comfort in knowing Rafael was there, he missed his son terribly. Having Miguel around was like an elixir for Juan, an invisible magic potion that would put his mind and body at ease.

With pained knees buried into the ground and body arched over a plant, Juan heard the unmistakable sound of thumping hooves. *Miguel must be in a great hurry*. Very slowly Juan rose to his feet, but he was immediately disappointed when the image of Rodolfo Hernández came into view. Juan did not need to see that devil of a man today or hear his annoying voice either.

Hernández deliberately drove his horse right into the finca, crushing valuable coffee plants in the process. He halted his horse only inches in front of Juan's face. Across the field, Rafael heard the sound of a galloping horse, and rose to his feet to witness the scene. Juan quickly noted Rodolfo's murderous eyes—eyes that glinted with rage and utter hatred. Rodolfo dismounted and walked straight toward Juan. "I will tell you this only once, Pítre!" he shouted. "Tell your son to stay away from my daughter, Rosalía! If I hear that your son has even looked at her, I will evict you from this land, is that clear?"

"What do you want me to do?" shouted back Juan, hands outstretched in a pleading gesture. "I cannot control him anymore! He is a grown man!"

"Then do whatever you have to do, Pítre. Consider this a warning, if I see him anywhere near my daughter I will kill him!"

For the first time in his life, Juan Pítre felt true rage in his heart, but it wasn't the kind of rage that Rodolfo harbored perpetually. Juan's rage swelled from the depths of his soul, and it was directed solely at *El Demonio*. When he heard Rodolfo speaking of killing his son, as if he had the right to do so, as if Miguel's life had no more value than that of an insect, the rage rose out of him like an erupting volcano. Rodolfo had clearly overstepped his bound. He had gone far and beyond anything evil he might have done in the past, into a dark realm where only demons dwelled. Juan's eyes widened angrily and he could no longer control his mouth. "Now you listen to me," he shouted at Rodolfo, "if you as much as touch one hair on my son's head, I will kill you, you goddamn son-of-a-bitch! How dare you come here and threaten to kill my son as if you were God, the Almighty? How dare you think you have the right to kill people? Now get off my plantation or I will get my rifle and shoot you to pieces!"

Rodolfo squinted at Juan, wondering if the peasant standing before him was truly serious. He considered Juan's threat for a few seconds but then he let out a burst of laughter, as if Juan's threat was too amusing to take seriously. Had he known that Juan Pítre kept his rifle close to him, Rodolfo might have thought differently. "You don't have cojónes big enough to kill anybody, Pítre. I will evict you and your goddamn son if he doesn't stay away from Rosalía!" Rodolfo then laughed loudly again, but as he placed his boot into the stirrup, he heard the distinct sound of a clicking rifle. It wasn't until he was firmly sitting atop his horse that he saw Juan Pítre's Henry rifle aimed directly at his heart.

"Get off my plantation or I will show you how big my cojónes really are!"

"You dare point a rifle at me, Pítre? You don't know what you've just done."

Juan Pítre fired his weapon, and the bullet whizzed so close to Rodolfo's ear, it caused him to flinch fearfully, but the gunfire was so loud it startled the horse. Rodolfo's horse whinnied and rose on its hind legs causing the landowner to tumble backwards and come crashing down on the ground. His boot still attached to the stirrup, Rodolfo tried to get up off the ground but then froze when he saw the muzzle of Juan's rifle pointed at his face.

Rodolfo ignored the rifle and stared at Juan from the ground. "Go ahead, kill me, and see how far you'll get. You will hang for murder, and so will your son."

"I said get off my plantation!" said Juan, ignoring Rodolfo.

Rodolfo finally removed his boot from the stirrup, rose to his feet, dusted himself and then remounted. "I will see you in court, Pítre!" Rodolfo spurred his horse and galloped away, shouting obscenities.

CHAPTER 37

Juan Pítre had waited all day and part of the evening for his son's return, but Miguel was too busy in town to come home. Juan's fear for his son's life was increasing by the hour, and it was so compelling that he felt no other recourse. He simply had to convince Miguel to stay away from Hernández's daughter. Finally, he decided to go into town. He knew precisely where Miguel was that night and he reasoned that if Miguel would not come home, then he would go to Miguel.

Juan knocked once but there was no answer. The fact that the colmado appeared closed for business did not seem to discourage him at all. He knocked repeatedly until Enrique Ramirez finally answered.

Enrique allowed Juan to enter the colmado, and escorted him to the back of the store where he asked him to sit directly behind the members of the cell. The cell had grown considerably, thought Juan. Carlos Peña had made enormous strides in so little time. Standing on a crate, addressing his audience, Carlos looked more like a priest at a sermon than a rebel at a rally. "...and the date for revolution has been tentatively set for the middle of October, so we really don't have too much time." As Carlos addressed the gathering, Juan's eyes strayed away from the African and focused directly on Diego Redondo, who sat on a crate facing the speaker. Juan shook his head at the image of Rodolfo Hernández's lawyer sitting in the midst of a rebel gathering. It just didn't seem right to Juan. Watching Diego sitting in a rebel gathering was like watching a fox in a hen house, but Juan kept his objections silent.

The meeting was over in less than an hour, and as the members slowly dispersed, Miguel saw his father for the first time that night. Juan nodded at him but didn't offer anything else. The fact that Juan said nothing bothered Miguel. It wasn't like his father to attend a secret rebel meeting just like that; there had to be something else, something of great importance to have made him ride into town. As Carlos shook hands with the members, he turned to Miguel who was standing next to him. "What is your father doing here?"

Miguel shrugged his shoulders, "I've been wondering about that myself."

Enrique bade Carlos, Miguel and Juan goodnight before latching the door to his father's colmado. Standing outside the colmado, Carlos looked down at Juan. "I'm glad you attended the meeting, Don Pítre. Will you become a member?"

Juan tilted his head up at Carlos and gave him a cold stare. "I have no intentions of joining the rebellion, señor Peña! I came here to see Miguel."

"What about, Father?"

"I know about you and that young woman, Miguelito."

Miguel raised his eyebrows at Carlos and uttered, "News travels fast, doesn't it?"

"Didn't I tell you?" replied Carlos with an all-knowing expression.

"How much do you know, Father?" said Miguel, turning back to face Juan.

"I know that you've been seen with her in town. It is my wish that you stop seeing her immediately. No good can come from that relationship, and you should well know that. She comes from a very different world, a world where you do not exist, and she is the daughter of Rodolfo Hernández. You must also disassociate yourself from the ridiculous notion of revolution. If you are caught, you will hang!"

"Pápi, I thought you agreed to go along with the revolution. What caused to you to change your mind?" Carlos took a step backwards and allowed the two men to talk. "I will not leave Porvenir, Father, and any attempts to convince me otherwise will be an exercise in futility. And as far as my association with señorita Hernández, it is purely platonic." Miguel hoped his response would convince his father to stop meddling in his affairs. But he detected something different in his father's eyes, something he had never seen before. "What's the matter, Pápi? Why did you feel you had to ride into town just to tell me this personally?"

Juan Pítre moved his eyes away from Miguel and trained them on the lantern-lighted ground. "Rodolfo Hernández paid me a visit today. He demanded that you stay away from his daughter, and if you refused, he would evict us from the farm."

"So, he's threatened us like that before," said Miguel uneventfully.

"He said he would kill you, if you persisted in seeing his daughter. When he said that, I picked up my rifle and made a shot so close to his ear, that I saw his face turn as white as a bed sheet. I told him never to threaten me like that again, but I fear that I have forced Hernández to respond, Miguelito. You must be very careful now." Juan suddenly turned to the tall African, "That man's got spies everywhere. Did you recognize Don Diego Redondo in your audience, Carlos?"

Carlos said nothing.

"He's been screened by our ruling committee," Miguel quickly answered.

"I'd be very careful around him, Miguel. After all, he is a lawyer and he works for *El Demonio.*"

Miguel turned to Carlos and nodded. "I agree with my father. I cannot ignore what Hernández has done, you know I can't."

Carlos finally rejoined Miguel and Juan. "I told you weeks ago that nothing good would come of your relationship with señorita Hernández. Now you cannot stop the consequences; it is like a wild river that flows without a damn. So what do you intend to do?"

"I'm going to pay that son-of-a-bitch a visit!"

"Foolish, Miguelito, very foolish!" replied Carlos.

"Yes, it's about as foolish as your rebel cause." Juan added.

Carlos chose to ignore Juan's comment. "What do you hope to accomplish?"

"Nothing, except to show him that we Pítres do not fear him and that we will fight him or any of his peninsular friends."

"Go home with your father and take the night to think about this," said Carlos. "Do not act upon the passions of the moment. You'll see that when you wake up tomorrow morning, you'll think differently."

"For the first time I am in total agreement with your friend," chimed in Juan.

CHAPTER 38

At four in the morning the next day, Juan stepped out of his shack to gaze up at the hill where Miguel stood every morning. He did not see the gas lantern on the ground, nor did he see Miguel's silhouette on the summit.

There would be trouble that day.

Determined to put Rodolfo in his place, Miguel left Pepinos early in the morning and reached the Hernández hacienda well before sunrise. He decided to wait in front of the house until Rodolfo emerged at daybreak. There was no way in hell that he would allow Rodolfo to get away with what he did to his father, and he'd been wide-awake all through the night and into the morning. He needed to show Rodolfo, in a very clear manner that he was not going to intimidate his family any longer. This stand Miguel had to make for pride and self-respect; a stand he needed to make to restore his father's dignity.

At around seven o'clock in the morning, Rodolfo stepped out of the hacienda and called out for his slaves to bring his horse to him. As he waited, Rodolfo saw the image of a young man pulling a horse behind him. "Stop right there, Pítre, and don't come any closer!" yelled Rodolfo, but Miguel kept coming. "How dare you present yourself to me, especially after what you've done?"

"How dare *you*, señor? How dare you come to my home and threaten my father and me with death?"

"You're associating with my daughter, and that is something you know can never be," said Rodolfo waving his hand in a negative gesture. Then a thought quickly rushed through his mind, perhaps a speedy resolution to the current dilemma. As a shrewd and successful businessman, he'd always find a solution to any problem, no matter how big; he was good at it, and he built his reputation upon it. Rodolfo quashed his anger for the moment and spoke passively. "What is your name again?"

"Miguel," the younger Pítre said impatiently.

"Look Miguel, I was wrong to ride to your farm and threaten your father, but I was acting as any normal father would have acted and nothing more. I do not wish to offend you, Miguel, but you are a jíbaro from the mountains, whereas Rosalía, well…"

"Whereas, Rosalía comes from an aristocratic family, right?" Miguel filled in. "I'm so sick of hearing that, señor. Have you asked Rosa how she feels?"

"I don't need to, Miguel. She is far too young to realize the consequences of being with someone like you. You know it, too. You know you can never make her happy. Well, perhaps in the beginning, yes, when the power of love in your heart and mind is so strong it blinds you to the realities of life. But after the spark of love has faded, Miguel, what will Rosa have left? The only things that will remain after the love burns out are the cold and hard realities of poverty and despair. Are you prepared to face those realties when the time comes?" Rodolfo let the words settle into Miguel's mind for a moment. Then he changed the tone of his voice to an almost whisper. "Young man, I am appealing to your common sense, and you know it in your heart that I am speaking the truth. As a loving father, I am pleading to you, and asking you to do this not for yourself, but for Rosa, for her happiness."

Miguel's intentions were to insult Rodolfo and scare him out of his wits for daring to threaten his father. Common sense, however, did finally prevail, and while standing before Rodolfo, Miguel contemplated the moral dilemma. He had to make a tough decision and knew the effects would either haunt him for the rest of his life or make him a happy man. While Miguel mulled over his decision, the slaves brought the horse over to Rodolfo, who quickly took hold of the reins. The ever-astute Rodolfo allowed Miguel enough time to let his words sink in. After several more moments, Rodolfo mounted his horse and trotted toward Miguel, who was still deciding.

Looking down at Miguel, Rodolfo nodded at him. "You see, if you think the matter through, you will reach the same conclusion over and over again. You will never make Rosa happy."

Miguel's eyes strayed away from Rodolfo's face and stared at the ground. Deep inside, Rodolfo's words seemed to take effect. There was no way in the world that he could ever make Rosalía happy. Miguel thought about his own family experiences growing up in a household without food or money, the constant arguing between his mother and father, and the misery of hard plantation work. No matter how much Juan Pítre tried to make his wife happy, she was always miserable, miserable because Juan could never give her what she wanted. Miguel thought about his own future with Rosalía and in that glimpse of time, he saw the same things that happened to his father happening to him, and he wanted no part of that. Presently, he saw how much his father still loved his wife, and how much he suffered every day, wondering what his true love was doing. He felt the hurt in his father's heart, knowing exactly where the love of his life was but never having the nerve to go see her. He slowly turned and mounted his horse. Settling into his leather saddle, he took one more look at Rodolfo but said nothing.

By his silence, Rodolfo understood that his words had finally sunk into the young man's heart. At this point, though, things might have turned out differently for the Hernández and the Pítre families. But Rodolfo did what he did naturally, what he did best, and that was to open his mouth at the wrong time and say the wrong thing. Rodolfo eyed Miguel with a steady gaze and said confidently, "To seal your agreement to stay away from my daughter, I will pay you three thousand pesos. You can give it to your father if you wish, so that he can pay off the debt, or you can keep it and leave San Sebastián altogether. What do you say? It's a fair offer."

All of a sudden, a torrent of anger began to swell inside Miguel, like the vortex of a tornado. It rose from the bottom of his spine to the back of his neck, and he glared at Rodolfo with unrestricted contempt and hatred. "You sorry sack of shit! And to think, you almost had me convinced! There is no love in your heart for Rosa—that much is evident. There is only the fear of losing your reputation, and your fear is so great that you're willing to pay just to get rid of me! Now I am thoroughly convinced that Rosa will never be happy in your world. I will make her happy in mine!"

"Don't be a fool, Miguel. Three thousand pesos is a lot of money. Besides, I will stop at nothing to prevent you from courting my daughter—you know that."

"Even murder, right? But no money in the world is enough to buy *me* off, Hernández, you've figured me wrong. I'm not Santiago Duran, or any other creole you might have bought off in the past."

"If you insist on courting my daughter, you will force me to evict you," insisted Rodolfo.

"Go ahead. Do it. But remember this: the time will come when your existence here, in Puerto Rico, will be nothing but a faint memory."

"What do you mean by that, Miguel? Are you a member of the rebellion? Just what are you up to?"

"I am no member of any rebellion, but there are rebel cells all over the island, waiting to pounce on all peninsulares and pigs from Spain. The creoles have a long memory and they will remember all of the abuses wrought upon them by Don Rodolfo Hernández. So if you don't want any reprisals, you better think twice before evicting us from the lands you stole from us!" Miguel glared at Rodolfo for a few seconds, before digging his spurs into the horse. The beast raised his forelegs, whinnied and took off like a bolt of lightning. Rodolfo sat atop his stallion in the middle of the dirt pathway staring at Miguel's image growing smaller and fading into the forest.

CHAPTER 39

Rodolfo Hernández sat still atop his horse, wondering whether Miguel was being truthful about a revolution or whether he was just another mindless peasant making empty threats. Though he dismissed Miguel's threat at first, it was the sound of his voice and the certainty in its tone that brought a shiver of fear all over Rodolfo's body, as if a cold wind had swept in from the south on a rainy night. In the end, however, it was the fear of losing his real estate empire that caused Rodolfo concern. He couldn't let anything, no matter how insignificant, go unchallenged. He dismounted and pulled his horse to the front of the hacienda. Once inside he called everyone downstairs, including the servants.

The women were still dressed in their nightgowns, yawning incessantly. Rodolfo ignored the yawns and the sleepy eyes and looked at no one in particular as he opened his mouth to speak. "I have important things to tell all of you. I have good reason to suspect that a rebellion is in the making, right here in San Sebastián." Rodolfo then shot a glaring look at Rosalía, "Your friend, Miguel Pítre, came here earlier with God only knows what kinds of intentions."

"Miguel was here?" asked Rosalía, curious but alarmed at the same time.

"That's right, dear Rosa. I convinced him to stay away from you, so you will not be seeing him anymore. During our conversation, though, he made it very clear to me that a rebellion is in the making. It is for this reason that I am instructing everyone not to venture into town. Should a rebellion begin, the first people the rebels will come looking for are the peninsulares and their families. I must go into town to finalize a couple of business transactions before heading back to San Juan. In the meantime, I will remain in San Sebastián to see if I can lend the mayor a hand."

"That is not your job, Rodolfo," said Maria. "Your job is to see to your family!"

"Hush now woman! I *am* seeing to my family by getting them the hell out of here and out of harm's way."

"May I stay, Father?" Rosalía asked humbly.

Laura shot Rosalía an incredulous look. With all that she had done to embarrass the family, how could Rosalía think that Father would allow her to stay? In Laura's eyes, Rosalía was the least deserving of all the Hernández children. Before she could open her mouth, her father yelled, "Are you jesting? You want me to let you stay in San Sebastian, *you*, the source of my current troubles? No, that is out of the question!"

"What about me?" Laura asked, grinning.

"No, no, no! What is the matter with all of you? You obviously do not realize the seriousness of what I am telling you. No, and that is my final answer! Now I have business to take care of in town, and I do not need to be distracted. I want everybody to start packing so by the time the wagons are loaded, you may leave right away!"

By the time Miguel returned home, Carlos and Juan were waiting for him. The somber expression they both gave Miguel told the young man they had not approved of his actions. For the first time, Carlos and Juan stood united against him, and the feeling was very unsettling for the idealistic young jíbaro from the mountains. He slowly trotted to the front of the shack and dismounted silently. "What in God's name did you do?" demanded Juan, wasting no time.

"You know what I did, Father, I went to see *El Demonio*."

"Miguelito, what exactly did you say?" Carlos ripped into him.

"What is this, an inquisition?"

"Miguel, what did I tell you last night?" yelled Carlos. "Did I not tell you to let things be? Now what did you say to the man?"

Miguel took his time and told both Carlos and Juan the entire conversation he had had with Rodolfo early that morning. As he recounted the story, Miguel could see their jaws dropping out of shock and disappointment. When he completed his story, there was dead silence for a brief moment before Carlos broke it. "Miguel, Miguel, if you went there to chastise him, then why did you have to plant a seed in his mind about a rebellion? It just wasn't enough to castigate him verbally, was it? No, you just had to put the fear of God in him, didn't you? And now, by doing that, you might well have jeopardized the revolution. You were very foolish today, Miguelito, very foolish!"

"Son," added Juan in a fatherly tone. "We should never act on impulse, especially during the heat of passion. Now we must prepare for eviction, and seek shelter somewhere in town."

"Señor Pítre," interjected Carlos. "Let us not be so hasty. Let us see what Hernández's next move will be, now that Miguel has given him something to think about, right? Evicting you might not be as important to him as before." The African turned to his young protégé and smiled in a brotherly sort of way. "I think that instead of giving your father a heart-attack, you'll give *me* a heart-attack! What am I going to do with you, you stubborn mule of a man? I must go into town to speak with Aguilar and Ibarra and seek their counsel on this matter."

Miguel looked up at Carlos and sighed. "My dear friend, I gave Hernández nothing useful. You should know that I would never consciously betray Porvenir or any of our rebel members. I was weak, Carlos. I allowed that bastard to drag me into his evil web and said things to him in the heat of the moment. I did insult the man, but I gave him nothing about our cause." Miguel turned to his father and with humble eyes said, "However, I must apologize to you, Father, because of my weakness." Turning back to Carlos he nodded, "And to you, too, my dear friend."

Juan Pítre climbed onto the porch, sat down on the school chair and stared aimlessly at the field of coffee plants. While Juan stared at his finca, Carlos eyed Miguel for a long while, and then stretched his face with a smile. “There’s no need for apologies, Miguel. Had this island been free of peninsulares, you and I would not be here, talking the way we are talking. It is their fault and their fault alone, and the sooner they’re out of Puerto Rico, the better.”

CHAPTER 40

Diego Redondo's door banged incessantly, causing the sleeping solicitor to rise in shock. When he opened the door, it seemed as if he had confronted the devil himself. Rodolfo did not wait for Diego to invite him in; he simply walked in and began his tirade. After explaining to Redondo everything that Miguel had said, he waited for Redondo's reaction. Redondo yawned deeply and spoke with a gravelly voice. "There is not enough evidence for you to go to the mayor with, or even to Colonel Ibarreta."

"What in heaven's name are you talking about, Diego?" yelled Rodolfo, unwilling to yield to his solicitor's somber evaluation. "He all but made it clear to me that a rebellion was going to start."

"You asked for my opinion, right? I gave it to you. Have a good day, señor." Redondo climbed onto his bed and closed his eyes.

"All right, Redondo, you've made your point. Now get up out of bed and offer me some counsel on this matter. Which rebel cell have you infiltrated?"

Redondo rose up out of bed. "Didn't you just asked me to counsel you on—"

"To hell with that! Have you thought about my offer? Well, to hell with that, too! I am prepared to renegotiate our deal."

"Deal, I don't recall agreeing to any deal, señor Hernández."

"Goddamn it, Diego, it's a fucking figure of speech!" yelled out Rodolfo, annoyed. "How in the world did you ever graduate law school?" Rodolfo reached into a leather pouch he had brought with him into the house, and pulled out a stack of neat bills bound together with a paper strap, as if he had just withdrawn the money from a bank. He looked at Redondo and passed on a hearty smile. "Do you see what I'm holding in my hand?" He saw Redondo nodding in total comprehension. "Care to guess how much I am holding?"

"One thousand pesos?"

"No. Sixty-five hundred hard-earned pesos, my boy, and I will gladly give it to you if you will agree to show me your dispatches to Governor Pavía. Sixty-five hundred pesos is enough to pay back the money you owe the governor, and still have plenty left over."

"Señor Hernández, you are a tenacious bull of a man," uttered Redondo, eyes gleaming at the sight of so much cash. "I suppose you don't want any legal papers binding this transaction?"

"A simple handshake will suffice, young man." Rodolfo dropped the stack of bills onto the small kitchen table, and then reached out to grab Redondo's hand in a firm handshake. Then he turned and headed for the door. Before opening the door, he turned back and gave Redondo a stern look. "When will you be sending your dispatches to the governor?"

"I plan to write them on Sunday, and then send them Monday morning."

"Good. Then I expect you at my house Sunday evening, is that clear?"

"Very clear, señor Hernández." Diego Redondo took the money without really thinking. Now he had to deal with the consequences. So where was the real Diego Redondo? Where was that boy from Barrio Flores, the one filled with an insatiable ambition to succeed? What had happened to one of San Sebastián's boys who made good, graduated university, and made all San Sebastiános proud? What was he doing for his brothers and sisters, for the mothers and fathers of his hometown? What good did he bring with his education, and with his legal expertise? Nothing! Diego Redondo contemplated the stack of bills sitting on his table not with the alacrity and avaricious zeal of a peninsular but with the melancholy of a creole beset by guilt and remorse. As much as he wanted the money and as much as he wanted to pay off his debt, a small measure of pride still lingered in his heart. But how much information would Diego Redondo reveal to his two masters? The matter was entirely in his hands, and Diego would have to be as crafty and as evil as they were.

CHAPTER 41

The fierce battle had lasted all night long and into the early morning hours. For much of the night, cannons roared, rifles and guns exploded and the darkened skies lit up occasionally with streaks of orange and yellowish light. But as the sun slowly rose that morning, the smell of seawater and the splash of rolling waves overtook the dreadful blasts of weapons and the lingering odor of gunpowder that hours earlier dominated the rebellious air in that region of Santo Domingo.

Doctor Betances and several of his Dominican friends, including Jose Maria Cabral and Gregorio Luperon, had narrowly escaped the battle last night. The leaders traveled all night long until they found their secret location and rendezvous point, a tiny beach house perched on a small bluff overlooking the Caribbean Sea. Every now and then, they would poke their heads through a tiny window and scan the seas for a small sailboat, the one that would bring Segundo Ruiz back from South America. It wasn't until close to midday that the boat finally appeared in the horizon and everyone breathed a collective sigh of relief.

As the sailboat eased slowly toward shore, Ruiz could not hide the fatigue and stress that had overwhelmed his body and mind the past few days. Traveling incognito through some of the most dangerous rebel areas of Santo Domingo, and under constant threat of death by the Spanish government, had taken its toll on the Puerto Rican rebel leader. As much as he tried to maintain his discomfort a secret, Doctor Betances recognized it upon shaking his trembling hand.

"How goes it, Segundo?" said Betances with an appreciative smile.

"The Chileans have agreed to help us with arms and ammunition," replied Ruiz, voice raspy and fatigued.

"What about Venezuela?"

"They're mulling it over, but we have no time to wait for them. Have you talked to our Cuban friends? Are they ready?"

"Yes, Segundo, but they will not begin their rebellion until we begin ours. We must keep in mind that unless we divide the Spanish forces, both rebellions will fail."

"Have you secured the ship?"

"Yes. It will be ready to take you back to South America. Everything depends on that ship, Segundo, for without arms, we may as well throw coffee beans at the Spanish. You must make sure that you leave Chile immediately after securing the arms deal."

Ruiz nodded and sighed deeply before rubbing his stomach. He grimaced briefly but found that he needed to sit. Betances eyed him with alarming concern. "Are you all right, my friend?"

Dispensing with the sudden malady, Ruiz quickly rose to his feet and waved his hand at Betances. "Yes, I'm fine; must've been something I ate."

"Let me examine you," insisted Betances.

"There's no time for that now, Emeterio, I've got to be on that ship."

"No, Segundo, please take a few hours to sleep. The ship isn't due to leave until nightfall, so you have plenty of time to rest—Doctor's orders."

Though Ruiz made a valiant effort to lie down on his own, Gregorio Luperon had to step in to assist him to bed. After only a few seconds, Ruiz had fallen asleep. All three men looked down at Ruiz, and their concerned eyes could not betray the fear that their only ambassador, the only man with connections to South America, would not last the night. Jose Maria Cabral spoke while casting downtrodden eyes on Ruiz, "Why didn't you tell him, Doctor?"

"There was no reason for him to know."

"The Dominican militia is serious this time, Doctor, they know that you've publicly supported both Luperon and me, and they're under orders from Governor Baez to arrest you."

"What can I do? Who is going to receive the ship when it arrives? Who's going to guide the ship into the port of Guánica? Both of you are too busy with your own rebellion here, so it is up to me to see our rebellion through."

Luperon turned to Betances, and with saddened eyes said, "It is no longer safe for you to stay in Santo Domingo. We will try to protect you as much as we can, but in the end, they will find you."

Diego Redondo had been snooping around the barrios of San Sebastián for several days but was unable to gather any intelligence worthy of the governor's interest. On one of his many trips to the barrios, he recalled rumors about a new cell forming in Quebradillas and wanted to verify whether the rumors were true before penning a new report to Pavía. Diego wondered if his old school mate was still a member of the militia at Quebradillas. He also wondered whether his friend remained loyal to the Spanish crown. Rather than mailing a letter to him, which would have taken days to reach him and several more days to receive a response, he made plans to travel to Quebradillas.

Diego took nearly all day to reach Quebradillas, and finally arrived late in the afternoon. Despite his horse stalling several times during the journey, he pushed on with his mission. Upon reaching the outskirts of Quebradillas, Diego finally dismounted and walked the rest of the way. About an hour later, Diego finally reached the barracks of the local militia. He tied his horse to a wooden post near the barracks entrance and stepped onto the porch, where a militiaman, with a rifle by his side, was standing guard. Diego introduced himself, and then inquired about his friend.

Redondo took a step backwards when he saw his friend stepping out of the barracks. He gave him a broad smile and shouted, "Let me look at you, you son-of-a-bitch!" He drew closer and shouted again, "Corporal Carlos Antonio Lopez, how the hell have you been?"

With equal enthusiasm, Lopez's eyes gleamed at Redondo. "You may not have noticed but I'm no longer a corporal. The powers in Arecibo have seen fit to promote me to Second Lieutenant—not bad after only a year. There will be a general exam next month for promotion to First Lieutenant and I plan to pass the test with flying colors."

"I'm proud of you, Carlos, truly I am," replied Redondo nodding his head.

"Well, I'm proud of you, Diego. Look at you! You are a goddamn lawyer! I'm sure if your parents were alive today, they'd be very proud of you, too." Carlos Antonio Lopez immediately detected Redondo's discomfort. "I'm sorry, Diego, I didn't mean to—"

"It's all right, my friend, it's been so many years since their passing," replied Redondo with a half smile. "So, how have you been?"

"I've been all right, Diego, except for the fact that we keep hearing rumors about a rebellion. There is a heightened sense of fear among the people of Quebradillas, and our commander, Colonel Iturriaga of the Arecibo militia, has placed us all on high alert."

"There are rumors flying everywhere. So what does a high alert mean?"

"It means that we are not allowed to leave the barracks at any time. It means that we have to drill three times a day and patrol the perimeters of town day and night. We will stay on high alert as long as Iturriaga deems it necessary."

"What have you heard?" Redondo asked, drawing closer to Lopez.

The lieutenant hesitated for a moment, looked around to make sure no one was within earshot of his voice and gestured Diego to walk away from the barracks. As they distanced themselves from the barracks, Lopez whispered, "It is believed that there is a rebel cell based in Camuy, not too far from here. Rumors are that the name of the cell is Lanzador Del Norte, and that the cell's leader is a man named Manuel Maria Gonzalez. We do not know exactly in which barrio the cell is based, although some say it is Barrio Palomar. But we have raided Barrio Palomar three times and found no caches of arms, seditious literature or any evidence to support the rumor."

"I see," said Redondo, rubbing his chin. "What about here, in Quebradillas?"

All of a sudden, Lopez furrowed his eyebrows and shot a pair of questioning grey eyes at his former schoolmate. "Why are you so interested in knowing about rebel activities, Diego? What are you up to?"

Redondo hesitated, and then he pursed his lips for a split second before answering his friend. "I am working in secret for Governor Pavía. I have infiltrated a rebel cell in San Sebastián and I've been sending reports on their activities since February of this year."

"You're a spy?" Lopez said amusingly. "Don Diego Redondo is a spy for Governor Pavía? How did you get this job?"

"Never mind that, Carlos, what else do you know?"

"Well, in answer to your first question, there are no rebel cells here in Quebradillas. But I have suspicions about my uncle."

"Which one?"

"Hilario, that skinny bastard."

"Hilario Martínez?" Redondo said, crunching his eyebrows. "Have you told anyone about your suspicions?"

"He's my uncle, Diego. How can I bring myself to accuse my own uncle of sedition? And even if I did, how could I do it without proof; he's too clever to let on about himself, at least when he's sober anyway."

"That's not too good."

"Yes, I know. Look, Diego, my uncle is a good man, but he is a follower, not a leader. If I am right about, Hilario, I think that some aggressive recruiter must have persuaded him into joining a rebel group. If I am right about my uncle, then he is unaware of the kind of trouble he's in already. Perhaps if I expose his rebel group it may save his life in the end right? I'd be helping him, right?"

Diego narrowed his eyes at the young lieutenant. "Yes indeed. You would not only be helping your uncle but also gaining recognition within the militia. There may be a medal or two on your lapel one day and perhaps more promotions. I may be calling you Colonel Lopez one day."

"That would be something, wouldn't it? But how can I get information from Hilario without raising suspicion?"

"I'll tell you how, Carlos. When in the presence of your uncle start talking about how much you hate being a militiaman under the Spanish. Talk about how much Spain is making the creoles of the island suffer and of how you wish you could do something about it. Just keep doing this until you are able to convince Hilario that you are a rebel in the making. Only then, will he open up to you and talk about the rebellion. In the meantime, I will gather enough intelligence on the San Sebastián cell, and then help you gather intelligence on the Camuyan cell. And maybe, together, we can quell the revolution before it even gets started."

Carlos Antonio López gave Diego Redondo a skeptical look. "Why would I want to do that?"

"Because you're a loyalist, just like me, plus…there is money involved."

"How much?"

"For you, I would say about one thousand pesos." Diego saw the look of interest in Lopez's eyes right away and knew he had a partner. "What do you say, Carlos, want to join me?"

Carlos nodded his approval. "All right, what exactly do you want me to say to my uncle?"

CHAPTER 42

Muted celebration marked the evening of Friday, April 3, 1868. Subdued cheers and congratulatory remarks went out to four men who stood in front of a small gathering in the rear of Ramirez's colmado. Among the four men facing the crowd stood Diego Redondo with a look of conquest rather than a look of humble appreciation. The trial period was over and he had finally become a member of Porvenir. Diego would be more privy to Porvenir's secrets now, and reasoned that it was only a matter of time before all thoughts of a revolution would fall by the wayside.

The meeting was over shortly after ten that evening, and though Miguel shook hands with the new members on their way out, he still felt uncertain about Diego Redondo. He stood outside the colmado, waiting for Carlos Peña to bid goodnight to both Aguilar and Ibarra. But the three men talked away, and at times, raised their voices at one other. About twenty minutes went by before the three men finally parted company. Miguel waited for Carlos to approach his horse. "Interesting conversation," said Miguel contemplatively.

"Aguilar is too emotional and impatient," replied Peña ruefully. He mounted his horse and smiled at Miguel. "I don't mind that so much, except that he's just very impulsive. He feels we should begin the revolution now, and not wait for Betances's ship."

"I'm glad *you're* the one leading this cell."

"Yes, but if something should happen to me, guess who'll be leading it."

"I know, so let us pray that nothing happens to you, right? I just hope the new members turn out to be all right. I still do not trust Redondo."

Carlos Peña let out a sigh of frustration. "We've gone over this point many times, Miguel. Look, Diego Redondo comes from a creole family who worked very hard to give him a sound education. Why should we mistrust him, because he works for Rodolfo Hernández? I cannot accept that, and I wish you would just take him at face value."

"I've seen too much to take anybody or anything at face value. If there is one thing I've learned it's that everyone has a price; anyone can be gotten to."

"Including you and me, right?"

"Given the right circumstances, yes; after all, we're all humans."

"Sometimes I wonder where your heart is, Miguelito."

CHAPTER 43

Saturday, April 11, began with the usual wave of humidity that stifled the air inside the Hernández country estate. As the sun began to rise, Rodolfo Hernández dressed quietly in his bedroom, going over in his mind the things he needed to do before day's end. It didn't take too long before his clothes began to moisten from sweat. His face gleamed with perspiration, forcing him to leave the oven-like house without eating breakfast.

Rodolfo had completed nearly all of his business transactions, and normally would have made plans to leave San Sebastián long before this day. But there were too many things, other than business, that remained unfinished. For one thing, the rumors about a revolution were growing stronger, and then there was the matter of his youngest daughter whom he felt was still infatuated with a peasant. Aside from that, Rodolfo had paid his solicitor an extremely large amount of money to spy on the rebels. Rodolfo felt that any insurgency, no matter how small, would be a direct threat to his business empire. Then there was the matter of Juan Pítre, an insignificant peasant that dared to raise a weapon against him. Finally, he heard rumors about armed rebels camping in the woods and attacking peninsulares traveling to and from San Sebastián. And although there were no official reports about the incidents, Rodolfo decided the roads were too dangerous to send his family back to San Juan and reluctantly ordered them to remain at the hacienda for a little while longer.

In her bedroom, awake and restless, Rosalía gazed out of her window with hopelessness and despair. It had been over a month since Rosalía had last seen Miguel, and she wondered incessantly over his well-being. Rosalía heard the front door as it creaked open, and then saw the back of her father's head. She watched the wealthy peninsular as he stood in front of the house, waiting for Candelario to fetch his horse from the stable. Her father stood motionless, while holding his walking cane in one hand and riding baton in the other. A few moments later, Rodolfo climbed onto his horse and disappeared into the woods.

Rosalía contemplated the pathway that led out of the hacienda and into the dirt road, and thought about venturing into town again, but she remembered her father warning against the idea, and his warnings were too strong to take lightly. She knew all too well the consequences of disobeying her father's orders. Yet somehow, the pangs she felt in her heart over seeing Miguel again were just as strong as her fear of disobeying her father was, if not stronger. Rosalía wanted to see Miguel's face again, she wanted to be held in his arms, feel his kisses, and hear his voice just like that memorable day in town one month ago. Deep, in the recesses of her heart, there was even more desire, and that desire was for Miguel to make love to her. That wasn't such a bad thing to desire, thought Rosalía. *Everyone has a right to fall in love, and it doesn't matter who or what that person may be, so long as the love for each other is genuine. Why is Father so reluctant to see this? Why must we present a different face to the world? Why must we pretend to be something different?* It angered Rosalía that her father wanted to stifle her emotions, quell her happiness as he had successfully quelled Maria's happiness and that of his family's.

Rosalía's heart beat rapidly as she dressed herself and quietly made her way down the stairs to the stable. At first, Agustín refused to bridle the horse because the master had left strict orders against it. But Rosalía had been kind to Agustín and Candelario, never raising her voice at them and always thanking them politely. Many nights, she crept surreptitiously along the side of the house toward the slave quarters just to bring Mamíta and Papá extra food and old clothing that her father would throw in the garbage. Candelario and Agustin appreciated those small gestures of kindness, and they grew to love Rosalía as a sister rather than a mistress. Had it been Laura, who would always yell at them and berate them in public, Agustín would never have even listened to the request. It wasn't until Rosalía told him that if her father inquired of the incident, she would tell him that she bridled her own horse and rode it out of the stable without Agustín's or Candelario's knowledge. It was only then that Agustín agreed to ready the horse. An hour later, she trotted quietly out on to the dirt road toward the pueblo.

Rosalía arrived in town just as the merchants began to open their market stands. There were just a handful of customers in the market square, seeking to buy milk and eggs for their morning meals. A few people noticed Rosalía entering the pueblo and stared at her for a long while before resuming their shopping. At first Rosalía felt uncomfortable, but her overwhelming desire to see Miguel instantly diffused any feelings of awkwardness she might have otherwise had. She dismounted and tethered her horse to a wooden post at the far end of Orejola Street, ignoring the townsfolk's occasional glare.

Rosalía walked along the narrow sidewalk, gazing with disinterest at the tiny storefront displays, slowly making her way toward the market square. On occasion, she would purposely stop and look at a dress on display, stroll up toward another window display and do the same thing. When she finally approached the market square, she noticed the arrival of more customers and the buzzing of conversations grow louder. Rosalía paced herself slowly and deliberately, and stopped at each stand, hoping to find Miguel.

Unfortunately, Miguel was nowhere in sight, and a sinking feeling quickly began to overtake Rosalía's heart. She walked past eight wooden stands, toward the end of the square, and then moved to the other side, where she passed over nine other wooden stands. At every stand, she could hear men and women shouting at her, beckoning her to their stand, convincing her that their fruits or vegetables were the freshest in town. With hopes dampened, Rosalía realized that Miguel was not in town that morning, and decided to leave. Perhaps none of Rodolfo's acquaintances had recognized her in town, and maybe her father would never know that she had disobeyed him. Maybe she could get home before her mother and sisters even woke that morning. Her reasoning was sound, and, with a little luck, no one would ever find out about her venture into town. But señor Diego Redondo had entered town at the same hour Rosalía had, and he immediately noticed Rodolfo's youngest daughter.

Diego Redondo spurred his horse into a soft gait, and caught up to Rosalía moments later. "Señorita Hernández!" he shouted while removing his top hat. Rosalía instantly froze, but then just as quickly she composed herself. She turned around and gently tilted her head up at the rider. "It is not safe for you to be in town by yourself."

"I keep hearing those words over and over, señor, but I cannot imagine why anyone would say that," replied Rosalía sharply, annoyed at his tone of voice. "I don't see the town square filled with lions or wolves, and I don't see bears or wild dogs. I see human beings, señor. I see people innocently going about their business. How can I feel unsafe?"

"You are right, señorita, they are human beings," said Redondo with apologetic eyes. He dismounted and walked toward Rosalía. "I didn't mean to imply otherwise, but you must know that the peasants of San Sebastián do not take too kindly to your father. They may want to hurt you just to get back at Don Rodolfo." The roar of shouting stand owners grew even stronger now as more customers began to arrive at the market square.

There was one person among the new influx of shoppers that stood out like an alluvial diamond partially wedged into the ground. His black head, bearing thick and nappy hair, rose above the crowd as if he were bobbing in the ocean up to his neck. Rosalía recognized Carlos right away, but she did not want Diego to know that.

Redondo drew closer to Rosalía and spoke as if he'd been a long time friend. "I would like to be your escort in town for today and perhaps accompany you back home, if you wouldn't mind."

"Thank you, señor Redondo," responded Rosalía with a polite smile. "But I'd rather be alone, if you don't mind."

"As you wish señorita Hernández." Redondo bowed courteously, put on his top hat and remounted. He gave Rosalía a wide smile, before turning his beast in the opposite direction. Although he rode away from the market square, he did not ride far enough to lose sight of Rosalía. Diego dismounted at the other end of Orejola Street and stood next to his horse, carefully watching Rosalía.

Carlos Peña had brought with him several baskets filled with an assortment of fruits and vegetables he had picked up off Don Blanco's farm. He was penniless but he would do what he knew best, and that was to sell scraps at the market at ridiculously low prices. He had taken up a position away from the legitimate sellers, and far from their annoying shouts, and began to call out for potential customers. He knew that his deep voice would carry further than the collective calls of his fellow vendors, and it wasn't long before he sold his first batch of ripe plantains. No sooner had he made his first sale than he noticed Rosalía walking out of the market square. He noted a look of frustration and sadness on her pretty, young face. He tied his bundle and swung it over his shoulder before making a dash toward Rosalía. "Señorita Hernández!" he shouted, as he caught up to her. "Señorita Hernández, what are you doing here?"

"Señor, I came to see Miguel, do you know where he is."

Carlos removed his pava, extended his hand at Rosalía and thundered. "It is a pleasure to finally meet you, señorita. My name is Carlos Peña, and I am a good friend of Miguel's."

Rosalía shook his gargantuan hand, and smiled. "Do you know where I can find Miguel, señor Peña?

"You may call me Carlos, and yes, I do know where you can find him."

"Then can you please take me to him?"

Carlos frowned at Rosalía, deliberately revealing his disappointment. "Why? Have you not caused him enough grief? You know that it is very dangerous if any of Rodolfo's spies see you and Miguel together in town. Your father has warned him to stay away from you, and has threatened him with eviction. Please señorita Hernández, for the love of God, leave Miguelito alone."

"Call me Rosa, I insist. I understand how you feel, Carlos, but God has nothing to do with this. I just don't think you know me."

"I don't need to. All I need to know is that you are a member of the ruling class and that we are nothing but garbage to you."

"Not true, Carlos, not true at all!" said Rosalía defensively. "I spent time with Miguel, and he took me deep into the barrios of San Sebastián.

He showed me how the majority of the people actually live, an opened my eyes to the truth. I admit: it is an unfair system—a sys that only works for the rich…and it must end. I no longer support father's views, or those of the ruling class. I want to join your cau and I want to see the people of Puerto Rico free of Spanish colonialisı free of the peninsulares' grip. I want to contribute to the revolution.

"It is not your fight, and it is not your struggle," Carlos replied.

"Why is that, Carlos?"

"Because you have never suffered in life."

"Don't be so quick with your assessment of me Carlos, I have indeed suffered."

"No you have not. You have never risen in the morning with a hunger so powerful that you could eat your own leather shoes, if you happen to have any. You have never felt the roughness of canvas sheets upon your delicate body, or caked up grime on your skin, or the smell of unwashed clothes. You have never walked by a restaurant and stood before the windows, glaring at a piece of meat, hoping and praying that someone would have the heart to give you their unwanted scraps. You have never walked for miles barefoot and felt the rocks or razor-sharp twigs jabbing at your feet. You have never felt the rain seeping through your tin, rusty roof and beading down on your face. You have never had the privilege of sleeping on wooden planks inside a shack no bigger than an outhouse, with no doors for privacy. How can your heart be into a revolution that you know nothing about?"

"Because I have been a witness to the suffering and the pain you so eloquently described. You are right, Carlos, I have not personally experienced such hardships, but do I really have to experience them? Must I actually live through them in order to be accepted by you and your fellow revolutionists?"

Carlos looked into Rosalía's blue eyes and, although he detected sincerity in them, he nodded his affirmation. "Yes; it is the only way. You cannot join our cause because you are merely a sympathizer."

"Then it is a pity."

"Why?"

"Because you need people like me. You need the sympathy of the ruling class, otherwise, you will not be able do it all by yourselves. A revolution costs money, and I know it is very scarce in San Sebastián. Let me help you, Carlos, even if it is only with money. I can be the voice of opposition among the ruling class."

Carlos shook his head this time. "Miguel would not approve of that; it is far too dangerous for you, Rosa."

"Will you at least allow me to see him?"

Carlos took in a deep breath and sighed heavily. "All right, Rosa, but only for this one time. And even if Miguel, by some miracle, approves your joining us, I will never allow it. Come with me."

Diego Redondo had been watching the scene with alarming interest. The moment he saw Carlos escorting Rosalía out of town, he mounted his horse and began to follow them. Diego trailed the pair until they reached Carlos's horse. After confirming his suspicions, he departed quickly, and headed straight for mayor Chiesa's office, where he knew Rodolfo was.

CHAPTER 44

Mayor Luis Chiesa kept fanning himself as Felipe, the head servant, poured the morning coffee into three cups. A droplet of sweat ran down the mayor's cheek as he picked up the cup and drank heartily. "I heard through the grapevine that you will be investing in Marquez & Co."

Rodolfo Hernández and Colonel Manuel Ibarreta sat before the mayor, and quietly sipped their coffees. "You must be addressing señor Hernández," said Ibarreta. The mayor nodded.

Rodolfo flashed a conquering smile at the mayor. "Rumors spread so quickly here in San Sebastián, don't they?"

"Ah…but are they true?" persisted mayor Chiesa.

"I have no idea how this rumor ever got started, Luis, I don't even know the Marquez brothers."

All of a sudden, as Rodolfo placed his cup down, one of mayor Chiesa's slaves entered the study. "Señor Alcalde, there is a Don Diego Redondo outside, and wishes to enter your office."

"It's my solicitor, señor Alcalde," said Rodolfo, somewhat embarrassed at the interruption.

"Let him in," said the mayor, unfazed by the new arrival. He sipped his coffee and smiled graciously at Rodolfo. He knew full well that Rodolfo was lying to him about the Marquez venture. Diego Redondo finally entered the mayor's study. "Good afternoon, señor Redondo, what can I do for you?"

"I apologize for the intrusion, señor Alcalde, but may I have a private word with señor Hernández?" Diego watched the mayor nod his approval. Rodolfo placed his cup down on the mayor's desk and rose to his feet right away.

The two men walked out of the mayor's study and stood face to face. Holding tightly to the brim of his top hat, Diego looked into Rodolfo's inquisitive, but steely eyes. "Don Hernández, I'm afraid I have very bad news for you."

"What is it? Come man, tell me!" yelled Rodolfo impatiently.

"I saw one of your daughters in town."

"Which one?"

"I believe it was the youngest, the one named Rosalía."

"Are you sure about that Redondo? I gave my daughters explicit orders not to venture into town, especially by themselves. Now, are you sure it was her?"

"Yes, Don Hernández, I even spoke to her."

"You spoke to my daughter? How dare you, Redondo!"

"It wasn't like that, señor, I advised her that it was dangerous for her to be in town alone, and that she should go home."

"And she refused?" Rodolfo inquired. He watched Diego nodding affirmatively. "But what the devil was she doing in town? Was that peasant Miguel Pítre with her?"

"No," replied Redondo. "But I saw her walking away with another man."

"Another man?" Rodolfo said shockingly. "Who?"

"I believe it was Carlos Peña," said Redondo trying hard to sound uncertain.

"Who is Carlos Peña?"

"He is a former slave, a freed man, and a good friend of Miguel's. He's also been associated with a rebel cell here in San Sebastián."

"Porvenir, the one you've infiltrated?"

"Yes señor Hernández," replied Redondo. He could have given Rodolfo more information. He could have told Rodolfo that Carlos was the president of Porvenir and that the rebels had already laid out plans for an armed conflict. But he decided to hold back that piece of information and use it for another occasion, a time when he would desperately need it. Diego waited for the usual outburst from Hernández, but there wouldn't be any this time. Instead, he noticed that his ruthless employer was smiling, and deeply calculating.

"Diego, I believe an opportunity has presented itself," said Rodolfo after considering the situation for several moments.

"What do you mean señor Hernández?"

"I believe that my daughter has been abducted by an African man. Heaven only knows what he is doing to her right now. He could very well be raping her in the forest or worse, he could be killing her right now!"

"But señor Hernández, I didn't see Carlos forcing your daughter away from town. I saw her willingly leave with him. I don't think that—"

"Shut your mouth, Redondo! You will tell the mayor that you saw the African abducting my daughter and beating her!"

"I cannot do that, señor Hernández."

"Oh yes you can, and you will. And if you don't, then I will expose you to the very same insurgent bastards you're spying on. You will do it because it is your duty, because you are a loyalist and…because I own your ass! Now straighten yourself up before we go back into the mayor's study."

Redondo let out a huge sigh of frustration before following his employer back into the mayor's study. "Alcalde Chiesa, señor Redondo has terrible news…" When the puppet solicitor finished telling the mayor about the incident, he watched the politician rise to his feet in a fit of anger.

"Colonel Ibarreta, if it wouldn't be too much trouble, could you round up some militia men and find this Carlos Peña? I hope to God that we are not too late."

There was a hint of skepticism on Colonel Ibarreta's face; a premonition that something wasn't right. Maybe it was the calm manner in Rodolfo's appearance as Redondo told the mayor about the incident. It did not give Colonel Ibarreta the feeling that he was too concerned about his daughter's safety; only the zeal of having a freed black man arrested. Besides that, the repentant look on Redondo's face gave the Colonel the impression that Diego might have been coerced into making a false accusation. But other than his feelings, there wasn't much proof to the contrary, and so he had to follow the mayor's orders. "Very well, señor Alcalde, I will have this Carlos Peña arrested."

"Yes, and you can arrest that Miguel Pítre, too," added Rodolfo calmly, "After that, I will begin eviction proceedings."

At that moment, Diego stepped forth and confronted Rodolfo. "Señor Hernández, perhaps that decision might be a little premature." Diego's confidence had suddenly resurfaced. "Allow me to continue my surveillance. It is only a matter of time before I can confirm Miguel Pítre's involvement in the rebellion, as well as provide you with the names of the other rebels. It would be wise, too, if you held back on evicting Juan Pítre off your land."

Rodolfo said nothing at first. He stood before the mayor and gave Redondo's suggestion careful consideration. Then, he looked down at the mayor and noticed him nodding his head, approving Redondo's plan. He turned to Ibarreta, who did not see a need for such melodrama, and noted his look of approval, too. Finally, Rodolfo gazed at Redondo and said, "All right, Diego, I will hold back the eviction of Juan and the arrest of Miguel, but you better come up with something concrete real fast."

Colonel Ibarreta was the first to leave the mayor's office, followed minutes later by Rodolfo and Diego. As Diego mounted his horse, he knew that he already had enough information about every member of Porvenir. He could have divulged everything he knew about the rebels to the mayor if truly wanted to. So why didn't he do it? Why was he holding back? Would he get the opportunity to release that information if the situation became too dangerous for him?

CHAPTER 45

The afternoon soon proved to be a terrible hardship for Rosalía. She had left her parasol home, and her smooth, delicate skin was at the mercy of an unforgiving sun. Riding alongside her, Carlos kept mostly to himself. He knew it was against his better judgment to bring Rosalía to Miguel, but somewhere in his hardened heart, there was a soft spot. The poet in him, the romantic side of him had taken over and had overturned his otherwise perfect reasoning. There were several more hills to overcome before reaching the Pítre farm and the road to the summits was less than perfect, but they trudged along as best they could.

With only one more hill to pass, the ground beneath Carlos and Rosalía began to vibrate. The low rumble of hooves furiously beating the ground was coming from the direction of town, and it began to stir their horses. Carlos, who was growing more uncertain, noticed it first, and as he turned around, Rosalía heard it for the first time. Facing the dirt road in front of him, a look of desperation had suddenly overtaken the calmness Carlos displayed only seconds earlier. He knew something was wrong.

In a matter of minutes, Rosalía and Carlos found themselves surrounded by twenty militiamen, all pointing their rifles directly at the African man. "Are you Carlos Peña?" shouted Colonel Ibarreta.

Carlos finally realized what was happening. Somehow, he just knew that his days as a free man were over. Carlos slowly turned toward Ibarreta and squinted at the golden shanks of his uniform, each button reflecting sunlight. He regained his composure and nodded at Ibarreta. "I am he."

"Then you are under arrest for the abduction and attempted rape of la señorita Rosalía Hernández!"

Rosalía's eyes widened from shock and she shouted as loud as she could, "That's a lie! Carlos Peña was merely escorting me to the Pítre farm, and he never laid a finger on me! Who issued the order for Carlos's arrest?"

"My name is Colonel Manuel Ibarreta, and I am acting upon the mayor's orders, and he's acting upon a complaint lodged by your father."

"This is madness!" shouted Rosalía. "It's utterly ridiculous. What's going to happen to Carlos?"

"He will be arrested, tried, and if found guilty he will hang," replied Ibarreta. Turning to one of his militiamen, he ordered. "Bind him and take him to the town jail." Ibarreta tipped his head at Rosalía and politely said, "My lady, I shall escort you back to your house."

"I don't need your goddamn escort!" growled Rosalía. She spurred hard into her beast and galloped furiously back into town.

Carlos kept silent as the militiamen forced him off his horse, bound his wrists and at gunpoint began escorting him back into town.

CHAPTER 46

Miguel had worked all day in the coffee field, but had spent the early evening hours watering and pruning plants in a patch of land at the far northern end of the field. It was his little plot, his idea to plant beans and cilantro, and it took him several months to convince his father to grant him that tiny indulgence. The sun was about to set for the day when he began to walk languidly back to his house. It had been a rough day for Miguel because none of the hired hands had reported to work. His father was unable to help either because he had been under the weather for the past few days.

As Miguel approached the house, he saw the figure of a well-dressed man standing next to his father. As he drew closer to the house, Miguel recognized the figure to be that of Manuel Cebollero Aguilar. Miguel also noted the distressed look on Aguilar's face; something he had never before seen in the rebel leader. That look triggered Miguel's consciousness into sensing something dreadful had happened. He dropped the small shovel he was holding, parted several bushes and quickly rushed toward the house.

"Buenas Tardes, Don Aguilar!" shouted Miguel, finally reaching the porch. He glanced at his father who also gave off the same look of distress. "Miguelito, I'm afraid Don Aguilar has bad news."

Miguel furrowed his eyebrows, and while turning to face Aguilar, he said, "Would you like some fresh coffee, Manuel?"

"There's no time for that, Miguel," said Aguilar hurriedly, shaking his head. "Carlos Peña has been arrested." Aguilar paused and watched Miguel as he ran his hands through the hairs of his head, eyes bulging in response to the shocking news. "He's been arrested on trumped up charges," continued Aguilar. "He was seen in the company of señorita

Rosalía Hernández, and someone accused him of abducting and raping her."

"Carlos would never do anything so hideous, you're damn right it's a lie!" said Miguel. "Was he arrested by the militia?" He saw Aguilar nodding his head. "Then they were acting upon the mayor's orders. And if I know that son-of-a-bitch, he issued the orders upon *El Demonio's* insistence."

"Oh come on now, Miguelito, that's a bit of a stretch. You don't know that for sure!" said Juan, fearing Miguel might do something rash.

"Someone must have seen her in town with Carlos," reasoned Miguel. "And it had to be one of Hernández's spies; it's the only logical explanation. But what was she doing in town today?"

"Maybe she was looking for you, Miguelito," said Juan Pítre. There was split second of silence as Juan's comment registered in Aguilar's mind. Now that Juan had unwittingly brought up the subject, Miguel kept his silence and waited for Aguilar's protestations against his relationship with Rosalía. Preoccupied with other more important matters, however, Aguilar chose to ignore Juan's comment for the moment.

"By the rules of our constitution, I am now acting president of Porvenir," Aguilar said humbly. But contrary to the expression Aguilar contrived to display, Miguel detected an air of restrained excitement, as if he had been waiting for this moment to materialize. "I am going into town for a meeting at Ramirez's colmado tonight and I want you to be there."

"But what are we going to do about Carlos?"

"We will discuss that at the meeting. Miguel, I need you there tonight, and I need your mind clear and alert."

"Goddamn peninsulares!" muttered Miguel. "I despise them so much!"

"Miguel!" shouted Aguilar. "Take hold of yourself!"

"Where are they keeping him?" Miguel demanded.

"At the town jail, but don't go there. The commander has deployed a contingent of more than fifty militiamen to guard the jail and changes the guard every two hours. Trust me: you will not get within ten feet of Carlos. But as lieutenants of San Sebastián's militia, Eusebio and I have access to the jail. We will see him tonight and get his version of the story."

"Carlos is my friend, and no one is going to stop me from seeing him!" fired back Miguel.

Miguel arrived in San Sebastián at around nine that evening. Gas lanterns posted along the shops' walls dimly illuminated Orejola Street, allowing Miguel to see at a distance the militiamen guarding the jail. He dismounted, tethered his horse to a post and decided to walk the rest of the way. As he approached the jail, treasured memories of Carlos flashed through his troubled mind. The Duran farm sat right next to the Pítre farm, and Miguel was an ignorant and uneducated boy when, at fifteen, he first met Carlos. Miguel's education never went past grade seven, and he might have been content with that had he not heard Carlos speaking with such commanding wisdom and intelligence. From then on, he yearned to possess the same knowledge that Carlos had acquired. Although he never conveyed his feelings to Carlos, the self-educated former slave understood him better than he did himself. Carlos took him under his wing, though Miguel never asked him, and willingly passed on his knowledge without seeking a thing from Miguel in return. When Miguel demonstrated his ability to read and write to Carlos's satisfaction, the African freedman next taught him philosophy and mathematics. Carlos embraced Miguel's insatiable desire to learn by compelling him to read the works of Aristotle and Plato, and the writings of Isaac Newton. Miguel pored through books that were so old that the pages would sometimes crumble if turned too quickly or brusquely. When Miguel turned eighteen, Carlos then introduced him to the ideals of freedom and democracy and his political ideologies concerning the independence of Puerto Rico. Suffering the miseries of poverty since birth, Miguel easily converted to the separatist movement and quickly became Carlos Peña's protégé. Aside from Carlos's mentoring, Miguel had spent time with his friend going on fishing and hiking ventures and doing things that only brothers did, so in every way Carlos played the role of not only a mentor but also a real brother to Miguel. Miguel had a profound respect and deep admiration for Carlos but more importantly, he truly loved Carlos as any brother would. Now he was about to see his dear friend, his hero and the pillar of rock upon which he leaned so heavily, as a wrongly convicted rapist, sitting inside a dank and musty jail, helpless for the first time in his life.

As Miguel neared the jail, he could hear the clicking of rifles and the rustling of men rising into their fighting stance. Then he heard the deep voice of a militiaman ordering him to halt. Miguel recognized the voice but he chose to keep walking.

"Miguelito what are you doing here so late in the evening?" demanded the militiaman.

"You know why I'm here, Alvaro. I want to see Carlos Peña."

After his brief encounter with Miguel, the sergeant hustled back into the jail. Moments later, an officer, bedecked in a sprawling blue and white uniform with sparkling buttons, emerged. He slowly paced himself toward Miguel, but the young man noticed something different about the officer's demeanor. There was no hint of malice on the officer's face, and no signs of pomposity or of superiority either. If he did possess those traits, reasoned Miguel, they were not as blatant as those he had seen in every Spanish officer that came to Puerto Rico prior to him. In fact, there seemed to be an aura of benevolence on the officer's face, something completely incongruous to the nature of peninsulares. Miguel remained silent as the officer came face to face with him. The officer paused momentarily, and then he looked straight into Miguel's green eyes, as if studying the face of a potential opponent. "So, *you're* Miguel Pítre," said the officer almost sounding admiringly. "My name is Colonel Manuel Ibarreta, and I was ordered to arrest your friend." Miguel kept his silence. "I must say," continued Ibarreta, "you're the only one who's given Rodolfo Hernández a good run for his money. You've done well, up until now, but I would like to give you a little advice for whatever it's worth. Though you may have won several battles here and there, in the end you will lose the war against the Hernández. They are simply too powerful for the likes of you, Pítre. I'm not telling you this because I'm a Spaniard or because I'm a peninsular, as the locals prefer to call us. I am telling you this because I'm just tired of the bloodshed, of seeing people maimed or killed, children without mothers and fathers, anarchy reigning wildly and every negative act associated with the class struggle. I am too damn tired of it, señor Pítre. Do you understand me? I came to Puerto Rico because I thought it was a peaceful land, where a man could make a future for himself. You have no idea how brutal a revolution can be. I have seen it first-hand, in Santo Domingo, where the fighting is so fierce that many people are dying." Ibarreta paused for a quick moment, and noted Miguel's indifference. He promptly concluded that Miguel had no clue of the horrors of a revolution, and further understood that the young man could never relate to his feelings about war. He nodded at Miguel. "Your friend stands accused not only of abducting the daughter of a prominent Spanish citizen, but of attempted rape; these are very serious charges. He is also facing accusations of being a rebel activist. I'm afraid that your friend has already been and will continue to face severe interrogation. He will have no choice but to give up the rest of his co-conspirators." Ibarreta kept his eyes on Miguel but Miguel smirked at Ibarreta, and other than that gesture, offered nothing more. "What about you, Miguel? Are you associated with Carlos in any way?" Again, Ibarreta paused for Miguel's response, but the young man remained silent. "It doesn't matter. A few more hours of intense interrogation and Carlos will tell me whether or not you're a revolutionist."

"Are you finished? May I see Carlos, now?" said Miguel finally.

Ibarreta narrowed his eyes at Miguel. "You have ten minutes."

Escorted by a militiaman, Miguel moved slowly into the tiny jail and saw Carlos sitting in a four-by-four-foot cell. The militiaman, another childhood friend of Miguel's, reminded him about the ten minutes before leaving him alone with Carlos. Miguel noted that Carlos's hands were clasped in iron bindings, which severely restricted his movements. A set of chains kept his feet bound together so that he could not even walk. There were numerous bumps and bruises on Carlos's face. He could not speak clearly because of his swollen lips and he could not see very well because the bruises to the left side of his face completely closed his left eye. Miguel frowned in despair, but there was nothing he could do to help his friend. He sat on the floor next to Carlos and watched him through the cell bars. "They're all lies, Miguelito, all lies. I never touched her. I was only taking her to see you because she insisted."

"I know, my friend, I know. We must hire a lawyer."

"What about Diego Redondo?"

Miguel shook his head. "No. I still don't trust that man."

"You may be right. We cannot afford to place too much trust in anyone anymore. There are too many spies and too many traitors. So, who else is there if not Redondo?"

"There are many lawyers in town; we could find you a good one."

"But the trial is set to take place in a fortnight, Miguel."

"Isn't that a little too fast? You won't have any time to hire a lawyer, and even if you did, it would take more than two weeks to prepare for a trial!"

"They want to get rid of me; it's the only logical explanation for such a quick trial. They intend to torture me, too, to give up the names of the members of Porvenir, but I will not talk. They have already sealed my fate, Miguelito. You must now look toward leadership of Porvenir."

"Aguilar has already claimed presidency, Carlos, there isn't much I can do."

"Aguilar…" Carlos muttered. "That man is too impulsive, too high strung to lead Porvenir. No doubt, he will push to make Ibarra his vice-president, and you will fall to the wayside. You must be aggressive and take up some form of leadership within the cell. Otherwise, there won't be much of a future for the cause."

"I'll try but what if they refuse?"

"Then leave the cell and go to Manuel Rojas. Tell Manuel that I asked you to join the Centro Bravo cell."

Miguel nodded. He rose to his feet and grasped the iron bars of the cell, looking down at his friend. "I'm going to see Hernández."

"Now why would you want to do that?" answered Carlos, looking up at his protégé.

"I'm going to convince him to drop the charges on you, to plea for your case."

"No, Miguelito, don't beg for my life. Please, if I am going to die, then let me die with dignity. Let them take my life away but don't let them take away my dignity; do that for me, please." Carlos saw Miguel's eyes shedding tears of sorrow, sparkling drops streaming down his face and dripping off his chin. For the first time in their friendship, Carlos saw the helplessness in Miguel but he could do nothing for him. "Do not weep for me, Miguelito, for I am a free man and I will die a free man." Miguel wept in silence as the militiaman entered the jail cell and commanded Carlos's only visitor to leave.

CHAPTER 47

It was two o'clock in the morning when Rodolfo Hernández stormed into his country estate, waking everybody at the same time. As he stomped his way up the stairs, he spewed every profane word stored in the evil repository of his mind. The tone of his voice, laced with so much anger, brought the fear of God in the souls of his slaves. He banged both of his fists against Rosalía's door, forcing Maria, Laura and Anita out of their bedrooms. This was going to be a very bad night for Rosalía, but a memorable one for Laura.

"Rosa!" shouted Rodolfo, banging away at the door. "Open the fucking door, or I'll break it down!"

"Rodolfo!" yelled Maria. "What's going on?"

Rodolfo Hernández stopped banging for a short moment, turned his head and narrowed a pair of wicked brown eyes at his wife. "That whore of a daughter of yours was seen in town with a goddamn negro! He abducted her and then tried to rape her! God only knows what really happened! And it's your fucking fault, Maria! I can't even trust you to watch the girls! Did I not give you orders to keep them here? Oh what's the use?" He turned back to the door and banged hard. "Rosa! Open the fucking door!" The doorknob slowly turned and Rosalía emerged from her room.

The moment Rosalía's eyes captured the evil glare in her father's eyes she knew he was going to beat her. She looked up at her father with an equal glare and shouted. "That's not what happened, Father, and you know it! I went into town to look for Miguel. Since I could not find him, I asked Carlos to take me to him. *I* asked Carlos, Father! And he was a perfect gentleman who never put a hand on me!"

"So everybody that saw you in town was lying, right?"

"They work for you, don't they?"

"That's got nothing to do with it!"

"It has everything to do with it, Father, and as the so-called victim, of this so-called crime, I'm going to testify in court that Carlos is an innocent man! I'm also going to testify that you coerced your witnesses, whoever they are, into falsely accusing Carlos!"

"How dare you?" shouted Rodolfo, swinging an open hand across Rosalía's face. Rosalía instantly fell backwards, a red blotch now covering the side of her face.

Horrified, Maria stepped in and pulled Rodolfo's arm back. "Stop it Rodolfo! You're going to kill her one day!"

"Get off me, Maria!" fired back Rodolfo, trying to loosen Maria's firm grip. Unable to break free of Maria's grip, he finally turned and swung an open hand across her mouth. Down went Maria, bleeding from a torn lip, but it was only the beginning. Rodolfo took two steps forward, and then he crouched in front of his ailing wife.

"You're an evil man, Rodolfo, I curse the day we were married," Maria mumbled through swollen lips.

Rodolfo swung again with an open hand, and this time blood began to flow freely from Maria's nose. "I, too, curse that day, because you've never been a wife to me, and have never been a mother to these bitches!" Rodolfo closed his fist and shot a punch across Maria's face. All of a sudden, he felt Rosalía on top of him, pulling his hair, punching his face. He tried to break free of Rosalía's grip, but she would not let him. Watching her father bent over her mother beating her with his fists somehow gave Rosalía a surge of energy that she had never before experienced. "Get off me, you bitch! I'm going to make it so that your mother will never walk again!"

"Leave her alone, you monster!" yelled back Rosalía. She turned to Laura and Anita, who were both witnessing the struggle, and pleaded with them. "Don't just stand there, help me!" Anita stood frozen, too shocked to do anything meaningful, but Laura obviously had her wits about her, and she just watched out of amusement. Unable to elicit help from her sisters, Rosalía reached over with her mouth and bit into Rodolfo's ear.

"Ahh!! You bit me, you goddamn whore!" shouted Rodolfo in pain. He rose to his feet and quickly shook Rosalía off his back. The second Rosalía fell to the floor she felt the tip of her father's boot on her thigh, and later, her face. Rodolfo kept kicking his daughter, burying the tip of his boot into her without compassion. Unable to muster any sense of courage, all Anita could do was cry. In contrast, Laura's eyes gleamed with joy as she watched her father brutally kicking her baby sister.

Tired of kicking Rosalía, Rodolfo knelt before her limp body and began smacking her delicate face. As he watched the blood trickle down Rosalía's mouth, he never noticed that Maria, despite the pain and dizziness overwhelming her at the moment, had risen to her feet. "This will teach you never to disobey me again!" Rodolfo said wickedly.

As Rodolfo mercilessly slapped and punched Rosalía, Maria's fiery eyes regarded him with utter contempt. Nothing evil had ever entered her mind, but at that moment all she wanted was to put a bullet into her husband's head, and if she'd had had a gun right then, she probably would have. As she balanced herself, Maria saw her image in the mirror across the hall. Rodolfo had wrecked her perfect hairdo. Wisps of hair went in every direction and streaks of grey were now visible from afar. The blood poured steadily out of her nose and mouth, but the matriarch was determined to stop Rodolfo from scarring Rosalía's face, or even killing her. As Maria moved along the walls of the bedroom hallway, she stopped by a medium-sized wall table where a ceramic pot, filled with flowers, stood innocently. By this time, Rosalía had fallen out of consciousness and no longer felt the wraps on her face by her father's wicked hands. Too mesmerized with the scene though, Laura and Anita never saw what their mother was doing.

Very gently, Maria picked up the ceramic flowerpot and placed it neatly on the floor. She stood in front of the table and grasped the mahogany structure with both hands. For a split-second, Maria nearly fell backwards as she lifted the mahogany table over her head. But she regained her balance and brought the table down with a force propelled by nothing but sheer hatred. The table hit Rodolfo's head, and sounded like a pop; it did not break apart as Maria thought it would. Instead, the table rolled down Rodolfo's back and careened off the wall down to the floor. A trickle of blood began to flow from the top of Rodolfo's head before he slumped forward and fell unconscious next to Rosalía. Seconds later, a gush of blood flowed down the back of Rodolfo's head collecting on the floor into a thick crimson puddle. Maria leaned against the wall for support and stood looking over the two figures. Tears of sorrow dripped down her face and mingled with blood that still poured from her nose and mouth. She shook her head before leaning against the wall. Moments later, she slid down the wall and passed out.

Later that day saw Rodolfo lying on his bed, eyes closed and a large cloth wrapped around his head. During the wee hours of that violent morning, Laura had sent Candelario to fetch Doctor Bartolomeo Cisneros, who lived a few miles down the road. The sixty-year-old Cisneros, with swirls of platinum hair cascading over his shoulders, narrowed his brown eyes at his patient. The wrinkles around his eyes and small mouth were more visible now as he grimaced at the thought of the violence that had taken place in the Hernández household. The short and thin doctor sat on the bed overlooking Rodolfo, making sure his pupils reacted to the candle fire he brought to his patient's eyes. There was brain activity, and this seemed to bring a sigh of relief in the good doctor. He had already stopped Maria's bleeding and had dressed her wounds. But he had been very concerned about Rosalía, because although her pupils had dilated, too, he noticed she was breathing heavily, and the warmth of her face told him she was suffering from a high fever.

Finally, after the doctor felt he had successfully attended to all medical matters, he turned to Anita and Laura. "Just what in heaven's name happened here?"

"Doctor Cisneros, I must ask you to keep this matter to yourself. You know my father, and you know how difficult a man he can be."

"Yes," agreed Cisneros. "I know of his reputation. It appears that your father and mother will recover, but I am little concerned about your sister. I suggest we take her to the hospital in Camuy, where she can be observed and monitored for anything unusual."

"I'm afraid my father wouldn't allow that," Laura insisted.

"Your father is incapacitated, young lady, and so too is your mother."

"I realize that, doctor, but in my parents' absence, I am in charge of the family. And I am telling you that Rosa is going to remain here."

Doctor Cisneros sighed before rising to his feet. "Very well, then I must ask you to send for me should señorita Hernández take a turn for the worse."

By late afternoon, both Maria and Rosalía had regained consciousness, but they remained in bed following Doctor Cisneros's orders. Lying still in her bed, Rosalía felt pain all over her body. Her thighs and her torso, riddled with red blotches that would later turn black and blue, hurt so much they sometimes made her cry. The excruciating pain on her swollen face was just as bad, and the haze in her eyes prevented her from focusing clearly on the image that had just entered her room.

"Mother, are you all right?" Rosalía said groggily.

"It's not Mother—it's me, Laura."

"Get out of my room, cabróna."

"You are an ungrateful bitch. And you shouldn't be, Rosa, because I was the one who sent for Doctor Cisneros."

"But you just stood there, watching Father beat me and Mother, and you did nothing about it."

"Neither did Ana, so why aren't you sore at her, too?"

"I'll have words with her later, but you know how mentally frail and helpless she can be. You, on the other hand, had the presence of mind to stop Father and you chose to do nothing about it. You've reached a new low, and I will never forgive you."

"You deserved it, Rosa. You have brought shame to our family by falling in love with a peasant, and now this business with that prieto slave will damage Father's reputation even more. And if Father loses his status and business connections as a result, he will disown you."

"What about Mother? Did she deserve to be beaten also?"

"Mother's a weakling, just like Ana, and besides, she was the one who stopped Father."

"What do you mean?"

"She picked up the wall table outside your bedroom and smashed it on top of Father's head. That was the only way she could stop him,

I suppose. Anyway, Father is lying in bed presumably in a coma, though Doctor Cisneros thinks it is only a concussion. But if I were you, I'd start praying that Father recovers, little sister, because if he doesn't, then señora Maria Hernández will be arrested for assault and attempted murder."

"Well, Laura, I'm sure we can count on your testimony in court."

"If it comes to that: absolutely. Then, with our parents out of the way, guess who's going to inherit the money?"

"Laura, you are ten times worse than Father. Know this: from this day forward, you are not my sister. You are not my friend, and you are nothing to me. From this day forward, I will never address you. You are now and forever will be my enemy."

"Oh get a hold of yourself you dumb cunt!" Laura growled. Standing just outside Rosalía's bedroom, Anita heard the entire conversation. It hurt her badly that everyone thought she was weak-minded, including her beloved Rosalía. Tears rolled down her face, but she decided to stand there, eavesdropping.

"Get a hold of myself? Oh, I have, Laura, and you will see how much I am in control of my faculties. You will see. Now, get out of my room!"

Realizing the conversation was over, Anita quickly dashed back to her bedroom.

Laura could not hide the chagrin on her face when she heard Rosalía's threat. "I'll go check in on Father."

"Yes, do that!" answered Rosalía disdainfully.

Moments after Laura left Rosalía's bedroom, Anita entered. She gazed at the bruises on Rosalía's face and closed her eyes remorsefully. "Forgive me, Rosa, for not helping you."

"I'm very sore at you right now. I am sore at you because you present yourself as a weakling. Ana, you must get stronger if you want to survive in this awful world. You must strengthen your resolve, especially against Laura. Now I do not know what Laura thinks she is doing, but we two have to be very mindful of her. I know she's plotting something against me and mother, and you must decide which side you want to be on, sister, right now."

"Oh Rosa, please forgive me!" cried Anita, falling to her knees by the side of Rosalía's bed.

Rosalía, with tremendous pain, sat up and petted her sister's head. "I forgive you, Ana, truly I do. But you must get stronger because in the coming days, you will have to make a stand. Now, what's it going to be? Will you side with Laura or with me?"

In between sobs, Anita looked up at her sister and said, "I'm with you, Rosa, I've always been on your side."

"Good," replied Rosalía with a forced smile. "Now this is what I want you to do. I want you to go see Miguel and tell him that I said Carlos is innocent. You must tell him that I had no idea that my father was going to have Carlos arrested. Tell him that the trial is fixed and that there is no way Carlos is going to be judged fairly."

"But Rosa, what about Father's spies, won't they see me in town?"

"Father's spies are fixated on me, Ana; they won't even blink an eye at seeing you. Just be careful that Laura doesn't get wind of this."

"When do you want me to see Miguel?"

"Right now, Ana."

CHAPTER 48

The sun had set for the day and dusk settled in for its brief life when Anita entered the town of San Sebastián. She had no idea how to find Miguel or any clue as to how she should go about it. Anita began to walk aimlessly up the street, scrutinizing every passerby with her eager, light-brown eyes. Frustration soon overtook Anita, and she began to doubt herself once again. Then, she remembered that it was at the market square where she had last seen Miguel, and she took off for the shopping district. When she arrived, she noticed that the merchants had closed their wooden stands and were mounting their wagons or horses for the nightly trek back home.

Anita began to run toward the last of the merchants, an older man with a protruding belly. As he climbed onto his horse with a great deal of difficulty, he heard Anita's clamoring voice. He turned around in response and confronted Anita's hopeful eyes. "Stop your shouting, señorita!" he yelled in annoyance.

"I'm sorry, señor, but can you help me?"

The man raised his bushy white eyebrows and said, "With what?"

"I'm looking for Miguel Pítre; do you know where I can find him?"

The man's dark eyes stared at Anita for a long moment, as he contemplated the idea of giving away such valuable information. "You're not from these parts, are you?" He watched Anita nod in agreement. "So what is it that you want from Miguel? Wait a minute, aren't you one of Rodolfo Hernández's daughters?"

"Si señor, I have a message for Miguel from my sister Rosalía."

"Hasn't your family caused him enough grief already? Has not your father done enough damage to us San Sebastiános? I'm not going to tell you where he is young lady, because you are a peninsular, and I simply do not trust the whole lot of you."

"I beg you, señor, please help me. I am Miguel's friend, and I must deliver an important message to him. It's about señor Carlos Peña."

The old man took several more minutes to study the young woman. While scrutinizing her, he sensed a kind of truthfulness about her. He pursed his lips, narrowed his eyes and uttered, "Miguel works for me from time to time, selling fruits and vegetables. I will take you to him, but if you turn out to be a spy, I will use this leather whip on your delicate peninsular body—this I promise you."

An hour later, the old man helped Anita off his horse, and pointed with his index finger toward a small hill. "The Pítre farm lies below the summit of that hill yonder. You must climb it to get to Miguel. Unfortunately, I am already late for supper and cannot take you there."

"Thank you, anyway, señor, I am deeply indebted."

The old man nodded emotionless. "Buenas noches, señorita."

Anita fell and slid down the hill several times before she was able to reach the summit. The summit was pitch-black, and the sound of coquís came from everywhere. Anita looked down the side of the hill and noticed a tiny fragment of light. Focusing her eyes on that light, she began to walk down the other side of the hill.

Anita finally reached the bottom of the hill and paced herself slowly toward the light, following a very narrow dirt pathway. As she drew closer to the light, she noticed it was a gas lantern attached to the outside wall of what looked like a tiny tool shed. Fully focused on the gas lantern, she approached the tool shed but quickly realized it was someone's home. She did not see a front door for privacy or protection, only a wrinkled and dirty curtain that covered the threshold.

As Anita drew closer, she could hear two men conversing. One was clearly the voice of an older man, but the other sounded youthful to her. The second she set foot on the porch, the wooden planks creaked loudly. She was just about ready to knock on the side of the house, when she saw a hand pulling the curtain to the side and a set of curious eyes starting at her. Juan Pítre stood frozen for a split-second before opening his mouth to speak. "Who are you? And what are you doing here, young lady?"

Miguel had already settled into his hammock when he heard his father apparently speaking to someone other than him. Someone had visited the Pítre home, and the thought made Miguel's heart flutter with excitement. He quickly rose to his feet and dashed toward the front of the house, but when he recognized Anita, his eyes saddened right away and his heartbeat returned to its normal rhythm. "It's all right, Father, I know her."

Juan turned completely around to give his son a quizzical look, "Who is she?"

"That's Anita Hernández, Rosalía's sister. Señorita Hernández, this is my father, Juan Pítre."

Juan turned back to face Anita and noticed her extended hand.

"A pleasure to meet you, señor Pítre."

With eyes widened and mouth muted for the moment, Juan extended his arm and shook Anita's hand. They stood there shaking hands for a long moment before Juan finally regained his composure. "Please come inside, señorita."

"I can't stay very long. I have a message for you, Miguel, from Rosa."

Juan shook his head vigorously, because despite his warnings to the contrary, Miguel had chosen to continue seeing Hernández's daughter and communicating with her, too. Miguel ignored his father and asked Anita if she wanted some coffee. Anita refused and immediately delivered Rosalía's message. Miguel took in every word and nodded to show Anita that he understood her message. There was a brief moment of silence before the roaring sound of Juan's snore filled the air inside the shack. Ignoring that awful sound, Miguel gazed at Anita while sorting things out in his mind. "Thank you, Ana, for bringing me the message. Please tell Rosa, that I already know what happened, and that I already know Carlos is not going to receive a fair trial. But you must tell her this, too: she is well aware that I am a member of a rebel cell, right here, in San Sebastián. We have vowed to revolt against Spain, and if the authorities discover my association with the rebel cell, I will most certainly hang for sedition. If the authorities discover that your sister is associating with a known revolutionist, they will arrest and hang her as well, whether or not she is Rodolfo Hernández's daughter. It is for this reason, that she must forget about me and that I forget about her."

"So that's it? You want me to break my sister's heart for you?"

"Do you think I want to break her heart? I love Rosa with all of my heart, and I will do anything for her. But I don't want to place her life in jeopardy for the sake of love. If I die, it would break her heart even more. I love her very much, and I long to see her and hold in my arms once again. Rosalía has become the very essence of my heart and soul, and I feel incomplete without her. But at the same time, I fear for her life, and I will not consciously endanger her. Tell her that I have already forgotten about her; in fact, tell her that I am with another woman."

"That is cruel beyond all measures, Miguel," Anita replied quickly, surprised at Miguel's words. "And I doubt very much that you want me to tell her that. No, I will tell her exactly what she needs to know and that's it." All of sudden, she reached out and took hold of Miguel's hands. "You are a man of conviction and honor, and I hope and pray that one day I am lucky enough to meet another man just like you. It doesn't have to end like this, Miguel."

"Yes it does, and it will," replied Miguel, letting go of Anita's hands. "Now, I must take you back home."

CHAPTER 49

Carlos Peña's trial took place on Monday, May 4, in San Sebastián's tiny courthouse, at the far end of Orejola Street. The Mayor delayed the trial for nearly two weeks so that a fully recovered Don Rodolfo Hernández could testify against Peña. The trial lasted only one hour, and the jurors, who were all peninsulares, took less than half an hour to deliberate on their verdict.

Everyone was there at the trial, from peninsular to creole, from merchant to jornalero, and from jíbaro to plantation owner. No one wanted to miss hearing the news first-hand. To the peninsulares, a guilty verdict would send a message to all Africans to stay away from their peninsular white women. A guilty verdict would send a clear message that it was the peninsulares and not the creoles who were in control of things, and that no matter what happened, the will of the elite would always rule San Sebastián and all of Puerto Rico, for that matter.

To the creoles of Puerto Rico, a verdict of not guilty meant that for the first time in the history of San Sebastián someone other than a peninsular had received a fair trial. It would have signaled a change in the courts for the common man. If the jury found Carlos Peña innocent, then he would become a symbol for democracy and a symbol for freedom. A victory in court would not only have crystallized the start of social change, but would have galvanized everyone's hope for the future, too.

Unfortunately, things do not necessarily go as planned or as hoped. The attorney assigned to defend Carlos found early on that his case was doomed from the outset. Though he protested vehemently against the lack of evidence supporting abduction and rape, he could not find anyone willing to corroborate his contention or testify on Carlos's behalf. He argued strongly but found it extremely difficult to reverse the judge's decision to suppress Rosalía's testimony. He didn't even know that Diego Redondo was the sole witness to the alleged crime; a fact that was never made part of the complaint against Carlos. Facing such terrible odds, there was no way that he was going to successfully defend Carlos, and he was right. In less than half an hour, the jurors took all the hopes and dreams of every common person and made them vanish along the winds of injustice.

Within half an hour, Carlos Peña's status among the creoles transformed from a symbol of hope and change to a symbol of struggle and pain. The former slave, who had educated himself and had become the champion of freedom, had unwittingly become a martyr for the cause of liberty.

The execution of Carlos Peña was to take place at dawn on Wednesday, May 6, 1868, and as the wrongfully convicted rapist sat in his cell, awaiting his death, Miguel Pítre was there to comfort him. "Do not look upon me with such sadness," Carlos said with a conquering smile. "You know I'm an innocent man, and so does everybody else. I am right with God, and I know that He will receive me with open arms."

"We have two more hours together, Carlos," said Miguel, trying to hold back his anguish. "Is there anything you need me to do before they come to execute you?"

"Like what?"

"Would you like me to fetch Father Delgado?"

"To do what exactly, receive last rites from a peninsular priest, another hypocrite? No, thank you."

"There must be something," muttered Miguel.

"Yes, there is something you can do for me. Now that Aguilar and Ibarra have legally assumed leadership of Porvenir, there won't be much for you to do there. I want you to stay clearly focused and move on with our dreams. You remember them, don't you? You remember our dreams of seeing the Spanish returning to Spain? You remember our visions of a new flag hoisted atop the capital building—a flag representing the new and free nation of Puerto Rico? You remember our talking at great length about how we would travel abroad, as ambassadors of Puerto Rico, and bring international industry here? You remember those things, don't you? You remember how we planned to open up schools in every town, and colleges and universities in the great cities. Do you remember how we talked about opening hospitals and about ridding the island of Cholera? Those dreams must never end, Miguel, they must be ingrained in your mind and soul and they must be the force behind your resolve to free Puerto Rico from the clutches of tyranny. You must take the mantle from me and push the cause of freedom forward! You must never relent, never falter and never regret your actions! As for me, I will be watching you from heaven."

"As soon as it is over," replied Miguel. "I'm going to stay at Manuel Rojas's plantation. I have already talked to him and he has graciously given me some farm work to do. Of course, my main work will be in the cell itself."

"Manuel Rojas is a good man, and although he may be a half Venezuelan, his heart is in Puerto Rico one hundred percent and his vision is singular and completely focused. He is fully committed to the cause, and I am certain he will guide you along the way." Carlos Peña stood up and grasped the iron bars his cell. He watched as Miguel stood up to face him. "You know something, Miguelito," Carlos continued, "during my trial, all I kept thinking about was the men of the American Revolution. Do you know what amazes me about them? Their incredible determination and confidence despite the odds, the terrible sacrifices they made for their beliefs in freedom and democracy for all Americans. If General Washington's troops had lost the war, all revolutionists would have hanged for treason. Do you think the thought of death ever left their minds? I'm sure the thought of capture and death resonated inside their very souls, Miguel, but they resolved to push forward and one day they saw the fruits of their sacrifices. It is that kind of resolve that we Puerto Ricans need right now. Things will be bad Miguel, but no matter how bad things get, you must never give up. I want you to become a leader, Miguel. I want you to lead our people to the next, logical phase in our evolution. If people like you choose to do nothing, then Puerto Rico will remain under Spain's yoke or maybe the yoke of another more powerful country."

The two men said nothing further for the next hour, until the jailers came to get Carlos Peña.

The gathering of witnesses, both peninsular and creole, stood before the gallows, and as the magistrate calmly read the sentence aloud, Miguel remained inside the jail. He pressed both knees to the floor and prayed for the soul of his dear friend, a mentor whom he loved so very much. The trap floor opened loudly and Carlos easily fell through it. He swung from side to side and twitched for several seconds. It was over. Carlos was on his way to meet God.

Several hours after the execution, Miguel Pítre finally received permission to retrieve Carlos's remains. After that, he searched high and low for the members of Porvenir, but he could not find anyone to help him bury Carlos. Frustrated, Miguel rode back home and begged his father for help. By late afternoon, Miguel had placed Carlos's body onto the wagon, and Juan, driving the wagon, led a small procession of onlookers toward the cemetery. Since most of the priests were peninsulares, Miguel found it very difficult to find one that could provide his dear friend with a benediction. In the end, no member of the clergy dared to volunteer the service, and so Miguel offered his own version, before laying the wooden casket into the ground.

CHAPTER 50

The late hours of the evening saw Miguel knocking hard on Manuel Aguilar's door. Aguilar opened the door slowly, and as he peeked through the narrow opening, his face could not betray the sudden shock at seeing Miguel. "Miguel! It is dangerous for you to be seen with me! You are not following protocol!"

"Where were you today? Where were the members of Porvenir?"

"We heard that the authorities have gotten wind about Porvenir, so we decided to suspend activities for the time being."

"That's horseshit! You were all just scared! If the authorities had known about Porvenir, we would all be in jail right now, or dead, just like Carlos. I saw none of you there and it shames me to know that you all show your fears so plainly!"

"That's not true, Miguel. We are not afraid. You know that I am a Second Lieutenant in San Sebastián's militia, and so is Eusebio; anything we do out of the ordinary can easily be detected by loyalist militiamen and reported to our superiors. I was not going to compromise Porvenir just to attend Carlos's execution. Carlos's death was painful to all of us, and though we wished we could have been there, the cause for freedom far outweighed our sentiments. Please, come inside so we could talk some more."

Miguel stepped inside Aguilar's house but refused Aguilar's invitation to sit and have coffee with him. "All I want to know now is where I stand in Porvenir!" Miguel demanded.

Aguilar hesitated for a short moment before answering Miguel. "By charter I am now the president of Porvenir. Eusebio Ibarra is now the vice-president, and Juan Mendez is our agent. All senior posts have been filled, but I still have need for a man like you, Miguel."

"In what capacity am I to serve Porvenir?"

"You can be the cell's secretary, under Mendez. You know the countryside far better than any of us do, and we could use that knowledge to send messages to Centro Bravo, Capa Prieto or even Lanzador Del Norte. You could be our eyes and ears out there."

Although Carlos's last wish was for Miguel to leave Porvenir and join up with Centro Bravo, the young idealist could not do it. It wasn't because Aguilar had relegated him to a mere messenger, and it wasn't because he didn't know anyone at Centro Bravo, other than Manuel Rojas, and it wasn't because he felt more comfortable staying with Porvenir. The fact that Porvenir was very close to his home also did not play into his decision to stay with the cell. Miguel based his decision entirely upon his desire to be close to Rosalía and nothing else. He knew that in heaven, Carlos was probably shaking his head at him wondering where the master had gone wrong with his pupil. Miguel nodded at Aguilar and uttered, "All right, señor presidente, when is our next meeting."

"Next Friday, but first I want you to ride to Centro Bravo and tell them exactly what happened to Carlos Peña."

Miguel Pítre rode like the wind on the morning of Thursday, May 7. He arrived in Lares by late morning and was pleased that his knowledge of the countryside had cut the travel time by one hour. Wasting no more time, he directed his steed toward the Rojas plantation just outside the town of Lares.

Mariana Bracetti greeted Miguel Pítre but she informed him that Manuel and his brother were out working on the plantation. Bracetti gave him general directions, and Miguel rode his horse wildly into the field.

He rode swiftly past several slaves toiling the fields, and then stopped by an overseer to inquire the whereabouts of the Rojas brothers. The overseer pointed toward the end of a long field, where Miguel managed to see two figures on horseback.

"Señor Rojas!" shouted Miguel as he approached the two rebels. Miguel pulled on the reins, stopped just short of Manuel's horse and quickly informed the Rojas brothers what had happened to Carlos Peña and about the subsequent restructuring of the Porvenir cell.

"I am deeply saddened to hear this grave news, Miguel. My brother and I had the utmost respect for Carlos Peña, but we know Aguilar and Ibarra well, and they are good men, too. I'm glad you chose to stay with Porvenir. Now, we have terrible news as well, and you should deliver the news to Don Aguilar of Porvenir and to Don Gonzalez of Lanzador."

Manuel Rojas's face spoke volumes to Miguel, as if the news he was about to give him would rock the foundation, the very core of their movement. Manuel Rojas gazed into Miguel Pítre's green eyes and spoke dryly. "We have learned that our dearest friend, Segundo Ruiz Belvis, has died in Chile, in the town of Valparaiso. From the cryptic letter sent by Doctor Betances, it appears that señor Ruiz died under mysterious circumstances."

Miguel closed his eyes and shook his head at the terrible news. His mind was swirling with confusion. Did the Spanish know that Ruiz was dealing with the Chilean people? Did the Spanish send agents to Chile to assassinate Ruiz? Had Ruiz's death signaled the end of their cause? "This is a serious blow to all of us, señor Rojas," uttered Miguel.

"There's more bad news, I'm afraid," added Manuel Rojas. He watched Miguel's eyes widen, bracing himself for more. "Santo Domingo's police force, at the orders of Governor Baez, issued orders for Doctor Betances's arrest. Fortunately, our friends there found out about the arrest orders and helped Betances flee Santo Domingo."

"Where is he now?" asked Miguel, narrowing his eyes at Rojas.

"He's in New York City, sharing an apartment with several Cuban nationals. He is awaiting Mathias Brugman's arrival, and the two plan to meet with Senator Morgan to plea our case."

"You think the United States will help us?"

Manuel Rojas shook his head, "I don't know, Miguel. At this point, I don't know where all the pieces of this great puzzle will fall. All I know is that we lost our most important and only connection to South America. I just hope Ruiz was able to secure an arms deal with the Chileans before his death. As far as the ship Doctor Betances promised us, I'm not too sure about that either. That is why I am going to Mayagüez to meet personally with Brugman before he leaves for New York. We must know where this revolution stands, and the only one who can tell us that is Doctor Betances."

CHAPTER 51

Several days later, on May 11, Diego Redondo arrived at the Hernández country estate at around two in the afternoon. By orders of Rodolfo himself, Diego walked around the house toward the rear, where he and his employer could talk in private. "Come inside!" commanded Rodolfo.

Redondo removed his top hat and obediently stepped into the house. "You've made a remarkable recovery, señor Hernández."

"Not really. I still get dizzy spells and sometimes my vision gets blurry."

"Perhaps you may want to consult a doctor in San Juan, it may—"

"Enough of this small talk, Diego. I hope that you bring very good news, at least enough to justify the sixty-five hundred pesos I gave you."

Diego hesitated briefly but then submissively gave his report. "The cell is called Porvenir, as you already know, but what you didn't know was that it was led by none other than señor Carlos Peña…," Redondo explained. He went on to brief his employer on everything he knew about Porvenir, including the names of Porvenir's leaders, where the cell meets and their plans for the future. As Diego spilled his guts out to his master, Rodolfo's eyes gleamed with excitement; his investment in Redondo had paid off handsomely.

"I knew that son-of-a-bitch was a rebel scum!" figured Rodolfo. "What about his father, Juan?"

"No. Juan Pítre refuses to get involved with the rebels. But I think I have even more important intelligence." Diego watched his master nodding his head at him, signaling him to proceed. "The rebels expect a shipment of arms to arrive soon from South America. The arms deal was negotiated by the two exiled leaders, Ruiz and Betances."

"Those two bastards should have hanged a couple of years ago," said Rodolfo angrily. He looked at Redondo and raised his eyebrows. "How are they getting this shipment of arms, and from whom?"

Diego narrowed his eyes briefly. "The arms are coming from the Chileans, by way of Venezuela, aboard the ship *El Telégrafo*."

"Anything else?"

"That's it, Don Hernández, that's what I'm going to write in my dispatches to Governor Pavía."

"Wait just a minute," said Rodolfo raising his hand at Redondo in a halting gesture. "Just give the governor the name of the rebel cell and the names of its members. Do not tell him yet about the shipment of arms. I don't want Pavía to send a horde of militia men here and screw things up for me." He flashed a devilish smile at Redondo, but Diego saw past the smile, deep inside his master's soul, and knew that Rodolfo was already calculating something devious. "You've done well, Redondo, I might even give you a bonus."

"Thank you, señor Hernández."

"You're welcome. Now get the fuck out of my house!"

From the second floor of the house, Anita saw Diego Redondo as he pulled his horse along the dirt pathway. She noticed that he did not mount his horse until he was on the trail leading out into the woods. She found it strange too that Redondo was looking everywhere, as if he felt someone was watching him. Anita did not give the matter another thought, and continued to gaze out of her window.

CHAPTER 52

Juan Pítre had been under the weather now for the past four weeks but despite his ailments, he had set out to plow a small parcel of unclaimed land next to his farm. He knew it was illegal to do that but since no one had laid claim to the land, he figured he could use it for now. As he pushed Candela forward, he began to breathe heavily. Chest tightening and sweat beads pouring down his face, he began to feel lightheaded.

He pulled hard on Candela's reins, removed his drenched pava, and wiped the sweat off his face with a weakened forearm. Juan had sent Miguel into town to buy a few vegetables for dinner that night, and now, feeling more ill, he regretted sending his son on the errand. Not long after pausing, Juan heard the sound of hooves thumping the ground at a rapid pace. He knew it could not have been Miguel because his son would always arrive slowly, inspecting the fields as he drew closer to the house. This was somebody else.

Sweating profusely now and breathing faster than before, Juan turned around to cast his blurry eyes at the oncoming figure. Blurred by salty sweat, his eyes could not make out the approaching figure. Finally, Juan heard the horse whinny as it came to an abrupt stop. Unable to focus on the imposing figure, Juan called out, "Who's that?"

"It's me, Rodolfo Hernández!" said the peninsular authoritatively.

"You've come to evict me?"

"No!" replied Rodolfo. "I came to tell you that I have received important information about your son."

Juan was still unable to see Rodolfo clearly, but he nevertheless addressed the fuzzy image in front of him. "What about my son?"

"I have learned that your son is a member of Porvenir, a rebel cell in San Sebastián. I have learned the names of all the rebel members and of their plans for a revolution. I came here just to tell you this, Pítre, because I wanted you to hear it from me. I also wanted you to know that I am going to tell the authorities everything about your son. Your son is going to hang for sedition, Juan. He will die as a traitor to his country. I told you not to fuck with me, Pítre, didn't I?" Rodolfo's eyes teemed with merriment, as if he truly enjoyed watching Juan absorb the catastrophic news.

Instead of begging for mercy, as Rodolfo might have expected though, Juan began to breathe even harder than before, and quickly reached over with his right hand to clutch the center of his chest. The inexorable pain that froze the left side of his chest plainly revealed itself on Juan's agonizing face. Taken aback by Juan's unexpected reaction, Rodolfo shot a curious look at him before watching him slump forward. "Pítre, are you all right?" said Rodolfo. This was bad, he thought. Rodolfo wanted Juan Pítre to suffer miserably, not to die. All of a sudden, Juan Pítre fell off the plow face forward onto the ground. Rodolfo remained seated atop his horse and, without any form of compassion, gazed at the lifeless body on the ground. Finally, Rodolfo dismounted and walked over to Juan Pítre. He crouched over Juan and placed a hand on his neck. Feeling no pulse, Rodolfo rose to his feet and climbed back on his horse. "A pity," he said looking down at Juan's body, unemotionally. "It would have been nice to have seen you suffer a while, old man." Rodolfo spurred his horse and disappeared from the Pítre farm.

Not long after Hernández had driven the final nail into Juan's life, Miguel had arrived with two canvas bags full of vegetables. Almost immediately, he sensed something wrong. His father would never leave the plow in the field, much less Candela still tied to it. And where was he? Miguel spurred his horse and galloped furiously toward the plow. When he reached the plow and saw his father lying face down on the ground, he jumped off his horse. "Pápi!" he yelled. Miguel buried both knees into the soft ground and turned his father's body around. Miguel placed an ear on Juan's mouth, but he neither felt nor heard his father breathing. Next, he put his fingers on Juan's neck but he felt no pulse. Realizing his father was dead, he tilted his head and looked up into the afternoon skies, as if he were about to talk to God. He closed his eyes, and from the depths of his soul came forth a deep, wailing cry that echoed throughout the coffee plantation. Even the crickets and coquís, birds and land creatures fell silent in response to Miguel's deafening cry of anguish. Miguel bent his body forward and hugged his father, weeping. The love for his father was profound and as immeasurable as the grains of sand on a beach. The admiration, respect and utter devotion for his father was equally incalculable, and now, the cavernous void in his heart, the abysmal vacuum left by the deaths of Carlos and his dear father, was filled with nothing but sorrow and despair.

Miguel Pítre was all alone now.

Miguel stood kneeling over his father's corpse for hours, crying and reminiscing. It wasn't until close to midnight that Miguel finally decided to take the wagon out of the barn. Very gently, Miguel picked up his father's body and placed it into the wagon. Through the early morning hours, Miguel washed his father's body, shaved his face, combed his hair and put on his Sunday clothes. He finished cleaning and dressing his father's body shortly after sunrise. Towards mid morning, he hitched Candela to the wagon and brought his father's remains into the town's cemetery for burial.

At around eleven o'clock, on the morning of May 12, those that knew Juan Pítre were shocked to see his limp body lying on a wagon bed, a wagon destined for the tiny cemetery at the end of town. Miguel purposely drove the wagon slowly through town, allowing Juan's friends and acquaintances a final glimpse and a little time to pay their respects. Miguel's eyes had dried out from crying so much during the night that he couldn't cry even if he wanted to. His reddened eyes burned every time he blinked. A long procession of San Sebastiános began to form behind the wagon, following it closely toward Juan's final resting place. Among the mourners were Aguilar and Ibarra, both of whom learned about Juan's death that same morning. Marching behind the wagon, too, were mostly all of the market square vendors who had closed their stands for the morning in honor of a fellow jíbaro. There were no priests to be seen anywhere in town, and Miguel quickly realized that San Sebastián's Roman Catholic Church, that bastion of love and compassion, had shut its doors out of fear. No priest in his right mind would willingly allow himself to be seen performing last rites and benediction to a jíbaro peasant or creole. Miguel did not bother to seek a priest this time, because he knew they were all hiding inside the church.

Atop his horse, watching the long procession with indifference, sat Rodolfo Hernández. Things could not possibly have turned out better for him. Good fortune had favored him that morning, and he would use the opportunity for personal gains. Rodolfo dismounted, and while drinking coffee at the Ramirez colmado, he waited patiently.

Two hours later, the mourners began returning to the market square, giving Rodolfo a clear indication that Miguel had finally interred Juan's body. Rodolfo stepped outside and waited until he saw Miguel driving his empty wagon now. The land master dashed out of the colmado and called out for Miguel, voice loud enough so that everyone else in town could hear. In response, Miguel pulled hard on the reins, forcing the wagon wheels to slide along the dirt road until they came to a stop. Miguel slowly turned his head and reluctantly focused his eyes on the face he hated with so much passion. "Miguel Pítre," said Rodolfo, "I wonder if we might have a word."

"What do you want, Hernández?" Miguel said impatiently.

"I wanted to express my condolences," replied Rodolfo with a half smile.

"Thank you. Is that all?"

"No, Miguel. Unfortunately your father's sudden death has left too many things open between us."

"You can have your land back, Hernández; I'm not interested in farming anymore."

"That's not what I want to talk to you about, Miguel. Please, come down and talk to me. Come, and let us walk over to Don Pagan's restaurant and have some coffee. How about it?"

Miguel nodded to accept Rodolfo's invitation. He drove the wagon toward Pagan's tiny restaurant and followed Rodolfo to a vacant table. Brushing away the flies off the table, Rodolfo demanded two cups of coffee from a thin and scrawny waiter. Moments later, the waiter brought two steaming cups of coffee and departed quickly. Rodolfo studied Miguel briefly. Miguel poured sugar into the coffee cup, picked up a spoon and stirred several times, but he never raised his hand to drink. Finally, Rodolfo spoke. "I am not your enemy, Miguel. I am sorry for your father's death."

"Damn you, Hernández, what do you want from me?"

"I want to renegotiate the deal on the farm. You're a good farmer, and you know how to grow coffee beans. I don't want to throw you off the farm anymore than you want to be evicted."

"For the last time, Hernández, what do you want from me?" yelled Miguel, banging both fists on the table, shaking some coffee out of both cups.

"Relax Miguel, and I'll tell you," answered Rodolfo. "I am willing to absolve your father's entire debt. That means that you will not inherit any of your father's financial burdens. I am further willing to give you the fourteen cuerdas back. I'll even throw in the parcel of land next to your farm, the one your father was plowing illegally."

"I know you, Hernández; you're not the kind to give something away for nothing. It's just not in your evil soul to do so. Why are you being so generous? What angle are you playing?"

"You're right, Miguel. Everything in life has a price and this proposal does come with a price. What I want in return for the land is your agreement to confirm the names of the leaders of Porvenir."

"You sorry sack of shit, how do you know about Porvenir?"

"There's no need for insults, Miguel, we're having a civil conversation here. Anyway, does it matter how I came by this information? The fact of the matter is that I do know about the rebel cell. I also know that Don Aguilar and Don Ibarra are the leaders. What I need is someone to corroborate the names, a bona fide rebel member, someone like you. If you agree to confirm the names, and later testify in court, I will give you the land free of any encumbrances. I'll even throw in a few thousand pesos."

Miguel sneered at Rodolfo, eyes glaring with utter hatred for the man. "You tried to bribe me once before and it failed. What makes you think you can bribe me again?"

"You're all alone now, you're penniless and you have no future whatsoever, that's why. Because you and I both know that everyone has a price, and you are no different. Ideologies and faith in a cause...they are noble things, but they do not put food in your stomach, clothes on your back or a roof over your head. All I'm asking is that you consider my offer, and take it for what it's worth."

Miguel shook his head angrily. "You think I can be bought, like your friend bought off Santiago Duran? If you're thinking that, then you're barking up the wrong tree, and I gave you too much credit. I will never sell out, especially to the likes of you." Miguel rose to his feet and looked down at Hernández. "I will go back to the farm but only to retrieve my personal belongings. The farm is yours, Hernández."

As Miguel began to walk out of the restaurant, Rodolfo shouted. "Don't be a fool, Miguel! Just think about the offer!" Rodolfo sat at the table, looking through the window, watching Miguel climb onto the wagon. "Damn fool," he muttered to himself. Rodolfo stepped out of the restaurant and stood gazing at Miguel's wagon until it crossed the bridge over the creek and faded into the woods. Standing across the street and watching Rodolfo, was one of his daughters who had gone into town against his explicit orders. Too consumed with his plans for destroying the rebels, Rodolfo never even noticed her.

Anita shook her head with confidence, knowing her father was too preoccupied to notice her. As her father departed town, a man atop a horse stopped in front of her. The horse grunted several times, causing Anita to turn her attention toward the rider. "Señorita Hernández, it is dangerous for you to be in town by yourself."

Anita smiled at the rider and spoke politely. "You are my father's solicitor, are you not?"

"Yes. My name is—"

"Diego Redondo, I know señor."

"If your father learns that you have gone into town by yourself—"

'What is he going to do, señor Redondo, beat me? Please, tell me something I don't already know." Anita watched Diego and waited for a response, but the young lawyer removed his top hat and simply gazed contemplatively at Anita. Before he could say another word, Anita spoke again. "Tell me: was that Miguel Pítre's father in the wagon?"

"Yes, señorita, he died yesterday," replied Diego, dismounting. He slowly walked toward Anita, but as he approached the young woman, something inside him began to stir. All those times he was in the Hernández hacienda and in spite of all his dealings with Rodolfo, he never even dared look upon any of Rodolfo's daughters. It wasn't out of respect but out of fear for his employer's wrath. This time, though, since Rodolfo was not around to see him, he felt no constraints and seized the moment to absorb and retain Anita's image. "May I escort you back to your hacienda?"

Upon seeing Diego, something stirred Anita, too; something she had never before felt. All of a sudden, Anita's yearlong wait for Ruben De La Cruz had become a faint memory, faded recollections quickly replaced by the fresh image of a young, tall and handsome solicitor. "You may señor."

"Please, call me Diego."

"Thank you. You may call me Ana." Diego took the reins of his horse and pulled his beast behind him. As the young couple walked slowly down the dirt street, Anita gazed at the ground thoughtfully. "I wonder what is to happen to Miguel now that his father has passed away."

"That matter is entirely in your father's hands," replied Diego.

Anita suddenly stopped and turned to face Diego. "What do you mean?"

Diego turned to look down at Anita but he hesitated. "I meant nothing, Ana. I really don't know anything."

"Yes you do, Diego," Anita replied quickly. "You're my father's solicitor, and you know every detail about his dealings." Then she flashed a coquettish smile at Diego, and grabbed both of his hands. "Tell me, Diego."

"Can you keep a secret?"

"Of course I can."

Diego hesitated again, but desirous of currying Anita's favor, he went against his better judgment and freely divulged everything he knew to Rodolfo's daughter. "Your father will evict Miguel Pítre off the farm. He has already found a new tenant for the property who will be moving in by the end of the month. Your father is planning to…"

CHAPTER 53

Many miles away from San Sebastián, traveling mostly at night through the town of Toa Baja, Manolo and Berta kept vigilant for posses of overseers out looking for them. Although the two runaways kept up their rigid vigilance, there really was no need for it because there were many white creoles in their midst who offered them protection. The creoles were ardent abolitionists who formed a secret society three years ago shortly after hearing news that the American Civil War had ended and that slaves received their emancipation. They created an underground highway, with many safe houses along the way, a freedom road that led them through the town San Sebastián and ended at the port of Guánica.

Cirilo moved along the long procession of runaways, toward the head of the column, where Berta and Manolo followed Don Justicio Serrano. "Don Serrano, we're approaching Don Miranda's house," said Cirilo cutting in front of Manolo and Berta.

"Good," replied Serrano smiling out of relief. "In about an hour the sun will rise, so we will stay at Don Miranda's farm and sleep during the day." He turned to face Manolo and Berta. "You will like Don Miranda; he's a muláto but he looks more like a creole hacendado. He's a compassionate and most generous human being."

"How long do you think it will take for us to reach Guánica?" Manolo asked innocently.

Cirilo, holding his torch up to illuminate his immediate area, turned to Don Serrano with a look of uncertainty. Don Serrano sighed. "I really don't know. I can only take you as far as Don Miranda's farm. From there, one of Miranda's men will guide you to your next stop." Serrano was quick to notice the apprehension and fear that suddenly surfaced on the faces of both Berta and Manolo. "Please, do not be afraid. We have successfully guided many runaways through this underground highway and not once has it been discovered by the Spanish authorities."

Feeling more reassured, Manolo nodded. "I just want to thank you, Don Serrano, and you, too, señor Cirilo. No one has ever shown us such kindness. My sister and I will never forget you."

"No need for thanks because you and every person in Puerto Rico ought to be free," Serrano replied quickly. "Now what I want is for you and your sister to find a spot in that red barn over there and get as much sleep as you can. The next leg of your journey is approximately two miles and you will be traveling through dense vegetation, probably the worst on the island. It will take you all night to reach señora Claudia de Sotomayor's hacienda in Dorado. From there you will travel through the towns of Vega Alta and Manatí, where you will stay at Pedro Caban's farm. From Manatí, you will travel west through Barceloneta and stay in a vacant house in Arecibo. Then you will travel westward again through Hatillo and Camuy, and stay at Fausto Cruz's house in Quebradillas. From Quebradillas you will turn south and pass through the town of San Sebastián. You will stay at Don Blanco's farm there, and then head down to the southern coastline, toward the port of Guánica. As you can see, this is only the beginning of your freedom odyssey. You must be brave and alert and you must listen to every guide assigned to you along the way."

CHAPTER 54

Diego Redondo could not hide his fears as he drew closer to the Hernández hacienda, but he had promised to escort Anita all the way there. As a gentleman, he had to keep his promise. But Anita sensed fear in him, the same type of fear the slaves back in San Juan exuded in the presence of Rodolfo Hernández. Moments before walking into the pathway leading to the house, she stopped abruptly to face her escort. "Thank you, Diego, for escorting me. I know that my father will get terribly upset if he sees you with me, so I won't ask you to take me all the way to the house."

"Your father can be a very difficult man at times, Ana."

"My father is a difficult man all the time, Diego, please don't make him out to be anything different; I'm not one of his cronies."

Diego laughed boisterously, truly enjoying Anita's candor. "You are right, señorita. Your father is a bastard!" This time Anita burst out in laughter. After several moments of laughter at Rodolfo's expense, Diego's mirthful face changed to show his true emotions. "It was nice to be in your company, and I would like to see you again, if you wouldn't mind."

Anita said nothing at first, but when she saw the sincerity in Diego's eyes, she could not bring herself to deny his wish. "Certainly, Diego, but we must be careful."

Diego Redondo began to feel butterflies in his stomach, as if he were a child expecting a toy from his parents. He reached out, grabbed Anita's hands, brought them to his lips and kissed them. After kissing Anita's hands, he smiled. "Buenas Tardes, señorita." Diego then mounted his horse and swiftly faded into the woods.

As she watched Diego's fading image, Anita chuckled, and muttered to herself. "Señor Diego y la señora Anita Redondo—I wonder how father would feel about *that*!"

Anita quickly climbed the stairs and rushed into Rosalía's bedroom. Rosalía remained mostly in bed the past few weeks, still nursing her badly bruised ribs, and still feeling the tips of her father's boots on her delicate, supple body. Rosalía had been awake when she felt Anita plopping herself on the bed and raising her eyebrows at her younger sister. "I went into town today, and I'm afraid I have very bad news."

Rosalía quickly sat up, ignoring a sudden rush of pain. She faced her sister eye to eye. "Is it about Miguel?"

Anita nodded. "Don Juan Pítre died yesterday, and Miguel took his body into town for burial this morning."

Rosalía shook her head. "Juan didn't appear sick to me and even Miguel didn't seem too concerned about his father's health, or else he would have mentioned it to me. What could have sickened him so much to have died so early in life, Ana? Are you sure about this?" Rosalía watched her sister nod at her with certainty in her eyes. "Poor Miguelito—he lost Carlos and now he has lost his father. He must be devastated."

"From where I was standing, he looked awful, Rosa, but that's not the worst of it, I'm afraid. I met Diego Redondo after the burial."

"Father's solicitor?" Rosalía asked curiously.

"Yes, he's quite handsome, don't you think?"

"Ana, don't be fooled by good looks. Diego works for Father, and you know that anyone who works for Father cannot be trusted."

Anita sighed deeply and dipped an eyebrow in annoyance. "Are you going to lecture me again?"

"No. Did Diego say anything to you?"

"Yes. He told me that Father intends to evict Miguel Pítre from the farm. He's not only going to chase him off the farm but—" Anita stopped herself when she noticed Rosalía's eyes watering with tears. "There, there now, Rosa, I'm sure Miguel's all right."

"No he's not, Ana," replied Rosalía in between sobs. "And it's all Father's fault. Heaven only knows where he is right now. I wish I could go to him and comfort him at this terrible hour in his life."

Anita squinted at Rosalía and finally saw something in her younger sister that she had never before known or experienced: love. Anita saw how much her younger sister was truly, genuinely and absolutely in love with Miguel. It was not only the tears forming in her eyes and dripping down her cheeks, but the expression on her face, too. Sitting across from Rosalía, Anita could feel the depth of Rosalía's emotion by simply looking at her melancholy blue eyes, but it was the profound wailing that told her just how much Rosalía loved Miguel. At that very moment, Anita coveted those emotions, and wondered at the same time why she never experienced those feelings in the presence of Ruben De La Cruz. She knew right then, that she was never in love with Ruben, and that all she wanted Ruben for was to get away from the house just like Rosalía said. Now, more than ever, she wanted to experience what love felt like, and something about Diego had sparked that curiosity.

Anita took Rosalía into her arms and stroked her back consolingly. "You poor thing, Rosa, you're so much in love." Rosalía found solace in Anita's arms but kept crying. "Is there anything I could do for you?"

Rosalía forced herself out of Anita's arms and quickly brought her fists to her eyes to clear the tears away. "Yes," she replied. "I need to know that Miguel is all right. I'm going to write a letter to him, and when you get an opportunity to go into town again, I want you to find him and deliver my letter to him. Can you do that for me, Ana?"

Anita sighed again, realizing the danger in fulfilling Rosalía's task, but she understood how deeply Rosalía felt about Miguel and that was the only reason why she nodded to show her compliance. "All right, Rosa. I will do it."

CHAPTER 55

On the morning of Friday, May 15, Rodolfo had left the house at seven o'clock with plans of reaching Camuy by early afternoon. Rodolfo was going to meet with Ignacio De La Torre and Francisco Frontera to discuss the investment in Marquez & Co. He brought along ten thousand pesos just in case De La Torre backed out of the proposed investment. Knowing the Marquez brothers to be successful men in the export business, Rodolfo realized a good opportunity had presented itself. He would not come back to San Sebastián without a firm agreement in his pocket. To solidify his negotiations, he decided to retain the services of a local solicitor in Camuy rather than the services of Diego Redondo, whom he deemed to be inept and lacking in business savvy.

Rodolfo's plans to travel to Camuy gave Anita the opportunity she had been waiting for, and she wasted no time in going about her business. As soon as her father cleared the pathway, heading north to Camuy, Anita dressed herself, took the letter from Rosalía and rushed down the stairs. She was able to convince Candelario to take her into town before her mother and Laura woke that morning. Rosalía was the only other person awake that morning, and she watched with hopeful eyes as Anita entered the coach. Moments later, the coach turned onto the dirt road outside the house and headed straight for San Sebastián.

Candelario drove the team of horses with a great deal of care. He was not only watching out for their only means of transportation but he was keeping vigilant for anyone that might present a threat to one of Rodolfo Hernández's daughters. He knew that by driving señorita Ana into town, he was already disobeying his master, but he also knew the importance of Ana's visit. Peninsular families had the habit of talking in front of their slaves as if they were part of the furniture. Perhaps that is why the previous day when Rosalía and Anita talked about Miguel's father and of the plans to deliver a letter to Miguel, they never noticed Candelario sweeping the floor outside the bedroom, nor bothered to close the door for privacy. They also were unaware that Candelario and his brother, Agustín, were secretly rooting for Rosalía, whom they liked most of all.

Candelario reached San Sebastián by nine-thirty that morning, and before he was able to stop the coach, Anita had already opened the door. When the coach finally stopped in front of Don Emilio Pagan's restaurant, Anita stepped out and looked up at Candelario. "Please wait right here until I return." She spun around and headed up the dirt street in search of Miguel Pítre. As she navigated the street, she asked people where Miguel Pítre was but no one responded to her. The creoles of San Sebastián knew exactly who Anita was, and wisely avoided her.

Undaunted, Anita ventured into the plaza and inquired about Miguel from several men sitting on park benches. None of them knew where Miguel Pítre was. Next, Anita decided to go to the market to see if Miguel was there selling fruits at his stand. She stopped at every stand but she did not see Miguel anywhere in the busy market.

As Anita headed for Ramirez's colmado at the end of the street, she felt someone tapping her shoulders. When she turned around, her eyes confronted the handsome Don Diego Redondo. "I heard you were looking for Miguel Pítre, is that right?"

Anita flashed a warm smile. "Diego! How are you?"

"Good, Ana, now that your image has graced my eyes," Diego replied while removing his top hat. He took comfort in seeing Anita smiling back at him. "So are you or are you not looking for Miguel Pítre?"

"Yes, Diego, I am. I've asked around but everyone seems to be afraid of talking to me."

"They don't trust you because you are Rodolfo Hernández's daughter."

"That's not fair, Diego, I am not my father," replied Anita defensively.

"It doesn't matter, you're still a peninsular."

"So what I am I going to do now? I need to find Miguel."

"You haven't asked me, now have you?" Diego said grinning.

"You know where he is?"

"Yes, but is it you that wants to see Miguel, or are you seeing him on behalf of your sister?"

All of a sudden, Anita's pleasant demeanor changed to show sudden concern. "Why did you ask me that, Diego? Do you know about Rosalía and Miguel?"

"Who doesn't Ana? It's the center of conversation here, in San Sebastián. I've heard about Rodolfo's methods of punishment, and I do not want you to get into trouble. I can deliver a message to him, if you like."

Anita thought about Diego's suggestion, but then she remembered Rosalía's warnings about Rodolfo's solicitor and quickly shook her head. "No, Diego. This is something I must do personally. Do you know where Miguel is right now?"

"Yes. He is staying at his great uncle's house a few miles from here. Let me take you there, at least you'll be safe in my company."

Anita's lips stretched with a wide smile. "All right."

Diego escorted Anita to his horse and helped her mount. Seconds later, Candelario, while feeding the horses some grain, watched Diego and Anita take off for the woods. He shook his head in disappointment as he kept his untrusting eyes focused on Hernández's lawyer.

About an hour later, Diego and Anita reached a small parcel of land filled with all sorts of plants. As they made their way toward the farmhouse, Anita looked across the field and recognized sprouting bean plants, yucca, batata and other vegetables. Diego dismounted first and then helped Anita off the horse. They walked slowly toward the house, where Juan's great uncle, Mateo Ramirez, immediately confronted them. "Buenos Dias," he said politely.

"Buenos Dias," replied Diego. "We are looking for Miguel Pítre."

"And you are?"

"My name is Diego Redondo and this is la señorita Anita Hernández."

The old man turned slowly to Anita and with a smug look said, "Are you Rodolfo Hernández's daughter?"

"Yes," replied Anita nervously, but before she could say another word, the old man put his hands to his mouth and called out for Miguel several times. Miguel, who was crouching somewhere inside the field inspecting several plants, suddenly stood up to acknowledge his great uncle. From where she stood in front of the house, Anita could only see Miguel's straw pava and white shirt, but she was certain the figure in the field was that of Miguel's.

Miguel slowly approached the visitors but could not hide the sudden feeling of mistrust when his eyes captured Diego Redondo's image, standing tall and confidently. When Miguel finally reached the front of the house, he removed his pava and looked straight into Anita's brown eyes. "Señorita Anita," he said, smiling. He looked at Diego and merely nodded. "Señor Redondo." Miguel brushed the sweat off his forehead with the back of his hand and turned to face Anita. "To what do I owe this visit?"

"I am here to deliver a letter to you," said Anita with a sense of relief, handing over the folded letter to Miguel.

Miguel took the letter and stepped a few paces away from Anita so that he could read it in private. He read the letter slowly, pacing further away from Anita. Then he stopped and read the letter again. Dying with curiosity, Diego studied Miguel's face. Unable to control himself, he walked over to Miguel and said, "Who's the letter from, Miguel? What does it say?" Feeling uneasy around Diego, Miguel wondered why the solicitor had been so interested in knowing the contents of the letter. It was not only rude of Diego but intrusive, as well. The only reason why Diego wanted to know about the letter was so that he could tell Rodolfo. Miguel always had his suspicions about Redondo, but now he felt very sure about Diego's intentions. "Señor Redondo, you are a fellow member of Porvenir but that does not grant you the right to poke your nose into my business. This is a private letter and its contents written for my eyes only. Now, if you would be kind enough to separate yourself from me, I would like to have a word with señorita Anita."

Redondo turned his back on Miguel, unable to suppress the embarrassment at Miguel's outright dismissal. He walked back to Anita. "He wants to speak with you."

When Anita confronted Miguel, she could see the sorrow that still lingered in his eyes, like a bad odor in the air. "Anita, tell Rosa that I miss her, too. Tell her that I think about her day and night, and that I long to see her again. Please tell her that I love her, can you do that for me?"

"So you've changed your mind then? Didn't you ask her to forget about you and that she should find another man?"

Miguel took in a deep breath and exhaled slowly, "I didn't believe that when I said it then, and I don't believe it now. I never changed my mind. I love her, Anita, truly I do."

Anita's eyes began to water with tears, and as she looked deeply into Miguel's eyes, she nodded. "Then I will tell her word for word."

"Thank you. Please tell her that I am all right and that I am living with my great uncle. Tell her that I want to see her again and that I wait for her arrival here."

"But Miguel, I don't know where this place is. How can I tell her where you are, how can she find you?"

"I will tell the people in town that Rosalía will come looking for me. Someone will take her to me."

"And then what? Are you two going to leave San Sebastián? Will you marry my sister? Where will you go? How will you live?"

Miguel held a firm grip on his straw pava, unsure of what to say. "I really don't know, Anita, I just know that I want her by my side, now more than ever."

Anita reached for Miguel's hand and held it tightly. "You are truly in love with her, aren't you?"

"With all of my heart, Anita; I cannot think of anything else."

Anita sighed, but it was out of happiness for her sister. "All right, I will tell her everything, I promise."

Miguel finally smiled. Then he leaned forward and planted a kiss on Anita's cheek. "Deliver that kiss to her, too. Thank you for your kindness."

Diego and Anita remained silent for most of their trip back into town. When Anita caught up to Candelario, she told him to return to the hacienda because she would ride back with Diego Redondo. Although Candelario agreed to return alone, he felt uncertain about leaving Anita in the company of a man he also distrusted. Since there was nothing Candelario could do about it, he returned home reluctantly.

On the final leg of their journey back to the Hernández estate, Diego and Anita decided to walk the rest of the way. As they walked along the dirt road, Diego Redondo's mind swirled with many protracted scenarios confronting Rodolfo about Anita. There was no doubt in his mind that he was attracted to Anita. She was very pretty, he thought, and he liked her personality, too. But, at the same time, he thought about Rodolfo Hernández's wrath and of his ideal choice for Anita's husband. It certainly would not be a local solicitor from San Sebastián, much less a creole. Rodolfo's high expectations centered on a member of the social elite, a son of a peninsular family with lots of money, and a husband that would have his stamp of approval like a Papal bull from the Vatican.

Anita chose to remain silent but she, too, felt curious. She wondered if the strange emotions she had felt for Diego the first time she spoke to him were the first glimpses into the world of love. She could not deny the fact either that she also felt attracted to Diego. The only thing that marred those new feelings was the distrustful look on Miguel's face when he and Diego talked. Since Miguel and Rosalía did not trust Diego, she could not trust him either, or even allow herself to fall in love with him, if that's what she was starting to feel.

"So, what was all that secret talk about?" Diego finally broke the long silence.

Anita turned to look up at Diego. "It was the last communication between my sister and Miguel. It would seem that Miguel has met and fallen in love with another woman. He no longer wants to know about Rosa."

Diego kept his silence. Though he wanted to believe Anita, he knew just how powerful love could be, and by the look in Miguel's eyes, he felt there was no truth to Anita's words. "Won't that message devastate your sister?"

"It'll crush her heart, break it into tiny pieces. But my sister is strong of character, and like every miserable episode in her life, she will survive this too."

Diego Redondo said nothing more and watched Anita as she made her way along the pathway to her house. He bid her farewell from afar. In his solitude, Diego would reflect on his actions thus far, and measure them against the new emotions he was feeling for Anita. Would he do the right thing for once in his life? What was the right thing anyway? Why was there a need in him to measure himself constantly against peninsulares? The innate desire of fitting in, of becoming a member of the elite had consumed him all of his life, forcing him to become something that he really did not want to become now. Was it too late to correct himself? Diego Redondo was at a crossroad in his life and he would have to think hard about what he was going to do from that moment on.

Anita Hernández entered the hacienda through the front doors, where she saw her mother, standing in the kitchen with arms folded, as if expecting an explanation. There was a sense of dread in her eyes, as if she knew Anita had been doing something her father would not approve. "Where have you been all day, Ana?" Maria demanded.

"I took a very long walk, Mother. Why do you ask, is that against Father's orders, too?"

All of a sudden, Laura entered the kitchen and said, "Who was that man?"

"Yes, who was he?" Maria added.

Anita walked into the parlor and sat on the wicker couch. Maria and Laura followed Anita into the parlor and stood in front of her with expectant looks. Anita sighed, realizing they were not going away without a response. She finally answered them. "Well if you must know, that gentleman was Diego Redondo. I was on my way back to the house when I saw him coming up the road from San Sebastián. Señor Redondo came looking for Father, but I told him that Father had left for Camuy early this morning."

"So why were you smiling so much?" Laura pressed. "What? Have you forgotten about Ruben De La Cruz already?"

Anita turned to her older sister, and with scornful eyes replied, "I'm not going to dignify that with a response, you cunt!"

"All right!" said Maria, turning to face Laura. "Enough! Laura, go back and finish your letter to Gregorio."

After Laura's departure, Maria turned her attention to Anita. "I saw the same thing, Ana. Is there anything going on between you and señor Redondo that your father and I should be aware of? Be careful Ana. Remember what Rosa's going through right now. Besides, you are practically engaged to Ruben De La Cruz, and he comes from a very good family. Your father will be greatly disappointed if you—"

"Father, Father, Father!" Anita spat out in fury. "It's always about pleasing Father, isn't it? What about my feelings, Mother? Don't they count, too?"

Maria's face contorted to express her sympathy, and with a motherly smile, she sat next to Anita. "Of course they count. For all you know, Ruben could very well be on his way here, you even said that yourself."

"Oh Mother, I didn't believe that when I said it. I just wanted to get Father off my back. The fact of the matter is that I have not seen Ruben in over a year, and he has written me only three letters in all that time."

Maria put her arm over Anita and spoke passively. "Be patient, Ana, you'll see that Ruben will come to the house and he will ask for your hand in marriage."

Anita did not turn to face her mother, but stared aimlessly at the floor. "If that were only true, Mother."

Maria rose to her feet and looked down at Anita. "I will go to Church on Sunday, and I will pray for you and Ruben. I will ask Monsignor Velez for a special prayer, too."

Anita watched her mother leave the parlor and then waited several more minutes before rushing up the stairs. She knocked hard on Rosalía's bedroom door and waited, but Rosalía took her time to rise from her bed. The right side of her rib cage did not hurt as much, and she was breathing a lot better today than yesterday, but, still, she could not rid herself of the lethargy that clung to her body like leeches in a swamp. When she finally opened the door, she confronted Anita's brown eyes, glinting out of excitement. Anita entered the room and quickly closed the door. "I found him, Rosa! I found Miguel!"

"I knew you would!" replied Rosalía, equally excited. "What did he say?" The two young women sat on the edge of the bed.

"Miguel said he that misses you, too, and that he loves you very much," answered Anita. Then she leaned forward and planted a kiss on Rosalía's cheek. "He told me to give you that kiss for him."

Rosalía smiled with satisfaction, as if it were Miguel himself who had kissed her, as if the kiss were the final token of his love for her. She gave Anita a curious look. "What else did he say?"

"He wants to see you, Rosa. He wants you to go to him."

"He did? So where is he? How can I find him?"

"He has taken up residence in his great uncle's farm a few miles west of San Sebastián proper," replied Anita. Then she frowned, "But, frankly, I don't know how to get there."

"What do you mean, Ana? You don't remember how you got there?"

"Well, no. It was Diego Redondo who took me to see Miguel."

"Oh no Ana, why did you have to ask *him*, why couldn't you find someone else?"

"Because he was the only person willing to help me and because no one in town would speak to me. You know, your little task was very difficult to accomplish, Rosa."

"I'm sorry, and I do thank you for the favor, but can you trust señor Redondo?"

"I believe I can."

"I wish you could have paid attention to the road as señor Redondo took you there," pondered Rosalía with a sense of nervous excitement.

"It doesn't matter, Rosa. Miguel said that all you would have to do is go into town and ask for him. He said that he would tell the townsfolk that you would be coming into town to see him and that any one of them should take you to his great uncle's farm."

"Clever," muttered Rosalía underneath her breath. She took her eyes away from Anita's face and thought deeply and carefully for a few seconds. Then, she quickly rose to her feet and with a grand smile said, "I will go to him tonight."

"No Rosa, not even I would do that; it's far too dangerous."

"But you said the townspeople would—"

"I know what I said, but I thought you would go to him in the daytime when Father would be away on business, not now, not when Father's about to return home. Believe me, Rosa, he won't be as forgiving as last time, and you know what happened to you last time, don't you?"

"He hasn't spoken to me in three weeks, and he hasn't come to see me, either. What makes you think he will want to see me tonight?"

"Rosa, Rosa, if you were a man, I'd say you have big cojónes. You've tempted that hat of fate enough times, already, and Father may reach a point where he might do serious harm to you. So think really hard about what you're going to do."

Rosalía walked slowly to her bedroom window and watched the sunlight as it began to fade into dusk. Neither she nor Anita said a word for a long moment. Then, Rosalía suddenly turned around to face Anita. "If anyone should come to see me, you must say that I was very fatigued and went to bed early tonight."

"That includes Father?"

"I'm not worried about Father, because he's too damn proud to come see me. I am not worried about Mother, either, because you can handle her, too. The only person I worry about is that bitch, Laura. She must not know anything about this, Ana, I'm depending on you."

Anita sighed heavily. "All right, Rosa, I'll do it for you. I will do it for the sake of your love for Miguel. Just be careful."

Rodolfo Hernández arrived at eight-fifteen that evening, and just like Rosalía predicted, he ate dinner by himself and had one drink of rum before retiring for the night. Rodolfo had been sleeping in one of the spare bedrooms ever since recovering from Maria's blow to the head. He had not spoken to any member of his family for weeks and his reclusive behavior did not seem to bother him or his daughters in the least.

Rosalía waited until nine-thirty that evening before boldly stepping out of the house. As she walked toward the stalls, she confronted a wide-eyed Agustín, who had raised his gas lantern high enough to see the figure standing before him. "Señorita Rosa, what are you doing outside the house so late in the evening?" All of a sudden, Candelario appeared from behind Agustín, holding a gas lantern himself.

"Agustín, Candelario, please go back to your quarters. I do not want to cause the two of you any trouble with my father. Please go back. You never saw me tonight."

"Señorita Rosa," said Candelario, stepping in front of his younger brother. "You must think we are blind and deaf, but we're not. We are very much aware of what you are going through with your father, and we pray to God for your protection. We knew Carlos Peña well, and we know he never laid a hand on you. You know that, too. You have been very kind to me and to Agustín. You have been very kind to our younger brother and sister, Manolo and Berta, and to our beloved Mamíta. We cannot allow you to go into town all by yourself."

"What will you do, call out for my father?"

By the light of the gas lantern, Rosalía could see Candelario smiling, white teeth glimmering. "No señorita, you know I would never do that. I will escort you into town."

"No, Candelario, I will not bring you into this. If my father finds out that you helped me in any way, he will beat you. Or worse, he will hang you."

Candelario turned to his brother. "Go get the horses and keep them quiet"

"Candelario you shouldn't do this," warned Rosalía.

"It's done, señorita, I will accompany you into town."

CHAPTER 56

Candelario and Rosalía arrived in San Sebastián at around ten thirty that night, and found many creoles still awake and walking about town. All commerce had shut down for the night except for the creoles' local bar, a tiny joint that easily filled with but only two or three patrons.

"I will wait for you in front of this bar, señorita," Candelario promised while watching Rosalía dismount. "I will wait all night if I have to, even until sunrise."

"Thank you, Candelario. I will never forget your kind gesture."

As Rosalía walked slowly up the street, she could sense Candelario's watchful eyes, still making sure that she was safe. She reached a group of middle-aged men, sitting at a square table playing dominoes. A gas lantern, hanging from a wooden post, illuminated the playing area, where the men took turns slamming domino pieces onto the table with professional authority. Sensing Rosalía's presence, one of the men turned up to face her. "Señorita, isn't it very late for a young lady to be out and about on the streets of San Sebastián?"

"Si señor, very late, but I am looking for Miguel Pítre. Do you know where I can I find him?"

Another man slowly rose from his seat, and walked over to Rosalía. His long, white beard seemed to shine against the gas lantern's yellowish light. His bright red face stretched with a smile, and his hazel-colored eyes beamed a sense of knowledge. Though he stood just slightly above five feet, he commanded a sense of respect, dignity and benevolence all at the same time. "Come with me," he said softly.

Escorting Rosalía away from the table of dominoes, he whispered to her. "My name is Don Rafael Blanco. My farm sits next to what used to be the Pítre farm. I knew Miguel's father and I have seen Miguel grow from a skinny, little boy into a fine and robust young man. It is a pity to see what has happened to the Pítre family over the years, a travesty, really. Anyway, Miguel asked me to take you to him. Personally, I did not think you would come that soon. In fact, I wagered Miguel that you would never come to see him. He was so sure you would come, that he bet his uncle's house against my finca. It was too big a bet for me, senorita, but now, after seeing you tonight, I am glad I did not place that wager after all. You will need a horse, señorita."

Rosalía rushed down the street to where Candelario sat patiently. "I'm taking my horse with me."

Recognizing Don Blanco from where he was standing, Candelario nodded approvingly. Rosalía would be safe in Blanco's company.

Don Rafael Blanco held true to his word and brought Rosalía to Mateo Ramirez's farm at around eleven o'clock. Rafael Blanco remained atop his horse and pointed with his index finger at a dot of light about one hundred yards away. "Miguel is there, señorita, he waits for you."

Guided by the flickering light of a gas lantern posted in the porch, Rosalía rode her horse all the way to the house. Her heart began to rattle, and she felt weakened by her anxieties. She dismounted quickly, and nervously walked toward the front door. Rosalía raised her right arm but before she could knock, the door opened to reveal the hopeful face of Miguel Pítre, holding a gas lantern to his face so that Rosalía could recognize him. "Rosa!" he said with great deal of relief. "I knew you'd come!" Miguel stepped outside, placed the lantern on the porch floor, and embraced Rosalía, scooping her off her feet. They kissed passionately for several minutes, wrapped in each other's arms. "Rosa, my love!" said Miguel in between kisses.

After their long kiss, Miguel stood back and took a few moments just to contemplate her beautiful face. Rosalía's eyes began to water with tears, but before she could say anything to Miguel, her lover raised his index finger to his mouth and said, "Shh, don't say a word my love." He picked up the lantern with one hand, and with the other hand grabbed hold of Rosalía's hand. He took her to the back of the house, where an even smaller house stood.

"Where are you taking me, Miguel?" Rosalía asked, but by look on his face, she knew exactly what Miguel had in mind. In fact, she had rather hoped it would come to that.

"This old house used to serve as slave quarters, Rosa. It can barely house two people. Can you imagine twenty slaves crammed into this little shack? That was nearly fifty years ago, when the ruthless Delgado family owned nearly all of these lands. My mother's uncle bought these few cuerdas from the Delgado family and when they left, they took all of their slaves with them."

"What happened to the slaves?" Rosalía asked sympathetically.

"I don't know," replied Miguel pensively. He quickly changed his somber countenance, and grabbed hold of Rosalía's hand again. The shack's entrance had a rickety, uneven door, which was a rarity in houses for that region of Puerto Rico, but which proved to be ideal for their needs that night. Miguel pushed the front door in and quickly entered the one-room house. The only furniture Rosalía could see was a bed neatly covered with fresh sheets. Rosalía followed Miguel into the house and waited for him to latch the door shut. Miguel placed the gas lantern down on the wooden floor, and then he took another moment to gaze into Rosalía's deep blue eyes. "I love you, Rosalía Hernández, with all of my heart."

"And I love you, Miguel Pítre, with all of my heart."

They kissed again for several minutes. As Rosalía's heart pounded with excitement, she felt Miguel's rough hands on her back, trying to unbutton her dress. After several moments, she felt the back of her dress begin to loosen. Very slowly, Miguel pulled the sleeves down, exposing Rosalía's milky-white shoulders. He gently kissed her neck and chest while slowly pulling down her dress. Rosalía could hear herself breathing heavily with passion. She tried desperately to mute her moans but found very early on that she would lose that battle. She wanted this to happen. She yearned to be held in Miguel's arms, and she wanted to surrender her virginity to the man she would love for the rest of her life. Her dress fell down to her feet, and Miguel quickly noticed she wasn't wearing a petticoat or corset. By the soft, flickering light of the gas lantern, which sat innocently on the floor as an inanimate witness to their love, Miguel gazed at Rosalía's breasts—pink nipples hardened and goose bumps covering the smooth, creamy white skin of her chest. He kissed her passionately from her neck down to her chest and further down to her breasts. He kissed her nipples and suckled them with care, as if not wanting to hurt her. In every way, Miguel was as gentle to her as the mountain winds of San Sebastián. He fell to his knees and kissed her belly, sticking his tongue into her navel. The more Miguel kissed her body, the more heavily Rosalía breathed. Rosalía placed her two hands on Miguel's head as he kissed her, her mind and body experiencing the art of love for the very first time.

Miguel continued to kiss her belly, holding Rosalía by her hips. He moved lower and kissed her thighs. Rosalía wanted to scream! What was Miguel going to do now? Miguel tilted his head and began to please the young woman orally.

Writhing in ecstasy, Rosalía could not hold back her voice, and she began to moan aloud. Miguel rose to his feet, unbuttoned his shirt and removed his trousers, exposing his hardened member to a woman for the first time in his life. He walked toward the gas lantern and turned the fire off. Then, in the darkness of night, he reached out with his hands until he felt Rosalía's trembling body. He walked her to the bed and made love to her for the next few hours.

CHAPTER 57

As the sun began to rise the next morning, Candelario, who was slumped against a wooden post, suddenly awoke to the drone of galloping horses. He rubbed and cleared his foggy eyes from sleep and was able to see Rosalía. He saw, too, that Miguel Pítre was riding along with her.

At six in the morning, the town of San Sebastián was devoid of people and seemed eerily quiet. Candelario had been the only person in town before the young couple's arrival. Rosalía gave Candelario an appreciative smile, as she slowed her horse. "Thank you so much, for waiting."

"You are very welcome, but I must urge you to leave immediately," Candelario replied hastily.

Rosalía nodded to agree with Candelario, and then turned to face Miguel. "When will I see you again, Miguelito?"

"You will see me soon, my love, very soon. In a few days, I will be making plans to leave San Sebastián for good. I am planning to travel to New York City and I want you to come with me. You know that neither of our worlds will ever accept us, so let us go to a place where nobody knows who we are. We can start our lives there and have our children there, too. We could learn to speak English in a few years and do things in the United States that we never did before. I had no plans on leaving Puerto Rico, this is my homeland, and where part of my heart will always remain. But my heart is with you, too, and I love you too much to forget you."

"Stop Miguelito, please don't say anymore. I will go with you. I will go wherever you go!"

"All right, Rosa. I will contact you within a few weeks with details of our voyage to America." Miguel faced Candelario and smiled at him. "We missed your presence at the meeting the other night, señor."

Candelario turned to face Rosalía and flashed an embarrassing smile at her. "So now you know about me, señorita."

"We all have secrets, Candelario, don't we? If you won't say anything about me, I won't say anything about you, agreed?"

Candelario nodded. "We must leave now, señorita Rosa."

Miguel nodded. "He's right, Rosa." He leaned forward and kissed Rosalía on her lips. "Go."

Rosalía spurred her horse and took off into the woods. As Rosalía's horse galloped away, Candelario gazed at Miguel. "She is a very good woman, so please don't cause her any pain."

"I would rather die than cause her any pain, señor Candelario."

Candelario and Rosalía arrived back at the Hernández hacienda around seven in the morning and took comfort in the fact that everyone was still asleep. The elder slave took the reins of Rosalía's horse before taking a brief moment to speak to her. "Señorita, I know it is not my place to tell you this, but are you sure that you want to go through with your plans? You know your father, and you know that he will never allow you to leave."

"It's all right, Candelario, you can speak freely. I know my father, and that is *why* I must leave with Miguel. He will never accept Miguel as a son-in-law and if Miguel tries to marry me, I know my father is capable of having him murdered. When the time comes, you must help me. Will you?"

"I promise I will help you, señorita." He glanced at the front doors of the hacienda, and then looked at Rosalía. "Will you be entering the house through the backside?"

"Yes."

"That trestle below your window looks difficult to climb, can you manage it?"

"I think so, but I may need help."

"Then wait until I put the horses back in the stable. I will come around to help you."

No sooner had Rosalía climbed through her open bedroom window, than her father had risen. She could hear his heavy footsteps as they pounded the hallway floor. Then, shortly after Rosalía jumped into bed, the sound of Rodolfo's feet suddenly vanished. She could see a shadow in the space between the bottom of the door and the floor of her bedroom, and knew that her father had stopped in front of her door. Rosalía quickly turned in her bed, making the sound of rustling sheets loud enough for her father to hear. Then she snorted a little to convince her father that she was in her room sleeping. Satisfied, Rodolfo ran his hands through his mussed up hair and walked down the stairs. Now that Rosalía felt certain her father was no longer present, she breathed a sigh of relief. She jumped out of bed and removed her dress. As she put on her nightgown, her small lips stretched with a pleasant smile. Despite the fact that she had not slept at all the previous night, her smile still complemented the exquisite features of her youthful face. Miguel had made love to her and she had made love to him. It was the best thing she had ever experienced in her life and she wanted to do it again. Rosalía crept into her blankets and closed her eyes with a smile.

CHAPTER 58

At around half past twelve noon, Rodolfo sat out in the front porch of his house, waiting for his solicitor—a look of impatience permeating his eyes. He had eaten breakfast by himself in the kitchen, and he felt certain he would not see any member of his family that day. Well maybe one, he thought, maybe Laura would come out to see him. If he had to make a choice, it would have been Laura.

Rodolfo quickly dispensed with family matters at the first sound of thumping hooves. He stood up, and while walking toward the edge of the porch, he shouted. "You're late, Redondo!"

Diego Redondo kept silent as he dismounted. He tethered his horse to the post outside the house and walked over to his master. "Buenos Dias, señor Hernández."

"Well? Do you have any news for me?" Rodolfo said impatiently.

"Yes. I met one of your daughters in town yesterday."

"Which one?"

"I believe it was the middle one."

"You mean Anita? What was she doing in town? I thought I gave them explicit orders not to go into town. Do you see, Diego? Do you see that despite my orders, they still fucking disobey me? Am I wrong to punish them? When you have children, Diego, you will see what I'm talking about—trust me. So what was she doing in San Sebastián?"

"Señor, I know this is none of my business, but I urge you not to punish your daughter."

"You're right, Diego, it's none of your business. So why do you wish that?" Rodolfo's skeptical eyes seemed to penetrate Diego's heart; and Diego could feel Rodolfo probing his mind with those evil brown eyes.

"Because, señor, you could use Anita to obtain more intelligence on Porvenir."

"You mean more than the usual bullshit you bring to me?"

Diego immediately resented that remark, and he wondered why he gave Hernández the liberty for such disrespect. "Yes," he said reluctantly.

"So what was she doing in town?"

"She wanted to deliver a letter to Miguel Pítre on behalf of Rosalía."

All of a sudden, Rodolfo transformed his nearly calm demeanor into his usual hideousness. His eyes bulged, and the tone of his skin quickly flushed with ire. "I knew it! That little bitch is still seeing that peasant!"

"Wait, Don Hernández," said Redondo holding both arms up in a halting gesture. He walked closer to Rodolfo, brought his arms down and nearly whispered to him. "It's not what you think." Diego told Rodolfo everything that happened the previous day.

Rodolfo calmed down considerably after hearing Diego's story. "So he told her he didn't want to see her again, that's good. He has more sense than his father ever did, I'll tell you that. And it didn't even cost me one centavo, too! To think, that I actually offered to buy him off; what a mistake *that* would have been!" Rodolfo beamed a conquering smile at Diego, believing in his heart that Miguel had feared his warnings and had decided to stop seeing his daughter. This was his moment of victory, his moment to reap the benefits of his status among the peasants of San Sebastián.

Unbeknownst to Rodolfo, this was a moment for Diego Redondo, too. Diego knew the time was coming, and it was here now. His life, his mind and his future had reached a crossroad, a fork in the road he had been dreading for some time. Which road would he take? Would he choose to take the easy road, where he would tell Rodolfo that Anita was lying to him about Miguel's secret message, or would he let Rodolfo continue believing that Miguel actually told Rosalía he didn't want to see her again?

Rodolfo stood laughing quietly, gloating over his victory with a sense of cheer that Diego had never before seen on his master's otherwise unpleasant face. In an instant, Rodolfo's eyes narrowed at Diego. "Is there anything else?"

Diego said nothing during those brief moments of decision-making. He kept his eyes trained on Rodolfo, aware that his employer despised all creoles and would never consider them his equals, even if they were lawyers. To Rodolfo, Diego Redondo was merely a servant that he could mistreat at his whim.

Rodolfo took two steps down from the porch and walked as close to Diego as possible. He looked into Diego's eyes, and with a powerful voice said, "Is there anything else?"

Diego Redondo looked right back into Rodolfo's eyes and replied evenly. "No, señor Hernández, there's nothing else."

"Then perhaps you may be right," added Rodolfo Hernández. "I should not punish my daughters. Instead, I want you to keep watching them, as well as all of the members of Porvenir. Hey Diego, you've finally done something right!" Rodolfo reached into his vest pocket and pulled out a gold coin. Then he flipped the coin at Diego, who caught it mid air. "Here's a little bonus for you. Use it to get a haircut!"

Diego Redondo held the gold coin tightly with anger. Rodolfo had tossed a coin at him as if he'd been a beggar in the street. It was hard for Diego to imagine Rodolfo's simple reasoning, for in his master's mind there was no distinction between a beggar in the street and a creole lawyer from San Sebastián. As Rodolfo turned back toward the front porch, Diego stood there, seething in anger, reeling from his master's actions. Diego remounted and slowly made his way out onto the dirt road. He rode his steed for several yards still fuming with anger. All of sudden, he brought his arm all the way back and flung the gold coin deep into the woods. "You piece of shit!"

CHAPTER 59

Rosalía had slept all morning and into the early afternoon, and had it not been for the annoying cackle of a large, colorful macaw, she might well have slept through the evening. The macaw was perched on the windowsill, but at the sound of Rosalía's rustling bed sheets, it took off into the air and soared majestically above the trees.

Rosalía watched the turquoise-feathered bird as it flew into the nearby trees, rattling its afternoon message. She rose out of bed with a pleasant smile, the memories of last night's events still fresh in her mind. She walked to a basin that sat on top of her dresser and washed her face. She dressed, walked downstairs and found her mother and her sisters sitting at the kitchen table, eating their midday meal.

Laura was the first person to sense Rosalía's presence, and by the glare in her eyes, Rosalía braced herself for whatever would come out of her sister's wicked mind that early afternoon. Laura bent her head, stared down at her coffee cup and muttered. "Well, well, the princess has finally awakened." Rosalía ignored her, took her seat at the table, and flashed a smile. It was a kind of smile that Rosalía's family had never before seen on her face, a tranquil and sublime grin that could only have resulted from a night of ecstasy, a night of sexual discovery. There was no other reason to explain why she did not immediately react to Laura's comment.

"Buenos Dias, Rosa," said Anita, with a curious expression. Maria looked at Rosalía too and nodded at her, but her motherly eyes could not hide the fact that she knew her daughter had done something secretive last night. "Buenos Dias, Rosa," she said. "You must be famished. Do you want me to fix you something to eat?"

"Oh yes, Mother, and some coffee, too."

Realizing her father was still sitting outside in the porch and within earshot of the kitchen, Laura saw another opportunity and she wasted no time in taking advantage of it. "You slept very well, Rosa, so well that you didn't even hear the loud noises early this morning."

Anita looked across the table and fixed her sights on Laura, knowing all too well that her elder sister's only motive behind that seemingly benign comment was to draw Rosalía into more trouble. Maria stood and walked over to the cast–iron stove to retrieve the pot of coffee. As she poured coffee into a ceramic cup, she remained silent and listened.

"I guess I did sleep well, Laura, because I didn't hear a thing."

"Well, the noises were loud enough to wake me. And the noises seemed to be coming from your room." Laura grinned at Rosalía, anticipating her sister's reply.

Sitting on his wicker chair outside in the porch, Rodolfo kept silent, too, but he paid close attention to their conversation.

"It must have been a rat," replied Rosalía.

"Yes," fired back Laura, "a very big rat."

Maria turned around and placed the coffee cup on the table. She looked at Rosalía and said nervously, "Don't be silly, Rosa, we have no rats in the house."

Laura looked up at her mother and laughed mockingly. Then she turned to Rosalía and with a sardonic smile said, "Then I don't know what else could have made such a noise. It sounded like something or someone was climbing up the side of the house. But you're right Mother, we have no rats. I guess it must have been my imagination."

"Must've been, Laura, because I heard nothing, too," added Anita.

Maria Hernández slowly turned and paced herself to the stove once again. She picked up two fresh eggs from a straw basket and cracked them over the frying pan. Within seconds, the smell of frying eggs overtook the air in the kitchen, and as Maria cooked Rosalía's breakfast, she recalled the events outside the house just a few hours earlier. Maria had not slept very much the past week or so and she would stay awake for most of her nights. The family vacation had become as torturous as life back in San Juan, and all hopes for a good time had vanished beginning with the beatings Rodolfo had given his daughters the first day. Despite the holiday shortcomings, Maria would deal with them as she had always dealt with the miseries of her life with Rodolfo. During one of her long intervals of deep thought early the present morning, she heard the unmistakable sound of horses and poked her head out the window. She saw Candelario and Rosalía, each holding a gas lantern, and each walking a horse back toward the house. Her motherly instincts immediately told her that Rosalía had been out all night long with Miguel, and that Candelario had helped her. Maria knew that if Rodolfo got wind of Rosalía's whereabouts last night, he would beat his daughter to a pulp and cause her serious physical damage, and she would not allow that to happen. She kept her silence instead. She kept silent not only because she feared for Rosalía's well being, but also because she realized Rosalía was truly in love and very happy, and she did not want to be responsible for ruining her daughter's happiness.

Laura rose to her feet and gave both Anita and Rosalía a scornful gaze. Then she left the kitchen in a huff. Meanwhile, Rodolfo sat outside and took in their short conversation, digesting every word. In those few moments, he put everything together in his mind, and he began to suspect that Rosalía was seeing Miguel after all. He then reasoned that Diego Redondo had not told him the truth, and that made him very angry. He rose to his feet and decided to ride into town to confront his solicitor.

Maria put a cooked green banana on the plate next to the eggs, and placed the meal before Rosalía. She watched intently as Rosalía devoured her food as if she had not eaten in days.

CHAPTER 60

Rodolfo Hernández arrived in San Sebastián late in the afternoon and headed straight for Diego Redondo's house. The impatient landowner banged on Redondo's door with authority, as if he were a soldier dispatched by Queen Isabel herself. "Señor Hernández," said Redondo, surprised to see his employer. "I wasn't aware that we had any business dealings today."

"I keep you on retainer, don't I? That means that you work for me every day, and that you're at my beck and call."

The fact that Rodolfo thought he could come to Diego's house any time without prior notice, angered the young lawyer. Nevertheless, Diego made the best of the situation.

"My apologies, señor, please come inside."

"No. What I have to say to you will only take a few minutes." There were a number of people outside Diego's home, and when they saw Rodolfo standing in front of their neighbor's house, many more people began to gather, all curiously speculating.

"Well then, what can I do for you?" replied Diego, fully aware now that his neighbors were watching.

"You can stop lying to me, you piece of worthless shit!"

Diego Redondo sighed in frustration, growing angrier by the second. "Señor Hernández, there's no need for that. What are you talking about, when did I lie to you?"

"Do not '*señor Hernández*' me, Redondo. You know damn well that you lied to me. How long has Rosalía been seeing that fucking peasant? And you better tell me the truth, or so help me God, I will see to it that you never get any business."

Diego's blood began to boil with anger and his eyes could no longer hide his frustrations. As the seconds ticked away in the presence of

Rodolfo, he could feel his resistance to his master beginning to dissolve against his own anger. "I've already told you the truth; I *do* work for you, don't I? Why would I want to jeopardize that?" Diego knew that as Rodolfo's lawyer and because of his verbal agreement to provide intelligence on Porvenir, he was bound to disclose everything to his client. The fact was that he just resented Rodolfo for treating him like an incompetent fool. He held back on information, not because of any moral sense of duty but because it simply gave him power over Rodolfo, and he actually liked that. "I was there, remember?" Diego continued. "I saw when Miguel told Anita that he no longer wanted to see Rosalía. I have told you everything, but if that is not satisfactory to you then you may break our contract, get your sixty-five hundred pesos back and happily go your way. But I will not stand here, in front of my own house and in front of my neighbors, and allow you to call me a liar! And if you persist on following this course of action, you will leave me no choice but to demand satisfaction, señor!"

It finally happened. For the first time in their business relationship, Diego Redondo had finally stood up to Rodolfo Hernández, and he began to feel good about it. On the other hand, Rodolfo, clearly taken aback, seemed unsure of how to respond. He gazed at Diego for a few moments before finally mustering his response. "You mean a duel, a real duel with pistols?" Neither of the two men paid attention to the swelling number of curious spectators moving closer to the front of Redondo's house.

"You have come to my house, unannounced, and you have insulted me, señor, in front of my neighbors. In what other manner do you expect me to respond? Now, retract your accusation or face me at dusk this evening." In reality, Redondo had never owned a pistol and though he had fired a pistol once, he rejected the idea of firearms. Nevertheless, this confrontation was different from all of the others he had had with his employer. This time it was a matter of honor, and he was willing to die in defense of that waning honor. It was a masterful bluff on the otherwise astute Hernández; one that Redondo knew had to succeed.

Sensing the gathering throng of spectators now, Rodolfo looked deeply into Diego Redondo's eyes, searching for fear. But Redondo kept his eyes firmly on Rodolfo's face, a face that seemed confused, and eyes that beamed at his potential opponent with uncertainty. Rodolfo nodded and grinned at Diego, realizing his solicitor was not going to back down, not this time. "All right, Redondo, there's no need for a duel. I retract my accusation." He abruptly turned around and mounted his horse. In that one instant, Diego Redondo wondered if the stance he had just taken against Rodolfo Hernández would change his life completely. In Diego's mind, Hernández would have to think twice now before insulting him again. In that brief confrontation, Diego Redondo regained his honor and respect, and from that moment forward, he would treat Rodolfo Hernández differently, as an equal and not as his master. He closed the door behind him and as he leaned against the door, he breathed a deep sigh of relief, and that's when it hit him. He had challenged another man to a duel—something, which he knew nothing about. He then realized how close he had been to death, and smiled at the success of his bluff.

CHAPTER 61

Several weeks later, on the morning of Saturday, June 6, delegations of the Porvenir and Lanzador cells rode out to Manuel Rojas's plantation in Lares. Greeting the delegation were the Rojas brothers, Mariana Bracetti, and Mathias Brugman who had stayed overnight as Manuel Rojas's guest.

Manuel Rojas escorted the members of Porvenir and Lanzador into an isolated shack deep in the woods near his plantation. The need for absolute secrecy was paramount on the minds of the rebel leaders, and no safety measures deemed too insignificant. There was hardly any furniture in the former slave quarters, and mostly everyone sat on the wooden floor. They focused their attention on Manuel Rojas and Mathias Brugman, both of whom stood facing the small gathering. The Porvenir delegation consisted of Don Manuel Cebollero Aguilar, Don Eusebio Ibarra and Don Diego Redondo. Aguilar had personally invited Redondo to the meeting because he felt a lawyer was a powerful thing to have in their midst. Although he wanted to invite Miguel Pítre, he knew that Miguel did not trust Redondo and felt there would be friction between the two men. Cutting Miguel off from all rebel meetings was a decision Aguilar would come to regret later.

"As you know," Manuel Rojas said remorsefully. "The Dominican militia has forced Dr. Betances to flee the island. The good doctor wrote to us from the United States Embassy in Santo Domingo, and informed us that the American government has granted him political asylum He has made it safely to New York City and he is all right. Aside from this terrible setback, you also know about the death of our esteemed colleague Don Segundo Ruiz Belvis."

"Yes, Manuel, Miguel Pítre gave us the news," said Aguilar. "But has Dr. Betances determined the cause of Ruiz's death?" Aguilar could not hide his fears for the success of their cause.

"No," replied Manuel Rojas ruefully.

"Do you think Ruiz might have been murdered by the Spanish?" asked Eusebio Ibarra.

"It is within the realm of possibilities, and even Dr. Betances has not ruled it out completely."

"So what does it mean for the rebellion?" Aguilar inquired.

"The loss of Don Ruiz has brought with it the loss of our political and financial connections with South America. It means that Dr. Betances will have to work harder to secure the shipload of arms. Dr. Betances has reassured us that negotiations are near the final stages and that the ship is ready. He urges us to set the date for the revolution for sometime in September of this year. We're thinking the middle or last week of September."

"We're in the beginning of June, why set such a late date? Why September?" Aguilar asked, unable to make any sense of the targeted date.

Mathias Brugman suddenly stepped in and addressed the gathering. "First of all, it is because the weapons are being transported from Chile to Venezuela, and that takes a great deal of time. Given the contents of the mule train, our friends cannot use the main roads but will have to make their way through the countryside. Second, because once the weapons arrive in Caracas, our South American friends will smuggle them aboard *El Telégrafo*, which we hope will arrive in time. And lastly, because *El Telégrafo's* charter calls for departure from Caracas on the 12th of August, there is nothing we can do to speed things up."

Comprehending the logistics involved in obtaining the weapons, Aguilar nodded with thorough understanding. Then he looked up at Brugman and said, "We must thank the Chilean people, for they will be among the first countries to acknowledge the free and independent nation of Puerto Rico, but what about the United States?"

Mathias Brugman nodded back at Aguilar and responded with a smile. "Last month I accompanied Dr. Betances to New York

City, where we met with the Cuban rebel leaders in an apartment in Manhattan. We then traveled to Washington, D.C. and met with señor Edward Denison Morgan, a Senator from New York. Señor Morgan is the former governor of the state of New York, and he is a member of a new political party opposed to slavery. They call it the Republican Party. We met with Señor Morgan over a two-day period and he assured us that if the Cuban and Puerto Rican rebellions succeed and if both rebellions are able to establish provisional governments, the United States will acknowledge the new nations and pledge its support."

Eusebio Ibarra suddenly rose to his feet and began to clap his hands appreciatively. "Well done, señor Brugman, well done indeed!"

Mathias Brugman held out his hand as if to quiet Eusebio Ibarra. "Wait just a moment. Before you go applauding and raving about this miniscule success, you must know something else. Although we have apparently received support from Señor Morgan, it is only the beginning. We must urge him to seek further support from the rest of the United States Congress, and that is a difficult task. A successful rebellion, together with a strong opposition to slavery will certainly give us the needed credibility in the American Congress. My friends, these are the keys to gaining support with the American senators and the American people. Let us keep one thing in mind, however: the current president, Señor Andrew Johnson, has vetoed many civil rights bills, and he may not support our new government. I urge you all to be patient. As you know, I am against the idea of a rebellion this year. I would rather wait until President Andrew Johnson's term of office is over. I would rather pin my hopes on Señor Ulysses S. Grant. Señor Grant is a man whom I strongly believe would be receptive to our struggles against Spanish tyranny; a former general that might even lend us military assistance."

Mariana Bracetti let go of her husband's hand and walked over to Mathias Brugman. "We all understand how you feel, Mathias, and your wisdom was appreciated in the past, as it is appreciated now and will be appreciated in the future, when the Republic of Puerto Rico is finally established. Given the change in circumstances, though, we cannot afford to wait any longer. We not only have the support of

Señor Morgan, but we have also received word from our representative in Europe as well, and he tells us that the French government will recognize our new nation pending the success of our rebellion. The timing is right, it must be this year or never."

The small gathering of rebels continued to hash out their plans for the coming revolution, and during all that time, Diego Redondo remained silent. He watched and studied every person in that small shack, absorbing every spoken word, committing to memory every nuance, every facial emotion and body movement. Then, when it was time to write his account to both Governor Pavía and Rodolfo Hernández, those reflections would easily transfer onto paper.

CHAPTER 62

The following Sunday, June 7, saw Diego Redondo moving past the center of town, past the barracks that housed the Puerto Rican militia of San Sebastián, and into the dirt road leading to the Hernández hacienda just outside town. In his hands, Redondo held the latest intelligence report on the band of rebels in western Puerto Rico. In his hands, Diego Redondo held the fate of the creole population.

Before Redondo could dismount, Hernández stepped out of the house and shouted. "Wait right there, Diego, let me get my horse!" Within minutes, Rodolfo mounted his horse and trotted over to Diego Redondo. "I would like it very much if you would accompany me to the Pítre farm!" Diego did not utter a sound but sat haughtily upon his steed. He did not even vocalize his usual morning pleasantries or offer the daily platitudes to his master, which usually fell on Rodolfo's deaf ears anyway. Rodolfo read into Diego's subtle insolence, noting a new demeanor in his lawyer that he could not ignore. For those few seconds, Diego exuded an air of confidence, an aura of newfound honor and a sense of earned respect. Despite his inner feelings, Rodolfo knew that he had to give Diego that respect or face another challenge to a duel; and Rodolfo, as always, took the path of least resistance. Contrary to his earlier comment, Rodolfo did not intend to travel to the Pítre farm; all he wanted to do was move away from the house so that he could talk privately to his solicitor.

Diego Redondo did not even smile, as he was used to doing in his former subservient days. Now he gave Rodolfo a firm look with barely a nod of the head. The two men rode their horses for a while until Rodolfo felt he was at a safe distance from the house. "I presume what you are carrying in that leather pouch attached to the pommel of your saddle is the latest report to Governor Pavía."

"You presume correctly, Don Hernández."

"Then may I see the contents of your report?"

Diego Redondo reached into the leather pouch and retrieved the letter. Then he extended his hand and gave the letter to Rodolfo. Rodolfo read the letter several times so that later he could recall every word. He gave the letter back to Redondo and with eyes revealing a great deal of concern he addressed his solicitor. "The ship that you mentioned in your letter is currently on its way to Caracas? This is a very good intelligence report, Diego. I must tell mayor Chiesa about this, I must urge him to maintain the militia ready. For all we know, the rebellion may take place tomorrow."

Diego smirked at Rodolfo. "Señor Hernández, you know that's not going to happen, because you know that I will give you plenty of warning. You forget that I have infiltrated the rebel cell and that I know everything that is going on there. So please, stop acting like a woman."

All of sudden, the blood inside Rodolfo's veins began to sizzle in anger. He squinted at Redondo with hateful eyes. "I am going to be honest with you, Don Redondo," said Hernández, now with conviction, "Don't think for one minute that just because I refused to engage you in a duel that I am afraid of you. Don't you ever liken me to a woman again, ever! If you do, so help me, I will take up your challenge in a field of honor, and you can bet on that. Now, don't *you* forget that you still work for me, and so I do expect you to give me fair warning of an impending rebellion. Send your letter to Governor Pavía; I'm sure he's expecting your report. I will meet with Mayor Chiesa and brief him on the rebel situation. Good day señor."

As Diego watched Rodolfo turn back toward the house, a surge of anger overcame him, too. He had allowed Hernández to regain control again and he hated himself for that. It was at that precise moment that Redondo decided to purchase a pistol in town. Later that day, he would practice in the woods, counting ten paces, then turning around and firing at an imaginary Don Hernández. He would practice every day until firing a pistol became second nature to him, because he knew now that Rodolfo Hernández would call his bluff the next time.

CHAPTER 63

For most of the night, Cirilo had led his band of runaway slaves through the forest until they reached the town of Manatí. Don Serrano had long departed his company back in Toa Alta, but had left Cirilo with enough money to purchase food for the sixty or so African men and women—enough for a few more days anyway. Cirilo knew that when the money ran out, he would have to obtain food from the various safe houses along the freedom highway. It was either that or forage for sustenance.

Cirilo had taken comfort that Berta and Manolo were always at the front of the procession. Over the past few weeks, he had come to know them well, and he began to take a strong liking to them. As he reached a clearing in the forest, Cirilo made a parting in the dense shrubbery and noticed the familiar white house owned by Don Pedro Caban. He took comfort that it was still dark enough that he could move the runaways toward the safe house. As he made sure there was no one in the immediate area, Cirilo sensed Manolo standing directly behind him, and knew that Berta was close by, too. Without turning around, he said, "There it is. Do you see it? That's Don Pedro Caban's house."

"I see the house, but, are we safe?" Manolo said with great concern.

"I believe so, but before I take you there, I must call on Don Pedro Caban. So please, give me a few minutes to do this."

Berta leaned closer to Manolo and placed her hand on his shoulder. "I'm scared, Manolo."

"Don't worry. Cirilo knows what he's doing."

Cirilo knocked several times on Don Pedro Caban's door and waited for what seemed like an eternity to Manolo. Meanwhile, Manolo could hear the rest of the runaways as they gathered behind him. He could hear their breathing and smell their musty perspiration. For most of their journey, the runaways were unable to use lanterns or torches to illuminate their way, not without giving themselves away. Many of them tripped over roots or rocks embedded in the ground and some walked into trees. Only when a full moon appeared on a clear night, could they see their way through the forest, but only through silvers of light that penetrated the green canopy above them.

From within the brush, Manolo could see that someone inside the house had ignited a gas lantern. Then he saw the door opening, and though he could see that Cirilo was talking, he could not make out the image of Don Caban. Manolo turned to Cirilo and saw him nodding and talking, as if Don Caban were giving him instructions. All of a sudden, the door slammed closed, and it was dark again. Manolo could hear Cirilo's footsteps as he began walking back to the forest.

Cirilo parted the shrubbery and rejoined the runaways, a hopeful look on his face that no one could see in the darkness. "Don Caban said we should wait here until sunrise," said Cirilo.

"Is it not safe?" Manolo asked.

"For the moment," whispered Cirilo. "It appears that several contingents of Spanish soldiers were making their way to Arecibo yesterday, but since they reached Manatí late in the evening, the Captain decided to stay the night right here, in town. They have taken lodgings in two of the town's inns. Don Pedro Caban insists that we stay here until the Spanish soldiers leave town."

CHAPTER 64

On the afternoon of Wednesday, June 10, Governor Juan Pavía sat calmly before his desk, reading Diego Redondo's latest dispatch. Across Pavía, Lieutenant Colonel Juan Manuel de Ibarreta looked on with concern and waited impatiently for the Governor to finish reading the dispatch. Ibarreta had just returned from his fact-finding mission in Camuy and San Sebastián, and faced the governor with eager eyes.

Governor Pavía placed the dispatch on his desk and looked at Ibarreta with furrowed eyebrows. "What were you able to find out, Colonel?"

"That you have a very reliable informant, Governor. I have attempted to elicit additional information from the locals, but they are too tight-lipped and simply do not trust anyone except for their own kind. The mood is tense and the ambiance is very strange in western Puerto Rico; something's about to happen, I'm sure of it. While I was in San Sebastián, I had to arrest a freed African accused of abduction and rape. Tried in the court of San Sebastián, the African's conviction compelled the judge to issue a death sentence as an example of Spanish law. I'm afraid the execution did not serve the judge's purpose. In fact, it was quite the opposite. Instead of scaring the creoles, it seems to have stirred them into a revolutionary frenzy."

"So you believe me now," said Pavía, ignoring Carlos's execution as if he were a dog rather than a man. "Did you meet with the Arecibo commander?"

"Yes, and he filled me in as to what he knows. Colonel Iturriaga feels that since the militia of San Sebastián and Lares are comprised of creoles, we should not place too fine a trust in them. He feels that Spanish soldiers should be stationed in those towns."

"We can't do that without tipping our hand, Colonel," replied Pavía wistfully. "They must not know that we are aware of their plans."

"Then what do you suggest, Governor?"

"Did Colonel Iturriaga tell you anything about a shipload of arms that's supposed to be sailing to the port of Guánica?" Pavía asked. He watched Ibarreta shake his head. "That damned Betances has apparently sealed an arms deal with the Chileans and Venezuelans. I am sending dispatches to Spain on the next ship, requesting naval and military assistance. Spain must respond or face losing yet another colony. In the meantime, we should prepare our forces and stand ready to crush any rebellion. I want you to go to Camuy and assume command of the militia there."

"You want me to take charge of the Camuyan militia in addition to the militia at Aguadilla, governor?"

"Yes. Since Arecibo is along the way, go see Colonel Iturriaga first and inform him about *El Telégrafo*, the ship that means to destroy us. Make plans and stand ready for war, and after our victory, we will hunt the rebels down, arrest and hang them all for sedition."

The next morning, a steamship bound for Spain left San Juan; its most important cargo was a letter written by Governor Pavía informing the Spanish government of an impending rebellion. About fifteen days later, the ship arrived in Cádiz, where the royal post received the dispatches and promptly delivered them to the Spanish Cortes. Four days later, two naval warships departed the port of Cádiz, en route to the Caribbean. As the Spanish government wanted no further conflict with the relatively new governments of both Venezuela and Chile, its former colonies, it ordered the two naval vessels to seize *El Telégrafo* in international waters.

The summer of 1868 was a tense period for Spain because of the insurrection in Santo Domingo and because of the numerous attempts that Queen Isabel made at regaining power in Perú. Adding to the Queen's problems, the political scene in Spain was a powder keg that would later explode into a violent revolution between the liberal and conservative elements. The Spanish government was also careful not to upset the United States government by invading its territorial waters. By the summer of 1868, the United States had become the beacon and symbol of freedom, independence and democracy to Latin America, and the American people were zealous defenders of liberty, especially in their own hemisphere. They simply would not tolerate a ship, representing the powers of tyranny, sailing too close to their homeland; an ideology they fought against one hundred years earlier.

It was on a cloudy day on the afternoon of Friday, August 14, when two Spanish warships confronted the merchant vessel bearing weapons and munitions to Puerto Rico. Spanish marines boarded *El Telégrafo* and detained the captain and officers while they searched the ship. The Spanish marines, quickly found hundreds of crates filled with rifles and bullets. They also discovered thousands of dynamite sticks, a dozen cannons, and provisions for a small army. They dumped everything overboard, released the captain and his men and then took off for a few days of shore leave in Havana before sailing back to Spain.

It wasn't until several days later, though, that word about seizure of the ship reached Doctor Ramón Emeterio Betances in New York City. It was a very sad day in that cramped Manhattan apartment on Wednesday, August 19, where the Puerto Rican and Cuban rebels had gathered to commiserate their apparent failure.

Doctor Betances removed his round spectacles and rubbed his eyes, the creases on his forehead clearly visible as he thought deeply. He sat on a worn out couch and looked up at the gathering of twelve men. "Gentlemen, we have suffered a serious setback but we mustn't allow this to dampen our resolve."

"Agreed, Doctor," said Carlos Seguin, a member of the Cuban delegation. "Our rebellion is on course, so we must proceed."

Doctor Betances gazed up at Seguin, who was standing in front of him, and took in his look of determination, his total belief in the Cuban and Puerto Rican rebellions. Unwilling to give up the cause without a fight, the resolute Betances leaned backward on the couch, closed his eyes for a brief moment, and then spoke in a whisper. "We need two volunteers to contact our brothers in Puerto Rico. I am thoroughly convinced that Spain is very worried, and I am determined to send word about seizure of our ship to our brothers. I need to encourage them to proceed with the cause."

Word finally reached Capa Prieto on August 31, where Mathias Brugman immediately called for a meeting of all of the rebel cells. Two weeks later, on the night of September 18, the leaders of Capa Prieto, Centro Bravo, Lanzador del Norte, Porvenir and other smaller cells met at Pedro Beauchamp's house in Mayagüez.

In all, there were forty men and seventeen women, and though they all exuded an air of determination, their faces and their eyes could not hide their sense of apprehension. Pedro Beauchamp gestured with his hand to quiet the thunderous chatter outside his house. After several minutes, he yelled at them to quiet down. "Please my brothers and sisters, allow señores Brugman and Rojas to address you!" The crowd slowly hushed into a silence.

"As you are all aware, the shipload of arms has been seized in international waters by the Spanish navy. There will be no arms for us!" shouted Brugman. "I have received word from Doctor Betances urging us to set a date for rebellion this month. Don Pedro Beauchamp has informed me that on September 29 hundreds of slaves will be celebrating in Mayagüez; some kind of African holiday. This date is ideal for us because they will be celebrating outside their masters' haciendas. This occasion will give us the opportunity to infiltrate their celebration and persuade them into joining our rebellion. Additionally, our Cuban friends have informed us that they have slated the start of their revolution for the same week. If we time our rebellion with that of the Cuban rebellion, it will force Spain to divert troops not only to Santo Domingo but to Cuba and Puerto Rico as well. Having the Spanish troops split into three fronts will weaken their forces and help us defeat them. The question is where do we begin our revolution?"

There was a long moment of silence before the gathering began to burst out with a loud chatter. Some rebels volunteered to begin the revolution in their hometowns, some resolved to abandon the idea in light of seizure of Betances's ship, and some said nothing at all. It wasn't until Manuel Rojas, accompanied by a robust man, stood before the crowd. Again, Pedro Beauchamp stepped in to quiet the gathering.

The crowd of rebels slowly hushed into silence. They watched Rojas as he gestured the stranger to stand closer to him. "You all know who I am but perhaps you may not know this man. This is Juan Ruiz Rivera. Señor Rivera was a colonel in the militia before his retirement. He is sympathetic to our cause and wishes to join our rebellion. With the approval of Doctor Betances, Señor Rivera, serving as General, will be leading one of our forces, so I ask you all to give him a hearty welcome."

At first, there were a few claps in the back of the gathering but slowly the rest of the rebels joined in until Rojas was finally satisfied. He waved the crowd off in silence. "Don Brugman and I feel that General Rivera should lead one of our columns into Camuy, where we will begin the revolutionary war." There was a loud murmur in the crowd, as if no one had expected the revolution to begin in Camuy.

It was then that Manuel Maria Gonzalez, the president of Lanzador Del Norte, stood up to address Rojas. "My esteemed colleagues, why have you chosen Camuy, not that we're afraid mind you?"

Rojas glanced at Brugman but his co-leader nodded back at him and by that gesture, Rojas understood Brugman wanted him to answer the question. "Don Gonzalez, you, most of all, should know the answer to that question. We have chosen Camuy because it is a Spanish stronghold, where a cache of weapons and ammunition is stored. There are three cannons there, too, and if we could overtake the stronghold, we will be better equipped to fight the Spanish. Camuy will sound the first cry of rebellion, then San Sebastián will second the cry, then Lares will sound the third cry. If all goes according to plan, other towns will sound the cry for independence, and we will be a free nation for the first time! We will become masters of our destiny and beholden to no foreign power. We will raise our new flag high and salute our freedom." All of a sudden everyone began to shout and stomp their feet, clap their hands and even sing their rebel songs. Rojas had lifted their spirits and now they were fully determined to succeed.

The members quickly ratified September 29 as the date for the rebellion. In the gathering stood Don Diego Redondo, mimicking the joy and excitement that the true rebels were experiencing. Not once did he ever take the time to survey his surroundings. Had he taken the time, as he had always done, he would have seen a pair of green eyes staring right at him. Several feet away from Redondo's left stood Miguel Pítre, scrutinizing the falseness that pervaded the face of a traitor. Though he could not prove it yet, he knew in his heart that Diego Redondo was the sole property of the much-despised Rodolfo Hernández. Aguilar did not invite Miguel to the gathering but Miguel had heard about it on the streets of San Sebastián. Realizing that Aguilar was going to keep him out of Porvenir's inner circle, Miguel decided he would start his own cell, without the Revolutionary Committee's sanction, and even without Dr. Betances's permission. It sickened him that Aguilar and Ibarra, both of whom stood in the gathering, shouting and dancing, never took interest in Redondo beyond his legal abilities. Miguel was the only member in the crowd that did not smile, laugh, dance or sing. The rebel mood was at a fever pitch and there was a new kind of excitement in the air, as if a new door stood before them, a door that would open up to a new world.

Miguel would not share in that excitement, for there was too much hurt in him. His mother abandoned him when he was child, and he never saw her again. He lost his beloved father to a heart attack, and he had grown remorseful that he was not there to comfort him during his final moments on earth. He had lost the only friend he had in this world, and the only home he had ever known, and he was uncertain about the outcome of the rebellion. Rosalía's image was the only thing that arrested his emotional collapse.

CHAPTER 65

On the afternoon of September 19, Rodolfo Hernández stood outside his hacienda, waiting for Candelario to bridle his horse. While he waited, he gazed at the woods and listened to the faint drone of a galloping horse. Someone had been riding hard and fast, and drawing closer to his house. Could this be the first warning of a revolution? His body tensed up for a few seconds, but then he managed to regain his composure. Rodolfo Hernández never considered the idea of staying in San Sebastián for so many months, but things had gotten so messy for him that there was no choice but to remain there and try to fix things. For one thing, too many hacendados owed him money, and he had to make sure that everyone understood how serious it was to owe a man like Rodolfo Hernández. He had to make examples; he would have to evict or incarcerate people for the crime of defaulting on a Hernández loan. Then rumors of a revolt were becoming stronger. Rodolfo realized that if a rebellion did succeed, the new regime would cast out all peninsulares. He would lose all of his land holdings and business ventures in Puerto Rico, and return penniless to Spain. Finally, there was the matter of Rosalía, who had fallen in love with a degenerate peasant from the mountains, a damn jíbaro; a lowlife that would destroy the Hernández reputation. Rodolfo had worked hard all of his life to attain such distinction, and he would fight brutally to keep it. It was a veritable certainty now that Rodolfo could not return to San Juan without the complete sense that everything was all right in San Sebastián.

As Candelario walked Rodolfo's horse over to him, Diego Redondo, riding fiercely, steered his stallion into the pathway leading to the hacienda. Rosalía, at her mother's insistence, had been reading passages from the Bible in her bedroom. Laura was in her bedroom, too, but she was busy writing another letter to her fiancé. Maria Hernández had been washing Rodolfo's trousers by the brook behind the hacienda, and she didn't hear Diego's horse. Anita was the only person in the house with nothing to do. Had she been doing something, she might not have heard the fateful conversation between Diego and Rodolfo.

Anita was downstairs sitting in the parlor when she heard the rumble of hooves slowing into a comfortable trot. She rose to her feet and parted the curtains of the parlor window to see who had arrived. Her face then stretched with a smile when her eyes fell upon the handsome Diego Redondo. At first, she thought to rush out of the house and greet her new friend, but then the mere thought of revealing her emotions in front of her father quickly changed her mind.

Rodolfo took his eyes away from the arriving Diego, and turned to Candelario. "Tie my horse to the post and leave us!" He watched as Candelario humbly obeyed his master's command.

Rodolfo looked up and took immediate notice of Redondo's face. It was a new look for Diego thought Rodolfo, a look that foretold gloom and danger. Redondo's horse grunted and panted heavily as it finally halted a few feet before the hacienda. "You look as if you've seen the devil himself!"

"Perhaps I have, Don Hernández!" shouted back Diego. He dismounted and quickly rushed to the porch, standing face to face with his employer. Meanwhile, Anita watched the two men through parted curtains, and listened.

"What's happened? What's so important it seems to have put the fear of God in you?"

"The rebellion, Don Hernández, it will begin soon!"

Rodolfo immediately grabbed Diego by his shoulders, eyes widened and staring directly into his soul. "Are you sure about this?"

"Yes," replied Diego while managing his sore body into a straight stance. "I was present at the gathering last night in Mayagüez. I rode all night long and all day today; I even had to purchase a fresh horse so that I could get here and tell you right away!"

Rodolfo let go of Diego's shoulders and shook his head. His worst nightmare had finally become a reality. "I will reimburse you for the cost of the horse, Diego. When will the rebellion start?"

Diego did not answer his master right away because he took in Rodolfo's facial expression at that moment and came to a sudden realization. Diego had to make his final decision. His fellow creoles had faithfully placed all of their trust in him, and he had betrayed that trust. It wasn't until that very moment, when he saw Rodolfo's eyes gleaming with desire to quash the rebellion, that Diego finally understood the cavernous separation between peninsulares and creoles; realizing at the same time that no matter what he did for Rodolfo and his kind, they would never accept him as an equal. It was the glint in the eyes that spoke volumes of revelation—an evil flash in the pupils that unwittingly showed Diego how much Rodolfo hated the creoles of Puerto Rico. From that moment on, Diego became a revolutionist in his heart and soul. He would quit working for Rodolfo Hernández and for all peninsulares. He would work hard for Puerto Rico's independence and help the creoles in every way possible. He would ask to become an ambassador for his new country, and in that capacity, gain worldwide recognition for his beloved nation. He looked straight into Rodolfo's eyes and answered him with outright conviction. "The revolution is set to begin on October 30, señor Hernández." It was an outright lie! But then again Diego's whole life up to that moment had been a lie. He had struggled all of his life to become something that he could never be. Now that he realized who he was and what his role needed to be, that lie was a good lie.

Rodolfo nodded angrily, acknowledging Diego's latest intelligence report. Then he turned and walked a few paces away to think hard and fast. After several moments of silence, he turned to face Diego. "I presume you will send word to the governor?" He watched Diego nod his head, affirming Rodolfo's presumption. "Then we have plenty of time to prepare for this rebellion. Thank you, Diego, thank you very much. I have been hard on you but I never thought you would ever come through for me like this. I will pay you a large bonus."

Anita's eyes watered with tears, as she put her right hand to her mouth in shock. How could Diego do this? How could he betray his own people? It hurt her so much to realize Diego was not the kind of man she wanted, and though she had started to fall in love with him, she had to fight her emotions against the idea. She could not bring herself to fall in love with a traitor, whether creole or peninsular. She eased the curtain back and slowly drifted away from the window. Then she quietly made her way up the stairs.

Rosalía placed the Bible down on her bed, rose to answer the door, and confronted Anita's brown eyes, reddened and teary. "What's the matter, Ana, you look hurt? What has Father done?"

"Nothing yet, Rosa, but I just heard a conversation between him and Don Diego Redondo."

Rosalía grabbed Anita's hand and pulled her inside the bedroom, slamming the door closed. "Tell me what you heard."

After Anita told her about her father's conversation with Diego, Rosalía shook her head. "Dear God, they will die if they go through with this revolution now that Father is aware of it. How could Redondo do this? I must inform Miguel right away!"

"You cannot do that, Rosa. Let me do it."

"Are you sure about that?"

"Yes, Rosa," replied Anita sadly. "Redondo is not the kind of man I thought he was. Besides, if Miguel is caught up in this, he will die, and I can't allow that to happen to you."

Rosalía smiled and began to cry. Then she leaned forward and embraced her elder sister. "Thank you, Ana, for doing this. You are the only person I can completely trust."

CHAPTER 66

On the night of September 19, Miguel Pítre's face revealed concern as he watched Anita Hernández riding into town. Unable to restrain himself, he ran toward Anita, anticipating yet another message of love from Rosalía. He noticed immediately that Anita wasn't her usual self, but that her brown eyes showed a look of gloom and despair.

"Miguelito, I have grave news for you."

Miguel stretched out his arms and grabbed Anita by her waist, helping her off the horse. "Is Rosalía all right? What happened?"

"Rosa's fine. We just want to tell you that you have a traitor in your midst."

Miguel's eyes squinted at Anita, and his hopeful expression suddenly changed to reveal his darker side, the side where all of his anger lay dormant, waiting to erupt like a volcano. "Who is this traitor?"

"Don Diego Redondo," answered Anita, quickly noticing the sudden change in Miguel's countenance.

"I knew it! I knew Redondo was a traitor! What has done, Ana?"

"He told Father all about the rebellion and the date it will start. Father knows everything, Miguel, and it is Rosa's wish that you not join the rebellion—she fears for your life."

"I had planned on leaving Puerto Rico and taking Rosa with me," replied Miguel. "But knowing about Redondo's treason now, I cannot consciously abandon the cause or my fellow revolutionists. There are too many traitors in San Sebastián, and I must do something about it."

"Oh Miguel, Rosa will be devastated if I should go back with this."

Preoccupied with Diego's treachery and clouded with thoughts of retribution, Miguel never pressed Anita for more information. Had he done so, he would have known that Diego had given Rodolfo a false date and perhaps Anita's life would have turned out better than she thought at the time.

Miguel had first decided to see Aguilar and Ibarra in the morning but then changed his mind. The information he now possessed was too important to let it wait until morning. He rode to Aguilar's house in San Sebastián that very night.

The look on Aguilar's face when Miguel informed him about Redondo told him how much Aguilar had trusted the young solicitor. There was a great deal of emotions in Aguilar's eyes, but the prevailing emotion Miguel saw was hurt; a deep hurt that could only have come from betrayal.

CHAPTER 67

Lieutenant Lopez arrived at the militia headquarters of Quebradillas at 9:30 on the morning of September 20. He had just returned from a two-week furlough in his hometown of Camuy. The young creole had undertaken the eight-mile trip in a little over two hours and though terribly fatigued and weary, he was still keen on seeing his commanding officer, Captain José Castañon. Five months earlier, Lieutenant Lopez had made an agreement with Diego Redondo to obtain rebel information from his uncle, Hilario Martínez. The agreed price for the information was one thousand pesos, which Redondo promised he would have readily available. Though Lopez suspected his uncle was involved with a rebel cell in Camuy, he never took the idea seriously, not until last night. Now he faced an even greater dilemma, and that was whether to sell out his uncle for one thousand pesos, or keep the matter to himself. There was no doubt in Lopez's his heart about his loyalty to Spain, but this involved his kin, and despite being a loud mouth, Hilario was still his uncle. He decided that rather than telling Diego Redondo about his uncle, he would tell his commanding officer, and maybe, just maybe, Castañon would confine his uncle to house arrest. Perhaps the captain would offer him a deal to give up his co-conspirators in exchange for his freedom.

Captain Jose Castañon had already been up and tending to his horse when he noticed Lieutenant Carlos Antonio Lopez dismounting and walking a terribly fatigued horse toward him. Castañon grinned and shouted, "I see that a two-week furlough just wasn't enough, eh Carlos!" The captain quickly dispensed with his jocular greeting when he noticed the young lieutenant's somber face. The young officer said nothing until he finally reached his dear friend. "Are you all right, Lieutenant?"

"No, sir," replied Lopez dourly. "I'm afraid I have disturbing news."

Castañon scrutinized his friend for a few minutes, and then he gestured with his head toward the barracks. "Come with me, Carlos." Lopez followed the captain into the barracks, where they spoke privately in one of two offices. Castañon closed the door to the office, walked over to his desk and sat on a chair facing the door. He turned to Lieutenant Lopez with a quizzical expression, "Tell me, Carlos, what's got you so spooked?"

"You know my uncle, Hilario Martínez, don't you?" Lopez began. He watched Castañon nod affirmatively. "Well, last night we were drinking and I guess the rum got the better of him."

"Yes, I've seen your uncle drunk—that cabrón's a light-weight when it comes to liquor."

"Right, Captain. He got so drunk last night that he began raving about the coming revolution. He told me that a conspiracy was being planned in the home of Don Manuel Maria Gonzalez."

"Are you sure about that, Carlos? The cabrón was drunk—how could you lend credence to a drunken man?"

"I do because in his drunken stupor, he gave me details, strong and reliable details about the rebellion."

"Like what?"

"He told me that there is rebel cell in Camuy by the name of Lanzador Del Norte, and that the leader of the cell is Don Manuel Maria Gonzalez. He also gave me the names of other rebel cells and the names of their leaders, too. He even told me the date that the rebellion is supposed to begin."

When he heard Lopez's reply, Captain Castañon rose to his feet, walked closer to his subordinate and stood nose to nose with him. "You really are serious, aren't you? So when is this rebellion supposed to begin?"

"September 29," answered Lopez resolutely.

"Do you believe your uncle, despite his condition last night?"

"Yes, Captain, why wouldn't I?"

"All right, then we must act immediately. Now tell me more about the conspiracy."

"I don't understand Captain, what else do you want to know?"

"Look, Carlos, I need to be very sure about the facts before I move to have your uncle and this Manuel Maria Gonzalez arrested for sedition. These are very serious charges."

"Captain, my uncle is not a very smart man; I think that's a well-known fact in Camuy. If you want to gather information about this whole rebel thing, then you could get it directly from my uncle. Believe me, Captain, just have him arrested and interrogated for a few hours, and he'll crack under pressure and fear."

"I understand he is your uncle, Carlos. I will give him every opportunity to come clean, and if he cooperates, I will set him free."

With the captain's assurance, Carlos Antonio Lopez told him everything he knew about the rebellion. As Lopez recounted last night's events, the captain sat down and wrote his every word on paper. Afterwards, he looked up at Lopez and nodded. "Have you told anyone else about this?" He watched Lopez shake his head. "Good. Then keep your silence and get your men ready. I will decide on what to do with this information."

Captain Jose Castañon, because of his prior experiences, where jurisdictional conflicts erupted between the military and civilian authorities, decided to share the intelligence report with the mayor of Quebradillas, Don Carlos Gonzalez, and enlist his help in capturing the conspirators of Camuy. At 10:35, on the morning of September 20, Captain Castañon began the chain of events that would lead to the infamous *Cry of Lares*.

"If what you say is true, Captain," said the thin, olive-skinned, fifty-year-old mayor of Quebradillas. "Then we've got to inform the mayor of Camuy as soon as possible!"

Captain Castañon was a veteran soldier, well acquainted with Spanish methods of interrogation. He spent five years interrogating prisoners, and he had come to recognize the look of primal fear in men. By the eager look on Mayor Gonzalez's face, and the general nervousness he displayed, Castañon sensed he was holding back information. He wondered very hard during those tense moments whether Mayor Gonzalez was truly following the protocols of jurisdiction or whether he was part of the conspiracy, too. Was there a sense of civil prudence in the mayor or was he merely attempting to buy time so that he could warn his fellow rebels about the revolution's discovery? Whatever the reason, from that moment on, Castañon felt he could no longer trust Mayor Gonzalez. He left the mayor's house with the understanding that Mayor Gonzalez would inform the mayor of Camuy about the conspiracy. For some strange reason though, Castañon never bothered to follow his standing orders, orders that implicitly stipulated the surveillance of all suspicious persons. Years later, in the silence of his solitude, he would wonder why he never ordered surveillance on Mayor Gonzalez.

On the other hand, Mayor Gonzalez was fully aware of the grave situation and the terrible events that would unfold later on. He waited until Captain Castañon departed, and then he rode out of Quebradillas en route to Camuy.

Mayor Carlos Gonzalez finally reached Casa Del Rey, in Camuy, at 12:15 in the afternoon. Upon entering Mayor Pablo Rivera's residence and much to Gonzalez's disappointment, the mayor of Camuy had company. In the mayor's home stood Don Francisco Alcazar, a tall and robust man sporting a long dark beard. Fully aware that Alcazar was captain of the Camuyan militia and subordinate to Colonel Ibarreta, Carlos Gonzalez hesitated for a moment before speaking.

"Buenos Dias, Carlos, to what do I owe this pleasant surprise from the Mayor of Quebradillas?" Rivera asked.

"Pablo, may we speak in private?"

Mayor Pablo Rivera quickly took note of the stress on Carlos Gonzalez's face. He gave Alcazar a curious look and said, "Captain, can you give us a few minutes?"

"Certainly," replied Alcazar without pausing to think about Carlos Gonzalez's request.

The two men entered a private room and closed the door behind them. All would have gone well, though, had the private meeting not taken so long. After fifteen minutes, Alcazar noted the two men emerging from the room with sullen faces. The wise captain waited until Carlos Gonzalez departed and then scrutinized Rivera's face as he returned to his office. Alcazar sensed the tension in Rivera's eyes, and knew there was something terribly important about that meeting. "So what was that all about? What's with all the mystery, señor Alcalde?"

"Nothing, Captain, ah…nothing at all." replied Rivera nervously.

"I don't believe you, Alcalde. Why are you so nervous all of a sudden and why are you sweating like a pig?"

Mayor Pablo Rivera had no idea how much the authorities knew about the rebellion, but given the tactics Spanish soldiers often used on the locals, he grew more frightened by his uncertainties. He wondered whether Alcazar was aware of the whole plan, too, and thought the captain might have been testing his loyalty. Pablo Rivera was afraid, very afraid, but the fear was not only for himself, but for his entire family, too. He knew the Spanish well and knew that they would treat his family harshly. Succumbing to his unfounded fears, he felt certain now that the Spanish authorities were already aware of the conspiracy and reluctantly decided to come clean. Wiping the sweat from his forehead, Mayor Pablo Rivera spilled his guts out to a jubilant and most surprised Captain Alcazar. "…it was then that Mayor Gonzalez sought advice from me as to how he and Captain Castañon should proceed," confessed Rivera, sweat pouring steadily down his face.

"And what did you tell him?" Alcazar pressed on, his face dry and his disposition calm.

"Since Colonel Ibarreta at the moment is somewhere between San Juan and Quebradillas, I told him to go see Colonel Manuel Iturriaga, who is the commander of the base in Arecibo." Again, Rivera wiped his forehead clean; his handkerchief drenched with sweat.

"Then you did the right thing, Alcalde Rivera," said Alcazar, but he remained convinced that Pablo Rivera, the respected mayor of Camuy, was still not being truthful. He stood in the middle of the parlor, watching Mayor Rivera as he sat helplessly before his desk. The mayor pulled out a sheet of paper and began writing furiously. As he studied the mayor's face, Alcazar wondered whether Rivera was a rebel, too, and the possibility that he might be sending word out to his fellow conspirators. Though he never questioned the mayor about the letter, he knew the letter's contents were terribly important. Indeed they were. The letter was probably the most important communication between the rebels since the formation of the cells. Rivera had addressed the letter to Manuel Rojas.

CHAPTER 68

At 1:30 in the afternoon, Miguel Pítre, brandishing a machete, led a thirty-man contingent to his great uncle's house. He wedged in the waist of his trousers a two-barreled pistol. It was so old that the walnut-finished grip was starting to fade away. How the Belgian Percussion Pocket Pistol ever found its way to Puerto Rico, Miguel Pítre would never know. He bought the pistol from an antique dealer in San Sebastián who told him the pistol belonged to a Belgian soldier. There was no doubt in Miguel's mind that the pistol, whose action contained an engraved floral design and marked with Belgian proofs, saw its first days of service in the early 1840's. The rarity of such a pistol was the reason why he took money that he saved for years and asked the dealer to send away for bullets and caps. He waited for months until the ammunition arrived from Belgium. Then he spent two consecutive Saturdays shooting at targets set behind his uncle's house until he learned how to use the dueling pistol.

The contingent of men was comprised of twenty creoles and ten Africans. Of the ten Africans, three were freed men and seven were still slaves. The slaves were all friends of Carlos Peña with ties to the farm formerly owned by Santiago Duran. They ran away from the farm the day the Spanish hung Carlos. They made their way through the forest until they reached the house where Miguel had been staying with his uncle Mateo.

Mateo Ramirez greeted Miguel and his men, and escorted them to a small shack several hundred yards away from the house, past the tiny shack where Miguel first made love to Rosalía. As Miguel walked past the shack, leading his men toward the far end of the farm, he gazed at the small wooden structure and reminisced about that night. He remembered how soft her skin felt to his callused hands, how wonderful her body smelled, how velvety smooth her hair felt in his hands and how the sweat of their heated bodies melded together in a tight embrace. He remembered her soft lips upon his lips and her deep moans of ecstasy, but in a sudden flash, Mateo's voice came crashing through his reverie. "Miguel!" shouted Mateo. Miguel snapped to attention and quickly turned to his uncle. "I swear boy, sometimes I wonder if your heart is fully committed to the cause!"

"I'm sorry uncle," said Miguel. He turned around to face his men and shouted. "Listen up, men! That shack at the end of the farm will be our new home until September 29. After that, you can choose whatever peninsular home you wish!"

The men of Miguel's contingent began to cheer wildly until Mateo raised his hands in the air in a halting gesture. "What's the matter with all of you? Have you gone mad? Don't you know there are loyalists everywhere, watching, waiting for the first sign of trouble, anxious to put an end to our cause? Now shut the hell up and walk silently to the shack. I will bring food and water every day until the time comes."

Miguel led the silent contingent of men to the shack where they would wait for the final word from the rebel leaders.

Captain Castañon had waited all day for Carlos Gonzalez, unaware that the Mayor had already returned from Camuy hours ago. Acting upon the rules of colonial governance, it was his duty as captain of the militia to inform the mayor of Quebradillas about the rebel conspiracy, but now he felt uncertain that he had done the right thing, especially after seeing the scared look on the mayor's face. He decided to wait no more for the mayor's word, and, at precisely 4:00 in the afternoon, paid Mayor Gonzalez a visit.

Castañon knocked repeatedly and waited for several minutes before Mayor Gonzalez received him. This time, however, Castañon noticed a calmer Gonzalez. Confidence and swagger had replaced the look of uncertainty and fear on the mayor's face, and perhaps, thought Castañon, there might have been nothing to this rumor of rebellion.

"Buenas Tardes, Alcalde. Has the Mayor of Camuy responded to your dispatch?"

Mayor Rivera paused momentarily, while carefully choosing the right words. "I decided to ride out to Camuy, rather than relying on dispatches, Captain."

Castañon narrowed his eyes at the mayor of Quebradillas, clearly demonstrating the lack of confidence in his reply. "Why didn't you tell me? Perhaps I might have wanted to come along with you to Camuy."

"It would have been a waste of your time," Rivera quickly replied.

"Why?" Castañon asked, prying like a true interrogator.

"Rivera thinks this talk of rebellion is nothing more than a silly rumor designed to scare the peninsulares. But, in keeping with our standing orders from Governor Pavía, we must give it our full attention."

"So, will Mayor Rivera issue orders for the arrest of Hilario Martínez and Manuel Maria Gonzalez?"

The mayor raised his hands and both eyebrows at the same time. "Not so fast, Captain. We are going to proceed the right way. First, I want you to give me a fully written report on how you came by this information together with your recommendation."

Castañon sighed heavily. "But that will take time, Mayor, valuable time. For all we know, the rebels might already be aware of our discovery. Why do you want me to waste time on a written report?"

"We must follow legal protocol, Captain. If we move to arrest these men without proper and legal cause, then charges of sedition may not hold up in court. This is not a military issue but a civil one; you do understand this, don't you?"

Captain Castañon's anger was visible through his fiery eyes. Resenting the mayor's condescending tone, he said nothing more to him and simply stormed out of his office. On his way back to the barracks, he knew that the mayor was merely stalling. Castañon felt certain that he was part of the rebellion. Had he known that Mayor Gonzalez, following Mayor Rivera's advice, was supposed to inform Colonel Iturriaga in Arecibo about the conspiracy, the civilian issue might have changed into a military operation. Nevertheless, Mayor Gonzalez never sent any messages to Iturriaga and he did not tell Castañon all the details about his meeting with Rivera either; important details that would surface during the inquest and subsequent trials.

CHAPTER 69

Diego Redondo felt he had done something right for the first time in his life, and the euphoria was intoxicating. As he made his way from the Hernández hacienda back to his small house in San Sebastián, he made the decision to throw all his energies into the cause for liberty. He felt good inside, as if he had shed a terrible burden off his shoulders, as if God had wiped his slate clean.

Diego Redondo entered his home at around 5:00 PM, removed his jacket and threw it on the bed. He removed his top hat and placed it on the table, where he would later sit to write an inflammatory paper on the injustices of Spanish imperialism. Then he would meet with Aguilar and Ibarra and move the rebellion forward. Redondo was a changed man, a convert, and a new champion for freedom. There was much work to be done and so little time before the September 29 revolution. He pulled out a clean sheet of paper from his leather case, as well as his favorite fountain pen and began to write his thesis.

No sooner had he put pen to paper than he heard several loud wraps upon his door. Diego calmly placed his fountain pen on the blotter and answered the door. He recognized the two men standing outside, and with a wide smile said, "Señores, please enter. I am writing a paper that will displease the establishment greatly." Before Diego could say another word, he heard two clicking sounds, and then saw several bursts of gunfire before feeling the whizzing bullets go past his ears. He quickly raised his arms in submission and shouted, "Wait! Do not fire!" The young lawyer gazed into the eyes of his shooters who began reloading their pistols. The two visitors stood before the open door and while quickly realizing they had succeeded in frightening Redondo, they bum-rushed him. Unable to react defensively, Diego Redondo felt the sting of a punch across his cheek. Diego fell hard. One of the men crouched and straddled the lawyer, then punched away at his face. As he writhed in pain, and while blood oozed out of his mouth, Diego looked up at his attackers and pleaded. "Why are you doing this?"

The man who remained standing took two steps forward and looked down at Diego. "This is how traitors are dealt with, Redondo!" All of a sudden, there was noise outside Redondo's house. Diego's neighbors had heard the percussion of the pistols and scuffle inside the house, and they began to investigate. The man who was standing turned and walked out to the porch, raising his pistol at the small crowd. "Get to your homes! There's nothing for you here!" He walked back into the house and addressed his partner. "Come, we've got to get out of here before the townsfolk alerts the militia!"

The man straddling Diego looked up at his partner and gave off a look of anger. "And what, leave this sack of shit to accuse us of attempted murder? We're not going to do that!" He took one more swing at Diego Redondo and knocked him out cold. The two men then picked up Redondo and rode away with him into the night.

CHAPTER 70

By 5:30 PM, Rosa had already packed her canvas bag and remained in her room waiting for the signal from Candelario. She had made the decision to ride to San Sebastián and join Miguel even it meant her father disowning her, even if it meant her death in the coming revolution. Rosalía had decided to become a rebel and be with her true love forever, even if forever meant a short time. But Rosalía had no clue that Rodolfo had given Laura explicit orders to keep an eye on her youngest sister.

Staring out of her window, Rosalía finally caught sight of Candelario pulling two horses behind him. That was the signal she'd been waiting to see for hours. Rosalía picked up her canvas bag and began making her way down the stairs toward freedom, far from her tyrannical father and the hell she had been living in since birth.

As she made her way to the stairway, she confronted none other than Laura. "And just where do you think you're going, you little bitch?"

"That's none of your business! Now get out of my way!" replied Rosalía angrily.

"That's what you think! Father!" yelled Laura.

Downstairs, Rodolfo Hernández rushed out of his study in his usual ferocity. "What the devil is all that goddamn shouting about?" When he looked up and saw Laura standing in front of Rosalía, apparently preventing her younger sister from leaving, his nostrils began to flair. He noticed the canvas bag over Rosalía's shoulder. "Well, well, Rosa, leaving us so soon?"

Rosalía turned to look down at her father but offered no response. Then she turned back to face Laura. "Get out of my way or I'll push you down the stairs!"

"You'll do nothing of the sort!" shouted Rodolfo. Hearing the commotion, Maria stepped out of her bedroom and stood at the top of the staircase looking down at her two daughters, unable to say a word. Anita quickly followed her mother and stood side by side with her.

Rodolfo climbed the stairs and pushed Laura aside. He confronted Rosalía with angry eyes. "What were you planning to do? Were you going to run away and be with that peasant scum? Have I not told you that he cannot give you the happiness you need? Have I not told you that all he can give you is a life of misery and poverty? You are not going anywhere, do you understand me?"

"I cannot live under your roof anymore, Father. I cannot live in this hell you call a home! I hate you! I hate everything you stand for and I hate what you've done to all of us! You are a monster! You are an evil man who beats up on defenseless people! You're a tyrant and a bastard!"

"A what? Why you fucking cunt! You're nothing but a spoiled little brat!" replied Rodolfo. Then he swung an open hand so hard at Rosalía it knocked her down. He scooped her off the stairs and placed her limp body over his shoulder. Then he plopped her on her bed and closed her door, locking it from the outside. An hour later, he took a ladder and a hammer and with long carpenter nails, sealed her window shut. Rosalía was now a prisoner in her own home.

Castañon remained in his barracks until 5:45 PM that afternoon. He attempted several times to write a clear and concise report for Mayor Gonzalez but the more he wrote the more he felt something was not right.

After several more minutes, he threw his fountain pen across the room, picked up the sheet of paper and tore it into pieces. He stormed out of the barracks and headed straight for the stalls, where Lieutenant Carlos Antonio Lopez had just put his horse in for the night.

As Lieutenant Lopez closed the door of the stall, he noticed Castañon walking over with a look of absolute determination. "Captain, sir, what's the matter?"

"That bastard's stalling, Carlos, and I know it good. But I'm going to go one up on the Mayor. I'm going to ride to Arecibo and inform Colonel Iturriaga about the rebellion."

"Captain, with all due respects, this is a civil matter, and you are breaking with procedures. You cannot go over the mayor's head or Colonel Ibarreta's head, for that matter."

"To hell with procedures, Carlos, if I fail in informing my superior's that a rebellion has started there will be more trouble for me. So get someone to fetch my horse! That's an order!"

Within minutes, a militiaman walked a fresh horse over to Castañon, but the effort of bridling and saddling the horse had given the captain enough time to think. He turned to Lopez, who was still standing next to him, and sighed. "You're right, Lieutenant. Perhaps I should not get too personally involved in this. For all I know, it could very well be a hoax. Instead of riding to Arecibo, I will send dispatches there, and avoid any embarrassment should this conspiracy turn out to be nothing more than someone's joke." He turned to the soldier. "Hold here for a few minutes while I prepare a dispatch. I want you to ride to Arecibo as quickly as possible and deliver the dispatch to Colonel Iturriaga"

CHAPTER 71

The sound of rolling waves brought a sense of calmness to Colonel Manuel de Iturriaga. Yet, in spite of such tranquility, the veteran soldier felt jittery. It wasn't so much that he was afraid, but something about that night had given him cause to heighten his sense of awareness. For one thing, the town of Arecibo seemed too quiet. Then there was the absence of gas lanterns that usually at this hour brightened the cluster of homes nestled behind the shore batteries. It seemed eerie to the colonel, so much so that it reminded him of the night he fought against a rebel crowd in Santo Domingo. He remembered how still the night was and how quiet it seemed before the first bursts of gunfire killed two soldiers standing next to him.

As the five-foot-nine colonel turned to enter the barracks, the drone of hooves seemed to overtake the steady crash of waves from the Atlantic Ocean. The figure of a militiaman riding a fatigued and near-to-collapse mare finally became clear to Iturriaga, who quickly stepped outside to confront the man.

"Colonel, sir!" shouted the militiaman, dismounting quickly. Sweating and panting heavily, the militiaman opened the pouch strapped to the pommel and retrieved a small handwritten letter. He saluted the colonel and handed the letter to him. "Colonel, sir, I have a dispatch from Captain Castañon, with his compliments."

Colonel Iturriaga returned the salute and took the letter from the militiaman's trembling hands. The blond haired Colonel then nodded at the soldier, and said, "Get some rest, and please wait until I have read this letter." The colonel limped over to his office inside the barracks and sat before his desk. While in the forests of Santo Domingo two years ago, a sniper took a shot at Iturriaga. The bullet ricocheted off a tree and buried itself into the colonel's leg. Although the surgeons removed most of the lead fragments, there was one stubborn piece that still lay somewhere in his leg bone. On occasion, it would cause him some pain, and remind him of how close he had come to death that day. The colonel opened the bottom drawer and retrieved a bottle of rum. He poured the brown liquid into a glass and then he unfolded the letter:

20 September 1868

To Colonel Manuel Iturriaga, Commander of the Arecibo base

My dear Colonel Iturriaga, it is with great concern and urgency that I write this letter to you. I have uncovered a conspiracy to overthrow the Spanish government in Puerto Rico. An armed revolution is set to begin in Camuy on the night of September 29 by a group that calls itself Lanzador Del Norte. The leader of this rebellion is a resident creole of Camuy by the name of Don Manuel Maria Gonzalez. This news has come to me by way of Lieutenant Carlos Antonio Lopez, whose uncle, Hilario Martínez, is a member of the same rebel group, and has told him of the plot. Colonel Ibarreta is currently in San Juan, but the militia at Quebradillas stands ready and awaits your orders. Please respond as quickly as possible.

Yours faithfully,

Captain Jose Castañon, Quebradillas Militia

Colonel Iturriaga's eyes never blinked as he read Castañon's message. He gently placed the letter down on his desk and slowly rose to his feet. "Sentry!" shouted Iturriaga. A young militiaman entered the colonel's office and stood at attention. "Send for Captain Sotomayor."

The colonel stepped outside the barracks and looked straight at Castañon's messenger. "Corporal, tell Captain Castañon that I am personally grateful for his prompt response to this crime. However, he is not to engage any of the rebels for the time being. I will arrive later tonight with soldiers and militiamen."

The messenger nodded and remounted his horse.

Moments later, another soldier appeared before the Colonel. "You sent for me, sir?"

"Yes, Captain, assemble one hundred and fifty colonial soldiers and fifty militiamen and have them ready to march to Camuy tonight. Have them pack plenty of ammunition and make sure they maintain a high level of alertness. While you're busy with that, I will obtain warrants for search and seizure from Judge Pizzaro."

"Yes, sir," replied the captain without even questioning the orders. Normally, military deployments consisted entirely of militiamen because the Spanish preferred to use locals first rather than their own colonial soldiers. What Sotomayor did not know was that Iturriaga took Castañon's message very seriously. If an armed conflict was to take place in Camuy, he did not want the militia to turn on him and side with the rebels. A three-to-one majority offered Iturriaga a stronger sense of security.

Colonel Iturriaga had made many mistakes over the past ten years, many of which were major embarrassments in civil courts. This time, however, he was determined to do everything by the book. Aware that this was still a civil matter, he was obligated to obtain proper documents to search the home of Don Manuel Maria Gonzalez, and authorization to interrogate the rebel leader. This time he wanted no mistakes and he wanted to make all charges stick. He despised all rebels and if Gonzalez resisted, he would have the legal right to execute him.

CHAPTER 72

At nine that night, Anita sat on the floor facing Rosalía's closed door, hearing her cries of anguish. Anita could not help but to cry along with her sister. She cried not only for Rosalía, but also for herself and for the misery and hell under which her father forced her to live. Anita wept because Rodolfo had controlled her for all of her life and cared nothing about her. She placed her hands on the door and whispered to Rosalía. "Rosa, please stop crying, you're breaking my heart."

Anita heard rustling on the bed and then a slight thump as Rosalía sat on the floor facing the opposite side of the door. "Ana, you've got to help me please! You've got to get me out of here."

"Rosa, I can't do that, Father will kill me!" replied Anita, terrified at the thought.

"No he won't, Ana, and if he beats you, then you can run away with me. One thing is certain, however: I no longer wish to remain here in this hell! So please, Ana, please help me!"

"Where will you go?"

"I will go to Miguel."

"How are you so sure that he will want you with him?"

"I know he will, and that's why you've got to help me. Please, Ana, unlatch the door. Where is that devil we call father?"

"He's gone into town to speak to the mayor about the rebellion. He wants to arrest Miguel and everybody associated with his cell."

"I hate him, Ana!"

"Rosa, he's still your father."

"No, Ana, he's never been a father to me or to any of us. Please, Ana, if you have an ounce of love, a small measure of pity, then please unlatch the door and set me free."

Anita's tears streamed down her cheeks and dripped onto her dress. No longer able to bear Rosalía's cries, she rose to her feet and unlatched the door. Rosalía turned the knob and poked her head through the opening. "Quick, come inside," she whispered. "Help me pack a few clothes."

Within minutes, Rosalía packed everything she needed, and while she dressed herself, Anita went down to fetch Candelario. Several minutes later, Anita came back to Rosalía and told her that Candelario had a horse ready for her. As she began walking down, with Anita closely following her, she heard Laura's voice from the top of the stairs. "Thank you Rosa, and thank you, too, Ana!" Anita and Rosalía both turned to face Laura. With arms folded, Laura looked down, grinning wickedly at her two sisters. "That's right, thank you very much."

"For what, puta?" Anita yelled.

"You have just cleared the way for me. Now I will be the only heir to Father's estate. He will cast you aside, Ana, for releasing Rosa, and he will disown you, Rosa, for running away. That will leave me as the sole heir."

"What about mother?" Rosalía said.

"She's no match for me. I can deal with her."

"You are a conniving bitch, Laura, I hope you die!" yelled Rosa.

"My time will come, Rosa, but you will have died long before me—this I assure you."

"So you're not going to stop us?" Anita asked quizzically.

"Why should I? Why should I interfere with something that's going so well; something I couldn't have planned any better?"

Laura's younger siblings turned and headed down the stairs. Candelario, who had just entered the house, stood by the door looking up at the two sisters. There was a sense of excitement on Candelario's face and he took no steps to hide it either.

Maria Hernandez, who was sitting in the parlor, in total darkness, finally stood up and walked toward the front door. All eyes suddenly turned toward the matriarch and watched her as she stood firmly with an imperceptible demeanor. Maria then showed her emotions. She frowned at Candelario, whose eyes remained unflinching. "I am disappointed in you, Candelario. Do you realize the consequences of your actions? You are helping my daughter run away from home, and you are clearly disobeying your master's orders not to bring his children into town."

Candelario removed his pava and gave Maria a humble and sincere look; his dark brown eyes as steady as before. "Señora Hernández, you have been very kind to me and to my family, but the time for masters and slaves is at an end. I am a human being, señora. I am not a dog, or a donkey or any other beast of the earth that white men might have the arrogance to own. I have a soul, a mind and a heart. I have feelings just like you. I have chosen to help señorita Rosalía because she is the only person in the Hernández household that has truly shown us compassion. Her feelings come from the heart, and her mind and soul are pure. You have been kind to us but you have always been afraid to stand up for what you believe, and that is a tragedy. Yes, my brother and I have been secretly helping your daughter and we are well aware of the consequences. That is why I must tell you now that I, and my brother, too, will be running away. You will no longer see us."

Maria shook her head and closed her eyes out of pain, pain from the heart; a kind of pain far worse than any of the physical abuses wrought upon her by Rodolfo. Where had she gone wrong in life? Why was God forsaking her? Tears began to roll down her face as she moved slowly toward Rosalía. She stood before her daughter and took some time to gaze upon her youthful but determined face. She wiped the tears from her eyes, embraced her daughter and then let out a deep wail. Maria held Rosalía tightly, as if somehow she knew she would never see her again, as if the authorities had already sentenced Rosalía to death and were leading her to the gallows. Rosalía held her mother and she too cried loudly for a few moments. Anita then stepped in, and hugged her mother and sister, bawling as well.

Standing at the top of the stairs, with arms still folded, Laura heard the wailing. She shook her head and muttered, "Please, spare me. I wish they'd all leave!" Laura turned, walked back to her bedroom and shut the door.

Maria finally let go of Rosalía and stood back to contemplate her face again. "Is this what you truly want? Does Miguel Pítre make you that happy that you are willing to give up all semblance of a normal life, even your inheritance?"

Rosalía wiped the tears from her face as Anita stepped back. "How can you call this a normal life? It isn't. And yes, Mother, Miguel truly makes me happy, and I will go to him. I will give up this so-called life of privilege, this so-called aristocracy that feeds off the lives of the poor. I will live my life in total simplicity. I will be Miguel's wife and we will have children. I will bring your grandchildren to see you, Mother, and you will see that I made the right decision after all. You know that I cannot live here any longer. Father is a monster and so is Laura, and they've made our lives a living hell."

"If Miguel makes you happy," said Maria, "and leaving home will make your life complete, then go with my blessings. Go, and be happy and never, ever look back." Maria then turned to look at Candelario and flashed a warm smile at her former slave. "I know that you're probably going to involve yourself in the coming revolution." Candelario furrowed his eyebrows and stared at Maria with newfound respect, as if all the efforts he had taken to keep his personal side a secret, were all made bare by Maria's wisdom. "Please don't look at me that way, Candelario," continued Maria. "Though I might have been quiet, I heard, I listened, and I knew the goings on between you and Agustín, as well as those of my daughters. All I ask you now, is to look in on Rosalía every now and then, and please see that she is all right. Can you do that for me?"

"I will, señora Hernández, until my last dying breath."

Mother and daughter embraced each other for the last time, and for the next several moments, the sound of moans, despair and tragedy filled the night air outside the Hernández country estate. Rosalía finally entered the stagecoach and soon, only the memory of her young, idealistic daughter remained in Maria's mind.

Anita, feeling helpless and at loss of self-control, shouted and ran upstairs to her bedroom.

CHAPTER 73

Miguel Pítre and his men had bedded down by 11:00 o'clock on the night of September 20. Not too long before Miguel had closed his eyes, his ears picked up the deep thudding sound of horses and the sharp pitch of coil springs from a stagecoach. The rumbling grew stronger, and Miguel had a very good idea as to where the coach was heading.

Miguel stepped out into the rare coolness of a San Sebastián night and waited for the approaching coach. He recognized Candelario right away and even recognized his brother who sat next to him. In that very instant, his stomach knotted and a feeling of nervousness and wonderment began to consume his being, as if a spirit of good had descended from heaven and had overcome his once troubled soul. Though he denied it to himself at first, his heart could not deny his suspicions and he just did not know what he would say when Rosalía would eventually step out of the stagecoach. He hoped Rosalía had taken his advice to heart and remained in her home, as he strongly suggested she do, and yet, despite all that he had told her, a part of him still wanted her to come out of that stagecoach.

The horses grunted as Candelario and Agustín both jumped down off the coach. Candelario reached out, pulled the handle and slowly opened the door. When Miguel saw the image of Rosalía, he closed his eyes in utter disbelief. He ran to her and put his arms around her, lifting her up off the ground. They kissed for a long moment, and, while they renewed their affection, Candelario smiled with a sense of satisfaction. Candelario felt deeply certain that he had done the right thing in delivering Rosalía to Miguel, and that God would be well pleased. The former slave turned around, met his brother and together they drifted away into the darkness.

"Why oh why did you come here, Rosa, especially after I told you it would be dangerous? I cannot continue with plans for the revolution knowing that you are here now. How can I fight and worry about you at the same time?"

"You don't have to worry about me, Miguel. I can take care of myself."

"That's not the point, Rosa!" shouted Miguel. "This is not a game, this is real life! If the rebellion fails and they capture us, the Spanish government will torture us without pity, without compassion, before killing us. They will not care in the least that you are Rodolfo Hernández's daughter. To them, you'll be just another rebel, another worthless piece of shit who has no business being involved in a revolution." Miguel raised his hands at Rosalía in supplication, "I don't want that to happen to you! I do not want to be the cause of your death! You have much to live for, much more than I do, Rosa. Why do you insist on throwing all that away just to be with me? Believe me, I'm not worth it."

Rosalía took two steps forward and gently pushed Miguel's hands down to his sides. "You are wrong about me and you are wrong about yourself. I love you, Miguel. I love you with all of my heart—that is true, but I also believe in the cause. I believe that Puerto Rico has the right to determine its own future, beholden to no foreign power. I believe in the notion of abolishing slavery and that all men are equal in the eyes of God the All Mighty. I believe that Spain will not listen and will continue to oppress the creoles of Puerto Rico. I believe that without an armed confrontation, without a revolution, Puerto Rico will never be free. You have shown me how the creoles live, and how hard they work just to eke out an existence. You have opened my eyes to the real world. You have shown me the great divide, the terrible imbalance between the rich and the poor. I believe in you, too, Miguel. When I look into your eyes, I see a bright fire burning against injustice and tyranny. I see the zeal, the fervor and the determination to change the way things are. In you, I see a complete and total revolutionary, a man fully committed to the destruction of imperialism, the expulsion of those who would seem fit to condemn the creoles to extinction by their financial wickedness and perversions. So do not stand there and ask me not to be with you. Do not stand there and ask me not to partake in the coming revolution, Miguel, because it's tantamount to my asking the same of you!"

Miguel just stared at Rosalía for a long moment, unable to counter any of her remarks. But even if he could, he was sure that she would have an answer for him, a much better response.

They made love for hours that night.

CHAPTER 74

Berta and Manolo had finally reached the outskirts of San Sebastián, much to their relief. It had taken so long to get there, and many times Berta thought about giving up and returning home. Despite her constant complaints though, Manolo, who felt reluctant to join her in the first place, had been the driving force behind the entire procession of runaways. By 11:45 that night, the townsfolk living along the dirt trail leading to San Sebastián had extinguished all gas lanterns. The sound of crickets and coquís were the only things that gave the runaways a sense of direction in the black of night.

At the head of the column, holding a swinging gas lantern in his hand, Cirilo forced the group to a stop so that he could look around the immediate area. He bade everyone stay low and out of sight while he took several minutes to survey the area in front of the procession. After several moments, the aging former slave scanned the fields once more, and made sure that the house he was looking at was the right one. He turned back to the runaways and whispered. "Do you see that house to the extreme left? That is Don Rafael Blanco's residence. Behind the house are three shacks, and that's where we will be staying until we receive word from our friends that it is safe to go on to Guánica." Cirilo heard nothing in response and he knew it was because they were exhausted and hungry. He could have shown them a Peninsular's house, and they wouldn't have known the difference. He could have told them Blanco was a peninsular and still they might have entered his house.

Cirilo escorted the runaways across the dirt trail, toward the wire fence that marked the Blanco and Duran boundary. He opened the gate, and while the runaways remained by the fence, he walked slowly toward the white house. After several wraps on the door, Cirilo confronted the muzzle of a Henry rifle aimed directly at his face. Cirilo gasped and then quickly raised his arms in submission. "Don Blanco, it's me, Cirilo."

"Who?" Blanco inquired, voice aspirated by a long night of sound sleeping.

"Don Serrano's friend," answered Cirilo nervously.

Don Rafael Blanco slowly lowered the rifle but kept it at waist level. He stepped out the house to get a better look at Cirilo despite the darkness, and after several more tense moments, completely lowered his rifle. "I was expecting you days ago. Where the hell have you been?"

With a sigh of relief, Cirilo lowered his arms. "It took longer this time, Don Blanco. We had to wait for several days in Manatí, at Don Pedro Caban's farm, until the Spanish militia departed the town."

"How many this time?" Blanco asked, concerned.

"Sixty."

"I don't have enough food for sixty people, nor do I have the space. Tell Serrano that he must cut back."

"But señor Blanco, they've traveled such a long way. They are very tired and they just want to be free."

"Wait right here," said Blanco. He went back inside the house and returned several minutes later with a lighted gas lantern. The runaways by the trail along the fence line could see the bright dot of light and the silhouettes of two men. "I have food," continued Blanco. "But the runaways must divide it among themselves. Usher them to the usual place behind the house, but be very careful. The farm next to mine, the one formerly owned by Don Santiago Duran, now belongs to a rich peninsular. I do not know if the bastard's moved in already and I do not want to know either, but that is not the end of it. The revolution is going forward and if it fails, there will be militia everywhere invading homes and arresting suspected conspirators. Should the revolution start before we are able to move your runaways out of here, will they join us in the fight?"

"I know I will, but I cannot answer for them."

"Well, they may not have a choice in the matter. In the morning, we will begin traveling south and when we reach Don Mateo Ramirez's house about five miles from here, we will rest. Take your group around back, and I will meet you there with food and water."

Berta had lost a lot of weight during her long journey, and at times felt faint and weak. She did take comfort that Manolo was always there to keep her from falling. Sometimes he would give her his daily rations so that she could retain enough energy to continue her freedom journey. Now, they had just one more stop to make before entering the world of liberty, and that stop was Guánica. Once there, they would board a ship and sail north to America, to the land of the free. Berta clung to Manolo as Cirilo led the sixty runaways to the back of Don Blanco's farm. Manolo, who was also hungry and tired, forced what little strength he had to keep Berta from sagging to the ground.

Cirilo divided the group into three sections and told them to occupy the shacks. Fitting twenty people in a shack that could barely house four was a difficult proposition, but to Manolo and Berta, it was a small price to pay for their freedom. It was hot and musty inside the shack, but Manolo found a corner where he and Berta could rest for a while. It wasn't long before Don Blanco came around with food and water. Cirilo chose three runaways to divide the food and parcel it out to the rest of their fellow runaways. Manolo took the portions and walked back to the tiny corner in the shack. He gave Berta two bananas and a grapefruit, which she devoured in minutes. Manolo only ate half of a cooked plantain; it was cold but he forced it down with a swig of water.

"You think Mamíta and Papá are all right?" Berta asked, now with added strength.

"I pray to God they are."

"It seems so long ago that we ran away. You think they miss us?"

Manolo squatted next to Berta and in the pitch dark, sighed heavily. "Of course they do, Berta, but I'm sure they are happy that we are free."

"Not yet, Manolo, we're not free yet."

"We will be…soon. I will find work in America and make enough money to buy Mamíta and Papá's freedom from that bastard. Then I will buy freedoms for Candelario and Agustín, too. We will all live in America and be free of slavery."

"So you think the revolution will fail?"

Manolo sighed again. "If the revolution starts before we get a chance to move on to Guánica, I will join them. But the Spanish are a ruthless people, and they will not give up Puerto Rico so easily. Besides, I don't know that the revolutionists have enough arms to combat the militia. Look, all I'm saying is that if we reach America safely, I will do everything to get our family out of Puerto Rico, regardless of the outcome."

"What should I do if the revolution starts?"

"I want you to go on with the journey. I know that most of the younger men here will join the revolution, but there are children and women among us. Some of the older men will have to stay with them. You just go with them, Berta, and if I survive, I will join you in America."

"No Manolo, either we go together or we do not go at all."

Manolo gave his sister a look of frustration. "I knew you were going to say that!"

CHAPTER 75

Colonel Iturriaga, with a contingent of two hundred soldiers, set out from Arecibo, determined to reach Camuy at all costs. Having failed to obtain a search warrant from Judge Pizarro because of jurisdictional conflicts, he marched his soldiers all night long and into the wee hours of the next day, until they finally reached Mayor Rivera's house in the outskirts of Camuy. At 1:47 on the morning of Monday, September 21, Iturriaga woke Mayor Rivera and forced him to sign a search and seizure warrant for the leader of Lanzador. Then he demanded Rivera join him in the arrest of Gonzalez. Mayor Rivera knew that any hint, any notion of a revolution was now dead; someone had talked, someone had betrayed them. There was no choice for Rivera now, he had to comply or risk having his name included in the colonel's search and seizure warrant. Rivera knew that he was walking a dangerously fine line, and any shift in that walk could spell doom for him and his family. Reluctantly, he agreed to accompany Colonel Iturriaga.

In Lares, where the seeds of rebellion in the Rojas plantation had blossomed into a real revolution, all was quiet that night. That is until someone banged hard on the door at 2:36 in the morning. Manuel Rojas and his brother Miguel came rushing to the door, half-naked, and armed with rifles. Was it over already? Was there a contingent of Spanish soldiers outside the house, ready to arrest them? Manuel Rojas opened the door slowly, sticking out the muzzle of his rifle first. Then he heard a familiar voice. "Don't shoot, it's me: Eusebio Ibarra!"

Manuel Rojas lowered his rifle and stepped outside, followed by his brother. "You have a lot of nerve to come here! It's nearly three o'clock in the morning, for God's sake!"

"Please, accept my sincere apologies, señor Rojas," replied Ibarra. "But I have an urgent message. There is a traitor in our midst and we know who it is."

"What? A traitor? Come inside, Eusebio."

Manuel Rojas placed his rifle against the wall and asked Ibarra to sit. While Miguel ran to his bedroom to tell his wife about what had happened, Manuel sat next to Ibarra and yawned deeply. Disappointed, he closed his eyes briefly and shook his head. "Who is the traitor?"

"His name is Diego Redondo," answered Ibarra. "We have him, señor Rojas. We're keeping him in a vacant barn in Señora Gutierrez's plantation about two miles west of San Sebastián. What do you want us to do with him?"

Miguel and Mariana rushed out of the bedroom and stood facing Manuel as he decided what to do with Diego Redondo. He looked up at his brother and uttered, "It's Diego Redondo, Miguel, and he has betrayed us all."

Mariana put her hands over her face in shock, and Miguel just looked on with mouth agape. Manuel turned to face Ibarra. "How much has he told and to whom has he been speaking?"

"We don't know yet."

"Then this is what I want you to do. I want you to interrogate him and try to get everything out of him. We need to know just how much the Spanish know about our revolution."

Ibarra nodded to acknowledge Rojas. "What do we do with him afterwards?"

Rojas lowered his head and placed his hands on his face for several moments. Then he brought his hands to his lap and gave Ibarra a decisive look. "Let justice prevail, señor Ibarra. He will receive a fair trial and a jury of his peers will judge his case. If found guilty, he will face punishment."

Ibarra chose to remain silent, but Rojas could easily read the uneasiness in his eyes.

"What's the matter, Eusebio, you do not agree with my decision?"

"Of course I do, but Aguilar may not want to wait for a trial."

Rojas narrowed his eyes at Ibarra and responded in a forceful tone. "We will not descend into a reign of anarchy, do you understand me?" He rose to his feet and cast a look of disappointment at Ibarra. "No señor. We will not do that. Don Diego Redondo may very well be a traitor, but he shall have the benefit of *Habeas Corpus* and the right of due process. Aguilar must adhere to these basic of human rights and he must abandon all disregard for the law. Do that, and we will all be better for it."

Looking up at Manuel Rojas, Eusebio Ibarra nodded. "All right, señor Rojas, I shall try to convince them."

"You must convince them, Eusebio," insisted Rojas, following Eusebio Ibarra to the front door. Holding the doorknob, Rojas looked into Eusebio Ibarra's eyes. "We will send word out to the cells for a meeting here later today. We would like for you and Aguilar to be here, as well."

Rojas closed the door and leaned against it with a hopeless look. Miguel studied his older brother but he didn't feel as dejected as Manuel appeared to be. Miguel Rojas wanted the rebellion to succeed, so much so that he had already resolved in his heart to die in the coming war. "What do you want to do, brother?" he said humbly.

"Send word out immediately, Miguel. We must convene here today and discuss contingencies!"

CHAPTER 76

Inside an old abandoned barn, deep in the woods of San Sebastián, a young man sat on a chair facing a group of other men standing menacingly before him. His hands, tied behind his back, were growing numb. His cut lips oozed out blood, and his swollen eyes could not betray the fact that a number of fists had severely beaten his once handsome face. The red blotches on his cheekbones and jaw were fresh and no doubt would turn black and blue over the next few days, if he lived that long. At 2:47 that morning though, Don Diego Redondo, had no illusions that he would survive even the next few hours.

The deep, physical pain on his face and body was so excruciating, it caused him to vomit all over his bloodied white shirt. It wasn't until several more men joined in the bashing of his face that the young lawyer, the boy whose academic successes became the pride of San Sebastián, finally relented. "Please, no more, I beg you."

"Wait!" shouted one of the men, one who had not partaken in the beating, but one who had clearly sanctioned the action. He was sitting near a table behind the group of men encircling Redondo. The group of six men, with their bloodied knuckles stepped to the side to allow their leader a clear line of sight.

The man rose to his feet and with arms folded walked slowly to Redondo. "Who else besides Rodolfo Hernández knows about the rebellion?"

Redondo looked up at the inquisitor with glassy eyes and tried to focus on his face. "You're all deluding yourselves if you think the rebellion is a big secret."

"I don't have time for this," said the inquisitor, throwing his hands up in frustration. He turned around and began walking back to the table.

"Wait!" shouted Redondo again. "Governor Pavía knows about the rebellion, too. In fact, he's alerted the militia."

The inquisitor dropped his arms to the side and shook his head. "You disgust me, Diego. You have betrayed your people for what—a few thousand pesos? Is that all we are worth? Is that all freedom means to you? You are an educated man, you could have been a valuable asset to us but instead of doing the right thing, you chose a different path."

"I am not proud of what I've done," replied Diego, blood dripping down his chin, "but I did not divulge the date for the rebellion, you must believe me."

"How so, Diego, and why would you want to do that if you had taken the money already?"

"I told both Hernández and Pavía that the date for the rebellion was set for October 30, not September 29," said Redondo, his left eye completely closed now. He spat out a wad of spit mixed with dark, red blood. "And yes, I took the money but in the end I did change my mind."

"And we're supposed to believe you? You? A spy? Amigo, you forfeited all credibility when you betrayed us!" yelled the inquisitor.

"It doesn't matter anyway," uttered Diego Redondo.

"Now why is that?"

"In the town of Quebradillas, one of your co-conspirators, a member of Lanzador, had already divulged your big secret months ago. His name is Hilario Martínez, a weak-minded fool and a weak-drinking lover of rum. In his drunkenness, he unwittingly told an old schoolmate of mine everything about the rebellion. It so happens that my schoolmate is a Lieutenant in the militia at Quebradillas. Following his standing orders, he informed his commanding officer about the conspiracy, and the good captain alerted the high command at Arecibo."

"You bastard!" shouted Diego's inquisitor, slapping the young lawyer's face several times. After several more swings, the inquisitor stepped back and wiped his hand on Diego's already bloodied shirt. He turned around and looked at his men. "Get him out of here!"

At 2:53AM on the morning of September 21, Colonel Iturriaga, in the company of Mayor Rivera and two hundred soldiers finally reached the town of Camuy. The low thunder of sixty horses pounding dirt, followed by the thumping boots of 140 foot-soldiers was loud enough to awaken the sleeping town of mostly Spanish loyalists.

Colonel Iturriaga led the contingent to the small plaza near the church in Camuy and then ordered his men to secure the immediate area. As he dismounted, he could see the darkened homes suddenly lighting up in intermittent waves. Colonel Iturriaga raised his gas lantern up at Mayor Rivera and with a determined look said, "You're coming with me, Rivera."

"Where are we going, Colonel?"

"You know very well where we're going. I'm taking a detachment of fifty men with me on foot to barrio Palomar and you know the way there. We're going straight to Manuel Maria Gonzalez's house."

Mayor Rivera dismounted and reluctantly accompanied the Colonel. His heart was beating rapidly but he was unable to stifle his fear. Mayor Rivera was so well entrenched in the conspiracy that he felt it was just a matter of time before Colonel Iturriaga would have him arrested as well. Nevertheless, he led the contingent of soldiers straight to his friend's house.

Colonel Iturriaga and his men reached barrio Palomar by 3:17AM and found everyone still sleeping. His soldiers had primed their weapons and stood ready to shoot at his orders, but the orders never came. Instead, Iturriaga saw a young man sitting on a chair in the front porch of Gonzalez's house. The young man, who was given the responsibility of sentry duty, had simply fallen asleep. No one would ever know that he and every member of Lanzador had gotten home just about an hour ago from a rebel meeting.

Colonel Iturriaga gestured with his hand, and four soldiers stepped fourth to accompany him. He turned around and motioned at Mayor Rivera to join him in the front porch. Mayor Rivera took a deep breath first, and then began walking to the porch right behind the four soldiers.

The twenty-three-year-old sleeping sentry felt a hard wrap to his head from the muzzle of a soldier's rifle. When he opened his eyes and saw four soldiers standing before him, he immediately reached for his own rifle, but it wasn't there, where he had left it.

"Looking for this?" Iturriaga said, holding the sentry's rifle and smiling wickedly. The young sentry could see only half of Iturriaga's face, the side that shone against the gas lanterns held by both he and Rivera. "Where's Gonzalez?" demanded the Colonel.

"He's inside, sleeping. They're all sleeping," answered the sentry fearfully.

The colonel narrowed his eyes at the door. "Break it down!"

The loud crash startled everyone inside the Gonzalez house. Gonzalez jumped out of bed wide-eyed, and began screaming profanities at the invaders, demanding to know the reason for the intrusion. Gonzalez's wife was even angrier than the mayor was. She walked up to one of the soldiers, faced him eye to eye, and demanded to know by what right they had invaded her home. Rivera's daughters cried and some male members of Lanzador rose to their feet to challenge the soldiers. "What is the meaning of this intrusion in my home?" shouted Gonzalez, putting on his robe. Then he recognized Rivera and shook his head at him. "Pablo, what are you doing here? What are these soldiers doing here?"

Mayor Rivera looked at Gonzalez but offered nothing more than a regretful gesture at him.

"We're here to place you and your co-conspirators under arrest," said Iturriaga with a commanding authority.

While Rivera's wife and daughters cried hysterically, and as the soldiers bound the three male members of Lanzador, the ones who had agreed to stay the night at Gonzalez's home, Iturriaga ordered Gonzalez into the kitchen where he began to interrogate the ringleader.

CHAPTER 77

The thudding of an approaching horse, at 4:05 in the morning, had rudely interrupted the sublime silence that still reigned over Don Rafael Blanco's farm. Reacting to the sound, Miguel and Rosalía both rose from their tiny bed and searched for their clothes. The low rumble came to a sudden stop right in front of the shack where Miguel and Rosalía had taken up their secret residence. Inside the three other shacks, situated about 100 yards to the north, the former slaves lighted their gas lanterns with hopes of catching a glimpse at who had arrived in such great haste.

Miguel put on his trousers and as Rosalía search for something decent to put on, he lighted a lantern. When he stepped outside, he recognized the rider. Several of the former slaves had already stepped out to investigate. "Señor Ibarra, what are you doing here so early in the morning?" shouted Miguel, curiously. "Has the revolution started?" He held his lantern up so that Ibarra could see his face.

"No!" yelled back Ibarra, dismounting. He approached Miguel and sighed heavily before speaking again. "Señor Aguilar wishes to thank you, for making us aware of Redondo's treachery. The Spanish have indeed discovered our rebellion, but we have Redondo!"

There was a murmur of gasps among the former slaves, and even Rosalía, who was standing behind Miguel, gasped loudly. Miguel shook his head at Ibarra. "What do you mean, you have him?"

"We have señor Diego Redondo," answered Ibarra, somewhat embarrassed. "You were right all along, Miguel. Redondo was a traitor. He was working as a spy for both Rodolfo Hernández and Governor Pavía. He sold us out for—" Ibarra hushed suddenly when he noticed Rosalía standing behind Miguel. "What is that woman doing here, Miguel? Are you out of your mind? That's Hernández's daughter!"

"I know who she is, Eusebio. Rosalía's with me, we're getting married after the success of our revolution."

"She's a peninsular, Miguel, how can you trust her?" insisted Ibarra.

"You questioned my feelings about Redondo, and you found out that I was right about him. Now you question me about the woman I love. Do you still not trust my judgment? Rosalía has abandoned her way of life and has joined our cause. She has joined the rebellion not only because of me but because she believes in our struggle."

"Señor Aguilar must know about this, Miguel."

All of a sudden, Rosalía stepped out from behind Miguel and shouted, "Tell him, señor Ibarra! Tell him to come see me, and tell him that I will answer any question he might have for me."

"You don't have to do that, Rosa," interjected Miguel.

"Señorita, while you joining the rebellion matters to our cell," said Ibarra more calmly now, "at the moment it isn't that important." Quickly turning to Miguel, he changed the subject, "Miguel, I came here to tell you that we have captured Diego Redondo. Aguilar dispatched me to Lares to inform Manuel Rojas about Redondo's betrayal, and it was Rojas's wishes that we try Redondo after the revolution. I'm afraid, however, that some of the more zealous members of our group will not heed his message. I conveyed Rojas's wishes to Aguilar but he has allowed the men to take matters into their own hands. If we don't get back there soon, I'm afraid they might kill Redondo."

"Isn't that a traitor's reward?" said Miguel shrugging his shoulders with indifference. "Why would I want to save the life of a traitor?"

"Because you're a decent and honest man, and you don't want his murder to mar the cause for liberty. You don't want his death in your hands anymore than I do. Convince them to set a trial for Redondo, but it must be after the revolution succeeds, once we have a provisional government in place."

Miguel sighed deeply. "All right, Eusebio. Let's go to them. I don't know how much influence I'll have, but I'll try to stop them from killing Redondo."

By 7:15 that morning, Mayor Gonzalez had undergone four hours of intense questioning about a supposed rebellion that required answers, truthful answers. Sometime during the interrogation, Colonel Iturriaga, frustrated that he was going nowhere, ordered Mayor Pablo Rivera to search the Gonzalez home. Gonzalez's daughters had found their sleep again, but their mother kept wide-awake, fearing the worst, fearing the arrest of all members of the Gonzalez household.

Iturriaga ordered two soldiers to search the house and demanded Rivera search Gonzalez's private study. The other two soldiers stood guarding the three male members of the rebel cell. As Colonel Iturriaga continued his interrogation, Mayor Pablo Rivera uncovered an old ledger inside Gonzalez's desk buried in a heap of papers. Rivera knew the exact contents of that ledger; he had seen it many times before in the company of Gonzalez. He had seen Gonzalez make numerous entries into that green book.

In the kitchen, Gonzalez sat uncomfortably and sweated miserably. He tried to peer into the parlor where his wife and daughters were, but he could not get a clear view of them. Finally, Iturriaga looked at him and said, "Your family is all right, we haven't harmed them at all. Contrary to whatever you may be thinking, we're not monsters."

"Colonel, why do you persist on following this course of action? I've already told you that I know nothing about a rebellion. My family is innocent and so am I."

"You're lying to me, Gonzalez," said the colonel. "I can feel it in my bones." He threw his hands up in frustration and walked out of the kitchen. When he entered the parlor, he noticed Mayor Rivera standing idle. "Well, did you find anything?" Rivera shook his head, but the look he gave Iturriaga did not convince the veteran officer. "And the men, did they find anything?" Again, Mayor Rivera shook his head. "This is hopeless. Look, I did not come all the way here to find nothing. Did you search the study, like I ordered you to do?"

"Why yes, Colonel, why wouldn't I? I found nothing of value," replied Rivera.

Iturriaga might have believed the Mayor, and he had already begun to walk back into the kitchen when he recalled the droplets of sweat on Rivera's forehead just a few seconds earlier. It didn't make sense to the colonel because it was too early in the morning for anyone to be sweating so heavily. He slowly turned around to face the mayor. Narrowing his eyes at Rivera, he walked over and faced him eye to eye. "You're lying to me, aren't you?

"No, Colonel, there's nothing of value in Gonzalez's study. Why don't you believe me?"

"I think you know the answer to that question, Mayor. Let's have a look, why don't we?"

Rivera followed Iturriaga into Gonzalez's study, where he fearfully watched the commander sift through a stack of papers scattered across the desk. The commander opened the drawers and pulled out envelopes and other documents. He read them briefly and then carelessly tossed them on the floor. With a look of frustration, the commander rose to his feet, lowered his head and stared at the floor, wondering, unable to explain the lack of evidence supporting the accusation. Then he noticed the corner edge of a green book that barely stood out from underneath a stack of papers under the desk. Following the commander's eyes, Mayor Rivera frowned and knew that Iturriaga had discovered the ledger. The commander did not reach for the damning evidence right away. Instead, he looked at the Mayor and gave him a look of disappointment. "What's that down there? I thought you said there was nothing of value here."

"I didn't see that, Colonel."

"Well, pick it up!" commanded Iturriaga angrily. The mayor bent his small body, reached underneath the desk and picked up the ledger. "Give it to me."

"It looks like some sort of record-keeping, commander, perhaps it is the town's finances," offered the mayor.

"We shall see," replied Iturriaga unconvinced. While the commander read and turned the pages, Mayor Rivera's heart pounded with fear. Several minutes later, the commander snapped the ledger closed and with a triumphant smile said, "Come with me!"

Mayor Rivera followed the commander into the kitchen and stood behind him as he addressed Gonzalez for the final time that morning. "Well, señor Gonzalez, you've been very busy." Gonzalez looked at the ledger Iturriaga was holding and closed his eyes. He knew the ledger had sealed his fate. "This green book shows me how well you've documented the rules and regulations of your rebel cell. I also note that your entries to the ledger are very clear, and well organized—nicely done, Gonzalez." The commander turned several pages and read briefly. "Let's see…the name of your cell is Lanzador Del Norte, cute. Oh, and I see here that you've written a reminder to tell the members about the need for obtaining arms for the revolution." The commander turned several more pages and then smiled at Gonzalez. "Here's something interesting, it's a list detailing the names of all of the members of your cell." The colonel closed the green book and smiled triumphantly. "Thank you, Alcalde, for being so meticulous." The commander turned around to face Rivera and gave him another disappointed look. Then he commanded one of the soldiers to bind Gonzalez. While the soldier bound Gonzalez's hands, Iturriaga narrowed his eyes at the conspirator. "Señor Manuel Maria Gonzalez, I am placing you under arrest for conspiracy to overthrow the Spanish government and for sedition as defined under the laws of the colony of Puerto Rico." Without taking his eyes away from Gonzalez, Iturriaga commanded, "Put him in the wagon and transport him right away to Arecibo."

Colonel Iturriaga's doubts about Mayor Rivera continued to gnaw at his conscience, but since there was no evidence, nothing at all to link Rivera to Gonzalez he had to let Rivera go. Now armed with Gonzalez's ledger, he would present it to Governor Pavía and obtain full authority to come back to Camuy and round up the rest of the conspirators. At 11:30 that morning, Colonel Iturriaga left Mayor Rivera in Camuy and began marching his contingent back to Arecibo with prisoner in tow.

CHAPTER 78

By 12:15 in the afternoon, news of Gonzalez's arrest had spread like wildfire, and because of the arrest, several members of Lanzador decided to meet at the home of Carlos Martínez, the cell's political instructor. The small gathering waited for the cell's vice-president, but he never showed up, and his absence caused them to think he had gone into hiding. As the cell's political advisor and the only person there with rank, everyone turned to Carlos Martínez for leadership. A foreman at a sugar refinery company in Camuy and known as a tough, no-nonsense man, Martínez easily assumed leadership and quickly hatched a plan to rescue Gonzalez. Martínez stood average in height with broad shoulders and muscular arms. His clean-shaven, angular face was pale and his amber-colored eyes seemed to give off a sense of determination. He walked with dignity and an aura of power that naturally attracted followers. At 12:35 in the afternoon, he and several men rode out to obtain additional help from other members of Lanzador, and along the way other members joined his ranks until his contingent grew to 45 men.

Carlos Martínez reached the home of José Antonio Hernández, another member of Lanzador who lived in barrio Ciénega and not too far from Gonzalez's home.

As the self-appointed new leader of Lanzador, Martínez demanded that José Antonio Hernández join him in his attempt to rescue Gonzalez. Martínez needed Hernández, not only because he and his men would strengthen his contingent, but also because Hernández was the cell's custodian of a cache of arms and gunpowder, which he kept secretly buried in his farm.

The plan was simple. Martínez and his men were to retrieve the weapons stored by Hernández, catch up to Iturriaga's marching contingent, rescue Gonzalez and kill the soldiers. Then he and his men would double back to Camuy, attack the small militia and seize the weapons and munitions stored in the barracks. After securing the weapons and munitions, the Camuyans would sound the first cry for independence. The revolution would start that very day in the town of Camuy.

José Antonio Hernández, however, thought much differently than the self-appointed leader of the cell did. He argued vehemently that Martínez was acting impulsively and hastily and that such poor planning would fail against a contingent of two hundred soldiers. He refused to join Martínez. Angered by his fear and lack of zeal, Martínez threatened to kill Hernández if he refused to join him. Fearing death, Hernández changed his mind and reluctantly agreed to join Martínez. Deep inside, though, he felt that Martínez's plan was weak and put together very haphazardly. It was for this reason that José Antonio Hernández would change his mind again, but he would not tell Martínez this time.

Satisfied now, Martínez ordered Hernández to dig up the cache of arms. Departing barrio Ciénegas, certain that Hernández and his men were going to catch up to Iturriaga's contingent, Martínez's confidence swelled. But as soon as Martínez departed, Hernández gathered food and water, and went into hiding. He advised his workers and some of the men under him to do the same.

At 2:37 on the afternoon of September 21, somewhere along the road to Arecibo, the Spanish army had taken time out to rest the horses. Camouflaged behind several tall bushes, Carlos Martínez and three of his men reconnoitered the enemy. Martínez's pale face suddenly flushed red with anger as he turned to face one of his men. "There are too many of them. Go back to the rest of our contingent and see if Hernández and his men have arrived. We need to do this now."

Ten minutes later, Martínez received his answer. Hernández had not arrived yet. Angered that Lanzador's captain-at-arms, the man trusted with the cell's ammunition, had disobeyed his orders, Martinez growled, "That goddamn coward is going to pay for this! There is no way we can attack them now, not without additional men and arms.

It is unfortunate that we cannot rescue our leader. We have no choice but to abort the mission."

"What do we do now?" one of his men asked humbly.

Martínez replied smugly. "Now we go back to Camuy, gather food and arms and join our brothers in Lares."

"Lares, señor, why go there?"

"The Camuyan cell has been exposed, and according to Rivera, Colonel Iturriaga seized Gonzalez's ledger, where all of our names is listed. We will go to Lares and hide there until the revolution begins in a few days. So for the short time we're in Camuy gathering our things, take the time to say farewell to your wives or sweethearts."

Martínez and his 45-man contingent arrived in barrio Puertos at 3:15 in the afternoon and immediately advised most of their fellow members about the coming militia. The stirring of men, their women and children, and the general commotion outside their homes gave the loyalists enough reason to think something in Camuy was brewing. A few wise peninsular men, noting the creoles outside their homes brandishing weapons and gathering stores of food and equipment, dispatched a messenger to Arecibo warning Colonel Iturriaga about an impending conflict.

With great haste Martínez and many members of Lanzador Del Norte, departed from the Camuyan barrios of Puertos, Palomar and Ciénegas en route to Lares.

At the same time Martínez left for Camuy, Don Rafael Blanco, Cirilo and the group of runaways finally arrived at Mateo Ramirez's hacienda. The walls of the shack were so flimsy that Miguel Pítre could clearly hear the commotion of people arriving. While Rosalía slept, Miguel stepped outside and recognized Don Blanco right away. He dashed toward his uncle's hacienda and with a smile greeted his long time friend. Concerned that loyalists would see the gathering outside his home, Don Mateo Ramirez cut their conversation off quickly. He offered Don Blanco a spare room in his home for the night and asked Miguel to find accommodations for the runaways somewhere in the fields behind the hacienda.

Cirilo, Manolo and Berta stood at the front of the gathering. They watched and listened to Miguel as he introduced himself and asked them to follow him into the fields. As Berta and Manolo moved past the shack where Rosalia was sleeping, they had no idea that Rodolfo Hernandez's daughter was there or that she had run away from home, just like they had done. The runaways followed Miguel until they came upon a shaded and secluded spot at the far northern end of the plantation. As Don Blanco followed Mateo Ramirez into the hacienda, Miguel gave the tired runaways a comforting smile and promised them he would come back with food and water.

CHAPTER 79

Colonel Manuel Iturriaga received the messenger from Camuy as the clock struck the hour of 4:00 in the afternoon. Iturriaga's second in command, Major Jorge Coronado, stood beside the commander as he read the handwritten note. "Well, Major, it would seem that we've stirred the viper's nest. The good citizens of Camuy are worried. They are claiming that a rebellion has broken out in the barrios of Camuy, and have requested military assistance to protect their lives and properties."

Coronado folded his arms and gazed at his commanding officer. "There is a young captain serving under your command, señor. His name is Captain José Pujols and he has been hounding me for an assignment."

"Well then, Major, let us not disappoint the man. Order him to assume command of the Camuyan militia, since Ibarreta is still making his way back from San Juan. But I don't want him to make more of the situation than necessary. Order him to talk to the loyalists and enlist their help in identifying the rebels. I want this to be a low-key operation and I want it limited to just a few men. If word gets out that we have sent soldiers out to Camuy in response to a rebellion, it will ignite the fires of revolution throughout the island. I want Captain Pujols to select just ten soldiers from here to take with him to Camuy. He can use the rest of the militia from Camuy, if necessary. The citizens will be more at ease if they see more of their own militia rather than colonial soldiers from Arecibo."

Captain Pujols arrived in Camuy at 6:15 that evening, where he proceeded to search barrio Puertos. He scoured the countryside as well, and then he traveled to barrio Palomar, but he and his men found no evidence of a revolution. Martínez and a good number of his men had long departed Camuy for Lares, and José Antonio Hernández had gone into hiding. The lack of evidence forced Captain Pujols to cancel the operation and return to the militia's barracks in Camuy. He decided to send word to Major Coronado and await further orders.

CHAPTER 80

Rodolfo Hernández had finished supper by 6:35 that early evening when he heard a loud knock on the front door. Maria was in the parlor, reading passages from the Bible, while her two remaining daughters were upstairs. Though Maria knew she had to tell Rodolfo that Rosalía had run away from home, she could not bear to do it. Maria knew that Rodolfo would blame her for Rosalía's disappearance, as he blamed her for everything else that went wrong in his life. Then he would cause such a stir in town and cause general grief that it would make her life even more unbearable. Maria decided not to mention a thing to Rodolfo until he found out about it on his own.

Rodolfo grunted as he rose to his feet to answer the door. When he opened the door, he saw the face of Mayor Chiesa's secretary, Don Pedro Ortíz. Ortiz, a short and pudgy man of forty-three, removed his top hat and entered the Hernández home without Rodolfo's invitation. Finding it odd that Ortiz had broken off with social protocol, Rodolfo ignored the slight when he noted the man's eyes. Breathing heavily, the wide-eyed Ortiz looked up at Rodolfo. "Señor Hernández, please pardon my intrusion, but I'm afraid I have disturbing news."

Rodolfo held up his hands and said, "Calm down, señor Ortiz. Now please follow me into the parlor, where we can talk in private."

"No señor Hernández, I must take my leave immediately."

"All right, then, speak."

"It is about your solicitor, señor Hernández."

"Diego? What about him, what's happened?"

"Don Diego Redondo is dead, señor Hernández, apparently murdered."

Rodolfo Hernández did not say a word, didn't even bat an eye; he just simply stared at Ortiz for several moments. Then he shook his head and sighed. "Where's his body?"

Ortiz cleared his throat. "A local jíbaro discovered him lying face down by the edge of a creek about a mile west of the pueblo. From the red blotches around his neck, it appears Redondo was strangled to death."

Rodolfo sighed again. "It is a sad day, then."

"There's more. This note was pinned on Redondo's jacket. It reads, 'Long Live Puerto Rico Free'."

Rodolfo sighed for the third time, "A sad day indeed. That note could only mean one thing, Ortiz. The rebels know that we are aware of their conspiracy. You must tell Mayor Chiesa to alert the militia in San Sebastián and be ready for war. In the meantime, I will gather as many men and arms as I can to combat the rebels. This coming revolution must be stopped at all costs, you hear me Ortiz, at all costs!"

"I will inform the Mayor, señor, good night."

Rodolfo Hernández closed the door and leaned against it, thinking deeply on what he should do next. He thought for a few minutes and then yelled for everyone in the household, including the slaves, to come downstairs. "Diego Redondo has been murdered," announced Rodolfo unemotionally. Maria and Anita gasped, and then held each other's hand. Laura stood beside Maria and Anita, but showed no emotions whatsoever. "We have to ready ourselves for a possible attack on our home. I'm sure this is the first place the rebels will attack. We need to—" Rodolfo suddenly stopped himself when he noticed Rosalía had not come downstairs. "Where is Rosa?" He looked at the recently hired cook and with fire in his eyes commanded, "Go upstairs and tell her to come down immediately!"

The cook rushed up the stairs but found Rosalía's room empty. She came back down and fearfully gazed up at her master. "Señorita Rosa is not in her room, Patrón."

Rodolfo's anger began to blister as he turned to his wife. "Where is Rosalía? Where are Candelario and Agustín?"

"I don't know, Rodolfo, I thought she was in her room, and I don't know where Candelario and Agustín are."

"Don't you fucking say that, Maria! I know you know! Where is she, damn it, before I put my foot through your goddamn mouth!"

Anita kept her cool while her mother lied about Rosalía's whereabouts. On the other hand, Laura was about to burst. She was just about ready to open her mouth, when Maria stepped closer to her husband and yelled back at him. "I told you, I thought she was in her room. Why should I lie to you?"

"You always lie to me, Maria. Your whole life has been a lie!"

When Rodolfo made that remark, something inside Maria finally snapped. Maybe it was the murder of Redondo, or the idea of how the life of a human being meant nothing to Rodolfo. Maybe it was because perhaps one day Rodolfo would kill her, and she would not get an opportunity to live her life as she truly wanted. But it was mostly because she was tired of his abuses that she finally got the nerve to speak up to him. "Don't you dare call me a liar, Rodolfo! If anyone has lived a lie, it is you! You are nothing but a bully and a wife beater. You are a devious and cunning bastard!" Both Anita and Laura turned to look at their mother. They could not believe what they were hearing from the mouth of Maria Hernández. "I know about your little secret, Rodolfo."

"What are you talking about, woman?"

"You know exactly what I'm talking about. Does the name Jorge Santos sound familiar? Or better yet, does Jorge Santos from Barcelona sound familiar?"

"You have a big mouth, Maria, and I advise you to shut it!" Rodolfo's disposition changed quickly. He dropped the argument and turned to everybody. We must prepare our defenses. Laura, Anita, you two will get plenty of water from the well and store it, for we may be under siege for days. As for the rest of you, prepare for the worst, now go!" As everyone in the Hernández household dispersed, Rodolfo called out for his wife. Fearlessly, Maria looked straight into his angry eyes. "How much do you know about Jorge Santos?" Rodolfo pressed her, "How did you come by this name?"

"Talk about having a big mouth, Rodolfo. It is you with the big mouth. My dear husband, you talk in your sleep. You talk so much that I—"

"All right, Maria, say no more. Have you told anybody else about me?"

"No."

"Good. Then we must keep this a secret between us. I know I have been a terrible husband, but if we get through this, I promise I will change. Do you believe me?"

Maria wanted so much to believe Rodolfo. She yearned to have that man back, the one who courted her and made her feel so loved. "We will see, Rodolfo. I will not believe you until I see you change."

"Fair enough, Maria. Now, can you tell me where Rosa's gone?"

"I have good reason to believe that she's with Miguel Pítre."

"Miguel Pítre, she's gone off with that piece of shit? Is that what you're telling me? That lowlife's gone too far! He's going to hang for this!"

Maria nodded. "Rodolfo, please do not harm Rosa, she's so young and so full of life. She is our youngest child and she deserves your love, not your anger."

Rodolfo placed his two hands on Maria's shoulders and nodded at her. "Hush now, Maria. I will not harm her, I promise. Rosa's just infatuated with Miguel, and Miguel doesn't even know what love is or what it takes to marry a refined woman such as Rosa. I will go to San Sebastián and convince the two of them. I will not exact any form of retribution on Miguel Pítre either. I will bring Rosa back safe and sound." Then Rodolfo did something completely unexpected, something he had not done in more than ten years. Rodolfo leaned forward and kissed Maria on the lips. Surprised, or better said: shocked, Maria recoiled at first, but then she leaned forward and kissed her husband passionately.

Rodolfo let go of Maria and gazed into her eyes. "When I come back from San Sebastián with our daughter, we will prepare for battle. After all this is over, we will take a trip to Spain. You can see your father and we will have a grand time."

"All right, Rodolfo. It sounds promising but many plans have a way of changing."

"Not this one, Maria. I promise you that I will not change the plan, and I will not allow anything to change it either."

Rodolfo stepped outside the house and mounted his horse. On the way to San Sebastián, he could not believe that he talked in his sleep. How could he have been so careless? Just how much information did he inadvertently reveal? But his secret was big, too big; so big that he needed to make sure it would remain a secret. While riding his horse toward San Sebastián he came to a sudden decision. Maria would have a terrible accident while sailing to Spain. He would inherit all of his wife's money, upon her father's death, marry off Laura and Anita, and place Rosalía in a convent in Spain. But before he could execute his plans for the future, he had to make sure that Miguel Pítre was out of the picture, completely and totally out of his family's life forever. He would convince Mayor Chiesa to issue an arrest warrant for Miguel under the charges of kidnapping and rape of Rosalía Hernández. He would accompany the militia to wherever it was that Miguel was staying, and he would personally hang the jíbaro who dared court one of his daughters.

CHAPTER 81

Carlos Martínez and his band of 45 rebels from Camuy arrived at the Rojas plantation at 6:45 in the evening. Surprised to see such a large gathering of armed men, Manuel Rojas stepped outside to investigate the commotion. He recognized Carlos Martínez as he dismounted a tired horse. "Carlos, what is the meaning of this?" shouted Rojas.

"My dear señor Rojas, I'm afraid I have bad news for you. Manuel Maria Gonzalez has been arrested for sedition and taken to Arecibo by a Colonel Iturriaga."

"Dear God!" exclaimed the half-Venezuelan farmer. "They're on to us!" The door to the house creaked open and out stepped Miguel Rojas and his wife. Manuel Rojas turned to face his brother, and with saddened eyes said, "Miguel, I want you to ride out to Mayagüez tonight. The authorities have arrested Manuel Maria Gonzalez and God only knows if troops are on the way to Camuy. We have no choice but to move the date for the revolution forward."

"How much forward, brother?" Miguel asked alarmingly.

"Tonight, if we can do it," replied Manuel Rojas, but even he knew that was impossible to do.

"We can't start the revolution tonight and you know that, Manuel," said Miguel while Mariana held a firm grasp on his arm. She had been up that night sewing, putting together the final pieces of the new rebel flag. "We need time to gather the men and ammunition," continued Miguel Rojas. "And we need time to form a plan of attack." There was no doubt in Miguel Rojas's mind that an armed conflict was a foregone conclusion, but he wanted to have better odds at success.

Manuel sighed, "You're right, tomorrow is a better day."

"That's still too soon, Manuel! Come now, man, you're not thinking right! You want me to ride out to Mayagüez tonight, and that's not across the road; it's pretty damn far. Then you want all of Capa Prieto to come here fully armed by tomorrow? I mean just listen to what you're saying, my brother."

"Miguel's right," said Carlos Martínez. "There's no way possible that the remaining members of Lanzador or that even Porvenir will arrive here fully armed by tomorrow, too."

Manuel took a few moments to think hard about the current situation. As the men of Carlos Martínez's contingent began talking amongst themselves, Manuel Rojas walked away from his brother and Carlos. He stood alone and thought hard for several minutes. Coming to a swift resolution, he walked back to them and nodded. "You're absolutely right, men, but we no longer hold the element of surprise and we no longer have the luxury of time. We will have all day tomorrow and all day Wednesday to gather as many men, arms and ammunition as possible. It is clear now that Camuy cannot sound the first cry of independence. That honor now belongs to Lares. Go now, my brother, tell Mathias Brugman what has happened, and tell him that the revolution will begin on Wednesday, September 23 in this year of our Lord 1868!"

Manuel Rojas watched his brother as he walked to the stable to retrieve a fresh horse. Rojas then turned to face Carlos Martínez. "I want you to ride back to Camuy, Carlos."

"When, tonight?"

"Yes Carlos, tonight, we have no more time. I want you to gather and organize the rest of your men at Lanzador. Then I want you to go to José Antonio Hernández's farm, dig up the stored cache of weapons and ride back here by tomorrow morning." Manuel noticed the sudden frown on Martínez's face. "What is it, Carlos?"

"José Antonio Hernández never did join me when I went to see if I could rescue Gonzalez. He has fled into the mountains and is presumably in hiding, that coward bastard."

"By God, is there anything else that could go wrong?" Rojas said in frustration. "Do you know where he buried the weapons and ammunition?"

"No, señor Rojas, only he knew that," Martínez replied apologetically.

Rojas sighed one more time. "Very well, then ride out to Camuy and bring back as many armed men as you can. We will make do with whatever is available."

Carlos Martínez chose three men to accompany him back to Camuy and took off that very night. On the road to Camuy, he would split up his company and send word out to the rest of the rebel cells in western Puerto Rico. About twenty minutes later, Miguel Rojas kissed his wife and he, too, rode out of the Lares plantation.

Manuel Rojas watched the gas lantern held by his brother until it faded into total darkness. Then he instructed the remaining men of Martínez's contingent to find a place behind the barn to lie down for the night. Manuel Rojas watched as the men slowly walked past him and into the darkened field. As they walked past him, he wondered how many of them would live beyond September 23. Manuel then turned and noticed that Mariana, who was still stunned at hearing the news, held on to the incomplete rebel flag she'd been sewing the past few days. He walked slowly to the porch and whispered. "It's going to be all right, Mariana, you know that Miguel can take of himself."

"Things are happening so quickly my head is spinning," replied Mariana.

Rojas smiled at her and slowly lowered his head to look at the forming rebel flag. "That piece cloth you are holding in your hands will become our flag. It will represent the sacrifices and the determination of our people to be free of tyranny. You must complete it tonight, so that when we have succeeded in our revolt, we will proudly hoist our new flag above the first public building we take over."

CHAPTER 82

Manuel Maria Gonzalez's face was barely recognizable, now that it had been the recipient of several blows at the hands of Iturriaga's soldiers. And yet, through that horrible night of pain and anguish, he held fast and refused to divulge a word about the Puerto Rican conspiracy. The leader of Lanzador held fast because he was a believer, a true believer in the cause for freedom. He had to reach down into the pit of his soul for the faith and strength necessary to withstand the punishment. He felt in his heart that God would reward him for such a noble act of defiance against tyranny, and against oppression and slavery. By 7:30 that evening, Gonzalez, zapped of all strength, could barely open his eyes and focus on his attackers. While the soldiers took turns on Gonzalez, Colonel Iturriaga attempted to decipher the encrypted entries he found in the back section of the green ledger. Although the Colonel tried many times, it proved to no avail. Colonel Iturriaga snapped the ledger closed and tilted his head up to look at the fine work his men were doing on Gonzalez's face. He rose to his feet with a sense of purpose. "Stop!" he commanded. The colonel paced himself slowly to his prisoner and contemplated his damaged face. "Had enough? Are you ready to tell me what the encoded writings are all about?"

Breathing heavily and blood oozing from his mouth, Gonzalez looked at Iturriaga out of his only functioning eye. "Colonel, how can I tell you about something for which I possess no knowledge?"

Iturriaga gave him a look of frustration. "Come now, Mr. President, the ledger was found on the floor of your study, buried under a pile of papers."

"And I'm telling you that I don't know how that book got there."

"It doesn't matter anyway," replied the Colonel. "We have the names of all your members. It's only a matter of time before we round them up, and I'm sure one of them will talk." He looked at his men and commanded, "Take him to the brig." What Iturriaga was not aware of though, was that Carlos Martínez was riding into Camuy that night to gather the remaining members of Lanzador Del Norte, leaving the Colonel with very little intelligence on the conspiracy, other than the green ledger. The colonel walked back to his desk and wrote orders for a contingent of soldiers to ride to Camuy and arrest all of the members listed in Gonzalez's ledger. It was now a race against time. Who would arrive at Camuy first?

CHAPTER 83

Don Mateo Ramirez answered the door at 8:05 in the evening. Standing before him was a young man, not much older than twenty years, with an anxious look about his face. Ramirez did not recognize the young man, but something about his appearance sent shivers up his spine. "Are you Miguel Pítre?" the young man asked.

"No. Who are you?" the plantation owner inquired.

"Gavino Mieles, but who I am is not important at the moment, señor." The young man took a step forward and looked down at his host. "May I come in?"

"Not until you tell me why you've come here," said Ramirez, standing defiantly in front of his home.

"Very well, then. Our plans for the revolution have been exposed, and as a result, the date for Puerto Rico's freedom war has been moved up to September 23."

Don Mateo Ramirez narrowed his eyes at the messenger and asked him to step into the house. "Please take a seat, young man, and tell me in detail what the hell happened?"

The young man calmly explained all the events leading up to his arrival that night at the Ramirez plantation. After recounting the events to Mateo, he contemplated the calm expression on the farmer's face. Mateo took it all in and accepted it matter-of-factly, as though he were accepting a coming rainstorm. At least it was the impression he gave the young Gavino Mieles. The messenger finally rose to his feet. "I must take my leave of you, señor, and deliver my message to our fellow rebels in other towns. Please inform the members of Porvenir that we are gathering in Lares, at Manuel Rojas's plantation."

Miguel jumped out of his makeshift bed and answered the hard banging on the door, trying not to wake Rosalía. But the knocking was too loud and Miguel wasn't fast enough. "What is it tío Mateo?"

"I have news from Camuy, Miguelito."

After relaying the news to Miguel Pítre, Don Mateo Ramirez stood watching his reaction. Instead of showing concern, as Mateo thought, Miguel flashed a smile at him. He turned around to face Rosalía who, by now, was sitting on the edge of her bed. "Rosa, the revolution will begin on Wednesday. I must gather our men and march to Lares tonight."

"Miguelito, I'm afraid."

Uncle Mateo stepped outside and with a calm demeanor addressed Miguel. "I will inform the rest of your men."

Miguel nodded, closed the door and walked slowly to Rosalía. He sat on the bed, put his hands on her delicate shoulders and whispered. "Don't be afraid, Rosa, we will have strength in numbers. But you must stay here."

"Don't ask me that, Miguelito. I cannot stay here. My place is with you now."

"Rosa, please don't make this more difficult for me. How can I fight knowing that you're with me in the middle of a war? How can I look out for my safety and yours at the same time? I love you too much to see you get hurt, and I don't want that. You needn't get yourself involved in our freedom war."

"No Miguelito, I am already involved, whether you like or not. I can help. You will need someone to care for the wounded; it might as well be me. I will go with you to Lares and I will wait for you at señor Rojas's plantation. That's final."

Miguel's eyes narrowed out of frustration, shaking his head at her. "You're so goddamn stubborn, Rosa. I suppose there's no way I can convince you otherwise?"

"No."

Miguel shook his head but wisely kept silent. He didn't want to get into an argument with Rosalía, and then leave for battle carrying the extra weight of a guilty conscience. As he donned his white trousers in silence, Rosalía suddenly bowled over and vomited all over the wooden floor.

Miguel turned and dashed over to her. "Rosa, are you all right?"

"I was feeling fine only a few minutes ago, Miguelito," replied Rosalía with hint of curiosity. She wiped her mouth clean. "I don't really know why this has happened. I don't feel sick."

At 8:45 that evening, Manolo and Berta stood in the middle of the gathering and watched Miguel Pítre address the crowd. Berta was the first to recognize Rosalía, and she gasped loudly enough for her brother to hear. As Miguel Pítre spoke to his contingent of men and women, Manolo turned to his sister. "Are you all right, Berta?"

"No. Look who's standing next to señores Ramirez and Pítre; it's Rosalía."

Manolo faced the front of the gathering and recognized Rosalía, too. "What is she doing here? It doesn't make sense."

At the front of the assembly, Miguel stretched out his arms in a pleading gesture, "So now that you're all aware of the latest events, we must look to gathering our weapons. Do this in an orderly fashion and remember that time is of essence. As soon as you are ready, please form three columns at the front door of the hacienda. We will be marching all night with very little rest. So make sure you have plenty of water and food!" Miguel nodded at the crowd and smiled with satisfaction. Then he opened his mouth wide and shouted. "Viva La Revolucion!" The crowd responded with cheers and cries of freedom.

While Don Mateo Ramirez parceled out morsels of food to the men gathering in front of his home, Miguel and Rosalía packed their horses with provisions and weapons. It wasn't very long before Miguel sensed a presence behind him. He turned around quickly and confronted Manolo. "Are you all right? May I help you?" Miguel asked.

"No, señor, I'm not all right."

Preoccupied with her own task, Rosalía did not notice Manolo, but when she heard his voice, she dropped a bag of oranges and spun around. "Manolo!" she cried out.

Manolo ignored her. "That woman you're with is a peninsular and the daughter of Don Rodolfo Hernández." Manolo could sense Rosalía staring at him in shock.

"I know very well who she is," replied Miguel. He was growing tired of having to justify Rosalía's presence all the time, especially to strangers. He felt Rosalía approaching him and reached out for her hand. He took her hand and held it tightly to show Manolo they were together. Then, out of the darkness, Berta appeared behind Manolo.

"Berta, you too?" Rosalía said shockingly.

Berta gave Rosalía a half-smile, unsure about Rosalía's motives for being there.

Miguel turned to the side to face his sweetheart. "You know this man and woman, Rosa? They arrived earlier today with Don Blanco."

Rosalía looked up at Miguel and nodded. "Indeed I do, Miguel. We were playmates a long time ago, when we were innocent children. They are Manolo and Berta. They were born on the Hernández plantation and they are the children of Claudio and Mamíta who are slaves purchased by my father before I was born. They have two older brothers, Candelario and Agustin, both whom you already know."

Miguel turned to face Manolo and Berta. "So you have run away from the plantation to fight in the revolution then?"

"That wasn't our intention, señor Pítre. We were on our way to Guánica to set sail for America."

"That was our intention also," replied Miguel.

"So what changed your mind?" Manolo inquired, feeling Berta closer to him now.

"The same thing that changed yours, Manolo: the revolution."

"What about you, señorita Hernández?" Manolo asked directly.

"I'm with Miguel. We're going to get married after the revolution, and before you ask me, I will tell you. Yes, I have run away from home, as well, and Father has no idea where I am. I believe that things in Puerto Rico must change and that is why I have joined the cause."

Manolo nodded at Rosalía. "Out of all of the Hernández children, I am glad it was you. You've always been kind to us señorita and you've always shown compassion."

"Call me Rosa, please, I insist. Berta, I would like it very much if you would join me. I will be helping with the wounded and providing general care to the men once the revolution starts. Will you help me?"

Berta was too shocked to answer verbally. She simply nodded her approval.

Miguel smiled. "Good, then it is decided. Rosa and Berta will remain at the Rojas plantation and provide care for the wounded. You and I, Manolo, will fight for freedom. Let us proceed to the front of the house, where I'm sure you will see your brothers."

By 9:50, Miguel Rojas had briefed Mathias Brugman, and while the leader of Capa Prieto sat back on his couch, he digested every word. "A secret that big could not be kept a secret for too long a time, I suppose," said Brugman ruefully. Miguel Rojas sat next to Mathias Brugman and watched the rebel leader sorting things out in his mind. Bruno Chabrier, who had been Brugman's guest that night, chose to remain standing. "Under the present circumstances," continued Brugman, "I have no choice but to agree with the Honorable Manuel Rojas. It is best to act quickly, now that the revolution has been exposed. Please tell your brother that I concur with his decision to commence the freedom war on September 23." Both men rose to their feet and shook hands. Miguel Rojas then mounted his horse and rode back to Lares that same night.

Standing idle, watching Miguel Rojas's image fade into darkness, Mathias Brugman wondered whether the revolution would succeed in light of the haste with which it began. He decided to dispense with his doubts and summoned Bruno Chabrier to the porch. Sensing Chabrier standing next to him, Brugman spoke without looking at him. "Well, my good friend, it would seem that the fight is on. I wonder if you could do me a favor."

"Anything, Mathias," said Chabrier willingly.

"I wonder if you could inform the members of Capa Prieto to gather here in my home as early as possible tomorrow morning. Could you do that for me?"

"I will die trying, señor Brugman,"

"No, Bruno, do not die yet. We will need you alive at least for the next few days. In the meantime, I will write a message to Doctor Betances advising him our change of date."

CHAPTER 84

On the morning of September 22, Governor Juan Pavía received Colonel Iturriaga and quietly escorted him into his private study. The governor closed the door surreptitiously, as if he could no longer trust the black house servants, and barely spoke above a whisper. "I trust your trip wasn't too much of a hardship, Colonel."

"It was a painful journey, and I haven't slept much in 48 hours."

Governor Pavía nodded. "I can only offer you my deepest sympathies and regret for the moment. However, if we do this right, there will be a reward for you. Now give me your status report."

"I've received word from my men that they found no rebels in Camuy. They scoured every barrio there and searched the countryside but found no evidence of an organized martial presence."

"Well," said the Governor, clearing his throat at the same time. "That could only mean that they were alerted to us and that they've gone into hiding."

"I don't think so, Governor," replied Iturriaga with a tone of hardened skepticism.

"What else could they have done but to run and hide like cowards."

"The conspiracy is greater than I thought, and much greater than you contemplated," said the Colonel. The governor noted the Colonel's brooding eyes and sensed the somber tone of his voice. "It stretches from San Sebastián to Mayagüez, and I feel there are hundreds, if not thousands of members in these cells already."

"If what you say is true, Colonel, then we must put the Gamir plan into action. I will personally write the official request and stamp it with my gubernatorial seal. There will be no doubt that your orders came directly from me. I want you to quell this rebellion quickly. Do not let this revolution get a foothold on this otherwise peaceful island. Make as many arrests as you deem necessary."

Colonel Iturriaga rose to his feet and nodded at the governor. "I will send word to Colonel Ibarreta."

"No, Colonel, I've reassigned him to the garrison at Aguadilla," replied Pavía tersely. "I've been working with Colonel Ibarreta on other matters, and he has not shown me the qualities of a type of man I need right now."

"Your Excellency, Colonel Ibarreta has been in some of the worst fighting in Santo Domingo. He's a hardened soldier and he could be useful to the counter-attack," insisted Iturriaga. He watched Pavía taking his time to answer, and wondered why the governor had been so reluctant to employ the services of a well-trained and decorated officer.

"Trust me on this, Colonel, I know men. I will have specific duties for Colonel Ibarreta, but they will not include things that I will ask of you. Aguadilla is on the western coast of the island, far from the den of vipers in Lares and San Sebastián, and precisely where I want Ibarreta to remain."

"That should make him happy. Anyway, what type of man are you in need of and what sort of things will you ask of such a man that you will not ask of Ibarreta?"

"Please take a seat and I will tell you what I want you to do. Have you ever pulled the nails out of a person's fingers?"

"Torture," Iturriaga said laconically.

"Yes, torture."

Colonel Iturriaga sighed deeply. "From my experience, alcalde, you can get anyone to say just about anything under torture."

"If it comes to that, maybe, but trust me Colonel, with these peasants you will never get that far."

CHAPTER 85

Miguel's contingent was reaching the outskirts of Lares. Although the town seemed quiet and non-threatening at 11:00 o'clock that morning, the fact that the Spanish authorities had discovered the rebellion, gave Miguel enough reason to look beyond the obvious. He chose to lead his contingent around the Pueblo of Lares, through very dense vegetation, and thus avoid scrutiny by some nosey loyalist who would no doubt inform the authorities about sighting an armed group of creoles and Africans. Upon sighting a clearing in the vegetation, Miguel raised his arm and asked everyone to rest for the next thirty or so minutes.

Miguel, Cirilo and Manolo walked to the base of a nearby Plumeria tree and sat under its leafy shade. The rest of Miguel's men found their own spot under other trees scattered within the woods. The men were mostly quiet, and Miguel found their silence a testament to their innermost fears, fears of the unknown, and perhaps fears of their own mortality. As Cirilo and Manolo watched the assembly of armed rebels resting, Miguel contemplated the skies. It had been a fair day, and he wondered if the rain clouds that were looming a few miles to the west, might dampen their resolve on the day of the revolution.

Rosalía and Berta were sitting by the edge of a winding brook, washing their faces, and as Berta dried her milky brown cheeks with a cloth Manolo had given her, she contemplated Rosalía. "Rosa, I still don't understand you. You had everything and you turned your back on it…why?"

Rosalía shrugged her shoulders and grinned. "I had nothing, Berta. I was just the daughter of Rodolfo Hernández; *he's* the one with everything, *he's* the one with money and power. Besides, having money does not make a person happy or fulfill a person's life. Before coming to

San Sebastián, I was miserable, and you know that. In fact, everyone in our household was miserable, including you, Berta. I grew up shielded from the realities of life in Puerto Rico, blinded by a domineering father, but everything changed the moment I met Miguel Pítre…and the moment he showed me the true Puerto Rico. I realized then that although this is a beautiful and enchanting island, something ugly was hiding just beneath its surface. I could not consciously live among the creoles knowing that the Spanish, my people, were exploiting them to further their riches."

Berta smiled and nodded at Rosalía. "You also fell in love."

Rosalía hesitated for a brief moment before her blue eyes flashed with a smile. "Yes, I did fall in love with Miguel. I did not plan to, but it did happen, and I am not going to deny it either. But my feelings for Miguel had nothing to do with my resolve to join the revolution."

Berta smiled again before rising to her feet. Looking down at Rosalía, she put her hands on her waist. "I have never seen you this happy and calm before, Rosa. Falling in love must be something truly special."

Rosalía stood up and gazed into Berta's inquisitive, brown eyes. "It is indescribable, Berta, and one day you will know the feeling."

CHAPTER 86

During the late hours of the previous night, while on the road to Aguadilla, Colonel Ibarreta received a message from Mayor Chiesa, urging him to ride to San Sebastián with all possible speed. He wrote nothing else in his letter, and the mystery behind it seemed to stir the Colonel's mind into action. Several hours prior to receiving Chiesa's message, though, Ibarreta had received new orders from Governor Pavía reassigning him from the Quebradillas militia back to the militia at Aguadilla. Ibarreta supposed reassignment to a far off post was the penalty for questioning the governor, a royal appointee. But somewhere in the back of his mind, there was a gnawing thought that perhaps the revolution had already started, and that the governor wanted him to take no part in the defense. Perhaps San Sebastián was already in flames and her citizens in desperate need of help. Since Chiesa had not written any details as to the reason why he wanted the colonel in San Sebastián, Ibarreta chose to ride there with a contingent of twenty soldiers and leave the rest of his company a few miles behind. He reasoned that if he should encounter no rebellion in San Sebastian, he would turn back and head straight for Aguadilla to assume his new position. If it turned out a rebellion had indeed started, then he would become the first defender of the island. The governor would have no choice but to acknowledge his success publically, and at the height of such vindication, he would respectfully resign his commission.

The experienced colonel arrived in San Sebastián by 11:30 in the morning and quickly discovered nothing out of the ordinary. There were no commotions of any kind, gunfire or blasts of cannons. It was just another normal Tuesday morning; a morning that saw the market vendors going about their business, people buying and selling goods, old men sitting on benches in the plaza feeding birds, church bells ringing and shopkeepers busy with their customers. Ibarreta saw nothing that would give him reason to request reinforcements, and that gave him a small measure of relief.

The small cavalry rode into town as quietly as they could humanly do, but the sound of twenty horses and the cloud of dust from their hooves were simply too much for the townsfolk to ignore. Distracted by the sudden convergence of twenty soldiers, they paused briefly to gaze at the military gathering and speculate the purpose for their sudden appearance. Colonel Ibarreta raised his arm, and all horses came to a halt right in front of the mayor's office. Realizing there would be no military action in their pueblo, the townsfolk resumed their activities.

Colonel Ibarreta entered the mayor's study and quickly noticed Rodolfo Hernández sitting across Chiesa. "Buenos Dias, señores," said Ibarreta. The second he stepped into the mayor's office, though, he immediately sensed something sinister in the air. Contrary to what the colonel was thinking last night, it was clear now that the mayor had summoned him there for highly questionable and perhaps illegal purposes. What gave him that impression was the anxiety in Rodolfo's face; the same look he displayed when Chiesa had issued orders for the arrest of Carlos Peña. Mayor Chiesa and Rodolfo Hernández both rose to their feet, and cordially tipped their heads at the Colonel, then they took turns shaking hands with him.

"Thank you for answering my message on such short notice, Juan Manuel," said Chiesa sitting back on his chair. Rodolfo, on the other hand, remained standing, wide-eyed, anxious and staring at the colonel. Mayor Chiesa opened the center drawer of his desk and pulled out a folded sheet of paper. He unfolded the letter and held it upright so that the colonel could see it. The writing was tiny, but the colonel could see the mayor's outlandish signature at the bottom of the page, as well as the mayoral seal just above it. It seemed to Ibarreta that the mayor had taken great pains to make the document look as official as possible—something which, naturally as mayor, he did not need to do. "This is an arrest warrant for señores Miguel Pítre, Manuel Cebollero Aguilar and Eusebio Ibarra. The warrant also lists the names of other Porvenir cell members. I want you to seek these rebels out and arrest them too.

Within this warrant, there are additional charges levied against Miguel Pítre and Manuel Aguilar. Pítre's charges include the abduction and rape of Rodolfo Hernández's daughter. Aguilar's charges include the torture and murder of Don Diego Redondo."

Colonel Ibarreta did not take the document from Chiesa's hand. Instead, he turned to Rodolfo, and said quizzically. "You really believe that, Don Hernández?"

"What, Colonel, that they're all rebels?"

"No. That Miguel Pítre abducted your daughter?"

"Of course I do. Rosa would never willingly run away with a goddamn jíbaro. She *had* to have been abducted by that rebel scum."

"That's not what I hear," said Ibarreta, now with growing skepticism.

"Oh, so now you hear things, Colonel?" Rodolfo uttered sarcastically. "What, have the jíbaros and creoles taken you into their confidence? How in the world did you accomplish that?"

Ibarreta sighed impatiently at Rodolfo, and then he shook his head. "Frankly, I'm surprised that you have not heard such talk from the townsfolk. With so many people spying for you, señor Hernández, how is that you are not aware of the scuttlebutt?"

"Well, Colonel, since you're so well entrenched in the community, why don't you enlighten us?" replied Hernández, nostrils flaring.

"Rodolfo, please, calm down," offered Chiesa meekly.

"No, señor Alcalde, I want to know what the people are saying," growled Rodolfo. "Well, Colonel?"

"The word is that your daughter is in love with Miguel Pítre, and that despite your wishes against their being together, she has been seeing him behind your back. Miguel Pítre did not abduct your daughter, señor Hernández. In fact, she is with him because she wants to be, not because he forced her into it. For these reasons, I am compelled to say that the charges of abduction and rape against Pítre are just as mendacious as those levied against Carlos Peña." Turning to Chiesa, the colonel continued, "What proof, other than señor Hernández's word, do you have for this charge? What proof do you have for the sedition and murder charges against Aguilar?"

Bothered by Colonel Ibarreta's response and sensing his reluctance to agree with the arrest warrant, mayor Chiesa quickly rose to his feet and raised his voice. "What the devil are you saying, Colonel? Are you calling me a liar? Are you calling Don Rodolfo Hernández, a respected member of the community, a liar? Watch yourself, Colonel, or you will find yourself busted down to a private. What do you take me for, a peon, a mindless bureaucrat? I have powerful connections in San Juan, and Colonel Iturriaga is a personal friend of mine."

Rodolfo did not say a word and simply allowed the mayor to spew his rage out on the upstart colonel. There were several moments of silence before Colonel Ibarreta decided to reply to the mayor. He did not feel the least bit intimidated by the two-faced politician standing before him or the opportunistic landowner next to him, staring at him with an evil glare. "Mayor Chiesa, I don't give a damn about your connections and I don't give a goddamn about your friendship with Colonel Iturriaga. I would just as soon be a private rather than a colonel forced to deal with the likes of you and Hernández. However, in light of the fact that the governor has seen fit to reassign me, I couldn't offer you my services even if I wanted to."

"Reassignment, what reassignment?" asked Rodolfo deflated now.

"I am to assume command of the militia at Aguadilla. I'm afraid the governor has banished me. You fine gentlemen will have to find someone else to do your dirty work."

Mayor Chiesa shot an angry look at Ibarreta, "It is not dirty work, Colonel, but official business. Now I do not know why the governor has reassigned you, and while I regret your absence here, there are others that can take your place."

Rodolfo nodded satisfactorily at Colonel Ibarreta before calmly sitting back on his chair facing the mayor. Mayor Chiesa nodded, too, and then he sat looking up at the colonel. "Very well, Colonel, had I been aware of your reassignment, I would not have sent for you. Who will be taking your place?"

"I do not know but I will write my intelligence report for the new commander. As you know, reports have been coming in about the rebels being well armed, and growing in numbers. The militia of San Sebastián, as you both know, cannot be trusted because they are comprised of San Sebastiános. My report will recommend the deployment of new troops from either the Camuy or Quebradillas militias since they are closer to you than my base at Aguadilla. You could have them here in three to four days"

"That's too long Colonel," said Rodolfo, concerned. "You don't think that by now the townsfolk have already alerted the rebels about your arrival here?"

"Señor Hernández," said Ibarreta with a huge sigh of tolerance. Aware that Rodolfo was a mere landowner, Ibarreta concluded that he had no idea about the logistics behind such a military action. "If we are going to quell this rebellion then our goal must be well planned and well coordinated. It is not going to be done haphazardly in order to appease your agenda."

"All right, all right!" said Mayor Chiesa, waving his hand at the colonel. "Do what you must do to get the troops here as quickly as possible. Here, take the warrant and pass it on to the new commander." The mayor handed the warrant to Colonel Ibarreta, who it took it with a great deal of reluctance. He turned around and without bidding good day to them, stormed out of the mayor's office.

"What do you think?" Rodolfo asked the mayor.

"He'll do what he is told, but I don't think I should put all of my eggs in that shaky basket. I haven't been too happy with the colonel lately, so a few days ago I sent Governor Pavía a letter of complaint. I sent a quick note to Colonel Iturriaga, too, just in case."

"One cannot be too careful these days, even with our own kind," answered Rodolfo.

Colonel Ibarreta stepped outside the mayor's office in a fit of anger. "Let's go, men, we're heading back to Quebradillas!"

Captain Collazo, a recent arrival from Spain, steered his horse closer to the colonel. "What's wrong, sir?"

"Goddamn politicians!" Colonel Ibarreta uttered. "They've issued orders for the arrest of several creoles here in San Sebastián. Well, I cannot think of a better way to ignite a revolution, Captain, than to levy false charges of sedition, abduction, rape and murder against respected townsmen of San Sebastián. I cannot think of a better way to galvanize the people, can you?" Colonel Ibarreta spurred his horse and began galloping away from the young officer. Collazo spurred his horse and caught up to the colonel. While bouncing atop his horse, Ibarreta turned to the side and gave the Captain a look of exasperation. "Ride ahead to Quebradillas and inform Captain Castañon to assume command of the militia until the new commander arrives in a few days. Give Castañon this arrest warrant, then gather my personal belongings at the barracks and join me along the road to Aguadilla. When we reach Aguadilla, I want you to alert the other officers there that I will be inspecting the troops within two hours of my arrival. Then I want you to coordinate the militia into action. We will not have too much time to do this, so I am counting on you to get it done. If those bastards think they're going to keep me out of this, then they've made a terrible mistake."

CHAPTER 87

Twenty miles southwest of San Sebastián, the sun was beginning its descent over the coastal town of Mayagüez. The Caribbean Sea was so tranquil that late afternoon, it seemed to purr like a kitten; the waves rolling onto the shores in sublime silence. It had taken nearly the entire day to send word out to the members of Capa Prieto, especially those dwelling in the outskirts of Mayagüez, but toward 6:30PM, they finally gathered at Mathias Brugman's colmado. The leaders, along with many of their seconds and regular members, all stood watching Mathias as he spoke to them with the zeal of a rebel. No one setback was big enough to dampen Brugman's spirits, and even if it did, he would never show it. "Brothers!" began Mathias. "I regret to inform you that the Spanish authorities have discovered our plans for a revolution. They have arrested Manuel Maria Gonzalez, the president of Lanzador and imprisoned him in Arecibo." Brugman noted the tone of alarm in the voices of the men as they began to murmur amongst themselves. The shock was so big that they simply could not hide their sudden fears. Mathias allowed them only a few moments to digest the news but then wasted no more time. "Listen to me," he said, raising his arms up in the air. "Please brothers, all is not lost!" He brought his arms down. "This is the plan: everyone is to go home tonight and retrieve his or her weapon. Tomorrow, we will march to Lares, where we will join forces with Centro Bravo, Porvenir and Lanzador Del Norte. Centro Bravo will sound the first cry for independence and take over the town of Lares. Then we will move northward and take San Sebastián. After securing San Sebastián, we will march on to Arecibo, free Manuel Maria Gonzalez and seize the stronghold as our base of operations. Once their cache of weapons and munitions are in our hands, we will march on to San Juan and then send Pavía back to Spain!"

The low hum of chatter grew louder. The rebels looked helpless and unable to hide their concerns about the sudden rush and haste with which the leaders were starting the revolution. One member in the back of the gathering raised his voice. “Señor Brugman, why are we planning to attack the base at Arecibo? Why not move slowly, and march on Aguadilla first?”

“Because Aguadilla is to the west and away from our final target, which many of you know, has always been San Juan. Arecibo is along the way to San Juan but, more importantly, it has the most concentration of weapons and ammunition other than San Juan. That is the reason, señor! It is very important that we take Arecibo first, before marching onto San Juan, everything depends on it.” Brugman gazed across the gathering of men and women and noted many distorted faces; some filled with apprehension and some with uncertainty and fear. He nodded at them, as if everything was going to be all right. “Brothers and sisters, the time has come. All of the things we talked about with such passion, the changes we planned to bring to Puerto Rico are closer to reality. We will change the current polluted economy that chokes us like a hangman’s noose, we will bring food to the hungry, and we will create hospitals with trained doctors devoted to the eradication of Cholera and other diseases. We will appoint bold new leaders that will address the suffering, and avenge the ravages of four hundred years of tyranny. But you have to be strong now, and you must have courage and determination. I will not lie to you. Many will die in the coming revolution, but your deaths, my death, will not have been in vain. All I ask is that you ignore the present, but look to the future and see what a free and independent nation can do for its people. This revolution is necessary because it is the only way that Spain and the rest of the world will listen to our cries for independence!”

Mathias Brugman said nothing more and simply stood watching the members of his audience. He felt his body shaking with nervous excitement, light brown eyes glittering back at the crowd, savoring the moment as if relishing the taste a cold flask of freshly squeezed orange juice. After several moments of silence, someone in the back began to clap his hands. Then, everyone in the gathering gave Brugman an ovation. The applause grew into a frenzy of loud cheers, causing Brugman to smile for the first time in weeks. Brugman turned to the side to look at Baldomero Baurer, and his dear friend returned an equally enthusiastic smile. Bruno Chabrier who was standing next to Baurer also flashed an uneven set of teeth at Brugman, pleased that the gathering of rebels were thinking as one, that their decision to fight had been unanimous.

CHAPTER 88

It took Colonel Ibarreta nearly five hours to organize the four hundred foot-soldiers and sixty cavalrymen into a cohesive unit. Now that his company looked more like a battalion, rather than a rag-tag outfit of men hastily put together, he rode his horse out to the head of the column to lead the march to San Sebastián. There was no question in his mind that the revolution was real. It was no longer an intangible set of ideals discussed at great lengths but never acted upon by its creators. Put forth by hundreds of peasants cramped inside stuffy, smoke-filled gathering rooms in the middle of the night, the plans to rebel against the mother country transformed into a battle for freedom. Political rhetoric and societal dogmas no longer encumbered the peasants' resolve to commit their hearts and souls to the cause. In the short time Ibarreta had lived in San Sebastian, he had come to recognize that inner cry of the human spirit, and in a strange sort of way, he understood their plight. He knew that the best fighters were those who fought for a cause, those who fought for their liberties and for their families. For this reason, he chose to prepare his men the second he arrived at the base in Aguadilla.

The highest-ranking officer at the Aguadilla barracks prior to Ibarreta's arrival was Major Francisco Navarro, who seemed less enthused about the colonel than the other officers were. Alongside Ibarreta, sitting atop his horse at the head of the first column, the major raised his hand and commanded the battalion to march forward.

Several miles into the march, a rider, a young militiaman, galloped to the head of the battalion to confront Colonel Ibarreta. Saluting Ibarreta, he said, "Colonel, I have a dispatch for you!"

Ibarreta ignored the messenger at first and continued to lead his soldiers, but the messenger's determination to fulfill his orders, forced him to keep close pace with Ibarreta. The colonel simply could not ignore him. Ibarreta sighed before moving away from the head of the army. Then he cast a pair of frustrated eyes at his second in command. "Take the lead, Major, I'll join up with you shortly. It's probably a letter from Colonel Iturriaga, wishing me good luck with the base here." He looked at the messenger and gestured to ride alongside him. Moving several yards away, Ibarreta flanked his column of soldiers, keeping pace with his men. He finally turned to the messenger and nodded at him.

"Colonel," said the messenger, reaching into his leather pouch. He retrieved a folded sheet of paper and handed it to Ibarreta. "It's from Colonel Iturriaga, with his compliments, señor."

Colonel Ibarreta took the paper from the messenger's hand and quickly opened it. While Ibarreta read the short message, the messenger noted the colonel's face stiffen with anger. Ibarreta crumpled the paper and threw it on the ground. Then he gave the messenger a stern look. "With my compliments, ride to the front of the battalion and inform Major Navarro to return to the base with the men." Disgusted with the sudden turn of events, Colonel Ibarreta spurred his horse and rode back to the militia's headquarters.

In a fit of rage, Colonel Ibarreta threw his riding gloves on the desk. He opened the bottom drawer and pulled out a bottle of rum. He filled the glass and drank several shots before leaning back on his chair. As he stared at the ceiling of his small office, he recalled the contents of the dispatch.

Colonel Ibarreta,

The Honorable Mayor Chiesa has called into question your recent actions in San Sebastián. Governor Pavia has also questioned your actions as of late and has expressed disappointment with your command. As your superior officer, I hereby order you to stand down and instruct the militia at Aguadilla to remain at the base and await further orders. In the meantime, make your way to San Juan with all possible speed, where you will meet with Colonel Gamir, Governor Pavia and me to explain and defend your actions.

Respectfully yours,
Colonel Manuel de Iturriaga,
Commander, Arecibo Base

Colonel Ibarreta rose to his feet and muttered to himself. "Damn politicians!" Standing by the open doorway, he noticed the battalion returning to the barracks, and Major Navarro riding toward him with a confused look in his eyes. From atop his horse Major Navarro looked down at Ibarreta, shaking his head. "Colonel, what's going on? Why did you order us to return to base, I thought there was a revolution to quell?"

"I don't know what's going on, Francisco. All I know is that I've been ordered to appear before the governor and my superiors in San Juan. Keep your men on full alert and wait here for further orders from Arecibo or San Juan." As Major Navarro watched Ibarreta mount his horse, he noted the frustration on his commander's face. "What is it, Colonel? Why are you being summoned to San Juan by the governor?"

"Politics, Major Navarro, bullshit politics!" answered Ibarreta. He spurred his horse into action and disappeared into the woods.

CHAPTER 89

At 8:15 on the night of Tuesday, September 22, news about the revolution starting the next day had spread through the barrios of every town in western Puerto Rico. It was a special night for the members of Porvenir because Lares was a sister town of San Sebastian, and they felt just as enthusiastic as those who would sound the first cry for independence. The excitement caused them to abandon their discretion and gather in the streets of Barrio Pepinos to celebrate the coming event. Without regard to secrecy, the assembly of rebels loudly hailed the names of both Aguilar and Ibarra. The shouts of merriment were loud enough that the Spanish residents, the few loyalists living in Pepinos, could clearly hear the celebration. From their windows, they could see the swelling number of rebels, some wielding machetes and some brazenly displaying pistols. Unable to quell their primal fears, they drew curtains, extinguished all lanterns and prayed to the All Mighty for deliverance. The loyalists all knew that the rebels would attack them first, steal their properties and perhaps kill them. Some of the loyalist men instructed their wives to hide all jewelry and money. Then they proceeded to barricade their doors, shut their windows and keep vigilant during the ensuing hours of the night.

The celebration went on for more than an hour, until Manuel Cebollero Aguilar finally raised his hands to quiet the gathering. "I want to thank you all and wish you good luck tomorrow. I don't know how many of us will live to talk about this great crusade we have undertaken, but to those men surviving tomorrow's revolution, please give honor to the ones that do not." Aguilar looked around the gathering but he could not find Miguel Pítre. He wanted so much for Miguel to be there, partaking in the celebration, but his most fervent member was not present. "And now," he continued, "let us gather our weapons and march on to Lares!" There was another cheer from the men before they began marching out of Pepinos.

Riding alongside Aguilar, Ibarra noted his pensive face. "Are you all right, Manuel?"

"Does anybody know where Miguel Pítre is?" Aguilar asked, turning to Ibarra.

"No one has told you?"

"Told me what? Did he abandon the cause?"

"No, Manuel, he would never do that. He marched on ahead to Lares. In fact, he might already be there. He knew that Porvenir would never approve his relationship to *El Demonio's* daughter, so he organized his own contingent and led them to Lares."

"I must meet this woman, Eusebio. Perhaps we might have been too harsh on the matter. Perhaps we should have given Miguel an opportunity to present his woman to us and explain his actions. Instead, our decision to reject her outright has driven Miguel away from Porvenir, and we need a strong man like him. When the revolution is over, we will reconcile with Miguel, and we will offer him a position in the new government."

"A wise idea, Manuel," said Ibarra, ginning.

The men of Porvenir marched through the night on their way to meet their destiny in Lares. Once again, Barrio Pepinos fell silent, but none of the loyalist residents would close their eyelids that night, for the fear of death far outweighed the temptation, the joy of reposing.

CHAPTER 90

Pacing back and forth in his study, Mayor Chiesa worried incessantly. He turned around to face Dario Pagan, a thinly man, whose face was constantly gleaming from sweat. He was a loyalist who heard every word at the gathering just minutes earlier at Barrio Pepinos, and had rushed to the mayor's office to bring him the news. "And you say they were armed?"

"Si, señor Alcalde, they are marching to Lares, even now as we speak. We could stop them, you know."

"With what?" Mayor Chiesa yelled, his face contorting to show the loyalist a disdainful intolerance for stupidity. "I've already written to Governor Pavía in San Juan and to Colonel Iturriaga in Arecibo. We cannot use the militia in San Sebastián because they're all creoles, and we simply do not trust the whole lot of them." Mayor Chiesa turned back to face the window, focusing on a gas lantern tied to a post. "Let us pray, señor Pagan, and let us ask God that the army arrives in time." He turned to face the loyalist. "Thank you and good night."

Chiesa watched the short, frail-looking man depart and another man enter. His name was Pedro Miguel San Antonio, a retired Spanish officer who had taken up residence in San Sebastián. The tall and husky former soldier stood at attention and waited for the mayor to initiate the conversation. "Please, take a seat, señor San Antonio." Mayor Chiesa walked back to his desk and stood looming over the imposing Spaniard. "You were a colonel before you retired from the army, isn't this so?"

"Si, Alcalde, why do you ask?" San Antonio shot a curious look at the mayor. Grey hairs now covered San Antonio's slightly balding head, and he sported an outlandish mustache, thick and unorganized. The square-jawed, broad-shouldered colonel nestled into the seemingly small chair, bringing his gargantuan legs closer together so that he could sit in relative comfort. The black pupils of his haunting eyes never dilated and never showed fear as he trained them on Chiesa.

"I would like to request your services for the next few days."

"In what capacity, señor?"

"I would like to reinstate your commission and retain your services as a Colonel once again…on a temporary basis, of course. I want you to assume command of the San Sebastián militia."

"Why, is the militia leaderless, mayor?"

"Let's just say I need someone in the militia that I can completely trust. The previous commander, Colonel Ibarreta, has assumed command of the militia at Aguadilla and the post in San Sebastián is now vacant. Rumors continue to stir amongst the creoles about a coming revolution, and I cannot take the rumors lightly. Fact is with Ibarreta's departure, there is no one at the base that I can trust because they are all San Sebastiános. That includes the one captain and three lieutenants, two of whom have already been charged with sedition but I fear they have already fled San Sebastián."

"I see. I heard about those rumors, too. I have just bought land and I am building a new house for my family. I will not allow any rebel to evict me from my home. When do you want me to assume command?"

"Right now, Colonel, I will have your papers drawn immediately."

The meeting was brief but the results for Mayor Chiesa would pay off in dividends. Now he had someone, a Spaniard, leading the San Sebastián militia, a man he could trust implicitly.

Colonel San Antonio rode his horse to the barracks and immediately assumed command. Known throughout his career as a man of action and very little words, San Antonio had earned the respect of his superiors as well as the men who served under him.

The moment San Antonio arrived at the barracks, he ordered a militiaman to his home to retrieve his military uniform. In the meantime, he checked the weapons and munitions stored in the barracks and informed the men to prepare for battle. Then he chose five militiamen to go into town and inform the peninsular merchants to gather all the gunpowder and dynamite and bring it to the barracks. Heeding the mayor's words about the militia being composed of San Sebastiános sympathetic to the revolution, he confined the rest of the militiamen to the barracks. Then he sent word to the loyalist men of San Sebastián to assist him by becoming armed sentries and watching the roads in and out of town.

CHAPTER 91

The night of September 22, 1868 would be a long one for everybody. Manuel Cebollero Aguilar would march his contingent of rebels during the darkness of that tense-filled night and would not reach Lares until 4:00 the next morning. As he marched his men along the edge of a creek, he kept his lantern at chest level—its undulating flames casting bursts of light along the way. He kept mostly to himself at the head of the column, and while he traversed the dark terrain, he ruminated over the past few months. His only regret was the fact that he was not able to defend Carlos Peña because of his status as a lieutenant in the San Sebastián militia. Then again, the constant reminder that he had taken in Diego Redondo without really knowing what kind of person he was, also played into his psyche. He felt guilty and sorrowful, too, that he did nothing to save Diego's life from his own men either, and that would gnaw away at his conscience for the rest of his life. But as he marched his men to Lares, he decided there was no time for feeling guilty, no time for remorse. The time for reflection would come later, after the revolution succeeded and after the fighting was over. Now, he would have to focus his energies on arriving in Lares with enough time for his men to rest. But would he get there in time? Would he arrive in Lares, only to find out that Rojas and all the rebels had gone off to fight? It was all in the hands of the All Mighty.

While Aguilar led his column during the night, inside a barn several hundred feet away from the Rojas hacienda, Miguel Pítre and Rosalía Hernández were kneeling before a priest. In that small barn, serving as witnesses to the wedding were Manuel Rojas, his brother Miguel, and Miguel Rojas's wife, Mariana. Among the witnesses, too, were Cirilo, all four of Mamíta and Papá's children, and a few African men and women. When the priest, an old creole and the only homegrown

Catholic minister in Lares, finished reading the passages from the Bible, he made the sign of the Crucifix and gave both Miguel and Rosalía his blessing. There was a loud cheer as Miguel kissed Rosalía passionately. But there was no time for celebration, and as soon as Miguel and Rosalía were married, the witnesses departed the barn. Only those rebels chosen by Rojas remained in the barn. The rest went back to other structures and shacks along the Rojas plantation.

Before long, everyone at the Rojas plantation had extinguished their lanterns and bedded down for the night. Almost immediately, Miguel heard snoring from one of the African men just a few feet away from him. Everyone had gathered hay and had thrown canvas sheets on top of their collections so that they could lie in relative comfort. It was a sacrifice not unlike the many they had made along their freedom odyssey, but they were all well worth it, for in their eyes they were small prices to pay for such freedom.

In a tiny corner of the barn, Miguel and Rosalía covered themselves with a blanket Mariana had given them. They held each other, kissed, caressed one another and whispered declarations of love for each other. It would be a long night for both Miguel and Rosalía, too. Though he kept his eyes shut, he wrestled with his conscience. Over the past few days, he'd been feeling distraught, his mind desperately coming to grips with the guilt he was harboring for taking Rosalía out of the comforts of a privileged life; a life where the want for nothing was a virtual guarantee. The guilt would always come back to him, haunting him like an evil spirit, persistently attacking him like a dreadful plague from which there was no cure, and sometimes he wondered whether she would have been better off without him. He did not know what the future had in store for him, but he was certain that he loved Rosalía with all of his heart. Rosalía was the binding glue that tied all of the fragmented pieces of his life together as in a great puzzle; she was the cornerstone of his happiness, the light of his soul, an angel sent from God. As he held Rosalía in his arms, Miguel vowed to himself that he would spend the rest of his life making her happy. He could not live without her, and if anything would ever happen to her, like dying, he would take his own life just to be with her in death.

Rosalía held Miguel around his waist and placed her head on his chest. She could hear his heartbeat pounding heavily. As the minutes of the night ticked away, she realized how much of her life her father had stifled. She had gotten a taste of freedom and now that she possessed such a hard-won liberty, she would never relinquish it. Rosalía had decreed her own emancipation and had resolved to leave home by her own volition. She would often tell Miguel that she did not base her decision solely upon her affections for him but because it would have been a matter of time before she would rebel anyway. Then again, she was glad that Miguel had come into her life, though she really did not expect to meet the man of her dreams in San Sebastián, much less a peasant jíbaro. She buried her face into Miguel's chest, feeling the heat of his body, and smiled. How quirky can life be, to have fallen in love with a peasant, a man representing the opposite of what her father dreamed and expected for her? But it was more than that, thought Rosalía. Miguel had a way about him that swept her off her feet. Miguel was very handsome and his lady-killer smile was unmatched by any of the men she had met before in her brief life, a smile that showed his perfect teeth, soft pink lips and wondrous green eyes. But the thing she loved most about Miguel was his fierce determination, his confidence and convictions about life. She loved the subtle whisper of his voice and the gentleness of his hands, though they were calloused beyond any kind of repair. Before Miguel, Rosalía's life was nothing but misery, melancholy, despair and loneliness. Before Miguel, Rosalía saw a bleak future, a future that saw her in an arranged marriage to a man she could never love. Before Miguel, she saw a future as a neglected and abused wife, a wife whose sole purpose was to have children and tend to the whims of an uncaring husband. Then one day, in a matter of only seconds, Miguel Pítre, a jíbaro from the mountains of San Sebastián would change that future. Rosalía loved Miguel so much that she would run away from home and give up all her rights to an inheritance.

Rosalía held Miguel tightly and kissed his chest. In the depths of her young soul, she knew that she could love no other man. And if for some strange circumstance she'd find herself back home, she would run away again just to be with Miguel. And if her father would send her away, or try to marry her off to a peninsular, she would kill herself rather than face a life of misery. In her arms, she held the only man in her life, the only man with the key to her heart, the only man who could ever enter the world of Rosalía Hernández. In her arms, she held the only thing in her life that mattered to her, and she would want to bear his children. She knew she was already pregnant, for it was the only reason why she had been so sick on the morning tío Ramirez came around with news of the rebellion. Now that they were legally married, and the fact that she had the papers to prove it, she would aggressively pursue her husband for more children. Rosalía struggled with her conscience that night. She wanted to tell Miguel that she was with child, but she refused to let her pregnancy get in the way of the rebellion. She also felt uncertain as to how Miguel would react to the news. That night was too long, and too important to tell Miguel he was going to be a father. Rosalía would wait until after the revolution.

As the night wore on, Rodolfo lay in bed wide-awake, wondering where his Rosalía was, and damning to hell all creoles of Puerto Rico. How could he have allowed a peasant to come into his life, so easily? Why did he not see it coming? Why was life being so cruel to him? Why did he talk in his sleep? Not once did he ever consider the notion that his actions might have been wrong. But Rodolfo had no conscience when it came to such matters, so in his mind he did no wrong at all. Things had gotten severely out of hand and he felt the tight control he once possessed on everything starting to slip from his grasp. There was so much that he needed to do and so little time to accomplish them. He needed to put down the coming rebellion. Then he had to find out who murdered Diego Redondo, but not because someone had committed a crime, but because someone had dared to kill his solicitor. He needed to find Miguel and find a way to kill the peasant, and then bring Rosalía back with him. If she refused, he would beat her into submission, and then ship her off to a convent. Then there was the matter of his wife, who simply knew too much about his past; Maria had to go. With the confusion and din of an armed conflict, he reasoned that he could use the excuse that rebels killed Maria during the height of battle; it was a plausible excuse and he would make it stick. In fact, it was a far better notion than the one about Maria falling off a ship was, and much simpler to explain, too. After dealing with Maria and Rosalía, he would send his two other daughters away to their own marriages. He would wait for two years to pass, and then he would start all over again. He would marry another woman, a healthy woman that would bear him sons, and he would continue with his life as if nothing ever happened.

Maria Hernández was wide-awake that night, too, unable to keep from recollecting the bad moments in San Sebastián. And to think that she'd been looking forward to a vacation away from San Juan, deep in the Puerto Rican countryside. With eyes staring at the moon through her open window, she convinced herself repeatedly until relief came to her troubled soul. Maria convinced herself that Rodolfo was going to change. Rodolfo said he would, so why would she not believe him? But it wasn't just the fact that he said it, but the way he said it. When he made that promise to her, the words flowed out of his mouth with a tone of heartfelt sincerity, raising her hopes of reigniting their marriage to new heights. When Rodolfo grabbed hold of her and kissed her on the lips, Maria felt that spark of love again, even though he had been a monster for nearly all of their twenty-five-year marriage. Maria had only enjoyed a short time of passion in that quarter of a century span, and she yearned for Rodolfo to hold her in his arms again. Maria wanted Rodolfo to love her, and she wanted to experience again what making love felt like. There was still a glimmer of hope for Maria. There was the promise that Rodolfo made to her. Then there was the kiss they shared passionately. And, finally, there was Rodolfo's gentle touch, the same touch she felt once before so many years ago. There was still love in her heart for Rodolfo, no question about it, and she would give him one more chance. In the recesses of her heart, she wanted to feel exactly how Rosalía felt about Miguel. She knew that wherever Rosalía was, she was truly happy. And if Rodolfo never found Rosalía, it would not matter to Maria because she knew that Miguel loved Rosalía and would never cause her any harm. Though she did not really know Miguel, she felt he was a good man, an honorable man who would make her daughter happy.

In the rooms upstairs, Laura also lay in bed wide eyed and staring at the ceiling. Her gas lantern was still on and she had trouble falling asleep. Her restlessness was not out of anger or despair, but out of happiness. Laura had succeeded in removing Rosalía out of her way, removing that stubborn obstacle between her and her father. Now with Rosalía out of the picture, Rodolfo would concentrate all his love on her. And as far as the other sister was concerned, Laura felt no threat from her, and maybe one day she would make friends with her. Anita was far too easy for Laura and she would manipulate her, mold her into something useful for her benefit only. Then, she would marry Gregorio and her wedding would be a grand one. She would give her father a grandson to dote on, give her father the boy he never had from Maria. Laura wasn't sleepy at all. Laura was too busy planning her future. It had been a good thing to travel to San Sebastián after all. She could hardly believe that she had been against the idea of traveling there, what a mistake *that* would have been.

In her bedroom, Anita was fast asleep. Poor Anita; she had been the middle child and the one most neglected by both Maria and Rodolfo Hernández. No one ever listened to her opinions and no one cared. Relegated to the same status as that of a doorknob, as she often thought of herself, Anita drifted into her own world, a world where she found solace, a world where she had respect from everybody and no one looked down on her. Perhaps one day she would find the right man, show everybody that she could think for herself, make sound decisions and not be judged inept in life. Perhaps one day she would come out of that perpetual fog that seemed to dominate her uneventful life. Perhaps one day her father would come to love and respect her. With those same dreams every night, she would fall into an abysmal sleep.

The hours of the night seemed to drag for Mayor Chiesa. Instead of spending the night at home, where he ought to have been, he decided to stay at his office in town. He paced back and forth, counting the minutes, nervously awaiting the arrival of Colonel Iturriaga from Arecibo. How would the events of tomorrow unfold, he had no clue. All he kept thinking about was the subsequent violence upon the loyalists should the revolutionists succeed. Deep inside, he felt like packing up and taking his family to San Juan, but his first duty was to the people of San Sebastián. The thought of rebel bandits prowling the streets of San Sebastián shooting loyalists scared the Mayor so much that he kept several rifles close by and constantly parted the curtain windows searching the streets below for any hint of trouble.

For many people in western Puerto Rico the night would be a dreadful one, a night where the long hours gave them too much time to think. The night of September 22 would be the last quiet night before the storm of a revolution would stir the towns of Lares and San Sebastián. It would be the last night where hope for a free and independent Puerto Rico would thrive. The revolution had to succeed not only for the sake of social and economic reform but also because the rebels knew that failure would result in certain death.

CHAPTER 92

On the morning of Wednesday, September 23, in a cluster of dwellings built in the center of Lares, a man named Frutos Caloca noticed something odd. At 9:22 that morning, the normally quiet, loyalist town was stirring about with action. A successful merchant himself, Frutos Caloca took pride in his growing business, and that morning he was thinking about expanding it and how best to entice investors into his new venture. At almost fifty, Frutos had no illusions about his appearance. A round protruding belly hampered all graceful moves he once had, and a thin crown of black and gray hair draped his head below the ears. A thick platinum line of bushy hair above his upper lip gave him a grandfatherly appearance despite the fact that his eldest child was only twelve-years-old.

All thoughts of expanding his business, however, vanished in an instant when Frutos noticed two of his closest neighbors outside their homes. What caused Caloca to take note of his neighbors, more so than on other occasions, was the fact that both Andres Pol and Francisco Santana had packed their wagons with trunks, suitcases and provisions. Caloca kept his eyes on his neighbors but immediately sensed something odd about the two men. Although Pol and Santana tried valiantly to appear as normal as possible, Caloca could easily read the sense of urgency in their eyes, which caused him to pay even more attention.

Frutos Caloca also noted both families doing exactly the same thing, and their goings on were reminiscent of a full-blown evacuation. Aware that such drastic actions were taken during a plague, war or hurricanes, Caloca thought hard, and came to the conclusion that a calamity was imminent, something much bigger than a hurricane, something truly monumental. Caloca stood in front of his home watching the two families climb onto their respective wagons. Neither Pol nor Santana took the time to look at their neighbor, though they were already aware that he was standing in front of his home watching them. Frutos Caloca moved his heavy-set body into his home, latched the door shut and told everyone in the house to be mindful of anything out of the ordinary that day. He told his eldest son to retrieve his two rifles upstairs and the pistol he hid in the top drawer of his dresser. He gave his wife specific instructions on how to answer the door should a stranger come knocking, and told his two daughters to hide in the attic should trouble arise. The Calocas were a tight-knit family, and they would faithfully heed his warnings. When he felt satisfied that he had taken all precautionary measures, he dressed and took off for work.

Frutos Caloca arrived at his shop at 10:17 in the morning, and again saw strange happenings. As he fumbled with the keys to his shop, he noticed Manuel Rojas in the bodega across the street. Rojas had one wagon already loaded with an inordinate number of blankets, gas bottles, and several new lanterns. Caloca also noticed a great number of burlap sacks containing rice, coffee and flour. In the other wagon, there was enough firewood to keep a cast-iron stove lit for months. There were crates of drinks, a few bottles of liquor and an assortment of dry goods.

Curious by nature, the middle-aged loyalist decided to cross the street and find out what Rojas was up to. Out of the corner of his eye, though, Rojas saw Caloca crossing and braced himself for the inevitable questions. Everyone in town knew just how nosey Caloca was, and many people took great pains to avoid talking to him, unless they needed to spread news quickly. In fact, Caloca knew things about people and events long before the local paper could publish them. The running joke around town was, *'don't waste your money on a newspaper when Caloca can give you the news for free!'* Rojas ignored the sound of Caloca's boots scraping the dirt road and continued to spread a canvas blanket over the wagon, fastening it by rope to the wooden frame.

"Buenos Dias, señor Rojas." Caloca said, stretching out his arm in a feeble attempt to shake hands with Rojas.

"What do you want, Caloca, I'm a little busy right now," said Rojas, ignoring Caloca's gesture.

"Nothing, Manuel, I was just wondering why you have made such a huge purchase. I hope you left something for the rest of us." Caloca searched Rojas's face but the rebel leader showed no fear and no hesitation.

"If you must know, Caloca," said Rojas, sighing impatiently. "I'm having a party in my house and I've invited many of my friends to attend. Now, if you would be so kind as to let me be, I would be much obliged. Oh, and one more thing, try not to spread this news too fast. I wouldn't want to have any uninvited guests."

Frutos Caloca narrowed his eyes at Rojas, unable to lend credence to his reply. "So what's the celebration for, your child, your birthday, what?"

"Caloca!" yelled Rojas impatiently.

"All right, all right, I won't pry," replied Caloca, waving his hands at Rojas.

Manuel Rojas tied the last knot on the rope and quickly turned his back on Caloca. As he mounted the wagon, he snapped the reins and uttered. "Buen Dia."

Frutos Caloca eyed the back of Rojas's head with skeptical, unnerving eyes. Something about the plantation owner's voice convinced Caloca that Rojas was lying to him. For one thing, Caloca had no prior knowledge of Rojas's party, and that was unusual. Then there was Pol and Santana, his two neighbors who left Lares in great haste. In his mind, he knew that Rojas, a known separatist, was up to no good.

Frutos Caloca would later prove his suspicions correct because in addition to buying supplies for the men stationed at his home, Rojas's trip into town would give him much needed intelligence about the militia in Lares. While in town, Rojas took note of the tiny barracks that housed the paltry number of militiamen, and made a mental note of the streets of Lares, especially those that led in and out of town. Upon his arrival at the plantation, he ordered several of his most trusted men to patrol all roads with access in and out of town, and to arrest any Spanish soldier attempting to enter the road leading to the Rojas plantation.

CHAPTER 93

At the home of Bruno Chabrier in Mayagüez, Eugene Bernard arrived to offer Chabrier assistance. He was one of the few rebels with a horse, and his appearance caused everyone at Capa Prieto to take notice. Brandishing a saber, revolver and rifle, Bernard's military appearance gave everyone a much-needed kick of confidence. Bernard's overseer, Pedro Segundo Garcia, also rode into Capa Prieto brandishing his own rifle and saber. After helping as much as he could, Bernard rode off to the Brugman hacienda, where he met up with his stepson, José Antonio Muse, who brought with him his slaves. Also at the Brugman hacienda, the brothers Beauchamp had arrived by 12:00 noon, along with a good number of their slaves. Bernard looked at the assembly thus far and guessed there were about 30 to 40 other rebel members already present, and he was surprised that they all possessed horses, revolvers and rifles, just like he did.

At 12:35 in the afternoon, Juan De Mata Terreforte arrived at the Brugman hacienda with an additional group of one hundred men. Terreforte's family was among the first Corsican families to settle in Mayagüez. Tall and lean, the square-jawed rebel had seen far too many creoles lose their lands over the years. Vowing to change conditions in Puerto Rico, Terreforte joined Doctor Betances's movement. Earlier that morning he received word from Chabrier to round up as many slaves and jornaleros in the nearby barrios and fincas of Mayagüez and march them to Lares later that afternoon, but his arrival at the Brugman hacienda gave the men already assembled there even more confidence.

Standing among the new recruits were two slaves, Candido and Polinario, their black faces gleaming from sweat and their lanky bodies exhausted from the long march that morning. Polinario, who was the property of José Antonio Muse, wiped the sweat off his forehead with the back of his hand and sighed in frustration. He turned to Candido and shook his head. "What did they tell you?"

"Not much," replied Candido. "They came on horseback and told us to join them in the revolution. They promised our freedom upon the success of the coming war."

"And you believed them?"

"It wasn't like I had a choice. After all, they were on horseback and they were well armed. How about you?"

"The same," answered Candido. "They simply told us to drop what we were doing and follow them." All of a sudden, Candido began laughing to himself.

"What's so funny?"

"Nothing, it's just that even in a rebellion there is still separation."

"What do you mean?"

"Did you notice that our group was split into two sections? One section has all the white creole hacendados on horseback, with rifles and swords, and the other has slaves and jornaleros on foot."

"Who knows, perhaps things will change for us."

Terreforte rode his white horse to the front of the gathering where he immediately commanded the men to assemble. He ordered twenty cavalrymen to lead the column, followed by sixty or so foot soldiers. He then ordered twenty cavalrymen to ride behind the foot soldiers in case any of them had a sudden change of mind and decided to turn back.

Terreforte's 18-mile journey from Mayagüez to Lares began with a joyous thunder of men joking and laughing, eager to face battle, but without a clue to its horrors. As the men marched along the dirt road, they even sang their freedom song, 'Long Live Liberty'. The only men who did not share in the good mood were Candido and Polinario, who kept their silence. As the singing continued, Santana, a twenty-two-year-old slave, moved up the column to march alongside Polinario and Candido. Santana had been watching them since the march began. "I too cannot share their sentiments," said Santana.

"And what makes you think we're not excited about this?" Polinario replied while looking straight ahead.

"I have seen nothing but gloom on your faces ever since I saw you two this morning. It amazes me that they seem so happy. Here we are, marching to Lares to face Spanish guns and cannons with only a machete in our hands. We have not eaten anything all day and no one even remembered to bring food. All we got at Chabrier's home were shots of rum, then a few crackers with cheese at the Brugman hacienda."

Polinario finally turned to face Santana. "It's all in God's hands now."

An hour into their journey, the procession of rebel warriors came to a halt by a nearby finca, where Terreforte noticed a number of jornaleros working the fields. With the purpose of recruiting additional soldiers, Terreforte ordered two of his men to ride into the field toward the working jornaleros. Minutes later, they came back with twenty-three willing field hands. Terreforte would make several more recruitment stops along the way to Lares until his band would swell to about one hundred and seventy-five men. On one occasion, though, he did not stop for recruitment purposes. Terreforte and his men had reached the home of a man called Manuel Gomez, a rebel sympathizer. At the Gomez home, the men drank more shots of rum, and with empty stomachs, the liquor became more effective, causing the men to become more jubilant, if not daring.

A few miles before reaching the outskirts of Lares, in a tiny, unincorporated and nameless pueblo, Terreforte and his band of rebels came across a store owned by a Spaniard named Coll. At 2:45 that afternoon, the pounding thunder of horses and foot soldiers permeated the walls of the store, prompting Coll to quickly step outside to investigate. Sadly, Coll would be the first loyalist to experience the wrath of the rebellion. He saw Terreforte raising his arm in the air to halt his army. The rebel leader stood atop his horse, gazing at Coll with hateful eyes. He spurred his horse toward the Spaniard and looked at him from top to bottom, as if he were sizing up an opponent. Narrowing his eyes at Coll, he said thunderously, "In the name of the new Republic of Puerto Rico, I am taking you as my prisoner!"

"What new republic?" shouted back Coll. `"This is a Spanish colony, and you are all subjects of Queen Isabel! The Spanish army will crush your pitiful band of rebels and you will all hang for treason!"

"Shut your goddamn mouth, you peninsular scum!" shouted back Terreforte. He turned to his second in command. "Arrest that pig and take as many provisions as you can from his store!" To say that Terreforte's men ransacked the store is to put it mildly. In fact, they took nearly everything edible, and when they had stolen all things possible, they turned the place upside down. They broke empty bottles, turned over shelves, and kicked down the door. Then, someone lit the curtains on fire. In a matter of minutes, yellowish-orange flames engulfed the wooden store and black smoke spiraled into the tropical blue skies.

With hands bound and a rag tied around his mouth, Coll marched behind Terreforte's white horse, sidestepping every now and then to avoid the horse's droppings.

CHAPTER 94

Terreforte and his army finally reach the Rojas plantation at 6:22 in the evening. The arrival of a new and large contingent caused the men already gathered there to stir with excitement. In all, there were approximately three hundred and fifty rebels at the Rojas plantation, and nearly all of them were eager to begin the war for independence. As Terreforte dismounted, Miguel Rojas rushed over to greet him. "Juan!" he shouted. "Thank God you're here! My brother will be very pleased. Where's Mathias?"

"He's gathering additional men and will arrive shortly. My men and horses are tired, Miguel. Is there any food and water you might give us?"

"Indeed, Juan, of that we have aplenty. Just tell your men to help themselves. But if I may steal a little bit of your time, my brother would like to see you."

Terreforte braced himself before entering the tiny hacienda. He had a plan of attack he thought was practical and efficient. His biggest worry, though, was whether the rebels would execute the plan as well as he had conceived it several days ago. He greeted Manuel Rojas, Aguilar, Ibarra and Carlos Gonzalez, who was the mayor of Quebradillas. Other leaders, such as Clemente Millan, Andres Pol and Francisco Ramirez were also present, and their somber faces revealed their commitment to the cause. Everyone stood before a table with a map spread over its surface, focusing their eyes on a tiny dot representing the pueblo of Lares. Terreforte greeted and shook hands with the rest of the leaders in the Rojas plantation, all except for Mariana Bracetti, who sat on the couch putting the final touches on the new flag of Puerto Rico. Terreforte took the time to gaze at Mariana's flag and smiled with a profound sense of satisfaction and national pride.

"Do you like it, Juan?" said Manuel Rojas jubilantly.

"It resembles the Dominican flag."

"A little, yes, but it is so much different. I'll tell you what, after the meeting is over, I want you to take a closer look at the flag and see for yourself how different it is. But for now, I need your undivided attention." Placing an arm over Terreforte's shoulder, Manuel Rojas said, "Juan, if you please?"

"Certainly," said Terreforte. Arching over the map, he pointed with his index finger. "These are the main roads in and out of Lares, here, here and here." Pointing to another section of the map, Terreforte spoke without taking his eyes away from the markings. "This is how we will form our attack, first we will…"

The meeting was over by 7:35PM and Terreforte took comfort in the notion that the leaders seemed to know their responsibilities. Nevertheless, Terreforte also knew he was leading mostly slaves and jornaleros, men who knew nothing about the military. He had served a number of years in the militia and was well acquainted with army tactics, but how many of his men would turn and run at the first sound of gunfire? How many of his cavalrymen would do the same? Indeed, it was all in God's hands. Everything was set in motion now, and like a runaway train, the rebellion was moving rapidly with no chance of stopping. Terreforte stepped outside and walked over to his men, where someone handed him a piece of beef jerky and a glass of rum. He sat on the ground, devoured the beef jerky and calmly sipped the brown, fiery liquid.

By ten in the evening, the men were starting to get restless. The leaders were well aware that they were powerless to contain the murmur of over three hundred men, and Rojas knew that he had to do something quickly. Standing idle, in front of Rojas's house, Miguel Pítre wondered why Rojas was hesitating so much and why was he displaying such a look of confusion? But was it confusion or was it simply fear? Rojas stood in the front porch of his house and while folding his arms, gazed at the rebel army. He never noticed Miguel standing next to him and trying to get his attention.

"I'm sorry Pítre, what were you saying?"

"I said now that we're all gathered here, when are we going to begin?"

Before Manuel Rojas could respond to Miguel Pítre, Aguilar and Ibarra hurriedly approached the rebel leader. It was then that Aguilar noticed the young Pítre for the first time that night. "Miguel!" he shouted. While holding his lit cigar, Aguilar searched Miguel's face, but Miguel maintained a placid, unemotional disposition.

Miguel Pítre turned away slowly from Rojas and focused his eyes on the new leader of the Porvenir rebel cell. Aguilar took in a puff from his long cigar and let it out slowly. "I heard you've been here for a while. Why didn't you present yourself to us?"

Refusing to interfere with cellular politics, Rojas said nothing and simply stepped to the side to contemplate the gathering. Miguel stared straight into Aguilar's eyes. "I no longer wish to be associated with Porvenir. In fact, I have my own cell. I have a contingent of forty-five men who are willing to fight to the death."

Aguilar glanced at Ibarra, flicked the ashes off his cigar and then looked at Miguel. "Is it because we did not attend Carlos's hanging and funeral? Is it because we did not see him in jail? Miguel, you know we couldn't do that without raising suspicion."

"And what were you afraid of? The very same people you are going to fight against tonight?"

"Yes. It wasn't the right time for Ibarra and me," replied Aguilar, visibly upset.

"Whatever!" Miguel said, throwing his hands up in the air.

"No, it's not whatever. We have to talk, Miguel. We have to figure out what role you're going to play in the new republic. We're going to need leaders, and you'll need to align yourself with me."

"I have no interest in politics, Manuel."

"No interest in politics? Are you crazy? You're a natural politician Miguel, and you could serve as a mayor, magistrate, judge or anything you desire."

"I will leave that to people like you. As for me, once the revolution is over, I will leave Puerto Rico for the United States. I am taking Rosalía with me and together we will live in America forever."

"You're turning your back on your own people, then?" interjected Eusebio Ibarra.

"My priorities have changed."

"I remember when you were a focused young man, full of ideas, hopes and dreams for a better Puerto Rico," muttered Ibarra.

Miguel laughed sarcastically.

"What? What's so funny, Miguel?" Aguilar asked.

Miguel sensed Rojas was far too distracted to pay any attention to their conversation. He looked at the two men with steady eyes. "Well for one thing, the ship that Betances promised us was boarded and detained by the Spanish. Second, we have no weapons to speak of, only a few men with rifles but mostly machetes. And, finally, the Spanish militia has plenty of guns, cannons and ammunition. Now I will give my heart and soul to the revolution, and I will pray for its success, but in the end, you and I both know that this is a lost cause."

Aguilar glanced over at Rojas, who was still busy contemplating the army. Then Aguilar turned back to Miguel and said angrily, "My young friend, the words you speak of are poison. If that is how you feel, then maybe it is better if you leave right now. I'd rather you be gone than have your poisonous words spread amongst the men; it's like a disease, a disease of fear and hopelessness."

"No, and I will tell you why," Miguel replied. "The reason why I have chosen to fight is because of the promise I made to Carlos Peña. If he were alive today, I might well have been a different man, and maybe, I'd be one of those politicians you speak of so enthusiastically. I will fight because of my father, because of the way things are in Puerto Rico. I will fight because if I don't, I will regret it for the rest of my life, and I have too much on mind for that!"

"Then you will not spread your thoughts amongst the men?" Aguilar asked humbly.

"No."

"All right, Miguelito, then where will you—" All of a sudden, someone in the crowd shouted, someone standing on the edge of the road, a sentry. At 10:15 that night, Pedro Pablo Gonzalez, a hacendado, arrived with a group of twenty jornaleros. Rojas, who was still standing aloof, took immediate notice of Gonzalez and for some reason the forces that caused him to hesitate seemed to vanish at sighting the arrival of Gonzalez. He stormed into his hacienda, much to Aguilar's and Miguel Pítre's surprise, and emerged moments later holding a red flag. Seconds later, another rebel leader, Clemente Millan, emerged from the Rojas hacienda holding a white flag.

As Miguel watched Rojas, he wondered what could have re-ignited him so much, why did he wait up until now to stir the rebels? He couldn't explain it, and when he looked across to Aguilar, even the leader of Porvenir had no answer. Then Miguel saw Terreforte and Colonel Ruiz Rivera making their way to the front porch, parting the sea of human bodies with their arms as if they were swimming a rough current. When they finally reached the stairs, they tilted their heads up at Rojas, removed their hats and changed their faces to a kind of reverence that Miguel could only compare to the vision of an angel.

Rojas, while holding the red flag, raised his eyebrows and addressed his fellow rebels. "Young men, old men and boys: Tonight we have gathered here in Lares for a singular purpose, to fulfill a singular goal, and to realize a singular dream! That purpose, that goal and that sublime dream I speak of is the liberation of our great nation from the clutches of imperialistic Spain, from the vile talons of two dreadful vultures we have come to know as tyranny and repression. Tonight we will set things right, tonight we will begin forging a new nation, a free and democratic society!"

Everyone in the gathering, including Terreforte and Colonel Ruiz, gave out such a rousing cheer and ovation that it lingered in the air for hundreds of yards in every direction. It went on for a while until Rojas waved his free hand, hushing them into silence. He paused briefly until there was only the sound of crickets, coquís and crackling torches. "Tonight we will take on the militia of Lares with our rifles, with our pistols, with our machetes and with our fists! For all eternity, history will remember the great sacrifices we make this evening! Many of you will die tonight, but many of you will survive and will live to tell your sons and daughters about the acts of a few visionaries who had the guts to stand opposed to tyranny! I have already resolved to give up my life in this noble quest of ours, for I choose to live free and beholden to no Spaniard or peninsular!" Again, there was another rousing cheer from the nearly four hundred men gathered in front of the Rojas plantation. This time, Rojas let the cheers and ovation simmer, like potatoes on a frying pan. Then, as the ovation subsided, Rojas stepped forward near the edge of the first stair. "After tonight, you will have your lands back, your haciendas, your money and most of all your dignity!" This time the cheers were even louder than before, and the mixture of low and high voices rang out in the night skies like a church choir singing hymns for the Lord. Hundreds of feet stomped the ground, hundreds of hands clapped thunderously, and hundreds of voices sang in prideful glee. Miguel stood on the second stair of the porch, mesmerized by the power of Manuel Rojas's speech. With but a few simple words, Rojas captivated his audience, filling them with a renewed sense of encouragement. He sensed when both Terreforte and Ruiz slowly placed their hands across their hearts, as if pledging allegiance to an imaginary flag. Miguel noted Rojas holding the staff of his red flag firmly in his hand as he looked across the band of eager men. To his left, he noticed the gleam on Aguilar's face, a boyish zeal that gave Miguel the impression he was about to burst with excitement. Rojas continued, "But there is one thing I will ask each and every one of you here tonight. Let us not sink into the same depths as that of our Spanish counterparts. If the enemy surrenders honorably to you, then you must give him quarter, for we shall not fall into anarchy but into deliverance! Now take your places among your leaders and may God bless each and every one of you!"

Unable to contain himself any longer, Aguilar took his cigar and crushed it into the top stair, extinguishing its light. Then, as the men began to sing their freedom songs, Aguilar climbed the last stair and rushed over to Clemente Millan. Miguel watched him, wondering what, in heaven's name, was the mostly sane Aguilar about to do. Even Rojas turned to take note of Aguilar. Aguilar confronted Millan and immediately grabbed the staff bearing the white flag. He crouched, placed the flag on the porch floor, and while the leaders gathered around him, he began writing on the white flag with the burnt out end of his long cigar. Upon the white flag, Aguilar inscribed *Liberty or Death! Long Live Free Puerto Rico, Year 1868!* Aguilar slowly rose to his feet and displayed the white flag to the already roused gathering. When the rebels saw the inscription on the white flag, they cheered louder than on all previous occasions that night. The jornaleros standing in the midst of the gathering reached into their jacket pockets, vests or trousers and retrieved their dreaded Libretas, the symbol that most represented their plight and repression. They held their Libretas high in the air so that everyone, including the leaders standing on the porch, could see them clearly. They tossed the Libretas into several fire pits, and sang loudly, cheered, stomped or clapped. As the fires consumed the hundreds of Libretas, Rojas stepped forth and with a thunderous voice made his proclamation. "In the absence of the Camuyan delegation, the Lares delegation will take the honor of sounding the first cry of independence!" But the rebels were too busy cheering and burning their Libretas to hear Rojas's proclamation. Unfazed by their lack of reaction, Rojas turned to Ruiz, Terreforte, Aguilar, his brother Miguel and several other unit leaders and addressed them with outright authority, as if he'd been an army general all of his life. "Colonel Ruiz, señor Terreforte, let us stick to the plan we discussed earlier tonight. My scouts tell me that resistance should be light. We must first take the barracks; everything depends on it. If we fail in taking the barracks, this whole venture will have been for naught." Rojas took a few minutes to look at his leaders, and then he sighed heavily, "Where is Mathias?"

"He'll be here soon," answered Terreforte. "He is gathering additional recruits and he is itching for a fight. He will come."

"I do hope so, my dear Terreforte, for his leadership is desperately needed." He then gazed into his brother's eyes. "Miguel, send a couple of messengers to Mayagüez."

"What for, brother? Mathias Brugman should not be reminded of his duties, something which he should well know."

"No, Miguel. That is not what I want. I want him to send word to Dr. Betances in New York City that the war for Puerto Rican independence has begun. More importantly, though, I want him to send word to our

Cuban friends, that they can begin their own war of independence. Do this, Miguel, with all possible speed."

Miguel Pítre sensed excitement amongst the leaders as they began to disperse. Stepping down from the porch, Aguilar noticed Miguel Pítre still standing, as if uncertain of what he was supposed to do. "Under which banner will you fight, Miguelito?"

"No banner, señor Aguilar. I do not need a banner, only a cause."

"Very well, Miguelito, I will be flying Porvenir's green and gold banner, and you're welcome to join us."

"Thank you, Manuel, and good luck to you, señor."

"Godspeed, señor Pítre," answered Aguilar. He extended his hand toward Miguel and both men shook for a little while. Then Aguilar reached into his vest pocket and pulled out his pocket watch. He looked at the time and with a serene smile, a kind of smile that did not give away any hint as to what he was thinking, he uttered. "Mark the time, Miguelito, for this will become history. It is 10:45 on the evening of September 23, 1868, the official time that the war for Puerto Rican independence began."

Miguel Pítre smiled back at Aguilar but offered nothing more.

CHAPTER 95

For most of the day, Rodolfo Hernández waited for word regarding Colonel Iturriaga's arrival. Miguel Pítre and the leaders of Porvenir were criminals requiring immediate arrests and prosecution, but he received no confirmation of the Colonel's arrival or the expected arrival of his contingent. Rodolfo rode into town early on the morning of September 23 with hopes of seeing Iturriaga rounding up the rebels of San Sebastián, but he saw nothing out of the ordinary, not even the market stand owners, whose shrilling voices would pierce the air and heard from deep within the woods. As he entered San Sebastián, the eerie silence was powerful enough to force the landowner to become acutely aware of his surroundings. San Sebastián did not look as it had always looked, vibrant, full of life, full of hope and dreams despite the current level of poverty. The only businesses open that morning were the ones owned by the peninsulares, and even they showed signs of peculiarity, as if wondering where all the townsfolk had gone off to, wondering why no one had stopped by their shops and spent at least one centavo or two.

Rodolfo spent the whole morning at Don Pagan's restaurant, then part of the afternoon at the Ramirez colmado. He talked at great lengths with Don Ramirez about rumors of a revolution, but even Don Ramirez could not tell where his two sons were that morning or what they were doing. The two men commiserated the current state of affairs in San Sebastián, and both agreed that the authorities needed to do something fast. In the end, though, Rodolfo and Ramirez did nothing either. Frustrated to find no one in town, and unable to ignore the fact that his plans for capturing Miguel Pítre were slowly dissolving, like sugar in a steaming cup of coffee, Rodolfo left town by 5:30 that afternoon. When he arrived at his hacienda, he quickly recalled the shame Rosalía brought upon the Hernández household. He took a moment to gaze up at the stairs leading to Rosalía's room. A vacant bedroom in a silent home gave Rodolfo much to contemplate. He shook his head, walked into the parlor and sat on the couch in silence.

A few moments later, Maria walked into the parlor and noticed a very dejected husband, a man perhaps in need of affection and love. Maria hesitated at first, but then her womanly instincts kicked in. She walked slowly toward him, sat down beside him and placed her arm around his neck. "You look very tired."

"I am, Maria, much too tired. I cannot stop worrying about Rosa going off with that peasant. Heaven only knows what he's doing to her right now."

Maria knew that Rosalía was all right, somehow she knew. Maybe it was because she saw and felt the sincerity in Miguel Pítre's eyes, or maybe the way Rosalía's face would glow at the mere mention of Miguel's name, or maybe it was just her motherly instincts that told her Rosalía would be all right, despite what Rodolfo thought. Looking at her husband, however—that bastion of power, that paragon of leadership—sitting on the couch all shriveled up like a wet dog, meekly staring at the floor, made Maria feel something for him, something she had not felt in a long time. "Forget about Rosa for tonight Rodolfo and let the militia do their work. I'm sure they'll find her and Miguel and justice will be served. Right now you should take a warm bath and then go to sleep."

"Yes, Maria, that sounds like a good idea."

Maria smiled for the first time in ages, and then she stood up to face her husband. She extended her hand at Rodolfo and said in a whisper, "Come, Rodolfo."

CHAPTER 96

In the woods behind the Rojas plantation, Berta and Rosalía peered through fronds of plantain trees, trying to get a clear view. Rosalía was very worried, now that the gathering of rebels were shouting and singing. She knew now that it was certain Miguel would go off to fight. Though she wasn't in denial about it, she tried to keep that possibility far from her mind. She held the long fronds back on her side of the tree while Berta held back the wide, fan-like leaves on the other side. Berta looked worried too, because she had more to lose than Rosalía did. Berta was a runaway slave, and if the revolution failed, she was sure that Rodolfo would flog her to death, hang or shoot her. She narrowed her eyes through the parting and gave off an exasperating gasp. "I don't see Manolo, and I don't know where he is right now."

Rosalía tried to sound reassuring to Berta, aware that Berta and her family had suffered greatly at the hands of her dear father. "Don't worry Berta. I'm sure Manolo is very close to Miguel. I think they're getting along just fine."

"Manolo is like my twin, Rosa. I don't know what's to become of me if he should die in battle."

Rosalía gazed at the raggedy dress Berta wore so proudly and felt pity for her. There was something strangely familiar about Berta, she thought, but she could not readily identify it. Was it her eyes or the curves of her small mouth? Was it her thin lips, high cheekbones or maybe even the long eyelashes? "Try not to think too much about that," she offered consolingly, "maybe it's just another rousing cheer to stir up the men."

"Are you not worried about Miguel, too?" Berta asked, somewhat surprised at Rosalía's calm demeanor.

"I am very worried," answered Rosalía politely, "but at the same time I know that Miguel can take of himself. I don't know why I feel this way but I do. I think the revolution will succeed."

"You have told me why you joined the revolution," said Berta. "You gave me many reasons, but for me there is only one, and that is to be a free person; free to walk the streets without a permit, free to come and go as I please without as much as a by your leave from a Spaniard or even a creole. I do not want to live in constant fear of a whip, a smack on the face, or feel the body of an unwanted man on top of me."

"You speak of my father; I know about that, Berta, and it pains me to know that you have had to endure such misery. Sometimes it is difficult to hide the moans of pleasure; sounds that everyone in the house has heard from time to time."

"Moans of pleasure? For your father, yes, but for me it was always an act," said Berta wistfully. Looking across the field, she smiled. "Well señorita, we shall see what tomorrow will bring. Look yonder and see that the men are starting to form into columns."

Rosalía turned toward the front of the Rojas hacienda and nodded approvingly. "Come, Berta, let us go to the shack and gather our things."

Rosalía stood and offered her hand to Berta, who took it and gently rose to her feet. The two women held hands as they walked back into the shack. Together they managed to gather rags, to serve as bandages, and other makeshift medical equipment. While the two women entered the shack, the deep vibrato of singing men carried through to them. The men were filled with high hopes, anxiety and fear, all rolled into a single, emotional tone. As they marched out of the Rojas plantation toward Lares, Rosalía heard their songs of liberty; a disparate, eerie battle cry that would haunt her for the rest of her life.

CHAPTER 97

Miguel Pítre and Manolo took up their positions at the head of Rojas's column directly behind the members of Porvenir. Although Miguel did not intend to march so close to Aguilar and his men, it was by sheer coincidence that the only spot in the column was behind his former cell members. Miguel thought nothing more about it, and chucked it to mere fate. The young man from San Sebastián could hear Aguilar joking with Ibarra and laughing loudly, as if he were marching to a party with drinking and dancing rather than to a battle with bullets and blood spatter. Miguel wished he could feel as relaxed as Aguilar appeared to be, but he kept thinking about Rosalía, and wondered if leaving her at Rojas's plantation was a good idea.

The night air had grown steamy and stagnant without as much as a breeze to cool the heated and much fatigued soldiers. Moments earlier a fast-moving shower had overcome the rebels, drenching them through and through, and while they marched along the road, Miguel glanced at Manolo. Manolo, whose face gleamed in the moonlight, glanced back at Miguel but offered nothing, not even a smile or gesture.

Candelario and Agustin were marching in front of Manolo and Miguel. Marching in between Manolo's two brothers was the young slave Santana who had parted company with Polinario and Candido earlier that evening. Manolo noted Candelario's stern face as he spoke to the young slave, and it seemed as if he was giving Santana specific instructions. Manolo watched Candelario's right hand as it dug deep into in his trouser pocket. Candelario took out a thick white envelope and pressed it into Santana's hands. Candelario gave Santana additional instructions and waited until Santana stuffed the envelope into his pocket. Manolo wondered what his two brothers were doing with Santana, and he would confront them later about that. He would never get the chance.

Rojas's column trailed Terreforte's column by about a hundred yards now, but even from that distance, Miguel could hear the men marching and their weapons clanking.

By 11:07 that evening, Miguel felt the column slowing. The rebels had reached a grocery store owned by Felipe Arana, a Spaniard. As the rebel army converged near the store, the commanders and their subordinate leaders quickly learned how difficult a job it was to maintain order in the ranks, and soon the two columns disintegrated into a mob. Hundreds of hand-held torches and gas lanterns moved about in random patterns, and a cacophony of male voices in desultory conversations transcended the usual sounds of the night. From atop his horse, Manuel Rojas ordered twenty men to storm Arana's store, and within minutes, the men took all of the machetes and knives off the shelves. Some of the men hauled away crates of beer and wine and one man even took Arana's horse and riding gear. When Arana woke to the sudden commotion, he confronted angry eyes and several arms groping his body. Rojas's men kept Arana at bay, and while he was unable to break free from the clutches of his captors, all he could do was shout profanities and threats at Rojas.

Within minutes of looting of Arana's store, a freed black man under Arana's employ by the name of Venero had shown up to investigate the shouting and general commotion that had awakened him. Gabino Plumey, one of Rojas's men, demanded that Venero join the rebels in their quest to free the island from tyranny. But enjoying his release from bondage and finding pleasure thus far working for Arana as a free man, Venero feared that the Spaniard might rescind his freedom and return him to slavery. Besides, Venero was not in the least bit impressed by the rebels. He stood defiantly before Millan and refused to join the revolution. As the crackle of hand-held torches and the murmur of hundreds of men filled the air surrounding him, Plumey gazed at Venero with utter contempt. Incapable of understanding or accepting Venero's recalcitrance, Plumey summarily dismissed him as a coward. As some of the men slapped and punched Arana, Plumey looked up at Rojas asking for permission. Rojas read Plumey's mind and shook his head, unable to pass judgment over a life and death situation. Helpless and daunted at committing his first field decision, he trotted over to Terreforte, who eyed him consolingly. As Rojas approached Terreforte, the popping sound of a pistol pierced the thick, humid air and rose above the murmur of soldiers. Rojas turned around quickly and noted Venero lying on the ground, blood oozing from his chest. Rojas looked at Plumey while shaking his head, but Plumey gestured at Rojas that he had not fired his weapon. Plumey pointed at a large gathering of rebels and shrugged his shoulders, unable to determine who had fired the shot. The men of both columns did not even react to the gunfire but continued their consumption of wine and beer. Miguel, Manolo and every member of Rojas's column who was standing idle, had witnessed the shooting. Miguel knew who had shot Venero but he chose to remain silent. He might have said something had Rojas and Terreforte made a concerted effort to investigate the blatant murder. Instead, the two leaders remained atop their horses, powerless to stop the mob.

Manolo turned to Miguel and sighed in despair. "Is this the way the revolution is going to start, by killing the very people we aim to free?"

Miguel gazed into Manolo's dark eyes and shook his head. "If our leaders fail to take control, I fear we will descend into total anarchy, Manolo, and we will lose sight of our goals. The mood is at a fever pitch and once the killing starts, we will lose control of the men. I pray that señores Rojas and Terreforte can keep a semblance of order."

"But if this turns out to be nothing more than just a night out for revenge, what will you do?" Manolo probed Miguel.

"I have made a commitment to fight for freedom, and I will keep my word."

"Well, I didn't sign up for this. I didn't sign up to commit murder and destroy property. If things get worse, I will abandon the rebellion."

Miguel placed both hands on Manolo's shoulders and nodded at him. "That is the smartest statement I've heard all day. Do what you feel is right for you, and do not worry what others may say. If you want to continue fighting, then look for me."

After the rebels had taken all that Arana's store had to offer, they proceeded to Lares, leaving Arana by the edge of the road close to death. It wasn't too long before other Spanish merchants along the road to the pueblo heard the gunfire. They all rushed out of their homes to investigate, only to confront their worst possible nightmare. When Rojas captured sight of the loyalists emerging from their homes and stores, he immediately issued orders to have them all arrested and their establishments looted as well. Then he commanded his captains and lieutenants to reassemble the men for the final push to Lares. Trailing the main body by a about a quarter mile, the two medical and supply wagons, pulled by old mules and sickly horses, trudged along as best they could.

At 12:03 on the morning of Thursday, September 24, nearly all of the stores in Lares, the ones owned by Spaniards, were in the hands of the rebels. Toward the center of town, Frutos Caloca's establishment remained untouched, but it was only a matter of time before the store would also succumb to rebel terror. Ever since yesterday morning, when Caloca saw his neighbors packing and fleeing Lares, and shortly after seeing Rojas buying provisions, he'd been wary. For this reason, he asked his friend, a Spanish druggist named Fidel Navas, to sleep the night at his store and watch over it.

For the past few weeks, Navas had been in the middle of constructing a new home and had been staying with friends at various houses in Lares. So when Caloca asked him to stay the night at his store, Navas readily agreed, partly because he would spend the night alone, and partly because he owed Caloca a favor. But as the door burst open and a stream of angry rebels rushed inside, he quickly regretted his decision. Navas rose to his feet immediately and saw the rebels breaking shelves and stealing merchandise. As they went about their business, they sang their songs of liberty. When they discovered Navas staring at them, shaking like a leaf, they rushed him and beat him to a pulp. They tied his arms behind his back and dragged him out of the store.

The darkened homes in the peaceful town of Lares soon began to light up, and curious loyalists awakened that morning only to confront the sad reality that anarchy had replaced the tranquility the townsfolk had always enjoyed. The rebels dragged the loyalist men out of their homes, bound them and held them prisoner as they made their way toward City Hall.

With prisoners in tow, the rebels finally reached the center of town, where they saw Rojas sitting atop his horse. “Lareños! Creoles! Hear me!” shouted Rojas. “I sound the cry for independence! Long live Puerto Rico free! Long live Puerto Rico free!” In response to Rojas’s cry for independence, the rebels yelled loudly, a deep cadence of male voices that seem to come together as one steady drone.

Rojas finally dismounted and walked over to Terreforte, who had been issuing orders to his men. “Juan, order a detachment to guard the roads in and out of Lares! Then join me and the rest of the leaders at City Hall!” Within minutes, the four hundred rebels fanned out across the tiny pueblo. While Terreforte’s detachment secured and patrolled all roads in and out of Lares, he and the rest of his men joined Rojas’s column at City Hall, where they formed another march toward the tiny barracks.

Terreforte and Ruiz moved their respective contingents from the north and linked up with Rojas’s unit in the center of town. Astounded by the lack of enemy gunfire, Rojas ordered the rebel army to form an arc facing the barracks. Within minutes, the men stood ready with loaded and primed weapons. A few moments later, the rebels fired a barrage of gunfire that easily consumed the barracks. It did not take much of an assault. In fact, after the second reload, Rojas saw the image of a man’s hand sticking out of a shattered window, nervously shaking a makeshift white flag. There were only five militiamen inside the barracks; the rest had fled at the first sight of the rebels.

Rojas secured the barracks, appropriated the weapons and ammunition in the name of the new republic, and issued orders to a few of his trusted men to arrest any Spanish loyalist attempting to flee Lares. After rounding up the few militiamen at the barracks, the rebels invaded every loyalist home until all of the appointed officials were in their custody.

From inside his home Frutos Caloca watched the terror in the streets of Lares. He saw his friend, Pedro Garandillas, forced out of his home half-naked and barefoot. Caloca also witnessed the arrest of Pablo Mediavilla, the mayor of Lares, the mayor's assistant, Lorenzo Camuñas, and two of his fellow merchants. It was then that reality set in, and Caloca began to fear for his life. The terror in his heart grew exponentially as he watched the rebels roam the streets of Lares, many of whose libretas he still held and kept in his house. He knew they would come looking for him to destroy his property, but, more importantly, to release the financial yoke he had had over them for a good number of years. From his window, Caloca saw wives clinging to their husbands as the hate-filled rebels dragged them out of their homes and took them to the city jail. He could hear their crying and their terrible lament as their children stood in front porches with confusion on their faces, clinging to their mothers' nightgowns. It was a terrible night for the Spanish loyalists, a long night of horror and fear. Squinting for a better look, Frutos Caloca was able to recognize a badly beaten Fidel Navas, and knew that the rebels had already raided his store.

Not long after witnessing Navas's dire bloody situation, Caloca saw about twenty or so rebels heading straight for his house. He thanked God that he had sent his family away to Camuy earlier in the day but he wondered now if there was a similar situation occurring there as well. All was lost, thought Caloca, all the money he had invested in the store, all the money he had put into his home, and all the work and sacrifice he had made for his personal success. Despite his tragedies, he was not going to allow himself to fall into the hands of terrorists. He would not allow them to beat him mercilessly, or gruesomely kill him or even allow them the satisfaction of rotting inside a tiny jail cell. Those were not the reasons why he had ventured to the New World. He reached for his rifle and jumped out of the back window. Wearing only his underwear, he trudged barefoot into a field of bean plants and hid there all night long. When the rebels busted down the door to the Caloca house, they found no one there. They ransacked the house until they found the libretas neatly stacked on a corner of Caloca's desk. They broke the desk into pieces, took the libretas and threw them out the door across the foreground. Using the libretas as tinder, they built a small bonfire. In the middle of the bean field, Caloca, sweating and panting heavily, could hear glass breaking inside his home and furniture thrown about, as if the rebels were taking immense pleasure in destroying his home.

By 1:52 in the morning, Rojas and Terreforte, accompanied by their lieutenants, stormed their way into City Hall. Secure in the knowledge that the rebels had arrested the mayor of Lares and the rest of the town's officials, and had taken them to jail, Rojas ordered his men to tear down all symbols of Spanish dominion.

Miguel Pítre and Manolo were part of the contingent assigned to the task, and both men readily accepted their orders. Miguel had waited endlessly for this moment, the moment when he and his fellow rebels would send all vestiges of tyranny and oppression into oblivion. He and Manolo, as well as the forty-man company assigned to the mission, swung their machetes across wooden signs, breaking them into pieces. They roamed the streets of Lares, targeting any hint of Spanish imperialism, and mercilessly disintegrated it. Walking up the street with a fierce determination, looking for something else to destroy, Miguel noticed a wooden block posted on the cement wall of a shoe store. It was a painting of the image of Queen Isabel. The very symbol that Miguel hated most was still nailed to the wall of a shoe store, as if it were emblazoned to the concrete, and made to insinuate itself into the collective conscience of Queen Isabel's subjects. Angered by all the suffering at the hands of the Spanish queen and her minions, Miguel ran to the shoe store. Powered by the forces of retribution, Miguel swung his machete and knocked the Queen's painting off the wall. He stood over it and gazed at the Queen's image for a while. Then he stomped on the picture before swinging his machete repeatedly until the wooden painting was nothing more than just tiny fragments of colorful wood. Consumed with the destruction of all things Spanish, Miguel did not notice Aguilar standing next to him, watching him. In his hands, Aguilar held the white flag bearing the inscription he wrote late last night. Miguel finally realized he had company and tilted his head up at Aguilar. Aguilar looked straight into Miguel's eyes and said calmly, "Where was that image posted?"

Miguel gestured with his head. "Right there, in front of the shoe store where it reminded everybody of Spanish tyranny."

"Good, then help me place this white flag where the image of Queen Isabel once stood."

Miguel nodded at Aguilar with a smile and then he reached for one end of the white flag. Using the butt of their pistols, Aguilar and Miguel nailed the white flag over the site where the Queen's picture once stood. The two men contemplated the white flag for several moments, as the streets of Lares rattled with vandalism and general mayhem. After several moments more, Aguilar shook Miguel's hand and both men quickly departed for City Hall.

CHAPTER 98

Many bonfires lit up the center of town but most of the fighting, if one could call it that was over. After the rebels arrested the male loyalists and imprisoned them in the local jail, they chose not to harm the peninsular families but instead left them in their homes to cry in misery. After the last gun fired, an eerie silence overcame the town. Only the crackle of bonfires and torches filled the night air as the 400 rebels slowly gathered in front of City Hall, awaiting the emergence of Manuel Rojas.

The doors finally swung open and out stepped Rojas, nodding and smiling at the rebels, a well-defined grin that revealed either his enthusiasm or his outright relief. But no one could tell the meaning behind Rojas's smile, not even Miguel who prided himself a good judge of character. Nevertheless, the men cheered Rojas on, as they had never before done, as if now they had something with which to be happy. The ovation and cheers lasted for more than three minutes until Rojas waved them off in silence. Finally, when the cheering subsided, Rojas stepped forth, and with a thundering voice said, "Hear me, my fellow revolutionists! I hereby declare today, September 24, 1868, as the birth of the Republic of Puerto Rico!"

The rebels jumped in the air and yelled, cried, clapped, stomped their feet and shot their rifles into the air in unrestrained joy. They had tasted freedom for the first time in their lives, they had accomplished what no other Puerto Rican had done before, and they had crossed over into a new world, a world filled with hope and change. Rojas again waved his hands at the crowd until they hushed into a reverent silence. As Rojas addressed his men, Miguel Pítre watched him with a profound sense of admiration and respect. "With the consensus of Centro Bravo, Capa Prieto, Lanzador Del Norte, Porvenir and the rest of our rebel organizations, I hereby appoint Don Francisco Ramirez as the first President of the Republic of Puerto Rico!" As the men cheered on, Francisco Ramirez stepped forth to acknowledge the appointment. He gazed at Rojas for a split second, and then he bowed humbly, as though he were bowing to the Pope in reverent acceptance of a pontifical appellation. Unable to stop the cheering, Rojas continued in a loud voice, "I hereby appoint, Clemente Millan minister of justice; Federico Valencia, minister of treasury; Aurelio Martínez, minister of foreign relations; and Bernabe Pol, secretary of state." As Rojas announced the names and each man stepped forward, the rebel cheers continued unabated.

Hiding inside a tiny closet in a small house at the edge of town, a Spanish loyalist bid his time while the rebels ransacked his home. After more than half an hour, they took everything of value and never once bothered to check the bedrooms or closets. To his great relief Rodrigo Ordoñez opened the closet door and found the house vacant. The rebels had gone off in the direction of City Hall and the area immediately surrounding his home was now devoid of people. Ordoñez walked out of the closet and quickly dressed himself. He rushed down the stairs, raised the living room window as quietly as he could and jumped out into the woods. When he reached the stable, he noticed the rebels had taken all of his horses, all except for one; a sickly mare, and the one he was going to put down later that morning. Ordoñez bridled the horse but he did not saddle her. He quickly jumped on her back and whispered, "Come on old girl. I've got to get to San Sebastián immediately or else everything will be lost. Do this for me and I will spare your life." Within minutes, the mare grunted softly and began to trot. Ordoñez disappeared into the woods and rode around the rebels guarding the road into Lares.

Ordoñez succeeded in avoiding the guards, but his attempts at evading the enemy forced him to ride eastward and around a cluster of homes where Rojas's plantation stood. It took Ordoñez nearly an hour to reach the road leading out of Lares, but as soon as he reached it, he heard the sound of heavy cavalry coming from the west. The sound was thunderous and it grew louder by the second. Curious, and with a deep sense of relief, Ordoñez dismounted, tied the mare to a nearby tree and walked for several hundred feet until he reached the dirt road. While taking cover within the brush, he could see a ten-man picket line spread across the road leading to Lares. He could see the men's faces begin to stiffen as the thundering cavalry drew closer. Ordoñez waited patiently and hoped that his mare would keep silent until he was certain the cavalry was indeed a Spanish contingent.

Deep within the brush, Ordoñez stood still and heard the cavalry slowing to confront the picket line. The leader of the cavalry held a torch in one hand while raising his other hand in the air to slow his column. As the leader's steed slowed to a halt, he noticed the barrels of ten rifles aimed directly at him, but rather than displaying annoyance, he gave the sergeant of the picket line a humble smile.

"Halt, and identify yourself!" the sergeant cried out.

Very calmly, the leader turned over his lighted torch to the man riding next to him and raised both arms in the air. "My name is Mathias Brugman, young man!"

Ordoñez, quickly realizing it wasn't the militia, raced back to his mare and departed the immediate area.

"Don Brugman!" shouted the leader. "I apologize, but we're under orders! We have taken over the town of Lares! Puerto Rico is free!" Turning to his picket line, he commanded the men to lower their weapons.

Mathias slowly brought his arms down and took hold of the reins. Looking down at the jubilant sentry, all Mathias Brugman could do was close his eyes, nod and sigh deeply. It had finally happened, all those years of endless speeches, all those attempts at stirring the people with his voice of opposition, and all the hardships of creating an ideology, planting the seeds of revolution had finally come to fruition. This moment of happiness, this moment of achievement would remain in his heart for the rest of his life. He would recall this feeling in detail and present it in a triumphal voice to his fellow members at the Masonic Lodge in Mayagüez. He would savor the moment, the excitement, the fear, the joy of victory, and the realization of dreams and hopes so that one day he would recount the story to his grandchildren. But realizing it was merely the beginning, he quickly returned to his senses.

"Will I find Manuel Rojas in Lares?"

"Yes, señor Brugman, but Commandante Rojas is planning to march on to San Sebastián very soon. It is his wish that you keep your troops here outside Lares proper as reserves. Your presence, however, is requested at City Hall."

Brugman frowned disappointedly at first, but he ordered his soldiers to stay outside Lares. After securing an escort, he and Baldomero Baurer rode straight to City Hall.

At 6:30 in the morning, President Ramirez had summoned Aguilar and Ibarra to City Hall. Manuel held a lighted cigar in one hand while removing his cap with the other. Eusebio, sweating and grimy from all the work he had done arresting people, followed Aguilar.

Francisco Ramirez sat on the mayor's chair, looking presidential. "Don Aguilar!" said Ramirez. Rojas and Terreforte stood behind Ramirez, and to the side of the new president, stood the members of his cabinet. "Thank you for your participation in the revolution. You too, Don Ibarra."

"It was our duty, señor Presidente," replied Aguilar. "You sent for us?"

"Indeed I did. Now that we have taken Lares, it is only the beginning. We are grateful now that our esteemed colleague, Mathias Brugman, has joined us with additional troops, but we have made plans to move in on San Sebastián. Don Manuel Rojas will lead his company there followed by the companies of señores Terreforte and Ruiz. Don Mathias Brugman and his company will remain here in Lares, and await Don Rojas's word for reinforcements should it ever come to that. The reason I have summoned you and Don Ibarra, is that you two were members of the San Sebastián militia. There is no doubt in my mind that as officers and as fellow creoles, you men exerted considerable influence among your men."

"That's correct, señor presidente. I know them all, they're all childhood friends, and they were all born and raised in San Sebastián.

They have no love for Spaniards, and they are fully committed to the war for independence."

"That is precisely why I want the two of you to ride to San Sebastián and gather the militia. Talk to them, and tell them that the revolution has begun and that we have declared a provisional government for the new Republic of Puerto Rico. Tell them that we need their help and that we need to get our hands on their guns and ammunition. Can you do this, Manuel? Can you do this Eusebio?"

"We will, señor presidente, when do you want us to leave?"

"Right now, Manuel. We must strike while the poker is hot! Señores Rojas and Terreforte will begin their march to San Sebastián later this morning by around eight or nine o'clock. This will give you plenty of time to reach the militia with the news."

CHAPTER 99

Ordoñez had left Lares long before Aguilar and Ibarra, but because of a sickly horse had arrived at San Sebastián nearly at the same time as they did. Not long after reaching the outskirts of San Sebastián Ordoñez's mare collapsed and died. A horseless Ordoñez, though no longer a young man, forced himself to walk along the dirt road until he came upon the first house he saw. It was a two-story colonial neatly tucked away and almost entirely camouflaged within the greenery of the woods. At 8:45 that morning, Ordoñez finally arrived at Rodolfo Hernández's home, having no idea who the homeowner was or his importance.

Startled by the loud knock upon his front door, Rodolfo quickly jumped out of bed and reached for the rifle he had carefully placed against the wall. Maria suddenly awoke and noticed her husband already up and reaching for the bedroom door; his other hand holding the death weapon. "What is it Rodolfo?"

"Someone's knocking on the door downstairs. Quickly, wake the girls and tell them to hide. You hide, too." Maria sprang out of bed, put on her robe and dashed to the adjoining bedrooms.

Downstairs, Ordoñez heard someone unlocking the door and was glad there was somebody in the house. Instead of receiving a polite greeting, though, all he saw was the muzzle of a rifle. "Who the hell are you, and what are you doing here so early in the morning," demanded Rodolfo.

"Please do not shoot. I have traveled from Lares, my horse collapsed and died about a mile from here. All I want is to advise the authorities in San Sebastián that a rebellion has started in Lares."

"What did you say?" Rodolfo said, wide-eyed.

"A rebellion, señor, the rebels have taken over Lares! They arrested the mayor and all of the loyalist men. Can you help me please? I need a horse. I need to get word out to the Spanish authorities."

Rodolfo nodded. "All right, come inside."

Within a half hour, Rodolfo, together with Ordoñez, rode into San Sebastián.

Aguilar and Ibarra reached San Sebastián but found the town eerily quiet. By this time, they expected to see jíbaros setting up their wooden stands, preparing for the day's sale of fruits and vegetables. It almost seemed like a Sunday morning, right before mass. Manuel and Eusebio rode their tired horses up the lonely street, and as their horses thumped the ground, they noticed that even the peninsulares had closed their shops. For a fleeting moment, Aguilar wondered whether Spanish soldiers were already there waiting for his arrival. As Aguilar and Ibarra rode slowly, they became more alert and mindful of anything out of the ordinary. At the opposite end of the street, they managed to see the figure of an elderly man, whose white beard seemed to glisten against the rising sunlight. Manuel recognized him immediately and quickly dismounted. Walking over slowly and cautiously, and as he extended his hand to shake with the elderly man, Aguilar could hear Eusebio dismounting, too. "Buenos Dias, señor Blanco."

Don Rafael Blanco did not extend his hand to shake, but merely sighed in anxiety. "Señor Aguilar, señor Ibarra, you are both in danger."

"Why, what's happened?" Ibarra said approaching Don Blanco.

"You two, along with Miguel Pítre and the rest of the members of Porvenir have been declared rebels and outlaws. There is an arrest warrant for all of you posted outside Mayor Chiesa's office. I don't know how they found out about Porvenir, but they did, and now they are searching the barrios of San Sebastián looking for you."

Aguilar knew how the mayor found out, but he didn't want Blanco to know it. It was bad enough that Rojas and the other leaders knew it was because of Redondo's treachery, and he didn't need to add Blanco to the list. "Listen to me, Don Blanco," said Aguilar animatedly. "It doesn't matter now because the revolution has begun. We have taken over the town of Lares and soon we will invade San Sebastián. Which of the militiamen are in the barracks right now?"

"All of them," answered Blanco dourly. "The word is that Mayor Chiesa has reinstated a former army colonel as the new commander of the militia. The good colonel has seen fit to confine the militia to the barracks and has taken extraordinary measures to protect San Sebastián."

"It still doesn't matter," said Aguilar confidently. "Once they see us marching into town armed and determined to fight, they will abandon their posts and join us. We have four hundred armed men ready to take San Sebastián. I know the men of our militia, and so too does Eusebio. They respect us as officers and they trust our judgment as well. You will see, Don Blanco, you will see. Now, how do we get in contact with the men in the barracks?"

Blanco just stood there looking up at Aguilar with incredulous eyes. "Are you deaf, señor Aguilar? Did I not tell you that the new commander has confined all militiamen to the barracks? You cannot reach them, señor! They are under constant scrutiny by the colonel's personally chosen men, and they're not even allowed to see their families!"

"What do we do now?" Ibarra asked somewhat deflated.

Aguilar turned to Ibarra displaying an upbeat grin. "Now we wait for Rojas's arrival. Let the militia see how strong we are, then they will join us."

"I hope you're right, Aguilar," said Don Blanco. "In the meantime, you must not be seen here in town. They will arrest you, and if you resist they will shoot you. Follow me."

"Where are we going?" asked Ibarra.

"We're going to Ramirez's colmado."

"Don Ramirez is a loyalist bastard, we cannot go there," cautioned Ibarra.

"The Mayor reinstated Don Ramirez as a militiaman. He is in the barracks watching your men. Apparently, the new colonel wants to make certain your men do not desert. However, Enrique is at the store. He was unable to join you last night because his father was at the store and demanded that he stay with him. His younger brother Raul is there too."

Aguilar and Ibarra followed Don Blanco into the Ramirez colmado, where Enrique and Raul greeted the cell's president and offered him a sound hiding place in the back of the store. There they would wait until Rojas's arrival.

Not long after Aguilar and Ibarra took up their hiding positions in the back of Ramirez's colmado, the sound of two horses galloping at top speed echoed through the streets of San Sebastián. The two riders halted their steeds in front of Mayor Chiesa's office. Determined to crush the rebellion Rodolfo jumped off his horse and rushed inside the modest public building.

Rodolfo found Mayor Chiesa sitting calmly before his desk, as if he did not have a care in the world. He also noted the mayor had company that morning. Unable to restrain himself any longer, Rodolfo did not wait for an invitation to enter the mayoral office. Ordoñez quietly followed Hernández. "Alcalde, I have very bad news. The revolution has begun in Lares!"

"Yes Rodolfo, I know. So?"

"What do you mean by that? Are you not in the least bit concerned about the safety of San Sebastián? Have you alerted the militia, not that we can put too much trust in them?"

"Relax, Rodolfo, now who is this man?"

Rodolfo turned to the man, "What was your name again?"

The man looked directly into the mayor's eyes and said, "Ordoñez."

Rodolfo turned back to Chiesa, crunching his eyebrows. "And who is this?"

The man rose to his feet and extended his hand. "My name is Jacinto García Pérez, and I am the Corregidor of Aguadilla. Colonel Iturriaga dispatched me here to investigate rumors about a revolution. Apparently the rumors are true."

Rodolfo shook hands with García Pérez.

"Now what seems to be the trouble?" the mayor asked, gazing into Rodolfo's eyes.

"Are you in some sort of a fog, mayor?" replied Rodolfo incredulously. "Didn't you hear what I just said?"

"A rebellion—right. Well, there is no need for you to be too concerned about a peasant rebellion. You won't lose any of your properties and none of your businesses, so please take a moment to breathe."

All of a sudden, Rodolfo realized why the mayor had been acting so calmly. He nodded at the mayor and glanced at Pérez. "They're here, aren't they? You sent for the army and they came, didn't they?"

"No, not exactly," replied the mayor. "The magistrate arrived very early this morning to make observations and report his findings back to Colonel Iturriaga. He has informed me that the Colonel is ready to deploy a force of two hundred soldiers to San Sebastián should we require it. For the moment, he issued orders for the militia of San Sebastián, which is now under the command of Colonel San Antonio, to stand ready for action. We have alerted every loyalist citizen of San Sebastián to take up arms in the defense of the town. Everyone here is ready, Rodolfo. If what the rebels are looking for is a fight, then a fight they shall get! Feel better now?"

"Oh yes, a whole lot better now," replied Rodolfo gleefully. A surge of confidence ran through his mind, now that Chiesa apparently had control of the situation.

"You can go back home now and see to your family," said the mayor reassuringly.

"No Alcalde. If it isn't too much of an inconvenience, I would like to remain in town today and wait for the rebels. I would like to participate in the fighting."

The mayor gazed into Rodolfo's eyes, shook his head and muttered quizzically, "Rodolfo, my dear Rodolfo. Now why would you want to do something like that?"

Rodolfo moved toward the vacant chair and sat facing the mayor, leaving Ordoñez by the door. "You know why." He sensed the magistrate from Aguadilla taking his seat but felt his eyes all over him.

"No, I really don't, so why don't you enlighten me? Why don't you tell me the reason why you'd prefer to stay here rather than home at your family's side?"

"Because I know that Miguel Pítre will be among them," said Rodolfo gritting his teeth in anger. His blood boiled every time he mentioned Miguel's name. "And I want to be rid of that peasant bastard once and for all."

"Rodolfo, they may not even come to San Sebastián!" shouted the mayor, annoyed now at Rodolfo's reasoning. "Why should they? San Sebastián has no arsenal to speak of, only a handful of rifles and one cannon—an old one at that. They could very well be marching on to Aguadilla or maybe even Arecibo, where the munitions are greater."

"Well if they do, then so be it, alcalde, I will go home. But what if you're wrong? It makes sense to reason that San Sebastián is on the way to Arecibo. Aguadilla is to the west and far off from a sound military path; even I know that. I'm betting they will march on to San Sebastián, and I'm betting you know that, too. Therefore, I request that you swear me in as a militia man."

Mayor Chiesa threw his hands up in the air in frustration. "I suppose I cannot convince you otherwise?" He watched Rodolfo shake his head. "Very well...Ordoñez!" Ordoñez rushed into the office and saw the mayor's angry eyes staring at him. "You and the Corregidor are going to stand as witnesses." The mayor slowly rose to his feet and looked into Rodolfo's eager eyes. "Now, before señores Ordoñez and Pérez, I want you to acknowledge that I have tried to dissuade you from joining the militia and fighting the rebels. Do you acknowledge this Rodolfo?"

"Yes," said Rodolfo impatiently.

CHAPTER 100

The fields of the Rojas plantation were extraordinarily quiet. Even the ubiquitous coquí's nocturnal music seemed to hush in deference to the uncanny silence; a silence replete with fear; a fear that pervaded the minds of the women and older men hiding in barns and shacks across the plantation. That blanket of fragile silence was nevertheless broken by the thrumming of a horse's hooves.

Rosalía stepped outside the shack and squinted through the darkness. A dim ray of moonlight, slithering through clouds obscured by the night, illuminated the field and gave Rosalía a glimpse of a shadow moving toward her. Rosalía kept silent and while she waited, she sensed Berta walking closely behind her. She could hear Berta's heavy breathing as the dark figure moved across the finca toward the back, where the barn and shacks stood.

As the rider's silhouette grew larger, like the rising shadow of a tree against the brilliance of sunlight, the doors to the other shacks creaked open and soon, nearly everyone emerged to investigate. Rosalía began to walk toward the rider, in an attempt to discern whether the rider was a rebel with a message or a soldier sent there with orders to kill everyone. She recognized the face right away, and with a broad smile shouted, "Agustín!"

"Señorita Rosalía!" Agustín shouted back with much relief. "I was afraid this might have been the wrong house. Señorita, I have good news, Lares is ours! It wasn't much of a fight!"

"Is Miguel all right?" Rosalía asked anxiously, fearfully, disregarding Agustín's glad tidings.

"Yes," replied Agustín, looking down at Rosalía. He tilted his head and fixed his sights on his young sister. "Berta! Candelario and I met

Manolo in Lares, and he told us where you were. It does me good to see that you are safe and sound!"

"How is Manolo? How is Candelario?" Berta shouted excitedly.

"They're both fine, we're all fine."

Rosalía finally reached Agustín, and flashed a set of bright and hopeful blue eyes at the former slave. "Is there any message from Miguel?"

"Yes. Miguel asked me to tell you that he does not want you to go to Lares under any circumstance."

"But why? Didn't you just tell me that Lares is in the possession of the rebels?"

"Yes, it is true but señor Miguel feels it is not safe because there are many Spanish soldiers in the surrounding towns, and because we are getting ready to march on to San Sebastián. It is not over, señorita, it is only the beginning."

Agustín noted Rosalía's smug expression and sensed resentment in her eyes. Making no concerted efforts to veil her disagreement with Miguel's banishment, she looked up and resolutely said, "Well I'm not going to stay here and wait all morning and afternoon! I'm going to Lares!"

"But señorita!"

"No! Please, Agustín, do not attempt to dissuade me, for I will not listen to you!"

Berta felt Rosalía's determination sweeping into her very soul, stirring inside her like the winds of a tempest. She put her fists on her hips and brazenly stood her ground looking up at her brother. Her eyes narrowed as she mentally communicated her intentions to him. Agustín saw her eyes glinting against the intermittent moonlight. But more importantly, he noted Berta's resoluteness as well, and realized she too had come to a decision. Agustín shook his head, "Oh no, not you too!"

"Yes, I'm going to Lares with Rosa!"

Later that morning, at around nine o'clock, Miguel, who had been resting on the ground with his back against a post near the walls of City Hall, captured the image of an angel riding into town. It was

Rosalía, his angel, the love of his life. While rushing to his feet, he tried desperately to suppress his emotions for his better half. His voice thundered through the streets of Lares, across the tiny plaza and into the delicate ears of his true love, forcing her to take notice right away. Many rebels sleeping in the streets awoke to Miguel's clamoring voice. "Rosa! This is not what I wanted! Go back to the plantation and stay there until I send for you, until it is safe for you to come out!"

Rosalía dismounted while shaking her head at Miguel. "I cannot do that, Miguel!" She dashed toward her husband, but all he could do was sweep her off her feet in a tight embrace. Rosalía, while still in the grip of Miguel's embrace, looked down at him and whispered, "It's only been a few hours but I've missed you so much already!"

"Rosa, Rosa, what am I to do with you now?"

Rosalía focused her eyes on the two peridots staring back at her. She wanted to tell him her secret right there, but she was frightened. Rosalía knew that if she told Miguel she was with child, he would abandon the revolution for the sake of her safety and that of the child's. Was the revolution more important than their child was? Was it more important than their love? Yes! But how much of their lives did they need to sacrifice in order to realize the jíbaro dream? How much of herself would she have to give up for Puerto Rico's dream of independence? Everything! The revolution *was* more important than hers or Miguel's life, and more important than the child sleeping, nourishing inside her womb was. The revolution was bigger than all of them, and if they had to give up their lives in the noble quest for freedom, then all their sacrifices will have been worth it. As she felt Miguel's grip loosening and felt her feet slowly touching the ground, Rosalía decided right then not to tell Miguel. Rosalía would wait until after the revolution, until Miguel's mind could easily take in the thought. It was simply not the right time.

After placing Rosalía back on the ground, Miguel shook his head at her to clearly demonstrate his disapproval. "I am marching in Manuel Rojas's column, and we are leaving very soon. Please stay here in Lares and try not to follow us."

"But Miguelito you know I can—"

"Listen to me, Rosa, if you value anything I say then please do not follow me. I beg you, from the bottom of my heart, from the very depths of my soul, stay here and wait for me." This time, there was no indication of forcefulness on the part of Miguel, only the humble pleas of a man in love, a man fearing for the safety of his beloved wife. This time, Rosalía felt the passion of his sincerity; his green eyes watering with melancholy, fear, excitement, happiness and love all at the same time. This time Rosalía would acquiesce to Miguel's pleas and stay in Lares…but for how long, she did not know.

At precisely nine fifteen in the morning, Rojas raised his arm and spurred his horse into a light gait. Although the march to San Sebastián began later than he had planned Rojas had high expectations that he could still catch the militia by surprise. The cavalry began to move slowly out of Lares, followed by the infantry and the two supply wagons. During the fight for Lares, many rebels were able to appropriate horses from the loyalists, and Miguel Pítre was now among the new members of the cavalry. He rode his horse closely behind Rojas, while Manolo, Agustín and Candelario rode alongside him, keeping watch on each other. Candelario had promised himself to look after Miguel Pítre. He wanted to repay Rosalía for her kindness to his mother and for her generosity over the years. Aside from that promise, he also made a secret promise to himself that he would watch over his two younger brothers. As the column of soldiers disappeared into the woods at the end of the street, the second column, led by Terreforte, began to march out of Lares. In the wake of the Lares take-over, spirits were high, morale was high and visions of a free Puerto Rico were starting to crystallize in the minds of the rebel soldiers.

Within minutes of Rojas's departure, Lares swiftly returned to that familiar, sublime silence of a rural town it once knew. The only sounds that morning came from chirping birds nestled in trees and colorful macaws soaring way above Rosalía's head. Yet, as peaceful as Lares appeared to be, the terror inflicted upon the loyalists by the rebels in the wee hours of the morning were still fresh in their minds. From where Rosalía stood in the center of town, she could see broken windows, empty wooden crates, clothing and various merchandize strewn across the dirt road. The wailing of a loyalist child, tugging at the hem of his mother's skirt and the helplessness on his mother's face were cruel reminders of the price of such conflicts. Rosalía stood at the edge of the road, watching an empty thoroughfare leading to San Sebastián, and worried over what dangers lay in store for her beloved Miguelito.

CHAPTER 101

Rosalía gazed broodingly at the main road for nearly half an hour, hoping that Miguel would somehow come back for her. During that time, she thought about her own family and wondered what her tyrannical father was up to, what stories her evil sister Laura had been conjuring up in her wicked mind, and what her dear mother and Anita had been doing. Rosalía's deepness of thought caused her to ignore the sound of fresh cavalry just arriving in Lares. She sensed Berta's presence behind her and was grateful that the former slave had chosen not to interrupt her thoughts. Ten minutes after the cavalry's arrival, Rosalía could hear the sound of distant voices coming from the direction of City Hall, of men arguing and sometimes shouting. Rosalía turned abruptly in response to a door bursting open. She noted the stout face of a tall man with a bushy mustache as he stormed out in the middle of that argument. The prominent facial features were that of Mathias Brugman, who while walking toward his men could not hide his reddened cheeks or the fire that raged from his dark, piercing eyes.

Following Brugman closely, President Ramirez called out for him. "But what if Rojas sends for reinforcements?" he yelled at Brugman.

"If I join Rojas and Terreforte now," reasoned Brugman, mounting his horse, "then perhaps there may not be a need for reinforcements, Francisco, but I simply cannot stay here and wait. I am compelled to fight; there is no other way for me."

"Then who will defend Lares?" Ramirez said pleadingly.

"I will assign 30 men to defend Lares; that's all I can spare," answered Brugman anxiously, sweat starting to accumulate above his eyebrows. "In the meantime, try to get Mediavilla to tell you where the town's coffers are kept."

President Ramirez watched helplessly as Brugman, followed by his longtime friends, Baldomero Baurer and Pedro Beauchamp, began to lead the troops out of Lares. A few minutes after Brugman's departure, Rosalía and Berta, riding together on a white horse, raced out of Lares to join up with Brugman's contingent. There was no way that she was going to stay in Lares, despite Miguel's pleas.

As Brugman and his men disappeared along the road to San Sebastián, all President Ramirez could do now was stand along the edge of the road and watch helplessly. Clemente Millan and Bernabe Pol approached Ramirez and stood side by side with the rebel leader. While gazing at the dust cloud forming behind the cavalry, Millan said consolingly, "It will be all right, señor Ramirez, you'll see."

"In any case, we must seek the Lord's favor in this," replied Ramirez ruefully. "Bernabe, kindly gather the men and ask Father José Vega to sing a *Te Deum* for us. This may also be a good time to confess our sins—we wouldn't want to go to our deaths without receiving absolution, now would we?"

After attending Church that morning, the men returned to City Hall and waited for news from San Sebastián. As they waited, the long stretch of time afforded them an opportunity to reflect on their actions thus far. They began to feel a swell of anxiety and apprehension, much like a dark rain cloud moments before a storm. Perhaps it was the sadness in Father Vega's eyes as he sung the *Te Deum.* Perhaps it was guilt over the manner in which the rebels had brutalized the loyalist men. Perhaps it might have been their fear of the consequences. One thing was certain though: they no longer felt the same enthusiasm as they once felt when they first arrived in Lares. The tidal wave of discomfort and the overpowering winds of fear were the main reasons that caused the scattering of the rebel minds. One by one, they began to abandon their posts and return to their homes, no longer wanting to participate in the rebellion.

While walking back to City Hall after church, Francisco Ramirez and Clemente Millan quickly noted the fear in the eyes of the men. Before they reached the municipal building, both Ramirez and Millan could see the men gathering their weapons and starting to walk back to their cozy lives. Ramirez stopped abruptly and cupped his hands over his mouth, shouting at the men to return. He promised them the success of the rebellion, promised them a different life as free men under an independent Puerto Rico, but it served to no avail. Nothing Ramirez or Millan could say would change their minds now. News from San Sebastián was not coming fast enough to stave off the exodus, and in less than a half hour, there were but only eight rebels left to defend Lares. The numbers were too miniscule, and Ramirez knew it. It was a mistake for Brugman to have taken off for San Sebastián. Ramirez dropped his hands in frustration and stared into Millan's brown eyes with a deep sense of loss.

"Should we send word to Rojas?" Millan asked, hoping Ramirez would do something quickly, something to change the minds of the deserters before they got too far.

"What *can* we do? The only thing that will get those men to turn back is news of a victory. I cannot afford to weaken any more our position by dispatching a man to San Sebastián. We have no choice but to wait it out. In the meantime, let us pay Alcalde Mediavilla a visit."

Twenty minutes later, Ramirez and Millan stood before Mediavilla's cell and demanded that he tell them where he kept the town's funds. But the mayor refused to divulge any information, and they were forced to return to City Hall empty-handed.

Fearing the authorities would discover rebels hiding in the back of Ramirez's colmado, Don Blanco waited until he saw the streets clear of loyalists. He told Aguilar, Ibarra and the Ramirez brothers to jump into his wagon. He covered the wagon bed with a canvass sheet and took the rebels to his farm, where he was hiding the remainder of Porvenir's cell members.

Inside a barn in the fields of Blanco's finca, thirty-one anxious men waited for news. At 11:15 on the morning of September 24, a fast-riding rebel arrived at Don Blanco's hacienda with news that Rojas and Terreforte were approaching San Sebastián. Ibarra could easily read Aguilar's utter relief the moment Don Blanco relayed the message. To Ibarra, Aguilar looked as if someone had removed the weight of the world off his shoulders. After Don Blanco told Aguilar from where Rojas would be arriving, Aguilar led his men straight to the rebel contingents.

They met with Rojas's column and greeted one another with joy and a kind of camaraderie that only soldiers shared moments before a battle. They were in it together, and together they would liberate the island or die trying. The leaders dismounted, and after reacquainting themselves, Rojas led Aguilar toward a secluded grove of mango trees. He stopped abruptly, turned to Aguilar and spoke above a whisper, "Were you able to contact the militiamen under your command?" There was no time for mincing words, and no time for hesitation. All communications had to be concise and clear.

Although Rojas tried to sound calm and in control of things, Aguilar easily read the uneasiness in his face. "We encountered a problem, Manuel. It appears that Alcalde Chiesa has reinstated a former army officer, a peninsular, to take over command of San Sebastián's militia. Upon assuming command of the militia, he confined the men to the barracks and assigned loyalists to guard them in case any of them had any ideas of desertion."

"Are you saying we will not get their help? Is that what you're telling me, Aguilar?" said Rojas, eyes steady, voice stronger now.

"No, Manuel. All I am saying is that both Eusebio and I found it very difficult to talk to our men. But rest assured, once they see us attacking the town, they will turn on the loyalists and fight along with us." Aguilar saw Rojas's skeptical face but he was powerless to convince his leader otherwise. In Rojas's mind, Aguilar was pinning his hopes on something impossible, something totally beyond his reach. Aguilar tried to reassure Rojas, but even in the deepest recesses of his own heart and better judgment, he knew that his chances of convincing the men formerly under his command were, at best, a 50-50 shot. "I know those men, Manuel," insisted Aguilar. "I grew up with them; they are like my brothers. You will see, once we storm the town, they will join us."

Rojas nodded at Aguilar but offered nothing more to him. All that Rojas could have said he said already, any emotion that he could have possibly conveyed either by voice or by gesture he had already conveyed. There were no more speeches left in Manuel Rojas, nothing else that he could offer to anyone except for action, except for the commitment of battle against an unforgiving, ruthless and uncompromising foe. Rojas simply turned and headed toward his horse. He mounted, took a firm hold of the reins and raised his arm to give the command to march on to San Sebastián.

CHAPTER 102

Rojas and his contingent of rebels arrived at the bridge leading into town, where they waited for Terreforte and Ruiz. All three companies finally reunited by the woodland side of the bridge at 11:50 in the morning. As the four-hundred-man-army gathered, Rojas gazed at them, and he could feel them all looking at him, waiting for his orders to charge. He nodded satisfactorily and issued his command.

The men of Rojas's column crossed the bridge first. They were followed by Terreforte's column and then by Ruiz's column. Rojas led his men eastward while Terreforte and Ruiz moved toward the western part of town. The fight for San Sebastián was on, and it began as the bells of the church at the end of the plaza struck the hour of twelve noon.

Positioning his men across Orejola Street on the western side of town, Terreforte waited for Rojas to begin the charge. Rojas ordered Ruiz's column, which presently flanked Terreforte's column, not to engage but to remain positioned there as reserves.

Rojas spurred his horse and rode out straight toward the barracks. He fired all six rounds of his weapon, and then he pulled out another gun and fired away. Then, anyone who carried a pistol or rifle began to fire upon the barracks. From his vantage point at the western edge of the road, Terreforte could see that Rojas's attack had started in total disarray. Instead of dismounting and organizing a line of fire with enough cover to protect his men, the rebel leader charged head on, shooting his gun at everything he saw.

At first, there was no answering fire from the barracks or from any direction in town. For several tense moments, Terreforte thought the militia had turned and run away, as it had done in Lares. But that glimmer of hope quickly vanished as the splatter of organized rifle fire overtook the individual pops that came from Rojas's pistol and from his men's uncoordinated attack. The militia fire had stopped Rojas and his men dead on their tracks, pinning them down in a hail of bullets. They quickly ran for cover.

On the western side of town, Terreforte had met heavy resistance that all of a sudden seemed to be coming from rooftops and from narrow window openings. Though Rojas ordered him to move his column toward the barracks, he learned very quickly that he could not complete the maneuver; a move that Rojas needed so desperately. Frustrated over the ineptitude of the attack, Terreforte told his second in command to form a line and suppress the fire against them. As the splenetic gunfire continued, Rojas could hear the bullets whizzing by him and over his head. Some bullets bounced off the ground, some buried deep into the soil, and some ricocheted with loud, pinging shrills, startling the horses and forcing them to scatter.

As Rojas captured sight of Terreforte, the gunfire became too loud and too much for his horse to bear. All of a sudden, the stallion rose on his hind legs and whinnied, forcing Rojas to tumble backwards and crash on the ground. Rojas fell down hard, puffs of dry, sandy soil rising into the air. Reacting to Rojas's dilemma, Miguel Pítre jumped off his horse as the bullets whizzed in every direction. He ran to Rojas, arched his body and gave the rebel leader the questioning look of a soldier: *Is he dead*? Miguel placed his hand over Rojas's neck and felt a pulse. "I'm all right." Rojas uttered above the whirring gunfire. Rojas's voice came across like music to Miguel's ears, all was not lost...yet.

Toward the west, Terreforte read the lamentable gesture in Rojas's eyes as the leader sat up off the ground. "This was unexpected," said Terreforte to himself. "There is considerable firepower in the barracks and everywhere else for that matter!"

Rojas slowly knelt, and while assessing the situation he said, "The men are pinned down; they've taken cover behind trees, wagons, and just about anything that can shelter them against bullets." Rojas reached for his hat. "I had been under the impression that Aguilar and Ibarra had the militia under control. Do me a favor, Pítre, and get a few of your men to send word out to Aguilar. Tell him to get his ass over here right now, before we all die!"

Sadly, for the rebels, the town of San Sebastián had been expecting the attack. They had prepared for days, and they had plenty of time to hide the munitions and set their defensive positions in key areas surrounding the town. In fact, bullets were coming from so many directions that none of the rebels could figure out from where the fire was coming.

Miguel Pítre had never felt so helpless before. Even after his father died, he knew exactly what to do. Now, with all the gunfire and all the confusion reigning rampant in San Sebastián, all he could do was just stand behind an oak tree trying to fire his Belgian Percussion Pistol at a well-entrenched enemy with superior firepower. For every bullet and cap he put into his pistol, the enemy would fire three and four bullets at the tree. Miguel could hear the wood splintering as the bullets pecked away at the bark, and as he reloaded, he wondered why he had opted for an ancient pistol from Belgium instead of a Winchester or Henry Rifle from America. Behind Miguel stood Manolo, Agustín and Candelario, all holding on to their machetes, as if by some miracle the enemy would allow them the proximity with which to make their weapons effective war tools. Yet, as hopeful as all those African and creole men holding their machetes were, the militia by maintaining a wide gap would give them no chance, no opportunity to use their weapons.

As the fight for San Sebastián continued, Mathias Brugman and his column arrived and began crossing the bridge. He positioned his men at the entrance of the bridge and scanned the field of fire until he managed to get a glimpse of Rojas.

Standing on the woodland side of the bridge, the crackle of gunfire penetrated Rosalía's ears and she began to shake with fear. The thought of not knowing where Miguel was or whether he was safe gnawed at Rosalía's conscience, crushing her heart with despair. Berta's eyes kept vigil for Spanish soldiers and militia that might otherwise come from their side of the bridge to attack the rear. She had resolved to cross the bridge and warn the rebels if she saw any hint of that. Berta could see Rosalía's nervous hands, as she held on to the railing, trying to get a better look at the field of fire. "There's nothing we could do but wait, Rosa."

"I have a mind to cross this damn bridge, Berta. I should have purchased a gun before coming here."

Miguel poked his head from behind the tree and saw the image of Aguilar making his way toward the center of Rojas's stagnant attack line. Every step Aguilar took between cover he timed perfectly, waiting until the next moment when the firing would pause for reloading, and then making the break for the next cover. Aguilar's movements from tree to wagon, to horse, and to sides of houses, were graceful and perfectly timed but terribly suicidal. He finally reached his leader, panting and sweating.

From his position, Miguel could hear Rojas's strained voice as he reproached the president of Porvenir for what seemed like hours. But it had only been just a few seconds worth of admonishment, a few seconds worth of frustration at a subordinate. After enduring Rojas's tirade, Miguel could see that Aguilar kept his cool and remained quiet. Then he saw Aguilar cupping his hands over his mouth. Amidst the crackling gunfire and through the growing yellowish clouds of gunpowder, Aguilar's voice came through like a lighthouse in the midst of a dense fog. "Mauricio! Ortega! Perez!" shouted Aguilar as loudly as he could. "Listen to me! Join us, for we have already taken Lares! Join us and together we can take San Sebastián! If we take San Sebastián, we will move in on Arecibo, then Camuy and then San Juan, and after San Juan, freedom will be ours! It is all yours for the taking! Remember your promise! Esteban, I can see you from here, come man, don't turn your back on us!" As much as Aguilar shouted at the militiamen, it was abundantly clear to Rojas that his efforts were in vain. The militia of San Sebastián was not going to join the revolution. They turned their backs on the rebels and there was nothing Aguilar or Rojas could do about it. Was it that Rojas saw fear in the militiamen, a cancerous fear that would spread to his men? Was it reasoning that caused the militiamen to conclude the revolution was simply a waste of time and energy, a folly? Were the Spanish authorities holding their families hostage, causing their reluctant turnaround, their betrayal against their brethren? Whatever the reason, thought Rojas, it was clear in his mind that they would not get the help they desperately needed.

The exchange of gunfire continued for about a half-hour, until Rojas's men began to clamor at the sight of empty ammunition bags. Making his way through the hail of rifle fire, a messenger came face to face with Manuel Rojas. "With compliments Commandante, from señor Brugman—he wishes to know if you want him to sweep the barracks from the east."

Rojas shook his head vehemently, "Brugman is here? I thought he was supposed to stay in Lares."

"He is here, señor Rojas, and he awaits your reply."

"Tell him not to flank the barracks. Tell him that we're going to regroup instead!"

"Where's the rally point, señor?"

Rojas glanced at Miguel then looked straight into the scrawny messenger's brown eyes. "We'll regroup on the woodland side of the bridge, got it?" The messenger nodded at Rojas, and then crept back to his column, avoiding the maelstrom of molten lead. Very slowly, Rojas crept along the ground, breathing in particles of dirt, tasting the ground with every desperate breath. Along the way, he ordered his men to regroup on the other side of the bridge. As Rojas made his way out of the hellish militia fire, he saw six rebels fearlessly riding their horses toward the mayor's office. Two of the rebels were brandishing sabers, while the others held their pistols at the ready. Rojas curiously watched the rebels navigate their way to the mayor's office through a storm of flashing bullets, as though they were invisible, as if their bodies were impervious to bullets. He turned to Miguel and uttered, "I do not know any those men. Where did they come from?"

Miguel turned to Rojas and in between heavy panting, said, "I believe they are part of señor Brugman's contingent. I think one of them is Bruno Chabrier."

Rojas smiled admiringly. "That's the kind of courage we need." He gave Miguel a fatherly smile. "Come, my boy, we need to get out of here and regroup."

As Rojas and Miguel Pítre hugged the ground for dear life, the other rebels followed closely behind them, mimicking their every move. While Rojas and Miguel crawled their way toward safety, they could hear the six rebels charging the mayor's office yelling their battle cries: *Death to the Spaniards, Death to the Queen, Long Live Puerto Rico Free!*

In the municipal building, Mayor Chiesa had just sworn Rodolfo Hernández into the militia, and had no idea that his town was under attack. As he and his company stepped outside, they heard a woman screaming. The plump woman, whose dark hair contrasted sharply with her pale skin, could not hide her primal fear. She yelled frantically, "The revolutionaries, the assassins are here!" She stuck her hands out of the window and reached for the shutters, slamming them shut. All of a sudden, the night watchman, Santiago Rodriguez, rushed over to the mayor.

The forty-seven-year-old loyalist, with sweeping black hair and dark brown eyes, announced the arrival of the rebels. Mayor Chiesa could see the panic in his eyes, and ordered him to take refuge inside his office, but Rodriguez refused and took a position next to the Corregidor. Mayor Chiesa ignored the night watchman and turned to Rodolfo Hernández whose eyes were gleaming at the six rebels charging the mayor's office. Rodolfo reached for his revolver, as did García Perez, but when the Corregidor heard the rebels' battle cry, he took immediate offense and rushed to confront them. Without thinking the matter clearly, Santiago Rodriguez, without a weapon, followed Pérez into certain death. Showing no sense of fear, García Pérez ran toward the charging rebels, raised his right arm in the air and shouted vehemently, "In the name of the Queen, I order you to cease this insurgency and give yourselves up!" The rebels continued to charge, however, and García Pérez could do nothing to stop them. Witnessing the Corregidor's bravery, Rodolfo dropped the revolver and rushed into the mayor's office. He pushed a cowering Ordoñez to the side and looked around the mayor's study. Rodolfo emerged seconds later holding a rifle. He squatted and took aim.

Leading the charge against the mayor's office was Bruno Chabrier who also showed no fear. He pointed his pistol at García Pérez but as he squeezed the trigger, he felt someone grabbing his arm and easily pulling him off his horse. Santiago Rodriguez had grabbed hold of Chabrier's arm, causing the rebel's bullet to veer off course. The lead projectile was intended for García Perez's head, but it whizzed past the Corregidor by just a fraction of an inch, lodging into the side of the office building. When García Pérez realized what Rodriguez had done, it gave him the opportunity he needed. He took aim and fired. The bullet streamed in a straightforward trajectory and wedged into the upper part of Chabrier's shoulder as Rodriguez finally pulled him down to the ground.

Chabrier's fellow rebels halted their charge only a few feet from the mayor's office and began firing their weapons. Everyone took cover as bullets pockmarked the mayoral building. Rodolfo fired his weapon but his first shot missed. The second shot, however, was good enough to graze a rebel's leg. The rebel dropped his pistol and grabbed hold of his bleeding leg. He shouted profanities at Rodolfo but in the end, he spurred his horse into a retreat. Three of the rebels continued firing away at the mayor's office, while the fourth one dismounted. At first, the dismounted rebel tried to pry loose the night watchman's grip on Chabrier's arm. After landing several blows to Rodriguez's face, he picked up Bruno Chabrier and placed him over his horse. He remounted and told his fellow rebels to retreat. Rodolfo kept reloading and firing but other than the one shot that grazed the rebel's leg, his shooting was as ineffectual as the rebel attack was on San Sebastián.

Rojas and Miguel finally reached a spot where they could lift their heads and assess the situation. It was bad. Rojas could see that Chabrier's charge, though brave, had failed. He saw them retreating toward the bridge, while miraculously evading the gunfire that came from everywhere. All of a sudden, Rojas and Miguel saw another charge of about 30 rebels on horseback rushing the barracks. This time, Aguilar was leading the assault. As Aguilar fired his pistol, he ordered his men to storm the barracks and take possession of the rifles and cartridges there. When Aguilar and his men got close to the barracks, a steady fusillade of lead gave them a hearty welcome. One horse collapsed after a bullet went through its head, throwing the rider to the ground. The rider, too, felt the sting of a bullet in his thigh, and as he agonized in pain, another rebel reached down and scooped him off the ground, saving his life. When he saw the militia firing on their own people, Aguilar raised his voice in supplication, "Milicianos! What are you doing? We are all San Sebastiános! Turn your guns on the Spanish and not on us!" The militia heard Aguilar's plea, and though it was powerful and sincere, they ignored him and continued firing. Unable to close the gap, Aguilar had no choice but to abort his brave charge and order a retreat.

Watching in dismay, Rojas shook his head. "Come, Miguel, let us regroup." Rojas turned around to the men still hugging the ground behind him. "Come men, we're regrouping at the bridge, down Orejola Street!"

Miguel followed Rojas until he reached a point where the range was too wide for any bullet to reach. Finally, they were able to stand without fear. Many of the horses were scattered and lost. In the midst of the chaos, though, Rojas did find his horse and quickly ran toward it. On the other hand, Miguel could not find his and reached for the reins of someone else's horse. Together, Miguel and Rojas galloped down the eastern end of town, toward the bridge.

Berta was the first to see the returning rebels and quickly jumped for joy. "Rosa! They're coming back!"

Rosalía was too nervous to be excited and could not allow Miguel to know that she was there. She shook her head at Berta and uttered, "If Miguel sees me, he'll be very sore at me. He will not be able to fight. I don't think Manolo will be happy either if he sees you, too."

"You're right, Rosa. Come, let us go into the woods and hide before anyone sees us." The two women turned and quietly walked into the woods. Though they hid in the brush, Berta and Rosalía kept vigil on the returning men.

CHAPTER 103

Terreforte, Brugman and Ruiz led their men across the bridge, where they reunited with Rojas near the edge of the creek. A look of frustration on Rojas registered in Brugman's eyes, something he had never before seen on his friend's face. As Miguel Pítre stood behind Rojas, he could not believe what he had just witnessed. The relative ease with which they had overtaken Lares only hours ago, was completely different from the difficultly they encountered in conquering San Sebastián. Was this the end for the revolution? How could it have come to this? It was not what he saw in town, but what he saw in the eyes of every rebel that had regrouped at the bridge, a look of utter defeat and unwillingness to go forward. Miguel thought about the mission Carlos Peña had undertaken, and wondered if he was watching from heaven and crying at their failure. *It cannot end this way, it has to have a different outcome, and that outcome has to be victory! Oh Carlos, how much I miss you! How much I wish you could be here right now!*

Sensing the leaders' wishes to speak in private, Miguel moved his horse away and dismounted. As he pulled his horse behind him, he noticed two women trying to hide in the brush. Knowing exactly who they were, he shook his head and quickly ran over to them. "Rosa, I told you to stay in Lares! It is dangerous for you to be here!" Rosalía did not respond to Miguel. Instead, she opened her arms, embraced her husband and kissed him. It was not a kiss of passion but a kiss that told Miguel of her relief that he was still alive. As Rosalía held him in her arms, and though he was greatly disappointed in her, he was glad to see her. "Rosa, I want you to go back to Lares."

Rosalía let go of Miguel and cast her blue eyes on his face. "I cannot, my love, not while you're still here. I can see now that the rebellion will not succeed. Come back with me and together we will leave the island for America, just like you said."

Miguel sighed, closing his eyes for a brief moment. "I cannot do that, not now. We are merely regrouping so that we could form another attack. I just cannot turn my back on the revolution, Rosa, you know that."

"Then I cannot go back to Lares, you must know that, too, Miguel."

Miguel sighed deeply this time. "You are so goddamn stubborn, Rosa! Why won't you listen to reason?"

"Señor Pítre," interjected Berta. Miguel turned slowly to Berta. "I will stay with Rosa, and I will see to her safety."

Miguel found little solace in Berta's reassurance. He turned back to Rosa, kissed her on the lips and took a brief moment to hold her tightly. He let go of her and with a look of determination said, "We *will* win this war, Rosa, and when the fighting is over in San Sebastián, we will march on to Arecibo. In the meantime, I want you to stay on this side of the bridge. Wait by that grove of orange trees until I send for you." Rosalía looked to where Miguel was pointing, nodded and kissed him one more time. Miguel returned the gesture and then watched the two women as they turned and headed for the orange grove.

Miguel grabbed hold of the reins, pulled his horse behind him and made his way back to the bridge, where he noted Rojas, Brugman, Terreforte and Ruiz discussing another attack on San Sebastián. There was a sense of urgency on their faces, a nervous energy, as if they needed to get this matter resolved quickly before more Spanish soldiers would pour into San Sebastián, a 'now or never' look which told Miguel that another attack was a foregone conclusion. To his left, he could see Bruno Chabrier agonizing as someone pried his wound open to retrieve the mangled led embedded in his shoulder. There were other rebels lying on the ground, wounded and moaning in pain. Miguel tried to ignore their cries but found early on that he could not do it because their wounds were real, the blood that poured out of their bodies was real, and their cries of pain and despair were real. Then it hit him! The notion of rebel invincibility had been a myth created in his mind. The fact was that the rebels were just as mortal as any other human being was. David had gone up against Goliath and this time Goliath had mortally wounded David. Now that the rebel weakness had been exposed, there was no doubt the Spanish would exploit it. *I guess you were right all along, Pápi. I guess the thought of gaining independence by revolution was indeed a pipe dream. Forgive me, Pápi, for not listening to you.*

At that moment, Miguel realized the only meaningful thing in his life was Rosalía, and that nothing else mattered. It was then that he began to regret his involvement in the revolution. But he didn't feel regret because he no longer believed in the ideals of freedom, but because he was madly in love with Rosalía, and realized there was something more to life than revolution. Prior to that pivotal moment the ideals of revolution had been the center of Miguel's existence, now Rosalía had assumed that position and she would remain there forever. Since it was too late to turn back, though, he had to bury his fears deep within his subconscious. As he stood a short distance away from the rebel leaders, he became a changed man.

Before Miguel could reach the rebel leaders, Rojas stepped away, and with the support of both Brugman and Terreforte, shouted his orders for another attack.

The rebels reassembled their ranks at 12:47 that early afternoon and crossed the bridge heading west onto Orejola Street. This time Terreforte and Ruiz led the first wave toward the impregnable barracks. They were soon followed by Rojas's contingent, and then by Mathias Brugman's column. And just like the first attack, the rebels confronted a steady stream of rifle and pistol fire. It never dawned on the minds of the rebel leaders that San Sebastián was not going to surrender, that unlike Lares, the rebels were not going to simply waltz in and take over a town without as much as a fight. To take San Sebastián the rebels were going to have to fight for it, they were going to have to earn that victory.

The second attack was more serious than the first one, not only because the rebels realized they were in a fight now, but also because this time the militiamen had emerged from their barracks to boldly confront their attackers. A line composed of six of Terreforte's men, angered that the militia would not join them, yelled profanities at them, calling them traitors and cowards. Terreforte could see his men's faces clearly, exuding a kind of hatred that he had never before seen on anybody. Now that they had seen the militiamen crouching with their rifles outside the barracks, without fear, the six rebels began to charge them.

Rojas waited anxiously as his brother Miguel Rojas, bearing a message, crept his way toward him. As Miguel Rojas took cover next to his brother, Manuel Rojas could see a look of desperation in his young eyes. He gave his brother a quizzical nod, "Who gave the order for those men to charge the barracks?"

"It wasn't Terreforte or Ruiz, and it wasn't Brugman, my brother. I think those men took it upon themselves to charge the barracks."

"Foolish, they're all going to die!"

"With compliments from señor Terreforte: the commander awaits your orders to flank the barracks. Señor Ruiz's column stands ready to provide cover to Terreforte's charge."

Rojas considered the request for several moments but as he mulled his decision over, he heard concentrated fire in the direction of the six rebels charging the barracks. He could see bright flashes of light as the men began to fall like apples off a tree. Down went Manuel de Leon; a shot to the head, his body still and blood oozing out of his forehead. Seconds later, Venancio Roman took a bullet through the center of his chest, and he too went down, his body twitching. As the third rebel, Manuel Rosado Gimenez, was shot in the abdomen, the remaining rebels began to pull back. While the bullets cascaded over them, like a torrent of rain, Gimenez and Roman felt someone grasping their hands and tugging them back toward the rebel camp. Watching the scene in horror, Rojas grew incensed and wondered why his four hundred-man army was unable to overtake such a small barracks. Years later, in the quiet of his solitude, he would ponder the reasons why he had not agreed to flank the barracks, as requested both times by Terreforte and Brugman.

Not far from Rojas, Miguel kept up a steady fire with his Belgian Percussion Pistol. But as he fired away, he could see that his weapon was ineffective because of the great distance. He paused for a short moment and scanned the field of battle. So many things were going through Miguel Pítre's mind as he witnessed Manuel de Leon's limp body on the ground several hundred feet away. As the retreating rebels drew closer to Miguel, he extended his hand and grabbed hold of one the wounded men, pulling him behind a wagon he was using as cover. When Miguel saw Gimenez's blood-soaked shirt, and when the wounded rebel's cries of inexorable pain pierced his ears, something stirred inside him. Watching Gimenez slowly die created a whirlwind of hatred in Miguel's heart, a vortex of raw evil that easily transformed Miguel. He dropped his antiquated pistol, grabbed Gimenez's repeating rifle and made sure it was fully loaded. He rose to his feet and began to fire at the militiamen squatting in front of the barracks. He fired mercilessly at them while trying to ignore the fact that he had grown up with and had known them all of his life. Before the conflict, they were his friends and he treated them as if they were part of his family. He played dominoes and drank beer with them, but now they were his mortal enemy. As he placed one knee on the ground to take aim, he could hear the bullets whizzing above his head or bouncing just inches off his feet, but he fired nonetheless, hoping that one of his bullets would hit the enemy.

Witnessing Miguel's bravado, the rebel men who had taken refuge next to him and those behind him began to rise to their feet as well, and even Rojas and his brother felt the courage. It was as if an invisible curtain of steel shielded them because no enemy bullets penetrated their exposed bodies. In what seemed like a coordinated attack, the rebels charged forward shooting their rifles and pistols, following Miguel as if he were an officer. From his position, Brugman saw the charge and quickly ordered his men to charge as well. To the left of Brugman's column, Terreforte felt Miguel's courage, too, and followed Brugman's charge.

As Miguel and his fellow rebels pushed forward, he could see that Clemente Borrero, a former schoolmate of his, was the first militiaman to go down. A shot to the leg, just above his kneecap, caused him to quickly drop his rifle and grab his leg in pain. Then, Aniceto Ahorrio fell with a wound to his upper chest area. Miguel used to date Aniceto's, sister and he used to work for his father sometimes. Miguel tried desperately not to feel any sympathy for Aniceto. All of sudden, as the rebels were beginning to show the results of their charge and as they were beginning to make headway on the barracks, Colonel San Antonio kicked open the barracks door and emerged with forty additional militiamen. With a cocked pistol in one hand and a bright saber in the other, he ordered the men to take up positions along the front of the barracks. There was a bright line of flashes before the explosion of unified rifle fire rocked the air. Within seconds, the screeching bullets felt like the howling winds of a hurricane.

Daunted by the militia's firepower, the rebels began to pull back again. As they pulled back, some of them felt the burning sting of hot lead. Even Miguel, who was showing no fear, could not avoid returning to his side without a bullet finding a target in his body. It was a .22 caliber bullet, fired by Colonel San Antonio himself. The bullet found its mark in the back of Miguel's left thigh. At first Miguel thought he'd been stung by a bee, but when he reached behind his left leg and felt a warm liquid he realized he'd been shot. It was not until he looked at his hand and saw it covered in dark, red blood that he began to retreat with a sense of urgency.

Unable to reach the rebel charge in time, both Terreforte and Brugman were stopped cold about two hundred yards from the barracks. Had they been quicker, the two columns might have made the difference. The firepower had been coming from rooftops and from open windows of every home at the hands of loyalist men. Unable to counter the attack, Terreforte and Brugman had no choice but to retreat. The two leaders moved their columns back toward Manuel Rojas with hopes of convincing the commander to make a concentrated head-on attack on the barracks with all of their men.

When Terreforte and Brugman reunited with Rojas, they briefly discussed the new plan of attack. But as they were preparing to mount the new offensive, a wave of new militiamen began to pour out of the barracks. Colonel San Antonio, confident now that the militia was doing its job, ordered the men to push forward and press a devastating counter-assault on the rebels.

San Antonio's counter-attack had taken Rojas and his co-leaders completely by surprise. The rebels had no time to gather themselves, and when they saw the militiamen advancing and firing their weapons, fear of death swept though their very souls. Unable to sustain a defensive line of fire, Rojas could see that the militiamen would overrun them in a matter of minutes. Reluctantly, Terreforte and Brugman agreed with Rojas, and together all three leaders gave the order for a retreat.

Colonel San Antonio, clinging to memories of past battles and the glory of victory, would not let them retreat so that they could regroup and mount another attack, not this time. This time he was going to mount a chase, and such was San Antonio's resolve that he would not stop until the rebels surrendered or died. Any rebel with a horse would be lucky that day. The infantrymen, on the other hand, would have to rely on the power of their legs. Caught up in the wave of retreat, Miguel had lost his horse to a fellow rebel. By now, Miguel had wrapped his leather belt around his leg but the makeshift tourniquet could not stop the awful pain, and he could not run as fast as the other men could because of his wound.

As Miguel hopped along, he could see the rebels running past him with a look of deathly fear in their eyes. The bridge was only a few hundred yards away, and Miguel could see it clearly, but in his condition, the bridge might well have been ten miles away. The sound of militia fire was growing louder now with each step Miguel took. He knew it was only a matter of time before someone would kill him. All of a sudden, Miguel saw three fellow rebels running back toward him, and when he recognized the three African men, he realized that maybe he would not die today. Candelario had been the first to reach him, and then Agustín, followed by Manolo seconds later. Candelario's forehead was gleaming from sweat and in between heavy panting, he said, "Miguel, can you run?"

Exhausted and out of breath, Miguel looked straight into Candelario's black eyes. "I can't even walk let alone run. Just leave me here and save yourselves!"

"No, Miguel, I promised Rosalía that I would protect you," said Candelario undaunted by the wave of militiamen approaching the bridge. He arched his strong body and scooped Miguel off the ground. Agustín and Manolo helped Candelario balance Miguel's body over his shoulders.

They finally reached the bridge but the militia was close behind them. As they began to cross, and as Candelario struggled with Miguel's body, Agustín and Manolo closely followed. The first wave of militiamen reached the San Sebastián side of the bridge and began to form an offensive line. They took aim and began firing. One shot entered the back of Agustín's head and pieces of his skull splintered, blood and brain tissue spattering in every direction. He came down face first and landed dead center on the bridge. "No!" yelled Manolo, watching his brother twitching involuntarily.

Hearing his brother's cry, Candelario turned around and yelled in anguish. He gently placed Miguel down and ran toward Agustín. As he cradled Agustín in his arms, he tilted his head up at Manolo and gave him a stern look. "Stop your damn crying and help Miguel off the bridge! I will take Agustín!" As the bullets whirred above his head, Manolo wasn't listening to Candelario; he'd been too horrified over Agustin's gruesome death. "Manolo!" shouted Candelario with urgency, as bullets began to ricochet off the bridge's wooden planks. "Get a hold of yourself and help Miguel to the other side!"

On the woodland side of the bridge, the rebels watched in horror. Atop their horses, Rojas, Terreforte and Brugman could see the militia had gathered at the other end of the bridge, and seemed to be getting ready to cross and continue the counter-attack. Finally, Manolo stood up and reached for Miguel. Candelario did not fully reach for Agustín until he was certain that Manolo and Miguel had made it safely across the bridge. Then, with bullets still soaring around him, he took hold of his dead brother. As he placed his arms around Agustín's limp body, two bullets entered Candelario's back and went through his chest. Blood spattered in the air like rain, and the eldest son of Mamíta and Papa fell forward on top of his brother.

Manolo gently placed Miguel on the ground but when he turned to face the bridge, the horror in his heart doubled. He screamed as loud as his young lungs could scream and began to make a dash toward the bridge. Almost immediately, he felt several hands pulling him down to the ground. Manolo fell backwards and hit the ground hard. "Don't be foolish, young man!" It was the voice of Manuel Rojas shouting from atop his horse. "They're dead!"

Manolo tried to free himself of the men groping him, but there were too many of them, and they insisted on pinning him down in an effort to save his life.

At the other end of the bridge, Colonel San Antonio smiled triumphantly. "That is how we deal with rebels!" he shouted. "We deal with rebels without compassion, without remorse and with total sense of purpose!" The militiamen said nothing in response, but deep in their hearts, they felt remorse and compassion for their fellow San Sebastiános. The Spanish had forced them into taking action against their countrymen because they had threatened to torture them and even kill their families if they did not cooperate. No sooner had Colonel San Antonio ordered the men to prepare for crossing the bridge than the observing Corregidor arrived unexpectedly.

At the woodland side of the bridge, the cessation of fire had given the rebels enough time to regroup and re-think matters. Rojas, Terreforte, Brugman and Ruiz dismounted their horses and took the time to assess the situation. The four leaders stood at the edge of the bridge and watched the militia. "What do you think, Juan?" Rojas asked Terreforte.

"They're preparing to cross the bridge—that's what I think."

"If those bastard traitors cross the bridge, then we will stop them cold," said Brugman forcefully, angered at the thought of retreat, bothered by the fact that the second attack had also failed miserably. Brugman would not allow the militia to cross to the other side, and he would die in that effort.

"I agree," said Rojas. "We will stack all of our men with rifles right here and greet them with fire. If they get through, then everyone with a machete will engage the enemy. Today, we will die here for freedom and for the independence of our beloved Borinquen!"

At the other end of the bridge, Colonel San Antonio could not hide his disappointment, and he plainly revealed his anger at the Corregidor. "But señor Pérez, we have them on the run, all we need to do is cross the bridge in an organized military manner and you will see that they will scatter."

"No," said the Corregidor sternly. "Take a look across the bridge and see that they are stacking their men. If you send the militia across the bridge, they will all die before they reach the other side. Think the matter through, Colonel, and remember your lessons from the academy. Remember what the Germans did to the Romans in the Teutoburg Forrest and what the Spartans did to the Persians at Thermopylae, but most of all, remember your lessons from the Battle of Stirling Bridge, where the Scots defeated the English. You've done an excellent job in defending the town, don't mess it up by sending your men to certain death."

"So you're just going to let them get away?"

"Yes, isn't it obvious to you what they're doing?" Pérez watched San Antonio nod his head to agree, but the colonel remained reluctant. "By now they must know that that their little insurrection is over," continued Pérez. "I will leave San Sebastián immediately for Arecibo, where I will request Colonel Iturriaga to deploy troops here to protect the town. In the meantime, post men here at this end of the bridge and make sure that no one crosses it."

"But they will return to Lares, señor Pérez."

"And then what? What will they do? They now know that we are on to them, and that it is only a matter of time before we capture them. Don't look so glum, Colonel, you've done a remarkable job here and I will see to it that Governor Pavía and Colonel Iturriaga know about it."

"Very well señor Pérez," replied Colonel San Antonio, angrily. He wanted to crush the rebels, destroy any a hint of a revolution, and erase the thought of rebellion for the next several generations. In the short time he had spent on the island, he had grown to despise the creoles and thought of them as nothing more than animals. Oh, by God, if it were up to him he would have executed every one of them. As he watched the Corregidor galloping back into town, he ordered the entire militia to remain there at the edge of the bridge. He would not redeploy them until the rebels left the area.

Rojas watched the action across the bridge, and as he witnessed the Corregidor's departure and Colonel San Antonio issuing orders, he knew that the militia was not going to cross the bridge. A sense of utter relief overcame Rojas, and the feeling was like pouring a bucket of cold water over his head after a long day in the finca. He heard Terreforte's voice, "You see that, Manuel? They're not going to cross." Rojas did not utter a word. He just gazed across the bridge with a slight grin.

Without taking his eyes away from the militiamen posted on the other side of the bridge, Mathis Brugman, who was standing next to Terreforte said confidently, "All right, now we should form another attack."

Almost immediately, Rojas and Terreforte turned their heads and gave Brugman a look of shock. Brugman turned to his co-leaders and wondered why they were so surprised. He was about to reproach them when a rebel, who was standing next to him with a bandage over his right arm and blood seeping through it, opened his mouth. "You're not serious, are you, Don Brugman?" His youthful, angular face could not hide the fear that his grey eyes plainly revealed. Then as if in a chorus, the rest of the men began to complain against a third attack.

Rojas slowly approached Brugman and whispered into his ear, "I wonder if we could have a private word."

The leaders left the men by the bridge and walked a ways down the dirt road. They slowly walked towards a Plumeria tree and stood underneath its stout, green leaves. A short distance away, by a grove of orange trees, Rosalía and Berta could see the leaders huddling for an intimate conversation.

Brugman folded his arms expectantly, knowing what Rojas was going to say. "Mathias, how can we mount a third attack when we can't even cross the bridge? The moment we get within distance, they will fire upon us and do to us what we were planning to do to them." He watched Brugman's unemotional face, his stern, unwavering expression, and knew it was going to be tough to convince his friend.

"There is another place where we can cross, Manuel; it is only several miles from here. Why are you so hesitant to fight? Our forces are still strong and we put up a good fight."

Terreforte shook his head at Brugman. "We put up a good fight? That tiny militia of San Sebastián routed us! Can you imagine our men facing the regular army of Aguadilla or Arecibo? Do you really think we could stand a chance against their cannons? Our mission was to secure the munitions in San Sebastián and we did not accomplish that. Besides, if we move our men to cross several miles upstream, we will run the risk of encountering Spanish troops."

"It must not end here, gentlemen, not like this," insisted Brugman proudly. "We've worked so hard for this day and now I cannot bear to see the look of defeat in the faces I trust most. I cannot bear to look at the men and see nothing but fear in their eyes. We must attack now before the army arrives. Manuel, you know that once the soldiers arrive, we will not have the opportunity again."

Rojas shook his head in frustration, but even he knew that if third attack succeeded, it still would not have mattered. They needed to secure arms and ammunition from San Sebastián, but they needed to accomplish that mission quickly, and then move on to Arecibo and by surprise attack the base there. Then they could get their hands on cannons, and more rifles and ammunition and then the people would start believing. Once the wave of rebellion caught on with the people, a full-blown revolution would sweep through the island. Thwarted at the outset of that dream by a tiny group of militiamen, Rojas could only conclude that all was lost. "I am very sorry, Mathias, but we must go back to Lares."

"You're making a big mistake, Manuel. Do you know what they'll do to us?"

Terreforte, Rojas and Ruiz all hesitated briefly before nodding, fully aware of Spanish methods of interrogation and torture. But they had made the commitment to rebel against Spain and they were well aware of the consequences. Rojas gave Brugman a sad look, an expression that revealed the pain of losing the belief in such an idealistic future. "Come, Mathias, let us gather the men and order an organized retreat."

As Rojas approached the bridge, Terreforte and Ruiz followed him closely, leaving Mathias Brugman under the Plumeria tree to seethe in anger for another fifteen minutes. Rojas reached the men, and while gazing pitifully at them, a young rebel by the name of Pablo Rivera y Delgado confronted him. He was only sixteen years-old but he was a robust young man, muscular with powerful broad shoulders. His long, brown hair had never felt the sharp edges of metal scissors and it ran down his back covering his shoulder blades. His light-brown eyes captured Rojas with a sense of pride. Somehow, Rojas felt that if he had given the order, Pablo would have stepped to the front and continued fighting. Rojas would never do that, not now anyway. "Señor Rojas, I have the casualty report."

Rojas placed a hand on the boy's shoulder and smiled at him. "Let's hear it."

The sixteen-year-old, voice crackling into manhood, spewed out the casualties. "One dead and forty-three wounded by the barracks. Two men were killed on the bridge and we lost nine horses."

Although the casualties in Rojas's mind were insignificant, the routing of the attack had been significant because it played into the psyche and heart of every rebel man. The rout had successfully weakened the rebels' resolve and had smashed a gaping hole in their morale—a morale which had reached its zenith in Lares the night before. Rojas took a brief moment to gaze at Pablo's youthful face and note the zeal that still lingered in his eyes, like a fire torch that never burned out. How could he send that young man to his death? How can he ask Pablo to go into battle now? How could he order that young man to fight for an ideal that was quickly becoming nothing more than a pipe dream? He decided right then to spare the young man. If the Spanish arrived before they could mount a successful retreat, then he wanted Pablo out of there. "All right, young man, thank you for the report. Now I want you to ride to Lares with a message for President Ramirez."

"But señor, I want to stay here and—"

"Listen to me," interrupted Rojas, "You fought well and bravely today. You are very young and you must survive this day so that you can tell our story to the world, to our children, so that the fires of liberation will never leave the hearts of Puerto Ricans, so that one day, when the people are of one mind, they can say no more to tyranny. Do this, Pablo, do it for your fellow rebels, for those who have paid with their lives. Do this for the many people of this island who face oppression and misery every day of their lives under the feet of their Spanish masters. Live to fight another day."

Pablo fell silent and though Rojas felt the young man did not understand his message completely, he knew that one day it would make sense to him. Pablo narrowed his eyes at Rojas. "All right, señor Rojas, I will do as you ask. What do you want me to say?"

"Tell the president to gather the prisoners in Lares and bring them to my hacienda. I want you to tell the rest of the men in Lares to ride to my hacienda as well, and tell them that we will arrive very shortly to discuss our next step."

CHAPTER 104

The town of San Sebastián fell silent once again, and it was due to the militia's efforts and, to a greater extent, the help of loyalist townsfolk. Their combined strength had repelled the rebel attack and had forced the revolutionists out of town. The busy reports of pistol fire and the loud crackles of rifles that dominated the airwaves only moments earlier had faded into oblivion, and only the harsh memories of the battle lingered in the minds of the loyalists. At first, there was only one woman who showed the courage to open her bullet-riddled shutters, but the longer it remained silent the more people began to open shutters or step outside to assess the damage to their homes. Before long, the town was busy again, filled with people observing the damages, commenting on the attack and commiserating for the one-day's loss of business.

Inside the mayor's office, Rodolfo Hernández grew more anxious as he waited for Chiesa to conclude his meeting with the Corregidor of Aguadilla. After the meeting, mayor Chiesa walked into the parlor where he noted the anticipation on Rodolfo's face.

As usual, Rodolfo wasted no time. "Alcalde, from the look on your face I can tell that we are not going to pursue those rebel fucks!"

"I must insist that if you continue to use profane language, I will not entertain you anymore, Rodolfo," said Chiesa angrily.

"Please accept my apologies, Alcalde," replied Rodolfo without hesitation but his face clearly showed no remorse. "So, why is García Pérez leaving San Sebastián? Why are we not mounting an effective chase against the rebels? Why are we letting Miguel Pítre flee?"

"The Corregidor is on his way to Arecibo to secure troops for San Sebastián," replied the mayor evenly. "And you should know that the rebellion is now over. It is only a matter of time before we arrest every one of the rebels. We'll get our hands on this Pítre fellow, don't you worry."

"Oh I'm not worried, Alcalde, I just want to be there when that peasant is finally captured," said Rodolfo gritting his teeth. "That is why I do not wish to go home. I will stay in town until the army arrives, and then I will go with them on the hunt."

"Why are you never satisfied, Rodolfo?" said the mayor, no longer taking great pains to hide his true feelings. The more he associated with Hernández the less he grew to respect him. Now he wondered if pandering to Rodolfo's charges against Carlos Peña was the right thing to do. Ever since Ibarreta had accused Rodolfo of making false charges, Chiesa kept second-guessing himself and wondered if Rodolfo had been truthful about Peña. He glared at Rodolfo with a touch of disdain. "Miguel's father is dead," he continued, "and you now have the land back without any legal encumbrances. You had that African man arrested and executed without a trial. We have crushed the so-called rebellion and the army is arriving soon to restore order in Lares. Yet, in spite of all this, you remain unsatisfied. Now you are setting your sights on Miguel Pítre who is just another jíbaro from the mountains. What more do you want Rodolfo? Why is it that you still feel threatened by him?"

Rodolfo's eyes drifted away from the mayor and focused steadily at the floor with a melancholy, almost weeping expression. "Because he's taken my daughter away from me and because if he is arrested and hung for sedition, I will get my daughter back. All I ever wanted was for my children to have a better life than what I had, nothing more. Now that peasant has poisoned my daughter's mind and heaven only knows if she is suffering right now."

Mayor Chiesa considered Rodolfo's words for several moments, but being a true politician and therefore too clever for the likes of Hernández, he could see through Rodolfo's façade of sadness and mask of hurt. He saw Rodolfo as nothing more than a symbol of avarice, a man that needed to satisfy an unquenchable thirst for money, and an unquenchable lust for societal position. The fact that Miguel had easily entered his life, coupled with the notion that Rodolfo did not foresee the untold damage he represented, threatened Hernández very much and scared him to the very core of his heart. So what was it that caused Rodolfo Hernández to fear a peasant so much? The mayor wondered hard about it and concluded that the great land owner, the infamous peninsular who feared no one, was hiding something about himself. What it was, the mayor had no idea.

CHAPTER 105

At 1:37 on the afternoon of September 24, Manuel Rojas mounted his horse and trotted to the edge of the bridge, where he saw Miguel Pítre lying on the ground amongst the wounded men. "How bad is it, Miguel?"

Miguel Pítre, whose wounds Manolo had been attending to, looked up at Rojas and shook his head. "I am unable to walk, señor Rojas, not well enough to keep pace with the infantry."

Rojas sighed pitifully. "We have no more horses, Miguel. Every man must make his way back to Lares on his own power. I'm afraid I have no choice but to leave the wounded here."

Manolo who had just completed wrapping Miguel's thigh with part of his shirt, turned to look up at Rojas. "Señor, you cannot be serious."

"I am, soldier," replied Rojas unemotionally. Rojas turned his attention to the rebel army and cupped his hands over his mouth. "Men, listen to me! Let us prepare for the march back to Lares!"

Two columns began to march, while a third stayed behind to protect the rear. In their wake, they left Miguel Pítre and twenty-six other wounded men. As the thudding sound of marching rebels dominated the airwaves, Miguel faced Manolo with sadness. "Go, Manolo, you're still fit to march."

"Rojas could have taken you on his horse," muttered Manolo.

Miguel frowned. "There were only a handful of horses. Why would Rojas take me and leave the others? You must go, Manolo."

"I cannot, Miguel, a promise is a promise. I must see to your safety."

"No," insisted Miguel, "that was a promise Candelario made to Rosa, not you. You are under no obligation to see to my safety. Go! I will be fine."

"But Miguel, they will arrest you."

"Yes, and they will arrest you, too. I need Rosa to know that I am all right and who better to tell her than you? Besides, if Rojas decides to attack again, he is going to need every able bodied man. They're here you know."

"Who?"

"Rosalía and Berta; they're hiding in a grove of orange trees just beyond the bridge. Go to them and make sure they return to Lares with you. You must keep up the fight."

"No Miguel, my fighting days are over. The deaths of my brothers were in vain—I can see that now." Tears began to well in Manolo's eyes as he focused his eyes on the two bodies that lay still at the center of the bridge.

"Not true, Manolo," said Miguel grimacing in pain, "not true at all. Candelario and Agustín died because they believed in the idea of freedom. Do not diminish their deaths but hold your brothers high in your mind for they are heroes, martyrs for the cause of liberty and justice."

"No Miguel," countered Manolo. "Their deaths were in vain. Now if you want me to abandon you, then that is your wish. I will find Rosalía and take her back to Lares, but I will take my sister and leave for America."

Miguel sighed thoughtfully and then forced a smile. "Very well." He noted the determination in the former slave's face as he rose to his feet. While standing, Manolo could hear the rear guard slowly making their way into the woods. Then without turning back for a final farewell, he marched toward the orange grove. As Manolo's body faded into the woods, Miguel could hear the moaning of his wounded fellow rebels. He placed his hand in the back of his thigh and felt the blood oozing out of the makeshift bandage. Miguel tried to move into a better position so that he could rest his wounded leg, but as he did so, the stomping of feet upon the wooden planks of the bridge startled him. He turned quickly toward the bridge and saw twenty militiamen running toward the woodland side; they were all aiming their rifles at Miguel and his fellow rebels. Miguel recognized all of them but he chose to remain silent for the moment.

"Can you stand, Miguel?" Sergeant Santos asked, still aiming his rifle at Miguel's chest.

Miguel looked up and shook his head. "Good Lord, Pedro, if you're going to shoot me, then do it! Otherwise, take that damn rifle out of my face!"

Shaking his head at Miguel, as if Miguel had been an unruly child who had disobeyed his parents, Sergeant Santos uttered, "Why did you do it, Miguelito? Why did you take up arms against Spain?"

Miguel gave the militiaman a look of intolerance. "Why didn't *you*? Are you not the son of Julian Santos, the man who lost his farm to the Marquez brothers? Are you not the son of the man whose family the Marquez brothers evicted from their home and forced them to live on the streets of Pepino for weeks before Don Blanco came to the rescue?"

"What do you want from me Miguel? I have a family of my own now, and they threatened to take reprisals on my wife and children if I refused to fight. It was easy for you to fight because you have nobody to care for, your father's dead and you have no family! Now, if you are not able to walk then I will help you."

"For what, so that you can put me in jail?" replied Miguel angrily. "Thank you, but no, I will go to jail on my own power."

"Then get up!"

Before long, the militiamen rounded up all of the wounded rebels and forced them to march across the bridge at gunpoint. When they reached the other side of the bridge, the rebels caught sight of Colonel San Antonio sitting atop his horse, gleaming victoriously. As the prisoners slowed their march, Colonel San Antonio dismounted and stood with arms folded waiting to take a closer look at the scum he had been fighting.

Forced to march at gunpoint, the weakened rebels collapsed after crossing the bridge. Only two were able to stand—Miguel and a young muláto with a shoulder wound. Colonel San Antonio unfolded his arms and drew his revolver before walking to the prisoners. As he moved closer he fixed his sights on Miguel, but it wasn't because the Colonel had singled him out, but because Miguel eyed him fearlessly. Colonel San Antonio finally reached Miguel and stood face to face with him.

He glanced at the muláto and shouted, "Take that half-breed out of my sight!" As the militiamen dragged the young muláto away, the Colonel looked into Miguel's green eyes, smiling sardonically. "You goddamn piece of worthless shit! Did you really think you could waltz in here and take over the town so easily?" Miguel Pítre remained silent but he kept looking at San Antonio with fiery, unblinking eyes. San Antonio moved even closer to Miguel so that his nose almost touched Miguel's nose. "And for what, to make us pay for your mistakes? If you peasants had an ounce of intelligence among you, then maybe you would be in a better position than the one you're in now. Maybe, this fucking island would be a center of commerce rather than the goddamn cesspool it is now!" He smiled wickedly at Miguel and whispered into his ear so that the militiamen would not hear him. "Do you know what's going to happen? At this very moment, the commanders of the Arecibo and Aguadilla garrisons are mobilizing, and so too are the garrisons of Mayagüez and Ponce. They are going to hunt down all of your co-conspirators and hang them for treason!"

Miguel, still with unflinching eyes, kept staring into San Antonio's hateful brown eyes. "You're a silly man if you think that by killing us you will rid yourselves of rebellion. Know this, you Spanish dog: for every rebel you kill ten more will take his place. Yes, you have the power to kill us, but never in your deepest imagination will you kill our dreams, our hopes and our patriotism!"

Incensed over Miguel's remarks, San Antonio swung his revolver across his face. The butt of the gun landed squarely on Miguel's right temple and caused him to fall backwards on to the ground. Miguel fell out of consciousness and in a dream-like state, a host of memories flashed through his mind. The first memory was as a ten-year-old child, hiding behind his father as his mother threw pots and pans to the floor, screaming in anger. The other was of his father crying when he came home and discovered that his wife had left him. Another was of his father, working the coffee fields and the hump on his back impeding his efforts. Then there was the memory of meeting Rosalía for the first time. Then, everything went dark.

Standing over Miguel, Colonel San Antonio heard the sound of a young woman screaming in panic. As she ran toward the bridge, the colonel noted the tears streaming down her cheeks and concluded she must have been the wife of one of the wounded prisoners.

CHAPTER 106

The young rebel dispatched to Lares by Manuel Rojas, arrived just past the stroke of two in the afternoon. He had driven his horse straight from San Sebastián without rest, and now his beast was near to collapse. After the horse buckled for several moments, Pablo decided it was time to dismount. He began walking the tiny streets of Lares, wondering where everybody had gone to; there was no one in sight. Perhaps the militia had arrived early in the morning and had already rounded up the rebels, or maybe even killed them. He shook his head, dreading the idea, and continued to walk along the desolate streets.

To his disbelief, the young rebel came upon a creole restaurant where he noticed Francisco Ramirez calmly having lunch in the company of Clemente Millan and several others. Pablo Rivera entered the restaurant with a sense of urgency and quickly interrupted the peaceful lunch party. He moved quickly toward Ramirez's table, removed his pava and spoke humbly. "Señor presidente, I wonder if I might have a private word with you."

Ramirez placed his fork and knife on the table, wiped his mouth and thick mustache clean, and then looked up at Pablo. "And who might you be, young man?"

"My name is not important, señor, but the message I have for you is," replied Pablo with forthright conviction, almost with the air of a seasoned warrior. He watched as Ramirez placed the tablecloth on the table and glanced quickly at his fellow diners.

Ramirez slowly rose from his chair, excused himself and then gently placed a fatherly arm around Pablo's shoulder, escorting him outside the restaurant. As soon as they stepped outside, Ramirez looked up at the taller man. "Now, tell me, what is the message?"

"Señor presidente, the attack on San Sebastián has failed." Pablo waited to see how Ramirez would react, but the president merely closed his eyes and sighed heavily. By Ramirez's simple gesture, Pablo understood everything. By reading the gloom on Ramirez's face, he finally understood the ideals preached by Dr. Betances, Manuel Rojas and Mathias Brugman, and the reason why the rebellion had to succeed. All of a sudden, Ramirez opened his chestnut colored eyes and cast a melancholy gaze at Pablo. "I do not want to hear details about the battle, so please spare me of the horrors. Is there anything else?"

"Yes. Señor Rojas requests that you remove all prisoners from the jail in Lares and take them to his hacienda."

Ramirez sighed again, but this time it was out of frustration. "I do not understand, young man. Why does he want to keep the mayor and everybody else prisoner? You have just told me that the attack on San Sebastián has failed, which means that our rebellion has failed. What does he intend to do, execute them?"

"I don't know, señor presidente, all I know is that Señor Rojas wants all prisoners taken immediately to *El Triunfo*. At this moment, he is making his way back home with all of the troops and he expects to see you there with the prisoners."

Confused and at a loss for a rational explanation to Rojas's orders, Ramirez threw up his hands in disgust. "Very well, I shall do what's best for everybody."

By 4:45 in the afternoon, Ramirez and Millan led the remaining rebel soldiers out of Lares proper with prisoners in tow. Midway through the three-mile journey to Rojas's plantation, though, Ramirez had had a sudden change of mind. He pulled hard on the reins, halting his miniscule column. Turning his horse around, he looked down at the keeper of the keys and said loudly, "Release the prisoners!"

The young private, who was riding alongside of Millan, instantly changed his demeanor. "Señor presidente, what are you doing?"

Ramirez slowly turned to the baby-faced soldier, and with a deadpan expression uttered. "Young man, there is no point in keeping these men prisoners since the rebellion has failed. Go home to your family and see to your folks. I will press on toward Rojas's hacienda and I will explain my decision to the Commandante."

"He will not be pleased, señor."

"It does not matter now, does it?"

Freed of the iron bindings, Mayor Pablo Mediavilla nursed his wrists for a short moment before looking up at a defeated Ramirez. "You think that by freeing us now you're going to receive a better treatment, señor Ramirez? You and your rebel friends have wreaked considerable damage in Lares. Your men have stolen goods and destroyed the establishments of hard-working loyalist men and, if I may, a few of your fellow creoles, too. I will see to it that you and all of your so-called liberators will face the maximum penalty of treason under the laws of Spain."

"Shut the hell up, you goddamn peninsular bastard!" shouted Clemente Millan. He turned to Ramirez. "Let me shoot this vulture!"

Without taking his eyes away from Mediavilla, Ramirez uttered, "No, Clemente. Contrary to what this man thinks, we are not animals and we are not anarchists. We are decent human beings forced to live under a repressive regime. The rebellion has failed today, but one day, we will rise again and we will be free!"

Within twenty minutes, the loyalist men were freed of their bindings, and as they slowly began to make their way back to Lares, Pablo spurred his horse. "Where are you going, young man?" said Ramirez.

"My name is Pablo Rivera y Delgado," shouted Pablo, glaring at Ramirez, "and I want you to remember it well. Remember this too: I am revolutionist, a true rebel and a believer! I'm going back to rejoin Commandante Rojas!"

Ramirez shook his head, disappointed, but then turned and spurred his horse into a trot. Clemente Millan, with fire still lingering in his eyes, quickly approached Ramirez and rode side by side with the defunct rebel president.

The young Pablo galloped furiously, determined to reach Rojas with news about Ramirez's awful decision. As fate would have it, Pablo would never reach his commander. Angry loyalist men, forced to take refuge in the woods during the Lares revolt, spotted Pablo and ambushed him. They tied his legs with a rope and dragged him along the road all the way to the Lares jail, a distance of two miles. There he would wait until Ibarreta's arrival and his subsequent trial.

CHAPTER 107

Colonel San Antonio focused his eyes on the young woman kneeling before Miguel Pítre, sobbing, trying to ascertain whether he was still alive. "Señorita, is this man related to you?"

Cradling Miguel's head in her arms, she replied, "Yes, he is my husband. Why did you beat him with your gun? Why did you beat a wounded and bound man?"

Colonel San Antonio ignored her inquiries, as the thudding of a horse's hooves grew louder in the distance. "If you are this man's wife, then you are a rebel, too, and you will be arrested along with him." San Antonio gave Rosalía a baneful stare before ordering a solider to bind her. The soldier stepped forward and grabbed Rosalía by her arms, forcing her to stand.

"What are you doing? Let go of me!" yelled Rosalía. She loosened herself from the soldier's grip and knelt again, reaching for Miguel's head. The soldier, unfazed by her devotion to Miguel, repeated his gesture. This time, he quickly brought Rosalía's arms behind her back and clasped her wrists in iron bindings.

Colonel San Antonio nodded satisfactorily as the approaching horse suddenly stopped. Turning around for a look, Colonel San Antonio noticed Rodolfo Hernández dismounting. In the distance, behind Rodolfo, San Antonio saw Mayor Chiesa approaching on horseback. Rodolfo walked slowly toward the bridge and while narrowing his eyes at his daughter said, "Release her, Colonel!"

"Who the hell are you?" San Antonio inquired, noting Rodolfo's fine apparel, concluding at the same time that he must have been a man of importance.

"Never mind who I am, I said release her! Now, Colonel, if you please!"

Mayor Chiesa finally arrived at the bridge, and as he dismounted, he addressed Colonel San Antonio. "It's all right Colonel, you may release her. This is Rodolfo Hernández, and that young lady is his daughter."

Refusing to release Rosalía, the colonel turned to Rodolfo. "Your daughter claims to be the wife of this rebel peasant. If that is so, then she is a rebel, too."

Rodolfo's leg hurt badly today, the old wound always seem to hurt him unexpectedly. Using his cane to brace himself, he walked over to the colonel. Rosalía's heart was pumping wildly, now that she came face to face with her father; something she thought would never happen again once she left home. Yet, at that moment, all she could think about was Miguel. Rodolfo's anger blistered over his face as he eyed the colonel with an unwavering determination. "Now you listen to me, Colonel. This man is a criminal! He abducted my daughter, took her against her will, and brainwashed her into joining his pitiful rebellion. If she is married to him, then he probably forced her into it, so the Church will not recognize the marriage. And finally, she is my daughter and I will use every resource at my disposal to free her, do you understand me?"

Colonel San Antonio turned to Mayor Chiesa. The mayor nodded in agreement. "That's right, Colonel. The mayoral office received a missing person report from señor Hernández a few days ago and we have been looking for her since then. Now kindly release señorita Rosalía."

The moment she felt free of the bindings, Rosalía knelt again and cradled Miguel's head, trying to wake him. Rosalía then noticed her father's familiar boot tips and knew he was standing over her. "Rosa," said Rodolfo in a peaceful tone, unlike his normal tyrannical and condescending tone. "Get up and come home with me, all is forgiven. Your mother is devastated by your running away from home and she is wondering where you are and whether you are all right. Let us go to her and show her that you are fine."

Rosalía knew her father was lying to her because her mother was there on the night she ran away and had even given her blessings, wishing her all the happiness in the world. Rosalía tilted her head and looked into her father's hateful eyes. "What's to become of my husband? Will you find a way to execute him, in the same manner as you did Carlos Peña?"

With much difficulty and strain, Rodolfo knelt so that he could face his daughter's weeping blue eyes. "Listen to me, Rosa. I can have the marriage annulled. The love that you seem to have for Miguel is merely an infatuation and nothing more. In time, you will see that the events of today will have mattered not in the least. You will become a woman of stature, a prize won by the best nobleman of Spain. You have filled your heart with an illusion of love, a dream that can never become true."

Gingerly cradling Miguel's head, Rosalía looked at her father. "No, it is not an illusion. My love for Miguel is real, and my marriage to him is real and sacred in the eyes of God. The fact of the matter is that you simply cannot live with the shame of my marriage, but I am not ashamed of it. In time, I will be glad that I chose Miguel as my husband because I will bear him a child soon."

Rodolfo's eyes suddenly widened out of shock. "What did you say?"

"I said I am with child, Father. Your grandchild is growing in my womb."

Rodolfo closed his eyes while shaking his head in disappointment, reluctantly absorbing the tragic news. Behind him, both Colonel San Antonio and Mayor Chiesa looked at one another, shaking their heads disapprovingly. "You have displeased me greatly, Rosa. I will never recognize that bastard as my grandchild—you must know that. However, I am willing to forgive your indiscretion if you agree to put the child up for adoption and annul your marriage to Miguel. If you do that, then I will turn the page on this sad episode in our lives. If you do it not, then I will turn my back on you. Now, at this very moment, you must make a decision, a decision that will affect you for the rest of your life."

Without hesitation, without pause for reflection, Rosalía eyed her father with conviction. "I choose to stay with Miguel."

Rodolfo sighed deeply, desperately holding back the hurt of his daughter's betrayal. "So be it, Rosa. From this moment forward, I disown you. You are dead now. That is what I intend to tell your mother and your sisters." Rodolfo rose to his feet, gasping for air at the same time, and slowly walked toward the mayor.

San Antonio gave Mayor Chiesa a questioning look. The Mayor knew what the colonel was asking by reading his eager eyes. He shook his head at the colonel. "No, do not arrest her, for we have had enough tragedies for one day." He placed a consoling hand over Rodolfo's shoulder and offered his sympathy. "Rodolfo, my dear Rodolfo. I am sorry to hear about your daughter's death; it was untimely. Come to my office, where we can have a drink of rum and see to a proper death certificate."

Sadly, Rodolfo mounted his horse and followed Mayor Chiesa. He never looked back at his daughter. As far as he was concerned, Rosalía had died in the battle of San Sebastián.

As the thundering beat of horses faded, Colonel San Antonio ordered his men to collect the prisoners and move them to the jail. The soldiers forced Rosalía out of the way, picked up Miguel's limp body and placed him over the side of a horse. Then a contingent of soldiers escorted the prisoners to the jail in San Sebastián, leaving Rosalía at the bridge, weeping in misery.

On the woodland side of the bridge, Manolo and Berta had seen everything.

Unsure of what to do now, Rosalía decided to cross the bridge and walk back to Lares together with Berta and Manolo. Perhaps the rebels were planning another attack. Perhaps Rojas had planned to come back for the wounded. If Rojas was planning another attack, then Rosalía wanted to participate in it. She decided that once she got to Lares, she would get her hands on a rifle and she would fight alongside the rebels. After explaining what had happened to Miguel, all three trudged their way back to Lares.

CHAPTER 108

The town of Lares lay in stillness, like a mountain lake without a ripple. The loyalists, unaware that the rebellion had failed and exuberant over their sudden release from jail, chose to remain in their wrecked homes and await the outcome of the day. At 6:05 in the evening they got their answer. It came in the form of a powerful thunder of rebel cavalry and the thumping of hundreds of retreating foot soldiers. The prodigious dust clouds they made through Lares's main thoroughfare gave the loyalists the impression that the rebels were in great haste. It took a mere twenty-five minutes for Manuel Rojas and his band of rebels to pass through Lares, and just as sudden, the town returned to its peaceful quiet. In spite of their optimism, the loyalists kept silent and remained in their homes.

Manuel Rojas and his defeated troops finally arrived at *El Triunfo* a little past seven that evening, where he first sought the president of the failed republic. Rojas dismounted, tied his horse to the post right outside his home and took a moment to look at his men. Almost immediately, he noted that many of them did not even bother to dismount but kept going. They were leaving for their homes, to reunite with their wives, children and sweethearts, and there was nothing he could do to stop them. Rojas felt a sense of loss, as if he were standing on a bridge and suddenly dropping something valuable into the water.

Rojas, closely followed by Brugman and Terreforte, reached for the door to his home but as he turned the knob, the door opened from the inside and out stepped Ramirez. Clemente Millan and several other men quickly followed Ramirez. "We received your message, Manuel. It is a sad day for Puerto Rico."

The men shook hands before entering the tiny house. Rojas seemed as though he had the weight of the world over his shoulders. With eyes reddened, mouth dry, face drawn and gloomy, he sat on his couch and looked up at Ramirez. "The militia fought against us, Francisco. We tried like hell to convince them to join us but they kept firing at us and we could do nothing to stop them. They were ready for us, must have been ready for days. It would seem that we were betrayed by Diego Redondo."

Ramirez, looking down at Rojas with melancholy eyes, shook his head at the rebel leader. "No, Manuel. That is not exactly what happened."

Manuel Rojas slowly rose to his feet. "What *did* happen?"

"I will let Clemente Millan tell you," replied Ramirez, turning to Millan. "Clemente, if you please."

Clemente Millan cleared his throat before speaking. "As you know, Don Aguilar and I interrogated Diego Redondo. Before his execution, Redondo admitted that a member of Lanzador had exposed our plans weeks before he gave his intelligence report to the governor. Diego also insisted that he provided disinformation to Pavía and that he never divulged the exact date of our rebellion."

Rojas looked straight into Millan's face. "And you believed his story?"

Millan nodded with certainty. "At first I thought he was lying to save his life. After his death, though, I began to put things together. If Redondo had exposed us, then Mediavilla in Lares would have requested assistance from Governor Pavia. That was not the case. In fact, the first person arrested for sedition was Gonzalez, the president of Lanzador, and that made sense with Redondo's story. Finally, if Redondo had exposed the true date for the rebellion, then I think that Lares, even with a small militia would have defended against our attack. No, señor Rojas, although Redondo was an unsavory character, shady and misguided, he did not betray us and I am remorseful over his death. That is something we must live with for the rest of our lives. The real traitor of our cause was Hilario Martínez, a member of Lanzador."

Rojas nodded at Millan showing thorough understanding and agreement with Millan's observations. "Tragic as it may seem, Diego Redondo was a casualty of war," said Rojas. Then he changed his demeanor and turned back to Ramirez. "So, where are you keeping the prisoners?"

Clemente Millan stepped backwards, allowing Rojas a clear line of sight to a cowering Ramirez. Ramirez felt a chill in his spine when he saw Rojas's inquisitive eyes, searching for truth. He stammered at first, but then took his time to answer. "I thought the young man you sent here with dispatches returned to you with my message."

"No, in fact, he never came back. Frankly, I thought he was still here with you," answered Rojas, growing curious. "So what was your message? Where are the prisoners?"

Ramirez hesitated, held his breath for a split second, and then uttered, "I released them." As soon as he said those words, he saw Rojas's optimistic face turn ashen and sullen.

"But why did you do that? I gave explicit orders to transfer the prisoners to my hacienda. Did you not understand my message?"

"Indeed I did, Manuel, but since the rebellion had failed, I thought it a moot point to keep them, and so prudence dictated that I release them."

Rojas brought his hands to his face in utter disgust. "Do you know what you've done? You've given away our only bargaining chip."

"I don't understand," said Ramirez, worried that Rojas might execute him.

Brugman and Terreforte showed nothing but disappointment on their faces, and Clemente, who thought Ramirez had erred in releasing the prisoners, expressed silent disappointment as well. Rojas rose to his feet, stepped forward and placed his hands gently on Ramirez's shoulders. "I had planned on using the prisoners to bargain for our lives in the event the rebellion would not succeed in San Sebastián. Now there is nothing to stop the Spanish from arresting us and hanging us for sedition." He let go of Ramirez and gazed wistfully at Brugman. "Mathias, it is truly over now."

Mathias Brugman, ever the optimist, eyed Rojas with confidence. "We could regroup and form another attack. We could start recruiting in the surrounding towns and plan a better offensive."

"Indeed," said Rojas with a tiny spark of encouragement. "But even now, as we talk about regrouping and attacking again, many of our men are leaving, and if I know the Spanish well, they are already on the hunt for us. To go into the countryside and recruit fresh men, would take a lot of time. This is what I propose instead: let us disband right away. We will flee into the mountains and seek out jíbaro sympathizers to keep us hidden and give us plenty of warning should the Spanish arrive. We will wait in the mountains until it is safe for us to come out, and then we will travel to the port of Guánica. There we will endeavor to secure a ship to Santo Domingo." The door suddenly opened and Manuel Cebollero Aguilar and Eusebio Ibarra both stepped into the hacienda. Rojas gave Aguilar a displeasing look, letting him know just how disappointed he was at his failure to convince the San Sebastián militia. Rojas moved his eyes away from Aguilar and looked at Brugman and Terreforte. "Is everyone in agreement with the plan?" Rojas found gratification in the knowledge that everyone had quickly agreed. Aguilar, who had come late to the meeting, was unaware of their decision and had to pull Clemente Millan aside so that he could learn the details.

Terreforte said dourly, "Many of my men began to leave long before we got here, Manuel. I think we should go in completely separate directions. I do not want to know where you are going, Manuel, you too Mathias. If the Spanish find me, I do not want to divulge your locations under torture."

Rojas nodded in agreement. "Very well, then let us disband right now."

CHAPTER 109

During the fearful moments the rebels were fleeing from *El Triunfo*, Governor Juan Pavía sat before his desk opening dispatches delivered only minutes earlier. The letter, written by the hand of Mayor Chiesa, informed the governor that a rebellion had begun in San Sebastián. Although the governor had sound intelligence about a rebellion in the making, and though he had made plans for counter-insurgency, he never thought it would really take place. Now, with Chiesa's letter requesting military protection and uncertain where Iturriaga's forces were at the moment, Pavía felt compelled to rescind Colonel Ibarreta's banishment and put the counter-insurgency plan into action.

Colonel Ibarreta, who was still in San Juan waiting for Iturriaga's arrival in order to explain his actions against Pavia's complaint, jumped at his new orders. He undertook the journey to Aguadilla by boat, and he would get there by way of Arecibo, but the trip would take twenty-four hours. The governor then sent orders to Lieutenant José de Arce of the Ponce militia to march his men northward. While de Arce's men marched northward, Colonel Iturriaga's troops marched southward from Arecibo, and Colonel Ibarreta's army would march eastward from Aguadilla. All troops would converge in San Sebastián. The hunt was on!

As Rojas made his way into the mountainside, he took one last look at his lush green fields, the plantation he fondly called *El Triunfo*. He turned slowly and began his retreat. In the Rojas party were Francisco Ramirez, Andres Pol, Manuel Cebollero Aguilar, Clemente Millan and Rudolfo Echevarria. Manuel Rojas's brother and his wife also fled but took a different course. Eusebio Ibarra parted company with Aguilar and chose to go elsewhere. They were completely unaware that the troops from Ponce were already marching late that evening and would arrive in Lares in the morning the following day.

The four hundred rebels hungry for change, desperate to see a better life for Puerto Rico, had made a conscious decision to take matters into their own hands. Behind their ideals and their noble visions, they set out to emulate the founding fathers of the United States of America. They took up arms against their Spanish masters in the same manner as that of the Americans against their British masters. They took up arms against four hundred years of repression, unaware that their battle had already been lost at the outset. Fear, desperation and a deep sense of loss had supplanted the eagerness, determination and patriotic fervor that had burned in their souls just one day earlier.

Thus ended the first and only Puerto Rican revolution, and thus ended the first and only cry for freedom.

CHAPTER 110

At half past nine on the evening of September 24, Captain José Pujols, of the Arecibo military base, found José Antonio Hernández hiding in the woods of Camuy. He arrested the rebel and brought him in chains to meet with Colonel Iturriaga who had made camp just three miles south of Camuy. With gleaming eyes, Iturriaga began to interrogate the frightened José Antonio Hernández, but the would-be rebel refused to talk. Wasting no time, the colonel placed the captured rebel in solitary confinement, and after several hours of solitude, reflection and mostly fear, Hernández caved in and spilled his guts out to Iturriaga. Hoping the colonel would release him in exchange for the information, Hernández gave every detail of the insurrection including the names of the members of Lanzador. In reality, Iturriaga did not need the member names because he had already obtained them from the green ledger back in Manuel Maria Gonzalez's home, but it was comforting to know that José Antonio had confirmed all of the names in the ledger. Hernández also told the colonel where, on his property, he had buried the cache of weapons; the very same weapons Carlos Martínez demanded he unearth in order to mount the rescue of the cell's president. Contrary to José Antonio Hernández's fleeting hopes, Iturriaga did not intend to bargain with any rebel, and he issued orders to have him transported to the brig in Arecibo. By September 25, Iturriaga had gathered sufficient evidence about the rebel conspiracy to show his superiors. Among the evidence seized from José Antonio's farm were two crates, containing 1000 sticks of dynamite, and a sack of gunpowder.

On September 27, the same day Ibarreta arrived in Lares, another column of soldiers departed the military base in Ponce. The column, led by the ruthless Colonel Francisco Martínez, consisted of 65 infantrymen and 20 cavalrymen. Determined in his resolve to capture as many rebels as possible, Martínez drove his men onward without rest until they reached their final destination of Adjuntas. While on the way to the village, several men of his advance party returned with rumors about two rebels hiding deep in the vast woodlands of Adjuntas. Since there were no roads or trails leading from Ponce to Adjuntas, and because the inclining land was steeped in dense vegetation, it would take Martínez and his column more than two weeks to reach his destination, and the long march there had further contributed to his festering rage. Colonel Martínez finally rested his men on October 6, but immediately made plans the next day to hunt down the rebels.

By October 7, Mathias Brugman and Baldomero Baurer had successfully evaded the authorities for two weeks. With the aid of a few friends and many jíbaro sympathizers, they held on to their secret position deep within several hills that ran north to south just a few miles west of Adjuntas. Every day, a different jíbaro would bring food, water and news to the two outlaws, and the more time passed, the safer Brugman and Baurer felt. The pair of rebels had just moved into their new camp on a hill called Garzas and had no idea that a relentless colonel, a man with a singular goal to root out all rebels, had just arrived in Adjuntas the previous day.

Sitting at the base of a tree, Mathias Brugman watched as Baldomero Baurer stoked the brilliant embers of a dying campfire. "It's been over two weeks now and we've heard nothing from Rojas or from any of the rebel cells. I wonder how they've fared in this tragedy, Mathias, truly I do." Half of Baldomero's face shone red against the dwindling campfire while the other half lay silhouetted against the darkness. "The ship of weapons could have made the difference, but the Spanish pigs seized it, and God knows where Betances is right now or if he's even heard about the failed rebellion."

"Is that what you think it is, Baldo, a tragedy, a failure?"

"What else can you call it?"

"A beginning, Baldo, a beginning," replied Brugman animatedly, eyes reflecting the reddish-yellow flames of their campfire. "Because even if our rebellion dies today, it will be reborn in the hearts of those we leave behind. We have already seeded the notion of freedom in the hearts of our young boys and girls, and there it will lie dormant until the day comes when we, as a unified people, will say with one voice: Freedom!"

Baurer dropped the limb into the ebbing flames and shook his head. "We've been friends for more than twenty-five years. We have shared the same political ideologies, the same societal views and yet, at this very moment, I cannot agree with you. We have seeded nothing, Mathias. All we've done is stir the viper's nest. How can you sit there and tell me that this so-called rebellion was a success?"

Mathias Brugman cast a disappointing look at Baurer, but as he was about to respond, he heard twigs breaking and the familiar sound of clicking revolvers. Before the two rebels knew it, Martínez and his men had surrounded them. "Stand up, you bloody rebel bastards!" shouted Martínez angrily. The colonel handed his torch over to the sergeant, who grabbed it with a shaking hand, and then turned to watch Brugman and Baurer slowly rise to their feet. "Identify yourselves!"

Brugman looked fearlessly into the Colonel's eyes, thumped his chest hard and said, "I am Mathias Brugman, president of the rebel cell you know as Capa Prieto! I denounce the four hundred years of Spanish tyranny over Puerto Rico! I denounce you, señor, as the instrument of such tyranny, the tool by which Spanish repression and brutality is enforced!"

"You're nothing but a clown pretending to be someone important," replied Martínez angrily. "Your pitiful insurrection is over and so are you! Prepare to meet the devil, you son-of-a-bitch!"

Standing next to Brugman underneath the tree, Baldomero came to the realization that Martínez harbored no intentions of arresting him or Brugman. He chose to remain silent and meet his death with dignity. On the other hand, Brugman refused to keep quiet. He gave Martínez, an unforgiving look. "Killing us is the only thing you *can* do, but you will never kill our hopes and our patriotism, commander. So live with that!"

"And so I shall," uttered Martínez. He took aim, cocked his revolver and shot. The bullet landed on Brugman's forehead and exited through the cerebrum, pieces of brain matter spattering onto the tree behind him and all over Baurer's face. Brugman fell instantly, body twitching for a few seconds before quietly expiring. Baurer did not look at his friend, and he did not need to see him either to know that he had died. Martínez cocked his pistol again, and shot Baurer though the chest, hitting his heart. Standing behind Martínez, both the sergeant and corporal made the sign of the crucifix and prayed for the souls of Brugman and Baurer. Hearing their prayer, and while waiting for his lieutenant to return, Martínez turned to face them. He cocked his pistol and aimed the weapon at the sergeant. "My report will say that we came upon the rebels and found them sleeping under the tree. I demanded their surrender but they refused and took up arms against us. In defense, I fired and killed Brugman, and you, Sergeant Diaz, shot and killed the other rebel. You and Corporal Fernandez will sign your names to my report as witnesses. If you do not agree with me now, I will do to the two of you what I did to the rebel scum you see there, lying dead. Will you sign your names?"

Martínez grinned with satisfaction as he watched the two militiamen quickly nodding their heads.

CHAPTER 111

For over two weeks, Rosalía pleaded with Colonel San Antonio, but the staunch Spaniard refused to let her see Miguel. Every day that Rosalía pled her case, the Spanish arrested more rebels, or anyone remotely suspected of the conspiracy. The jail's population had swelled to the point where the militia had to make extra room in the adjoining buildings. On occasion, Rosalía would see her father ride into town, and it hurt her that Rodolfo ignored her as if she were a mangy dog roaming the streets. On other occasions, she would visit Mayor Chiesa, but in deference to Rodolfo's wishes, the mayor refused to acknowledge her and oftentimes chased her out of his office. Frustrated and helpless, she agreed with Manolo's suggestion that they go back to Lares and seek help from the Centro Bravo members.

As they crossed the bridge out of San Sebastián, Berta, who was trailing Manolo and Rosalía, saw a pistol lying on the ground. The weapon, apparently discarded by a wounded rebel, had three bullets in it. Without hesitating, Berta picked up the gun and stuffed it inside her dress. As she drew closer to Manolo, she decided to keep it for now and later present it to him as a gift right before boarding the boat in Guánica.

By the time Rosalía, Berta and Manolo had reached Lares, the rebels were gone. Entering Lares through the main road with hopes of seeing the rebel flag hoisted somewhere, above a municipal building, a school or even a store, Rosalía's hopes began to vanish. There were no signs of a flag or signs of any rebel activity or even any evidence that Lares had suffered any violence. It was then that Manolo suggested they go to Rojas's hacienda.

Rosalía and her two companions arrived at Rojas's hacienda an hour later only to find the farm empty and unattended to, and all of its occupants gone. Rosalía began to weep uncontrollably because she had made Miguel's dreams her own dreams, because she had made Miguel's ideologies her ideologies, and because now those dreams and visions were gone. There was a deep sense of loss in Rosalía's heart, a pain far worse than any of the beatings she had ever suffered at the hands of her father, and a feeling of hopelessness and despair. Rosalía dropped to the ground on her knees and wept like a motherless child.

As she buried her face into her hands, she felt Berta's fingers caressing her back in a consoling gesture. Then she heard Manolo's voice. "Señora Rosalía, please get up, for we cannot stay here any longer. We are runaway slaves and we are your father's property. If you have any kindness still left in your heart, please get up and let us leave this place at once."

Rosalía wiped the tears from her eyes and slowly rose to her feet. She gazed at Berta and Manolo and smiled at them. Reading Rosalía's eyes, Berta and Manolo both felt her sincerity and the genuine care she still had for them. "I will head back to San Sebastián to see Miguel. I will entreat my father for his freedom. You two, however, must complete your journey. You must go to Guánica and get on the first boat out of Puerto Rico. Go to America and live the rest of your lives in freedom, the way you ought to have lived from the time you were born." Even as Rosalía spoke, she could see Berta's head shaking against the idea.

"Rosa, we cannot abandon you. How can you ask us to leave you now in your darkest hour?"

"Though it pains me to say this," replied Rosalía with a tone of sadness, "I am a white woman, in a white world, whereas you, well you are…"

"We are black," responded Berta. "You think we are not aware of that? Peninsulares and Creoles remind us of that fact every day, Rosa. Yet, despite the risks, we are willing to accompany you to San Sebastián." Unable to convince them, Rosalía had no choice but to welcome their company along the road back to San Sebastián.

CHAPTER 112

By October 8, the Spanish militia had rounded up a great number of insurgents. The militia arrested many of the rebels on the say so of vengeful loyalists, and arrested many more on the word of other rebels saving their own necks. The jails of San Sebastián, Camuy, Lares and Arecibo had no more room for new prisoners. The stifling air in the tiny cells had ripened to the point where it became the breeding ground for scurvy, dysentery, cholera, and hepatitis. The unbearable humidity combined with the heat of hundreds of human bodies in such close proximity was enough to make any sane man stir with madness. The intolerable conditions gave rise to several fistfights a day. Every day soldiers would bring in someone arrested on the remotest suspicion of rebellion, and there seemed to be no end in sight.

In one such jail, in the municipality of San Sebastián, Miguel Pítre languished along with eleven other men in a cell originally designed to house two people. He lay on the concrete floor curled into a fetal position, agonizing in pain. He had not eaten for several days now and the wound to his leg had gotten worse. Although the bleeding had stopped, the bullet, still lodged in his left thigh, had caused the wound to fester with germs. Miguel had also begun to feel the first symptoms of a fever and if he did not get immediate medical attention, he knew he would not live for much longer.

Polinario sat against the iron bars of the cell, and he was so close to Miguel that he could not avoid skin contact with him. Yet, as discomforting a situation as it was for Polinario, he knew that Miguel's situation was far worse. He studied Miguel for a short while and heard his muted moans. "I could smell your rotting flesh from here, señor Pítre," said Polinario.

"Please, call me Miguel," replied the young idealist, forcing a smile.

"If you do not get that wound fixed by a doctor, I'm afraid you will die here, inside this hell." Polinario had been watching Miguel for days now, and he had grown to admire him in a way. Miguel did not complain much, kept to himself most of the time and tried to make the best of his miserable situation. Polinario, however, noted a profound sadness in Miguel's eyes in spite of that calm and collected appearance.

"I don't think the Spanish are too much in a hurry to heal any of the wounded rebels, Polinario," replied Miguel, grimacing. "In fact, I think they would rather let us die."

"I do hope you're wrong, Miguel."

Two rough-looking militiamen were hastily approaching Miguel's cell. When they got there, they gagged and quickly covered their noses. The stench of human excrement and urine was so overpowering that one of the militiamen bowled over and vomited. The other one eyed Miguel and shouted, "Pítre, you have been summoned to the barracks. Get up!"

Polinario rose to his feet and looked at his captors with pleading eyes. "This man is wounded and cannot stand on his own." The militiamen looked at each other, and then one of them studied Miguel briefly. He turned to Polinario and commanded, "Then you help him, prieto!"

Polinario crouched and placed an arm under Miguel's shoulder. Miguel slowly rose to his feet and wrapped his arm around Polinario's waist. One of the militiamen opened the gate, while the other steadied his rifle at the prisoners in case they had any ideas of escaping. But the prisoners were too weak to do much of anything. As Polinario helped Miguel walk toward the barracks, he could hear him moaning, and thought he would die within the next few hours. They finally arrived at the barracks, where they confronted Mayor Chiesa, Rodolfo Hernández and Colonel San Antonio.

Polinario eased Miguel into a chair facing the three Spaniards and then stood behind him, but the mayor wanted no witnesses of any kind. He cast a set of angry eyes at Polinario and waved him off, as if he were a bothersome fly. "Leave us, now!" The mayor waited until Polinario left the barracks before addressing Miguel.

"I will make a deal with you, young man," the mayor offered. "We are going to ask you a few questions, and if you give us favorable answers, we will see to it that you receive proper medical care for that wound in your leg. Think about it real well, señor, because from where I'm sitting that wound smells like rotting fish."

Miguel studied the three faces staring back at him, knowing his fate lay in their hands. With every fiber of energy still left in his body, Miguel answered the mayor. "I already know what your questions are going to be, so don't waste your time because I will not answer them."

"What is it with you goddamn creoles, anyway?" Rodolfo said, unable to restrain himself, and much to the annoyance of both Chiesa and San Antonio.

"Rodolfo, please, let me handle this," insisted the mayor.

Ignoring the mayor, Miguel glared at Rodolfo. "The question ought to be: what is it with *you* Spaniards? Isn't time for you to return to Spain and let us rule our own country?"

"Oh stop it, Pítre," Rodolfo replied angrily. "That's the same song I've been hearing for more than twenty-five years, and, frankly, it's getting a little tiring. Why don't you sing a different tune, you fucking peasant!"

"All right, that's enough!" shouted Chiesa. "If you don't keep quiet, I will have to ask you to leave the interrogation, Rodolfo."

Rodolfo narrowed his eyes at Miguel while gritting his teeth in anger. He said nothing further, and allowed the mayor to continue his business.

The mayor re-assumed leadership and directed his voice at his young prisoner. "The offer still stands, Miguel. Look, I know what you and your family have gone through, and I know that you blame us Spaniards for much of it. I just want you to know that not all Spaniards are the same, but on the other hand, I think you would agree that not all creoles are the same, either. It is time for you to come to terms with the fact that your rebellion has failed. It is time for you to realize that unless you get medical attention, you will die."

"Unlike you, I am not afraid of dying, Mayor," answered Miguel. The unbearable pain in his thigh kept stabbing at him like a sharp knife.

"Don't be a fool, young man," insisted Chiesa. "Tell me where Manuel Rojas and Francisco Ramirez are hiding and I will see to it that you get immediate medical care. Not only that, but I will personally see to it that you get a favorable word at your trial." As Chiesa spoke, Miguel could feel Rodolfo's hate-filled eyes all over him.

"Before they disbanded," said Miguel, closing his eyes from the pain, "they agreed not to tell each other where they were going."

"How do you know this? You weren't in Lares after Rojas's retreat?"

"Some of my fellow patriots who were there that day were arrested and brought to this jail. I have spoken to them," Miguel answered calmly. "They do not know where the leaders are, and neither do I. But even if I did know, I would not tell you, señor."

"Fellow patriots?" Rodolfo interjected, "don't you mean fellow criminals?"

"Rodolfo, please!" said Mayor Chiesa.

Miguel opened his eyes and tried to focus his blurry vision on Rodolfo Hernández. "You are the criminal, Hernández, you and your fellow peninsulares who come here to squeeze us out of everything we own. You take our land away, our livelihoods and our dignities, and you perpetuate the domination of African men and women to serve and enrich you. You care nothing about Puerto Rico and her people! Yes, señor Hernández, you and all your fellow peninsulares are the real criminals."

"Tell me something Miguel," said Chiesa, narrowing his eyes. "If the revolution would have succeeded what would you have done to the so-called peninsulares?"

Miguel gasped in pain before answering. "We would have tried all peninsulares for the exploitation and brutality they wrought upon the people of this island. Depending on the degree of the crime, a guilty verdict would have resulted in a long jail term or a public hanging. As for the rest, we would have given them a choice to become citizens of the new republic or return to Spain."

"I see, so your measure of justice would have been the same ours," reflected Chiesa. "You see, young man, you wouldn't have acted any different."

"Perhaps."

"Well, do you have any information for us?" Chiesa said, downplaying Miguel's answer. He waited for several seconds, but Miguel kept his silence. "Very well, then Colonel San Antonio, would you be good enough to escort this prisoner back to his cell?"

Fully detached from any form of compassion, San Antonio grabbed hold of Miguel with all of his strength and forced him to stand. Then he dragged him outside of Mayor Chiesa's office all the way to the jail. A few steps before reaching the jail, San Antonio stopped abruptly and scowled at his weakened prisoner. All of a sudden, he swung his arm back, closed his fist, and thrust his arm forward punching Miguel in his belly. Miguel bowled over in pain, and as he bent over to heave, nothing but a clear, sticky liquid came out of his mouth. It was the lukewarm water he drank only moments before the mayor summoned him to the barracks. San Antonio, however, did not allow him to finish throwing up and forced Miguel to stand, causing the bile-laden water to spill over his tattered and dirty white shirt.

Inside the crowded jail, the rebels witnessed San Antonio dragging Miguel to his cell. Gaunt-faced and pale, Miguel had an aura of death that was difficult to ignore. With two militiamen aiming their rifles at the cell, San Antonio pushed Miguel back inside, forcing him to crash on top of several sleeping men. As soon as San Antonio departed, Polinario reached over to Miguel and turned him over. "Miguel, you're in very bad shape."

Miguel felt Polinario's hands grappling his body and propping him up against the concrete wall. He took in several deep breaths before turning to look at Polinario. Smiling, he said, "Christ, Polinario, tell me something I don't know."

Polinario smiled back at Miguel, and then he let out a hearty laugh.

In the mountainous region known as the Sierra Alta, deep inside the densely wooded forests, Manuel Rojas, Francisco Ramirez, Andres Pol, Manuel Aguilar, and Clemente Millan were among other rebels taking refuge from the Spanish authorities. They had been there since September 30, living off the meager scraps that nearby jíbaros brought every morning. Strangely, though, no one had come around to them with food and water for the past two days. The men of Rojas's company were starving, thirsty and hopeless. Any possibility of resurrecting the rebellion had faded away in light of their weakened condition.

The fugitives had lost considerable weight and the reality of spending every waking hour deep in the forest, way up in the mountains, doing nothing all day and night, drove them mad with boredom. A few of them wanted to return to Lares or Mayagüez, to surrender to the authorities, spend some time in jail and move on with the rest of their lives. Manuel Rojas, however, would intercede every time someone dared mention such a notion. He would insist that as leaders of the revolution, the Spanish would torture and execute them, make them examples of the consequences of rebelling against Spain. The men would listen to Manuel Rojas's words and heed them, and no one ever dared venture beyond the confines of their meager encampment.

Rojas had no idea, no hint whatsoever, that the unforgiving, ruthless and hateful Colonel Martínez, from the Ponce militia, was on his way to his location. Rojas had no idea also, that the colonel leading the militia there, detested all creoles and wanted nothing more than to erase all rebels off the face of the earth. He had already started by killing both Brugman and Baurer, but he wanted more blood.

CHAPTER 113

Rosalía had finally made it to San Sebastián along with Berta and Manolo. While on the road to San Sebastián, she went over all of the options available to her. Aware that her husband's wound did not affect any of his vital organs, she knew the Spanish would not be too eager to give him medical attention. Somehow, her woman's intuition told her Miguel was still in prison and suffering from his wound. But Miguel was still alive and that was better than nothing! Behind her, she could hear Berta huffing in an effort to keep pace. Realizing it would take longer to wait for Berta to catch up to her, Rosalía decided to continue on ahead. Manolo tried to stay in the middle, keeping watch on Rosalía ahead of him and Berta behind him.

Sitting in the parlor talking with Rodolfo Hernández, Mayor Chiesa seemed startled when his servant came in to announce the arrival of Rodolfo's daughter. Both Chiesa and Rodolfo quickly rose to their feet and dashed toward the front door. Between the two men, Rodolfo showed more emotions initially, but then he quickly stowed them away. "Who are you, young lady?" Mayor Chiesa inquired innocently.

"You know damn well who I am señor Alcalde, you've played this charade for more than two weeks, and it's getting a little tiring."

Turning to Rodolfo, Mayor Chiesa said quizzically, "Señor Hernández, do you know this lady?"

Rodolfo shook his head and cast a scornful glare at his onetime daughter. "No. She must be a jíbara from the mountains, Mayor, another piece of shit rebel."

"What do you want, young lady?" Mayor Chiesa demanded.

"I want to see my husband, Miguel Pítre, Mayor, if it isn't too much trouble," replied Rosalía, ignoring her father for the moment.

"I'm sorry, but I must tell you that your husband has been arrested for sedition and will be tried very soon. I cannot allow him any visitors until the judge arrives and approves it. You'd do well to go back home and await the outcome of his trial."

"Mayor Chiesa, my name is Rosalía, and you know very well that I am Rodolfo Hernández's daughter."

"No you're not!" interrupted Rodolfo. "My daughter died weeks ago in the battle of San Sebastián! I have been mourning her death ever since, and I'll be damned if I allow you to ruin my memories of her. Now be gone, you worthless peasant!"

Shaking her head at her father, Rosalía showed her disappointment. "How could you, Father? You're a heartless and cruel man, and I am sorry to be your daughter!"

Rodolfo was about to respond when out of the corner of his eye, he noted Manolo off to the distance. He dismissed Rosalía and moved to the edge of the porch. "Manolo!" he shouted. "What the devil are you doing here, in San Sebastián?"

Manolo stood still, glaring at Rodolfo with all the hatred he had stored up in his heart since birth. For the first time in his life, he felt unafraid of his master. He stood his ground and waited for Rodolfo to do something. Rodolfo blinked twice, appalled by Manolo's lack of response, lack of respect and insolence. Berta had been trailing both Rosalía and Manolo and never saw the confrontation until she turned the corner. When she came into full view of the scene, her heart nearly stopped in terror.

To Rosalía, everything began to move slowly as she witnessed her father turning his back on her and rushing into Chiesa's office. She could see the mayor and Colonel San Antonio slowly turning their heads to see what Rodolfo was doing. A few moments later, Rodolfo emerged with a rifle in his hands. He raised it slowly and aimed the weapon at Manolo. Then, without pausing to ponder the notion whether or not he was justified in the act, Rodolfo pulled the trigger. Rosalía slowly turned her head, and noted Manolo grasping his chest. Manolo fell to the ground, blood pouring out of a gaping bullet hole. Standing next to Rodolfo, San Antonio reached over and grabbed the rifle's muzzle, shaking the weapon loose from Rodolfo's hands.

Stunned by Rodolfo's actions, Mayor Chiesa shook his head. "Damn you señor, you cannot take matters into your own hands! That's why we have laws!"

Rodolfo let go of the rifle and stood in front of the Mayor's office, unemotional, detached from any compassion or remorse. To him, the act of killing Manolo was no different from the act of killing a horse with a broken leg. He needed to put Manolo down. As Rodolfo glared at the fallen young man, he never heard the sudden cries that came out of the mouths of Rosalía and Berta. Standing high and mighty, like one of his overseers, Rodolfo folded his arms, turned to the mayor and said, "That beast was my property, Alcalde, and I can do with him whatever I damn well please!"

Berta ran over to Manolo, yelling hysterically, but when she turned him over and saw the blood pouring out from the grape-sized hole in his chest, she fell silent with rage. Her hands, covered in Manolo's blood, trembled uncontrollably. Strangely, though, her trembling hands did not result from fear, but from eternal hatred. As her brother lay on the ground, mortally wounded and with the last gasps of air left in his lungs, he noticed Berta retrieving something. Berta reached under her raggedy dress, in a place no one was privy to except for Rodolfo Hernández from time to time, and drew the .45 caliber revolver she'd been hiding. Although she had planned to give the gun to Manolo as a gift, she never conceived the notion that she might have to use it.

By the hateful look on her face and by her strange body language, Manolo easily discerned that Berta was going to do something terrible. With tremendous effort and pain, Manolo gave his sister a brotherly gaze. "Berta, I can see the gun you're holding, and I am begging you: do not use that weapon. Do not shoot señor Hernández. You mustn't do that."

"Why? That pig must die!" Berta replied. She placed the gun on the ground next to her, and while she gazed at her brother, she kept her finger on the trigger.

"Listen to me Berta, you cannot shoot el Patrón."

"How can you ask that of me?" said Berta, frowning. "Look at what he's done to you, look at the years of misery he's caused our family. He doesn't to deserve to live."

"No Berta, with my last dying breath, I am imploring you not to kill him, please listen to me."

"Why, Manolo, why?" pleaded Berta. She shot a curious look at her brother as Rosalía came rushing over to them.

"I'm so sorry, Manolo!" cried out Rosalía, kneeling on the ground beside Manolo, tears streaming down her cheeks.

Ignoring Rosalía for the moment, Berta kept pressing her brother. "Tell me why?"

Rosalía took hold of Manolo's hand and tried to comfort him during his final seconds on earth. Though she could hear Berta questioning Manolo, nothing seemed to register in her mind.

Gasping for air, Manolo reached out for Berta with his other hand. Berta took hold of his hand and felt him pulling her toward his mouth. She put her right ear over Manolo's mouth and made every effort to listen, but her brother kept gasping for air. "You cannot shoot him because, my dear sister, he is…"

Berta kept her ear over Manolo's mouth, waiting for the completion of his sentence, but there was nothing more. Berta straightened herself, and while still kneeling, made certain her hand was still firmly holding the gun.

Rosalía finally noticed the weapon Berta was trying to conceal, but thought Manolo had given it to her. She gently placed Manolo's hand over his chest and gave Berta a sorrowful look. "Please forgive me, Berta."

"Forgive you, for what?" came back Berta's response. "You have done nothing to me, Rosa." Berta tilted her head and cast her saddened eyes upon the approaching Mayor Chiesa. Directly behind Chiesa, ran San Antonio followed by Rodolfo Hernández.

The world suddenly became silent for Berta, as if she were inside a large glass jar with a tightly closed lid, just like one of the preserves Mamíta kept in a shelf back in San Juan. Although Berta could feel herself slowly rising, keeping the gun hidden behind her, she could do nothing to stop herself. She beheld her Patrón's face as he gazed at her brother's remains without a measure of emotion, and that look of indifference is what she hated most about her former master.

The three Spaniards stood hovering over Rosalía and Manolo, watching the bloody corpse without any form of compassion.

Rodolfo finally said, "Colonel, would you be good enough to place that slave in chains and store her in the barracks until I leave San Sebastián?"

San Antonio did not respond to Rodolfo but glanced at Chiesa for approval. Mayor Chiesa, with saddened eyes, nodded approvingly at San Antonio. The colonel made a move toward Berta, but when he took the first step, Berta drew the revolver. Though San Antonio kept a sidearm, he froze instantly because Berta had been too quick and he did not know which of the three men she would shoot first. "You're a goddamn vulture!" Berta cried out. "I'm not going back to San Juan!"

"Put that fucking gun away, you don't even know how to use it!" Rodolfo yelled angrily.

Rosalía, stunned at Berta's action, quickly rose to her feet and approached the former slave. "Berta, please do not fire that gun. We have shed enough blood today. If you fire that gun, they will kill you."

"That monster is responsible for enslaving my family, for beating us, raping me and killing many other slaves that you don't even know about, Rosa. He must die!" Berta raised the revolver and aimed it at Rodolfo.

"Berta, he is my father, please don't do it," pleaded Rosalía.

"He's never been a father to you, Rosa, and you know it. He's beaten you badly, and has always treated you like one of us. Why do you ask me to spare his miserable life?" Berta was a woman possessed with evil at that moment, and her only resolve was to kill the tormenter of her life.

"Young lady," interjected Chiesa, "Put down that gun! You must know that if you shoot Don Hernández, you will most certainly hang."

"I don't give a damn anymore!" answered Berta, glaring at Rodolfo.

A few seconds of silence elapsed before Berta's index finger squeezed the trigger. Then, the gun exploded and a bright flash emanated from its muzzle. The bullet whizzed by Rosalía and San Antonio, and found its target in Rodolfo's body. The landowner let out a loud yell, and then fell on his back, grasping his belly with both hands. Wasting no time, San Antonio swung his arm and punched Berta on the cheek. Berta went down unconscious.

Rosalía could not believe what she had just witnessed in only less than ten minutes. She stood catatonically for several moments before letting out a devastating shout of horror. Rosalía quickly recollected herself, ran to her father and knelt before him. A steady downpour of tears streamed down her cheeks as she took hold of her dying father's hands. "Father!" she yelled, but Rodolfo was out cold and bleeding badly. Though Berta might not have intended it, the .45 caliber slug entered Rodolfo's belly and exited through his back, leaving a hole the size of an acorn. In her stupor, Rosalía could still hear Mayor Chiesa barking orders at San Antonio, demanding he bring Berta to the jail and take Rodolfo to Doctor Cisneros. To Rosalía, it all seemed surreal, and though she was fully cognizant, the sound of other people shouting and moving about drifted faintly into her ears. Then, as if in a dream, memories of her young life flashed through her mind. There were clear images of sitting on her father's lap, making him laugh with silly remarks, and of her father introducing her to the new tutors and reminding them how much he wanted his daughter to excel in her studies. Then, as if a dark cloud suddenly appeared before a coming rainstorm, the images turned toward her father's dark side, and the brutal beatings she had been a victim to since her prepubescent days. How could her father's life end that way? Why couldn't Rodolfo been a better father, a better husband? Time was running out for Rosalía, and she needed to talk to her father, explain why she married Miguel and convince him to accept legitimacy for her unborn baby. Now, seeing her father lying on the ground, bleeding and helpless, she felt nothing but pity for him. Weeping, she cradled her father's head in her lap and caressed his hair. "Don't die, Father, please don't die."

"Señora, please move aside so that we may take your father to the doctor." A male voice, no doubt, but who it was, Rosalía did not know, but she did move to the side. Two soldiers picked up Rodolfo's limp body and placed him on a stretcher. They carried him for several yards until they reached a wooden wagon. They placed him on the wagon and took off for Doctor Cisnero's house—a three-and-a-half mile journey on a rough and bumpy road.

As Rosalía sat on the ground weeping, two militiamen grabbed hold of Berta's arms and dragged her all the way to the jail. Realizing she could not do anything for her father, for Miguel and for Berta, Rosalía felt utterly helpless.

After watching the wagon disappear, Mayor Chiesa crouched so that he could talk to Rosalía eye to eye. "Señora Pítre, Rodolfo is in danger of losing his life. Yes, he is your father, I know. Go to him."

"Oh, so now he's my father?"

"I am sorry, but I was merely appeasing your father's wishes. After all, he had disowned you."

"Thank you señor Alcalde, I will, but I would like to see my husband afterwards. Can you please arrange that for me?"

"I'm not going to promise anything, but I will try."

CHAPTER 114

Doctor Cisneros had done his best to patch the two bullet holes in Rodolfo Hernández's abdomen. He administered medication and hoped that Rodolfo would recover quickly, but the land owner remained unconscious for two days, and Cisneros's hopes were fading quickly. The short and thin doctor incised Rodolfo's belly, removed several lead fragments and made a valiant attempt at stitching the large intestine, but the laceration to the stomach was large and there was too much blood and bile to allow him to complete the medical procedure. Rodolfo was dying, and the white-bearded physician could do nothing to save his life. There was no need to tell a sobbing Maria Hernández, who sat on Rodolfo's deathbed for the past two days, that her husband was dying. The look of total resignation on her face was enough to convince the doctor to remain silent. Cisneros gave Maria an elixir, fresh bandages and unguent to make the next few days of Rodolfo's life on earth as bearable as possible.

On the tenth day of October, Rodolfo finally opened his eyes. The pain resulting from the internal infection, however, caused him to grimace and shut his eyelids again. Bursts of pain would come and go, like ocean waves, and every time there was a lull in the action, Rodolfo would open his eyes and try to speak. Anita and Laura rushed upstairs as soon as they heard Rodolfo had awakened, but when they saw their father's gaunt face, the large bags under his once fiery eyes, and how much the wound had greatly accelerated the loss of weight, they, too, felt the end was near. Rodolfo's eyes moved slowly away from Maria to Laura and then to Anita. Holding his hand tightly, Maria prayed in silence.

Despite all the beatings at the hands of her domineering father, despite the verbal abuse and the constant disagreements, Anita gazed at her father with pity as he lay helplessly on the bed, a mere shell of what he once was. Tears streamed down her cheeks, and as she moved to the other side of the bed to take hold of her father's hand, Laura remained standing. It wasn't that Laura didn't love her father, but, like her father, she was incapable of displaying such weak emotions. As she took in her father's image, other images formed in the back of her mind, and those images were of the aftermath of Rodolfo's death. There was much that she needed to do, and she would hire the best solicitor from San Juan to squeeze out as much as she could from her father's estate. She would fight bitterly against her mother and sisters because in her mind, she felt the most deserving of Rodolfo's children, and she felt even more deserving than her own mother. It simply did not dawn on her that by undertaking such action she would exhaust a great deal of the inheritance, as well as drive her mother and Anita to the poor house. Laura folded her arms, and though a glint of genuine sorrow stirred in the pit of her heart and begged for exposure, her pride and determination thwarted it, stuffed it back down into the dark bowels of her misguided soul.

CHAPTER 115

In the mountains of Sierra Alta, word reached Manuel Rojas's camp that the vicious Colonel Martínez was leading a column of soldiers there. Although some of his fellow fugitives panicked at the news, Rojas remained calm, confident that the mountains offered them height advantage and would enable them to see Martínez's men for miles. Aguilar's reasoning was vastly different than Rojas's was. From Aguilar's point of view, Rojas had either grossly miscalculated his odds or had made an outright lie to quell his compatriots' fears. For one thing, the forest was densely populated with tall pine trees that impeded their view of the valleys below and the nearby mountains. Then he failed to acknowledge the fact that there were so many loyalists in the surrounding towns and villages, it would take little time before someone would see the white smoke from their campfires. Finally, everyone knew about Colonel Martínez's reputation, and by dogged determination, Martínez would lead his men on a relentless search and would stop at nothing until he found the rebels.

Aguilar searched Rojas's eyes for truth, but found nothing but apprehension in them. How could he disagree with the rebel leader? If he offered an opposing view, the fragmentary cohesion that held the camp together would vanish in an instant, and the rebels would disperse in every direction and caught within hours. Aguilar had to remain quiet and keep his thoughts to himself. That night, though, Aguilar went to sleep with the intentions of secretly leaving camp the next day.

As the sun showed its first inkling of light on the morning of October 10, Aguilar rose from his little place under a tree he shared with Clemente Millan. He yawned deeply and stretched his arms, but when his eyes captured sight of soldiers surrounding the camp, he knew he wasn't going anywhere that day. Within minutes of Martínez's arrival, the rebels woke in utter shock, all turning to Rojas for leadership, for explanation...and for blame. The soldiers quickly formed a circle around the encampment and aimed their rifles at the rebels. Rojas looked at the soldiers, in an attempt to discern which one of them was the notorious Colonel Martínez, but no one stepped forth to identify himself as the leader.

"Manos arriba!" Rojas heard someone say.

Rojas's co-conspirators slowly stood, groggy-eyed, and raised their arms in the air, uncertain of their immediate future. One soldier broke ranks and began to search the camp and the rebels for weapons. He seized several handguns, found a few machetes and four rifles neatly placed on the ground. With hands up in submission, Rojas pressed his search for Martínez but no one stood out as the leader. When his fellow rebels came to their senses they quickly realized their days of freedom had ended.

As Rojas studied the soldiers, no one appeared menacing enough to warrant the Colonel's reputation. Rojas hoped the soldiers were from another contingent and not from the one Colonel Martínez was leading from Ponce. Rojas pinned his hopes on the notion that the soldiers might have stumbled upon the encampment and perhaps would not even recognize the leaders of the rebellion. His hopes quickly disintegrated when Colonel Martínez finally made his foreboding appearance. Bedecked in a neat, clean and fashionable dark blue uniform, Martínez's stern demeanor sent a wave of fear in the hearts of the rebels. Though he appeared to Rojas as the infamous colonel, Rojas still felt uncertain about him; that is until the Spanish officer stepped forth to announce himself. Very slowly, he eyed each of the rebels standing before him. "My name is Colonel Francisco Martínez, and I am from the Ponce garrison. If you did not know me before, then, by God, you will know me by day's end—this I promise you. Now, which one of you is Manuel Rojas?"

Without hesitation, without an ounce of fear, Manuel Rojas kept his hands up in the air and shouted. "I am he, señor." He watched Martínez's cold, dark eyes turning toward him and knew his fate lay in the colonel's hands.

Martínez began to walk over to Rojas, and as he moved closer to his prized prisoner, he commanded, "Put the rest of the rebels in chains and get them out of here!" Flanked by just one soldier, Colonel Martínez stood face to face with Rojas, eyeing him from top to bottom as if he were sizing up an opponent. Rojas noted the repulsion on the colonel's face and knew he stood no chance of mercy. The utter disdain and contempt with which Martínez regarded his prisoner foretold the soldier standing next to the colonel that Rojas would most likely die that day. Ironically, Martínez's reputation as a cold hearted, sadistic and unforgiving man to his enemies, a fact witnessed by nearly all of the militiamen in Ponce and by anyone who served under him during his tour in Santo Domingo, had earned him the governor's praise. Today, however, Martínez was not seeking glory or praise from the governor, and he was not performing a special task that would earn him a promotion. Today, Martínez was looking to make an example of Rojas. Today would be the day that all thoughts of rebellion against his country would end.

"Who gave you the right to take up arms against your Queen and country?" demanded Colonel Martínez, eyes bearing down at Rojas with sheer loathing.

Rojas looked straight into Colonel Martínez's eyes and responded. "No one here, on earth, gave me the right, Colonel. It was God, The Almighty, who gave me the right! Spain and her monarchs have neglected us for four hundred years, and now, because of the rebellion in Santo Domingo, she has begun to pay us some attention. For hundreds of years, we have had to endure the insults and abuse from all Spaniards that come here. You come here with your arrogance and greed and squeeze us out of every centavo we earn and yet there is no hint of satisfaction. You have drawn an impregnable line between Spaniard and Creole and have reduced us to nothing more than beasts of burden. You have imprisoned many innocent people and tortured them mercilessly. You have killed many creoles and have stolen their properties. You perpetuate slavery and thrive upon an industry abolished by all of the European nations. You ask me, who gave me the right, Colonel? Take a look at it yourself, take a look at your Queen and your government in Spain, and then ask me who gave me the right."

Martínez nodded at Rojas for a few seconds, smiled and then let out a sarcastic chuckle. Then he stepped closer to Rojas, opened his mouth and spat at the rebel leader. Rojas, with hands still up in the air, closed his eyes, and felt Martínez's warm saliva drip from his nose down into his beard. "That's what I think about your rights, you peasant son-of-a-bitch!" yelled Martínez. He turned to his left and commanded, "Bind this piece of shit and put him in with the rest of the rebels. I will join you in a few minutes."

The soldier escorted Rojas down the road to where the rest of his companions were waiting. Martínez stood alone now, examining Rojas's camp, looking for evidence that he might use against the rebel leader. He looked under every blanket left by the rebels, near the bases of trees, but found nothing. Finding no papers or documents of any kind, he concluded the rebels had retreated hastily in the wake of the rebellion's failure and probably took off with nothing but the clothes on their backs.

Martínez walked back to his column with a sense of accomplishment, and with gloating eyes took satisfaction that his men had bound the rebels together by rope and chain. The colonel mounted his horse and commanded his men to move northward, toward Lares, but Martínez had different plans. Though he would eventually arrive in Lares, he would take a necessary detour first.

The column of soldiers reached a house where the colonel learned Rojas had been hiding for several days. He ordered twenty of his men to take the rebel prisoners into the house, and commanded the rest of the column outside to stand vigil. Inside the small house, huddling closely together, the rebels wondered if Martínez was going to execute them right there. "This is it, Manuel," uttered Francisco Ramirez. The former president's eyes gave no hint of fear, only resignation about his fate.

Manuel Rojas turned to Ramirez and whispered, "Was it worth it?"

Ramirez smiled gratefully. "For those few hours, I felt like a free man, Manuel. Yes, it was worth it."

All of a sudden, Colonel Martínez, entered the house, and everyone turned their attention to the Spanish officer. Gesturing to Manuel Rojas, Colonel Martínez commanded, "String that bastard up to one of those beams up there."

Two soldiers quickly put down their rifles and pulled Rojas away from the rest of the prisoners. They looped ropes around Rojas's wrists and then hoisted him by his arms until he was dangling from the beam. Rojas's feet stood about two inches off the floor, and the pain caused by the tight rope around his wrists was unbearable. Very shortly, his hands began to go numb. Martínez walked over to Rojas and grinned at him. Then he cracked his knuckles before slowly removing his pistol from the holster. He placed the pistol on top of a nearby table, and then walked even closer to Rojas. The colonel paused for a second, before backslapping Rojas across the face. The smack was so powerful, it tore Rojas's lip, and blood began to seep through the opening, dripping into his long and curly beard. With the same hand, Martínez swung forward and smacked Rojas's face again. This time, Rojas felt the ring on the colonel's hand as it hit his cheekbone. Rojas gasped in pain while Ramirez, Millan, Aguilar and the rest of the prisoners plainly revealed their horror. Even the soldiers felt repulsed by Martínez's actions. Aguilar wondered whether he would suffer the same fate, but he stifled his fears during those awful, terror-filled moments.

"It hurts, doesn't it?" Colonel Martínez taunted. Rojas gasped in pain, but his tenacious pride prevented him from talking, and he would not show Martínez any kind of weakness. Martínez swung another backslap at Rojas, followed by another forward slap. His right hand, covered now with Rojas's blood, came across the rebel's face two more times. Then he spat again at Rojas. "You have to learn and understand that your place is beneath us!" yelled Martínez. "We rule you, and you are Spain's subjects!" Martínez reeled his arm backwards, closed his fist, and punched Rojas in the belly. Rojas yelled in pain and soon afterwards, began vomiting. The white liquid that came out of Rojas's mouth was mixed with blood and dripped down to his already cluttered beard. Ramirez and Aguilar could do nothing to help Rojas; they had to stand there and witness the colonel's unrestrained abuse.

Taking a moment to rest, Martínez removed a handkerchief from his pocket and wiped his hand of Rojas's blood. "If you did not learn your lesson before, then as God is my witness, you will learn it today!"

Despite the swollen lips and chunks of undigested food in his mouth, Rojas managed to provide a response to the colonel. "Tell me, Colonel, do you honestly think that by beating me and perhaps killing me that you are going to end our cause? For every rebel you kill, ten more will take his place. You will never destroy the seeds we have planted today, for the day will come when Puerto Rico will become a free nation, free of all Spanish domination. I will become a symbol for freedom, a martyr, whereas you, colonel, will become a mere footnote."

Martínez narrowed his eyes angrily at Rojas, turned and reached for his pistol on the table. He swung the butt across Rojas's face and heard the slight crackling of his cheek bone. He swung the butt of his pistol three more times until a wide laceration on Rojas's eyebrows caused a deluge of blood. The blood streamed down Rojas's face to the point where he was barely recognizable, and yet the colonel showed no hint of relenting. Angered so much at Rojas's words, Martínez placed the pistol back on the table and punched the rebel on his belly, chest and face. As Martinez pummeled his body, Rojas no longer felt any pain, and he knew he was close to death. Still, Martínez's anger had not subsided, and he felt that he had not done enough to kill Rojas's passion for rebellion. He still felt he had not caused the rebel enough pain and humiliation. The colonel's anger and hatred for Rojas ran so deep he felt like biting the rebel's face, cutting off his ears or doing something extraordinarily brutal. Then he looked at Rojas's beard. Without hesitation, he grabbed a firm hold of the rebel's long facial hairs. Rojas sensed Martínez's hands on his beard, and when the colonel pulled, it felt like a thousand tiny daggers stabbing at his face. Rojas yelled loudly in excruciating pain. The colonel pulled Rojas's beard so hard that when he looked at his hands he noted Rojas's flesh still attached to the whiskers. Millan gasped, and Ramirez and Aguilar both turned away at the terrible sight. The militiamen witnessing the act also turned away in repulsion. A puddle of Rojas's blood seeped through the cracks on the wooden floor, but the macabre scene did not stir the colonel's emotions in the least. He swung away at Rojas with a closed fist, until Rojas finally passed out. Unable to inflict any more pain and humiliation to Rojas, Martínez's anger finally subsided. He turned around to face the other prisoners and said, "Let that be a lesson to all of you." He raised his bloodied hand at them, and with his index finger rocking left to right, he said, "Never rebel against the mother county and your sovereign Queen Isabel! Long live Spain!" Martínez took the blood-soaked handkerchief and wiped his hand again. "Remove him and see that he is given medical attention. I do not want him to die just yet. As for the rest of the rebel scum, take them out of my sight!"

CHAPTER 116

On the morning of October 16, two new columns of soldiers converged in the town of Lares, one from Ponce, led by Captain Prats and the other from Mayagüez, led by Captain Resano. Thought to have been relieved of the violence, as well as all other matters involving the revolution, the citizens awoke in panic at the sound of cavalry and thundering soldiers marching into town. Contrary to their misguided apprehensions, though, the soldiers did not fire a single shot.

The two captains reported to Colonel Ibarreta that morning, where he briefed them on the current situation and gave them new orders. Using information from a confidential informant, Ibarreta instructed the two captains to round up the last of the rebels in Lares. Among the five prisoners taken into custody by the two captains were Gabino Plumey and Eusebio Ibarra.

Taken to Arecibo, Miguel Pítre lay on a hospital bed for the past two days. Gangrene had begun to ravage his leg and the surgeons had no choice but to cut the limb off right below the hip. In the end, though, it did not matter because Miguel had already contracted yellow fever and his body had turned jaundice. When Rosalía received news that the authorities had transported Miguel from the jail in San Sebastián to a hospital in Arecibo, she begged Mayor Chiesa for help in getting to Arecibo as quickly as possible. After two days of constant pleading by Rosalía, Mayor Chiesa finally relented and asked his personal secretary to take her to Arecibo just so that he could have peace of mind once again.

The moment Rosalía saw Miguel, her heart shattered into pieces. There he was, the love of her life, reduced to a mere shell of what he once was. She sucked in a deep breath of hospital air, and as she slowly exhaled, she accepted Miguel's loss of limb. In her eyes, losing a limb was far better than the losing a life. Miguel was still alive and that was all that mattered to her. But when the doctors told her that Miguel was suffering from yellow fever, her world came crashing down. The doctors at first refused to allow her access to Miguel because of his prisoner status, but when Rosalía begged, cried, hollered and screamed, the doctors caved in just to shut her up.

Rosalía had not bathed in days, and the refined clothing she once wore, was now reduced to tatters. It didn't faze her in the least. In fact, she was proud of her appearance because now she felt like a true jíbara from the mountains. Rosalía crept slowly into the ward, where several other similar patients dwelled. The chatter of so many conversations was overwhelming to Rosalía. Wives talking with their husbands, husbands with their wives, young children crying, doctors issuing orders to nurses, orderlies shouting at other orderlies and all noises associated with a hospital ward was deafening. Ignoring the drone and clatter, Rosalía reached Miguel, and though she tried valiantly to hold back her tears, they cascaded down her face.

"Do not cry, my love," said Miguel in a whisper. He felt pain all over his body, but he was determined not to show Rosalía how much he was suffering.

"Your skin has turned yellow, my love. Even the whites of your eyes are yellow. Is there anything the doctors can do for you?"

"I'm afraid the disease is at an advanced stage. There's nothing else they can do." Miguel reached over and took hold of Rosalía's hand. "I have no regrets. I am thankful to God, though, because he gave me you, Rosa, and for the brief moments we were together, I was truly a happy man. I will leave this world knowing that I experienced true love, and that is more than many a good man can say."

"What will I do without you? I cannot go on living anymore if you should die."

Miguel noted the sadness in Rosalía's eyes, and the bleak outlook she had on life without him. He looked at her consolingly. "You are strong, Rosa, much stronger than I was or could ever hope to be. You must carry on with the struggle, because you are now a true rebel."

Rosalía squeezed Miguel's hand, debating whether she should tell him her secret. With eyes filled and reddened by tears, she reached down and planted a kiss on his lips. Then she looked deeply into his eyes and decided to do it. She reached for Miguel's hand and placed it on her belly. "Do you feel that?"

Miguel gazed at her with a set of inquisitive eyes, but nothing seemed to register in his mind. "Feel what?"

"Miguel, your child grows inside of me." She noted Miguel's eyes widen and his mouth stretch with a smile. Then he gasped, "Is it really true?"

"Yes it is, your child, our child."

"Oh Rosa, I'm so very happy. How many months are you pregnant?"

"Not sure, but I'm very much with child."

Miguel suddenly changed his disposition, turned his face to look up at the ceiling and sighed deeply. "How much I wish I could live long enough to see our child, if only for a few seconds, but I know that will never happen." Miguel gazed thoughtfully at his young bride for several moments. Then, as if reaching a quick resolution, he smiled at Rosalía. "Can you do something for me, Rosa? Can you help me write a letter to my son or daughter, will you do that for me?"

Brushing away her tears, Rosalía smiled back at Miguel and nodded. "Yes, my love."

CHAPTER 117

On the evening of October 16, Maria held Rodolfo in her arms. Sitting on his deathbed, Anita wept uncontrollably. Laura sat next to Anita, but kept her emotions in check, never revealing them to her father or to her mother. "I do not have any more time left," uttered Rodolfo in between heavy gasps of air, "so you must listen to what I am about to say." He let out a deep breath, and in a whisper said, "I am not who I claim to be."

"No Rodolfo, there's no need for confessions," Maria protested.

"Yes, my beloved wife, there is for me," Rodolfo countered quickly. He turned to his two daughters and smiled uncharacteristically. "My real name is Jorge Santos, and I was not born in Seville but in Barcelona. As a young boy…" Rodolfo took twenty minutes to confess to his family but after revealing his secret, he felt as if he had lifted a huge burden off his shoulders. He gazed sorrowfully at Anita, and tried to comfort her despite his own pain. "That is why I was so hard on all of you, because I never wanted to go back to poverty." He turned back to look at Maria. "But then, you knew who I really was all the time, didn't you? Yet, you never told me, until recently. Why did you keep my secret, Maria?"

Maria raised his hand to her face and rubbed it against her cheek. "Because of my love for you, my sweet Rodolfo, because I knew that frail and sensitive man behind the mask he wore daily. I loved you from the very first day I laid eyes on you and I have never stopped loving you."

Laura nearly threw up when she heard her mother's reply. The emotions in the room were palpable and as alien to her as her abilities to show compassion and love. Unable to deal with her own wicked emotions, as well as her new identity, she shook her head, stood up and stormed out of the bedroom. Maria noticed her abrupt departure and beckoned her to come back.

"Let her be, Maria," interjected Rodolfo, "She must come to terms with the fact that she does not come from aristocratic blood."

Maria smiled at Rodolfo, "Not completely, but at least half of her does."

Rodolfo smiled back at Maria, "Indeed." As he gasped for air, he gave Maria a pleading look. "Please forgive me for deceiving you and your family. Please forgive me for all the abuse and humiliation."

"There's no need for forgiveness, Rodolfo, but if you insist, then I forgive you."

"Good, that makes me happy. Now, you must take heed. I have already signed my last Will and Testament, and it is in the hands of Mayor Chiesa. In the Will, I have—" Rodolfo began to cough, while gasping for air. He took a long and deep breath, coughed once more, and let out the last fragments of air 7:43 that evening.

Maria would hold Rodolfo in her arms for hours, crying, wailing and moaning. During those mournful hours, Anita, confused about her own identity, would cry in the solace of her room. On the other hand, Laura quickly overcame her identity shock, and while she stretched across her bed in a blissful state of mind, she began planning the takeover of her father's estate.

CHAPTER 118

While Maria held her husband in her arms in San Sebastián, Rosalía held Miguel in her arms in Arecibo. By now, Miguel's urine was tainted with blood, giving the doctors clear indication that Miguel had lost the use of his kidneys. In his weakened condition, Miguel took longer to speak, pausing for long intervals of time in between breaths. With an infinite amount of patience and love, Rosalía tried her best to comfort Miguel as much as possible. "If it's a boy," whispered Rosalía, "I will name him Juan Miguel, and if it's a girl, I will name her—"

"Rosa!" Miguel filled in, straining himself for energy.

"If that pleases you, then it shall be Rosa," replied Rosalía. She gave Miguel a pitiful smile. "Do you want me to reposition the pillow?"

Miguel furrowed his eyebrows and shook his head. A short moment of silence passed before Miguel opened his eyes to reveal the horrible pain. He moaned deeply. "The pain, Rosa, I can't stand the pain anymore. It hurts so bad, I wish it would go away."

For the first time, she saw a tear in Miguel's eye, and felt a horrible sense of helplessness. Miguel was suffering badly from the pain and Rosalía could do nothing to alleviate his misery. Rosalía decided to fetch one of the doctors to see if he could help Miguel, but when she turned to look for the doctor, she heard Miguel gasping. Rosalía spun around and noticed Miguel's shock-filled eyes, as if he had seen a ghost. Rosalía arched over Miguel and watched him closely, "What is it Miguelito?"

"Rosa, I love you with all of my heart..." Those were the last words Rosalía heard out of Miguel's mouth. Miguel's eyes rolled up, and he let out a long and final last breath. "No!" cried out Rosalía. She grabbed hold of Miguel and cradled him in her arms for a few moments before several nurses and doctors rushed over to the bed. Miguel was no more, his body lay motionless and all Rosalía could do was hold him close to her. The only thing Rosalía took solace in was the fact that Miguel was not suffering anymore, that even though he had passed away, his face seemed to glow in a peaceful state. How could she go on living without him? What would she do now? As she held Miguel in her arms, she could not hear the doctors and nurses yelling at her, or feel their fingers prying her loose from her husband's body. After several tense moments, the doctors and nurses pulled Rosalía away from Miguel and escorted her to a waiting room, forcing her to sit on a wooden chair. Rosalía cried incessantly, fell off the chair and curled into a fetal position. The doctors and nurses watched her but decided to leave her there and see to the removal of Miguel Pítre's body. There were plenty of sick patients needing a bed, and since Miguel was already dead, his body simply had to go.

CHAPTER 119

Sitting inside a tiny jail cell by herself, Berta understood that she would die soon. She had killed a peninsular, her master and owner, and that was an unpardonable crime in the colonies of Spain. Every night she begged God to take her spirit away and free her from her miserable existence, but every morning she would wake only to find herself back in that tiny cell. After three weeks of isolation, someone had come around to see her, a militiaman.

She was going to hang that morning.

Considered sub-humans by the Spanish, slaves were never entitled to a trial by their peers. As the militiaman entered the cell, he commanded her to stand. He bound her hands and escorted her out of the cell.

When Berta stepped outside the jail, she saw no one, and this gave her reason to think. There were going to be no witnesses to her death.

"Do you know why I'm here?" The soldier questioned. Berta turned to her executioner and nodded. "Good, it will save me the trouble of explaining." He mounted his horse, and then reached over to pull Berta onto his saddle. He spurred hard and rode down Orejola Street, crossing the bridge at full speed.

The militiaman rode for a short distance into the woods until he was certain there was no one in the immediate area. He dismounted quickly, and left Berta atop the horse while he strung up a rope around a thick branch of a nearby tree. He had already prepared the noose, and made sure the rope was at the proper length. He walked back toward Berta, pulled the horse to the tree and centered her head underneath the noose. Then he climbed the horse, sat directly behind Berta and placed the noose around her neck. As he tightened the noose, he uttered, "I am under orders."

"I know you are, señor, and that is why I have already forgiven you."

As he dismounted, he heard the clicking of a rifle trigger and froze. At the same time, he heard a loud pop and caught sight of a flash of light from inside the forest ahead of him. A second later, he felt the sting of a bullet ripping through his chest. The militiaman dropped to the ground dying instantly. The gunfire startled the horse Berta was sitting on, and it began to gallop in fear. Berta felt her body fall off the horse and the noose horribly choking her. Her body rocked back and forth as she writhed in an agonizing slow death. The shooter rode his horse out of the woods and reached out for Berta's swinging body. He quickly removed the noose and cut the ropes that had bound her wrists. Berta began to cough while holding her throat with her two hands. After several minutes, she regained her composure and cleared her throat. It was then that her brown eyes confronted the face of a black man, exposing his white teeth in a wide smile. "You are free, Berta."

Berta tilted her head at the skies and shouted, "Thank you God!" Then she looked at her earthly savior and smiled. "Thank you too, señor, for with God's help you have saved my life! Who are you?"

"My name is Santana, and I met your brothers on the freedom march. We fought together in Lares and in San Sebastián. Your brothers made me promise that if something should happen to them I should look to your safety. Today I have fulfilled that promise."

"I thank you so much, Santana."

"You are very welcome, but right now I think we should get out of here. First help me pull this soldier's body into the woods, and then you will take his horse for as long as he is willing to go. Your brothers left some money for you and their wish was for you and Manolo to use it for the journey to America." Santana gave Berta a thick, white envelope.

When Berta opened the envelope, she could not believe what she saw. She pulled out a stack of bills and though she did not know how to count, she knew it was a lot of money. With gleam in her eyes, she looked at Santana and shook her head incredulously. "Do you know how much money is in this envelope?"

"Of course," replied Santana quickly. "They were the life savings of Agustin and Candelario. There are 5,200 pesos there, and please do not ask me how they got it. Just go to America and be free."

"I cannot go alone," said Berta ruefully, "I just can't do it."

Santana nodded at Berta, and with confidence said, "Yes you can, and you will. You are the sole surviving child of Claudio and Estella, whom you lovingly call Papa and Mamíta. Your brothers wanted you to have this money so that you can be free. Don't let them down, Berta, use the money and get away from this hell."

"I just don't know what to do or where to go once I get to America," insisted Berta.

Santana reached over and placed his hands on Berta's shoulders, "Look at me," he thundered. Berta slowly moved her head up to face him eye to eye. "Your brothers sacrificed their lives to achieve something they believed in, and that was freedom. They have bought your freedom with their lives and have given you the means by which to obtain that freedom. Now please try to keep that in your mind and heart and do not allow their sacrifices to become a total waste."

"What about you, señor Santana?"

"Me? I must return to my master's finca soon before he finds out that I ran away."

"Why don't you come with me to America? There is plenty of money here for the two us."

"I have nothing to contribute, and I'd only be a burden to you."

"No señor, you would provide me with valuable company and assistance. Besides, if my brothers trusted you with their money, then I think they would approve your accompanying me to America. Perhaps Candelario saw something in you when he gave you the money and made you promise to look for me."

Santana smiled and nodded at Berta. "All right, señorita Berta, I will leave it in God's hands. There is a ship docked in Guánica that is captained by a former member of the Capa Prieto cell. His name is José Benitez and he's a well-known abolitionist who ferries people to America from time to time. He charges a small fee, but that is only to cover food and boarding expenses and he asks no questions. He is due to leave port by the second week of November, so we must hurry to get to Guánica."

Berta smiled and hugged Santana as if he were one of her brothers. Santana helped her mount the soldier's horse and together they rode all the way to Mayagüez. From there, they hired a sympathetic coachman to take them to the port of Guánica.

The runaway couple departed Guánica on November 12 and arrived in New York City on November 28. When Berta and Santana set their eyes upon the harbor and gazed at the growing Manhattan skyline, they knew they had finally made it to America.

In time, Santana and Berta would part company. Within weeks of her arrival in New York City, Berta landed a job shining muddied boots for horse travelers, and then she moved into a tiny apartment in Harlem. One day, two years later, Berta met a distinguished African American man. He was from New Hampshire but he was in New York that day to attend his uncle's funeral, and stopped by the shop to polish his boots. His name was Vivantyne Jordan and he was one of a very few number of Blacks living in New Hampshire at the time. Gifted with a mechanical inclination and with ambition, he left South Carolina shortly after the end of the Civil War and found employment with the Wells Fargo Stagecoach Company as an assembler. After a whirlwind courtship, Mr. Jordan married Berta and took her with him to live in New Hampshire. Berta's descendants still live in the United States but have no idea that a part of their ancestry originated in Puerto Rico.

The rebels Berta left behind would face weeks of investigation and interrogations, ending in various trials throughout the western part of Puerto Rico.

CHAPTER 120

During the months of October and November 1868, many disputes arose between the civil and military branches of the government. Chief among the disputes was jurisdictional authority over the rebels. The military branch wanted to court-martial all rebels proven to have taken up arms against Spain, and allow the courts to try those that did not.

To quell the growing and unceasing dispute, Governor Pavía, decided to let the militia perform their court-martial. He decreed that only the nine prisoners captured by Colonel Martínez would be court-martialed. On November 17, the military authorities, appeased in a small way by Governor Pavía, court-martialed the nine prisoners, found seven of them guilty of sedition and sentenced them to hang. Among the rebels sentenced to hang were, Clodomiro Abril, Rudolfo Echevarria, Pedro Garcia, Ignacio Ostolaza, Andres Pol, Leonicio Rivera and, to no one's surprise, Manuel Rojas. Lacking sufficient evidence for a successful conviction, the military court issued lighter sentences to the former rebel president, Francisco Ramirez and to Manuel Cebollero Aguilar.

Although Governor Juan Pavía capitulated to the military commanders, and though he had signed the death warrants for the seven rebels, certain events caused him to delay the executions. During the latter part of November, Governor Pavía received many letters from the clergy and from women throughout the island pleading for mercy. They argued vehemently against the punishment, claiming it was too harsh a sentence for first-time offenders. Governor Pavía also received letters from five of the seven rebels condemned to hang, asking him for clemency and compassion. In addition to the pleas, the Spanish government sent word to Pavía on November 13, cautioning him against employing harsh punishment. Six days after signing the death warrants, Governor Pavía commuted the sentences for five of the seven rebels to just 10 years in prison. Sentences for the two other rebels, namely Rudolfo Echevarria and Manuel Rojas, were left unresolved due to conflicts between the civil and military branches.

Reluctant to imprison the five rebels on the island itself for fear of another rebellion, Governor Pavía decided it would better serve the colony if he transferred them to prisons in Spain.

On December 16, the five rebel prisoners boarded the Spanish ship *Santander*. Among the ship's cargo, there was a letter written by Governor Pavía explaining his reasons for commuting the sentences. After dealing with the rebels to his satisfaction, Governor Pavía ended the military proceedings in Lares. He concentrated next on the civil trials, which had been dragging on for nearly two months.

Governor Pavía, however, would not have time to close the civil proceedings because by the end of December, Spain removed him from office. The Spanish authorities awarded governorship of the island to José Laureano Sanz, who immediately ceased all civil proceedings in January 1869. That same month Sanz granted all prisoners a general amnesty. At the time, Spain was embroiled in a war against Cuba, and could not afford to let things go unresolved in Puerto Rico. Moreover, there were rumors that relatives of over five hundred prisoners were planning to storm the jails and free the rebels, causing fear of yet another revolution. In an effort to pacify the colonists, in February of 1869, Spain's overseas minister issued orders to the governor of Cádiz to release the five prisoners at once. He informed the governor that should the rebels, upon their release, desire to return to Puerto Rico, their trip would be at the expense of the state.

In all, the militia had rounded up and imprisoned 523 confirmed and suspected rebels. Of the 523 prisoners, 79 died in prison of yellow fever, 68 died in the Aguadilla prison and 11 died in the Arecibo prison.

Although the rebellion of September 23-24 failed miserably because of its poor planning and leadership, it nevertheless opened the eyes of Spain. In 1869, Spain extended to the island a part of their liberal constitution. Spain awarded the colony provincial status and Spanish citizenry to its creole population. Spain also granted political reform, allowing the citizens to participate in special elections and to legally organize and seek membership into political parties. That same year Spain addressed the issue of slavery, and though reforms on the island were slow, slavery finally met its demise in 1873. The latter part of 1869 also saw the end of the dreaded libreta system, causing much joy and relief to thousands of jornaleros.

Manuel Rojas was released from prison and returned to Lares, and though he came back as a free man, he was penniless. He returned to his plantation but quickly realized he could not live there any longer. The plantation simply held too many bad memories, recollections that were still fresh and painful to him. The ill treatment he received from the loyalist Lareños also made him feel unwelcomed, and these factors proved too much for Rojas. He had to leave Lares. Two months later, Rojas sold his plantation to a jubilant peninsular.

Rojas moved to Mayagüez where, two years later, he opened up a tiny fish store on the coast. There he lived in quiet solitude, a bitter man, beset with ruminative dreams of what could have been. He often visited the grave of Mathias Brugman, and he would talk to him as if he were still alive. He would sit in the porch of the small house he shared with his brother and often talk about the events of September 23-24, which many people by then were calling *El Grito De Lares*, The Cry of Lares. It bothered Manuel Rojas that people called the uprising The Cry of Lares. It wasn't just one cry and it didn't take place in Lares only. To Manuel Rojas, the dream of freedom started with the Cry of Lares, but it was in San Sebastián that those dreams came to a crashing end. The real cries came from San Sebastián. They were the passionate cries of freedom, hopes and dreams, but they were also cries of failure, despair and death. Manuel Rojas would dwell on the rebellion's failure until his death in 1897.

Maria Hernández waged a war against Laura that ended up in court and dragged on for two years. Having obtained a ruling in her favor, she gave Anita part of the estate but gave Laura nothing. Maria tried to reach out to Rosalía but besieged with pain and despair, Rosalía would not respond. In the summer of 1872, Maria decided to sell the properties in Lares and San Sebastián, as well as the house in San Juan, and moved back to Madrid. Anita accompanied her mother to Spain, where she met and married a Barron from Valencia. Maria moved in with Anita and her husband, where she lived the rest of her life in a mournful state, always wearing black, always attending church. She died in December of 1883, and upon her death, gave her entire estate to the church.

Undaunted, Laura went out to seek Captain Sánchez and found him stationed in Santo Domingo. Discharged by the army in 1873, Captain Sánchez quickly married Laura and moved to Ceiba, Puerto Rico, where he bought a sugar cane field. Laura hated the country and despised farm life, and she would make Sánchez aware of it every day. The fighting between them was so fierce, that one day, in a drunken stupor Sánchez picked up his rifle and shot Laura. Though the bullet did not kill her, it paralyzed her, and she became bedridden for the rest of her life. During the years that Laura was immobile, Sánchez ran around, and his reputation as a womanizer was a well-known fact in Ceiba. Laura would bear Sánchez no children, and one day in June of 1890, Laura was no more. Though there was talk among the neighbors that Sánchez had finally killed his wife, the local authorities found no evidence to support the rumors.

Rosalía Pítre buried Miguel in the local cemetery in San Sebastián de los Pepinos, right next his father. She carried his child in her womb for nine months, and on the morning of May 16, 1869 gave birth to an eight-pound, rosy-cheeked girl. When little Rosita opened her eyes for the first time, Rosalía smiled at the two emeralds staring right back at her. She cried and then she laughed, and then she cried again.

Rosalía had no money since she refused her Mother's offer. With child in tow, Rosalía went to see Mayor Chiesa to plead for a job. The Mayor refused to see her at first, but Rosalía's indomitable spirit would bring her back to the Mayor's office day after day. Rosalía was poor and hungry, and once she stopped producing milk, little Rosita became hungry too.

For the time being, Rosalía was staying at Don Blanco's farm, but she knew that soon she would wear out her welcome. She needed to get her life going, just as Miguel knew she could, and she would stop at nothing to fulfill Miguel's vision. For the next two weeks, she would knock on Mayor Chiesa's door sometimes two and three times a day. Finally, Mayor Chiesa, having no more patience, offered her a job.

Rosalía worked at the Mayor's office until his term ended two years later in August of 1871. Rosalía lost her job but with the help of one of Chiesa's friends, she went to work for a sugar refinery in the outskirts of San Sebastián, where she would labor for the next 11 years. Then, in July of 1882, a woman came to see her.

The woman, flanked by her husband, two daughters and a son, froze when she beheld Rosalía's worn out face. At first, Rosalía did not recognize the woman, but the moment the woman spoke, tears ran down Rosalía's cheeks. The two women ran to each other and embraced one another, crying out of happiness. Anita could not believe how much Rosalía had aged. Her younger sister looked beat up, and ravaged by the harsh existence of rural life.

That day, a thirteen-year-old Rosita met her three younger cousins from Spain, as well as her aunt and uncle. Rosalía invited Anita and her family to her little house in San Sebastián, where she cooked a big meal for them. The two sisters sat in the front porch of the house after dinner, drank coffee and talked for hours and hours. The next day, Anita tried to convince Rosalía to go back to Spain with her so that she could see her mother who was dying. Rosalía refused, insisting that her life was in Puerto Rico, and that she would never leave the island. Anita knew Rosalía's refusal to leave the island was because she was still clinging to Miguel's spirit nearly fourteen years after his death. Saddened by Rosalía's refusal, Anita returned to Spain. Before leaving, though, she gave Rosalía her share of her father's inheritance, money she had been holding on to for many years. At first, Rosalía refused to accept her father's money, but Anita insisted, and was finally able to convince Rosalía that little Rosa needed a sound education, and new clothes rather than tattered, hand-me-downs. It wasn't until Anita told her about Rodolfo's confession on the day of his death that Rosalía finally agreed to accept the money.

The inheritance made Rosalía one of the wealthiest women in San Sebastián. She constructed a modest home, and bought many farms back from peninsulares. Then she sold the farms back to the original landowners at rock-bottom prices. One day, when Rosita turned 14, she asked her mother if she could go to Spain to see grandmother before it was too late. Rosita, who was just as indomitable as Rosalía, persisted in her wishes to go to Spain. It finally paid off in 1883, when Rosalía decided to visit Anita. There was one thing Rosalía needed to do first before going to Spain, however, and that was to pay someone else a visit. For some time she had heard rumors about Doctor Betances still being alive and living in Paris. Through her connections with many of the old rebels still living in Mayagüez, she was able to obtain Betances's address. She waited for more than a month for a reply, and when it finally came in early October, she booked a voyage to Europe.

Rosalía and Rosita arrived in France by late November and found autumn in Paris a delight. Rosalía instructed her daughter to remain in the hotel room, while she made plans to see Betances. There were many things she wanted to talk to Betances about and she did not want to expose her daughter to her conversation with the good doctor; at least not until it was time for her to know them. Rosalía finally met Doctor Betances, had dinner with him and talked nearly all night long with him.

EPILOGUE

Doctor Betances finally put his fountain pen down on the blotter. He had written all day and night and well into the wee hours of the morning, and to his left stood a neat stack of papers. He rubbed his chin thoughtfully, shook his head in amazement and smiled deeply.

Rosalía was an amazing woman, he thought, but then again, they were all amazing. Perhaps Manuel Rojas, Mathias Brugman, Manuel Cebollero Aguilar and the rest of the rebels were ahead of their time. Maybe they were past their time and should have existed during the 1820's, when South America was rebelling against Spain. Perhaps Puerto Rico might have been a free nation by 1868.

Doctor Betances took the stack of papers and read each page to his satisfaction. He read the pages two more times, until the skies above Paris began to brighten. He rose to his feet after reading the papers for a third time, and walked over to the window. Far off into the distance, he could see undulating dots of light from numerous hand-held lanterns. Men were starting to climb up the steel frame of Eiffel's tower to begin riveting new frames. A new day was beginning.

Betances turned slowly back to his desk, picked up the stack of papers and looked at it for a long while. Then he placed the stack back on his desk, picked up the first sheet and tore it into tiny pieces. He repeated the same procedure until the torn pages filled the wastebasket next to his desk.

It was a clear and bright Saturday morning and Dr. Betances was glad to have closed his medical office for the weekend; even doctors needed to rest. Today, however, his mind was just as clear as the Parisian skies were, and with newfound energy he easily wrote his long awaited essay. By Monday, he would have it ready for his publisher. After his meeting with the publisher, he would hire a coach to take him to Six

Rue de Châteaudun, where he would open his new medical office, and continue to serve the poor people of Paris. The following week he would vacate the flat on Saint-Dominique and move closer to his new office. He sat back on his chair and began to write his new essay.

GLOSSARY OF TERMS

Alcalde (Ahl.kahl.deh) - Mayor
Borinquen (Bor.een.kehn) – Native Indian (Taino) name for Puerto Rico.
Cabróna (Kah.broh.nah) - Derrogatory word meant to hurt someone or incite a fight.
Calle (Kah.jeh) – Street.
Camuy (Kah.moo.ee) – A town in northwestern Puerto Rico.
Ciénegas (See-eh-neh-gahs) – A barrio (neighborhood) in the district of Camuy.
Cojónes (Koh.hoh.nez) – Testicles.
Cuerdas (Kwer.dahs) – A unit of land equivalent to 3930 square meters.
Estancia (es.stahn.seeah) – An estate designated for cultivation.
Finca (Feeng.kah) – Farm.
Hacendado (Ah.sen.dahdo) – Land owner.
Jibaro (Hee.bah.roh) – Hick.
Jornalero (Horl.nah.le.roh) – A field worker, farm hand.
Muláto (Moo.lah.toh) – A person of mixed race (European and African).
Pava (Pah.vah) – A staw hat.
Pendeja (Pen.de.ha) – Pubic hair, derogatory remark.
Peninsulares (Pen.eehn.soo.lah.rez) – European settlers.
Pepinos (Peh.pee.nohs) – A barrio of San Sebastián.
Prieto (Pree.eh.toh) – Black.

Breinigsville, PA USA
29 March 2011

258701BV00001B/13/P